M000283929

"A powerful and wonderfully perceptive author."
—Mary Jo Putney

"Ms. Kelly writes with a rich flavor that adds great depth of emotion to all her characterizations."
—*Romantic Times*

Mrs. Drew Plays Her Hand

"Another superlative character study from the wonderous pen of Carla Kelly . . . another precious gem in the Kelly treasure chest of extraordinary Regency romance." —*Romantic Times*

Miss Grimsley's Oxford Career

"One of the Regency genre's most innovative writers ever returns with another 'instant classic' for our bookshelves. . . . Ms. Kelly masterfully explores the roots of feminism in an earlier age with keen perception and stylish prose. Indeed, the last portion of this novel is nothing short of magnificent. . . . Brava!"
—*Romantic Times*

SIGNET

REGENCY ROMANCE
COMING IN AUGUST 2003

The Defiant Miss Foster and
A Highly Respectable Widow
by Melinda McRae
In two novels of love, one classic and one new,
Valentine Debenham seeks a match for his ward, never
thinking that he may be the best man for the job...And
a pompus Earl's ego is shattered by a wise widow.

0-451-20950-8

The Major Meets His Match
by Blair Bancroft
Lady Vanessa could not think of a worst match than a
common engineer. And Major Charles Tyrone would
sooner return to battle than marry this shrew. But when
fate throws them together, the pair wonder if this is
more than a mismatch.

0-451-20939-7

Three Wishes for Miss Winthrop
by Shirley Kennedy
Since Lucy Winthrop refused his offer of employment,
Lord Granville can't seem to get the minx off his mind.
And when he grants her three wishes, Miss Winthrop will
keep him guessing until the last.

0-451-20938-9

Available wherever books are sold, or
to order call: 1-800-788-6262

Mrs. Drew
Plays Her Hand

AND

Miss Grimsley's
Oxford Career

❦

CARLA KELLY

A SIGNET BOOK

SIGNET
Published by New American Library, a division of
Penguin Group (USA) Inc., 375 Hudson Street,
New York, New York 10014, U.S.A.
Penguin Books Ltd, 80 Strand,
London WC2R 0RL, England
Penguin Books Australia Ltd, 250 Camberwell Road,
Camberwell, Victoria 3124, Australia
Penguin Books Canada Ltd, 10 Alcorn Avenue,
Toronto, Ontario, Canada M4V 3B2
Penguin Books (N.Z.) Ltd, Cnr Rosedale and Airborne Roads,
Albany, Auckland 1310, New Zealand

Penguin Books Ltd, Registered Offices:
80 Strand, London WC2R 0RL, England

Published by Signet, an imprint of New American Library,
a division of Penguin Group (USA) Inc.
Mrs. Drew Plays Her Hand was originally published by Signet in December 1994,
copyright © Carla Kelly, 1994
Miss Grimsley's Oxford Career was originally published by Signet in March 1992,
copyright © Carla Kelly, 1992

First Signet Printing (Double Edition), July 2003
10 9 8 7 6 5 4 3 2 1

All rights reserved

 REGISTERED TRADEMARK—MARCA REGISTRADA

Printed in the United States of America

Without limiting the rights under copyright reserved above, no part of this publi-
cation may be reproduced, stored in or introduced into a retrieval system, or
transmitted, in any form, or by any means (electronic, mechanical, photocopying,
recording, or otherwise), without the prior written permission of both the copyright owner and the above publisher of this book.

PUBLISHER'S NOTE
These are works of fiction. Names, characters, places, and incidents either are
the product of the author's imagination or are used fictitiously, and any resemblance to actual persons, living or dead, business establishments, events, or locales
is entirely coincidental.

BOOKS ARE AVAILABLE AT QUANTITY DISCOUNTS WHEN USED TO PROMOTE PROD-
UCTS OR SERVICES. FOR INFORMATION PLEASE WRITE TO PREMIUM MARKETING DIVI-
SION, PENGUIN GROUP (USA) INC., 375 HUDSON STREET, NEW YORK, NEW YORK 10014.

If you purchased this book without a cover you should be aware that this book
is stolen property. It was reported as "unsold and destroyed" to the publisher
and neither the author nor the publisher has received any payment for this
"stripped book."

The scanning, uploading and distribution of this book via the Internet or via any
other means without the permission of the publisher is illegal and punishable by
law. Please purchase only authorized electronic editions, and do not participate
in or encourage electronic piracy of copyrighted materials. Your support of the
author's rights is appreciated.

Mrs. Drew
Plays Her Hand

*With love to Mary Ruth,
Sarah, Liz, Sandhya, and Jyoti,
daughters and nieces*

Who does not tremble when he considers
How to deal with a wife?

—William Shakespeare
Henry VIII

Chapter 1

Roxanna Drew was not a lady to trespass on anyone's property, even if the landlord was out of the country, but she had a blister on her foot, and the grass in Moreland Park looked so inviting. If she took off her shoes and stockings, she could cross that field barefooted and cut three miles off her return route.

"This is the folly of wearing new shoes," she said out loud as she sat on a log at the edge of the woods. She rubbed her heel and contemplated the gentle river of grass that flowed around well-spaced boulders and emptied into a larger meadow. She snapped open the watch that was pinned to the front of her dress. Seven o'clock in the morning. Helen and Felicity would still be asleep, curled up next to each other, and Meggie Watson would be lying awake and thinking about putting on water for tea.

She sniffed the breeze, enjoying the scent of wild roses still blooming into September. Somewhere behind the fragrance was the sharp odor of the sea. She closed her eyes, thinking of the sand dunes, and how wonderful it would be to walk barefoot there. Through the dismal spring and uncertain summer, Helen had wanted to visit the ocean at Scarborough. Perhaps next summer would be soon enough. Winter was coming, and with it, decisions enough to push a seaside visit into the background again.

She took off her shoes and stockings and stretched her toes in the dewy grass. I am not the prodigious walker I once was, she thought as she made no move to rise from her comfortable perch. She smiled to herself—grateful she had reached the point where she could smile about it—and thought of her husband, the dedicated walker. When she was expecting their first baby, he had gently bullied her into walking with him as he made the rounds of his parish. Even when she was awkward with child, he continued to insist on her company. He only smiled when she grumbled about delivering the baby under a hedgerow on one of the miles of country lanes, and was there at her side when Helen made her ladylike appearance in their own bed.

Roxanna leaned forward and rested her chin in her hands. "You were right as always, dear Anthony," she said. Her eyes misted over, but the moment passed quicker than it would have in April or May, when the ground was still raw over his grave.

They had continued to walk together through her next pregnancy, and on until the morning when he sat her down under a distant tree and told her the doctor's suspicions. She knew she would never forget the calm way he looked at her and said, "And if he is right, my dear, he doubts I will see another summer."

He lived another summer, and then another one, but it was from his sickbed that he watched their second daughter, Felicity, take her first steps. He was much thinner by the time Felicity called him Papa and crawled up on the bed to sit beside him. He died as quietly as he had lived, when Felicity was almost four and Helen six, an astonishment to his doctor, who had given him less than a year.

Through a mist of pain that was only beginning to recede now, Roxanna thought of the doctor's surprise at the vicar's ability to hold off death so long. *None of you suspected what a tenacious man he was,* she thought as she looked at the meadow stretching before her. *You saw only a quiet, self-effacing man, never strong, but lit from within by a flame so difficult to extinguish. We Drew ladies took such good care of him. And there is that matter of constant prayer, which most of you regard as sheer foolishness in this age of reason.*

Throughout that long, dismal winter as she watched Anthony fade before her eyes and gradually melt away, she promised herself that she would take long walks again, and breathe other air than sickroom air. When he finally breathed his last in her arms, her relief equally balanced her grief. It was time for Anthony Drew, vicar of Whitcomb parish, to quit this life and let his beloved wife see if she cared to go on living without him.

She had taken short walks at first, a mile or two here or there, not far from the village of Whitcomb. Invariably some parishioner in gig or cart would stop and insist that she ride to her destination. Roxanna had not the heart to tell them she had no destination, not really, so she invented enough little errands that filled her drawers with unnecessary notions from the cloth merchants, and more bread than they could eat from Whitcomb's bakeries.

A glance at her dwindling resources convinced her that she had better begin walking across fields, where the danger was reduced of encountering well-wishers and more sympathy than she needed. In rain or shine, she would look in on her sleeping daughters and then walk until she was pleasantly tired. She wore out one pair of walking shoes and started on another, which brought her back to her current difficulty. There was a definite blister on her heel. "New shoes are such a trial," she murmured, and stood up.

She had walked farther than usual, but she knew whose land she trespassed on. It was one of the numerous estates of Colonel Fletcher Rand, Lord Winn, currently on occupation duty in Belgium. Anthony had always made it a point to know something of his parishioners, even those far distant, or those who never attended services, even when they were in the vicinity.

Lord Winn fit both categories. She remembered mailing a Christmas note to Lord Winn in Brussels, begun in Anthony's spidery handwriting and finished in her own firm script. She knew Lord Winn was a colonel of one of the more distinguished Yorkshire regiments. There was more, of course, but she never repeated scandal, and did not think of it, either, beyond a sad shake of her head. "For who of us has not fallen short of the mark?" Anthony would say, and she could only agree.

She started across the field, her eyes on the larger, more distant meadow, ringed about with trees and noisy with birds throwing back their challenge to autumn and shortening days. During the long months of Anthony's illness and death, she sometimes wondered if the Lord was scourging her for thoughtless years of overmuch laughter and quick temper. All emotion had been drained from her now. She lived life on one plane only, and sometimes wondered what it would be like to laugh until her sides ached, or even get really angry. It seemed impossible.

But I know what it is to worry, she thought as she strolled along, breathing in the fragrance of fields ready for harvest. Where are my girls and I to go? And how soon can we get there?

She knew from the day she buried Anthony in the parish cemetery that his older brother Marshall, Lord Whitcomb, would be wanting to give the parish living to another vicar. Until yesterday, Lord Whitcomb had not even spoken to her about the matter, and she was grateful for his unexpected forbearance. He had given her almost six months to collect her shattered thoughts and ruined dreams, and put them away for safekeeping.

His visit yesterday had not been a surprise. He sent a note that he was coming to discuss personal matters. Meggie Watson, Marshall, and Anthony's old nursemaid reminded her little charges that she had promised them a visit to the creek behind the vicarage, where Helen could bait a hook in imitation of her father, and Felicity could churn up the water farther downstream as she searched for pebbles.

Roxanna frowned and sat down on one of the boulders. All things considered, perhaps it would have been better for the girls to have run in and out of the parlor during Lord Whitcomb's visit. "Roxanna Drew, you have earned your suspicions," she told herself out loud, then looked around, afraid the wind would carry her words too far. No one was in sight, not even a cow or horse, so she relaxed again, going so far as to hitch herself up on the boulder and sit cross-legged. She knew it was undignified, especially for a woman dressed in black, but she had more on her mind than decorum.

"I have decided to give this living to Thomas Winegar," her brother-in-law told her over tea and biscuits of her own making.

She nodded, pleased. Mr. Winegar, newly released from Cambridge and ordained, had been filling in during the last year of Anthony's life, even though he had duties of his own of a subordinate nature at nearby St. Catherine's. And hadn't he said something about a new wife soon? Roxanna knew that the future Mrs. Winegar would be as satisfied with her surroundings as the Drews had always been.

"This brings us to you, Roxanna," Lord Whitcomb had said next, as he set down his cup and brushed the crumbs from his impeccable waistcoat.

"I had thought to find a small place in the village," she replied.

Roxanna shivered and then looked around her in surprise. The sun was shining down on her particular boulder, warming her shoulders. Perhaps the chill came from within. Perhaps she did not want to think about Lord Whitcomb.

He had seemed shocked, angry almost, that she would consider such an independent step, reminding her that he had promised Anthony on his deathbed that he would take care of her and the little ones. "I will not hear of such a thing, Roxanna," he said, looking into her eyes and moving closer on the sofa. "You will come to us at Whitcomb."

"I think not, Marshall," she had replied gently. "I do not believe Lady Whitcomb would enjoy my little Indians running about the place, not with her nervous temperament."

There wasn't any need to add that Agnes Drew, Lady Whitcomb, had never reconciled herself to her brother-in-law's somewhat eccentric choice of a wife. On more than one occasion, Roxanna had overheard her to say that "Pretty is as pretty does, but why in a vicarage?" And there was no distinguished family pedigree to render even a pretty face acceptable. "Better a stout dowry in a vicarage than a trim ankle," had been Lady Whitcomb's remarks upon that subject, spoken, as were all her jibes, just loud enough to be overheard. But this was nothing that Lord Whitcomb had probably not already heard late at night in his own bedroom, when husbands and wives discuss their relatives and laughed over them.

Her unexpected resistance, after years of gentle obedience to his brother, seemed to set off Lord Whitcomb. He got to his feet and paced back and forth in front of the window as she stared at him and wondered at his agitation.

"Roxanna, my wife's nerves are her best friends," he had admitted finally, stopping in front of her. He sat beside her again, closer this time, his knee nearly touching hers. "They are her excuse for neglect of all marital duty." Shocked, she moved away slightly, hoping he would not follow, and wishing suddenly that Meggie would return from the creek.

To his credit, Lord Whitcomb picked his words with great care, even as he inched closer on the sofa. "I was thinking that we might consider a special arrangement, Roxanna," he said, his voice quite soft.

It was not in her nature to be suspicious, she thought as she slid down from the slowly warming boulder and continued at a more rapid stride across the field, unable to sit still at her memory of yesterday's searing interview.

"Marshall?" she had asked. "Whatever do you mean?"

He only moved closer until their knees were touching again, and she could not slide any farther away on the sofa. "I know you have been missing the comfort of a husband for several years at least," he had told her, his voice conversational, as though they chatted about the price of silk or the prospect of a good harvest. "I can provide that special comfort, and a good roof over your head, Roxanna." His hand was on her knee then. "And if there was a son, why, that would be more than Agnes has ever grudged me. No one would ever need to know that it was not hers."

Roxanna stopped in the middle of the field. She could not remember what had happened next, beyond the fact that in only a matter of seconds, Lord Whitcomb was standing in the doorway, his palm against his reddened cheek, his hat in his hand. "I do not think you fully appreciate your situation," was his only comment as he mounted his horse and galloped away.

Later in her room, as she retched into the washbasin and then tried unsuccessfully to pour herself a glass of water with shaking hands, she reflected on his words. She knew with painful clarity that he controlled whatever stipend she would receive as Anthony's relict. She also knew that her parents were dead and her brothers both in Bombay with the East India Tea Company. She could also assure herself that these circumstances suddenly rendered her even more vulnerable than Anthony's most bereft parishioner.

She hurried faster, grateful at least that they were newly into the quarter, and she still retained a substantial amount of her stipend. If she could find a place to live, and live cheaply, they could probably stretch it to December. Out of wounded vanity, Lord Whitcomb would probably reduce her stipend; surely he dared not eliminate it entirely.

She sighed. So many worries, and now this one, an anxiety so dreadful that she could only question if she had heard Lord Whitcomb right yesterday. Roxanna paused in the field, wondering if at any time in the last three years of Anthony's illness she had ever indicated her longings for marital comfort to Lord Whitcomb. Surely not. No matter how much she yearned for Anthony's love, she had never done anything to make her brother-in-law suppose she was that desperate.

Even if I am, she thought, and then tried to push away that imp from her mind. She forced herself to face the reality that more than once at night she had awakened beside her slowly dying husband and wished he was still capable of making love to her. But I never gave any hint to Lord Whitcomb, she thought. I would never.

Her uneasy reflections took her into the larger meadow, where she could see a dairy herd grazing. As she passed, the Ayrshires looked up at her with that curiosity typical of the breed. Some started toward her. She smiled to herself and hurried across the field, looking back to laugh out loud. Helen would be amused to see a string of spotted cows all following single file in her wake, intent upon knowing her mother's business.

Everyone wants to know my business it would seem, she thought as she came to the fence and climbed over it as gracefully as she could with her shoes still in her hand. She sat on the fence a moment until she had her directions again, and started through the larger meadow.

A short walk showed her that she had reached the lawns of Moreland Park. Sheep grazed around her as she admired the order she saw everywhere. If Lord Winn was still out of the country, he certainly had put his faith in the hands of a loyal bailiff, she thought. She skirted around the manor, observing that no smoke came from the chimneys, Nowhere was there any sign of habitation, and she thought it a pity. The honey-colored stone glowed in the morning sun, and if some paint was needed here and there, it only added to the air of shabby country charm that seemed to reflect from the walls of Moreland. She could imagine the interior, all ghostly with Holland covers on the furniture, and cobwebs and mouse nests. The building cried out for someone to throw open the draperies, raise the window sashes, and get on with the business of turning it into a home again.

She admired Moreland for another moment, smiling to herself at the thought of approaching the bailiff with fifty pounds and asking for a year's lease on the place. He would think me demented, she observed with a chuckle. Still, it was a shame for such a building to remain idle when her need was growing greater by the minute.

She looked at her watch again. Eight o'clock. The girls would be up now, and pestering Meggie for breakfast. And so I should be home, she thought. Oh, I hope Lord Whitcomb does not call again today.

She was crossing the park behind the estate, her eyes on the road that would lead back to Whitcomb, when she noticed the dower house tucked in the shade of Moreland's large trees. She started toward the house as if drawn there by magnets, then stopped and looked toward the road again. I must hurry, she thought, even as she continued until she stood on the front steps of the two-story house.

It was of honey-colored stone, too, and more shabby than the manor, with crumbling mortar, and rain gutters stuffed with debris. She noticed several broken windows as she walked around the house, wishing for a box to stand on so she could peer into the rooms. She found a wooden bucket with the handle missing, and turned it over to balance on it and peer into the front room. She rubbed at the glass with her sleeve until she cleared a small spot and then raised herself up on tiptoe.

"Mrs. Drew, if ye overbalance yourself, I'll be blaming myself."

Roxanna gasped and dumped herself off the bucket and into the arms of an old man scarcely taller than she. With a chuckle, he set her on her feet again.

"And barefoot, too? Beware of broken glass."

She did not know him, even as she held out her hand and allowed him to shake it. "You seem to know me, sir."

He released her hand and after sweeping off a winter's accumulation of rotting leaves, motioned for her to sit on the edge of the porch. "I'd feel better if you put on your shoes, ma'am," he said. "My name is Tibbie Winslow, Lord Winn's bailiff. And I've seen you walking about the place before, Mrs. Drew."

"I hope you do not mind," she said as she pulled on her stockings as discreetly as she could and pushed her feet back into her shoes. "I am not really one to cause alarm."

He chuckled again and looked carefully as she tugged her stockings to her knees. "I belong to St. Catherine's parish, ma'am, and let me tell you we were as sorry to hear about your husband's death as the folks in Whitcomb parish."

"Thank you, Mr. Winslow," she said quietly, touched by his matter-of-fact words.

When her shoes were tied, he stood up and patted his pocket. "Now then, Mrs. Drew, would you like to look inside?"

It was ridiculous, she told herself as she smiled into his face and nodded, her eyes bright. "If you please, sir," she said. "I like old houses." And I am desperate to find a place, she did not say.

He opened the door, leaning his shoulder into it when the key was not enough to allow entrance. "Warped," he grumbled, and then stepped aside to let her in.

There was a parlor, dining room, kitchen, and library on the main level, with floors buckled by rain from broken windows. She skirted carefully around a gaping hole of burned timbers in the parlor floor.

"Gypsies," Winslow muttered, and motioned toward the second level, where she found three bedrooms and a modest dressing room. The roof leaked in all these rooms and the wallpaper hung in sorrowful tatters, dismal evidence of neglect. As she gazed about her with growing interest, Roxanna could see what twenty-five years of off and on war with France and absentee landlords had done.

Then she did what she never should have done, but what all women did in a deserted house. As she walked from empty room to empty room, she began to put her furniture in each place, imagining the girls' bed next to that window, and Helen sitting on that floor with her dolls and a cozy fire in the rusty grate. She would

take the front bedroom, with its view of the park behind Moreland. She could pull up her chair to the window on cold days and
watch winter birds at the feeder she would hang right under the
eaves.

"I wonder how many fine old homes have been ruined because
too many men have been too busy fighting Napoleon?" she
mused out loud as she mentally rearranged her furniture and put
curtains at each bare window. Broken glass crunched underfoot as
she folded clothes into imaginary bureaus and placed flowers in
phantom vases.

"More than I care to mention," Winslow stated and closed the
bedroom door behind them. "Mind yourself on them stairs, now
then, Mrs. Drew." He laughed. "In fairness to Old Boney, I think
Moreland was deserted long before Lord Winn left Yorkshire. He
got this property by default through a cousin. He has never lived
here. Ain't it a sight how the rich get richer?"

"Oh," she said, stepping carefully around a tread rotting away
from the leaking roof.

She stood on the porch again in a moment, and the bailiff pocketed the key. "Pretty sorry, eh, Mrs. Drew?"

If she had been in a calm mood, she would have nodded, made
some throwaway comment about the sad state of ruined things,
said good-bye, and hurried toward the road that led to Whitcomb.
Instead, she took a deep breath.

"It can be repaired, Mr. Winslow. Oh, sir, how much would
you charge me for a year's rent?"

Chapter 2

Thank God Napoleon is banished to St. Helena, brother. You
have no more excuses now to avoid your family duty."

Fletcher Rand, Lord Winn, colonel late of His Majesty's 20th
Yorkshire Foot, looked up from his newspaper. He settled his
spectacles slightly lower on his long nose and peered over them at
the woman who had administered this opening shot across the
bows.

"Amabel, I wish you would drop yourself down a deep hole,"

he replied, and returned his attention to corn prices in Yorkshire. He cared not a flip for corn prices, but there was no need for his sister to think she had his attention. Corn it would be, until Amabel wearied of the hunt.

"Look at it this way, Winn," said his other sister. "Your eyes are going. Who knows what will go next? I wish you would marry and provide this family with an heir before it is too late."

"Lettice, there is nothing wrong with my virility," he commented, turning the page and directing his attention to pork and cattle futures. "I can refer you to a whole platoon of high flyers in London who were almost moaning to see me return from Brussels."

It wasn't true at all, but that should do it, he thought, in the shocked silence that followed. He returned to pork and waited for the reaction.

It was not long in coming, taking the form of several gasps from Lettice. He waited behind the paper, unable to resist a slight smile. Now she will fan herself, even though the room is cool. Ah, yes. I can feel the little breeze. Now Amabel will approach her with a vinaigrette. He took a deep breath. Yes, there it is. I wonder if Clarice will intervene now. She will clear her throat first. There we are.

"Winn, you are vulgar. I wish you would not tease your sisters like this. You know we are concerned about you."

He put down the paper to regard his older sister, who sat with her mending at the opposite end of the sofa. She returned his stare, unruffled, unblinking.

"Perhaps you are, Clarice," he said. "But that is because you are married to the juicy Lord Manwaring, and you do not need my money." He glanced at Amabel, who was chafing Lettice's wrists and making little cooing noises. "Amabel, on the other hand, hopes that I will burden some female with a son, and cut out Lettice's oldest, who is my current heir."

"I never considered it!" Amabel declared, dropping her sister's hand. "I only want what is best for you."

The fiction of that statement was not lost on any of the sisters. Clarice turned her eyes to her mending again, while Amabel and Lettice glared daggers at each other. Lord Winn waited for the next statement. It was so predictable that he had to resist the urge to take out his watch and time its arrival.

"It is merely that I do not think it fair that Winn has all the family money," Amabel exclaimed to her sister.

Lord Winn put down the paper, removed his spectacles, and

glared at his youngest sister, who pouted back. Hot words boiled
to the surface, but as he stared at her, he was struck by the fact
that although almost ten years had passed since he went to war
for the first time, the arguments had not changed. Amabel was
still feeling bruised because more of the estate was not settled
on her; Lettice was smug because her son, a worthy if prosy
young fellow, was heir; and Clarice did not care one way or the
other.

Nothing has changed, he thought. Nations rise and fall, and the
Rands remain as predictable as ever. We continue as we did before, getting each others' backs up, thinking ill thoughts, nursing
private wounds that we will throw at each other every time we are
together. Next Lettice will give me an arch look and ask if I have
heard the latest scandal about my former wife. We dig and hurt
and pry and wounds never heal.

Lettice looked at him and motioned to her sister to help her up
again from her semi-recumbent position. "Poor man," she began,
"you have only just returned, and there is more scandal. Did you
know—"

"Stop, Lettice," he commanded. "I do not want to hear any sor-
did anecdotes about Cynthia. She is no longer my concern."

"I think she is your concern!" Lettice burst out. "She goes
about the fringes of our circle, telling whoever will listen that you
beat her regularly and"—she gulped and blushed—"and forced
her into unnatural acts."

Even Clarice's eyes widened at this news. Amabel sniffed at
her own vinaigrette and looked everywhere but at her brother.

Lord Winn rose and went to the window, wishing with all his
heart to exchange rainy English skies for the heat and dust of
Spain, just one more time. "Sisters, let us not split hairs. I should
have beaten Cynthia regularly, but I never laid a hand on her in
anger. Never. I do not prey upon women, no matter how they deserve it."

"I didn't really think so, Winn," Amabel assured him.

"And as for unnatural acts—"

"Really, brother," Clarice protested quietly.

"The only unnatural act I ever required Cynthia to perform was
to keep within her quarterly allowance," he said, and then grinned
into the window, in spite of himself. "I suppose that *was* an ob-
scenity to her." He turned around to face his sisters, struck again,
as he looked at them, how lovely they were, and how discontent.
"And so, my dears, I trust I am exonerated?"

Lettice nodded. "It is more than that."

"It always is," he murmured.

"My dear brother," she began, in a tone almost loving, "Cynthia does you such disservice. There is not a mother in London who would allow you to come within a furlong of her daughter. I do not see how you can possibly find another wife."

He went to the door then and rattled the knob, giving any servants listening time to scatter from the hall. "As I have no urge to ever marry again, this concerns me not at all. Good day, ladies."

The hall was a welcome relief, but it was only a brief sanctuary. The door opened and Clarice stood beside him. "Fletcher, surely you wish to leave all this to a child of your own someday," she said, gesturing grandly to the ceiling, the floors, and the wider world beyond.

No matter his own disgruntlement, he could not overlook her obvious concern. Lord Winn touched her cheek with the back of his hand. "Why would I want to leave a child quarrels, pouts, and wounded feelings? No, Clarice, that argument does not move me. I shall remain childless."

Clarice was not a Rand for nothing. She followed him to the front door. "Fletcher, you can surely find a woman to love you."

He opened the door. "Ah, but can I find one I can trust? That, it appears, is the difficulty. Excuse me now. I think I will hide in the shrubbery until your sisters find some other target."

Lord Winn strolled down the front steps, his hands deep in his pockets. He frowned up at the gray skies and let the misty rain fall on his face, then turned around and walked backward across the lawn, staring at his home and remembering his arrival, only weeks ago. He had taken up a traveling companion in London, a fellow officer heading home to Nottingham. It was an easy matter to travel that way; although he was not much of a conversationalist himself, Lord Winn did not relish long silences. Major Peck was pleased to chatter on about this and that as the miles rolled by. By mutual if unvoiced consent, both avoided the war.

As they neared Peck's home, the major fell silent, watching for familiar scenes. Before they turned onto the family property, Major Peck looked at him. "Do you know, Colonel, I always wonder if she will want me again as much as I want her."

Winn had chuckled then, a dry sound evidencing no humor. "Well, sir?"

"She always does," Peck replied. "But still I wonder. Is any man ever sure?"

And then they were at Peck's home, a comfortable manor by

the river Dwyer. Before the carriage rolled to a stop, the major's wife threw open the door and hurled herself down the steps and into her husband's arms. Feeling himself a voyeur, Winn looked away from the Pecks as they kissed and clung to one another. He waited a moment, then spoke to the coachman, who unloaded Peck's kit, mounted to the box again, and drove away, while the Pecks still devoured each other in the front yard.

Winn leaned back in the carriage and remembered his last homecoming four years ago after the triumphant march across the Pyrenees. There had been no greeting from Cynthia. He was there for the trial of divorce and his best friend was one of the correspondents.

"Damn," he said softly as he looked up at his home, a pile of gray stone that meant almost nothing to him. His welcome three weeks ago from Brussels had been so different from Major Peck's, with servants lined up in front to drop curtsies, and tug forelocks. His sisters and their husbands had all been there, too, plus their children he could not remember, and who only knew him as the man with the money. Chaste kisses from his sisters, handshakes from his brothers-in-law. There was no one who cared to throw herself into his arms and eat him alive. But he had only a moment ago declared to Clarice that he did not need anything like that ever again, and it must be so.

He found a bench in the shrubbery and sat awhile, wondering what to do with himself. His first inclination on returning to England had been to sleep for a week and eat all his favorite foods, in the hopes of putting on some lost weight. But his good old English cook had retired and been replaced with a French chef, who only rolled his eyes and fanned himself when Lord Winn ventured to suggest that he would like a good roast of beef and Yorkshire pudding.

He had forgotten that Cynthia had replaced the old comfortable furniture with a style he could only call Demented Egyptian. His bed was the same, however. Cynthia never slept in it anyway, and even Amabel, who lived the closest, lacked the courage to replace it. Other than his bed, with the homely sag in the middle, the only thing that was the same was the view from his window. Cynthia had begun one of those ridiculous fake ruins, but his bailiff, in his infinite wisdom, had seen to its removal when the divorce was final.

"And so it goes." he said as he sat in the rain in the shrubbery, waiting for his sisters to occupy themselves with matters other

than his own welfare. All he wanted to do now was leave again.
His brothers-in-law had made their excuses two weeks ago, mum-
bling something about duty calling, when he knew it did not.
They were men of leisure, even as himself. Lord Manwaring at
least had the grace to wink at him as Winn walked him to his carriage. "Don't let'um get on your nerves, laddie," Manwaring had
said. "Put Clarice in a post chaise when you can't stand her another minute."

I think I will take myself off, he thought, and started a slow
walk to the manor. Unlike that of my wife, I have never
doubted the loyalty of my bailiffs, but it is time to see if there
is any heart left in my land. He strolled along, his own heart
lifting at the idea. He would travel to Northumberland, and
make his way back to Winnfield, stopping at his estates along
the way. He knew there were some he could let go. Others were
willed upon him, and according to law he must keep them, but
he would look them over and decide what use to put them. The
war was over at last. Napoleon would not be returning this
time.

He knew there were homes in Yorkshire where he needed to
visit. He would condescend to sit in smoky kitchens and speak to
work-worn mothers and fathers of valiant sons, buried now under
Spanish and Belgian earth. The good people of Yorkshire would
never understand that the condescension was theirs, and not his.
He owed his own life to their sons, and not the other way around.
All he had done was direct their dying. But they would never understand that, so he would let them make much of him, even as he
thanked them for their sacrifice at Quatre Bras and Mont St. Jean
and Bussaco and Ciudad Rodrigo, and a hundred other unglam-
orous forgotten places that took lives as readily as the horrific battles schoolchildren would still be studying, when he was clay in
hard ground.

And then he was hurrying faster, this time to the stables. The
horse he had just bought at Tattersall's wickered at him as he entered the low-ceilinged stable, but he went first to the chestnut
eyeing him from the best loose box. "Now then, Lord Henry," he
murmured to his horse in his best Yorkshire accent, " 'av ye summat to tell me, awd lad?"

"Only that ye 'av put t'lad on a brawny pasture, my lord," said
his groom from his perch on the railing in the box.

"Mind that Lord Henry's comfortable, Rowley," Lord Winn
admonished. "He took me from Lisbon to Brussels, and I won't
forget."

The groom only nodded and grinned at his master. "Carrots anytime he says, and sugar tits at Christmas?"

"I'll be back by then, Rowley, but yes, of course." He ran his hand down the old horse's long nose. "And if you should ever see the knackerman eyeing ta' Lord prematurely, you have my permission to shoot the man."

The groom cackled in appreciation and rubbed his hands together. "I'd love to shoot a knackerman!"

Lord Winn laughed for the first time since his return. "I'd like to see that, too. You know what I mean."

"Indeed, I do, my lord. Carrots and sugar tits for the old warrior."

He looked at the groom, struck by the fact that he was an old warrior, too. "Aye, Rowley. And have my new bay saddled and ready to go tomorrow morning early."

The groom nodded. "Have ye named him yet, my lord?"

"Not yet. I'm sure I'll think of something."

He chuckled to himself as he left the stables, remembering last month's final gathering of the regiment in London, when his staff and line officers presented him with a plaque that read, "Colonel Fletcher Rand, Lord Winn—From 1808 to 1816, we trusted him to think of something."

The phrase had become legendary among the regiments. In battle after battle, with the 20th up against many a tight spot, he had ridden Lord Henry up and down the ranks, assuring his men that he would "think of something" to get them out alive. It had worked, too, until Waterloo, when the 20th was almost blasted into a distant memory. Somehow they had survived. When they took him off the field on a stretcher after that endless day, he was still muttering, " . . . think of something."

He shook his head as he went into the house again. It's time to put those memories to pasture, he thought. Now I am a full-time landowner again. I wonder if I will remember how?

His sisters were kind enough to leave him alone for the rest of the day. Over dinner, he told them of his plans.

"I will start in God-help-us Northumberland before it gets too much colder, and see how things are."

"I do not know why you have to leave so soon," Amabel protested. "Your bailiffs have managed well for all these years. Surely after Christmas is soon enough, or even Easter."

"No, Amabel, it is not," he replied quietly. "I want to start now. I will look in on my tenants, too, and be back here before Christmas, I am sure." He looked at Lettice and Clarice. "I am certain you want to return to your own homes, too."

Clarice twinkled her eyes at him. "Tired of our company, Fletcher?"

He winked at her. "Does anything I do ever escape your sharp eyes, madam?"

She made no comment beyond a sharp laugh and a toss of her head.

"When will you leave?" Amabel asked.

"Tomorrow morning."

Amabel's eyes widened. "I am sure that is not time enough to make preparations, Fletcher!"

"Madam, I am ready right now. Pass the bread, please."

"It is not bread, Fletcher, but croissants," Lettice corrected.

"My God, Letty, give it up!"

He left before anyone was up except his groom, pleased with himself to have escaped even Clarice's notice. Beyond a change or two of clothes and linen, he traveled light, remembering that all his estates had the rudiments of soap, razors, and combs. And if he chose to light anywhere for a while, he could always summon a wardrobe from Winnfield.

He thought about stopping in York to visit friends, but changed his mind, the closer he came to that spired city. The friends he had in mind had two eligible daughters, and he did not wish a repeat of his recent experience in London. "No," he told his horse, "I do not need to be cut direct twice in a month. Once will suffice."

The memory smarted. The London Season had ended months before, but Lord Walmsley, his next-door neighbor on Curzon Street, had invited him to a small dinner and dance after his return from Brussels. The dinner passed off well enough, but when he asked one of the Walmsley chits to stand up with him for a country dance, Lady Walmsley had swept down upon him and declared that her daughters never danced with divorced men. She also added that no one would likely receive him, no matter his war record.

His mind a perfect blank, he had bowed to her, nodded to his host, who watched in horror, turned on his heel, and stalked across the ballroom floor, slamming the door behind him so hard that he had the satisfaction of hearing glass break somewhere inside. The next morning, he put his town home up for sale. He looked down at his horse then, grateful right down to his boots that his sisters had somehow not got wind of that development yet.

"So I shall not attempt York, my nameless horse," he said.

But the pull of the place was irresistible. He rode into the cathedral city, remembering happier days when the regiment marched through in full color, blooming with the flower of Yorkshire's finest sons. He had also attended boarding school in York before three years at Oxford, and then the army. He rode slowly past St. Giles, wondering if young boys still scaled the walls late at night. He would not stop to inquire. After his divorce, he was informed in a letter that his name had been removed from the list of trustees for that fine old institution. "Horse, it is a good thing I will never have a son who wants to go to St. Giles. I fear he would not be allowed admittance," he murmured.

He stopped at the cathedral and dismounted, left his horse in the care of a street urchin, and slowly climbed the steps, pausing to admire the facade. The familiar saints gazed down at him with the sorrowing mien of medieval holy men. He shook his head and went inside to the cool gloom, redolent with centuries of incense.

It took a moment for his eyes to adjust to the dimness and then direct their gaze to the loveliness of the rose window over the high altar. He had stood before that altar with the beautiful Cynthia Darnley leaning on his arm as York's archbishop joined them together. Even now his heart turned over at the memory of Cynthia, her hair brighter than guineas, her eyes bluer than cobalt, looking up at him as though her entire future happiness depended on him alone.

What a fool I was, he thought as he sank into a pew and propped his long legs on the prayer bench. Too bad he had to be married before he discovered that she looked at every man that way. Too bad he had the impolite timing to return from Spain unexpectedly and find her in bed with his former roommate from Oxford and best man. Even now his stomach heaved at the memory of her scooting out from under that good friend, opening her eyes wide as she covered herself with a sheet and declared that he should knock first.

And then the bed had turned to blood when he fired at his friend, who sobbed and pleaded for mercy. His hand was shaking; his aim was off. The doctors declared his friend a lucky man. Of course, he would likely never father children now, but that had elicited only a dry chuckle from Colonel Rand as he read the letter from his solicitor over a Spanish campfire six months later. The letter had also included information about the anticipated writ of divorce, which gradually worked its way up to the House of Lords while he fought through Spain and Lady Winn fornicated

through at least a platoon of former friends and relatives, his and
hers. She continued to spend his money at a dizzying speed that
infuriated him almost more than her blatant infidelity. He wasn't
a Yorkshireman for nothing.

The actual trial and divorce decree had ended all that. Somehow Lady Winn had the misguided notion that he would be a
gentleman and let her go after a slap on the wrist. To her furious
dismay, he had paraded that platoon of lovers before the House
of Lords and watched without a muscle twitching in his face as
they described in great detail her peccadilloes. He sat there im-
passively, decorated in his medals, his arm in a sling from Bussaco, a betrayed hero, while the Lords threw her to the dogs.

But now he was a divorced man, and no one would receive
him, either. He stared at the lovely window a moment longer,
watching it change color as the clouds maneuvered around the
noonday sun outside. I suppose I should have kept her, he
thought. At least I would still be received in places where I used
to go with some pleasure. I could have done like so many of my
generation and taken a mistress of my own. So what if our dis-
honor stank to heaven?

He lowered his glance to the altar and knew that he could never
have done that. Lord Winn rose to his feet, yawned and stretched,
overlooking the frowns and stares of the few others at prayer in
the cathedral. The trouble was, I actually listened to the archbishop when he spoke of loving, honoring, and obeying, he reflected to himself. They were more than words or hollow form to
me, thank you, Lady Winn. Damn you, Lady Winn.

He stalked down the center aisle, his hands clasped behind his
back. The glow of candles at the side altar caught his eye and he
went toward it. He tossed a shilling in the poor box and lit a candle from one already burning and replaced it carefully in its slot.

For the life of him, he could not think of anything to propitiate
heaven for. His existence was over at thirty-eight, and it only remained to keep going until death eventually caught up with that
reality and relieved him of his burdens.

But as he stood there, hypnotized a little by the flames, he
knew that it was a sham. He could tell his friends and family that
he never wanted a wife again, but he still could not lie to the
Almighty. "A good woman, Lord," he said out loud. "Someone I
can trust. Is there one anywhere?"

He waited a moment for an answer, got none, turned on his
heel and left the cathedral.

Chapter 3

To his credit, Tibbie Winslow did not stare at her as though she had lost all reason and was frothing about the mouth. He rubbed his chin.

"Come now, little lady?"

The words tumbled out of her. "Oh, Mr. Winslow, please let me rent this place from you!"

He shook his head. "I could'na do such a thing, Mrs. Drew! People would think me a sorry creature to rent you this run-down pile. I am sure if Lord Winn ever visits, he'll just tell me to put a match to it. No, Mrs. Drew." He waved a hand at her and started for the manor house.

She hurried after him, resisting the urge to pluck at his sleeve and skip beside him, as Felicity would have done. "Please, Mr. Winslow. If you can replace the windows that have broken, and just fix the roof, I am sure I can do the rest."

He stopped to stare then. "Mrs. Drew, that's a man's work!"

"Well, sir, I have been doing a man's work for three years and more now," she insisted. "The vicar was too ill for home repair, so I . . . I did it. I can paint and hang wallpaper. I might need some help with the floors, though." She stopped, out of breath, and embarrassed at her own temerity.

She held her peace then, watching Winslow's face as he seriously considered what she was saying for the first time. "You could put it to rights then, Mrs. Drew?"

"If you can fix the roof and the windows, I know I can," she declared, her eyes on the Yorkman as she considered what he would find most appealing about the arrangement. "And all at practically no expense to your landlord. We will save this lovely old house for him, and pay him rent besides."

Winslow looked back at the dower house, which glowed, honey-colored, in the early light of the autumn day. "No doubt Lord Winn would be tickled to find the place cared for," he mused out loud. "And I am thinking there is paint and wallpaper left over from the last renovation at the main house." He took a good look at her and slowly shook his head. "You're such a little bit of a thing. How can you do all that?"

She stood as tall as she could. This is my last chance, she realized, recognizing the look on his face from her own years of living with a man of York. Oh, Anthony, what would you do? She took a deep breath. "My husband always used to say that the dog in a fight was not half so important as the fight in the dog. Mr. Winslow, I can do it, and my girls need a place to live."

"Lord Whitcomb won't take you in?" he asked, his voice quiet, as though someone eavesdropped.

"He will, but I do not wish to live under his roof. I think he would try to make me . . . too dependent." There, she thought as she blushed. Read into that what you will. If you are a man with a conscience, I will not need to say more.

Winslow resumed walking, and her heart fell into her shoes. But he was talking as he walked, and she listened with hope, even as she hurried along and tried not to limp with her blister.

"I've heard rumors about your brother-in-law, Mrs. Drew. Didn't believe them then, but happen I do now," he said carefully, walking casually ahead of her, sparing her the embarrassment of his scrutiny during such a delicate conversation.

Roxanna watched his back as he walked before her, and silently blessed that tenderness of feeling she had noted before in other rough Yorkmen. She waited a moment before she spoke again.

"Well, then, sir, you understand my need," she said at last.

"P'raps I do, miss, p'raps I do," he said, still not looking at her. "Would ten pounds for the year suit you? I would blush to charge any more for a ruin. I can have that roof fixed by this time next week, and the windows sooner."

She was close to tears, but she knew better than to cry. "It will suit me right down to the ground, Mr. Winslow."

He turned around then, his hand stretched out, and shook her hand. "Done, then, Mrs. Drew. And it's just Tibbie to you." He took out the key from his vest pocket and placed it carefully in her palm. "You're not getting a bargain, mind."

"Oh, yes, I am!" she said. "We don't mind roughing it as we fix the place room by room."

He nodded, his eyes bright. "And it might be a project to occupy your mind, if you don't object to my saying that."

She could not speak then, and he looked beyond her shoulder, his own words gently chosen. "Now then, Mrs. Drew, we both have a good bargain. And only think how this will please Lord Winn. I don't remember much about him, except that he loves a good bargain."

Roxanna nodded, clutching the key in her fingers and memorizing its contours. "So do I, Tibbie," she said, smiling at him. "When can we move in?"

Tibbie looked back at the house, his eyes on the roof. "No reason why it won't be ready this time next week, Mrs. Drew. No reason at all."

Her heel scarcely pained her as she walked the remaining three miles to the vicarage. I have a place to live, she wanted to sing out to the farmers she passed, already out in their fields. Instead, she nodded to them soberly, the picture of sorrowing rectitude in her widow's weeds. Inside, her heart danced. She passed the parish church, too late this morning to stop in and see how Anthony did. She blew him a kiss as she passed his gravestone. "Anthony, it won't be as good as it was, but it will be better than it could have been," she whispered as she hurried by.

The girls and Meggie Watson were waiting at the table for her when she hurried to the breakfast room, flinging aside her bonnet and pelisse. Felicity, brown eyes bright, looked up from an earnest contemplation of her cooling porridge.

"Mama, you are toooo slow," she chided. "Didn't you remember that I am hungry in the morning?"

Roxanna laughed and kissed the top of her younger daughter's curly head, still tousled from a night of vigorous sleep. Like herself, Felicity did nothing by half turns.

"Silly mop," she said, her arms around her daughter's shoulders. "You are hungry at every meal. Helen, you seem to have all the family patience."

"Papa and I," Helen corrected gently. She smiled briefly at her mother, a smile that went nowhere, and then directed her gaze out the window again.

Roxanna released Felicity and put her arms about Helen's shoulders. How thin you are, she thought. And how silent. She rested her hands on her daughter for a moment more, thinking of the many whispered conversations that Helen and Anthony had granted each other in those last few months, when he was in continual pain and scarcely anything soothed him except the presence of his older child. Did you absorb all that pain? she thought, not for the first time, as she touched Helen's averted cheek, then sat down at the head of the table.

"We were wondering if a highwayman had abducted you, Mrs. Drew," Meggie Watson said.

"And what would he do with me, Meggie?" Roxanna teased. "I have no money and no prospects."

"Mama, perhaps a highwayman would give *you* something?" Felicity stated as she picked up her spoon.

Roxanna laughed out loud for the first time in months. Tears welled in Meggie Watson's eyes at the refreshing sound, and Helen looked around, startled. Roxanna took her hand and kissed it. "My dear, we do need to laugh. But now, let us pray over this porridge, and then I have such news."

She waited until Felicity was well into her bowl of oats, and Helen had taken a few bites, then put down her spoon. Roxanna picked up Helen's spoon again and put it back in her hand, wishing, as she did at every meal, that she did not have to remind her daughter to eat.

When Helen had taken a few more bites, Roxanna put down her own spoon. "My dears, I have rented the dower house at Moreland Park for us. We will move in a week."

Meggie stared at her in surprise. "Mrs. Drew, didn't that burn down several years ago?"

"It is most emphatically standing, but it does need considerable repair. Tibbie Winslow assures me that the roof will be repaired by this time next week, and the windows replaced."

"Good God," Meggie exclaimed, her voice faint. "Next you will tell us that the floors have rotted away and the walls are scaling."

"I was coming to that," Roxanna said, wondering for the first time at the wisdom of her early-morning rashness. "We'll have to walk carefully until the floors are repaired, but there is nothing wrong with the walls that I cannot fix with paint and paper."

"Mama, I know that Uncle Drew promised us a place at Whitcomb," Helen said. "He told me I could have a pony," she added as she pushed away the rest of her porridge.

He promised me a great deal more, Roxanna thought as she regarded her daughter, but it is nothing I dare tell anyone. "I know he did, my dear, but I want so much for us to have a home of our own."

"We can stay here," Felicity declared as she finished her breakfast and eyed Helen's bowl. "This is where my pillow is," she added, with a four-year-old's unassailable logic.

Roxanna smiled at her younger daughter. "We can move your bed to Moreland, and your pillow. Besides that, my dear, Thomas Winegar is going to be moving in here to become the new vicar."

"Oh," Felicity said, her voice resigned, but only for a moment. She brightened. "He can sleep with you in your bed, Mama."

"Felicity, don't be a dunce," Helen said.

"I think it is a good idea." Felicity pouted as Meggie Watson tugged at her chin, and tried to hide a smile.

Roxanna laughed again. "Daughter, our dear Mr. Winegar is about to marry. He would probably have other ideas. No, we will move to Moreland as soon as we can."

Felicity was never one to release a topic without a good shake. "But will I like it there, Mama?"

Roxanna looked around the table at her daughters, Helen withdrawn again, and Felicity demanding an answer that would create order in her world, topsy-turvy with her father's death. She thought of Anthony, who used to sit in the chair she now occupied. When I leave this lovely home, I will leave part of Anthony behind, too, she reflected. The thought jolted her, and she fought to keep the pain from her face.

"Lissy, you will probably like it as much as you want to," she said finally. "That goes for you, Helen, and . . ." her voice faltered, but she raised her chin higher and waited until the moment passed. "And it goes for me. We will make the best of what we have left."

They were all silent a moment, then Meggie Watson rose. "So we shall! Girls, it is time for lessons."

Roxanna remained where she was as her daughters left the room. Meggie Watson told them to go to the sitting room, but she closed the breakfast room door and sat beside Roxanna. She took her hand.

"Mrs. Drew, did Lord Whitcomb say or do something improper yesterday?"

With a startled expression, Roxanna looked at the older woman and returned the pressure of her fingers. She nodded, unable to speak of something so monstrous. Meggie put her arms around her, something she rarely did. Roxanna allowed herself to be hugged, wondering that the starchy nursemaid would allow such a familiarity, but grateful beyond words for her comfort.

"I feel so helpless, Meggie," she said finally. "There is no one here who can extricate me from this mess, so I must rescue myself." She let go of the other woman. "I wish it were possible for women to make their own way in the world."

Meggie reached out to straighten Roxanna's lace cap, tucking her hair here and there as though she were a child. "There are two of us here, Mrs. Drew."

Roxanna smiled at the dear face before her, grateful again that Meggie Watson had come out of her well-deserved retirement when she learned of Anthony's illness. She felt a twinge of conscience, and took a deep breath. There was no sense in putting off a matter she had been agonizing over for months now.

"As to that, Meggie, I cannot pay you any longer," she said in a rush of words. "I will certainly understand if you choose to leave us, for it will not be profitable for you to remain here." She sighed. "Not that it was before."

Meggie blinked. "Leave you?"

"I can think of no way to pay you now. Lord Whitcomb controls my stipend, and I fear that after the way he left yesterday, he will not feel inclined to keep me from the poorhouse." Roxanna felt the tears prickle behind her eyes. She had spent the last three years keeping bad news to herself to spare Anthony more pain. To spill it out now into Meggie Watson's lap seemed like cowardice.

Meggie's eyes narrowed. "He cannot cut you off!"

"No, he cannot do that," Roxanna agreed. "There are laws. But he can reduce my stipend, and I fear he will." She got up and went to the window, her hands on each side of the frame, hanging on as though the room spun about. "I cannot give Helen a pony, or either child any luxuries. It will be everlasting porridge for breakfast and twice-turned dresses, and no hope of dowries." She leaned her forehead against the glass. "I admit I thought about his offer last night when I should have been asleep, and I was almost tempted . . . Oh, Meggie!" She burst into tears.

The nursemaid was beside her in a moment, hugging her as she sobbed. "There now, Mrs. Drew."

"You must think me terrible to even consider such an offer!" Roxanna gasped and covered her face with her hands.

"No, not at all," said Meggie. "It's easy to think crazy thoughts when you are desperate." She took Roxanna's hands and gave them a little shake. "But you're never going to be that desperate, because I won't leave you."

Roxanna closed her eyes and gathered herself together. "I can promise you nothing in exchange."

It was Meggie's turn. Her eyes filled with tears. "Tell me, Mrs. Drew, what do you think is so attractive about a little rented room in Brighton? I do not think you could get me to leave now, even if you tried." She hugged Roxanna again, then went to the door. "And now if I do not hurry, Felicity will think I have declared a holiday."

As if in response, the doorknob rattled. "Miss Watson, we are getting ever so weary of waiting," Felicity said on the other side of the door.

Miss Watson smiled. "She's your daughter, Mrs. Drew!"

Roxanna smiled and nodded. "So Anthony always reminded me. Thank you, Meggie. Words don't say it."

Meggie put her finger to her lips. "Then don't try. I do think you should get that ten pounds to the bailiff as soon as you can. When Lord Whitcomb gets wind of this, and you know he will, there could be trouble of a legal nature."

"So true," Roxanna agreed. "I suppose we have our morning's work cut out for us."

She gathered up the dishes and left the breakfast room with them when she composed herself. The warm water in the dishpan was soothing to her jangled nerves as she washed dishes and dried them, and thought about the dower house. With the exception of the girls' bed, they would have to leave behind the other furniture. She put away the dishes, mentally sorting out which utensils she had brought to the vicarage as a bride, and which would have to remain. She had her mother's china, of course, but beyond a few pots and pans, the rest belonged to Lord Whitcomb. "And I will not be dependent on you, Marshall Drew," she said out loud, her voice low but fierce.

She separated ten pounds from the pouch hidden behind the row of ledgers in the bookroom, trying not to notice how meager was the amount remaining. She looked out the window at the farmland surrounding the vicarage, ready for harvest now, ripe with the bounty of a Yorkshire summer. It wouldn't be possible to depend upon the farmers bringing her fruits and vegetables now. They would go to the new vicar and his wife. Somehow we will manage, she thought again as she retrieved her bonnet and pelisse, found the old pair of shoes and a gum plaster for her heel. In a few minutes, she was hurrying toward Moreland again.

As she almost ran up the long, elm-shaded lane toward the manor house, it occurred to her that she had no idea where Tibbie Winslow would be. Anthony had told her that Lord Winn controlled several estates in the vicinity, and Winslow was responsible for all of them. "Oh, please be there," she said, out of breath, as she resisted the urge to pick up her skirts and race along.

To her immense relief, Winslow stood on the gravel drive that circled in front of the manor, hands on his hips, waiting for the shepherd to herd his flock to the overgrown hay field that was probably the front lawn in better times. She stopped to catch her breath and look around, then sighed with pleasure.

Moreland's yellow stone glowed like rich Jersey butter in the cool autumn noonday. It sat on a small rise, overlooking fields in all directions, fields aching for harvest. An orchard lay to her right, the boughs heavy with fruit. She smiled to herself, thinking of Felicity marching there and climbing up for apples. Perhaps I will join you on a branch, my dear, she thought. Moreland was a working farm, burdened with a manor house at once pretentious and absurdly dear. The building had obviously grown to meet the needs of an expanding family that had also scaled a few rungs up the social ladder. I wonder they did not tear it down and build something in the grand manner, she thought. I am so glad they did not.

Winslow had seen her by now. He waved to her and motioned her closer. She walked rapidly up the gravel drive, noting the deep pits where rain and winter snows had washed away the pebbles. As she came closer, she noticed the gray paint peeling from around window frames and under eaves, and windows with no curtains.

"Change your mind, Mrs. Drew?" Winslow asked when she stood beside him.

"Oh, no," she declared, and held out the ten pounds to him. "I wanted you to have this right away so you would not change *your* mind!"

He smiled and took the money, motioning her to follow him. They went into the manor, and she looked around with interest. It was much as she had expected from her first traverse across Moreland's lawns only that morning. Everywhere was furniture draped in holland covers. She sneezed from the dust, and sneezed again.

"Needs some work, think on?" was Winslow's only comment as he ushered her into the bookroom and pulled down a ledger. He carefully wrote out a receipt and handed it to her. "I'll write to Lord Winn and let him know what I have done." He looked up at her from his seat at the desk. "He may not care for this arrangement," he warned.

"Well, then, it's a good thing I have a receipt," she said as she pocketed the paper. "And I'll hold him to it."

He paused then, and frowned down at the ledger. "There's summat else you should know, Mrs. Drew. Lord Winn has a rather checkered past."

She blew off some dust from the wooden chair facing the desk, sneezed again, and perched on the seat. "I had heard something about a divorce, Tibbie, but cannot see how that concerns me. This is just one of his many estates, isn't it?"

Winslow nodded. "He may come here after Christmas to look over the property. Beyond that, I don't think we'll see him overmuch."

"Mr. Drew told me there was a scandal of startling dimensions, but, sir, who of us does not sometimes fall short of the mark?" she said quietly, thinking of her own temptation only the night before.

"If he had the wisdom to hire you as his bailiff, I am sure he shines in certain essential areas."

Tibbie beamed at her. "Mrs. Drew, not everybody can dispense two compliments in one sentence! I've done my best here."

"It shows, Tibbie." Roxanna looked out the back window at the dower house beyond, noting, to her extreme gratification, that the front door was off its hinges and being planed to remove the warp. Another man walked on the roof, testing it carefully.

The bailiff followed her gaze. "I wish I could put more than one man on that roof right now," he apologized. "The harvest is on us, and that's even more than I can spare."

"I am grateful for whatever you can do," she said, and held out her hand as she rose.

He shook it and walked her to the front door. "Would it help if the girls and I came over here and swept out the house?" she asked.

Tibbie shook his head. "No need in the world, Mrs. Drew. We'll have it all right and tight by next Thursday. See you then."

When she arrived at the vicarage, pleasantly tired from her second vigorous walk of the day and thinking along the lines of a brief nap, she was met at the door by Meggie. The set of Meggie's thin lips, and the crease between her eyes were warning enough not to enter. She grasped Meggie by the arm and pulled her out onto the stoop. "Whatever is the matter?" she whispered.

"The very worst thing, Mrs. Drew," Meggie whispered back, barely able to contain her rage. "I sent Helen to Whitcomb for her pianoforte lesson. Lissy tagged along, and told her uncle about the scheme to move. You know how open she is! He's waiting for you in the sitting room. He looks like a leopard ready to pounce."

Roxanna leaned against the door frame, her stomach fluttering as though the breath had been knocked out of her body. "I suppose I was foolish to think that we could keep this a secret until we stole away like gypsies," she murmured, "but I did hope for a few days!"

Meggie shook her head. "We never thought to warn the girls." She sighed. "They wouldn't have understood, anyway."

Roxanna nodded. "Lord Whitcomb is an indulgent uncle to them," she said, her bitterness surprising her. "And he is an upstanding landlord, and an exemplary parishioner, a justice of the peace noted for his fairness! Oh, it galls me, Meggie!"

"Now what, Mrs. Drew?" the nursemaid asked, after the silence had stretched on too long.

Roxanna squared her shoulders and opened the door. "I suppose it cannot be avoided." She stood for a moment outside the closed door to the sitting room, trying to borrow courage from some unknown quarter.

"Should I go in with you?" Meggie asked, her eyes anxious.

Roxanna shook her head, took a deep breath, and opened the door.

Lord Whitcomb was on his feet in an instant, his eyes targeted on her face with a look of such outrage that it took all her willpower not to bolt the room. In her whole life, no one had ever looked at her like that. She forced her feet to move her into the room, advancing even as her brother-in-law strode toward her.

He stopped directly in front of her, so close that she could feel the heat from his body. Roxanna gritted her teeth but refused to step backward. You cannot have that satisfaction, she thought as he stared down at her, his breath coming in short bursts. To her intense satisfaction, he was forced to take a step backward when she refused to move.

"Have you taken complete leave of your senses?" he roared at her.

Roxanna covered her ears with her hands. "We do not shout in this house," she murmured.

Without a word, Lord Whitcomb yanked her hands off her ears and held them pinned to her sides, then grasped her by the shoulders and shook her until the pins fell from her hair. "You idiot! You imbecile!" he shouted as he shook her. "That house is a perfect ruin and I will not allow you to move there! What can you be thinking?"

With a strength she did not know she possessed, she wrenched herself from his grasp. "You have no say in what I do with my family," she said, wishing that her voice did not sound so puny and frightened.

He grabbed her by the neck then, his fingers pulling her unbound hair until she cried out. "Oh, I do not?" he whispered. His face was so close to hers that she could see the pores in his skin. "I am meeting my solicitor at Moreland's dower house within the hour," he hissed at her. "Tibbie Winslow is a reasonable man. I'll send a cart Monday to move you and your goods to Whitcomb. Be packed and ready, you simple woman."

He released her then and threw her back against the sofa, where she doubled her legs under her and put her hands to her face to protect herself. She shuddered as he came closer, then held her breath, praying for Meggie to open the door. But he only stood looking down at her, and when he spoke, his voice was different. It was softer, the malice cloaked in something much worse than rage. It was the voice of a lover, and it filled her with more terror than the fear of a beating. "Oh, Roxanna, you will be such a challenge to me."

And then he was gone.

Chapter 4

Roxanna stayed awake late that night, fearing to sleep because she knew she would dream about the dreadful interview with her brother-in-law. She had sat awake discussing the matter with Meggie until the nursemaid finally looked at her with bleary eyes and said that she had to sleep or she would drop down. Roxanna nodded and took herself off to bed, too, hoping that she was tired enough herself to fall into dreamless sleep.

She could have saved herself the bother of undressing and putting on her nightgown. There was no opportunity to dream, because she did not sleep. She lay in her bed unable to relax, her eyes wide and staring into the dark, listening to the clock downstairs chime its way around the night. Every little murmur and groan of the old house as it settled sent her bolt upright in bed, clutching her blankets to her breast, terrified that it was Marshall Drew, returning to subdue her in a way that made her sob out loud at the mere thought.

Her hands tightly clenched at her sides, she lay still, wondering what she had ever done to encourage her brother-in-law. Had she ever acted in a fashion that would make him think she was interested in him beyond his position as her husband's brother? True, he took occasion to tell her what a pretty ornament she was to the vicarage, but others had told her that, too. She always smiled and blushed, and passed it off. Only when Anthony told her how beautiful she was did it move her. She sighed into the darkness. Of course, when he said that, he was usually in the process of relieving her of her clothes, or kissing her in places that would have amazed his congregation.

She got out of bed and sat at the window, dismayed at the direction of her thoughts. *I am so vulnerable right now,* she thought. *Somehow, Marshall knows this. Do some men possess a shark's* instinct for blood in the water? Does he know that I am very ready for a man's body again? This will never do, not if I am to remain an independent woman, with my own say in the future of my body and soul. What he is suggesting is devilish, and I will not yield, no matter how much I want to.

There, Roxanna, you have thought the unthinkable, she told herself, and felt the first stirring of hope. You are a widow of some six months, but your husband has been dead to you for more than two years. You would very much like what no lady talks about, but not from your brother-in-law, and most certainly not as his mistress. You can wait for a better offer. Somehow, you can hold him off, even though you don't really want to. Is that it, Roxanna?

She was still sitting in the window when the sun rose. Her spirits rose too, unaccountably. She had seen herself through another long night in three years of long nights. It was different earlier, she thought as she stared through exhausted eyes at the dew-covered fields and the river shining in the distance as the sun's rays struck it. Before, you mourned your coming loss. Now you mourn your loss and fear for your self-respect. Which is harder?

"Oh, bother it," she said out loud. "Anthony, you were a beast to leave me. How dare you?"

The question took her breath away and left her quivering in the worst pain she had ever known. To think ill of the dead, especially her beloved husband, harrowed her already raw flesh in a torment that was exquisite and brutal by turns. She forced herself to consider her feelings for the first time. Anthony was a beast to leave her with two small children, no home, no money, no prospects, and a lustful brother-in-law. She sat calmly in the window and stared down this living nightmare. The pain settled around her shoulders like an unwelcome shawl, wrapping her tighter and tighter until she could scarcely breathe.

And then when she thought she could not manage another moment, her mind cleared. "But you couldn't help it, could you, Anthony?" she said, remembering his long struggle to remain alive and with her, and the gallantry with which he compelled himself into the pulpit on Sunday mornings when he should have stayed gasping in bed. She remembered the hours he lay listening to her ramble on about this and that, when he was probably screaming with pain inside.

"Oh, Anthony, you did what you could," she said, her words no louder than a whisper. She closed her eyes then, and unaccountably, the pain began to recede, unfolding itself gently, softly, from her shoulders. She leaned against the windowpane, and thought of the everlasting card games she had played with her brothers when they were growing up in Kent. They showed her no mercy, compelling her to play terrible hands to the end, instead of folding the cards and running away to her dolls. At first she cried and complained to Mama, but then she learned to play the hand dealt to her. Sometimes she won, sometimes she lost, but she never threw down a dealt hand again.

"Do your worst, Marshall," she said to the window. "I will beat you at this hand." She smiled then, and resolved to finally write that long letter to her brothers in Bombay that she had been putting off. She owed them something.

But first I must face the lions, she thought as she got up and went to the washstand. The water was cold, but she did not care as she stripped off her nightgown and washed until she was a pin-cushion of goose bumps. Ruthlessly she looked at herself in the mirror, raising her arm over her head and noting how her ribs stuck out. You have taken perfectly dreadful care of yourself, Roxanna Drew, she thought. You are a skeleton with breasts. This will never do. She dressed quickly, and then looked into the mirror again at her face. It was still pretty, an older Felicity with flashing brown eyes and curly hair, and that relieved her. I would like to hear compliments again, she thought as she pulled her hair back and tied it with a white ribbon. I am sick of black. Surely a ribbon will not matter?

Dressed in black again, she looked out the window and saw a man hurrying across the field from the direction of Moreland. Well, Marshall, did you and the solicitor get to Tibbie as you promised? she asked herself. If the dower house is not to be mine, I will throw myself and the girls on the dubious mercies of the parish poorhouse before I will end up laid in your bed.

Blunt words, she thought as she went calmly down the stairs and opened the front door, smiling her welcome as coolly as though she greeted the ladies of the parish sewing circle.

It was a man she did not recognize from the parish. He tipped his hat to her and thrust a note into her hands, then blinked in surprise when she invited him in.

"My boots is summat muddy," he apologized.

Roxanna smiled wider. "Come in anyway, sir. I do not have any water on for tea, but—"

"We haven't no time for that, ma'am," he interrupted as he stepped inside and she closed the door.

As he waited, cap in hand, Roxanna opened the note from Tibbie and read it quickly. "He has something to tell me?"

"Yes, ma'am," said the worker. "Told me to walk you back. Says there's some ugly John in the neighborhood he doesn't trust."

"Well, I have not had an escort in some time, sir," she said. She wrote a quick note to Meggie, warning her not to let the girls out of her sight, and then wrapped a shawl around her shoulders. "Let us not waste a moment of Mr. Winslow's time, shall we?"

He may have been an escort, but the worker was not a conversationalist as they hurried across the fields. The farm laborers were at work everywhere, scythes flashing rhythmically in the dawn's light, as landowners stole every bit of light for a Yorkshire harvest. She breathed in the wonderful smell of the harvest, and pushed the poorhouse into the back of her mind. Time enough and then some, to think of that.

At least Tibbie is man enough to tell me bad news face to face, she thought as she hurried to keep up with her protector. He could have written it, and sent back the ten pounds with the letter. I hope I do not beg and plead and look foolish.

They hurried up the lane, and she was grateful to be spared the sight of the dower house in the rear of the estate. Tibbie sat on the front steps, waiting for them. "Now then, Mrs. Drew," he said as he stood up and held out his hand.

She shook it. "Well, sir, I thank you for what you tried to do," she said, determined to blunt the knife before he had time to plunge it into her chest. "I am sorry you had to face Lord Whitcomb yesterday. I don't suppose your interview was any more pleasant than mine."

He nodded and smiled at her. "Ooh, he was in a pelter, wasn't he? That's why I have asked you here, Mrs. Drew."

Roxanna squared her shoulders and imagined herself six feet tall at least. "Lay it on, sir," she said calmly. "I can take it."

He blinked at her. "Take what, Mrs. Drew?" He touched her arm briefly, his eyes boring into hers. "You don't think I have cried off?"

"I understand perfectly," she said, and then stopped, her eyes wide. "Tibbie?"

"I should give you a shake for your thoughts, Mrs. Drew!" He sighed. "Although I doubt me that you have a kindly regard for men right now. Come here."

He led her into the house and directly to the bookroom, where he took her arm again and walked her to the back window. She looked out, and felt the tears well in her eyes, just when she was so sure she was too tough to cry ever again.

Four men worked on the roof, with another two at the windows, removing broken shards of glass. Inside the front room, she could just make out other carpenters tearing up the floor. She could not look at the bailiff.

"He came here yesterday with his solicitor, breathing fire," Tibbie said, his voice quiet, but with an edge to it. "Told me I was to return your money and stop work on the dower house immediately. Told me if I did not, he would personally contact Lord Winn and demand it. Said I would lose my job and never find work evermore as a bailiff in Yorkshire."

"Sir, those are hard words and these are hard times. I think he can do what he says."

Tibbie touched her shoulder and she looked at him. "I told him I would die before I would stop work. Told him I had taken your money and signed a paper. Told him to go to hell, ma'am, if you'll excuse me. I also told him to do something else, but I don't think he can."

Roxanna let out a breath she felt she had been holding since she first spotted the man coming across the field to the vicarage. "I would like to have done that, Tibbie. I can say thank you, but the words seem a bit flimsy after what you have done."

The bailiff stuck his hands in his pockets and rocked back and forth on his heels, immensely pleased with himself. "You'll be a good tenant, I am thinking. Maybe there'll be zinnias in the spring in front of t'awd house?"

"Oh, at least," she agreed, determined not to embarrass this man with tears. "I would like to start some ivy on that west wall. It will take a while for ivy, of course, but I intend to stay in this game, sir."

"Ten pounds a year, and you're in, Mrs. Drew," he said and laughed. "And now, I have some harvesting to oversee. True, it may go a bit slower because of the urgencies on the house, but I don't care."

They shook hands again, and he walked her to the front door. "During his volcanic eruption, Lord Whitcomb lathered about having a cart at your door on Monday morning to remove your things to his manor."

"That he did, sir," she agreed.

"Well, how about if I just happen to send a cart Sunday afternoon?"

Roxanna grinned at the bailiff. "I think we could fill it and be off Lord Whitcomb's property before he has time to blink. I really should pay you for that service."

He shook his head. "You've paid your ten pounds, Mrs. Drew. That got you in the game, think on."

The leaves had been stripped from Northumberland trees by arctic winds when Fletcher Rand received the packet of letters. Amabel had forwarded them to the estate he left a week ago, and it had taken another week for them to catch up to him here at High Point.

He wrapped his many-caped driving coat tighter around him and wished he had resisted his sisters' endeavors to see him into a more modish wardrobe before he left Winnfield. He longed for his army overcoat, warm and totally without style. A fire burned in the grate of High Point's master bedroom, but it was a forlorn hope, competing with the wind that insinuated itself through every crack in the window frames. Lord, how do people live here? he thought as he shivered and opened the packet. Especially in October.

He set aside the letter from Amabel, not feeling sufficiently strong to read it until the chill at least was off his feet. The letters from his solicitor could wait, and there were no invitations to anything. He propped his boots on the grating and considered the remaining letter.

It was from Marshall Drew, Lord Whitcomb of Whitcomb Manor. He slit the envelope and spread the closely written pages on his lap, keeping his fingers pulled up into his overcoat as much as he could. He vaguely remembered Lord Whitcomb from his first and only visit to Moreland after the death of a distant cousin twelve years ago, but could form no opinion as he sat and shivered in a drafty manor in Northumberland. He recalled that their North Riding lands marched together across the eastern property line, and that was all.

Fletcher Rand sighed and leaned back in his chair, thinking dully of property lines, entailments, mortgages, summary leases, and quitclaims. His brain was crammed to overflowing with *de donis conditionalibus*, and today's unbarrable entailment—or was that a *quia emptoris*?—on High Point. He longed to leap on his horse, still nameless, gallop to the nearest port, and take a ship to Spain. He seemed to recollect a seaside town on the Mediterranean side of Gibraltar where the food was good and the women more than willing. He could leave all his dratted property in the hands of capable bailiffs and never look a remainder and fee tail in the face again.

But the letter in his lap wouldn't blow away, despite the steady breeze from the closed and bolted windows, so he picked it up and read it. When he finished, he looked into the flames. "My dear Lord Whitcomb," he murmured, "what the hell do I care if a widow is living in my dower house, as long as she pays rent?" He glanced at the letter again, wondering at Whitcomb's obvious bitterness, directed so acutely at Tibbie Winslow and this poor widow and her two daughters. Probably old maid daughters, without a groat between them for a dowry. Too bad.

Winslow had sent him a short note a month ago, describing the results of September's harvest on the North Riding estates, and mentioning at the end that he had leased Moreland's dower house to a vicar's widow, after making a few necessary repairs. And did Lord Winn mind if he took some furniture from the estate to put in the dower house? The widow was bereft of almost any benefit from her former vicarage. Lord Winn did not mind. Lord Winn could not even recall what furniture reposed in Moreland in the first place, so how could he possibly mind?

He sighed, crumbled the letter into a ball, and pitched it into the flames. He would go see Lord Whitcomb in two weeks, drink tea in his sitting room, and maybe offer Moreland for sale to him. He held that property fee simple, thank the Lord, and could dispose of it as he wished. Then he can do what he wants with that wretched widow, Rand thought. Lord knows I do not give a rat's ass for Moreland, or any of these northern estates. I wonder if I give a rat's ass about anything?

He picked up Amabel's letter when he could no longer avoid it. "And what scheme have you hatched for me, dear sister?" he said, addressing the envelope.

The first page contained a breathless description of the activities of her children, none of whom he could remember. The next page made him frown and mouth obscenities even before he reached her "ever yours in sisterly affection," at the bottom. "Damn you, Amabel," was the most polite thing he muttered as he sent the letter into the flames after Lord Whitcomb's tirade. At least she had not asked for money this time, he had to admit. She had informed him that Louisa Duggett and her parents, Lord and Lady Etheringham, would be spending the Christmas holidays at Winnfield. "I will be pleased to act as your hostess and present you to this diamond of the first water," she wrote.

Lord deliver me from the Etheringhams, he thought. Their son had bought a colonelcy and managed to kill himself and most of his regiment at Waterloo, and the only daughter he remembered was rising thirty by now, and gap-toothed. He smiled unpleasantly into the flames, thinking of the Etheringhams, who were without question the most impecunious family in the peerage. *Lord E. must think he can get enough money out of me to stay afloat, and offer his daughter as a sacrifice to a divorced man, in exchange for my respectability again.*

Thank you, no, Amabel, he thought, and then began to wonder where he could spend Christmas this year. His best friends were dead on Spanish and Belgian battlefields. Perhaps Clarice could tolerate him, and resist the urge to dangle a woman his way. Clarice could probably be depended on to keep his whereabouts a secret from Amabel. He would write her in the morning.

Lord Winn reconsidered. The ink was probably frozen in the bottle in this cursed estate. He would finished up his business as fast as possible, direct his horse to Moreland, and write his letter there. It would be a simple matter to clear up this mess with Lord Whitcomb, assure Winslow of his undying affection, visit a few more estates, then beat an incognito retreat to Clarice's manor for the holidays.

Good plan, he thought, rubbing his hands together and blowing on his fingers for warmth. He cursed Northumberland roundly and stalked to the window. There was snow flying in the air, and despite his ill humor, the sight made him smile. *And so another season turns,* he thought, *and I am older. Still alone, too,* he considered, and leaned against the cold window frame.

But I was alone when I was married, he told himself. In all fairness to Cynthia, he could not blame her for that quirk in his character that isolated him from others. He had always enjoyed solitude. The war only made it worse, he knew. There was something about watching friends blow up on battlefields that led to a certain melancholy, he told himself wryly as he stared out at the snow, which was beginning to stick to the ground now. Others drank their way through the war, or wenched, or took fearful chances. He had withdrawn inside himself until he was quiet to the point that Amabel called him a hermit.

"And so I would be," he said out loud as he went to the bed. He thought about taking off his clothes, but it was too cold. He removed his boots and crawled under the covers, overcoat and all. He shivered until he fell asleep, thinking about Spain, and heat and oranges, and getting the hell out of Northumberland.

He left early in the morning, after scrawling out a note for his bailiff, vowing that he would return in the spring and try to figure out the legal tangle over High Point that had been festering since the days of the first Bishop of Durham, at least. "If it has waited five centuries, it can wait until spring," he wrote in big letters, and signed his name with a flourish. "After all, I am the marquess," he said out loud to the letter as he propped it against an ugly vase on the sitting room mantelpiece. "I can do what I want." He was still chuckling over that piece of folly as he mounted on Young Nameless and pointed him toward Yorkshire.

Lord Winn rode through snow all day until his head ached from the glare of white against the bluest blue of any sky he had seen. And there in the distance, and coming closer, were the Pennines, the spine of England, tall and brooding, and then a delicious pink against the setting sun. There wasn't an inn to be found on the lonely road, but he was welcomed into a crofter's cottage for the night, where the ale made his eyes roll back in his head, and the bread and cheese was far finer than the haute cuisine of his French cook. He slept three in a bed with two of the crofter's children, and was warm for the first time in a week.

The snow began again in the morning, but he rode steadily through the day and into the evening hours, telling himself that Moreland was only over the next rise. He wondered if Tibbie Winslow would have a welcome for him, considering that he was two weeks ahead of schedule, but shrugged it off. He rode doggedly on, thinking of Napoleon's retreat from Moscow.

It was nearly midnight when he rode wearily up the lane to Moreland, lighted by a full moon that came out from behind a bank of clouds like a benediction. The house was dark, which was not surprising, considering the lateness of the hour. To his dismay, he discovered that it was also empty, and he did not have a key.

"Blast and damn," he said out loud into the still night, irritated at himself for crowding on all sail to get to a deserted house in the middle of the night. He cleared off the snow and still holding the reins, sat down on the broad front steps of his property. Despite his disgruntlement, he had to admit that it was beautiful in the moonlight, the snow shimmering here and there like diamonds, the air so still that the trees were diamond-encrusted, too. The orchard to his left was dark and brooding, giving no hint of the promise of apple blossoms in the spring.

"Well, you brilliant man, now what?" he asked himself. The cold was seeping through his coat and his leather breeches, and his toes were beginning to tingle.

He thought of the dower house then, and got to his feet, wiping the snow off his cold rump, then swinging into the saddle again. Perhaps if the old widow wasn't too hard of hearing, or too much of a high stickler, she might let him in to sleep on her sofa. He rode around to the back of the estate, vaguely remembering the direction of the smaller house.

There it was, under the bare trees, smaller than he remembered, but a welcome sight. There was no smoke in the chimney there, either, but a lamp's light glimmered in an upstairs bedroom. That is at least hopeful, he thought as he encouraged his horse with a little dig in the ribs.

He knocked on the door and waited. After a long moment, he heard light footsteps on the stairs.

"Who is it, please?" came a small voice behind the door. She sounded apprehensive, and he couldn't marvel at that, considering the lateness of the hour. The old widow probably didn't have much male company, especially with two spinster daughters.

"I am Lord Winn, and I own this property," he said a little louder, in case she should be hard of hearing. "Could I come in? I think Tibbie Winslow was not expecting me so soon."

The key turned in the lock then, and the door opened upon the prettiest woman he had seen in years, perhaps ever. Her eyes were brown and round like a child's, with high-arched eyebrows that gave her flawless face a surprised expression. *My God, I have never seen skin like that,* he thought as he stared at her loveliness. She was all pink and cream, with dark brown hair tumbling out from under her nightcap. She was dressed in nightgown and a robe too large for her. It looked like a man's robe.

"You may come in, my lord," she was saying as he stood there gaping at her like a mooncalf. "It's too cold to stand overmuch on ceremony, if that's what you are expecting."

He laughed and came into the house after dropping Nameless's reins. "Oh, no, no ceremony. Now tell me, is your mother still up? I must ask a favor for the night."

She tilted her head in a way that he found perfectly adorable. "I am the mother here," she said. "What were you expecting?"

He stared at her in surprise, and she gazed back with that natural inquisitive look that was growing on him by the minute.

"Well, I mean, Tibbie mentioned a widow, and I thought, of course . . . well, you know . . ." he stopped, tongue-tied and feeling like a bumpkin.

"Oh." She looked down at the floor a moment, then back at his face. "My lord, young men die, too. As a former soldier, I am sure you are much acquainted with this phenomenon."

"I am sorry, Mrs.— Mrs.—" he stammered.

"Drew," she said, and held out her hand. "My husband was vicar of Whitcomb parish. Let me help you off with your coat, my lord."

They shook hands. Before he could protest, she grasped his coat from the back, and he had no choice but to pull his arms from the sleeves. For a little woman, she was a managing female, he thought as he obliged her. "I was wondering, Mrs. Drew, if I could sleep on your sofa for the rest of this night?"

She hung his coat on the coatrack by the door. "That will be difficult, my lord, as I do not have a sofa." She picked up the lamp she had carried downstairs with her and held it high so he could look into the sitting room, with the floorboards new and raw, but unpainted, and the wallpaper in tatters. "We're redoing it room by room, and the girls' bedroom was more important."

He looked around the bare room, cold and cheerless in the moonlight that streamed through the uncurtained window. "I certainly hope Tibbie is not charging you too much rent."

She laughed. "Oh, no. I am sure I am cheating you, my lord." She paused, as if trying to gauge his mood. "In the morning, I can show you what we have done with some of the other rooms. They should meet with your approval." He noted the touch of anxiety in her voice, but made no comment upon it.

He took his coat from the rack and carried it into the sitting room. "I can manage all right here on the floor," he said, spreading out the coat.

Her delightful eyes opened wider at that and she shook her head vehemently. "I won't hear of it, Lord Winn," she said, her voice a bit breathless. "I have a much better idea. You may take my bed."

It was his turn to open his eyes wide and stare at her. "I wouldn't dream of that, madam!" he insisted, and felt his cheeks grow warm.

"It's the only solution I will consider," she said firmly, and again he felt himself yielding without complaint to her competent management. "I can sleep with my daughters. There is even a hot water bottle for you." She peered at his face, her eyes filled with concern. "You look as though you have a headache."

"I do," he replied simply, charmed that she would notice, and quite forgetting his headache. "It's hard to ride in snow."

"I have headache powders in my room on the bedside table.

You will feel much better in the morning if you take some. Come, my lord. My feet are bare and the floor is cold."

He shook his head at her forthrightness, then remembered his horse. "Is it too much to expect a stable behind your house?"

"I am sorry, my lord. There is a little shed. You could stable him there until Tibbie arrives in the morning."

She sat herself on the bottom step while he went back outside, hurried his horse around to the shed, and tethered him there. "It'll do, 'awd lad," he said in his broadest Yorkshire as he removed the saddle and covered his back with several pieces of sacking. "We'll find better accommodations for you in the morning."

Mrs. Drew was still seated on the stairs and leaning against the banister, her eyes closed, when he came back in. He stood there a moment, taking in her loveliness, admiring her full lips and the absurd length of her eyelashes. This was a vicar's wife? My God, he thought, in reverent impiety.

"Mrs. Drew?" he said softly.

She opened her eyes, and he almost chuckled at that natural look of surprise on her face. I wonder, can you ever frown? he thought in delight.

"Well, now, perhaps you will come upstairs?" she said. "Duck your head halfway up. The ceiling gets a little low there where the stairs turn."

He followed her up obediently, ducking where he was bid, and breathing in the pleasant odor of lavender that trailed behind her. She hurried up the stairs, her bare feet quiet on the treads. At the top, she held up the lamp for the rest of his ascent.

"This way, my lord," she said, and motioned him into the first room.

There was only the paltriest fire in the grating, but it glowed a welcome at him as he went straight to it to strip off his gloves and warm his hands. While he stood there, she gathered together some clothing from the tiny dressing room off the bedroom, then joined him at the fireplace.

"Good night, my lord," she said softly. "You should sleep very well here. Tibbie arrives around nine at the manor house, so you will have time to breakfast with us before you go, providing you like porridge."

"I love it," he lied, perjuring his soul without a whimper. "Thank you for your kindness, Mrs. Drew. This is such a shocking intrusion."

She gave him that wide-eyed look. "Not in a vicar's household," she said. "We've sheltered many orphans of the storm who

looked more weary than you. Good night then, my lord. If you
need anything, why, you'll probably find it about where you
would find it in your own house."

She closed the door behind her, and he smiled at her ingenuous
reply. Still smiling, he looked under the bed, and laughed out
loud. Sure enough, there was the chamber pot. You are a diplomat, madam, he decided as he shed his clothes and crawled gratefully between Mrs. Drew's warm sheets. They smelled
wonderfully of lavender, too, and he relaxed and felt the tension
leave his shoulders. You cannot imagine how weary this orphan
is, he thought as he closed his eyes in sleep.

Chapter 5

He slept soundly and well, stirring only once when he
dreamed that someone was pounding on his back. "Stop it,
Threlkeld," he muttered, dreaming of his aide-de-camp, dead now
this year and more at Waterloo, who used to wake him up for urgent messages with a thump to the kidneys. "Stop it," he murmured again, and dropped back into dreamless sleep. The bed was
firm in all the right places, and he was warm for the first time
since he had laid eyes on Northumberland in October.

When he woke finally, the sun was streaming in the window as
though yesterday's snowstorm had been a bad dream. He lay
comfortably on his side, drowsily gazing at the bare branches that
tapped on the window glass, and imagining them full-leafed and
green in summer. His back was deliciously warm and he started
to close his eyes again.

They snapped open and he sucked in his breath. Who *was* that
cuddled so close to him? He pulled the sheet up higher across
his bare chest, looked over his shoulder, and found himself staring into a second pair of lovely brown eyes, round and wide
open.

"Where did you put my mother?" she asked, sitting up and
tucking her flannel nightgown down over her feet like a proper
little lady.

She couldn't have been much over four, but as he smiled into her charming face, Lord Winn was delighted with her calm air of competency, so like her mother. You were certainly fashioned from the same mold, he thought as he tucked the blankets about his bare body and sat up in bed, propping the pillow behind him. I wouldn't have thought it possible.

But she was obviously waiting for an answer. In fact, she was getting a little impatient. She pursed her lips in wondrous imitation of her mother, then to his delight, sighed and laid her head on his blanketed thigh. "I wish you would tell me," she muttered, then closed her eyes again.

She was irresistible. I must remind myself that I do not care for children, he thought as he touched her curly hair tentatively, then rested his hand on her small shoulder. She sighed again and snuggled closer.

"No wonder I was so warm last night," he said softly. "My dear, I did not put your mother anywhere. In fact, do you wager?"

She looked at him with those big eyes and frowned. "I don't know what that is," she asked, her voice full of suspicion.

He grinned. "Of course you do not. You are a clergyman's daughter," he said quite matter-of-fact. "Well, I would be willing to lay down good money that your mother is going to come running in here any minute, looking for you. Can you reach my watch there on the night table?"

She sat up again and found his watch next to his reading spectacles, which she put on. He laughed out loud at the sight, and she peered at him over the top of the glasses. She held out the watch to him, but he shook his head.

"You open it, my dear. Can you tell the time?"

After a moment of concentration, with his glasses dangling on the end of her short nose, and her tongue between her teeth, she snapped open the watch, and held it up in triumph.

"Excellent! Now, do you know your numbers?"

She nodded. "The little hand is by the seven, and the big hand is on the six."

He winced. "Seven-thirty! You certainly keep army hours here."

She put the watch to her ear and kept time with the ticking. He took his spectacles from her. "I will give your mother another five minutes to come bursting in here. What do you think?"

She grimaced and snapped the watch shut, dangling it in front of her face by the long gold chain. "She will be here sooner."

"Well, I say five minutes. This is a wager, my dear, a bet. If she comes in after five minutes, I win. If she comes in before, you win."

"What do I win?" the little one asked, flopping onto her back and resting her head on his thigh again.

"What do you want?"

She thought a moment, still dangling the watch from its chain. "I would like a pony for Helen."

Her answer moved him beyond words. He thought suddenly of Amabel and Lettice, and their constant bickering. He touched her hair again, winding a curl around his finger.

"It's too much, isn't it?" she said, more to herself than to him. "Then I would like a skein of yarn, instead."

"For what?" he asked, marveling at the size of the lump in his throat.

"So Mama can make me some mittens. It snowed last night." She handed back the watch, and then her eyes opened wide. "But suppose you win?"

He couldn't think of anything he wanted more than just to stay where he was, but was spared the necessity of an answer. He heard a door open, and someone calling, "Felicity? Felicity?" in a low voice.

"I lost," he said. "Here she comes. You are Felicity?"

She nodded. "I could hide under the covers."

He clutched his blankets. "Not a good idea, Felicity! It's too late to duck from the wrath. By the way, my name is Fletcher Rand. Perhaps we should shake hands."

"That is a strange name," she said as she solemnly shook his hand and Mrs. Drew knocked softly on the door.

"So I have always thought," he agreed. "Call me Winn. Come in, madam. I think I have what you are looking for."

The original pair of round, brown eyes peeked into the room. Mrs. Drew, still in robe and nightgown, opened the door, her marvelous complexion a deeper pink at the sight of his bare chest.

"I am so sorry, Lord Winn . . ." she began, then let her gaze go to the window. "I never thought . . . Felicity does that . . . Oh, I hope she didn't push on your back with her feet! She nearly tumbled me out of bed once."

He laughed out loud and slid down under the covers again to spare the widow his hairy chest. "So that's what it was! I had an aide-de-camp who used to wake me up with a chop to the kidneys. I'm a heavy sleeper, ma'am, or so he used to tell me. Felicity and I have already introduced ourselves, and I have taught her to wager."

"Such dissipation!" Mrs. Drew exclaimed. "I suppose you were wagering how soon I would miss her?"

He nodded. Felicity, still resting against his thigh, nodded too. "I won, Mama."

"Of course you did, you scamp! You know me a little better than our sorely tried guest." She held out her hand to her daughter. "Come, my dear. Let us leave this gentleman in peace."

Felicity sat up and looked back at him, her eyes merry. "Yarn and a pony, or just yarn?"

To his intense amusement, Mrs. Drew put her hands on her hips and pursed her lips. "Felicity! Next you will tell me you wagered for a castle in Spain!"

"Mama, I would never. What good is that?"

Mrs. Drew turned away for a moment to hide her smile. "Spoken like a true Yorkwoman!" she murmured, then shook her finger at him. "Lord Winn, if you have set Felicity on a life of dissipation and crime, I will lay the blame entirely at your door."

"I think it will not come to that," he protested. "And truly, I have been marvelously entertained. "Don't be too hard on her."

"She is a scamp!"

Felicity stood up on the bed and opened her arms wide for her mother, who came into the room, picked her up, and whirled around with her, nuzzling her neck until she shrieked. She carried her to the door, set her down, swatted her lightly on the bottom, and pointed her in the direction of her own room.

"Lord Winn, really, forgive us."

"Nothing to forgive, Mrs. Drew," he assured her. "She's better than a hot-water bottle."

Mrs. Drew smiled then, and went to the door. "Lord Winn, in a few minutes I will have a can of hot water for you. I'll knock on the door when it is ready. There will be some coal, too. Not much, I fear, because it is so dear this season." She turned to leave, then looked back, hesitating. "If you wish, you can find Anthony's shaving gear in the dressing room. I . . . I left it there."

"Thank you, Mrs. Drew," he replied, rubbing his chin. "I must have left my saddlebags in the shed last night."

"Well then, please use what you can find here. We'll eat when you are ready."

She closed the door, and in another moment, Lord Winn heard her admonishing Felicity in firm but quiet tones. He lay still another moment, considering his early-morning bed partner. I wonder if Felicity would like red mittens or green ones? Red, I think. And where can I find a pony? He got up and pulled on his small-clothes and breeches. Soon there was a knock at the door. After waiting a modest moment for her to retreat, he opened the door and brought in the hot water and a very little coal.

"So coal is dear," he said as he dumped the hot water in the washbasin. "I think I shall save this, then."

He washed his face, but couldn't bring himself to use the razor belonging to the late vicar. He stood a moment in the dressing room, breathing in the lavender fragrance from Mrs. Drew's clothing, then pulled on his shirt.

Still tying his neckcloth, Lord Winn came downstairs and followed his nose to the kitchen, where Mrs. Drew, dressed in black with her hair pulled back tidily under a lace cap, was stirring the porridge. Felicity counted spoons, while a tall, thin woman brewed the tea and eyed him with vast suspicion.

"Lord Winn, this is Meggie Watson. She was Anthony's nursemaid, and came to help us out when . . . things were difficult. Now I do not know what I would do without her. Meggie, Lord Winn."

He nodded to her, then ruffled Felicity's hair. "And you are in charge of spoons? Did you count out an extra one for me?"

She nodded, intent upon her work as she gathered up spoons and napkins. "I am to behave myself, Lord Winn, if you do not make it difficult."

Mrs. Drew laughed out loud, then covered her mouth with her hand. "Felicity! Be a little kinder to our landlord!" she insisted, and gave her daughter another gentle swat. She looked at him then. "Couldn't you find Anthony's razor? I was sure it was in the dressing room."

"As to that, Mrs. Drew, a man would always rather use his own blade," he said as he finished tucking in his shirt and pulled on his riding coat, which someone had thoughtfully draped in front of the fireplace. "I'll retrieve my gear from the shed and shave after breakfast, if the sight of a day's growth doesn't upset anyone's appetite."

"I think we can manage," Mrs. Drew allowed as she removed the pot from the stove.

"My lord, perhaps you could hurry along Helen," Miss Watson suggested. "I sent her outside with a bucket of water for your horse."

"She still isn't back?" Mrs. Drew said. "I don't wonder. She gets dreamy-eyed around horses."

"So do I, madam," he said as he opened the back door.

The back steps were deep in snow, except where Helen had walked, so his first task of the morning was to clear them off.

When he finished, the air was moving briskly through his lungs and he looked about in appreciation. There was no wind, and not a branch or bush rustled. The diamonds of snow and ice still jeweled the trees and the ground, and the silence was almost as intense as the blue sky. I wonder why people live in cities? he asked himself as he followed much smaller tracks to the shed.

There he found Helen, nose to nose with his horse, saying something to the big gelding that was generating a wicker of appreciation. He paused in the doorway, unwilling to intrude on the formation of a friendship, and content to admire this other daughter of the lovely Widow Drew.

You must be the image of your father, he thought as he leaned against the door frame and regarded the young girl before him. Her hair was blond and free around her shoulders. She had pulled up a box to sit upon and her posture was impeccable. He could almost imagine her in a riding habit and seated sidesaddle upon a fine horse of her own. She was slim and elegant, with a profile almost regal.

She turned then, and her blue eyes were nearly the color of the sky outside. "I like your horse," she said, then got down off the box, suddenly shy. She remained beside his horse, but Lord Winn had the feeling that had he not been standing in the door, she would have bolted.

He stayed where he was, unwilling to see her disappear. "I like him, too. Are you Helen?"

She nodded, her eyes on his face. He regarded her calm beauty, and found himself irrationally jealous of her dead father. Mr. Drew, you must have been a handsome man, he thought as he smiled at the vicar's elder daughter.

"Thank you for watering my horse," he said, moving closer slowly, as he would approach a skittish colt. "I hope Tibbie has some corn in the stables behind the estate."

"He does, because he puts his own horse there when he comes," she offered. "There are no horses now, my lord." Her voice was wistful, but he did not remark on it.

She couldn't have been more than six or seven, but there was a maturity in her voice that saddened him, somehow. Perhaps I have seen too many children in Spain growing up faster than their years, he thought. I recognize that voice, no matter what the language. Helen, you hide your loss with dignity.

He joined her beside his horse, rubbing the animal's nose as Helen stroked his shoulder with a sure hand, standing on tiptoe to reach him. He slowly moved the box closer to the horse, and to his delight, she allowed him to give her a hand up onto it.

"What do you call him?" she asked as she ran her fingers through the horse's mane, straightening the tangles.

"I haven't named him yet."

Her blue eyes widened at such neglect, and for a moment, he saw her mother's expression in them, too.

"Perhaps you can think of something," he offered hastily, unwilling to suffer her measuring regard. I am short of the mark, he thought with amusement. "I will entertain any and all suggestions."

She nodded, her face serious. "I will ask Mama. She names everything." The briefest smile lit her face, then was gone. "She even named our pigs, which Papa said always made it rather hard to eat them."

He smiled at her. "Did she name them Ham and Bacon?"

Again, that brief smile. "No, my lord! One was Columbine and the other Cynthia."

Lord Winn burst into laughter, transfixed by the idea of his former wife as a sow rooting in a vicar's barnyard. "Magnificent, my dear!" he said, when he could speak. "That is more amusing than you know. We shall apply to your mother for a name. And now—"

"Lord Winn! Helen!"

Helen sighed. "We are both late to breakfast, my lord."

He nudged her shoulder gently. "Does this mean we are in the basket?"

She regarded him candidly. "I think I would be, if you were not here, too, my lord."

He helped her down from the box. "Strength in numbers, Helen, is an element in military strategy. Shall we?"

Mrs. Drew waited for them at the back door, with Felicity beside her, looking impatient.

"Lissy does not like to wait for her meals," Helen confided in a whisper that he had to bend down to hear. "She even likes oats."

Lord Winn smiled, pleased to be taken into this quiet child's trust. He wondered what Tibbie Winslow would say if the first thing he inquired about at Moreland was where he could buy a pony. And some coal. And red yarn for Felicity.

Helen skipped ahead, walking in the wider tracks he had made, her blond hair rippling and shining in the cold, clear air. "Mama, you must think of a name for Lord Winn's horse!"

Mrs. Drew twinkled her eyes at him, and his heart nearly stopped dead in his chest. "I'm sure I'll think of something," she said, and she touched Helen's face briefly and helped her unbutton her coat.

He nodded, remembering his plaque at Winnfield from the 20th Foot with those very words inscribed upon it. And how is your generalship, madam? he wondered as he followed Helen into the kitchen.

Felicity tugged Helen toward the breakfast room, and he stood with Mrs. Drew a moment as he removed his coat and she regarded her daughters.

"You have met my family now, sir," she said.

He looked down into her laughing brown eyes, and his heart started to beat again, but a little faster. "Charming, Mrs. Drew, simply charming. And I don't even like children very much."

She stared back at him. "My lord! Everyone likes children!"

"I do not," he said firmly. "My sisters' children fight with each other and only greet me to ask for things. Dreadful brats."

Mrs. Drew lowered her gaze from his face. "Oh, dear, and didn't I hear Felicity petitioning you for yarn?"

He took her by the elbow and guided her toward the breakfast room, where Felicity was standing at the door, her head tilted and her hands on her hips. "My dear Mrs. Drew, that was a wager and she won it fair. I am always scrupulous in gambling debts." He stopped her and leaned closer to her, breathing in her lavender fragrance. "Tell me, how much yarn does it take to make a little pair of mittens?"

He could almost feel her reluctance. "Oh, I wish you would not."

"Mrs. Drew, you would have me avoid a gambling debt? You wound my honor. How much yarn? I insist."

"Oh! One skein, my lord."

He bowed in her direction. "Done, then, madam. Of course, the labor will be yours. I wish all debts were so easily discharged."

She only smiled and shook her head, then helped Felicity into her seat with the books on it. "Sit over there, my lord. If we wait much longer, Felicity will rise in open rebellion, and it is not a pretty sight."

He did as he was told and was startled when Mrs. Drew took his hand on one side, and Helen on the other. He looked at the widow, his eyes questioning her.

"My lord, we always pray this way. Will you say grace?"

"It's been years, Mrs. Drew," he protested, even as he clung to her fingers.

"I can help you, Lord Winn," Helen offered.

His eyes were still on Mrs. Drew. To his amazement, they filled suddenly with tears. She swallowed several times, and bowed her head. Moved beyond words, and not understanding, he bowed his head, too.

"Yes, if you please, Helen," he said. "I'm a bit rusty. No one prayed much in Spain."

"Please bless us, Oh Lord, and these thy gifts," she said softly.

"Amen," he finished. When he opened his eyes, Mrs. Drew was in control again. She filled their bowls and Felicity tackled hers at once.

He had never eaten better porridge.

While Helen was clearing off the table, Mrs. Drew looked out the window. "Ah! Tibbie is at the estate now, Lord Winn," she said.

The news did not please him particularly. He rubbed his chin. "I really need to shave first," he temporized.

"Certainly, my lord. Meggie, will you pour another can of hot water for Lord Winn? Helen, when he finishes, perhaps you will show him to the right entrance?"

Helen smiled shyly and nodded. Felicity regarded her mother. "I am to come, too."

Mrs. Drew knelt beside her younger daughter, and put her forehead against Felicity's. "My dearest, you would disappear in a snowdrift. This is Helen's duty."

They looked at each other eye to eye until Lord Winn wanted to laugh. He touched Felicity's head. "Felicity, perhaps you could get that leather pouch with my razor and shaving bowl from my coat pocket and carry it upstairs?"

She nodded, mutiny forgotten, and skipped into the kitchen. Helen grinned and followed her. He gave Mrs. Drew a hand up.

"Masterfully done, my lord," she said. "One would think you had practice."

He winced. "I have already told you my feelings regarding the infantry, madam! It is but a fluke."

She only smiled, then touched his arm as he started from the room. "I must apologize for my weakness a moment ago."

He started to protest, but she shook her head. "My lord, Helen has said more this morning than she has since . . . well, in months. I do not know what magic you are working, but it makes me happy."

"It is horse magic, madam, that is all," he said, keeping his voice light, even though he felt another lump rising in his throat. "And you have promised us a name."

He could see tears threatening again, and he felt an absurd desire to pull her close and let her weep, but he did not. "And now I must shave. Excuse me, Mrs. Drew, or Felicity will become impatient."

So that is it, Mrs. Drew, he thought as he mounted the stairs, untying his neckcloth. I wish I had time to be drawn into your little circle here in the North Riding. Too bad I do not.

Felicity perched herself on the bed and watched as he pulled down his shirt and draped a towel around his shoulders. Her face was serious, her lovely eyes wide as he lathered up and began to shave himself. He propped his shaving mirror on the bureau, and watched her through it.

When he was halfway done, another pair of brown eyes regarded him from the open doorway. "Felicity! Leave Lord Winn in peace!"

"I do not mind, madam," he said as he tilted his face up to shave under his nose.

"Mama! He is shaving himself! And he is standing up!" Felicity whispered, her voice filled with wonder. "Can you imagine?"

He laughed and flicked some soap at her. "Of course I am, you absurd child! How else would I shave?" he said, and glanced at her mother. To his consternation, her eyes were filling with tears again. This time, she turned away and her shoulders began to shake. Quickly, he wiped the soap from his face, and picked up Felicity, depositing her outside the door and closing it behind him. Without another word, he took Mrs. Drew in his arms. She buried her face in the towel around his neck and sobbed.

My God, what a strange family this is, he thought as she cried. He wasn't sure what to do, except put his arms around her and let her weep. Her tears seemed to come all the way up from her toes.

In another moment, she pulled herself away from him and wiped her eyes on his towel. Her face was fiery red. "I am so ashamed of myself," she said at last.

"Mrs. Drew, what happened? I don't understand," he asked, lathering up again to finish his face. "I wish you would tell me."

"I used to shave my husband and Felicity always watched," she said, her words coming out in a rush. "In her young life, she has never seen a man shave himself while on his feet."

"I had no idea," he murmured.

"I know you did not, my lord. She never knew her father as a well man. Excuse my tears, please. I don't know what's the matter with me," she said as she opened the door. "I should be beyond this by now."

Felicity came back in, her face cloudy with hurt feelings. Lord Winn set her back on the bed, took some lather off his face, and liberally deckled her cheek. To her delight, he laid the blunt side of his straight razor against her cheek and scraped it off. She shrieked with laughter and then ran from the room to show her sister. He looked around. Mrs. Drew was gone.

To his disappointment, she did not reappear after he came downstairs again, dressed and ready. Helen held his riding coat by the front door.

"I hope you are not upset, Lord Winn, but I led your horse to the front door."

He grinned at her and opened the door, then picked her up and set her on his horse. "We'll come back for the saddle later," he said as he took the reins and walked alongside as his horse broke a trail from the dower house to the estate.

"That's the door to the back entrance by the bookroom," Helen said.

"Well and good, my dear, but let us go to the stables first," he said. "I feel certain you can show me where they are."

The stables were substantial, but only one horse resided within. "That is Mr. Winslow's horse," Helen offered, then leaned down confidentially. "He's not really much of a horse." She touched his shoulder, her eyes lively. "But Mr. Winslow is not much of a rider."

They chuckled in conspiratorial fashion and then he lifted her off his horse. Helen skipped ahead to a loose box and opened the gate. "You could put him in here, my lord," she said.

He led his horse into the box and Helen closed the gate. He leaned on the gate, regarding his horse. "My dear, surely this box already belongs to another horse. It is all set up with hay, corn, and water. I thought you said there were no horses here usually?"

Helen blushed and looked at her feet. "I fixed it that way. I like to pretend I have a horse." She looked up at him then. "Mama thinks I am helping the housekeeper over here, but sometimes I come to the stables instead."

"I'll never tell," he promised, and crossed his heart. In another moment, she was gone.

"Helen, you are a fairy sprite," he murmured, and turned back to his horse again.

"Lord Winn! I thought I saw you from the bookroom window!"

He turned around to see his bailiff, Tibbie Winslow, standing in the door of the shed. Winslow came toward him with that dignity that he recognized as pure Yorkshire, and held out his hand. "It's been a few years, hasn't it, my lord?"

Winn nodded. "A few, Tibbie." He looked around him. "You seem to be well in control here."

"I can show you better in the bookroom, my lord. Ledgers are all right and tight, and we had a good harvest, we did. Will you join me inside? I know you're a busy man, going from estate to estate. I'll not hold you up here at Moreland."

"Certainly, Tibbie. I will only be here a few days, and I do need a prompt inventory." Lord Winn followed his bailiff to the stable door, then stopped. "Tell me, where can I find a pony?"

Chapter 6

From an upstairs window, Roxanna watched Lord Winn and Helen leave the dower house, her heart lifting to see her daughter lean down from atop his horse to speak to him. She hugged herself and shivered, even as she smiled. Oh, Helen, how good to see you in conversation with someone again, Roxanna thought.

She made Helen's bed quickly, fluffing the pillows, then went to her own room. Lord Winn was obviously not there, but she felt a moment's reticence in opening the door. In a way she could not understand, it seemed to be his room, too, and not hers alone.

"Of course, Roxanna, this is his house," she reminded herself as she opened the door and closed it behind her. She bit her lip in dismay. The coal she had rationed out for him was still sitting in the scuttle. "Lord Winn, you will think I am such a nip-farthing."

Well, you are, Roxie, she thought as she went to the bureau. You have another month to go in this quarter, and then you can face the reality of what damage your brother-in-law will have done to your next quarter's stipend. It was a discouraging thought, so she forced her mind into other channels. Bad news could always keep.

Lord Winn had left his shaving mirror on the bureau, and there were his soap and brush. She swished the brush around in the washbasin, breathing deep of its fragrance, trying to remember when she had last smelled shaving soap. Toward the end, it had been too painful to shave Anthony, so she had stopped. She

picked up the soap container. " 'Limón de España,' " she read,
" 'un jabon de hidalgos.' The soap of gentlemen." She sniffed
again, enjoying the lemon fragrance, more than slightly tart, and
as subtle as a bolt of lightning. "Nice," she decided as she
screwed on the lid, dried the brush, and replaced his shaving gear
in its leather pouch with the razor. Helen would probably enjoy
another trip to the estate to return it to him.

She looked around to make sure he had not left anything else,
and discovered his spectacles on her night table. There was no
case for them, so she wrapped them in a handkerchief of hers and
placed them on the bureau, where Felicity could not reach them.
He had left his shirt in the dressing room. She fingered the material. "Fine linen, my lord," she commented. "Nicely made, too."
She rubbed the material against her cheek, breathing in the slight
lemon fragrance and a pleasant combination of sweat and
woodsmoke. The fabric was soft from many washings, and as she
held it out, she noticed a European cut to the design. "How long
have you been away?" she asked as she folded it carefully and
added it to the pile on the bureau.

She made her bed, noting the indentation of Lord Winn's head
on the empty pillow next to hers. I wonder if men have an instinct
about these things? she thought as she fluffed her pillow and
straightened the blankets. After Helen was born, she had claimed
the side of the bed closest to the door, so she could be up quickly
in the night. She started to fluff his pillow, but changed her mind.
She traced her finger over the indentation, then pulled the bedspread over both pillows. I really should change the sheets, she
thought, but knew she would not.

Roxanna went to the window again, looking for Helen, and
wishing she had not made such a fool of herself in front of Lord
Winn. He must think me a certified ninnyhammer, she thought, to
cry over a man with shaving soap on his face. I must learn not to
let little things set me off, or else life will be a misery. I must
learn to go to bed at a decent hour, and not read myself into a stu-
por until I am too tired to do anything but sleep without dreaming.
And I really must go through Anthony's things and see what I can
give away to those in need. When Helen asks for spice cake, I
must not keep making silly excuses, just because it was Anthony's favorite dessert. I have to move on.

She gazed out the window with dull eyes, seeing not the
sparkling winter landscape, but the years yawning before her like
an endless cavity with nothing to break her fall. She stood another
minute at the window, then hurried from her room. Today she had

promised Meggie they would strip the remaining wallpaper from that last wall in Meggie's bedroom. Soon the upstairs would be done, and she could tackle the sitting room at last. By spring, the dower house would be finished. And then what will occupy my mind? she wondered.

Glowing with the cold, Helen returned from the estate, and skipped back just as happily with Lord Winn's property, while Felicity glowered from the breakfast room window. "It's not fair," she declared to her mother, who only smiled and kissed her cheek.

"Of course it is, my dear," she told her daughter, taking her on her lap, and hugging the warmth of her. "Didn't you get to spend the night with him? Lissy, you are such an imp! When will you learn to stay in your own bed? I cannot imagine what he thinks of us."

"Well, he has promised me red yarn," Felicity allowed at last. She leaned back against her mother, pacified. "And do you know, I first asked for a pony for Helen?"

Roxanna rolled her eyes and held her daughter closer. "No more wagers with Lord Winn," she said firmly. "I doubt he will be here much longer than a day or two, but I will not have you making any more wagers!"

The yarn arrived in early afternoon with Mrs. Howell, the housekeeper who came occasionally to Moreland for basic maintenance. Roxanna welcomed her in, shook the snow off her cape, and sat her down to tea in the breakfast room.

"Mrs. Drew, this is for you, with Lord Winn's compliments," she said, pulling out a red skein from her bag. "And this blue skein is for Helen. He told me to match her eyes."

Roxanna blushed and took the skeins on her lap, looking up into Mrs. Howell's inquiring face. "Oh, it was a foolish wager he lost with Lissy. This is his payment, and I am to make mittens."

Mrs. Howell laughed. "He seems a most pleasant man, for all the stories I have heard about him." She paused, and took another sip of her tea, regarding Roxanna over the rim of the cup.

"There was some scandal, wasn't there?" Roxanna said carefully, looking around to make sure that Felicity was still napping upstairs, and Helen engaged in lessons with Meggie. This is none of my business, she thought. Why do I care?

Mrs. Howell pulled her chair closer, eager to continue. "Aye, indeed, Mrs. Drew! A mighty scandal. Worthy of them Romans, think on. 'Twas five or six years gone now, I recall. Something about Lady Winn servicing half the bucks in London whilst he, poor man, fought Ney and Soult in Spain!"

"Mrs. Howell!" Roxanna said, her cheeks on fire. "Dear me! Was it that bad?"

"That and more, lassie," she stated, pouring another cup as calmly as though scandal was mother's milk. "If that wasn't embarrassing enough, instead of just hushing it up and demanding crim. con. money from the more flagrant offenders, what did Lord Winn do but parade them all through the House of Lords for a regular trial. Complete with juicy details."

"No!" Roxanna gasped. "How dreadful for him!"

"Him? Him?" Mrs. Howell demanded. "I hear the entire Winn family was mortified nearly to death. It put old Lord Winn over the edge and into his coffin, it did!" She looked about her. "I hear that no one in London receives him for showing such bad manners. It could have been a quiet divorce. I guess them earls and lords and what-alls do it all the time."

"He must have been grossly offended by his wife," Roxanna said quietly. She thought absurdly of the lemon shaving soap. "Some people are not subtle, Mrs. Howell. Perhaps he really loved her."

"Oh, aye, lassie, happen he did," Mrs. Howell agreed. "I am sure it tickled his male pride, at the very least and all. But to do such a thing to your family?" She was silent, finishing her tea.

"No one receives him?" Roxanna asked. "That seems wrong. What of the former Lady Winn?"

Mrs. Howell snorted, and pushed back the teacup. "The ways of the aristocracy is beyond the ken of you and me, missie, I don't mind saying. What does the former Lady Winn do but marry one of her lays? She's Lady Masterson now, and isn't she seen everywhere?"

"Sounds as though she was before," Roxanna murmured, then blushed again. "Oh, excuse me, but that was a rude comment. But it isn't our business, is it?"

"Well, it might be a little, Mrs. Drew," said the housekeeper. "I've promised myself to Moreland for these next few days for an inventory of the estate's contents."

"Yes, I hear he has been looking over his estates," Roxanna agreed, relieved to change the subject. "Does he own much land around here?"

Mrs. Howell stared at her with wide eyes. "Mrs. Drew, where have you been? He owns half of the North Riding, I am thinking, plus land in Northumbria and Durham, not to mention his own seat somewhere to the south of York."

"Goodness, no wonder he wants to get out from under some of that," she said. "Imagine the responsibility. Well, I only hope he does not decide to sell Moreland."

Mrs. Howell stood up and held out her hand. "As to that, I do not know." She looked around her at the pleasant breakfast room. "It would be a shame, with all the work you have done."

Roxanna thought of her brother-in-law. "You don't know what a shame it would be." She shook herself mentally. "Well, let us hope Lord Winn leaves Moreland alone. Thank you for the yarn, Mrs. Howell."

The housekeeper put on her cloak again and opened the front door. She breathed deep of the cold. "The snow's melting. It'll likely be gone before too much longer."

"Until it settles in again and winter begins in earnest," Roxanna reminded her. "Mrs. Howell, if you need any help with that inventory, I will gladly offer my services."

The housekeeper put her hand to her mouth and laughed. "And wasn't that the other reason I came over here? I must be in my dotage, my dear. Yes, would you help? Tibbie and Lord Winn are riding to Retling Beck tomorrow to check the books there, and I am beginning then. Eight o'clock? And wear an old dress."

Roxanna smiled. "That's all I have!" she teased, then her face fell. "But it isn't black."

Mrs. Howell patted her arm. "Don't worry, dearie. I'll never tell. Tomorrow then?"

"Yes. Eight o'clock."

She was there before eight, wearing a dark green wool dress and accompanied by Felicity and Helen, each with new mittens. Mrs. Howell received them in the warm house, and Roxanna could not overlook Helen's smile of pleasure.

"It's so warm here, Mama," she said.

Roxanna ignored Mrs. Howell's inquiring gaze and held her chin up higher. "Yes, my dear. We do keep our home rather cool, don't we? Perhaps Lord Winn is used to Spain."

Felicity twirled herself around. "I think I would like Spain then, Mama."

Roxanna laughed. "I think you would like any place with hot sun and opportunity for mischief! Now then, Mrs. Howell, tell us what to do."

Mrs. Howell gathered the girls to her. "First, there are cinnamon buns in the breakfast room. Lord Winn said to leave them there for you two. When you finish, stack the dishes, and then find us. I think you can start dusting. The scullery maid will show you where the rags are."

Roxanna followed the housekeeper into the main hall. Mrs. Howell had removed the holland covers from the furniture and she looked about her in delight. "What a fine old piece," she commented, admiring the pianoforte in the sitting room. She played a chord, wincing at the sound. "A bit out of tune."

"I wouldn't know, Mrs. Drew," the housekeeper said. "It all sounds the same to me." She ran her hand over the newly polished wood. "Lord Winn was in here last night. He played something, and told me to have it tuned before it gave him a headache."

"He plays? How delightful," Roxanna said. "See there, Mrs. Howell, he can't be all bad!"

"Well, I wouldn't care to get on his dark side," Mrs. Howell said. "Come, my dear. You can tackle the linen room. I'll inventory the silver. Tibbie says there's enough of that to pay even the Prince Regent's debts."

She spent all morning in the linen room, writing down in her careful hand the sheets, pillow slips, bedspreads, towels, and handcloths, and culling out those obviously lost to mice. She admired the ornate embroidery on some of the sheets, wondering if they dated back to the days of Queen Anne, herself. When she couldn't stand to look at another sheet, she walked through some of the upstairs bedrooms, her eyes wide with wonder at the stately beds, most of which would be too tall for her to crawl into without a stepladder. Felicity and Helen tagged along with her.

"Helen, think how high we could jump on these beds!" Felicity said to her sister.

"Mama would not approve," Helen admonished, even as she grinned at Roxanna.

"Lord Winn wouldn't mind. I am sure of it," Felicity declared.

Roxanna took a firmer grip on her younger daughter's hand. "And you, you ragamuffin, are destined to never know!"

They returned to the dower house when the shadows were lengthening across the back lawn, pleasantly tired and eager for the dinner Meggie had promised them. Roxanna looked at Felicity. "I insist that you take off your mittens for dinner," she said firmly.

Felicity looked mutinous until Meggie brought in the covered roasting pan. She sniffed the fragrance and looked at her mother.

"No food until your mittens are off, Lissy," Roxanna said, trying to subdue the laughter that welled inside her. Oh, Lord, was I this difficult as a child? she thought. Probably.

Felicity did as she was told. The nursemaid, her eyes lively, made them close their eyes. Roxanna opened them to see a roasted leg of mutton before her, the meat moist and ready to be carved. She gasped in surprise.

"Meggie, where did this come from?"

"Mrs. Howell said she bought too much and Lord Winn told her to see that we got some for our dinner."

Roxanna frowned. "We can't make such generosity a habit," she said, hesitating even as she held the knife in her hand. "What will people think?"

"Roxanna, he's only going to be here a couple of days!" said Miss Watson.

"Mama, it's been a long time," Helen added.

She sighed and looked at Felicity, who already had a finger in the gravy that pooled in the bottom of the platter. "Very well," she grumbled. "I may have to take Lord Winn to task, but we will eat to bursting tonight. Pass your plate, Helen. Lissy! Wait your turn. Oh, we are forgetting grace!"

It was a good dinner, complete with Yorkshire pudding covered in gravy so creamy that Helen sighed. "Mama, you know what Papa would say," she commented as she leaned back finally and pushed away her empty plate.

Roxanna looked at her daughter. You have never spoken of him, she thought as she set down her own fork, fearful that her hand would tremble. "You tell me, dear," she said, her voice low with emotion.

Helen sat up straight, and put both elbows on the table in an imitation of her father that made Roxanna close her eyes for a moment. " 'Well done, Mrs. Drew. It couldn't possibly be any better, not even if the Lord Almighty himself sat for dinner,' " Helen said, pitching her voice lower.

Felicity laughed and clapped her hands. Helen burst into tears, and then they were all crying, and laughing, and hugging each other, until Meggie hurried in from the kitchen where she was removing the plates, and joined them. Roxanna pulled both girls onto her lap and held them close to her, feeling better than she had in a long time.

Helen blew her nose vigorously on a table napkin. "Mama, do you mind?"

Roxanna shook her head, her lips on her daughter's hair.

"Somehow, it makes me feel better to talk about Papa."

"Me, too, dear," Roxanna said. "Let's do it whenever we feel like it."

After the girls were in bed, she went onto the front porch, breathing deep of the cold air, more content than she had felt in months. She drew her shawl closer, surprised at her own peace of mind. For someone with such an uncertain future, Roxanna Drew, you certainly are as merry as a grig. She smiled to herself, then found herself listening, her head tilted to one side.

She could hear the faintest sound of a piano coming from the estate. She listened harder, and her grin widened. The piano tuner must have found his way through the melting drifts, after all, she decided, as she strained her ears and concentrated until she identified a Beethoven sonata. It ended with a flourish and a crash of chords, just before her toes started to tingle from the cold. She clapped her hands softly, and went inside, closing the door behind her.

Her teeth chattered as she undressed and crawled into bed, wishing almost that Felicity would climb in with her for warmth. But I must not encourage that, she thought. Gradually, the heavy blankets warmed her and her eyes closed. Before she drifted to sleep, she ran her hand over the indentation in the other pillow. The scent of lemon shaving soap was long gone from the room, but she imagined it anyway, and places like Spain where it was warm.

Lord Winn and Tibbie returned from Retling in the afternoon, when she was trying to count the sheets and stack them back on the shelves. At the sound of horses' hooves on the gravel drive outside, Helen set aside the towels she was folding and looked out the window.

"Mama, can I go to the stables? Maybe Lord Winn will let me curry his horse!" she asked, her eyes lively.

" 'May I,' not 'Can I,' " Roxanna corrected absently as she began her count again. She looked up as Helen tugged on her arm. "Of course, my dear. Only do not make a nuisance of yourself."

"Mama, I would never!" Helen declared. She looked at Felicity, who slumbered on a pile of rejected linen, still wearing her red mittens. "Now, Lissy might."

Roxanna put her finger to her lips. "Then don't wake her, silly!" She returned to her count, stacked the sheets, and opened yet another carved chest. At least it is the last one, she thought. I wonder if the inmates of Moreland ever threw out anything? She opened the chest and gasped out loud, then looked around to make sure she had not wakened Felicity.

The chest was full of lace, beautiful lace, old and yellow now, but still possessing the power to amaze. She carefully lifted out a tablecloth and napkins, tracing over the delicate design with one finger, almost afraid to touch it. I wonder if any of this is salvageable? she thought as she set it aside and turned her attention back to the chest.

There was a smaller tablecloth, and then a christening dress. She sighed with pleasure and held it up, admiring the tiny stitches in the wool and the lace edging around the tiny cuffs and hem. How many generations of babies have worn this? she wondered. And what a pity it is to stick it unused in a chest. She looked about her at the shelves and chests, full to bursting with so much to offer. Such bounty for an empty house, she thought.

She heard firm footsteps in the hall outside, and looked up from her contemplation of the christening gown in her lap. She smiled. It was Lord Winn.

"Good afternoon, my lord," she said, and put her finger to her lips, indicating Felicity with a nod of her head.

He was dressed in riding clothes, the top boots and leather breeches of the country gentleman he was, his coat open and his neckcloth comfortably loose. You don't stand much on ceremony, do you? she thought as her glance took in his graying brown hair, with the indent where his hat had rested, and his handsome green eyes. I did not notice before how green they were, she thought as she returned his smile with one of her own. He was just tall enough, and just broad enough to look substantial, without any suggestion of overweight. You look healthy, she thought, and then blushed at such a foolish observation.

"Now what did I do to make you blush?" he whispered, coming closer.

She shook her head in confusion, not about to admit to her thoughts. "I am still embarrassed over my piece of foolishness yesterday," she murmured. There. He didn't need to know that she was measuring him, and not finding him wanting in any way.

"Already forgotten, Mrs. Drew," he said cheerfully, then peered at Felicity. "Nice mittens."

"She refuses to take them off, except for meals," Roxanna said, happy to change the subject.

He shook his head and grinned at her. "What's that?" he asked, pointing to the bit of lace in her lap.

She held it up for him to admire. "It is a christening gown, my lord. Imagine all those little stitches for one wearing."

"Beyond me," he said. "Most children should be drowned at birth, anyway."

"Lord Winn!" she exclaimed, then pursed her lips when he told her to shush and looked at Felicity.

"I have already told you my opinion of children," he whispered. "I intend never to have any." He watched Lissy. "She won't take them off, eh? Did you make them too tight?"

She put her hand to her mouth to keep from laughing out loud. "No! Lissy finds you 'top 'o the trees,' my lord. If she were a puppy, she would follow you from room to room, I am sure! It's a good thing for you that your stay here is not long."

He nodded. "I suppose," he said, without any particular enthusiasm.

The silence made her uncomfortable, but he did not seem to notice as he walked around the little room, his hands behind his back. "Damned lot of sheets," he commented finally, when he finished his circuit. "Take anything you want, Mrs. Drew."

"I could not—" she began.

"Of course you can," he insisted. "Take that christening gown, too. You'll likely marry again won't you, Mrs. Drew? You'll find a use for it, unless I am grossly overestimating the abilities of most Yorkmen."

"I—I hadn't really thought of it," she stammered in confusion.

"I'm sure that once you are out of black, the men of the North Riding won't waste any time," he said, and strolled back into the hall, leaving her to stew in her muddled thoughts.

Roxanna blinked and stared after him. You have such a nice walk, Lord Winn, she considered as she watched him. It's somewhere between a saunter and a . . . Oh, Lord, Roxie, mind your thoughts.

She pulled out the rest of the chest's contents, suddenly eager to be done with the inventory and back in the dower house. She applied herself to her task, finished the list, and was about to wake Felicity when she heard more steps in the hall, light steps, Helen's steps, and she was running. She tiptoed into the hall in time to catch Helen in her arms.

Her daughter's breath came in rapid puffs as Helen grasped her about the waist. "Is something wrong?" she asked anxiously, kneeling beside her daughter.

"Oh, Mama! You cannot imagine! Mama!" Helen said, her eyes shining.

"What, my dear?"

"It's a pony! Lord Winn says it's part of Felicity's wager. Oh, Mama, come look!"

Chapter 7

O h no!" she exclaimed. "My dear, we can't possibly . . ."

But Helen was tugging her down the hall. She took a last look in the linen room to make sure that Felicity still slumbered, then hurried down the stairs and out to the stable with her daughter.

She paused in the stable's entrance. Lord Winn was leaning comfortably on the gate of a loose box, resting his arms on the top rail. He looked at her and winked at Helen. Roxanna sighed and came closer, her lips set in what she hoped was a displeased expression. Lord Winn moved over obligingly and she stood next to him, too angry to look in his direction. Helen clambered between the rails and put her arms around the little animal's neck.

"Oh, Mama, he's the most beautiful horse I have ever seen!"

Roxanna stared straight ahead at the pony. "Lord Winn, I ought to call you out for this!"

"You and who else, madam!" he said, his voice full of amusement. "I told you I always pay my gambling debts."

"My lord!"

"Are you swearing or addressing me?" he asked, and then laughed, turned around when she gasped, and leaned against the railing with his hands in his pockets. "Name your second, Mrs. Drew. I would recommend Felicity. Is it swords or pistols at twenty paces?" He peered at her face. "You know, the way your face is so nicely arranged, it's hard to tell if you're truly angry at me."

"I am angry, my lord," she assured him.

He leaned closer and nudged her shoulder. "What could I do? There was this little pony at Retling Beck, and the stable keep there is half blind and past ready to retire from my services. I couldn't leave him there. And what better hands could he be in than your daughter's?"

"You know this won't do!"

He took her by both shoulders, his touch gentle but firm. "Why not? I have an empty stable here, and someone who will take excellent care of my property." He peered closely at her. "What is it, Mrs. Drew? Do you not relish being under obligation to a man who is not a relative?"

"It is rather improper, my lord," she said. "Surely you must see that?"

He released her, and resumed his casual position against the gate again. "Perhaps you would like it better if I gave the pony to your brother-in-law Lord Whitcomb, then he could bring it over here, or you could keep it in his stables. Would that be better?"

He spoke casually enough, and she knew that he was sincere, with no idea what his words meant to her. Still, she could not repress a shudder. She felt nauseated then, and desperate to leave the stable before she disgraced herself yet again before this well-intentioned man.

"No, that would be much worse," she managed. "I would far rather be under obligation to you. Excuse me, my lord."

Her anguish must have showed in her voice, because as she started from the stable, he turned quickly to look at her, and grabbed for her arm.

"Hold on, Mrs. Drew!" he called after her, but she ignored him and walked faster, her hand to her mouth, her whole aim in life at that moment centered on getting out of the stable before she threw up.

She made it, but barely, hanging her head over some bushes around the corner of the building. Luckily, her stomach was nearly empty, so she was wiping her mouth with the edge of her apron when Lord Winn caught up with her. He stood there in open-mouthed surprise as she calmly patted the sweat from her forehead and turned to face him.

"My lord, I do not wish to discuss my brother-in-law with you or anyone else. And yes, Helen may keep the pony on your property. Excuse me." Please don't stop me, she thought as she looked at him.

To her chagrin, he took her by the arm and gazed into her eyes. "Mrs. Drew, what is the matter?" he asked, his voice firm.

She glanced away, wishing that her voice did not sound so puny. "It is not something I am prepared to discuss with you, my lord." She tried to pull away, but he tightened his grip. She looked into his eyes again, remembering her dreadful interview with Lord Whitcomb, and his hand on her arm. "Oh, stop!" she pleaded.

He released her arm immediately, his face flushed. "Mrs. Drew, if I am not mistaken, there is something quite wrong here. I wish I knew what it was."

She shook her head. "Lord Winn, this is a matter between me and Lord Whitcomb. I cannot see how it can possibly concern you, especially since you will be leaving any day now. Please let it go at that."

He wanted to say more, she knew he did, but Helen came out of the stable then, and he stepped back.

"Mama, you must name the pony," Helen insisted, tugging her toward the stable.

Roxanna glanced around at Lord Winn, who stood regarding her, a frown on his face and his hands thrust in his pockets again. "It seems I am needed elsewhere, sir," she said, her voice calm again.

"What do you think, Mama?" Helen asked as they stood in front of the loose box again.

Roxanna gathered up her skirts and climbed up a rail for a better look. To her surprise, Lord Winn picked her up and set her on the top railing. She rested her hand on his shoulder to steady herself, and tried to look stern. He gazed back at her, his eyes innocent.

"You are a difficult person to remain angry with, my lord," she murmured.

"Oh, well, you need only ask my former wife about that," he said mildly.

She blushed. "And you are exasperating." She looked down at the pony. "A name, Helen? Let me think."

Lord Winn moved slightly, and rested his arms on the railing again as she took her hand from his shoulder. "I am sorry, Helen, but you will have to wait in line. I believe your mother had promised to name my poor nameless beast," he explained. "I have a prior claim. Isn't that right, Mrs. Drew?"

He smiled up at her, and she nodded. "Yes, I did," she agreed, and shifted herself to regard the big hunter in the other loose box. She started to smile. "Of course! Why didn't I think of it sooner?" She looked down at Lord Winn, "You should call him Ney, my lord."

Helen frowned and shook her head in disappointment. "Oh, Mama! That will never do. You cannot name a horse Neigh."

But Lord Winn was chuckling to himself. "N-E-Y, madam?"

"Exactly. I assume you have a working knowledge of that foxy Frenchman, and after all, this is a hunter."

"Happen I did know Ney reet well," he said, looking at her then but not seeing her. "He was a worthy opponent the length and breadth of Spain, and I must admit to a mild regret when Louis had him executed. Well, only a mild regret. Ney, it is, Mrs. Drew. It is an excellent name for an old Peninsula man's horse." He reached out and touched Helen's head. "You're right, my dear. Your mama has a facility for this."

Roxanna held out her arms to Lord Winn. "And now, please help me down, my lord. If Felicity wakes up and finds me gone, I know she will rush upstairs to try to bounce on one of your beds. It is a temptation no four-year-old can resist."

He helped her down. "Or forty-year-olds, madam. That almost sounds fun."

"You are hopeless, my lord," she murmured as she straightened her dress, then laughed in embarrassment. "That was rude of me. Excuse it, please."

Why do I seem to say and do the most stupid things around Lord Winn? she asked herself as she hurried into the manor again. Thank goodness he is not staying here beyond a few more days, or I would make a complete cake of myself. As it is, I have cried all over his bare chest, and thrown up in his bushes, and now I call him names. Oh, dear. She stopped outside the linen room door and leaned her forehead against the cool wood for a moment. I could almost tell him about Lord Whitcomb.

Felicity still slumbered on the pile of rejected sheets, her red mittens a splash of color against the yellowing fabric. Roxanna sat down, her eyes soft as she regarded her younger daughter. There had been enough yarn left to make a little cap. Another evening would see it finished, and then Lissy would have something else she could not bear to take off. She thought about Lord Winn, wondering how it was that someone so adamantly opposed to children could be so good with them at the same time. Drown them at birth, indeed, she thought. You could no more do that than fly to Madagascar, my lord. Or could you?

She gave herself a little shake. Roxanna Drew, you know next to nothing about Lord Winn, beyond the fact that he is your landlord, and kind to your daughters. And he was the center of a huge divorce scandal. He is not received in his former social circle, or

so Mrs. Howell says. She thought about her husband, wondering
how he would treat someone with Lord Winn's reputation. Anthony was kind to everyone, but even he had his limits. "And so
should I," she said as she kissed Felicity and woke her up.

The snow was gone by morning, but a bone-chilling cold settled in. It was almost a relief to hurry to the much warmer manor
house to complete the inventory with Mrs. Howell. Even Meggie
Watson came along this time. Lord Winn and Tibbie were already
out riding, and Helen quickly disappeared into the stable, after assuring her mother that she would keep her coat well-buttoned, and
her mittens and cap on. With a determined expression, Meggie
headed for the library to begin her inventory. Lissy followed Mrs.
Howell into the breakfast room to see what Lord Winn had left
behind, and Roxanna continued her inventory with the second-
story bedrooms, writing down the contents of each room.

There were six bedrooms, so she went quickly to work. She
would have worked faster, but each room presented the temptation to stand gazing out the south-facing windows, looking down
from their situation on Sutton Bank to the Great Plain of York. It
stretched away, resting now in winter's early grasp, but fertile and
only waiting for spring and the bite of the plow in the soil. There
would be lambs dotting the landscape, too, and calves, and long-
legged colts that Helen would exclaim over, and follow with her
eyes as they trotted, stiff and clumsy, along the fences. Both of
her babies had been born in the spring. I must be quite in tune
with the land, she thought as she sat in the window seat, put aside
her paper and pencil, and rested her chin on her gathered-up
knees.

"I do that, too, Mrs. Drew. Lovely view, isn't it? Moreland is
more charming than I remembered."

Startled, she looked around in surprise and reached for the inventory pad again.

"No, no. Don't let me disturb you," Lord Winn said as he sat
on the edge of the bed. He still wore his riding coat, but he held
his muddy boots in his hand.

"Well, I am hardly discharging the duty Mrs. Howell requested
today," she said, even as she turned her gaze outside the window
again. "Do you know, sir, this view reminds me that there is not a
season in Yorkshire that is not beautiful."

"Even winter?"

She nodded, and looked at him, still resting her cheek on her
knees. "I like the holly on the snow, and the sky so blue it looks

as though it will crack with the cold. Stars seem larger in the winter, or have you noticed, my lord?"

"You're talking to someone who campaigned outdoors through too many winters," he said. "Now I prefer a fire, and a good book, and a comfortable chair a bit sprung in the seat, like me. Ah, yes, Mrs. Drew, I was waiting for that smile! You would have to show me what was so enchanting about a tromp through the snowy woods."

She stood up and reclaimed the pad and pencil again. "All you require for that are two little girls who need to wear off endless energy before they can sleep."

"Or you, madam?" he asked. "I seem to notice a lamp in your window rather late at night."

"Perhaps," she replied, suddenly shy. "Excuse me, my lord."

"Don't bother with the next room, Mrs. Drew. It's mine, and I am not particularly tidy."

"Very well, my lord."

He stood up, still tall in his stockinged feet. "Would you call me Winn?"

"That's rather too familiar, my lord,"she murmured, and left the room.

He followed her into the hall. "What's your first name, or may I be so bold?" he asked.

"It is Roxanna, and no, you may not be so bold," she replied, trying to suppress a smile. Here I am in my oldest dress, with an apron wrapped practically around me twice, my hair probably dusty, and you are trying to flirt. How absurd.

"Anyone ever call you Roxie?"

She shuddered. "Only my brothers! Don't remind me."

He laughed."Very well, Mrs. Drew." He opened the door to his room and tossed in his muddy boots. "If I dare not call you Roxie—"

"You dare not," she interrupted.

" . . . and you intend to 'my lord' me to death—"

"I do," she interrupted again. "My lord."

"You are a bit of a trial, Mrs. Drew," he said. "Look now, I have completely lost my train of thought."

"I have not lost mine, sir," she said as she opened the door to a bedroom across the hall.

He followed her into the bedroom, and she laughed out loud. "Sir, leave me to my duties! You are so persistent!"

"Yes, rather like Felicity," he said. "I remember what it is, Mrs. Drew. Could I ask Helen to ride with me this afternoon? I am going into the village to see my solicitor, and it would be a good distance for her pony."

"Your pony," she reminded him.

He rolled his eyes at her. "You know, your perpetually pleasant expression is exasperating! Just when I think you will return an unexceptionable comment, you surprise me. Let us call it a loan, madam!"

She smiled again and looked around the room. "Let me see, a bed, a bureau, a clothes press." She wrote them down. "Yes, my lord, Helen may accompany you. A wing-back armchair, a foot-stool . . . Very well, sir, a loan."

He was gone then, whistling down the hall. What an odd man, she thought as she continued the inventory. After a quick lunch in the kitchen, Meggie took Felicity home for a nap, and Helen left for the village, riding alongside Lord Winn's tall hunter. Roxanna watched them, proud of the way her daughter sat so erect in the saddle. Lord Winn had found a sidesaddle somewhere in the stable loft, Tibbie had polished it, and Helen sat it like the lady she was. "I wish you could see her, Anthony," she said as she watched from an upstairs window.

In the final bedroom, she made the mistake of sitting down on the bed to rest a moment. Before she knew it, she was lying down. Lord Winn is right, she thought as she closed her eyes. I do stay up too late each night. I wonder if it will ever be easy to sleep without Anthony there?

When she woke, the room was in shadow. She got up quickly, finished her inventory, and hurried down the stairs. Mrs. Howell waited for her at the bottom, her hands on Helen's shoulders.

"We were about to send out a search party for you," the house-keeper said. "Helen's been eating macaroons this past hour with Lord Winn." She tittered behind her hand. "Lord Winn was of the opinion that you were asleep on one of the beds. I told him that was ridiculous."

"Oh! Yes, ridiculous," she agreed, holding out her hand to her daughter. "Come, my dear. If we delay much longer, Felicity will be tapping her foot by the front door and reminding us that she is starved."

They hurried along, almost gasping with the cold. "How was your ride, Helen?" Roxanna asked.

"Oh, Mama! It was such fun!" Helen exclaimed, and Roxanna blessed Lord Winn for the enthusiasm in her voice. "Because I was so good in the solicitor's office, Lord Winn took me to the Hare and Hound for trifle and ladyfingers."

"And now macaroons here?" Roxanna teased. "We'll have to roll you into the house, if you keep up such dissipation!"

"Lord Winn ate more than I did, especially the trifle," Helen confided. "He says his French chef at Winnfield hasn't a clue about 'reet good Yorkshire food with bark on it.' "

Roxanna widened her eyes. "A French chef? Oh, my! Somehow, I don't think that was his idea."

Helen nodded, her eyes merry, then she stopped. "Oh, but, Mama, he said he is leaving tomorrow."

Roxanna digested that news as they walked along in silence. "I will miss him," she said finally. Yes, I will, she thought. It had been a pleasant diversion to have someone as interesting as Lord Winn tumble into their limited society.

"Mama, do you think I could write him?" Helen asked as they scraped the mud off their shoes on the edge of the back porch.

Roxanna considered the question. "If you were older, I would say it was too forward. Since you are six, perhaps it will be unexceptionable, my dear."

"Mama, you could write him, too, and I could add a letter to yours."

Roxanna shook her head, amused at her daughter's enthusiasm. "Now that would *not* be proper! Besides, my dear, what could I ever have to say that would interest a marquess?"

She opened the door, then stepped back outside in surprise, wondering for the briefest moment if she had stumbled onto the wrong property. The dower house was warm. She and Helen stared at each other, and she opened the door cautiously this time.

It was still warm, deliciously so. They hurried inside to keep the cold out, and Felicity looked up from her contemplation of the silverware destined for the dinner table. Meggie Watson smiled at her from the fireplace, where she was lifting off the kettle of mutton stew.

"Meggie, what is this?" she asked as she removed her cloak and bonnet.

Meggie ladled the soup into bowls and managed a rare joke. "I believe it is called heat, miss! I was just sitting here this afternoon, when a coal wagon drove up. The man dumped a load of coal in the shed without so much as a by-your-leave."

"It must be a mistake," Roxanna said, even as she stood before the massive fireplace that covered one end of the kitchen and turned around, reveling in the warmth. "I have no hope of paying for this. Do you think he meant to deliver it to Moreland?"

"I asked him, Mrs. Drew," Meggie said. "He wouldn't say. You'd have thought he was deaf. Or addled."

"It cannot be correct," Roxanna insisted.

"I am sure you are right." Meggie looked her mistress in the eye and set her lips in a firm line for a brief moment. "But all the same, I brought in enough to warm this house tonight. You can take it up with Lord Winn in the morning."

"I will take it up with him tonight!" Roxanna said, already dreading the interview. "He is leaving tomorrow morning."

I wish I were not one to put things off, Roxanna Drew told herself two hours later after she tucked her daughters in their warm bedroom, told them a story about a prince rescuing two little girls in distress, and then knelt on the floor for their prayers without freezing her knees. She knew she should have gone over much sooner, but she couldn't bring herself to leave the warmth of the dower house. I could even do my mending tonight, she marveled. My fingers are still nimble.

Instead, she pulled on her cloak again and girded her loins to face a rather different lion. He will probably tell me some cock-and-bull story and insist that I keep all that lovely coal, she thought as she hurried along, her head down against the wind that grabbed her about the neck and shook her. This much solicitude borders on impertinence, and so I will tell him.

Mrs. Howell answered her timid knock. "Mrs. Drew, nothing is wrong is it?" she asked, holding the door open wide.

Roxanna came inside gratefully and laid her cloak on the hall table. "No, not really. Well, yes, actually. I need to speak to Lord Winn. He hasn't gone to bed yet, has he?"

Mrs. Howell chuckled. "Oh, my, no! He stays awake till all hours, prowling about the house, standing by the window, or just looking into the flames." She tilted her head toward the sitting room. "And now since that pianoforte is tuned, he has a new toy."

Roxanna smiled in spite of herself and listened to the sound of Mozart rippling through the closed door. "He's rather good, isn't he?" she asked.

Mrs. Howell walked with her down the hall. "As to that, I wouldn't know." She took Roxanna's arm and leaned closer. "Sometimes he even sings." The two of them chuckled together.

Mrs. Howell knocked on the door.

"Come in, please," Lord Winn said.

Roxanna took a deep breath and raised her chin higher. Onward, Roxie, she told herself.

He was standing by the piano, his pocket watch out, when she came through the door and Mrs. Howell closed it behind her. He regarded it a moment, then snapped it shut.

"Felicity should be here, my dear Mrs. Drew. I think I would have lost another wager."

"Oh, now, see here, sir . . ." she began, coming toward him, fire in her eyes.

He sat down at the piano again, straddling the piano bench this time. "You see, I thought you would come right away to scold me. But look, you have waited at least three hours." He put on his spectacles. "Pull up that stool, Mrs. Drew. You can turn the pages while I play. My Mozart is rusty and I need the music."

She sighed in exasperation, and he looked at her over the top of his reading glasses. "You don't read music?"

"Of course I do!" she said. "My lord—"

"There you go again, swearing. I am distressed at such laxity in a vicar's widow," he said smoothly as he turned toward the piano.

"I would like to thump you! No wonder you can't stay married!" she burst out, then gasped at her impudence.

Lord Winn leaned forward and rested his forehead on the piano, laughing. He laughed until he had to clutch his side. "Oh, Mrs. Drew, that hurts my Waterloo souvenir!" he managed finally. "And don't frown at me like that, or blush. Your face just won't let you look serious."

"Oh, you! What I said was dreadful," she admitted, sitting on the stool beside the piano. "I don't know why that came out."

"You were upset with me for dumping coal all over the yard and warming up that glacier," he said calmly. "And I *am* exasperating." He began to play an allegro, and her eyes went automatically to the music as he played. "Watch closely now. You need to turn . . . ah, very good. You'll do, Mrs. Drew."

She stared at the notes before her, wondering what to say. This will never work, she thought as she turned another page. "I cannot accept that coal, my lord."

"Hush, Mrs. Drew. I have to concentrate on the allegro passage. You can scold me during the andante. Heap coals on my head during the largo, eh?"

She couldn't help herself. She snatched up the pages he was playing, rolled them into a tube, and struck him over the head with them. He laughed as he played doggedly on from memory, and she hit him again, then collapsed with the giggles on the stool. "You would try a saint!" she protested as she laughed and hit him one more time for good measure.

He rescued the music while she laughed, and continued playing, a grin on his face and his eyes on the music. "I do like a hearty laugh, Mrs. Drew. When you are through, we can get down to the business at hand."

She wiped her eyes on her sleeve finally. "Oh, forgive me! I haven't laughed like that since . . . Well, it's been a long time. And I still can't take that coal. Will you pay attention to me, my lord?"

He stopped playing, and straddled the bench again, looking into her eyes until she wanted him to start playing instead. "Mrs. Drew, there is a clause in your contract. As your landlord, I am required to provide coal."

"That is a hum, and you know it, my lord," she said quietly.

He took her hand. "Dear lady, I have spent the last two miserable months—or is it three now?—traveling from estate to estate, staring at deeds and titles and clauses until I am practically blind with it, and if I tell you that the Moreland holding has a clause about coal, you can bank on it that I am right. Cross my heart and hope to die."

"You had better show me the deed," she said, pulling her hand away.

He put his face close to hers. "It is in Latin, you exasperating female!"

She did not back away. "Next you will tell me you found it in your personal copy of William the Conqueror's Domesday Book!"

His eyes brightened and he took off his spectacles. "How did you know? Have you been in my library?"

She leaped to her feet, resisted the urge to thump him again, and took a turn about the room. "Very well, sir, we will accept your coal. Arguing with you is like trying to stop water flowing."

He turned back to the piano and played a wonderful minor chord. "Now you understand! Excellent, Mrs. Drew. There is hope for you yet. Pull up that stool. Do you know Mozart's Piano Duet in C sharp minor?"

She stood looking down at him. I could go home right now, she thought. I probably should. But I am tired of worrying and contriving. Very well, sir, let us play a duet. She sat down and pulled the stool closer while he spread out the parts.

"Just the andante, please, my lord," she said, her back straight, her hands poised over the keys. "I need to get home to my girls."

"Very well, madam," he agreed, his voice gentle. "I know you do. Are you ready?"

"Not too fast," she cautioned. "I have not done this in a while."

"I will take my time," he said, and smiled at the music. "And then when we are done, we will discuss your brother-in-law, who paid me a visit tonight. He wants to buy this place from me."

Chapter 8

Her hands faltered on the keys. He reached over and touched her wrist lightly, then continued the melody.

"Keep playing, madam," he said, his eyes on the music. "The first rule of dealing with such men is not to show any fear."

"But I am afraid," she said. "I am terrified."

"You must not show it. I suspect a deep game here, but we're going to finish this andante first. Excellent, Mrs. Drew. You're a steady one."

The andante concluded. She put her hands in her lap, and continued to stare at the music. Lord Winn closed the piano and put away the music in silence. He shifted to face her, but she could not bring herself to look at him.

"Do I go first, or you?" he asked quietly.

"I wish you would, my lord," she replied. "I want to know what happened tonight before I say anything." You are sitting too close to me, she thought, and felt that same panic that had nearly overwhelmed her during that quelling interview with her brother-in-law.

To her relief, he got up and stood before the fireplace. "I ran into Lord Whitcomb in the village this afternoon. He was surprised to see Helen with me. By the way, Helen was delighted to see him."

Roxanna looked up for the first time. "I am sure she was. He has always been kind to her, and to Felicity."

"And to you, Mrs. Drew?"

She nodded, unable to speak.

"He asked if he could visit tonight on a matter of business." Lord Winn poured himself a glass of port from the table by the fireplace and offered her one. She shook her head. "He wasted not a minute in telling me that he wanted to buy Moreland. Said he would pay any price."

Roxanna shivered, and met Lord Winn's eyes. "Come closer to the fire, my dear," he urged. "Or is it cold that you are feeling?"

She shook her head and remained where she was.

"I asked him why he was so eager to have Moreland. Told him I would gladly sell him Retling Beck, but he wasn't interested in that property."

He came closer and leaned against the piano. "Mrs. Drew, he said he wanted Moreland so he could keep a better eye on you. It seems he made a perfectly kind offer to move you into Whitcomb Park, but you would have none of it." He sat down again by her on the piano bench. "He wonders if you possess all your faculties."

She sat absolutely still as her insides churned. She could feel the color draining from her face. The room seemed too hot and too cold by turns and she closed her eyes. In another moment, Lord Winn had raised his glass of port to her lips. She drank, and felt her color return. He set it beside her on the piano.

"You need this more than I do, Mrs. Drew," he said. He touched her cheek, and withdrew his hand quickly when she flinched and pulled back from him.

"I think I am beginning to understand what is going on," he commented. "But you need to talk about it, my dear."

Roxanna looked into his eyes again. Can I trust this man, she asked herself, or is he just another Lord Whitcomb? God knows his reputation is much worse than my brother-in-law's. To everyone in the North Riding, Marshall Drew is an excellent landlord, husband, parishioner, and friend. On the other hand, Lord Winn is a wild card, a man steeped in scandal, someone mysterious from farther south. What do I really know of him?

He returned her stare without wavering. "Mrs. Drew, you already trusted me enough this afternoon to take your daughter riding," he said. "I strongly suspect that your daughters mean more to you than your life."

She nodded. "They *are* my life now. Very well, sir, I have to trust you, don't I?"

"I believe you do."

She took a deep breath and let it out slowly. "Lord Whitcomb wants to get me into his bed." She shivered again. "That's bald, isn't it?"

He nodded. "Bald, but it covers the subject," he said as he got up and took a light blanket off the sofa, which he wrapped around her shoulders. She clutched at the fabric until her knuckles were white, but he made no comment.

"His own wife is a disappointment to him, or so he told me. He thinks I should . . . accommodate him, in exchange for a pleasant life at Whitcomb Park. My daughters would have every advantage." She turned away because she could not bear to look at him. "And if . . . if I had a child, we could pretend it was his wife's. It seems she cannot have children, and I am obviously capable of this."

She jumped up then and stalked to the fireplace to grab hold of the mantelpiece and stare into the flames. " 'We will keep you in the family,' he told me, as though I were a plaything, a man's bauble! Oh, God, what could I do but leave?" The words were torn from her and she shivered again. "He controls my parish stipend as Anthony's relict. He cannot eliminate it, but he can reduce it, and probably will, out of spite. I thought if I could rent the dower house, I might be able to make ends meet, no matter how much he shaved from my allowance."

"Have you no male relatives to apply to for protection?"

She shook her head. "My parents are dead these five years, and my brothers are both officers in the East India Company, situated in Bombay. I have no one in England to turn to, Lord Winn, and no one would believe me if I told them what Marshall was planning.

"Probably not. On the face of it, he seems as upstanding as your late husband must truly have been."

She walked to the piano to stand in front of him. "Do you believe me?" she asked, her voice barely audible to her own ears.

"I do, most emphatically," he replied, his voice as quiet as hers, but filled with a conviction that made her sigh with relief.

"I'm so cold," she said suddenly. "I cannot seem to stop shivering." She tried to smile. "Since you have arrived, I have done nothing but make a cake of myself. What you must think!"

"I think you are quite a valiant lady, but far out of your depth, Mrs. D.," he said as he tugged the blanket tighter around her shoulders.

She questioned him with her eyes. "What do you mean? What can he do beyond what he has already done, if you will not sell him Moreland?"

"Rest on that, at least, Mrs. Drew. I will not sell him Moreland. And so I told him."

"Was he angry?"

Lord Winn smiled. "Oh, a little. Less than you would suspect. I think he must have another plan, but I do not know what it is. I cannot think he has power to harm you here, and I've never been one to borrow trouble from tomorrow."

Roxanna nodded. "I remember a sermon once along the lines of 'sufficient unto the day is the evil thereof.' "

"Matthew 6:34," he said absently, then noticed her wide-eyed gaze. "Yes, I read the Bible, Mrs. Drew! I've even been known to go to church! Not recently, however," he added. "I don't think the Lord is too pleased with me lately."

She sipped the port, then handed it back to him. "Perhaps you are too hard on yourself, Lord Winn."

"Perhaps," he agreed. "At any rate, you needn't worry about your situation here."

"I feel safe enough, as long as you do not sell Moreland." She frowned. "But . . . but I cannot dictate the terms, my lord. This is your property, and if you choose to sell it, then we will leave. It's as simple as that."

"My dear, seldom is anything simple."

She did not know what he meant. He wasn't looking at her, but beyond her and out the window. Somewhere a clock chimed. She counted the chimes in the quiet room, and got to her feet.

"Oh, it is so late! I am sorry to have burdened you with my problems, Lord Winn, but then, you did ask," she said as she held out her hand to him. "I certainly wish you a happy journey tomorrow. Are you returning to your principal seat?"

He nodded, and shook her hand. "I think so. I have to strategize where to spend Christmas this year. It must be a place where I will not get into any trouble, and my sisters will not try to manage me."

"Good luck! My girls will miss you."

He nodded. "Tell Felicity I said to take off those mittens occasionally, and assure Helen that I will answer any and all letters."

"I hope she will not plague you," Roxanna said.

"I don't she how she could," he said, then looked into her laughing eyes. "And you, Mrs. Drew, will you miss me?"

She considered his question, and chose to answer in the spirit of its asking. "Why yes, I will," she replied promptly. "I've laughed with you, cried on you, thrown up in your bushes, and thrashed you with your own music score." He started to laugh, and she held up her hand. "It is nice to know that I can feel something again, my lord, even if it is merely rage and nausea!"

He was still laughing when she hurried down the hall, pulled on her cloak, and opened the back door. She waved her hand at him. "I enjoyed the duet, my lord," she called. He bowed to her and she thought him charming.

It was even colder than when she left the dower house, but Roxanna walked slowly home. Poor Lord Winn. You will wish you had never set eyes on Moreland, she thought as she picked her way carefully through the hardening ground. Widow Drew and her daughters are rather a lot of trouble for ten pounds a year.

She let herself in the front door, and stood for a moment in the empty sitting room. I will tackle this room right away, she thought. I can have it done and furnished with a sofa and chairs from Moreland by Christmas, if I can beg those items from Tibbie. Oh, dear, Christmas. I fear it will be sparse this year.

It was easier than usual to sleep, she discovered. Meggie had thoughtfully provided a warming pan between the sheets, and the grate was furnished with enough coal to keep the chill away. She snuggled into the blankets, thankful to be warm for a change. As sleep came closer, she stretched out from habit to put her feet on Anthony's legs, and drew back when no one was there. "Oh, drat!" she said out loud. "When will I stop doing that?"

Lord Winn stood by the bookroom window and watched until Mrs. Drew was safely inside the dower house. He locked the door and sauntered back to the sitting room, where he poured another glass of port and sat down at the piano again. He held the wine up to the light.

"Here's to you, Lord Whitcomb," he said. "I can empathize completely with your desire to slide Mrs. Drew between your sheets." He drank it down, and poured another drink. "And here's to you, Mrs. Drew. Truth to tell, Roxie dear, I'd like to see you between mine."

He drank the second toast more slowly, playing one-handed through the andante of the duet, wondering why he had been chosen, out of all the people on earth, to be such a fool. "I am an ass, Roxie Drew," he said softly as he concluded the andante, then went back and played her part. "You would no more consider this divorced man as prospective husband material than walk naked through York."

Restless, he went to the fireplace and stared into the mirror over the mantelpiece. Discounting all that, Winn, if she possibly could, you are nearly forty, with graying hair, catty green eyes, and a sharp tongue. A bit of a misanthrope. Mrs. Drew would want children, and you cannot abide the idea of ushering little ones into a miserable world of greed and squabbling relatives. It's a good thing you told yourself that you don't wish to marry ever again, because it's not going to happen with Mrs. Drew, be you ever so in love.

He winced and looked away from the mirror as he remembered the times he had told Cynthia he loved her. Well, you did love her, Winn, he reminded himself. He poured another drink, sloshed the wine onto the carpet, and wondered why the decanter looked farther away from his arm than before. "And here's to you, Cynthia," he said, and drank steadily. The thought of you kept me alive through many a battle, when I wanted to run screaming from the field, he considered. I owe you that.

He picked up the decanter and drank from it. Damn good thing I didn't know what you were doing in our bed while I was thinking noble thoughts in Spain, though, he told himself. Damn good thing. He sat down on the floor by the fireplace. "You are drunk, Lord Winn," he observed, and reached for another bottle on the table. It was too far away, so he abandoned the idea, contenting himself with the last drops from the decanter.

His mind was clear enough. He lay down on the carpet in front of the fireplace, enjoying the warmth on his back, and stared up at the crumbling plaster swirls in the ceiling overhead. Roxie Drew, I was a dead man from the moment you opened your door to me at midnight. I should have just put a gun to my head and blown out my brains on your doorstep. I could look at you, listen to you, watch you for the rest of my life and never get bored. I wonder what you look like when you sleep. When you're angry. When you make love. I would like to know.

Lord Winn put his hands behind his head. This will never do, he thought. A man can go crazy thinking things like that. I can understand Lord Whitcomb's predicament. "Poor sod," he murmured. "You've had to admire her for years and not touch. Did you hold her in your arms to comfort her when Anthony died? How did you manage that, Lord Whitcomb?"

His eyes started to close. Well, at least you are safe from that pile of dirty laundry, Mrs. Drew. I'll never sell Moreland. And since I'm leaving tomorrow, you're safe from another ugly customer.

When he woke, the coals glowed dull red in the grate and the candles had burned down beyond the wicks into waxy puddles. He sat up and rubbed his head, wondering what campfire he had nodded off beside, what battlefield he rested on. In another moment, he recognized his surroundings. He stood up, stretched, and found an unlit candle, which he lighted from the coals.

The hall was dark. Mrs. Howell had long ago gone to bed below stairs. He raised the candle to look around the hall. "A bit shabby, my lord," he told himself. "Could use some refurbishing, rather like you."

He mounted the stairs slowly and walked down the upper hall to his room. "Good night all," he called to the empty rooms. "Sleep well, everyone."

Mrs. Howell woke him in the morning with a can of hot water, coal for the grate, and a reminder that breakfast was ready, and wasn't he leaving? He dragged himself onto his elbow, uncomfortable in his clothes, and wishing he had possessed enough dexterity last night to have at least unbuttoned his pants. Mrs. Howell folded her arms and regarded him with the proprietary disfavor that was the particular gift of female servants old enough to be his mother.

"I know. I know. I am disgusting," he growled. "I'll be down in a minute, Mrs. Howell."

"Take your time, my lord," she muttered as she left the room. "You can only get better."

He took his time, shaving carefully, dressing with more care than usual, and wishing he had time for a haircut. That could wait for Winnfield, he thought, where his valet languished. He combed his hair, glad at least that while it was graying, it was not thinning. Chickering could scold him for being such a shaggy beast, and probably would. Then Amabel would descend again, full of plans for Christmas and her palm up for money. He winced at the thought and put his hands to his head, pressing hard against his temples.

He pulled on his boots, packed his saddlebags, and took a last look around the room. Mrs. Howell could put the books back in the library, he thought, then he looked at the one on top. He pulled out the handkerchief he had been using for a bookmark and sniffed it. Mrs. Drew had wrapped his spectacles in the handkerchief, and he had been meaning to return it. The lavender was gone now, but he tucked the dainty square out of sight in his pocket.

Mrs. Howell waited for him outside the breakfast room. "You have a visitor, my lord," she whispered.

He hauled out his watch. "At seven o'clock in the morning

someone has come calling?" He groaned, pocketed his watch, and went into the room after squaring his shoulders.

He looked around and could not see anyone. "Hello?" he called. "Anyone here?"

Felicity peered out from one of the wing chairs. She grinned at him, and he smiled back, unable to resist her any more than he could resist her mother.

"I thought you would never come down," she scolded, and took a napkin from the table. "I am starving."

He laughed out loud and looked down on her over the back of the chair. She tipped her head up to return his stare. He rested his arms along the back of the chair and admired her red cap, noting that she had removed her mittens at least. Red was definitely Felicity's color. Probably her mother's color, too. He took her plate.

"What will you have, my dear?" he asked, peering at the sideboard. "I don't see any porridge."

"That's all right," she said generously. "I can have that at home. I would like some bacon and a cinnamon bun most especially."

"Very well," he said as he grinned and selected her choices, adding a baked egg. "You'll eat an egg, too."

He set the plate before her and filled his own, marveling how rapidly his headache had disappeared. When he sat down, she took his hand for the blessing, and his cup nearly ran over.

They ate in silence. When Felicity finished her bacon and bun, she wiped her hands carefully on her napkin and looked at him with those eyes that made his heart crack a little. "Aren't you going to wager?" she asked.

He let out another shout of laughter and she grinned at him. "Do you know that you are a certified rascal?" he asked.

"Mama says I am a scamp."

"She's right," he agreed. "No, I am not going to wager. If I do, and lose, your mama will ring such a peal over my head."

"She would never!" Felicity said, shocked, her eyes wide.

"Trust me on this one, Lissy," he said. "She would." He leaned back in his chair and looked at his breakfast guest, who tackled the egg last. "You know, if you had eaten the egg first, then it would be out of the way, and you could have saved the best for last."

She nodded. "Mama puts things off, too."

"Oh?" he asked, hoping for more information about Roxie Drew from such an unimpeachable source.

"She says bad news always waits. So do eggs." She finished the egg and looked at him expectantly. "And I am depending on you to give me another cinnamon bun!"

He laughed again, then heard rapid footsteps coming down the hall. "Lissy, I think your tenure in my breakfast room is about to end."

"I had hoped she would wait until I had another cinnamon bun," Felicity commented, her disappointment evident.

He leaped up and put another one on her plate and then opened the door as Mrs. Drew had raised her hand to knock on it. "Mrs. Drew, what a delightful surprise, and so early!" he commented as she just stood there, looking at her daughter.

She was dressed, but her hair was still down around her shoulders, wavy and brown. Although his brush with marriage had been brief, he knew better than to make any remarks upon her appearance. She would smite me if I told her how beautiful she looked with her hair that way, he thought as he ushered her in and pulled back a chair for her to sit in. Or at least, Cynthia would have. Of course, Cynthia never got up before eleven o'clock, so what do I know?

"Lord Winn, I hope you have not been making any bets," she said as she glared at her daughter. "Felicity, you are enough to try a saint!"

"Have a cinnamon bun, Mrs. Drew," he said, and brought the whole dish over to the table. "I told Lissy that her credit wasn't that good at present, so we had better not wager on your approximate arrival."

"Thank heavens for that!" she declared, and to his delight, sat down in the chair he pulled out. "I would love a cinnamon bun. Lissy tells me they are wonderful." She took a bite and rolled her eyes, to his infinite enjoyment. When she finished it, she turned to regard her daughter. "I thought I sent you upstairs to get Helen out of bed, and what do I find but that you have escaped!"

"I wanted to say good-bye to Lord Winn," Felicity said, then grinned. "And eat his cinnamon buns."

Mrs. Drew laughed. She ruffled her daughter's curly hair, then looked sideways at him. "Only think how much more peaceful your life will be soon with no little scamp to plague you!"

Dead dull is more like it, he thought, but returned her smile. "The funny thing is, I haven't minded it," he said, then put his napkin on the table and pushed back his chair. "But I do have to leave."

Mrs. Drew rose, too, and held out her hand for Felicity. "Then we will see you off from the front steps, sir. By all means, my dear, put on your mittens!"

"Then to earn your breakfast, you can carry my saddlebags out to the front," he told Felicity and pointed to them by the door.

He chuckled as she tugged the saddlebags down the hall, intent on her duty, then strolled along more slowly with Mrs. Drew, savoring every moment of her presence. "Mrs. Drew, I have instructed Tibbie to spend more of each day here at Moreland. I think Retling Beck will be sold within the month, and I prefer that he spend more time here."

"Why, sir?" she asked. "Are you worried about my brother-in-law?"

He took her by the arm, holding his breath that she would not bolt from such familiarity. To his relief, she did not. "Let us say, I am cautious, Mrs. Drew. If he tries anything, Tibbie can get me word."

She nodded and moved along slowly at his side. "Very well, my lord. I will be finishing the sitting room at the dower house now, and if there is anything you wish done here, I am at your disposal."

How I wish you were, he thought. I would take you upstairs and we wouldn't come down until spring. "Do remind Tibbie when the coal gets low," he said instead. "That clause in Latin covers coal until the warm weather returns."

She stopped and looked up at him. "Don't try me, Lord Winn!" she began. "Yes, I will let him know. And thank you."

Felicity had tugged the saddlebags out the front door, where his horse waited, saddled and bridled. He took them from her and fastened them onto Ney, who whinnied and stepped about at the prospect of removal from Moreland. "Slow down, lad," he cautioned. "We haven't left yet."

There was nothing to remain for. He had finished his business at Moreland. He could return to Winnfield and suffer any variety of plaguey attention from his relatives, now that he had visited this estate. Mrs. Drew stepped back inside and came out with his riding coat and hat. He shrugged into the coat and rescued his hat from Felicity, who was trying to put it on. "Fits me better than you, Lissy," he said as he clapped the low-crowned beaver hat on his head and moved toward his horse again.

"Wait one minute, Lord Winn!"

He turned around, his heart pounding, as Mrs. Drew came toward him.

"You can't leave here without buttoning your coat!" she scolded as she stood on tiptoe and started at the top. "Don't you have a muffler? Suppose you get a cold?"

Felicity looked up at him. "She does that to me, too," she commiserated.

His eyes lively, he allowed Mrs. Drew to button him into his coat. "There!" she said and stepped back. "Now you can leave." She held out her hand. "Thank you again for all you have done."

He took her hand, wanting to sweep her into his arms and kiss her until she begged for breath. "It's been a pleasure, Mrs. Drew."

Felicity leaned against his leg, so he knelt down and kissed her cheek. "Take care of your mother," he said. "And don't make any bets with strangers. Give Helen a kiss for me." And your mama, he told himself, as he swung into the saddle. I feel as though I am leaving my wife and child, he realized with surprise. We have discussed mundane affairs, she has made her last adjustments to my person. We will say good-bye, except that I am not a husband or a father, and there will be no return anytime soon. I am imagining what isn't there.

"Can I finish the cinnamon buns?" Felicity called to him.

He laughed and waved his hand, then put spurs into Ney's ribs.

Don't look back, you idiot, he told himself as he set his face south down the lane of bare-boned elm trees, ragged now with descending winter. He would write Clarice and tell her he was coming for Christmas, the Etheringhams be damned. He could stop back here in the spring on his way to Northumberland to straighten out that pernicious deed on High Point. By then, Mrs. Drew should be out of mourning, and probably the center of attention of several of the North Riding's gentlemen. If not, at least he should be sufficiently recovered from his brush with love to risk a brief stop here on his journey to nowhere.

He reached the end of the lane and stopped. It was safe to turn around, he thought. They would be inside by now, and he could savor one last look at an estate that was infinitely more dear to him than any other he owned. He turned around for a last look, and they stood there yet, mother and daughter, far away now, but watching him still. He could make out the red dashes that were Felicity's mittens.

As he looked, Mrs. Drew raised her hand again.

"That does it," he said. "Ney, I hate to disappoint you, but we're not going anywhere today."

He wheeled his horse about and started back up the lane. He wanted to gallop, but he forced Ney into a sedate walk, trying to give himself more time to think of a plausible reason that he would be returning. Mercifully it came to him as he traveled the lane again. He reined in his horse in front of Mrs. Drew and Felicity, who could hardly contain her excitement.

"Mrs. Drew, I am the veriest coward," he said as he dismounted. "I find that I cannot face my relatives for Christmas. I have a proposition for you. And don't look wary! How would you like to direct the refurbishing of Moreland? It's a lovely old home with much promise." Like me, he thought. Please, Mrs. Drew.

Chapter 9

"Mama, I think Lord Winn is not easy to argue with."
Roxanna looked up from the baseboard where she was peeling away the last of the sitting room wallpaper, tattered from years of neglect. She laughed in Helen's dirty face and touched another smudge from the end of her finger to her daughter's nose. "My dear, he is impossible!" She leaned closer, her eyes twinkling. "Perhaps he is deranged. Let us do what he says before someone hauls him away to an asylum and we do not have a sitting room."

"Who is deranged, madam?" asked Lord Winn from the entrance, where he was scraping his muddy boots. He draped his coat over the newel post and came into the room dressed in a faded shirt and patched breeches.

"You are, my lord," she replied as the wallpaper came away with an enormous rip and a showering of plaster that left Helen gasping. "Oh, dear, Helen, come out of there! Lord Winn, you do not need to do this before we start on Moreland. And surely you don't have to help with this work."

"Of course I do," he replied as he dusted the plaster off Helen's head and pointed her in the direction of the kitchen and Meggie's attention. "I think it's in that old Latin contract," he said and grinned at her.

"You will remind me," she murmured.

"Of course! Besides all that, Mrs. Drew, I hate to leave things unfinished, and I enjoy this kind of work. We'll have this room plastered and repapered by the end of the week, and then you can turn your attention to Moreland, where I will use you unmercifully until that grand old place is up to snuff." He grinned and ripped off the piece above her head that she could not reach. "At least now you'll have a sitting room to collapse in every night after I've wrung you out!"

"I suppose that is fair warning," she said, ducking from under his arm and turning her attention to another section of the wall. "I recommend that we tackle the sitting room and library at Moreland first. That way, should you choose to entertain during the holidays, at least they will be done."

"Oh, I won't be entertaining, Mrs. Drew," he said as he pried off the rest of the baseboard under the window and the glass shivered. "Don't you know I am not received anymore?"

"I had heard," she replied cautiously.

"Hasn't everyone?" he replied, his voice affable. "I am a beast and an ogre for creating a scandal where there did not need to be one." He stood the baseboard in the corner. "I should have been a gentleman about my former wife's numerous indiscretions, and I was not."

This is not a conversation for my ears, Roxanna thought as she pulled off the layers of wallpaper. Why is he telling me this? she thought, knowing that her face was rosy with embarrassment.

"And now I have embarrassed you," he said quietly, looking at her. "Perhaps I am still not a gentleman." He turned back to the wall to pry up another section of baseboard.

She watched him in silence for a moment, admiring how easy the work was for him, and remembering how hard it was for Anthony to even hold a spoon in his hand toward the end. I wonder, Lord Winn, do you work hard all day so you can fall asleep without dreaming at night? I know I do. But he was speaking to her, and she forced her mind back to the present.

"Your silence tells me that you agree," he said, putting his back into the pry bar.

"Oh, no! I wasn't thinking of that," she apologized, speaking louder to be heard over the creak of the wood.

He stopped and leaned against the wall, shaking his head at her. "Mrs. Drew, here I give you the perfect opportunity to learn all the unsavory details, and you are not interested! You are a disappointment to your sex!"

"Really, Lord Winn!" she protested.

"Yes, really! Or is it that you have already formed your opinion of my character?" he asked, his voice subdued now.

She looked at him then, considering his question seriously.

"Why, yes, I suppose I have." She paused, watching him, and the way his eyes never seemed to leave her face. "I think you are very kind, sir," she concluded, wondering what it was about her that always seemed to take his whole attention. I must have plaster in my hair, she thought. Is my bodice too low? Surely not.

"You should have seen me in the House of Lords, passing that legion of lovers in review by some very startled peers," he said. "No one thought me kind then."

"You were hurt, weren't you?" she asked. She looked into his green eyes, calmly observed the pain there, and plunged ahead. "I personally think infidelity is a dreadful circumstance. Perhaps that makes me old-fashioned, but—"

"That's two of us then, Mrs. Drew," he interrupted. "I took my marriage vows seriously. Too bad Lady Winn did not."

"You must be a rare member of the peerage, indeed," she said before she thought.

He laughed. "You have definitely formed an opinion of my class! And you would be right, in the main, Mrs. Drew." He ripped up the rest of the baseboard, then sat back on his heels. "But, no, I am not kind."

She smiled then, thinking of red and blue mittens, and a pony, and coal, and a leg of mutton. "Well, as to that, I suppose you are entitled to your opinion and I to mine."

They worked in silence then. In a few moments, Lord Winn was whistling under his breath, absorbed in his efforts. When she finished stripping the wallpaper, she paused to watch him a moment, admiring the play of muscles under his shirt as he strained at the baseboards, and remembering when Anthony would have thought nothing of such a task. She remembered their first year in the vicarage, and the times he carried her upstairs for an afternoon romp in their bedroom that would have scandalized his parishioners. She sighed, and then looked guiltily at the marquess, hoping he had not heard.

To her chagrin, he turned around with that searching regard that further discomfited her. "Mrs. Drew, if you have time to sigh like a schoolgirl and be so idle, give me a hand here."

She hurried forward and grasped the board he indicated. "You pull while I pry, and if the whole wall doesn't come down, I'll be through with this."

Roxanna did as she was told, gritting her teeth against the shriek of the wood. One more deft nudge of the pry bar and the whole baseboard came off in her hands. She sat down with a thump as the dust and plaster swirled around them.

"Are you all right?" he asked, kneeling beside her. "Nothing injured?"

"Just my dignity," she said and remained where she was on the floor. She gazed around the room in dismay. "Oh, my. You really think it will be done by Friday?"

He wiped his hands on his breeches. "I am certain of it. Which reminds me"—he looked toward the entrance to the front door—"do my eyes deceive me, or is that a clean child in the doorway?"

Felicity giggled. "Meggie says I am not to enter this room," she reported to her mother.

"Sound advice," Roxanna said.

"Lissy, let me engage your services," Lord Winn said as he settled on the floor, his long legs crossed. "Hand me that scroll of wallpaper by my coat."

"Just toss it in, love," Roxanna said.

He caught the roll of paper and spread it out between them. "What do you think?"

Roxanna leaned forward, careful not to touch the paper. It was a floral pattern, delicate and springlike, the lightest shade of blue, and obviously expensive. "It's beautiful, my lord," she breathed.

"Good! I thought so, too."

"Is it for your sitting room?" she asked. "What an excellent choice."

"It is for yours, madam," he said. "I was in Darlington earlier this morning, and this caught my eye in the warehouse."

"Oh, dear, Tibbie didn't tell you?" she asked, dismay and regret mingled with equal parts in her voice.

"Tell me what?"

"We've been doing the rooms here with leftover paper from earlier renovations at Moreland. This is much too expensive, my lord."

"But I like it," he said. "I bought it for this room because it reminded me of you and your girls. And I don't like to be argued with."

"He doesn't, Mama," Helen agreed from the other doorway into the dining room and kitchen.

"My lord!"

"There you go again," he said as he rolled up the paper and tossed it back to Felicity. "You really have to let me use it on the walls here, because it matches the carpet I purchased at the same time."

Impulsively she touched his sleeve. "And yet you will tell me that you are not kind?" she asked, her voice low.

He got to his feet and held out his hand for her. "Kindness has nothing to do with it, Mrs. Drew," he assured her as he lifted her up. "It is mere expediency. How would it appear if the carpet did not quite fit with the sofa and chairs I ordered?"

Roxanna glanced at Felicity. "Lissy, hand me back that roll of paper. I intend to beat Lord Winn over the head with it!"

Felicity laughed and clapped her hands. "Can we watch, Mama?" she asked, while Helen opened her eyes wider. "Mama, he is a marquess!" she reminded her mother.

"He is a scoundrel," Roxanna said. "And now you will say it is in the Latin charter."

To her further embarrassment, Lord Winn ruffled her hair. As she coughed from the plaster dust, he went to the entrance and pulled on his coat. "I wouldn't dare, Mrs. Roxie Drew," he declared. "If you and the girls will wipe down those walls, I'll send the plasterer over here this afternoon. Good day, Mrs. Drew. Don't get in a snit over small things."

And he was gone, shouldering his roll of wallpaper like a musket, and leaping lightly over the muddy spots in the front yard. Helen watched him go, then closed the front door. "He likes you, Mama," she said quietly. "Do you like him?"

Roxanna sat down on the stairs and held out her arms for her daughters. "Of course I like him," she said, hugging her girls, even as they sneezed from the plaster on her dress. "You'd have to be made of stone not to like Lord Winn."

Felicity nodded, and rested her head on Roxanna's lap. "Mama, do you think Papa would have liked him?"

Why that should bring tears to her eyes, she did not understand. "I am sure he would have, my dear," she said, and kissed Felicity, and then Helen. She hugged her girls close, comparing and contrasting. Physically, they were two completely different men, she thought, Anthony tall and slender, Lord Winn shorter by a little, and built sturdy like a Yorkshire barn. She rested her cheek against Helen's hair, reminded of Anthony's blondness and his graceful ways as she looked at her elder daughter. He had been everything she wanted in a husband. Too bad he was gone before they had time to do more living together.

But both men were kind. She considered her dead husband a moment, aware for the first time that his kindness everyone took for granted, because he was a vicar. With Lord Winn, such kindness was unexpected. Roxanna ran her hand through Helen's silky hair. Why is it that I suspect he is selective in his kindness? she thought. And why on earth has he singled us out?

She closed her eyes a moment. When she opened them, Felicity was watching her. "Mama, are you sad?" she asked, her voice anxious.

Roxanna hugged Felicity. "I don't know what I am, Lissy, but I don't think I am sad."

The plasterers descended on the dower house after a hasty rubdown of the walls that left Meggie retreating upstairs to nod over a book, and Roxanna and the girls sneezing even as they withdrew to the kitchen. "Why does every home improvement seem to fill a whole house?" she asked Tibbie as he got the workers started.

"That's what my wife always wonders." He pulled a folded note from his pocket. "It's from Lord Winn. He said he won't take no for an answer."

Roxanna glanced at Helen's expectant face as she opened the note. "My dears, it seems we are to dine at Moreland tonight." She sighed and looked at Tibbie as her daughters clapped their hands. "We are such an imposition on that man!" She pointed to the note and read out loud. " 'I do not think you would care for stewed plaster, or fricasseed plaster, or plaster hollandaise, which, I believe, is on the menu in the dower house tonight. I will request cinnamon buns for Lissy.' "

"Mama, he will spoil us," Helen declared solemnly as she read the note in her mother's hand, then ruined the effect by grinning at her sister. "I like it!"

Roxanna shook her head at Tibbie, who shrugged his shoulders. "Think of it as getting a wonderful return on your ten pounds, Mrs. Drew!"

Lord Winn dressed more carefully for dinner than usual, changing waistcoats several times, thinking that he ought to write to Chickering for more clothes. He combed his hair and wondered if the village had a barber. Not that it would help much. Cynthia used to complain that no matter how elegantly he dressed, he always looked as though he belonged on a farm. "Happen I do," he murmured to the mirror. There was no question that he was seriously wanting in high looks. "But I am rich," he told himself. "I can have anything in the world I want—except Mrs. Drew." He raised his chin and tied his neckcloth. "And that, Fletcher, is the cruelest kind of poverty."

He considered Mrs. Drew as dispassionately as he could, comparing her to Cynthia, who was without question the most beautiful woman he had ever seen. He was only one of many suitors that season who'd dangled after Cynthia Darnley, second daughter of Sir Edwin Darnley, enraptured by her ash-blond beauty and eyes the color of cornflowers. She was tall and elegant of form, with an aristocratic curl to her lips that he'd thought enchanting at first. Her nose was chiseled from the palest marble, and Brummel himself had rhapsodized over Cynthia's profile until little portraits of her appeared, white against a blue background, all over London. "Chiseled" was certainly the operative word, he thought. Cynthia, you were chiseled from an entire block of marble. Lucky me. Thank God there was a war on and I had to leave you. I can only wish Lord Masterson good luck.

He sat on his bed, wondering for the thousandth time if things would have been different if he had been able to devote all his time to her. He concluded, as always, that it would have made no difference. "Cynthia, you were just bound to be too much trouble," he said, and got up to change waistcoats again.

Mrs. Drew, on the other hand, has more than beauty going for her, he considered as he looked in the mirror, tugged on the waistcoat, then reached for his coat. If anything, she was thinner than Cynthia, as though she didn't take any thought to her own health. While Cynthia's fashionable slimness was due to a daunting regimen of vinegar and boiled potatoes that used to take away his own appetite, Roxie Drew was thin because she worked too hard, slept too little, worried too much, and wasn't loved sufficiently.

But, oh, those eyes. He knew, as sure as he stood there in his stockinged feet, that he could look at her all day and never grow weary of the view. In fact, when they were working in the sitting room, he'd caught her questioning gaze when he stared too long. It would never occur to Roxie Drew that she was worth a second and third glance, he decided. Her marvelous skin was not a city pallor, but a rosy country hue, and her wonderful high-arched brows and brown eyes, round as a child's, made him want to take her in his arms and just hold her until moss grew over them both and they blended into the landscape.

"Rave on, Lord Winn," he said as he looked at himself one more time. He was reminded then of Cynthia's favorite pose in front of the mirror, and was immediately disgusted with himself. "At least she thinks I am kind," he said as he closed the door behind him and went downstairs. But I would rather be a dashing lover, he thought as he shot out his cuffs and hoped Mrs. Howell had remembered cinnamon buns for Felicity.

After a few minutes of standing in the hall, he opened the back door at a tentative knock coming from rather low on the door panel.

"It's me, Felicity," he heard on the other side of the door, "and we are cold!"

Helen and Mrs. Drew were laughing at Felicity when he opened the door. It was easy to bow and usher them in, mouthing something about "three of the prettiest women in England on my doorstep," and meaning each word utterly. He looked into Mrs. Drew's enchanting eyes. Cynthia would have simpered at such a compliment, but Roxie just grinned at him and said "Thank you," quite prettily.

Dinner was a remarkable success, and it gave him the greatest pleasure to lean back in his chair, admire the diners around him, and pretend they were all his own. Mrs. Drew ate a healthy serving of everything, and he felt himself relaxing as she leaned back, too, her hand on her stomach.

"Mrs. Howell is a wonder," she said finally as she wiped cinnamon glaze off Felicity's cheek and nodded to Helen.

With another glance at her mother, Helen got to her feet and stood beside his chair. "Mama says I should play a song for you on the piano, Lord Winn," she said.

He pushed his chair back. "Aha, you are to be the evening's entertainment, my dear?" he asked.

"Not precisely," Helen replied. "You are, sir. Mama is going to cut your hair while I play for you."

He laughed and looked at Mrs. Drew, who was taking a pair of scissors and a comb out of her reticule. "You're serious," he said.

Mrs. Drew stood up and took Felicity by the hand. "Of course I am, my lord," she replied. "I never say anything I do not mean. Tomorrow I will be struggling with wallpaper again and you do need a haircut. It will have to be tonight, if you are to pass yourself off with any credit in this neighborhood."

He allowed himself to be led along the hall by Felicity, with Helen beside him, her back straight, her lips firm, as though she contemplated an execution rather than a recital. After soliciting a dish towel from Mrs. Howell, Roxie Drew joined them.

Helen stood by at the piano bench while he adjusted the height. She played a tentative chord and smiled at her mother. "Mama, only think how fine it will sound when I can reach the pedals!"

"Oh, most emphatically yes, Helen. Take off your coat, now then, Lord Winn," Mrs. Drew commanded.

Anything, he thought. She pulled out a straight chair and made him sit in it while Helen began "Fur Elise" and Felicity settled herself on the sofa, her ankles crossed and her hands folded in her lap. He watched her, then glanced up at Mrs. Drew, who stood behind him. "Do you wager?" he asked, his voice low.

She chuckled. "I would not give her beyond thirty seconds of such gentility." He watched in amusement as Felicity sighed and flopped back on the couch to stare up at the plaster swirls in the ceiling.

"The civilizing process is a long one, Lord Winn," Mrs. Drew commented as she removed his neckcloth with a practiced hand and unbuttoned his top button. "I don't see Lissy rushing it, either, do you?"

My God, he thought as her warm fingers tucked the dish towel around his neck. *I could die right now and be in paradise, breathing lavender and listening to "Für Elise."* To his continued delight, Mrs. Drew stood in front of him, pursed her lips with that expression that made him want to shout "Yes!," and stared at his hair. She combed his hair carefully, smoothing it with her hands, then stepped behind him and began to snip. "This is certainly the least I can do, after all your many kindnesses," she said, and he felt her breath on his neck as she clipped away. He closed his eyes with the bliss of it all as Helen launched into something that sounded like Vivaldi and Lissy watched him, her eyes slowly closing.

"We have a casualty from all those cinnamon buns," he whispered.

"I am sure I will be the second one," she said. "I ate too much, but then, Meggie Watson insists that I need to put on some weight."

As a former husband, he knew that any addendum to that statement would have got him into trouble. He remained silent, relishing Mrs. Drew's proximity, and the heavenly way her bosom brushed his head once or twice as she cut his hair and hummed along with Helen's performance. She was soft beyond belief, and he closed his eyes in gratitude to a merciful God who was sometimes surprisingly kind to miserable sinners.

When she finished, she rested her hands on his shoulders for a brief moment. He could have cried when she removed them and walked to the mirror over the fireplace. "Come here, my lord, and tell me what you think," she said.

He followed and gazed into the mirror at the two of them standing together. *I think I would like to kiss you,* he told himself. "It's fine," he said, running his hand along the back of his neck. "In fact, much better than my valet usually does."

She grinned into the mirror at him. "I am happy to have the chance to do something nice for you."

I have so many other suggestions then, he thought, each of which would earn me a slap in the chops. Instead, he returned some comment, and to take his mind off Roxie, glanced at Felicity, who was sleeping soundly on the sofa. Helen played the last chord of the Vivaldi.

"Shall I play some Bach now?" she asked.

Mrs. Drew shook her head, and he wanted to cry out in disappointment. "No, my dear. I think it is time we were leaving."

"It's a lovely piano," Helen said, her voice wistful.

"Then I think you should practice on it as much as you like," he said, extending his arm to Roxanna. "And do play the Bach, Helen. Mrs. Drew, may I just take you upstairs to show you what I have in mind for the second floor?"

He didn't have the slightest idea what he wanted for the second floor. Perhaps if they strolled through the rooms, her lavender scent would linger after she was gone. He looked up at the crumbling plaster scrollwork in the ceiling. "I think you can see what needs to be done down here."

"Oh, yes," she said, and after a slight hesitation, took his arm. "I would like to use that same wallpaper in here that we are putting into my sitting room. It's just the right touch. We'll be only a moment, Helen."

Upstairs, he took her through the room and babbled something about colors and heavy furniture that must have sounded more intelligent than he thought, because she nodded and seemed to regard his comments seriously.

"Exactly so, my lord," she said, standing at the window in the last bedroom. "Moreland is a wonderful old farmhouse that woke up pretentious one morning. I would like to strike a happy medium and return some of that innocent quality to it."

Anything, anything at all, Mrs. Drew, as long as it takes you months and months. Her next words were a cold water bath.

"This won't take any time at all, sir," she said, fingering the ornate damask draperies. "I will lighten the walls with more modern paper and paint, and replace these drapes with lace, or even muslin." She sat on one of the unyielding beds. "You might want to reconsider these mattresses, my lord. And I know of a warehouse in Darlington with lovely bedspreads, too."

He watched her as she perched on the bed and felt the sweat start down his back, even though the room was cool. "I bow to your judgment," he said, his voice calm, his mind in outrageous turmoil. "Just make it look like a home."

She laughed and got off the bed, to his relief. "That's easy, my lord! I'll loan you jackstraws and blocks to trip over in the middle of the night, enough clutter to drive you distracted, and suspicious marks and rings on things that no one admits to."

He tucked her arm in his again and picked up the lamp from the bureau. "Well, new bedspreads and curtains will do, I suspect, and more modern furniture."

"Oh, that's right," she returned, closing the door behind them. "Didn't you say something once about children being the curse of the earth?" She looked about the hall, doubt in her eyes. "I do not know that a house without children is really a home, but I'll do my best to make it so here at Moreland. And now I really must be going, my lord."

Felicity was still asleep on the sofa when they returned, and Helen was gathering up her music. "Just leave it there, my dear," he said as he helped her into her coat. "If we can convince your mother that Ney and your pony need some exercise, we can ride tomorrow, and then you can come back here to practice."

Helen, her eyes dancing, looked at her mother. "Oh, please!"

"I am sure that will be fine," Mrs. Drew said. "You can work on that Mozart piece you were practicing"—she paused, then continued smoothly enough—"at your Uncle Drew's house."

"I can help her if she needs it," he offered.

Mrs. Drew widened her eyes in mock surprise. "Why, Lord Winn, how *kind* of you!"

He smiled at her little joke, and picked up Felicity. "I am kindness itself," he said, grateful that at no point in the evening could she read his thoughts. *Actually, I am wondering how on earth I can convince you to marry me, and coming up absolutely dry.* The reflection pained him.

Some of this agitation must have crossed his face then, because Mrs. Drew touched his arm. "Lord Winn, are you all right?" she asked. "Is it a war injury? I can wake up Felicity. You needn't carry her."

"Oh, no!" he assured her. "It's nothing. Perhaps I shouldn't have pried so energetically on those baseboards. Lead on, Helen."

Snow was in the air again. Mrs. Drew turned her face up to the heavy clouds in the night sky. "I think there will be snow by morning," she said softly. "And I do not think it will leave much before spring now, my lord."

"Winter comes early to the North Riding," he said, loathing

himself because his conversation could go no deeper than the weather, or the price of bedspreads.

"It's November," she said. "Not so early."

He carried Felicity upstairs to the bedroom that she shared with Helen, and stood watching as Mrs. Drew deftly removed her shoes and stockings, slid her out of her dress, and tucked the blankets around her. She kissed Helen good night and then joined him in the doorway.

"I sometimes stand here and wonder how I got so lucky," she whispered to him.

"Lucky, madam?" he said. "Some would say you were not so lucky." It sounded bald to his ears, but it was honest. He wanted so much to touch her, but he could only make bracing statements.

"Lucky," she said again, her voice firm. "I have my girls."

Her quiet words humbled him as nothing else could. I have more estates than ought to be legal, and more money than some countries, he thought. Mrs. Drew isn't even sure if she will have a quarterly allowance after December, but she is lucky and I am not.

Her head came just past his shoulder. How easy it would have been to kiss her, but he knew he did not dare. A few more perfunctory words, a nod or two, and he was outside again, looking up at the dower house. He walked back quickly as the snow began to fall, resolving to write Amabel in the morning and tell her that he had no intention of spending Christmas at Winnfield this year. The Etheringhams could go to hell, for all he cared. Perhaps he could spare a day or two with Clarice and Frederick, but that was open to debate.

To his gratification, the upstairs hall did smell faintly of lavender yet. He was a long time getting to sleep.

Chapter 10

The sitting room was done by Friday afternoon, true to Lord Winn's prediction. Roxanna sighed with pleasure and wiggled her stockinged feet in the carpet, then leaned back on the sofa. The only bad moment had come during the unloading of the furniture. She knew enough about quality workmanship to know that Lord Winn had squandered what Meggie called a king's ransom on the sofa, chairs, and end tables now placed so companionably in the compact room. It was the kind of furniture that she and Anthony would have admired in a warehouse, but never selected, no matter how much they wanted to.

"I think he's up to something," Meggie said from her perch on one of the wing chairs before the fireplace.

"Lord Winn?" Roxanna asked. "Oh, Meggie, that's preposterous!" She patted the cushions into place. "I do own to some guilt that he spent so much, but, Meggie, he has the money. If he chooses to do this, I wouldn't argue." She smiled. "Even Helen will tell you what a waste of time it is to argue with him. And truth to tell, it *is* his house."

"All the same, Roxanna, be a little wary," Meggie warned. She settled herself in the chair, and in a moment was snoring.

Roxanna tucked her legs under her and gazed out the window, curtained now with lacy strips the same pale blue as the wallpaper. If I want to worry about something, Meggie, let me worry about my brother-in-law, she thought. She had not seen Marshall Drew since her removal to the dower house, but he was on her mind more than she cared to admit.

She had known him for eight years, since her marriage at age nineteen to his younger brother, and while she did not study his career about the North Riding, she knew that Lord Whitcomb never failed to get what he wanted, whether it was a parcel of land, or a colt to train for the Scarborough races. It was a quality that Anthony shook his head over more than once, then confessed to her that he did not know if what he felt was envy or approbation at this doggedness in his brother.

We are safe here at Moreland, she reminded herself, then stood to put more coal in the grating because she felt a chill. She remained at the window, hugging herself, and admiring the shocking blue and white landscape of a Yorkshire winter that never failed to move her. A child of Kent, she had been raised in a milder climate. The bite of December in the North Riding, with trees iced and streams silenced, and hills almost grotesque with drifted snow, awed her. Everything seemed to hibernate, in the hopes that deep sleeps would produce spring sooner. Even Felicity slowed down, and offered less objection to an afternoon nap.

She was discovering that she thought of Anthony more in the winter, waking up at night to wonder how cold the graveyard was, and how deep the snow there. He seemed farther away under that additional burden of snow, as though the distance now was more than miles. She had cried yesterday when she couldn't remember whether his birthday was January 16 or February 16. What else will I forget? she wondered as she stood before the window.

I wish I were not so restless, she thought. I wish I could relax like Meggie, and sit in one spot without leaping up to pace about a room, or search for more to do, when I have already done everything around here that needs to be done.

She knew what she missed, what drove her to ceaseless activity, but there wasn't anyone to discuss the matter with. Meggie had never married, and Mrs. Howell, well, Mrs. Howell would only stare at her. Proper ladies didn't talk about what she needed. For the first time also, she found herself wishing she had been less interested in Anthony's body when he was alive, and able to gratify her love. Roxie, if you had been a bit less eager then, perhaps you wouldn't feel such a sharp edge now, she scolded herself.

"Oh, bother it!" she said, then put her hand over her mouth when Meggie woke up and looked around. "I am sorry, my dear," she exclaimed, contrite.

Meggie watched her, but she could not help herself as she paced in front of the window, feeling like a pet mouse on a wheel. She stopped finally and lifted her cloak from the peg by the front door. "Meggie, I am going for a walk. Lissy is napping on my bed, and Helen is reading in her room." She was out the door before Meggie could ask any questions.

She swung the cloak around her shoulders and took a deep breath of the bracing air. All was silent now, the stream by the house quieted by ice, the birds far south. The only sound she heard was the impatient crunch of her shoes on the crusty snow.

The lane that led from the main road to the manor house was

free of snow, something Lord Winn insisted upon. She started down the road, feeling better already as the cold circulated through her lungs and her cheeks began to tingle. I shall become a champion walker, she thought, and giggled at the notion. Anthony, the lack of your husband's comfort will turn me into the healthiest woman who ever strode the hills of the North Riding. The doctors will have to take my heart out and beat it to death so I can die at a decent old age.

She was still smiling when she reached the end of the lane and started back. As her mind cleared, she considered Christmas, which would be sparse, but not impossible. Someone, probably one of her husband's former parishioners, had sent her an anonymous five pounds, so there would be a goose and other good things, and perhaps enough for a small gift for each girl. She would like to have afforded something for Mrs. Howell, Tibbie, and even Lord Winn, but that was out of the question, particularly for Lord Winn. What could she possibly give to a man who had everything?

"Mrs. Drew, are you practicing for a footrace?"

Startled, she looked over her shoulder and up into Lord Winn's eyes, as he sat on Ney.

"You should not sneak up on a person like that," she scolded.

He reined in his horse and she stopped, too, as he hitched his leg over the saddle. "My dear Mrs. Drew, I was whistling something rather loud from *The Magic Flute!* This was not a sneak approach. What is occupying *your* mind?"

"None of your business!" she said crisply, then repented. "Well, actually, I was wondering what I could give you for Christmas since you already have everything."

To her amazement, Lord Winn began to blush. She laughed out loud. "Well, whatever it is, I am sure it must be illegal or immoral! Surely nothing a vicar's widow could possibly satisfy."

He had to laugh at that, but it sounded rueful to her. He peered down at her as he swung his leg back in the stirrup. "Mrs. Drew, you are a rascal. I think I understand Felicity better now!"

"I am no such thing, sir!" she protested, and walked alongside his horse. "You are the rascal."

He was silent for most of the lane, then he reached inside his coat pocket. "Mrs. Drew, you'll appreciate this," he said as he pulled out a sheet of paper and handed it down to her.

She looked at it with interest. "Very good, my lord. You've ordered enough wallpaper and paint to get the whole job done. Tibbie told me this morning that he has arranged for the plasterers to return. They promise to tackle the ceiling in your sitting room the first thing on Monday morning."

"Well, then you'll have to suffer my presence in your sitting room occasionally until it is restored," he replied and pocketed the paper again.

"You may drink tea with us this afternoon, my lord," she offered. "Everything is finished, just as you promised, and Helen and I made gingersnaps this morning."

"Tea *and* gingersnaps?" he quizzed. "Strange isn't it, Mrs. Drew? Two years ago, I was dining on puppies—don't tell Lissy—and strained pond water somewhere in the Pyrenees."

She made no comment as they continued slowly up the lane. What a different life you have lived, she thought. "I should think that after all those years of deprivation, you would seek out the company of your friends, or at least your relatives, at this time of year," she said finally as they approached the curving drive before the manor.

He dismounted and handed the reins to his groom, who must have been watching for him. "My dearest friends lie dead on battlefields all over Europe, and I only quarrel with my sisters. Oh, now, Mrs. Drew, don't take it so to heart!"

"I'm not!" she declared, even as her eyes filled with tears.

She held her breath as he took off his glove and touched her cheek, then leaned close to whisper in her ear. "Don't ever cry over me, my dear. I'm not worth that. I have everything, remember? You said so yourself."

She dabbed at her eyes, embarrassed. "I say stupid things, don't I?"

"No more than I," he replied, his voice suddenly hard. "I have the advantage over you, my dear. I *do* stupid things." He took off his hat and bowed to her. "I think I will skip tea this afternoon, Mrs. Drew. Some other time."

And then he was gone, hurrying inside the manor without a backward glance. She stood a moment longer in the driveway, her heart even heavier than before, then turned and walked back to the dower house.

I must have said the wrong thing, Roxanna Drew told herself many times in the coming weeks before Christmas. I wonder what it was? she asked herself as she threw herself into the renovations at Moreland. She removed paintings, shifted furniture, stripped wallpaper, and learned to patch with plaster as the work proceeded in the manor. At the end of each day, she was deliciously tired and no good for anything except a quiet dinner, and then blissful sleep.

Lord Winn did visit in her parlor on several occasions while his own sitting room was a tattered ruin. He drank tea, played cards with Helen, read to Felicity, and even listened to Meggie Watson's animadversions on the current government. He spoke but little, and too many times, Roxanna could almost feel the sadness in him. No one else seemed to notice, and she wondered if she was just imagining his low state, because he said and did all that was proper.

Or perhaps because I feel low, I have imagined others are so afflicted, she considered one afternoon as she straightened up from scraping paint from a window frame. She backed up against the wall to straighten her spine, wondering why the closer Christmas came, the worse she felt. As she stood there, she remembered something Marshall had said to her just after Anthony's funeral. "My dear, the holidays and birthdays will be the worst," he had told her. As much as she disliked thinking about Marshall, she had to agree with him.

Christmas without Anthony would not be Christmas, not really, she reasoned as she tackled the frame again. They always decorated the sitting room with greens, and hung a wreath, but she had not bothered yet. Meggie had reminded her only last night that it was time to start on the Christmas cooking, but the conversation had drifted off to nothing.

I simply must exert myself for the girls' sake, she thought as she left Moreland that evening. She thought of her brothers, glad that she did not have to report to them how badly she was playing her hand right now. "We will make gingerbread cookies tomorrow," she said out loud. But no mistletoe this year, she added to herself, remembering the sprig that dangled last year over Anthony's bed. The stockings would have to go up. Maybe if she spaced them wider apart on the mantelpiece, Anthony's wouldn't be missed. "Oh, God," she cried out loud, and stopped in the snow. "I can't face it."

She stood there in the snow until her feet started to grow numb, then continued into the house, ashamed at her own whining. I still have so much, she thought. Why must I dwell on what I do not have?

Helen met her at the door with the news that Lord Winn was in the parlor and would stay to dinner. Roxanna sighed. Why tonight, when all she wanted to do was go to bed and curl up in a little ball?

"I gather from that sigh that you wish I would take my mutton at Moreland, Mrs. Drew," Lord Winn said from the doorway into the sitting room.

He was still dressed in his riding clothes, and leaning comfortably against the door. She did not want to look at him because she knew her face was bleak, but courtesy demanded some response. She glanced in his direction and mumbled some pleasantry, and then he promptly straightened up and spoke over his shoulder to Helen, who had been out riding with him.

"Helen, I think you and Lissy should see what Meggie needs in the kitchen. Come, come, march like soldiers."

When they were gone, he came closer and took her arm. To her vast relief, he didn't say anything, only gave her a little shake. It was enough. She squared her shoulders and came into the parlor, grateful to sit down before the fireplace.

"If Moreland is too much, I can get some more help," he said as he sat in the other wing chair.

She shook her head, not looking at him. "It's not Moreland, my lord, and you know it. I will be glad when it is January and this holiday is behind us."

"There will always be something else, my dear Mrs. Drew," he commented, pushing the footstool her way. She propped her feet on it, sharing it with him.

"I know," she agreed. "And I will take each event as it comes and not think too far ahead." She smiled into the flames. "I refuse to be defeated by death."

"Bravo, Roxie Drew," he said softly. "I get through days like that, too."

She looked at him in surprise. "Somehow I never thought . . ." she began, then stopped.

"That I loved her?" he finished. "Oh, I did, Mrs. Drew. I suppose I mourn a little too, wondering if Cynthia and I were casualties of the war, or if all this dirty business would have happened, anyway. I conclude it would have, then I kick myself for loving her."

Impulsively she touched his sleeve, then drew her hand away, embarrassed at her forwardness. "I'm sorry," she said simply. "It's hard to let go, isn't it?"

She cried then, leaning back in the chair and letting the tears slide down her cheeks. To her relief, Lord Winn said nothing, but let her cry in peace. He left the parlor in a moment, and she heard him supervising her daughters in the breakfast room. She dried her eyes, blew her nose, and settled more comfortably in the chair. Her eyes closed and she slept.

When she woke, the house was quiet, and the fire much lower in the grate. She looked around in surprise, and saw Lord Winn in the other chair again. "Goodness, what time is it?" she asked, sitting up in alarm.

"Nearly midnight, Mrs. Drew," he said. "Meggie and I put the girls to bed. Lissy cut up a bit stiff because I did not carry you up to bed and tuck you in, too, but I assured her you would rather not wake up that way."

Roxie chuckled. "Trust Lissy to worry. You could have at least wakened me for dinner."

He shrugged. "Why? You needed a nap."

"Why, indeed?" she agreed. "Do you think there is any food left?"

"Mrs. Drew, I made you a sandwich, and found a bottle of ale from somewhere, if that won't disturb your gentility."

She laughed as he went to the kitchen and returned with the sandwich and a dark brown bottle.

"Do you require a glass?"

"Of course, my lord! I am not dead to propriety,"she teased, and accepted the glass that he pulled out from behind his back.

The sandwich was delicious. "I am always amazed that sandwiches taste better when someone else fixes them," she said between bites.

"You should try my horse meat on a stick over a cow dung fire," he said. "You don't even need seasoning."

She laughed again and he joined her, after taking a swig from her bottle of ale. "You are a man of many talents, Lord Winn!" she exclaimed.

"Oh, I am," he agreed affably, putting his booted feet on the footstool again. "I've decided to go to Clarice's for Christmas," he said, changing the subject. "She's not too far from here, but far enough from Amabel, who, by the way, wished me to Hades in her last letter."

"Your sisters!" she said. "Of course, I am certain you wrote Amabel a perfectly gentlemanly letter explaining why you did not choose to entertain the Etheringhams and their daughter," she continued, trying to keep the amusement from her voice.

"Of course!" he stated in mock seriousness. "How could you doubt it? I only mentioned casually that I would not stud for the Etheringhams to cut Lettice's son out of my succession. I do not understand why she took offense at that."

Roxanna rolled her eyes, grateful that the gloom in the sitting room hid the color that she felt rush to her cheeks. "Lord Winn! You are a trial to your sisters!"

"Yes, ain't I?" he agreed cheerfully.

"You know, you could always fall in love again and marry," she commented as she finished her sandwich and set the plate on the floor. "What then?"

He was a long time in replying. "I doubt marriage is possible," he said finally as he stood up to leave. He bowed over her hand. "Mrs. Drew, go to bed. Tell Helen we will go riding in two days. I'll leave Christmas Eve morning for Clarice's place."

She walked him to the door. "Very well, sir! We will take good care of Moreland while you are gone."

He paused in the doorway, his overcoat half on. "By the way, I have taken the liberty of purchasing presents for your daughters."

She started to protest, and he put his finger to her lips.

"A riding crop for Helen and some rather pretty barrettes for Lissy. That is completely unexceptionable, Mrs. Drew."

"Well . . ." she stalled.

"All you need to do is say 'Thank you, Lord Winn, you shouldn't have,' and leave it at that." He shrugged into his coat.

"Thank you, Lord Winn, you shouldn't have," she repeated.

He winked at her and closed the door.

She shook her head and climbed the stairs. "Telling his sister he wouldn't be a stud . . . ," she muttered as she opened her bedroom door. "Brothers are a dreadful trial."

Roxanna saw Lord Winn only briefly in the next two days, and then from the window as he rode out to Retling Beck with Tibbie and his solicitor. They must have returned long after she finished chipping paint for the day, and by then she was involved in the Christmas baking she had been putting off and did not think about him much.

At any rate, she tried not to, but this was rendered difficult by the discovery of a large goose on her doorstep the following morning. Lissy stared at the plucked and bound bird and looked up at the sky, her eyes big. Roxanna turned away to avoid laughing at her daughter. "My dear, I think it may be a gift from Lord Winn," she said, when she could speak.

Lissy nodded. "Not from heaven?" she asked.

"Well, not precisely, my dear! Here, help me carry it in."

Lissy's "goose from heaven" found its way to Meggie in the kitchen, and then onto the cold side porch with the other perishables she had baked earlier.

"It will be cookies today, girls," Roxanna announced to her daughters over porridge. "Your favorite kind."

Helen looked up from her bowl, her eyes troubled. "Papa's,

too?" she asked. "Please, Mama, I don't want to forget him," she burst out when Roxanna hesitated.

Helen pushed back her chair and ran from the room. Roxanna bit her lip, poured the rest of her oats into Lissy's bowl, and followed Helen upstairs. The door was closed, so she knocked on it quietly, and then entered.

Helen lay on her side, facing the window, staring out at the bleak landscape. Roxanna sat beside her, rubbing her back as Helen cried. "I thought I would like Christmas," she said at last after she blew her nose on the handkerchief Roxanna held out to her. "Why is it so hard this year?"

Roxanna leaned against the headboard. "Helen, I think it is hard because we want to remember Papa, and we want to go on, at the same time."

Helen looked at her through red, swollen eyes. "Will it be any easier next year?" she asked as she rested her head in her mother's lap.

"I suppose we won't know until next year, my dear," Roxanna said honestly. "We won't ever forget Papa, but I suspect our feelings will change and mellow."

Helen was silent. Roxanna hugged her close, looking forward to the dark and cold of January as never before. "My dear, we will make those cookies with almond paste that Papa liked so well. I wish we could gather holly and greens like we used to, but we don't have a gig."

Helen blew her nose again and managed a watery smile. "Oh, it will be all right if we just have the cookies. And will we read from the Bible on Christmas Eve?"

Roxanna smiled at her daughter, because she knew it was expected of her. "I don't see how we can possibly avoid it!" she teased, keeping her voice light. "Now you wash your face, and we'll go downstairs and start on the cookies." She gave Helen a little pat. "Didn't you promise to go riding with Lord Winn this afternoon?"

Helen nodded. "Five Pence needs the exercise."

"Five Pence?" Roxanna asked. "You finally named your pony?"

"Lord Winn did, Mama," Helen said from the depths of a washcloth. "He said my pony was as fine as five pence. He's almost as good at naming as you, Mama."

The morning was devoted to cookies, and the whole dower house smelled divinely when Lord Winn rapped on the door that afternoon for Helen. He stepped inside the house when Roxanna opened the door, took a deep breath, and staggered back against the doorsill while Felicity laughed and clapped her hands. Even Helen grinned, to Roxanna's relief.

He took Helen by the shoulder. "My dear, you cannot possibly expect me to take you riding without a little restorative. I'd like at least one of each of those smells, please."

She and Felicity hurried off to the kitchen for some cookies as Lord Winn watched them go, an appreciative smile on his face. "Charming," he murmured. "Mrs. Drew, you and the late vicar are to be congratulated on your offspring."

"Why, thank you!" she exclaimed. "Now, you will eat with us tonight? I know Mrs. Howell has left for Darlington already."

He bowed and accepted promptly as the girls returned. He scooped up a handful of the cookies Helen held out to him. "Come, my dear. Our horses are turning into hay burners. Race you?"

They returned just as dinner was ready. Roxanna spooned up bowls of potato soup, Lord Winn said grace this time, and they began dinner. Lord Winn ate in silence, then held out his bowl for more.

"Mrs. Drew, Helen has informed me that the sitting room is quite bare without greenery," he said as he lifted his spoon again. "I have advised her that we will take the gig on that road toward Whitcomb tomorrow morning for holly and whatever else appeals to us."

Roxanna looked at him in surprise. "But you're leaving for your sister's tomorrow, aren't you?"

"Well, I was," he temporized, dipping a chunk of bread in the soup. "I rather think the greenery is more important than an early start. Clarice can wait a few hours for my scintillating appearance."

"Very well," Roxanna said dubiously. "I wish we were not such a chore to you." He opened his mouth to speak and she interrupted. "And this is *not* in the Latin charter!"

"My dear, I didn't know you had read it," he said smoothly, then returned to the soup.

"It really is a trouble to you," she said later as he came downstairs from telling the girls good night.

"Not at all, Mrs. Drew," he insisted, and gently took her by the elbow to steer her into the parlor. "Helen needs to have some continuity right now."

Roxanna went to the window and stared out at the darkness.

"She was feeling in the dumps this morning about forgetting her papa."

"So she told me."

She turned around to face the marquess. "I seem to get deeper into your debt each day. But we do need to gather greens tomorrow." She hesitated. "I feel it, too."

He nodded and picked up his overcoat. "Excellent, Mrs. Drew! How pleasant you look when you do not argue with me!" He was gone with another wink, and she had no time to feel sorry for herself.

They didn't leave before afternoon, because Lord Winn discovered another paper he had to sign at Retling Beck to secure the sale of that manor. When he returned with a gig, they piled in and left Meggie waving at the front door and giving all manner of cold-weather advice that no one remembered.

It was almost too cold to talk. "We'll keep this short," he assured her as he reined in on the Whitcomb road. "Mrs. Drew, if you would oblige me by driving this horse up the lane and then back, the girls and I will hunt the wild holly. Come, Felicity."

He tucked Felicity, shrieking, under one arm, and broke a trail through the snow for Helen, as Roxanna sat in the gig, blessed him, and wiggled her toes to keep them warm. *I wish you would not leave,* she thought. *It's too cold and I will worry.* Then she scolded herself for being a ninny. *Roxie, he crossed the Pyrenees on foot once with a starving army,* she told herself. *Surely he is beforehand enough to negotiate the distance to his sister's estate without coming up against disaster.*

She took the horse and gig up and down the lane twice before they returned with a burlap sack bulging with greenery. It was a tight fit in the back now for Helen, so Felicity sat on her lap for the return journey. In a moment Lissy was asleep, her face turned into Roxanna's warmth. The marquess glanced at her. Roxanna flashed him her most appreciative smile.

"I'll leave right away and spend the night in Wisner. I'll be at Clarice's by the middle of tomorrow afternoon," he said, still looking at her.

I wonder why he does that? she thought, then took his arm to point out the fact that the gig was wandering from the road. *I know I am not a beauty. He must be lonelier than he lets on.* She stared ahead, hoping that Clarice would find one or two interesting women to drop in on Boxing Day, for her brother's benefit.

"Well, are you expecting company?" Lord Winn asked as they approached the dower house.

She looked at the horse, blanketed and miserable, tied to a tree in the dower house yard, and shook her head. "I can't imagine anyone who would visit on Christmas Eve. Come, girls, let's see who our company is."

"The horse looks familiar," Lord Winn said. He stopped the gig and jumped down to help Roxanna with Felicity. Helen pulled the burlap bag from the back and accepted a hand down. "I think I will help Helen with the bag, if you don't mind."

"You're just nosy, my lord," Roxanna teased, "wanting to know who visits a widow on Christmas Eve!"

"Guilty as charged," he said cheerfully.

Helen and Felicity ran ahead, calling to Meggie to hurry with the string and shears to create a wreath, and Roxanna came more slowly. The marquess closed the door behind them. She came into the parlor, shaking the snow off her cloak.

She did not recognize the man who sat on her sofa, but he leaped up the moment she entered the room, and then looked in surprise at Lord Winn, who followed her in.

"Lord Winn! I was told . . . I thought you were gone for the holiday," he said as he tugged a wax-stamped document from his overcoat pocket.

Roxanna looked from the man to Lord Winn, curious about the frown that appeared on the marquess's face. "No," he began, and she wondered at the wary tone. "Should I have been?" Lord Winn turned to her. "Mrs. Drew, since he has no manners, let me introduce the sheriff of this district, Reggie Cowans. Mr. Cowans, is your business with me or with Mrs. Drew?"

She frowned at the marquess. *I wish you would be a little more friendly,* she thought as she reached out to shake hands with the sheriff. *And here he is, impatient with waiting. I wonder if he would like tea?*

She gasped as Cowans slapped the document into her outstretched hand and bolted for the door. "It wasn't my idea!" he shouted over his shoulder as he ran from the house.

"Good God!" the marquess exclaimed. He took her by the shoulder as she stared down at the papers in her hand. "I don't know what this could possibly be, Mrs. Drew, but I think you ought to sit down before you open it."

"Nonsense!" she exclaimed as she broke the seal and spread out the pages. She read a few words, then sank to her knees before Lord Winn could grab her. She dropped the document as thought it burned her fingers, and covered her face with her hands.

Lord Winn snatched it up, his face white. "My God," he said softly as his eye scanned the first page. "Mrs. Drew, this is a writ of removal." He sat down hard on the sofa, running his finger down the document. He sucked in his breath and stared at her, dumbfounded. "Lord Whitcomb means to take your children in three days!"

Chapter 11

There was a great roaring in her ears, blocking out what Lord Winn was saying to her, even when he grasped her by the shoulders and spoke right into her face. She noticed finally that she was sitting on the sofa, and that someone—it must have been Lord Winn—had placed her hands in her lap.

She sat there, and finally heard someone, his voice urgent, saying, "For God's sake, make a wreath in the kitchen and keep the girls out of here! Meggie, do you have any brandy?"

As her vision cleared, she saw Lord Winn holding out a glass to her. She tried to reach for it, but it seemed miles away and her hand was shaking too badly. In another moment, Lord Winn gripped her shoulder, put the cup to her lips, and made her drink.

"You were saying something," she managed to gasp, after the brandy began its work.

He sat beside her, his arm tight around her shoulders, as though to stop her trembling. "You simply must get hold of yourself, Roxie," he ordered softly. "The girls cannot know what is going on. It would destroy them."

She nodded, clenching her jaw closed to keep her teeth from chattering. She knew she should remonstrate with him for calling her Roxie, but it suddenly seemed so unimportant. He could call her anything, and it would not matter. Marshall Drew was coming for her children. She closed her eyes and leaned against the marquess.

Her senses on edge, she jumped and opened her eyes at the rustling of paper. Lord Winn had spread out the pages on his lap, reading them quickly, turning the pages. "Damn," he said several times softly, but with great venom.

"Tell me," she said, wishing that he would put more coal on the fire. She was numb with cold. But how could that be? A fire roared in the grate.

He shook his head. "No time now." He looked at his watch. "Roxie, we have to decorate this room with greenery and help hang a wreath. Then we'll eat dinner. What do you do then on Christmas Eve? Roxie? Come on, my dear. Speak to me."

"We read something," she said, her voice dull to her ears. "I wish I could remember what. Something."

"The Bible?" he suggested gently.

"Bible?" she repeated. "Oh, yes, the Bible. Something in St. Luke. I can't remember what. Why would we read Luke? I wish I knew."

She stared at the marquess. He put his hands gently on her neck and gave her a little shake and then spoke distinctly, as though to someone deaf.

"Roxie, you've been dealt a dreadful hand by your brother-in-law," he said. "Are you going to play it?"

Am I going to play it? she asked herself and thought of her brothers, teasing her when she threw down a bad hand and ran from the room. "Of course I am going to play it," she replied automatically, and took his hands from her neck. "Of course I am."

She sat still a moment, and gradually began to feel warm. She sighed and burrowed closer to Lord Winn, grateful for his warmth. She could hear the clock ticking over the mantelpiece now, and the girls laughing with Meggie in the kitchen. I cannot lose them, she thought. I must be in control. She sat up straight then, and the marquess relaxed his grip.

"We read the story of the First Christmas from Luke, my lord," she said calmly, even as her stomach churned and roiled. "We hang our stockings, and the girls go to bed."

"Good girl," he said. "When they're in bed, we're going over to Moreland to take a real look at this and figure out what we're going to do."

To her indescribable relief, he said, "what we're going to do," and not, "what you're going to do." She turned to look him in the eyes. "Thank you for not leaving me in this alone."

"I wouldn't dream of it," he replied, standing up, and pulling her to her feet. Her legs buckled under her, but he held her up until she could stand on her own.

"Mama?"

It was Helen, and she was holding out a red ribbon. "Mama, are you all right?" she asked anxiously.

I am dying, she thought as she squared her shoulders and smiled at her daughter. "Of course I am," she lied smoothly. "I think I was just a little too cold out there. Do you need me to make a bow?"

Helen nodded. Lissy came into the room, struggling with a wreath as tall as she was. Roxanna sat on the edge of the sofa as Meggie hurried to Lord Winn, a question in her eyes. There were whispered words between them, then Meggie gasped and turned away to face the window.

"Now, my dears, let us go in the kitchen, so I can lay out this ribbon on the table," Roxanna said as Meggie began to cry softly.

Startled, the girls looked at Meggie, then followed their mother into the kitchen. As they watched, she willed her hands to stop shaking, and made a bow for the wreath. It took three tries, but received Helen's approval finally. Under her direction, Helen threaded a needle and bound the bow to the wreath with a few careful stitches.

"Excellent!" Roxanna declared and took a step back for the full effect. "I am certain we can get Lord Winn to hang it over the mantelpiece. Is there enough holly left for a small wreath at the door? Hand it to me carefully, Helen. I can do that."

She fashioned a holly wreath, surprised that she could not feel the sharp pricks of the leaves. It is as though I am watching someone else do this, she decided. Nothing hurts, because it is not happening to me.

"Mama, it's beautiful," Lissy cried, her arm resting on Roxanna's leg as she worked at the kitchen table.

Roxanna bent down and kissed the top of Felicity's head, breathing deep of her child's fragrance. She rested her head against her daughter's curly hair for a moment and closed her eyes, trying to imagine life without her.

"No," she said firmly. "It is not possible."

Lissy looked at her with those brown eyes so like her own. "Mama, *I* think it is beautiful!" she argued.

"Oh!" Roxanna said. "Of course it is. I was thinking of . . . something else. Let's put it on the front door."

By the time she returned to the sitting room, Meggie was fully in possession of herself and helping Lord Winn arrange the large wreath over the fireplace. Roxanna hung the holly wreath over the knocker. It was beautiful, she thought, the shiny green and red contrasting so elegantly with the white door. I will not think about the end of the week, when my brother-in-law will knock on this door to take my daughters from me.

She and Meggie prepared dinner in tight-lipped silence while Lord Winn and the girls sang carols and draped the holly and greens about the sitting room. Meggie looked up once from the onion she kept mincing over and over. "He's a cool one, Mrs. Drew," was all she said. Roxanna could only nod her head in agreement.

She did not attempt dinner, knowing that if she raised her fork to her lips, she would throw up. By pushing the food around on her plate, she managed to look busy enough to fool Lissy, who was always involved in her own meals anyway. Helen regarded her with a frown.

"Mama, you should eat," she scolded. "Don't you like fricassee?"

Roxanna patted her stomach. "What I really need is a glass of soda and water. I think I ate too many cookies this morning."

Helen nodded, accepting this reasoning, and finished her food. Lord Winn even asked for seconds. "You're a good cook, Mrs. Drew," he said. "I could grow stout with my legs under your table."

She smiled at him. "Don't blame me! It's all those cinnamon buns that Lissy insists on at your house."

There, she thought, that was a reasonable volley of conversation. We almost sound normal. She glanced at the clock. Another two hours of this charade and I can put the girls to bed and fall apart.

After dinner, while Meggie cleaned up in the kitchen, Lord Winn settled himself on the sofa, took Felicity on his lap, and accepted the family Bible. "Luke 2, my lord," Roxanna reminded.

He looked up at her in genuine amusement. "I know where it is, Mrs. Drew!" he declared. "You must not persist in thinking that I am a heathen." He turned the pages. "Ah. Here we are. 'And it came to pass in those days that there went out a decree from Caesar Augustus that all the world should be taxed . . . ' "

Her arms around Helen, Roxanna leaned back against the sofa and closed her eyes, the majestic words like a balm flowing over her whole body. As Lord Winn read, his voice that interesting combination of Yorkshire brogue and cultured diction so familiar to her ears now, she forced herself to think about that first Christmas. She thought next of her eight Christmases with Anthony, then folded them in her memory and tucked them away in her heart. Next year will be better, she thought. It has to be.

Helen was disappointed that there was no stocking for Lord Winn to tack onto the mantelpiece. "You could take off your boot and let me have that one," she reasoned as Roxanna hung the Christmas stockings.

"Oh, you wouldn't want either one," he assured her. "I believe there is even a hole in the toe of one and in the heel of the other."

Helen's eyes opened wide. "But you are a marquess!" she exclaimed.

Lord Winn laughed. "A title has nothing to do with it! You should have seen me in Spain. Even my breeches had holes in them there. Let me bring over a clean sock in the morning." He looked down at Felicity, who slumbered in his lap. "Here, Mrs. Drew. Take the Bible and let me get Lissy upstairs."

She and Helen followed him up the stairs. The floor was cold, so Helen's prayers were short. Felicity didn't even wake up as Roxanna dressed her in her nightgown and tied on her sleeping cap. Lord Winn stood looking down on her. "If that were anyone but Felicity, we could call it the sleep of the innocent," he whispered. Helen giggled, and crawled into bed beside her sister. She held out her hand.

"Good night, Lord Winn. I hope you have a happy Christmas."

As Roxanna watched, he turned away, the muscles in his face working. Tears started down his cheeks. She touched his shoulder and sat on the edge of Helen's bed as he left the room. "I am sure he will," she managed to say. "Perhaps the holidays are hard for him."

"But he has us," Helen asserted, keeping her voice low to avoid disturbing Lissy.

And such a lot of trouble we are for ten pounds, Roxanna thought. She kissed her daughter good night. "When you wake up in the morning, you will smell Lissy's heavenly goose cooking."

And my goose is already cooked, she thought as she hugged Helen, then closed the door behind her. Lord Winn was already down the stairs and into his overcoat, the writ in his hand, his eyes red.

"Get on your cloak, Roxie," he ordered. "We're going to Moreland. You can cry in peace over there and I can throw things."

She nodded and let him help her into her cloak. "I'll be back in a while, Meggie," she said. "Please try to sleep."

"I couldn't possibly, Mrs. Drew," Meggie said.

Lord Winn took her hand and hurried her through the snow to Moreland, his face grim. She half-ran to keep up with him, and then he shortened his stride. "Sorry," was all he said as they traversed the distance.

The estate was dark and cold. He let her into the bookroom and lit a lantern, then dumped coal in the grate and started a fire. "I'm going to the stable to wake up my groom," he said as he looked at the little flame. "I'm sending him for Tibbie."

"Tibbie?" she asked.

He nodded. "He may be the only cool head in the bunch, Mrs. Drew. I'll be back."

She pulled up a chair close to the fire and reached for the document that Lord Winn had thrown down on the desk. The Latin phrases mingled with the English words and leaped out at her like little imps to torment her. She shuddered and pushed it away.

By the time Lord Winn returned, the fire glowed in the grate, and her hands were warm for the first time all day. He sat down heavily in the chair and swiveled it around to face her. "Did you read it?" he asked.

She shook her head. "I can't bring myself to touch it."

"I understand that, Roxie," he said simply. "He has been granted a writ of removal by the lord magistrate in York."

"York?" she questioned. "Why there? It's so far away!"

"Exactly," he said, scooting his chair closer until they were knee to knee. "The writ can only be answered in York, my dear."

"Then we will start out tomorrow," she said, her eyes on his face.

He shook his head. "To enter a pleading you have to have a court hear you. There's nothing in session right now." He leaped to his feet and slammed his hand on the desk. "Damn that man! There are no Common Pleas, or Assizes, or even Chancery Court open between now and at least January 6," he shouted. "Quarter sessions doesn't start for another three weeks! Mrs. Drew, he has humbugged you!"

She sagged back in the chair, her mouth open. "My God," she said softly. "Can I not at least bring a plea before a justice of the peace?" she asked.

He grasped her by the shoulders. "And who is this district's JP?" he demanded, his eyes fierce.

She began to cry. "It is Lord Whitcomb!" she sobbed. "But . . . how can he do this? Why can he take my children?" She cried as he took her in his arms and held her close.

"It's in the document, my dear," he said, holding her off a little to look at her face. "He claims you are an unfit mother because you moved your daughters into a dilapidated house with floors and roof missing. As the only living relative in England, he is empowered to take your daughters from your influence."

Roxanna stared at him, her tears forgotten. "But the house is beautiful now! How can he say that?"

Lord Winn was thumbing through the document. "Look you here. 'The house is in execrable condition, with peeling wallpaper, parts of the roof missing, and the floor entirely gone in the sitting room. The structure is unsound and dangerous for children. By reason of the fact that Mrs. Anthony Drew, relict of Anthony Drew, is obviously of unsound mind, I claim her children as my own to raise.' "

"How can he do this?" she murmured, looking over his arm at the words. "It is not true now about the house."

He sank down in his chair again. "And how is a magistrate in York to know that?" he asked quietly. "And why would a magistrate in York have cause to doubt Lord Whitcomb's testimony to the state of your house? He is a district justice of the peace, and by everyone's acknowledgment, a gentleman." He spit out the word like venom.

She let the words sink in as she read where he pointed, looking up finally. "I have no legal recourse, have I?" she asked.

"None whatsoever, Roxie," he agreed. "None that I can see, at least."

"I have to turn my daughters over to him on Friday," she said, her voice calm. "And myself, too, I suppose. He will have me after all, because he knows I would never let them go without me. And I cannot do a thing about my upcoming ruin."

They were both silent, staring into the fireplace. In a few minutes, Lord Winn put more coal on the grate, then rested his boots against the fender. He reached for her hand. "We can enter a pleading in the middle of January when quarter sessions convenes."

"That will be too late," she said. "He's a strong man, Lord Winn. I do not think I will have much of a chance to resist him." She shuddered. "I am already afraid of him. Excuse my blunt words, but I know he will hurt me," she said frankly. Her voice broke then. "We can't do anything? Oh, God, tell me there is something we can do!" She sobbed into her hands.

"You could grab them and run, but why do I think he will be watching the roads?" he said, handing her his handkerchief.

"Of course he will," she said, her voice muffled in the handkerchief as she blew her nose angrily. "And when I am apprehended, it is only one more indication that I am of unsound mind. Even a January pleading in quarter sessions would not convince a judge that I was a fit mother. I cannot run."

"No," he agreed, "you cannot. And I doubt anyone would take the word of a woman suffering from derangement of grief against Lord Whitcomb's calm testimony. As far as the world knows, all he wants to do is offer you and your daughters a good home with him and his lady, and you have irrationally resisted his good offices by moving into a ruin." He sighed. "I might add, the house is on the estate owned by a notorious divorcé of dubious character. Humbugged," he repeated. "Trussed up better than a Christmas goose."

"Oh, don't say that!" she pleaded.

"If I weren't so angry, I could almost admire his cleverness," he said, then sat up, listening. "I believe Tibbie is here. Roxie, light another lamp and go to the kitchen. I think there is a bottle of rum on the table. Bring it back here with some cups."

When she returned, the marquess was sitting on the edge of the desk, telling Tibbie the story. She calmly poured rum for the three of them. Tibbie accepted his absentmindedly, his eyes on the document before him. He looked up finally.

"I think I understand how he could give such a description," he said, and held out his cup for more.

"Say on, sir," Lord Winn declared.

The bailiff looked at Roxanna. "Remember when he and his solicitor came here to talk me out of renting you the house?"

She nodded. "Yes. And I was so afraid you would yield."

"Well, after they left in such a fit, one of the workers came to tell me that they were going through the dower house, room by room. He said the solicitor was taking notes!"

"That explains how he knew so much," Lord Winn said. "Well, Tibbie, any suggestions? We're fresh out of ideas."

The bailiff shook his head. "You need to see a solicitor, my lord."

Lord Winn managed a laugh with no humor in it. "He left yesterday for Edinburgh for the holidays. The only other solicitor in the village is retained by Lord Whitcomb." He rose heavily to his feet and paced in front of the window, his hands behind his back. "I cannot believe how cleverly we have been diddled!"

"Yes, and the sheriff even thought you would be gone today," Roxanna said, joining him at the window. She leaned her forehead against his arm for a brief moment. "I am so grateful Helen had to have her greenery. I could not face this alone."

He put his arm around her. "I can't see that my presence here is making one scintilla of difference, Roxie dear," he admitted frankly.

As they stood at the window, staring out into the snow, Tibbie Winslow began to chuckle. It started as a low rumble in his throat, then welled into such a hearty laugh that they turned around to gape at him. As they watched, he reached for the handkerchief Roxanna had abandoned and dabbed at his eyes.

"Have you lost your mind?" the marquess snapped.

Tibbie looked at Roxanna and then at Lord Winn. He nodded. "It'll do in a pinch," he said to himself. "It'll do."

"What will do?" she demanded. "Oh, Tibbie, you are driving me distracted!"

He spread his hands out on the table and looked up at them with glittering eyes. "It's simple. Lord Winn, all you have to do is marry Mrs. Drew! Then Lord Whitcomb can't touch her or the girls. It's so simple."

She gasped and released her hold on Lord Winn. "Tibbie, that is out of the question!"

"Why?" he asked simply.

"Well, because it just is," she said, looking at the marquess for confirmation. "Surely Lord Winn will agree. Tibbie, I believe you owe him an apology for such an absurdity."

To her bewilderment, the marquess was looking back and nodding, his expression completely unreadable.

She stared at him. "You can't be considering this seriously!"

"And why not, Mrs. Drew?" he said at last. "Tibbie, you may have hit upon the only thing that will humbug Whitcomb."

Tibbie agreed, his eyes bright. "Just the way you two were standing there, you know, like she fits under your arm, made me think of it." He looked at Roxanna. "He's a good man, Mrs. Drew."

"A bit shopworn," Winn said, his eyes light now with something besides despair. "But I could be the answer to your current dilemma."

Roxanna sank down into the chair. "Surely you don't want to do something that drastic, my lord. I mean, what a crazy notion this is!"

"It's not so crazy," the marquess argued, sitting on the edge of the desk. "If you and your daughters are my chattel, according to law, Whitcomb can't do a thing. That would solve your problem."

"Yes, but—" she began helplessly.

"And if you marry me, then Lettice, Amabel, and even Clarice will be off my back forever," he continued with relish, unable to disguise his growing enthusiasm. "I would count that a blessing!"

He reached out to shake Tibbie's hand. "Sir, you are a genius! I am sure I do not pay you enough!"

Tibbie glanced at Roxanna and allowed himself a little smile. "My lord, I think this will require some convincing on your part." He grinned at Roxanna. "I think something in the stables is needing my attention."

"What?" Roxanna snapped. Everything was happening too fast. She wanted to curl up somewhere and think about matters, even as they were racing toward a conclusion she had no control over.

"Happen I'll find out when I get there," he said quickly as he nodded to Lord Winn and backed out of the room with the speed of someone half his age.

Lord Winn closed the door behind his bailiff and strolled to the window again, his hands clasped behind his back, not looking at her. He waited a long moment to speak, as though choosing his words with impeccable care. "Mrs. Drew, I need hardly remind you that you are at *point non plus*, if ever anyone was."

"I suppose I am," she agreed, her eyes lowered, the words dragged out of her.

There was another long silence. He finally turned around and looked at her. She couldn't bring herself to meet his glance, so he knelt by her chair and raised up her chin with his fingers until she had no choice.

"Marry me, Mrs. Drew," he said softly. "And let me assure you from the outset that this will be a marriage of convenience."

"That is hardly fair to you, sir," she protested, when she could speak.

He continued to look into her eyes. "Oh, Mrs. Drew, it is entirely fair. I really have no desire to commit any more matrimonial folly. You already know my ideas on children of my own. I will deed Moreland to you upon my death and provide you with an income now. Beyond a few visits a year to make sure that all is well, I'll not trouble you with my presence. It will drive my sisters crazy, but what can they say, really?"

She was still silent, staring at her hands now.

"And Mrs. Drew, should you form a more agreeable attachment in a year or so, I am sure we can arrange a very quiet annulment."

"But this is all so cold-blooded!" she burst out, unable to contain herself. "Fletcher, I cannot do this to you."

He smiled. "Well, at least you acknowledge that I have a first name. That is a step in the right direction. And yes, you are right.

It *is* cold-blooded. We are trying to save your daughters and your virtue," he reminded her.

She nodded, unable to dispute his line of reasoning. "But—"

"Do you like me even a little bit, Roxie Drew?" he asked suddenly.

"Oh, of course!" she said. "How could I not like you?"

"Well, you need only ask Cynthia for a whole list of reasons why not," he replied, a twinkle in his eyes. "My dear, this will solve your problem and mine, too. Marry me."

She looked him in the eyes. I am not even a year through my mourning, she thought. My God, I am still in black! The village will be scandalized. His relatives will be aghast. A sudden smile played around her lips. The girls will be delighted, and we will be safe. The smile left her face. And I have no choice, none at all, but by God's blood, I will play this hand.

"I will marry you, sir," she said.

Such a light came into his eyes that she gazed at him in surprise. When he saw her expression, his own became more sober again. He held out his hand and they shook on it. He sat at the desk again, and leaned back in his chair. "Very well, Mrs. Drew. We certainly haven't three weeks to cry the banns. It will have to be by special license."

His chair came down with a bang and he slammed his fist on the table. "Damn!" he shouted, and she jumped. He touched her arm, his eyes filled with distress. "I'm sorry, my dear. I just remembered. I cannot get a special license. The only way I can remarry is with a writ from Chancery Court and with the approval of the Archbishop of Canterbury himself."

He went to the window to stare out at the snow as her heart sank again. She was beyond tears. And so even this wretched plan will not work, she thought. I am doomed to be Lord Whitcomb's mistress. God help me.

She watched with dull eyes as Lord Winn paced the little room, pausing at last in front of a map of England and Scotland. He stared at it, and as she watched, his shoulders relaxed and his hands came out of his pockets. He picked up the lamp and moved closer to the map.

"Oh, Mrs. Drew, we'll get that bastard another way," he said, the note of triumph undisguised in his voice.

"How?" she said at last, afraid to hope.

"We're about seventy miles from the Scottish border," he informed her, his voice filled with enthusiasm again.

"I know that! I do not think I need a geography lesson right now, my lord," she said. "How will this solve our—"

She stopped, leaped to her feet, and hurried to join him in front of the map. "You are not thinking for one minute . . ." she began.

He was nodding as his finger traced the route. "Oh, yes I am, Mrs. Drew, think on. If we can catch the mail coach, we can be in Gretna Green on Boxing Day. My dear, we will have to marry over the anvil."

She blinked her eyes and leaned against the wall, the breath knocked out of her. "Sir, is that legal?" she asked.

"Most assuredly. It's just a bit . . . well, the word *ill-bred* does come to mind."

She was silent, contemplating the enormity of such a step. What will people think? she asked herself, then shook her head. What did it matter? Her girls would be safe, no matter how scandalous the wedding.

"I will do it, my lord," she said slowly. "I have no choice."

"No, you do not, my dear," he sympathized. He held out his hand again and she extended hers slowly until they were clasping hands. He gave her hand a shake, but did not release it.

"Well, Mrs. Drew. In for a penny, in for ten pounds, in your case. Let's go find Tibbie."

Chapter 12

Sleep was out of the question that night. After a lengthy conversation with Meggie, in which they both cried and clung to one another, she filled the girls' stockings and sat in the parlor until even the coals grew dull in the grate. What have I done? she asked herself over and over. Did I have any choice? The answer was always the same. She was as much at the mercy of Lord Winn as Lord Whitcomb.

It distressed her that she knew even less about Fletcher Rand than she did about her brother-in-law, and yet she was ready to join her life to his in the most intimate bond. I could say I was taking him on faith, she thought, but that almost seems like blasphemy. I am doing this because it is the only way I can save my daughters. I must trust my future and my daughters' futures to someone I scarcely know.

She went upstairs to bed finally, knowing that she needed at least part of a night's sleep before the trip tomorrow. The marquess had warned her that it would be a difficult journey. She undressed and brushed her hair, then crawled into bed.

She was still awake when the room began to grow light again, lying there thinking about the night before her wedding to Anthony. She had stayed awake all night then, too, but with a difference—excruciatingly in love with the vicar and wanting him so much that she did not know how she could contain herself until the wedding.

This time was different. Her friends and Anthony's former parishioners would be scandalized at her hurried marriage over the anvil to a divorced peer. Sweet Roxanna Drew, who never spoke a word out of turn or did an improper thing in her life, was eloping to Scotland when their beloved vicar was hardly settled in his grave. Will they think I married Lord Winn for his wealth? she asked the ceiling. Will they conclude that I had to get married to beat the stork? Will they call me deranged? An opportunist?

She knew she could always start a story circulating about Marshall Drew and his infamous offer, but that was even more repugnant to her than what the villagers would be thinking of her marriage to Lord Winn. Suppose Lissy and Helen heard the rumors about their uncle? She sat up in bed and pulled the covers around her. They must never know what an odious man Lord Whitcomb was. She refused to betray Anthony's memory and the Drew name that way. Better that people should wonder about her, and not lose faith in the Drews, and what they meant to the North Riding.

Roxie, you are not being fair to yourself, she thought. You are getting security, but at the price of a warm man in a warm bed. Lord Winn has made it perfectly clear that he does not covet your body. You are going to be taking a lot of long walks for the rest of your life. She knew that once she said her vows over the anvil, there would never be anyone else. She could no more look around for another husband and seek an annulment from Lord Winn than fly. Her word, once given, was given.

I have made an empty bed, and now I must lie in it, she told herself as the sun came up. But did I ever have a choice? Lord, you have dealt me another wretched hand. Is that any way to treat someone?

The room grew lighter. There was no wind outside, and she

could not see any snow falling, which was a relief. At least we will not be frozen in a blizzard in the Pennines, she thought as she lay back and listened for the girls. I am making such a sacrifice for them, and they must never know. Anthony. I trust this is what you would have me do. I can think of nothing else, and as God can witness, I have thought all night.

Her eyes closed then in weariness. She slept for a few minutes before she heard the door open, and Helen and Lissy threw themselves on her.

"Happy Christmas, Mama!" Lissy shouted as she pried open Roxie's eye to make sure she was in there.

"Felicity, have a few manners," Helen scolded, and then crawled into bed with her mother.

Roxanna held her close, and pulled Lissy up beside her. "Happy Christmas to you, too, my darlings."

"Can we go downstairs now, Mama?" Lissy begged.

Roxanna took a deep breath and cuddled her daughters on either side of her. "First I must tell you something. I do not know if you will understand, but you must know." She paused, then plunged ahead. "Lord Winn and I are going to Scotland this afternoon to be married."

"Oh, Mama, how famous!" Lissy exclaimed as she clapped her hands. "Can we come, too?"

Roxanna shook her head. "I am sorry, my dear, but it's too cold, and we have to hurry." She looked at Helen, who lay still, staring at the ceiling, even as she had earlier. "My dear?" she asked.

Helen was silent a long moment before she spoke. "Mama, why do you want to forget Papa so soon?"

Roxie felt her heart break as she gathered Helen closer. "Oh, never even think that, my dear! I could never forget Papa."

"Then why are you doing this so soon?"

Why indeed? she thought. It is for your protection, Helen, but I cannot tell you that. "Let us say, it is for our benefit."

Lissy sat up and looked across Roxie to her sister. "Helen, you know you like Lord Winn!"

"Yes, of course," she agreed. "But I do not understand."

Roxie could only kiss the top of her head, hold her close, and say, "You'll have to trust me, Helen, that I am doing what is best for all of us. Please believe me."

Helen nodded finally. "I trust you, Mama," she said at last, but her voice was wistful. "But, Mama, do you ever wish things were different? Why is life so strange?"

Roxie could not speak as she held her daughter. Is this what we do now? Do we take life an hour at a time? Do we wish for what once was, or do we move ahead on this new path? She held her daughter off from her so she could look into her eyes. "My dearest child, we move forward," she said firmly. "The less we look back, the better."

It felt like betrayal, like a corkscrew spiraling into her heart, each turn more painful than the one before. She calmly stared down the hurt in Helen's eyes, even as she wanted to run around the room screaming and pulling at her hair.

"Forget Papa?" Helen whispered, and Roxie felt another turn of the corkscrew.

She shook her daughter gently. "Never! But, my dears, we must put him in a special place now and turn a page in our book."

Helen sighed and leaned against her mother again. "I wish I could understand," she sighed.

So do I, Roxie thought as she forced a smile in Felicity's direction. I am glad you are too young for this, Lissy.

"I do not have to call him Papa, do I?" Helen asked.

"No, my dear. I expect he will want you to call him Winn, though."

Felicity tugged at her mother's nightgown, then rested her head in Roxie's lap. "What will you call him?"

Roxie fingered Lissy's dark hair. "I really don't know. He has always been 'my lord,' or Lord Winn."

"His name is Fletcher," Lissy offered.

"It seems a little strange."

Lissy brightened and sat up. "Mama, you can name him like you did Ney!"

Roxie laughed. "I do not think he would take kindly to that!" She kissed her daughters. "Come, my dears. Let's go see if Father Christmas found us here in the dower house."

The house was smelling wonderfully of cooking goose when Lord Winn knocked on the door. Felicity let him in, wearing all four of the barrettes he had left in her stocking. She twirled around so he could admire the dress Roxanna had made. He smiled and covered his eyes. "Such beauty if positively blinding, Felicity." He handed her another package. "Open this now, and remember, you have to share."

Roxanna knew she should have come forward when she heard his knock on the door, but she felt suddenly shy. You are a goose, Roxanna, she thought as she stayed in the sitting room and watched Lissy and the marquess. He was dressed more elegantly than usual, his boots polished and his neckcloth arranged with more thought than was typical. She watched as he knelt beside her daughter to talk. Lord Winn, for all the things you say about children, you have the good instinct to speak on their level.

Lissy ran into the room, holding out the box she had opened. "Mama, it is chocolate! Oh, please, may I have one?"

"Of course you may. Did you tell Lord Winn thank you?"

Lissy put her hand to her mouth in dismay, turned, and curtsied. "Thank you, Lord Winn," she said breathlessly as she popped a chocolate in her mouth, then dashed into the kitchen calling for Helen.

"I had no idea the effect of chocolate on that one," Lord Winn mused as he watched her go and rose gracefully to his feet. "Is there anything she doesn't like?"

His tone was light, and she knew it was her duty to match it. "She is not overly fond of aubergine in any form. I cannot disguise it enough."

"Then she and I are at one on that issue," Lord Winn agreed as he sat beside her on the sofa. "You don't ever need to serve it, except in times of famine." He reached in his pocket and pulled out a narrow package. "Happy Christmas, Roxanna," he said.

She took the package after a moment's hesitation. "I do not have anything for you, my lord," she said.

"Next Christmas will be soon enough," he replied somewhat enigmatically. "I would be happy enough now if you would call me Winn."

"Very well, Winn," she replied as she opened the package. She held her breath as she opened the box, dreading something expensive. She stared, then took out a tin-stamped medal on the end of a leather string. "What is it, my l—Winn?"

He grinned and took it from her. "It's a good luck charm I got from a Portuguese fisherman when he fished me from the water three parts drowned after our ship sank off Cabo San Vicente. You've earned it."

Her eyes lively, she held still as he draped it around her neck. He kissed her on the forehead with a loud smack that made her giggle, despite her discomfort at his nearness.

"I didn't think you'd accept anything else, and by God, it got me through eight dreary years without a fatal injury."

She fingered the medal then looked at him. "Thank you," she said simply as she tucked it inside her dress. "I don't know that there's anything I need more right now than a little good luck."

"That's what I thought. You're welcome," he replied, then stood up and held out his hand for her. "Let's hurry up that goose in the kitchen. We want to catch the mail coach."

Tibbie and Emma Winslow arrived just as Lord Winn began to carve the goose. Roxanna showed them to their seats, apologizing for this shocking intrusion on their holiday.

"Think nothing of it, Mrs. Drew," Tibbie said as he tucked a napkin under his chin. "Emma and I will be delighted to keep an eye on things while you're gone." He tilted his head toward Meggie Watson. "I think between the three of us that you can count on it."

Roxanna nodded, her eyes serious, then looked down at her plate. This is all a dream, she thought. In a moment I will wake up, and Anthony will be carving the turkey. Then she touched the leather thong around her neck and sighed.

"White meat or dark, Roxanna?" Lord Winn was asking. He swallowed as he watched her, and she realized he was keeping a check rein on his emotions, even as she was. The thought comforted her as nothing else could. In for a penny, in for a pound, indeed, she thought as she held up her plate and asked for white meat, please.

Tibbie turned to Helen and Lissy. "My dears, go into the kitchen a moment. You'll find a pudding that Mrs. Winslow brought along. Can the two of you bring it in here?"

Helen and Lissy both jumped up from the table. "Mind you take it out of the bowl and find a plate," Tibbie called, then turned back to Lord Winn when they left the room, his eyes serious. "Lord Whitcomb has his people watching the inn where the mail coach stops, my lord. He doesn't mean for Mrs. Drew to even try to get through to York."

"Damn!" Lord Winn exclaimed. "That means we have to catch the coach in Richmond."

"I'm not even so sure the road north is open," Tibbie continued. "I heard something about a road crew at work."

"We'll manage either way," Winn said, his expression grim. "Damn that man. With someone watching, we can't go south or north on the highway, at least until Penrith, on the other side of the Pennines."

The girls returned with the pudding and he smiled at them, joking with Lissy that the pudding was bigger than she was. You're a cool one, Lord Winn, Roxanna thought as she forced herself to smile, too. No wonder Soult and Ney lost Spain for Napoleon, if the other soldiers they fought against were anything like you.

After the dinner, Lord Winn and Tibbie returned to Moreland, their heads together, engaged in earnest conversation. Her heart pounding, her thoughts on the journey ahead, Roxanna read to Felicity and tucked her in bed for a nap. Helen and Mrs. Winslow were busy in the kitchen with dishes. She listened to the comforting domestic sounds as the clock struck one.

She pulled on her warmest dress, a woolen petticoat, several pairs of stockings, and her riding boots that she had not worn since well before Helen's birth. Something old, she thought, looking down at her boots, and something new to me, as she fingered her necklace. She went into the dressing room and found Anthony's woolen muffler, wrapping it around her neck. "Borrowed and blue," she whispered as she leaned against the wall until she had the strength to stand upright.

She looked in at Felicity one more time. The barrettes caught the fire's glow and twinkled back at her. I would die for you, she thought. Is that what I am doing? She closed the door quietly.

Lord Winn returned on horseback, bundled in his military greatcoat and wearing boots with no polish and deep scratches in the leather. He dismounted as she opened the door.

"I thought we'd both ride Ney," he explained. "Helen tells me you're not much of an equestrienne."

"She's right," Roxanna agreed as she pulled on her mittens. "Is Ney up to this?"

"Roxie, you don't weigh much," he said. "And he has a grand, brawny heart. Besides all that, we'll keep each other warm. Are you ready?"

No, she thought, I am not. She hesitated at the door, and knew that he could tell exactly how she felt.

"Ready or not, madam, you haven't a choice," he reminded her, his voice firm, even a little hard.

She took a deep breath and closed the door behind her. "Then I am certainly ready."

He mounted again, then held out his hand to her, pulling her up in front of him in the saddle. "It's a tight fit," he said in her ear as his arms went around her and he grasped the reins tighter. "Too many cinnamon buns, Roxie."

She chuckled because he expected it, then stared in surprise as Tibbie came toward them in the gig, dressed in Lord Winn's greatcoat and low-crowned beaver hat. He waved a gloved hand at them, and turned the gig toward the lane overlooking the Plain of York.

"He says he and his missis were followed to Moreland," Lord

Winn said as they watched the bailiff drive slowly south. "Let's watch from here a moment."

He backed Ney off the lane and into the orchard, with its concealing hedgerow. "Happen he was right," he whispered in her ear. "Your brother-in-law is not taking any chances," he observed as two horsemen followed the gig at a distance. "He still thinks either you or I will be making a break to the magistrate in York, and he means to stop you even before you reach the mail coach."

"But why is Tibbie doing this?" she asked.

"Diversionary tactic, my dear. He'll give the men someone to follow while we try another road." He wheeled Ney around toward the hills nearby. "We will ride east for a few miles then turn west and north, in case anyone else is curious." His cheek was next to hers. "I trust you know some back trails, Roxie."

She nodded. "I can guide us through to Richmond without getting on the main road."

"Good girl! You'd have been an asset in Spain."

They entered Richmond as the clock in the church there chimed two. The road was closed, true to Tibbie's prediction. Without even pausing, Lord Winn ignored the warning of the road crew and continued steadily toward the great bulk of the Pennines, that spine of England so green and inviting in the summer, but white now, and stark with winter. The road was a narrow lane between shoulder-high drifts, a mire of freezing mud that Ney picked his way through carefully, slipping occasionally, but guided by Lord Winn's firm hand on the reins. He steered mainly with his knees, digging in sometimes with his spurs when Ney hesitated. Roxie admired his horsemanship, even as she blinked at the glare of the snow and kept her chin down in Anthony's muffler.

She had never been so cold before, even crammed up against Lord Winn in the saddle they shared. The inside of her nose prickled; she tried to breathe through her mouth, but that pained her lungs. She gasped for breath several times, and then Lord Winn pulled her muffler up over her nose.

"Breathe through your nose," he ordered, his own voice muffled. "Keep your head down. And let me know if you can't feel your fingers or toes."

They continued steadily upward, never looking back, but concentrating on the road before them that wound past villages sleeping in the grip of winter. As they plodded toward Scotland, Roxanna imagined people in their houses decorated for the holiday, toasting the season with loved ones, warming themselves with a Yule log. In the distance, through fields bare now of roads, and with stone fences scarcely showing above the snow, she saw lonely crofters' cottages, the smoke brave against the sky.

The sun was low and still they had not reached the summit. She protested when the marquess handed her down and made her walk. He joined her as he led Ney along, his arm tight around her shoulders. "My feet were getting numb," he said. "Keep your head down, Roxie." She nodded, too cold to speak, until he prodded her. "Yes," she replied distinctly, knowing that he wanted to hear her voice.

It was dark when they reached the summit. The wind picked up then as the sun fled from the freezing Yorkshire sky, and whipped around them until her head began to ache. Can we see to go on? she wondered, and then noticed the full moon rising.

"Think of it as the retreat from Moscow," Lord Winn said as they struggled on in the early dusk. "Speak to me, Roxanna."

"You weren't there, were you?"

"Lord, no, my dear. That was Napoleon's little blunder. It was cold enough over the Pyrenees." He managed a dry chuckle. "And here I thought my campaigning days were behind me." He put his cheek next to hers for a moment. "At least you smell better than my lieutenants."

They rode slowly into the night then, the air so cold that it almost hummed around them. Lord Winn pummeled her once to point out the northern lights. She gazed at their green splendor, her mind too dull to appreciate the beauty before her. She thought of Helen and Felicity asleep in their bed, and closed her eyes.

He wouldn't let her sleep, but prodded her awake again and again. "Keep your eyes open, Roxie, or I'll make you walk," he insisted, his own voice slurred with exhaustion.

The moon was beginning its descent when she finally noticed that they, too, were traveling down hill. The thought gave her heart and she sat up straighter in the saddle, grateful for what little warmth Lord Winn gave off. Minutes or hours later—she could not tell—he pointed with his riding crop.

"Penrith," he said, a note of triumph in his voice. "By God, Roxie, we've done it."

Penrith before dawn was as still as the crofters' cottages on the high passes. They traveled the quiet street and Lord Winn dismounted before an inn proclaiming itself The King and Prince. He pounded on the door a long time before the keep stuck his head out of an upstairs window.

"Come back when it's morning," the man protested. "I've got no room."

"Typical for Christmas, wouldn't you agree?" Lord Winn murmured as he stepped back in the street. "Let us in, anyway," he ordered. "We've come from Richmond tonight."

The window slammed shut, and Roxanna's heart sank. To her vast relief, the door opened in a few minutes.

"Richmond?" the keep asked as he tucked his nightshirt into his breeches. "You must be daft. The road is closed."

"It certainly is," Lord Winn murmured. "For God's sake, build us a fire."

In a few more moments, they stood before a roaring fire, ale in hand. The landlord pointed to the settle against the wall. "No room, but you can rest there. I'll take your horse around back."

"Stable him there for a day," the marquess said as he reached slowly into his coat. "Lord, but my fingers hardly work," he grumbled as he took out a handful of coins with stiff hands. "When does the mail coach from the west road come through to Scotland?"

"Two hours. You can rest here."

Lord Winn made her drink the ale, then led her to the settle. He sat down and pulled her head into his lap. She protested, even as her eyes closed. "Shut up, Roxie," was the last thing she remembered hearing.

The mail coach was late, and she hardly recalled climbing onto it. They slept, leaning against each other, until they crossed the Scottish border. When she finally opened her eyes, the sun was blinding on the snow, and they were in Gretna Green. She looked over at Lord Winn, who still slumbered. Here we are, she thought. I will hold hands with this strange man and be married by a blacksmith. She pulled out the charm he had given her and held it up to the light, hoping the luck had not disappeared with the end of the war.

"Well, so far our good fortune is holding," Lord Winn commented as he watched her.

"I thought you were asleep," she said, shy again. She tucked the necklace back into her dress, where it rested against her skin.

"No, no, madam," he said lightly. "I've got wedding jitters." He smiled at her and gave her shoulder a squeeze. "Well, let's get off and find the blacksmith."

The village blacksmith was dawdling over a late breakfast when they interrupted him. He came to his door with his napkin still tucked into his shirt and a thick slice of ham in his fist. Roxanna stared at the meat as her mouth watered. She remembered goose, but it seemed years ago.

"Come back tomorrow," he growled and started to close the door.

Lord Winn stuck his foot in the door and shouldered his way in. He strode to the table and slapped down a handful of guineas. "Now!" he demanded, his voice full of command. He leveled a stare at the blacksmith that probably had struck terror into many a soldier from Spain to Belgium. Roxanna felt herself standing up straighter.

The blacksmith stuffed the ham in his mouth and strolled to his table. He fingered the coins, letting them drop through his hand. "Maude," he bawled over his shoulder finally. "We've got some customers. Look lively." He glanced from Lord Winn to Roxanna. "You must really want to get married today," he commented. He winked at Roxanna as he still chewed the ham. "I like winter weddings, myself, dearie. Good cuddling afterward."

Roxanna blushed and he laughed, his mouth still full. "Oh, Maude, you've got to see this one! When did we last have a blushing bride?"

"That's quite enough," Lord Winn snapped.

The blacksmith almost came to attention. He swallowed the great lump of ham. "Hurry up, Maudie!" he called, when he could speak.

The blacksmith's wife joined them from the kitchen, wiping her flour-covered hands onto her apron. She nodded to Roxanna and then riveted her eyes to the pile of gold coins on the table. She nudged the marquess. "Pound for pound, couldn't ye have snabbled a bigger one for all that money?"

His jaw working, the marquess stared at her until she retreated to stand beside the blacksmith, muttering, "I didn't mean nothing by it."

Her nose in the air, she pulled out a piece of paper and plumped herself down at a writing desk by the fireplace. She dipped the quill in the ink and looked at Roxanna. "Name and age?" she demanded.

"Roxanna Maria Estes Drew, twenty-seven," Roxie said, her voice a whisper. She reached for Lord Winn's hand and clutched it in her fear. The pen scratched on the paper.

"You, laddie?"

The marquess's hand tightened around hers. She looked at him in surprise. You are as frightened as I am, she marveled.

"Fletcher William George Winfrey Rand, Marquess of Winn,

thirty-eight," he said, and repeated it when the blacksmith's wife looked up in surprise.

"We don't get too many lords up here," the blacksmith commented, rubbing his hands together. "Spinster or widow?" he asked Roxanna.

"Widow," she said.

"You, sir? Bachelor or widower?"

"Does it matter?" Lord Winn asked, his voice grating like sandpaper.

"For the book, my lord."

"I am divorced." He reached in his pocket and slapped down an official-looking document.

The blacksmith read it through carefully as the marquess's grip tightened around her fingers. He looked down at her hand and loosened his hold when he noticed her pained expression. "Sorry," was all he said.

"So this is why you came to Scotland?" the blacksmith asked as he gestured to the document.

"Why else, sir?" Lord Winn answered, trying to keep a lid on his irritation.

"It appears in order," the man said at last. He looked toward the door. "It's too cold for the anvil, my lord. Do you mind?"

"Of course not," he replied. "Just marry us."

The blacksmith motioned to his wife to hand him his jacket. He pulled it on, trying to brush off the more obvious stains, and picked up a well-thumbed book from the table. He looked at his wife in irritation. "For God's sake, Maudie, take off your apron! This is a marquess!"

Lord Winn turned his head slightly, and Roxanna felt his shoulders shake.

"I could sing a wee hymn," Maudie offered.

Lord Winn couldn't help himself. He started to laugh, then looked down at her. "Oh, my," he said. "Roxie, were you ever in a stranger situation?"

She shook her head and took a firm grip on his hand. "Marry us, sir," she told the blacksmith. "We'll manage without the wee hymn."

It was the service of the Church of England, read with the glottal stops of a lowland Scot, standing before a peat fire. The stately words rolled off her like rain and she admired them all over again, despite the bone weariness that was even now making her eyelids droop. She only had the courage to glance at Lord Winn once and discovered, to her embarrassment, that he was looking at her with an expression that, if it was not tenderness, was a close relative.

We are safe, she thought as she murmured yes, and the marquess answered in the affirmative, too, his response more confident. The blacksmith assured them that they were man and wife now, and was there a ring?

The marquess reached into his waistcoat. He held the ring out to her. "Will this do?" he asked.

It was a plain gold band, wide and softly glowing in the light of the fire.

"I am sure it is too large," he apologized. "We can have it cut down later." The marquess slid the ring onto her finger, where it dangled. He took it off and placed it on her thumb instead. "For now," he assured her.

The blacksmith nodded in approval. He clapped the marquess on the arm. "She's all yours, laddie, my lord. Take good care of her."

"I intend to," Winn replied, a slight smile on his face.

"You can kiss her, my lord," Maude suggested as she put on her apron again.

Roxanna stood still as Lord Winn grasped her by the shoulders. She closed her eyes and raised her face to his as he kissed her. It was such a brief kiss that she felt a slight disappointment.

"Well, laddie, you've done it now," the blacksmith said as he removed his coat and looked at his breakfast table with some longing. "I always offer a little advice." He paused. "That is, if you don't mind, my lord."

"Say on, sir," Lord Winn stated in amusement, his arm tight around Roxanna's waist.

The blacksmith cleared his throat. "It's good advice, my lord, especially since you've ridden this hobby horse before."

"Don't remind me," Winn murmured.

"It's this, laddie," he said, leaning closer and winking at Roxanna. "Always do what they want."

The marquess grinned. "Very good, sir," he said. "And now if you can direct us to an inn, we are falling down with exhaustion."

The blacksmith winked at Roxanna and grinned as she blushed. He handed the marriage lines to her. "Try the Bonnie Charlie," he suggested. "Down two blocks. You'll see it. I hear the sheets are usually clean."

He was sitting down to his meal before they even closed the door. Roxanna handed the marriage lines to the marquess. "Here you are, Lord Winn."

"Nope. Try again, Roxie," he said as he tucked the paper in his coat.

"Oh, very well, then! Fletch," she replied, her eyes straight ahead, her lips firm. "That's what I'll call you."

The keep at the Bonnie Charlie found them a room near the eaves, apologizing because his wife's relatives were visiting for the holidays from Fort William. "It's a good room," he assured them as they climbed the narrow stairs. "Not much view, but then, not many of my patrons waste time on that!"

Roxanna turned away in embarrassment and the marquess handed another coin to the landlord.

"When does the next mail coach to Carlisle come through?" he asked.

"Three hours."

"Knock on this door in two and a half hours then, and have some food ready."

When the door closed, Winn turned around. "Well, my dear, if I do not lie down I'm going to fall down." He took off his coat and waistcoat and loosened his neckcloth. "Could you help me with my boots?"

She did, tugging them off, then sitting down so he could help with hers. He pulled back the covers, unbuttoned his breeches, and lay down with a sigh. His eyes closed and he was asleep in minutes.

Roxanna arranged his clothes over the back of a chair and unbuttoned her dress. She lay down next to the marquess, gradually relaxing as his warmth spread to her. She touched the ring on her thumb and closed her eyes.

Chapter 13

She woke to loud knocking on the door. Go away, was her first thought, then she raised her head slightly. "Yes, thank you," she said, and the knocking stopped. She lay back down again, held firmly in Lord Winn's grasp. He had pulled her up close against his chest while they slept, his arm draped over her.

She lay still and looked at his hand, admiring the handsome

signet ring he wore. He was warm, so warm, and she was more comfortable than she had been in ages. The pillow was soft, and she felt her eyes closing again. No, she told herself, just before she drifted off to sleep again. We have to catch that mail coach.

Roxanna eased out of the marquess's grasp and tried to tug down her dress. In another moment, Lord Winn rolled onto his back and continued to sleep. She looked down at him. Why is it that men look like little boys when they sleep? she wondered.

His eyes opened and he smiled at her. "It's time to get up," she said.

"Damn." He sighed, and closed his eyes. "I'm finally warm for the first time in at least a day. Thank you for not digging me in the back like Lissy."

"I would never—" she began, then laughed. "You're quizzing me."

"Ah, yes. How astute you are, Mrs. Rand."

Mrs. Rand. She got out of bed quickly, pulling down her dress and looking for her boots. Get used to it, Roxie, she told herself. At least it sounds less formidable than Lady Winn. "My goodness," she said out loud.

"That's pretty strong language, Roxie," Lord Winn said mildly as he ran his hand over the stubble on his chin. "Did you just have a vision I should know about?"

She blushed as she pulled on her boots. "It just occurred to me that I am a marchioness, my lo—Fletch." She stood up and looked out the window. "I don't feel like one."

Lord Winn laughed. "That is funny. Cynthia always felt like one. Damned near ruined me, too. I'll call you Mrs. Rand, when you get tired of hearing 'Roxie.' "

She turned to regard him. "Well, it is not as though it will be much of an issue."

"No," he agreed. "I'm heading for Winnfield as soon as this matter with your wretched brother-in-law is taken care of. Despite her serious irritation with me, Amabel did inform me that I have piles of correspondence on my desk at home and daily notices from my solicitors." He winked at her. "But if you do get any mail at Moreland addressed to Lady Winn, don't send it back, hear ye? I do intend to write you."

They ate quickly in the tavern, bolting down their coffee when the coach announced its arrival from Dumfrees with a blast on the tin horn. The coach was crowded. By putting his arm around her and crowding in close, they managed to stay together. I wish I could talk to you, Roxanna thought as they bowled along. She glowered at the other occupants of the coach and wished them elsewhere, but no one disappeared.

As they traveled steadily south, the sunny morning gave way to clouds that drooped lower and lower. Lord Winn's attention was taken up with the weather, but she snuggled in closer to his chest, preferring to ignore it. *And what if it is snowing?* she thought, then shut the idea from her mind. *Time enough to worry about that later.* She chuckled.

The marquess leaned toward her. "What?"

"I was just thinking that if I don't look out the window I won't be frightened. Helen accuses me of putting off bad news."

"Do you?"

"I suppose I do, Fletch," she replied. "I've noticed in the last few years that you can put off anything, because bad news is always still there when you have the strength to face it."

"I have a better idea, Roxie," he said. "Let me worry about it for you."

His face was close to hers. Impulsively, she kissed his cheek. "Thank you, Lord Winn," she replied. "That's quite the nicest thing anyone has said to me in a long while."

It was his turn to blush this time. He squeezed her shoulder and looked out the window again. "Roxie, you're a funny thing."

Snow was falling by the time they reached Penrith. As the marquess handed her down from the coach, Roxie looked up at the sky in dismay. Winn touched her cheek. "I told you to let me worry, my dear," he murmured.

"This could be tricky," she said, unable to help herself.

"I have faced worse things, and so have you, Mrs. Rand," he told her. "What's a little snow?"

Little snow, indeed, she thought four hours later as they dismounted yet again to flounder through drifts too deep for Ney to carry them. They toiled toward a summit that seemed to move farther and farther away the more they struggled. Only through strenuous effort could she keep herself from looking back to see if Penrith was still visible. *That would be discouraging in the extreme,* she decided, *so I will not do it.*

Lord Winn walked Ney ahead of them to break a trail. "You know something, my dear?" he asked as they labored along, out of breath.

"What?"

He reached behind for her hand and she took hold of him. "In addition to being rather nice to look at for extended periods of time, you don't complain."

"Your compliments are so charming," she replied, amused, as she slipped on the snow and he stopped to steady her.

"Well, I don't tell just anyone these things. Ah, Roxie! The summit. Let's rest a moment and consider this situation."

There was nothing visible for miles around except snow. The sky was blue again, and the wind only idle puffs. Roxie put her hand up to shade her eyes from the glare. "It's beautiful," she said. "Do you feel like we're the only two people on earth?"

He draped his arm on her shoulder and leaned on her a little. "Yes, nice isn't it? Except that I am cold and my feet hurt, and my stomach is growling, and my eyes are starting to burn from the glare. Unlike you, wife, I do complain."

She leaned against his arm. "For a marriage of convenience, this one is certainly taking on adventurous overtones, my lord."

She felt rather than heard his chuckle. "Things can only get better, Roxie," he said as he straightened up and whistled to Ney. "Let's see if this noble beast will carry us for a while."

They continued into the afternoon, traveling a little faster when they reached the area cleaned by the road crew, then slowing down when snowdrifts claimed even that narrow passage. She felt stupid with sleep as she lay back in Lord Winn's arms. He rested his chin on the top of her head as they inched along.

"I should tell you," he said as the sun set, "I wrote to Clarice before we left, advising her of my marriage. If I know Clarrie, she will pass the word to my other sisters." He tightened his grip on the reins and dug in with his knees as Ney slipped onto his haunches. "I expect that will solve my problem. Since I am no longer matrimonial fodder, that will keep shabby genteels like the Etheringhams off my back."

She sat up a little, until he pushed her back gently with his hand against her chest. She relaxed again. "Did you tell them . . ." She paused, not knowing how to phrase her question.

"That it is a marriage of convenience?" he finished. "No. That's none of their business, is it? What we have done is between us, Roxie. You need suffer no embarrassment over this from my family."

"I owe you such a debt," she said softly. "If ever I can repay you, only tell me how."

He was silent, and she wondered if he heard her. "Oh, Roxie," he said finally, and nothing more.

There was no question of stopping for the night, even though they passed crofters' cottages with lights in the windows, and saw, in the distance, the comfort of two farmers herding in their cows from some desolate pasture.

"My God, my hands are cold," the marquess said finally, after an hour of silence. "Roxie, can you take the reins for a while?"

"Of course," she said as he handed them to her. "Maybe I should make you some mittens like Lissy's, instead of those leather gloves."

"I recommend it. Mind you make them brown, though, and not Jezebel red. Now if you don't object, I'll get really forward, Mrs. Rand," he continued, stripping off his gloves with his teeth.

When she said nothing, he reached inside her cloak and under her sweater. He wrapped his arms around her breasts, tucking his hands up under her armpits. "That helps," he said after a few minutes, the relief evident in his voice.

"I can hold the reins as long as you need," she said, enjoying the warmth of his fingers, too, as they gradually thawed.

"I remember killing a horse once in a blizzard and opening him up to tuck my hands in his entrails," he said, his tone conversational. "I won't do that to you, however."

"Thank you, Fletch," she responded.

As his hands grew warmer against her body, he became more conversational again. "Roxie, we used to dig up French graves, dump out the corpses, and burn the coffins to keep warm."

Roxanna shuddered, more wide awake than she had been for miles. "Those days are over," she reminded him.

"I hope so. If you keep prodding Ney, he might not have to give up his guts."

"You wouldn't . . ."

"Of course I would, Roxie. We have some business this morning with your brother-in-law. Do you think I would let my affection for a horse stop me?"

No, I do not, she thought. You are a hard man, Lord Winn. How grateful I am that you are on my side.

They walked past Richmond just as the sun was coming up. She staggered through the snow as Lord Winn kept a firm grasp on the back of her cloak. Once he slung her over his shoulder and kept walking doggedly along, until she cried, pounded on his back, and made him set her down.

Past Richmond the road was clear and they mounted Ney again. There were even farmers on the road now bringing goods to market, who stared at them as they rode slowly by. Lord Winn rubbed his chin.

"We must look like desperate characters," he told her.

"Speak for yourself," she said, wondering why it was so difficult to even move her mouth. She felt frozen solid, Lot's wife in wintertime, turned to a pillar of ice.

The sun was up, illuminating the Great Plain of York as they reached the end of Moreland's tree-lined avenue. Lord Winn reined in his horse. "I have never been so grateful to see anything as these elms," he told her as he sat there a moment, then gathered up the energy to dig his heels into Ney again. "Come on, old champion. Let's get Roxie Rand home before we have to chip her out of my saddle."

The dower house looked unbelievably welcome as Lord Winn twitched on the reins and Ney stopped, his head down, the journey over. Winn let the reins drop, but made no effort to dismount. "I can't move, Roxie," he said finally. "Can you throw your leg over the saddle and get down?"

She shook her head, too tired to speak, too exhausted to cry. As she sat there in misery, wondering if they would die from the cold just outside her door, she saw Helen's face in the window, and then jumping up and down, Lissy, too. "Oh, thank God for early risers," she murmured as the door opened and Helen ran out in her nightgown and bare feet, calling for Tibbie.

In another moment Tibbie followed. He stared at them in openmouthed amazement. "We heard the roads were all closed from Scotland to Carlisle. Did you manage?"

In answer, Lord Winn tugged Roxie's mitten off her left hand and held it up in triumph so the bailiff could see the ring stuck firmly on her thumb. "It was a grand wedding, Tibbie," he said. "Only don't ask!"

Tibbie chuckled as he reached up for Roxanna. "And I suppose you can't move, Mrs. Drew . . ." He paused. "No, it's Lady Winn, now, isn't it?"

"It is, indeed," Lord Winn said. "Any sign of Lord Whitcomb yet?"

"Not yet. We'll give him another hour to drink his tea and put a silly smirk on his face, damn his hide."

"Tibbie, no!" Roxanna murmured, and looked meaningfully at her daughters. Tibbie pulled her from the saddle and she gasped at the pain. She sank into the snow and just lay there as Helen hugged her and Lissy knelt beside her, touching her face.

"Oh, Mama! Couldn't you have waited until it was warmer?" Helen asked, her eyes filled with concern. "Lissy, feel how cold she is."

Roxie shook her head and managed to reach her hand up to

touch Helen's face. "I've never been better, my dearest," she whispered, meaning every word.

With a groan that seemed to well up from the soles of his boots, Lord Winn dismounted and leaned against Ney. He regarded Roxie as she lay in the snow at his feet. "Mrs. Rand, you truly have been more trouble than any tenant I ever encountered." His eyes smiled into hers. "And I would do it over in a minute." He groaned again and leaned away from his horse, reaching down for her hand. "But not in the next one hundred or two hundred minutes, let us say."

His arm around her waist, Helen and Lissy right beside him, they tottered into the house, collapsing onto the sofa. Roxanna stared at the wreath over the fireplace. Was it only three days ago that they had decorated the sitting room? It seemed like years. She uttered no protest as Meggie pulled off her boots, then stood shaking her head at the sight of her feet.

Lord Winn leaned forward and pulled up her skirt to her knees, even as she protested feebly. "Don't worry, Meggie," he said. "No white patches. I recommend that you set up the tub in front of the kitchen fireplace and start warming some water. That should thaw out Mrs. Rand." He shivered involuntarily. "And I'll see what I can find at Moreland."

"It'll have to wait."

They looked at Tibbie, who stood at the window. Summoning strength from somewhere, Lord Winn got to his feet and joined him.

"He's not wasting a moment," Winn said as he removed his overcoat, wincing at the exertion. He reached into the pocket for the marriage lines, and held out his hand for Roxanna. "On your feet, my dear. Let's not forget our manners. Helen, I want you and Lissy to go upstairs and stay there with Meggie and Mrs. Winslow until your uncle leaves. Give me no grief, please."

There was something of firm command in his tired voice that stopped any argument the girls might have offered. He helped Roxanna out of her cloak and sweater, slowly unwinding the muffler from her face, and then leaned against her, forehead to forehead, as Lord Whitcomb's carriage drew to a stop in front of the dower house. He straightened up as Lord Whitcomb rapped sharply on the knocker.

"Open it, Tibbie," he said, very much the colonel commanding.

Lord Whitcomb came in, followed by the sheriff. He stopped in the open door, staring from Lord Winn to Roxanna.

"I told you he was still here," the sheriff murmured to Lord Whitcomb.

Marshall Drew came forward. He removed his coat, looked around for someone to take it, then shrugged and draped it over a chair. He walked farther into the room, past Lord Winn, until he stood before Roxanna, who dug her toes into the carpet and refused to step back.

"Where are they? I have come to claim your daughters, Roxanna." He paused and then coughed delicately into the back of his hand. "Of course, you may accompany them, if you choose, but they are mine now by consent of law."

"No, they're not," Lord Winn said. "And I'd like you to leave."

With a nod, Lord Whitcomb indicated the sheriff to come closer. "This may be your property, Lord Winn, but you can have nothing to say about this matter. It is between Mrs. Drew and me."

Lord Winn limped from the window to stand beside Roxanna. His arm went around her waist. "I have every right to speak, sir." He smiled at her and handed her the marriage lines. "Perhaps you'd like to have the honor, my dear."

"With pleasure," she said, her voice low but carrying an intensity that filled her whole body, driving out the exhaustion and the pain and the worry of the last few days. She slapped the document into her brother-in-law's outstretched hand. "I have a writ of my own, Marshall."

His eyes widened as he read once through the brief paper, then again. "This is not possible," he said, throwing it down.

"Pick it up before I break your neck," Lord Winn ordered.

Whitcomb pushed it aside with his foot. "It can't be official," he protested, his voice rising even as his face turned red.

"Ask any magistrate. Take it to the House of Lords, if you choose," Winn replied, biting off each word. "At least we will not fool you and diddle you and frighten you with an unanswerable writ delivered the day before Christmas! Lord Whitcomb, how dare you terrorize this woman like that?"

His words hung in the air between them, the loathing unmistakable. Roxanna trembled at the fervor of the exhausted man who stood beside her. I do not know why you are fighting my battle, she thought as she looked from him to Lord Whitcomb, but thank you. I can never repay you, Lord Winn, not if I live a thousand years.

"You're really married?" Whitcomb asked, as though he could not believe the paper still at his feet.

"It was the only road you left open to your sister-in-law!" Winn shouted. "She and her daughters are my chattel now and if you do not leave this house at once, I will ask this sheriff to arrest you!" He came forward and took Lord Whitcomb by the neckcloth, jerking him off his feet. "They are my property now!" he snapped, each word distinct.

With a gesture of revulsion, he released Lord Whitcomb. "You offend me, sir," he said finally. "I don't ever want to see you again."

Whitcomb made no reply. He picked up the marriage license and read it again, shaking his head. He handed it to Roxanna. "I hope you have no cause to regret this piece of folly, Roxanna," he said at last, his voice heavy with disdain.

"I regret not one thing, Marshall," she said, hoping she sounded as determined as Lord Winn. "Please leave."

He stared at her another long moment and she gazed back, her spine straight, her shoulders squared. You will have to blink first, for I will never do it, she thought. Never.

He looked away finally, and groped for his overcoat, as though he could not see it. She let her breath out slowly as he pulled on the coat and walked to the door. He turned back suddenly and she held her breath again.

"What do you know of this man?" he asked. "I could tell you things."

Roxanna reached for Lord Winn's hand, grasping it to her stomach. "I know he will never let me down, or scare me, or threaten me, or take what is mine, or violate my mind, as you have tried to do." Her voice trembled with emotion. "Go, Marshall. We can have nothing more to say."

Without a word he turned on his heel and stalked from the room, leaving the door wide open. In another moment, the carriage was retreating down the lane. Tibbie closed the front door. "Some people have no manners," he murmured.

Lord Winn raised Roxanna's hand to his lips, kissed it, then rubbed her fingers against his two-day-old beard as she laughed and tried to pull away. "Now who is humbugged?" he said as he released her.

Roxanna sat down in relief, holding the marriage lines tight in her hand. She wanted to say something else to Lord Winn, but her eyes insisted on closing. In just a moment I will open them, she thought as she fell asleep sitting on the sofa.

She vaguely remembered a warm bath in front of the kitchen fireplace, with Meggie scrubbing her back and scolding her for taking such chances, even as the old nursemaid cried with relief that "her girls" were safe. She dimly recalled the smell of lavender shampoo, and then the delicious feel of a rough towel on her skin, and the pleasure of sliding between flannel sheets with a footwarmer at the bottom of the bed.

She slept solidly for the rest of the day and then all night, waking in the morning only with the arrival of Dr. Clyde, who had come at Lord Winn's insistence. He thumped her soundly, listened to her breathe in and out, and scrutinized her fingers and toes.

"You'll do, Mrs. Drew—no, no, Lady Winn," he corrected himself. "Nothing wrong with you that a good rest won't cure, and some of Mrs. Howell's cooking. She's back, by the way, with her sister to help cook." He tucked the blankets up to her chin again. "Of course, I assured Lord Winn that you were stronger than a French pony and more fit than most crofters, but he insisted I put you through your paces."

She rose up on her elbow. "Is Lord Winn all right?" she asked.

"Well, he lost a toe, madam. Told me not to tell you."

"No!" she exclaimed, feeling a wave of extraordinary guilt. "Nothing else?"

"No. You were both lucky, in my estimation." He replaced his listening tube and closed his black satchel. "I can't see why the hurry, but then, I never argue with the aristocracy."

And I'll never tell you, she thought. Lord Whitcomb may be a scoundrel of the first water, but that Drew name still means something to me. "You are sure he is all right?" she asked.

"He's already up and using a cane. Says he's leaving in a day or two for Winnfield." He shook his head, as if questioning the wisdom of the entire peerage. "I almost don't doubt him. Good day, my dear. Stay out of snowdrifts, mind."

She lay back as Meggie fluffed the pillows behind her. "Where are the girls?" she asked, when the house seemed too quiet.

"Helen is riding with Tibbie, and Lissy is jumping from one foot to the other outside the door, waiting for me to let her in."

Roxanna held out her arms. "Lissy! Come here at once, my love. I need a hug!"

As she hugged Lissy, she noticed that her wedding ring was gone. "Meggie, did I lose my ring?" she asked in sudden alarm. "I thought it was on my thumb when we arrived here."

"It was," Meggie assured her. "Lord Winn removed it before Tibbie took him back to the manor. He said he would have it sized."

Lissy napped with her that afternoon until Meggie carried the sleeping child to her own bed with the whispered announcement that Lord Winn was coming up the stairs.

Oh, dear, she thought as she reached for a brush, wondering what her hair looked like. He should not be climbing stairs, with his foot so uncomfortable. She brushed the tangles from her hair and listened to his slow tread on the stairs. In another moment, he rapped on the door with a cane.

"Come in, please," she said, setting down the brush and wishing she had on something more attractive than faded flannel. Don't be a goose, Roxie, she scolded herself. He couldn't possibly care.

He opened the door and leaned on his cane, wincing as he crossed the threshold. He stopped to admire her. "Mrs. Rand, you look as fine as five pence," he said. "How do you do it?"

"At least I have all my parts," she replied. "Do sit down, Fletch."

He ignored the chair she indicated and sat heavily on her bed. "I suppose the doctor told you," he grumbled.

"Did you really think he would not?" she questioned. "Will you be all right?"

"Certainly! It was only a toe," he assured her. "And don't look so wide-eyed! Well, do, actually. I like your expression. Seriously, Roxie, at Waterloo I spent the better part of a long afternoon in the middle of a square, holding my insides in. I think I can suffer the loss of my little toe without getting too worked up." He leaned closer. "Anyway, I should know better than to wear socks with holes in them."

She touched his arm. "You're pretty tough, Lord Winn," she said.

"So are you, Roxie. I can't fathom any other woman going through all that and then sitting here looking so pleasant." He chuckled. "And the doctor assured me downstairs that you are right as a trivet." He considered a moment, then plunged on. "He also assured me that no one has babies as nicely as you do, and he wished me happy."

Roxanna grasped the blankets and slid down in the bed until her face was covered. She started to laugh then, despite her embarrassment. In another minute she sat up again. "You'll have to forgive Dr. Clyde," she said, apologizing for the doctor, and unable to look him in the eye. "Only think how glad you will be to leave in a few days. This neighborhood could become unbearable."

"Yes, only think," he agreed, sounding anything but cheerful.

She watched his expression. "Does your foot pain you?" she asked, forgetting her own discomfort.

"I suppose," he agreed, his thoughts obviously concentrated somewhere besides his little toe. After a moment he reached into his pocket and took out her ring. "Hold out your hand, my dear."

She did as he said, and he slid her wedding ring on her finger, where it belonged.

"Perfect," she said, holding her hand up to the light. She clasped her hands in her lap. "I truly do wish I knew how to thank you for all you have done." She shook her finger at him. "And even you are not so brazen as to tell me it's part of the rental agreement!"

He twinkled his eyes at her then, his momentary melancholy forgotten. "Happen there is something you can do, Lady Winn," he said as he reached into his pocket again and pulled out a letter. "Read that."

She eyed the letter while he rested on the bedcovers. "It's not from Lord Whitcomb, is it?" she asked with suspicion.

"Oh, no! Nothing like that. Apparently since we suffered your relative yesterday, it's my turn tomorrow. Read it, Roxie."

She picked up the letter and read it through once and then again, her eyes wide. "Does this mean . . ."

He nodded and laughed at the look on her face. "Most assuredly, my dear wife. My sisters, husbands, and children are descending on us here tomorrow."

"Oh, no," she said in dismay.

"Oh, yes! And you thought a trip over the Pennines was bad!"

She gulped and twisted the ring on her finger.

"Happy New Year, wife," he said as he winked and kissed her fingers. "You are in for a real scrutiny."

Chapter 14

Lord Winn propped his aching foot on the chair next to Roxie's bed. What he really wanted to do was lie down beside her, breathe deep of her lavender fragrance, work up his nerve to kiss her, and see where it led. She looked so adorable sitting there, staring at the letter, her mind already going a thousand miles an hour.

"You could have warned me this might happen," she accused.

He wanted to laugh. Have you any idea how very married you sound right now? he asked himself as he shook his head and looked serious. "I really had no clue they would do this, my dear," he replied, remembering contrition as a useful tool from his first marriage. Not that it ever worked for long with Cynthia, he thought as soon as the words were out of his mouth.

"I am sure you did not," she replied, to his intense gratification. "Please do not think that I am blaming you. These things happen, don't they?"

Oh, excellent. No blame, and does she appear concerned at *my* discomfort? As he tried to look casual and admire her at the same time, Lord Winn was struck all over again that Roxanna Rand was a distinct cut above any woman he had ever known before. He wondered if he dared rest his hand upon her leg, which had produced such a shapely outline under the blanket. After a moment's reflection, he concluded that his credit was not that high yet, despite this promising beginning. He would attempt something else.

"Roxie, you'll have to excuse me if I lean back," he said. The wince was genuine, he was sure of it.

His cup nearly ran over when she helped him lie back at the foot of the bed, and tucked one of her heavenly lavender-scented pillows under his head. Surely it wasn't his imagination that her hands lingered a moment longer than necessary on his neck as she positioned the pillow. Since his long legs dangled off the bed, she leaped up and pulled the chair closer, resting his wounded foot in the seat again. He had never seen such an attractive flannel nightgown. It was worn from many washings, and the fabric was thin enough now to exhibit the outline of her hips to great advantage.

"Much better," he managed.

"I should scold you, of course," she said, trying to look stern, and failing utterly because her face was not constructed upon stern lines. She went to the bureau and rummaged around until she found a pencil and paper. She plumped herself back in bed while he watched appreciatively, then crossed her legs Indian-fashion. She poised the pencil over the paper.

"All right now," she said. "What do you want me to do to get ready for this onslaught?"

Roxie, you are amazing, he thought as he put his hands behind his head. He took a deep breath, wondering how far he would get.

"Roxie, they think we are happily married newlyweds, and not, you know, pursuing this as an arrangement of convenience."

She pursed her lips and regarded him, and he fought the urge to take her in his arms and damn the pain in his former toe. "The girls and I will move to Moreland at once to perpetuate this notion," she said, and wrote on the page. "There are six bedrooms there, one of which is in the depths of renovation and not suitable for anything." She looked up and blushed. "The girls will take one room." She hesitated. "And I suppose I will have to share your chamber to accomplish this subterfuge."

Better and better. Roxie, you are a sensible woman. "I suppose," he replied, keeping his voice offhand. "There is a cot in the dressing room which I can use for the duration of the vis—"

"I won't consider that!" she interrupted, indignant. "I will take the cot and you can have the bed!"

"Wrong, Roxie. I'll take the cot," he said, grateful right down to his bandage that she was still consenting to sharing the bedroom.

"I insist," she said. "After all, I have all my parts."

He laughed. "Roxie, it's only a toe! I still have nine others, plus all my fingers."

She looked at the paper. "Well, I suppose we can fight this out tomorrow night."

Oh, God, Roxie. "I am sure we can."

She wrote on the paper. "That will free up the dower house. Who do you want the farthest away?" She grinned at him over the paper and his heart seemed to change rhythm.

"Amabel, without question," he said with no hesitation as she wrote. "Clarice and Frederick and their children will occupy two more bedrooms at the manor, and that will leave—"

"One bedroom for Lettice," she said. "Did you not say she was a widow?"

"Yes. Edwin, her only child, is my heir. I do not believe he will be coming."

"Well, it's a good thing," Roxie said. She unlimbered herself from the covers and flopped down next to him on her stomach, pointing to the paper. "See here? That fills the bedrooms. Their servants can go below stairs. Amabel and hers will be in the dower house and I'll sleep in your dressing room!"

"Roxie!" he declared as he turned sideways to face her. He surrendered to her good-natured expression. "Oh, very well. Have it your way."

To his delight, she leaned her head on his arm for a moment.

"Good for you, Fletch. Didn't that blacksmith advise you to always do what I want?"

He groaned and ruffled her hair before she could move away. "I suppose you will remind me of that now and then!"

To his dismay, she grew quiet. She left his side and returned to her own pillow. "There won't be much opportunity for that. Didn't the doctor tell me you were leaving in a couple of days?"

"Yes, I am," he said, forced to agree. "I have a mound of correspondence at Winnfield, and most of it concerning these pesky deeds of title to all my land. Was ever a man so cursed with wealth?" He chuckled and put his hand over his heart. "So if you want to get anything out of me in the next few days, that will be your golden opportunity."

She regarded him with an expression he was unfamiliar with. "You know, I will miss you," she said frankly.

He raised up on his elbow, unable to allow that to pass unanswered. A thousand witty things came to mind, but none of them were fine enough to say to this woman he loved. "Thank you," he said simply, cursing himself for the lameness of his delivery. "I don't know when anyone has ever missed me before."

To his further amazement, tears came to her eyes. She reached out and touched his arm, then sat back. "Now you'll have to leave," she said firmly as his heart sank. "I have a lot to do before your sisters get here, and I need to get dressed."

"Oh, very well," he replied, relieved that she was not ejecting him forever. "You'll have to help me up."

He didn't need any help. He remembered a time after the battle of Bussaco when he had sewn up his own arm because the surgeons were too busy. But, Roxie, you don't know that, he thought as he allowed her to help him to his feet. He leaned on her, breaking into a sweat as his fingers just brushed her breast. It was almost more than he could bear when she came closer and dabbed at the perspiration on his forehead.

"Oh, you are in pain!" she said, her voice filled with remorse. "I wish you had not climbed the stairs!"

He should have been ashamed of himself, but he was having too much fun to feel any remorse of his own. "I'll be all right," he managed, trying to sound gallant, and grateful that none of his former comrades in arms were around to hoot at him and make rude noises.

"I'll be fine," he assured her, feeling just a twinge of guilt at his performance. "If you can arrange affairs here, I can have Tibbie marshal his forces to move your things next door anytime you say."

"Very well," she agreed. "I can put Meggie on it right now, and I'll be at your house in a moment." She turned him around and gave him a push toward the door. "Is Mrs. Howell about? She and I will need to discuss menus and make beds. Go along, now, Fletch. I'll see you soon enough."

He descended the stairs carefully, a smile on his face. He stopped halfway down and looked back at the closed door. I am married to that magnificent creature, he marveled. The impossible has happened, and I really can't thank Lord Whitcomb enough for his perfidy. My stars, life is strange.

True to her word, he soon found Roxie at Moreland, deep in consultation with Mrs. Howell and her sister, Mrs. Hamilton. He peeked in on them in the kitchen and was shooed away by all three ladies. It may have been wishful thinking, but he thought Roxie winked at him. He was content to limp to the sitting room and play through Haydn's Second Piano Sonata, the perfect antidote for a disordered mind. Cadence and calm, Fletcher, he told himself as he followed the score. Spain wasn't won in a day; neither will Roxie be.

"Take your time, Fletch," he heard from the doorway and stopped, startled, wondering if she could read his mind. Please no, he thought. In another moment Roxie stood beside him, her hand resting lightly on his shoulder, her other arm full of sheets.

He continued, almost overwhelmed by her lovely presence as she looked at the music then sat down beside him on the piano bench, the sheets clutched in front of her now. "You need a metronome," she said, then glanced at him, her brown eyes merry. "What's the hurry?"

I am thirty-eight and deep in love, he thought. That's the hurry, my dear. "I always seem to rush Haydn," he temporized, racing one-handed through the rest of the page as she laughed. "There! Can I help you now?"

They made beds until Meggie and Tibbie brought over the clothes from the dower house, Lissy and Helen trailing behind, their arms full of possessions.

"You will be in here," he said to Roxie's daughters as he opened the door to the room next to his. "Will this do?"

Helen gazed around the room, open-mouthed. "It is so large!" she declared. "Oh, Mama, I do like this wallpaper you chose."

Roxie was already putting clothes away in the bureau. "Actually, I think Winn picked that out in Darlington. Oh, and the bed is so soft, Lissy. You'll find that most agreeable."

But Lissy was already sitting in the window seat, looking out as dusk tinged the Plain of York far below. "Is this the whole world?" she asked in awe of the view.

He limped over to sit beside her. She patted his arm, looking up at him for an answer. "I think it must be," he replied as he looked into her brown eyes and fought an absurd urge to cry.

"Then I am glad we are all here," she said, leaping up to jump on the bed before he disgraced himself with tears. He sat there a moment longer, trying to regain some measure of control.

But Roxie was watching him, a frown on her face. She told the girls to carry their boxes into the dressing room, then joined him at the window. "That look on your face tells me that we are already too much trouble," she said, the anxiety evident in her voice. "I am sorry. Sometimes Lissy is rambunctious. I'll remind them to be a little calmer while you are still here."

"It's not that," he said, wanting to spill out his heart to her.

She touched his forehead. "Oh, it's your foot, isn't it? I think you should lie down until dinner."

He nodded. "Yes, I am sure that is it." He rose and she took him around the waist, as though she had done this a hundred times before. "Lean on me and I'll get you to your room."

He did as she said, marveling at her resilience. *I suppose you have done this often with Anthony,* he thought as she helped him into his room and off with his shoes. *Mrs. Rand, I am no invalid, except that my heart has been pierced through and through as never before.*

He did sleep, which surprised him, and gave him some slight justification in his own eyes that perhaps his foot was partly the culprit. To his delight, Roxie and the girls brought their dinner upstairs and ate with him in his room. When they finished, Lissy tucked herself under his arm and insisted that he tell them all about his nieces and nephews who were coming to visit. He remembered as many names as he could, wishing that he had paid closer attention to his sisters' various birthings. Roxie rescued him finally.

"Have a heart, Lissy!" she scolded and sat down beside him, gathering her daughter in her arms. "He was away in Spain for eight years fighting Napoleon. Perhaps Lord Winn needs to become reacquainted with his own relatives!"

Lissy considered that and nodded. "Do you think they will like us?" she asked.

"I like you," he replied. "Who cares what they think?"

"We do, Fletch," Roxie said, her voice firm. "And I think you should, too. Come along, girls, let's go home for our last night in the dower house."

Lissy blew him a kiss as Roxie led her out of the room. Helen remained behind, sitting quietly in the chair beside the bed. She began to gather up the dishes, then set them down and came closer. He watched her, again struck by her quiet dignity, and afraid to break into her silence. He took his chances and held out his hand to her.

He smiled when she took his hand. Still she was silent.

"It's difficult, isn't it, Helen?" he asked at last. "Please don't think that I will ever try to take your father's place. That will never be my intention."

She was still silent, but as he held his breath, she sat on the edge of the bed, and for the briefest moment, touched her cheek to his hand. It might never have happened; he could have dreamed it, except that her eyelashes brushed the back of his hand and he knew he would never forget the feeling. In another second she was darting to the door. But she paused and raised her hand to him in a gesture of friendship.

"Good night, Winn," she whispered. "I hope you feel better tomorrow."

He never slept more soundly in his life.

The Rand sisters came in one steady invasion the next afternoon. Lissy had bounced in with the news that a whole train of carriages was trundling down the lane. "Mama, there are so many of them!" she said, then hurried to the window.

Lord Winn peered over his spectacles at Roxie, who sat beside him on the sofa, darning his socks. "I can't face it," he moaned as he put down his book.

Roxie only laughed and threw a sock at him. "We are supposed to love our relatives," she said, then amended under her breath, "except for Lord Whitcomb."

"Well, he loves you, Roxie," he joked, and ducked as she dumped the basket of socks on him.

Helen stared at her mother in amazement. "Mama!" she gasped. "You've never done anything like that."

Roxie paused, surprised. "No, I suppose I have not," she agreed. "But I enjoyed it, Helen." She threw a last sock at him. "And he deserved that. Oh, foul!" she exclaimed as he threw the socks back.

They were still gathering up socks, sitting on the floor and laughing when Mrs. Howell opened the door to announce Amabel, Clarice, and Lettice, with husbands and children in tow.

"Oh, dear," Roxie said under her breath when Lettice raised a lorgnette to her rather prominent eyes.

Winn grinned at his sisters, and threw a sock at Amabel. "Happy Christmas!" he announced, flopping back on the carpet to toss another sock over his head at Roxie.

Clarice stared at him, then began to chuckle. "Winn, you're certifiable," she declared as she came forward and stepped over him, her hand outstretched. "You have to be Roxanna, my dear. No one else but a wife would stay in the same room with this lunatic. I am Clarice and this is my husband Frederick. Fred, help up your brother-in-law. He seems to have done injury to his foot."

Roxie raised up on her knees and shook hands as though she did this every day. "Welcome to Moreland," she said, tucking her hair under her lace cap. "I was darning socks and your brother was being outrageous."

"I'd like to know who began this attack," Winn said as he held out his hand to his brother-in-law.

"You deserved it," Roxanna replied.

Lord Winn allowed his brother-in-law, Lord Manwaring, to help him back to the sofa. "My God, Winn, where did you find one that juicy on such short notice?" Fred whispered.

"It was just the most bare-faced piece of luck, which I will never explain to you," the marquess whispered back. "Good to see you, Fred," he said out loud, then turned to Roxie. "Fred, meet my wife, Roxanna. And these are her daughters Felicity and Helen."

Lord Manwaring bowed, then kissed Roxie's cheek. "Welcome to the family, m'dear. You're a brave one."

Amabel still stood in the doorway, transfixed. Lord Winn grinned at his youngest sister. Never saw me have any fun before, did you, Amabel? he thought. He waved her in. "Cat got your tongue, Amabel?" he asked. "This is a rare occasion, indeed. Let me make you known to my far-better half. Roxie, this is Amabel. And Lettice. Sisters, such a pleasure to undergo your scrutiny! I hope we measure up."

"I cannot imagine what they must think of us," Roxie told Lord Winn that night as she sat at the dressing table in his chambers and brushed her hair.

"Let me answer for Fred," he spoke up from the bed, where she had fluffed his pillows behind his head and given him his book and spectacles. "He wonders where I found such a beautiful wife."

She clapped her hands in genuine delight. "Really? He thinks me beautiful? How diverting."

"Roxie, sometimes I think you have cotton wadding where your brains should be," he remarked, putting down his book. "Don't you ever stand still long enough to look in a mirror? I wish I had a sock to throw at you."

She rolled her eyes and looked at him through the mirror. "Don't remind me! I do not think Amabel was impressed."

"Amabel has had a poker up her bum as long as I have known her," he responded, sinking lower and returning his attention to the book.

He sighed with pleasure as she sat in the chair by his bed. "And you would say all those outrageous things at dinner!" she scolded. "You needn't look so pleased about it, either."

Lord Winn took a last look at the page and closed the book. *I do not know what I have been reading anyway,* he thought as he watched his wife's lively face. *It might be the records from last year's Corn Exchange or merchant marine lading bills. Roxie, I see only you. I'm the one with cotton wadding for brains.*

"Well?" she was prompting.

He drew his legs up, wincing a bit. "I don't think our reproductive proclivities are any of her business, do you? Lettice's son is my heir, and I intend to leave it that way. You know my views on the subject."

He knew she would blush, and she did, the rose coming into her cheeks as he watched. "But did you really need to make those remarks about stud fees among the peerage?" she persisted. "And now Helen is asking me questions. Dear me, Fletch. She's only six."

He took her hand, running his fingers over her wedding ring. "I am sorry, my dear. It was rude of me." He sat up straight again, wishing he had the nerve too pull Roxie onto his lap. "But Amabel is such fair game!"

Roxie sighed and rose to her feet. "My brothers were just the same!" She shook her head at him. "Fletch, they will be here one more day and so will you. Do try to be pleasant."

She went back to the dressing table and tied on her sleeping cap. His heart sank. *And now you will leave me for the other room,* he thought. "What will you do for me if I am a model of rectitude tomorrow?" he asked, stalling her.

"I will probably sink into a coma at your feet," she responded promptly and kissed her hand to him. "Good night, Fletch. I hope you sleep well."

I would sleep better if you were in my bed, he told himself as he nodded to her and smiled. She went into the dressing room and closed the door behind her. He listened, but she did not turn the key in the lock. At least you trust me. Damn, what a burden.

He took off his glasses and turned down the lamp. If I must leave the day after tomorrow, how soon do I dare return? At what point will she look at me and see a husband, and not a convenience? Anthony, you must have been quite a fellow.

He tried to make himself comfortable, but all he could think of was Roxanna Rand in the next room. And Clarice and Fred in the room beyond, and Lettice, and Amabel in the dower house probably complaining to her mouse of a husband about the accommodations. He wished he could evict them all and woo his wife in the day remaining. I know so little of the sensual arts, he thought as he stared at the ceiling. There was only argument as I grew up, and then war, and bitterness and divorce. He remembered a Spanish proverb then, and smiled into the gloom—"Patience and shuffle the cards." But I am not a patient man.

The next day began in a more promising fashion, with the company lured to the breakfast table by Mrs. Howell's cinnamon buns and a ham that suited even the critical Amabel. While he sat at the table after breakfast chatting with Fred, Roxie organized a snowball fight on the front lawn. He went to the window to watch, finally opening the window quietly to scoop snow from the ledge and plaster his wife when she wasn't looking. He barely closed it in time, laughing as a snowball splattered onto the glass by his head.

Lord Manwaring watched him from the breakfast table. "She's a ripe one, Winn," he said, and nudged his wife. "Don't you think so?"

Clarice only smiled and finished her tea before speaking. "She's a delight, Winn. But why do I think there is much more here than meets the eye?"

I cannot fool you, he thought as he regarded his older sister. He sat down beside her. "Because there is."

"Tell me, brother," she asked quietly. "I won't say anything to my sisters."

He looked from his sister to her husband, leaned back, and told them the whole story, leaving nothing out. He was relieved that Clarice had the good sense not to make any comment as he spoke quickly, hurrying to finish before the snowballers trooped indoors for a continuation of breakfast. "And that's it," he concluded. "She's sleeping on a cot in my dressing room, and we are trying to present a good face to all of you. I wish you had not come, actually."

Fred chuckled. Clarice touched Lord Winn's hand. "You love her, don't you?" she asked, her voice soft for a sister of his.

"Clarrie, I can't begin to tell you how much I love her," he replied. "That's the damnable part. If she were merely agreeable, this would be an easy arrangement. But she is a darling and I want her so much." He shook his head. "But I have to be patient now, and return to Winnfield, and leave her here. It chafes me."

He heard the front door slam, and excited voices in the hall. "Well, now you know. Wish me success, Clarice. Maybe I can return here in the spring . . ." His voice trailed off.

To his surprise, she came up behind his chair and hugged him. "We do wish you well, my dear." The door opened and his nieces and nephews tumbled into the room, snowballs in hand, to continue the fight indoors. "But now I would duck, if I were you, Winn!"

As the day wore on, the thought of leaving sank him lower. His mood was not improved when yet another post chaise rolled to the front driveway at Moreland and released from its confines Lettice's son and his heir, Edwin Chandler. If that was not enough to throw him into despair, the carriage also disgorged two of Edwin's Cambridge friends, all watch fobs and seals and too-tight pantaloons.

"Uncle! What a pleasure!"

Why must he be so cheerful? Lord Winn thought as Edwin shook his hand vigorously, introduced his friends whose names he promptly forgot, then toddled off to find refreshment, looking about with interest as though he already owned the place. *I wonder he does not follow me from estate to estate, counting the silver,* Winn thought sourly. *Why did I never notice that about him before?*

Roxie was the perfect hostess, smiling at the new arrivals, and even listening with what appeared to be interest at yet another of Edwin's prosings about life at university, the price of things, and other bits of noninformation that made Lord Winn's head and toe throb simultaneously.

The only crisis passed quickly enough. Roxie whispered to Mrs. Howell to clear up that yet-unfinished chamber, and try to locate a third bed from somewhere. Mrs. Howell thought a moment, assured her that she could find something, and hurried off to do her duty.

He managed to capture Roxie for a private word before dinner as she was hurrying to make a tisane for Amabel's headache, brought on, Amabel was sure, by "all these children shouting."

"This is not what I had in mind for a peaceful holiday," he said, draping his arm over her shoulder as she headed for the kitchen. "Hold still a minute, Roxie," he ordered, when she remained in motion.

She slowed down to oblige him, and looked up into his face, a question in her eyes.

"Why isn't this driving you crazy?" he asked, out of sorts with her that she could be so cheerful in the face of relentless relatives.

"It's simple, Fletch," she replied, offering no objection when he put his hands on her waist to stop her. "I like Clarice quite a bit, and Fred, too. Lettice is a prosy windbag but she means well, and Amabel was put here on earth to test mortals."

He let out a shout of laughter and smacked a kiss on her forehead. "You're a wonder!"

"No, I am not," she argued and gently moved out of his grasp. "I would trade you one Lord Whitcomb for at least ten of these people. Twenty. Thirty."

He could not disagree. "Never thought of it like that." He resisted the urge to pat her on the fanny as she hurried off to the kitchen.

He suffered Edwin's after-dinner chatter, and couldn't hurry through the brandy and cigars fast enough. He was starved for a glimpse of Roxie. Somehow, when she was close by, he felt less inclined to speak his mind to his relatives. Do I just feel *safe* around that little lady, I who have fought Napoleon's legions across half of Europe? I wonder how soon I can tear a page from Amabel's book and plead a headache? he thought as Edwin blew another puff of smoke in his direction.

But when they rejoined the ladies in the sitting room, Amabel was on one of her rampages. She lay on the sofa, wincing as Helen softly played a rather fine Scarlatti he had been teaching her. Roxie turned the pages and Lissy leaned against her. Roxie patted the chair beside her, but Amabel was too quick.

She dragged herself upright. "Brother, I have something to say to you about the sale of your London house," she began.

"Don't start on that, Amabel," he warned. "There is nothing for me in London anymore."

"You might have considered the rest of us," she burst out, holding her head and ignoring the twitterings of her colorless husband seated beside her. "It is just another example of your selfishness!

If society sees fit to cut you direct, I don't know why you need to take it out on us! Wasn't it enough for you to tumble Papa into an early grave? Perhaps Cynthia was justified."

"Damn you, Amabel."

"No, Winn! You are the villain here," Amabel shouted.

Lettice gasped and dug for her smelling salts. The air was thick with tension as he felt his own anger rising. Out of the corner of his eye, he could see Clarice starting toward her sister, but a calm voice interrupted them all.

"No, Amabel, not here," Roxanna said. She rose from her seat at the piano and stood in front of him, leaning back against him as if daring him to move. "I cannot permit you to rip at my husband that way. You may return to the dower house now, or silence your tongue. This is our home, not yours, and we do not speak that way."

Her words were quietly spoken but they carried to the far corners of the room. My God, Roxie, he thought as he gently rested his hands on her shoulders. She was trembling, but she did not take her eyes from Amabel. Helen continued with the Scarlatti invention, and soon his relatives were conversing with each other again. Amabel said nothing more.

Roxie returned to the piano bench and soon Edwin reclaimed his attention, demanding to know what it was really like at Waterloo. When he looked around finally, she was gone, and so were her daughters. Clarice was regarding him with something close to fondness.

"I think we can see ourselves to bed, Winn," she said. "Good night."

Chapter 15

Roxie wasn't in their bedroom so he knocked quietly on the next door, and opened it when Lissy called out. She lay in the girls' bed, a daughter on each side of her. Lissy sat up and motioned to him. "Mama tells the most wonderful stories," she said. "You can lie down, too."

He did as she said, finding himself a spot at the foot of the bed where he could grab Lissy's toes and make her shriek. Soon even Helen was laughing. When Roxanna finished her story, she kissed her daughters and sat on the edge of their bed as they said their prayers.

"Good night, my dears," she said as she snuffed the candles and then closed the door behind her.

He followed her to their room, chagrined that she had not once looked him in the eye. You must be so disgusted with my relatives, he thought as he closed the door behind them. I am so ashamed of them. And myself.

"Roxie, I . . ."

She turned around then, her eyes bright with tears. "You have every right to be upset with me," she began, raising her glance to meet his. "I just couldn't bear to hear Amabel go on that way, digging at you like a harpie. I know I have no right."

He pulled her close to him. "You were wonderful, my dear. Thank you."

She stepped back to look at him, astonished. "You're not angry?"

"Heavens, no," he said and released her. "I don't know when any husband has ever been so adroitly defended. Anything you want from me? Just name it, up to one half my kingdom."

She laughed then, relieved laughter. "I have my limits, sir," she said. "I do not think Amabel and I will be on speaking terms, but perhaps she will not harrow you up again in my presence. Here, let me help you off with your shoes. I noticed you've been gritting your teeth since dinner."

"It was the company, not the toe," he assured her, but allowed her to assist him. She took off his sock, and stared in dismay at the blood on the bandage.

"Sit right there," she ordered, and went to the washbasin.

"Roxie, I can take care of it," he insisted.

"I am sure you can," she agreed, returning with a tin of water and a cloth. "You've been taking care of yourself for far too long. Do allow me my penance for getting stern with your relatives."

"Really, Roxie," he protested as she knelt by the bed and carefully lifted off the bandage.

It looked disgusting, but she did not even flinch as she dabbed at the crusted blood around the sutures. "I suppose you will now bluster and protest and tell me that you rode your horse all across Europe with your bowels hanging out, and your nose on by a flap of skin only, and your backbone open to the spine," she murmured as she worked, her hands expert.

He laughed. "Yes, I do go on like that, don't I?" he agreed. "How insufferable for you."

She stopped and sat back to look up at him. "There's no shame in letting someone do for you, Lord Winn. Hold still."

He looked down at her in self-conscious amusement. "It doesn't look too appealing."

"It is nothing, really. You should have seen Anthony's bed-sores before he died," she murmured as she dried off the wound. "His skin was breaking down and we couldn't do a thing about it," she said, her voice matter-of-fact. "I cried a lot, but not when he was conscious."

There wasn't anything he could add to her artless statement, but admire her sensible courage in silence. He pointed out the fresh dressings on his bureau and let her re-bandage his foot. "That should keep you until morning," she said as she stood and gathered up the old bandage. "Let me look at it again before you leave."

"Yes, doctor," he replied.

She grinned then. "I do become somewhat managing, don't I?" she said.

"Yes, you do," he agreed as he untied his neckcloth. "But I am tired, and don't intend to worry about it tonight." *I feel old, too,* he thought as she helped him from his coat and arranged it over the back of a chair. *And bitter, and disgusted with myself, and missing you already.*

"Well, good night, Fletch," she said and went into the dressing room with her lamp.

She was out in a moment, her eyes wide. "Do you know where Mrs. Howell found that extra cot for Edwin's friend?" she asked, her face red.

There is a God, he rejoiced. *Play this carefully, Fletcher,* he told himself, as he continued unbuttoning his shirt. "Your bed?"

She nodded. "I suppose I can find enough blankets in the linen room to make a pallet on the floor."

He shook his head, trying to appear casual. "I'm afraid you're out there. I'm sure Mrs. Howell gathered up the last of the blankets to make up those beds for Edwin and his friends." He pulled out his shirttails. *Do this right, Winn,* he thought. "Do you trust me, Roxie?"

"Yes," she said. "But . . ."

"Well, then, I will share my bed, as long as you promise not to touch my foot. I'd probably shriek and then my sisters would come running." He shuddered elaborately.

She stood there at the door of the dressing room for a long moment as he regarded her.

"In for a penny . . ."

" . . . in for ten pounds," she finished. "Oh, very well! It seems I do not have a choice. Why has this become my Christmas refrain?"

She returned to the dressing room and he hurried into his nightshirt, wishing that his hands would stop trembling. Winn, you are too old to be coy, he thought as he put on his dressing gown, took out his book, and lay down on the bed.

Roxie came out in a moment, wearing Anthony's dressing gown with the sleeves rolled up that he remembered from his first sight of her two months ago. She went to the dressing table and took the pins from her hair, shaking it out with a sigh. She started to brush her hair, and the crackle was pleasant to his ears. He put down the book and watched Roxie over the top of his spectacles as she brushed out her long hair and hummed to herself.

He screwed up his courage and closed the book, going to stand behind her at the dressing table. "Hand me your brush," he said as she watched him in the mirror, her eyes wary. She did and he brushed her hair, pulling the brush vigorously through the length of her hair from root to stem. It fell nearly to her waist in a glorious wave of dark brown, lively with electricity.

"Oh, much better," she sighed. "Helen tries, but she doesn't have the force to make that feel so good." She closed her eyes in pleasure. "I've thought about cutting it."

"Don't you dare," he said, his whole body on fire, hoping that he did not sound like he was panting. "There now."

She pulled the mass of hair over her shoulder. "Wonderful. This excuses all your social blunders of this evening, Fletch."

He laughed and sat down beside her on the bench. "Roxie, you're too easy to please."

She tied on her sleeping cap and went to the bed, standing there a moment in reflective indecision. "This really isn't a very good idea," she said dubiously.

He took a deep breath and removed his dressing gown and got into bed. "Well, the floor's too cold to stand there ruminating too long, Roxie," he said, and blew out the lamp. "Maybe you'll lose a toe tonight."

He held his breath as she still stood there. "Oh, bother it," she said at last and took off Anthony's robe. She crawled into her side of the bed and punched down the pillow, wrapping her arm around it and looking remarkably like Lissy.

He turned to face her. The moonlight came in through the draperies he had forgotten to close, and her skin was lit by the soft glow from the window. She chuckled. "Do you know, I almost laughed out loud this morning when Lissy threw a snowball at Lettice!"

"She has a good throwing arm," he agreed, relaxing and letting the mattress claim him. The fragrance of lavender surrounded him and he felt more peace than at any time he could remember. "But I don't think she expected Lettice to throw one right back!"

They laughed together. He took her hand. "Good night, Roxie," he said softly. "Thanks for coming to my rescue."

She gently eased her hand from his loose grasp. "Someone has to save you from yourself," she replied, her voice sleepy.

He lay there a moment, contemplating all manner of mischief, and rejecting it. Ah, well. "Good night, Roxie," he said again. He raised up on one elbow to kiss her chastely on the cheek. She had started to turn away from him as he leaned over, and they cracked heads.

He thought about it later, recognizing the event as a pivotal moment similar, somehow, to Wellington's decision to attack Quatre Bras and bring on Waterloo. Once begun, inescapably engaged. They could have laughed, said good night, and turned over again, but they didn't, and the chance turned into something wished for but not expected.

Even moments later, he couldn't be sure who began it. Did she grasp him around the neck and pull him closer? Did he kiss her on the lips, and then do it again when her arms went around him? Her lips were as soft as he imagined, gentle and demanding at the same time. She sighed and moved closer, her hands in his hair now, her body sliding under his as though she belonged there.

He hesitated a moment, his thoughts wild. I will not regret this, he considered as he tugged up his nightshirt, but, Roxie, will you? He rested lightly on her then, his mind screaming one thing, his body another. And then she said, "Please," her voice filled with as much desire as he felt himself, and he understood perfectly.

He gave her time to divest herself of her nightgown, helping with the buttons, and then he was captured in love, devoured by it, overwhelmed as never before—and his memory was excellent. She was a woman starving, and it gave him the most exquisite joy to pleasure her over and over again until they were both boggled with exhaustion. Even then, she allowed him to leave her only with the greatest reluctance.

"Roxie, I weigh too much," he said finally.

She relaxed her grip then even as she protested. He lay beside her, his mind completely blank. Then the cool night air reminded him that the blankets were somewhere and he searched for them. She lay watching him as he covered her. He smiled and picked up her hand, letting it drop to the mattress again, limp as a rag doll.

I shall not say anything, he thought as he lay back next to her. I shall lie here and breathe lavender and Roxanna, and it will be enough. Everything I ever did in life before this moment is of no consequence. I have been baptized with love and I am clean as never before.

Roxie sighed, and he turned his head to look at her, raising up on one elbow.

"I should be ashamed of myself," she murmured. "I can't imagine what you must think." As he watched her lovely face, tears slid onto the pillow.

Careful, Fletcher, he thought. Say the right thing for once. Don't laugh off her genuine remorse at breaking so thoroughly your idiotic marriage of convenience, or at giving me a glimpse of the intensity of female love I wasn't sure existed. There's more here than even she understands.

He touched her face. Please God, the right thing. "Tell me, Roxie, and tell me frankly: when was your husband last able to pleasure you?"

She closed her eyes. "He's been dead nine months now, and before then . . ." She sighed again. "It was two years before then that he had the strength. I suppose nearly three years."

"That's a long time for a healthy young woman, Roxie," he said.

She hesitated, then thought better of speaking.

"Tell me, my dear," he urged. "Please don't be shy."

"I enjoy making love so much," she whispered, and then covered her face with her hands. "Oh, God, so many nights I wanted to touch Anthony and turn him into someone healthy, anyone. I cannot tell you how many miles I have walked over these hills, trying to wear myself out!"

He did chuckle then. "I seem to remember surprising you once on one of your forced marches."

To his relief, she laughed softly. "Yes." Her voice turned serious again. "But this is not something good women talk about, I suppose."

"You can talk to me," he replied. "Let me say that I feel . . . oh, I don't know . . . honored almost, to have given you something you needed. And Roxie, there's no shame in wanting what I gave you."

She shivered, and sat up to find her nightgown, buttoning it slowly as she looked at him in the moonlight. "Then I thank you, sir," she said, quite serious. "I do regret that I trampled on our convenient agreement."

"No regrets, Roxie," he commanded. "I don't think either of us had much control over this circumstance. We can overlook it."

"I know, but . . ."

She lay down again. He put his arm out, inviting her into his embrace, but she shook her head, clutching her pillow again, but still looking at him. "I feel such relief," she said finally and then closed her eyes.

He watched her, loving her with all his heart. At some point, Roxie, he vowed silently, you'll consider me and see a real husband. I can wait until that happens. He touched her hair and she moved a little closer, more into his warmth.

"Roxie, are you still awake?" he whispered.

"H'mmm."

"If you wish more refreshment again before morning, I'm a light sleeper."

Her voice was drowsy. "But you said once that your aide-de-camp had to punch you awake," she murmured, her face in the pillow.

"He wasn't Roxie Rand. Good night, dear."

She woke him before morning, rubbing his back, and her love was even more thorough. At first, he hoped everyone at Moreland was a sound sleeper, and then he didn't care.

When he got up and dressed in the morning, Roxie was still sleeping, her arms thrown out like a child, her hair fanned around her face. He built a fire for her, wincing at the noise the coals made, but chuckling to himself at the soundness of her slumber. Roxie, not only are you rendered boneless by intercourse, but deaf also, he thought, a smile on his face. And I feel like I will live a thousand years now. Such immortality you bestow, my love.

They were all assembled and deep into breakfast before she came down. Winn patted the chair beside him. "My dear, I was afraid you would sleep through our departure."

"Oh, no," she replied, not looking at him as he poured her coffee, just a hint of unruly color in her cheeks. "You're all leaving at once?" she asked.

"Winn is ever so far behind on *our* family affairs at Winnfield," Amabel said, effectively snubbing Roxie from the family circle.

"I am sure he is," Roxie replied smoothly, smiling at him as he handed her a cinnamon bun.

"I think you should join him there, my dear," Clarice said.

Don't meddle, he thought. Let her take her time, Clarice. "Oh, sister, this is a delicate matter," he said out loud. "Helen and Lissy need some time to work around to this change in their lives. We'll take things as they come."

"I suppose it was rather a rush," Amabel said, her eyes on Roxie. "Are you even out of mourning yet?"

Winn could hear everyone take in a breath and hold it. He looked at his wife, who calmly set down her knife and fork. Go get her, Roxie, he thought.

"Yes, it was a rush, Amabel," she replied. "And no, I am not out of mourning yet. You can think what you choose. I really don't give a hearty damn." She nodded to Clarice to pass the eggs as Amabel choked on her tea and left the room coughing.

Edwin giggled. Fred grinned at the departing Amabel, and Lettice glowered at him. "You're a quick one," Clarice said, smiling at Roxanna. "It's hard to render Amabel speechless."

Roxie blushed. "I don't make a practice of that," she assured her sister-in-law as she touched a napkin to her lips. "Now, can I help anyone pack? Amabel, perhaps?"

I do not know what is coming over me, she thought as she allowed Lord Winn to pull back her chair from the breakfast table. I don't make a career of setdowns. She glanced at her husband. And I don't, as a general rule, leave fingernail tracks all across a man's back. I certainly hope I didn't draw blood. Oh, my. What must he think of me? The sooner they are all gone, the better for my piece of mind. Or what's left of it, at any rate.

"Roxie, come with me to the bookroom a moment," Winn was saying to her. "We need to discuss a little business."

She allowed him to take her arm and stroll with her down the hall. She noticed that he barely limped now.

"Your foot is better this morning?" she asked.

"Yes, and everything else, too," he replied, a slight smile on his face.

Better let that one pass, she thought as she sat next to him at the desk and he indicated the ledgers in the glass-faced cabinet.

"Tibbie handles all the estate matters, planting, lambing, and so forth," he was saying, when she dragged her thoughts back from last night to the present. He held out a smaller book. "I've settled a yearly allowance of five thousand pounds on you, Roxie. You can keep a record here."

She gasped. "Five thousand pounds?" she repeated. "Fletch, I was managing on two hundred pounds!"

"A paltry sum," he declared as he replaced the ledger. "You'll be wanting a new wardrobe when you're out of mourning in a few months."

"Yes," she agreed, "but I was thinking more in terms of muslin, and less of cloth of gold and ermine!"

He laughed and took her hand. "You really are a wife after a Yorkshireman's heart, Roxie dear! I'll bet you even turn up your petticoats, and scrape butter off bread to conserve."

"Doesn't everyone?" she asked blithely, grateful for his light tone, especially after last night's heavy doings. "I am sure that will be more than ample for my needs, and see to the finishing of the renovation here."

"My dear, that comes out of estate funds." To her relief, he looked up from his contemplation of her when Lord Manwaring called to him from the front hall. "Use your allowance on yourself and the girls! No arguments. Fred is anxious to be off. He knows it's best to travel with Amabel on a full stomach."

She allowed him to help her up, but she held him back for a moment. He looked at her and shook his head.

"If you intend to apologize again for what happened last night, I won't listen," he said softly. "I had a delightful time, and so did you, and let's leave it at that for now."

She sighed.

"And don't sigh and flog yourself," he continued. "What I do want you to do is write me occasionally, and let me know how things go on here." He led her into the hall, her arm tucked through his. "See my solicitor in the village for funds, and I think his wife knows a good piano teacher, if you find you haven't time."

"Aye, sir," she said, amused.

"I'm trying to think of everything," he protested and tugged at the loose hair under her cap. "I've left our marriage lines with him, and a fair copy of my divorce papers, and a statement of chattel. I can see no further difficulty from Lord Whitcomb on that head."

"Very well," she said, hurrying to keep up. "Ah, here comes your farewell committee. Good morning, my dears!"

Lord Winn picked up Felicity, who was still rubbing sleep from her eyes, and continued down the hall beside her. He looked across Roxanna to Helen. "Helen, I trust you will continue riding. I have arranged for a rather gentle little mare to be delivered to your mother. With saddle, of course."

"You needn't have—" she began.

"Roxie, it is so hard to do nice things for you!" he protested, amusement evident in his voice. "Well, nearly always," he amended, his eyes roguish. "Helen, teach your mother to ride. She might find it useful."

"Yes, sir," Helen replied, taking her commission quite seriously. "And I will practice my Scarlatti."

"You'll be back in a few days?" Lissy asked, her hands on his face.

He stopped then and gave her his full attention. "No, my dear, I won't," he said at last.

"But when?" she persisted as he set her down and opened the front door.

"I don't know," he said.

Roxanna knelt beside her daughter, hugging her close, and feeling an absurd urge to join in Lissy's sudden tears. "Lord Winn has a lot of business to attend to," she explained. "We were . . . lucky to have him here as long as we did, Felicity."

Lissy sobbed, stopping only when Lord Winn picked her up again and held his handkerchief to her nose. She blew, and then threw her arms around him in another flood of tears.

Roxanna looked away, the pain of departure suddenly real. *I owe you so much, Lord Winn,* she thought. She gathered together her own disordered thoughts, and tried to smile and nod at Edwin Chandler and his friends, standing there with baggage in hand. *You've rescued my daughters for me, and given me enough income to live on for the rest of my life. I have a beautiful home now, and nothing to fear or worry about. Why do I feel so dreadful?*

It was an unanswerable question. Lord Winn, his face a study in discomfort, gently pried Lissy's hands off his neck and handed her daughter to her. Lissy watched him. "I want to know when you are coming back," she stated, each word distinct, the model of her mother.

Yes, Roxie thought, *tell us when.*

"Lissy!" he began, exasperated. He looked at Roxanna. "That depends on a lot of things," he said, "none of which you will understand."

"I want to know," she demanded.

Clarice stepped to her brother's side then and nudged him. "As a parent of some years, I recognize that tone, Winn, even if you are unfamiliar with it. Four-year-olds want answers, brother."

Roxie nodded to Clarice in complete agreement. "Yes! Don't they?" So do I, she thought, and I am much older than four.

Lord Winn thought a moment then cleared his throat. "Very well, Felicity Drew," he said and put his hand on her shoulder. "I will make a flying trip back here in March with my York solicitor. We have to return to Northumberland to settle up a rather pesky deed, and I trust the snow will be gone then." He knelt by her again. "Now. Will that satisfy you?"

Lissy was silent a moment, tears forgotten. She blew her nose again on Winn's handkerchief. "Mama, can we mark a calendar?" she asked.

"I am sure we can, my dear. Now don't plague Lord Winn anymore."

"I am not a plague, Mama," she replied with dignity. "I am merely a trial."

And so the Rands were laughing when they entered the carriages drawn up for them. Lord Winn tied Ney's reins to the back of his brother-in-law's carriage, then came up the front steps again, walking slowly, reluctantly, almost. He took Helen's hand in both of his hands.

"Take good care of your mother," he said, his voice strained.

Oh, dear, she thought. I hope you are not getting a cold, too, from all these comings and goings.

"I will," Helen assured him. "And I will write."

"Excellent!" he kissed the top of her head, then picked up Lissy again. "You are not even a trial, Lissy. Admire that view of the Plain of York for me," he told her. "I live at the other end of it, think on."

She nodded, and touched his face again. "March?"

"Just three months, Lissy."

And then it was her turn. What do I say to you? she thought as he took her by the arm. I like you a lot. God knows I have used you down to a burned wick. It's even quite possible that you know me better than Anthony did. You've seen me through one of my worst experiences.

"I don't know what to say," she admitted, tears in her eyes.

He hugged her close, taking her breath away with the strength of his grip, and then he released her.

"You'll think of something someday, Roxanna," he said.

"You're sure of that?" she murmured.

"No, I am not," he replied, his words honest. "But then, I always was a fool where women are concerned. Take care, Roxie. Think of me occasionally."

He kissed her then, put on his hat, and took another long look at the three of them standing close together on the front steps. He turned his back on them, hurried down the steps and into a carriage. He did not look back, but they stayed on the front steps until the carriages were only a speck on the road.

"Well, my dears," she said at last, when she finally noticed that Lissy was barefoot and Helen shivering. "Let's finish the cinnamon buns and find Meggie. There's much to do."

The hall was so empty, with no quick, firm steps of a military nature. There was no Haydn played too fast in the sitting room. The cinnamon buns didn't taste the same, and even Lissy left the last one unfinished on her plate. When she suggested that Five Pence needed some exercise, Helen shrugged and continued to sit there until Roxie reminded her.

"We are feeling sorry for ourselves," she declared finally. "Come, girls, it's time to get dressed."

She shooed them upstairs to their room and went into the room she shared with Lord Winn. The bed was a mess, she thought, but what fun. She sat on his side a moment, wishing that it was still warm and still smelled of him.

It did not. She peeked in the dressing room, but all his clothes were gone. So was his shaving gear, his book, and his spectacles. She straightened the bedcovers and noticed something white under the bed. She pulled out his nightshirt and laughed softly. So that was where it ended up, she thought as she hung it on a peg in the dressing room.

There was a calendar next to the clothes hamper. She found a pencil stub and drew an X through December 30.

"January, February, March," she said. "And what then, Roxie? What then?"

Chapter 16

If it wasn't the snowiest winter on record in the North Riding, then it was second cousin to the snowiest, Roxanna decided as she marked the last X through January 31 and crumpled the page into the fireplace. She sat on the hearth and poked at the coals. February would be long, she knew, fifty days at least. Then would come March, and Tibbie and the shepherds would be on the alert for ewes snuffling about, looking for a likely spot on the thawing ground to drop their lambs. And the wind would blow, and she and Lissy would continue to spend too much time at dusk looking across the Plain of York.

Helen seemed to adjust quickly to Lord Winn's leaving. She devoted long hours in the stable to Five Pence, and cajoled Roxanna into currying the Empress Josephine, her mother's new mare and parting gift from Lord Winn. Roxanna had to admit that she was looking forward to a break in the weather so she could ride the pretty animal.

"Mama, she likes you," Helen declared.

"Well, I do believe I like her," Roxanna replied, stroking the horse's nose.

"I am going to draw a picture of the Empress to send to Lord Winn," Helen said as she handed Roxanna a bucket of grain. "Do you think he will like that?"

"I am sure he will," Roxanna said.

"You'll mail it?"

"Of course. But don't tell Lissy. It think it almost makes her more sad to send letters because it reminds her that he is not here."

Helen turned back to Five Pence and began to curry the pony. "She'll get over him, Mama," she said, her voice matter-of-fact, a little cold, almost. "I have."

"My dear, you sound a wee bit bloodless," she scolded, startled from her contemplation of the Empress.

Helen leaned against her pony. "Mama, I do not want to like

someone else who will just be leaving, like Papa," she said calmly. "It's too hard to do."

Roxanna sat down on the grain bucket and pulled Helen close to her. "Oh, my dear, I wish you did not sound so adult," she whispered into Helen's ear.

Helen only cuddled in close to her mother, her eyes filled with misery. "Mama, I miss him, too." She sat up. "Why, Mama? He wasn't here that long. Why do I miss him?"

Roxanna cradled her daughter close again. "Well, he had a way of filling up a room, didn't he?"

"He did." She moved off her mother's lap and back to Five Pence again. "I am forgetting things about Papa, too. Will I do that with Lord Winn? Why does that have to happen? I try and try to remember . . ." Her voice trailed away.

I have no answers, my love, she thought that night as she sat in the bookroom, long after the girls were asleep. She picked up the picture of her horse that Helen had drawn, folded and addressed to the marquess. "My husband," she said out loud, wondering why it seemed so distant now. He had been gone a month and more. Even their tumultuous night together was fading around the edges now. She put her head down on the desk. *I shall have to start taking long walks again when the snow stops. If it ever stops.*

He wrote once a week, in response to their letters. Lissy usually received pictures he had drawn, sketches of Winnfield, mainly. One sketch was of the picture gallery with a series of forbidding, pop-eyed faces glaring down from the cobwebbed walls, and a note, "Wish you were here," scrawled across the top in spooky handwriting that made them all laugh.

To Helen he wrote horse advice, and sent along music, one sheet a Mozart exercise, and another a work of his own creation that Helen played over and over. "So you do not care?" Roxie said to herself as she heard Helen humming the tune and rehearsing it endlessly.

Her own letters from Lord Winn could have been read from the pulpit on Sundays, prosaic bits of news about Parliament's latest blunder, or more often, the business venture he was involved in that took him to London for several weeks. "Mind you," he wrote, "soiling my hands with business makes me smell of the shop to some of the high sticklers I know; but since I seldom have any dealings with the *ton* anymore, it hardly matters. They can be proud; I choose to be richer."

It was an intriguing venture, and so she wrote him, asking for more details about the canal system he was investing in. He responded promptly with maps and schematics of the canals. She pored over them, feeling complimented some how that Lord Winn would not dress them down or simplify them because she was a woman. He seemed to know that she could follow them, and she did. To Lissy's delight, one of the canal maps had a small boat sketched in, with a pirate on a plank who looked something like Lord Whitcomb.

His letters to her were nothing special, no intimate references to make her tuck them under her pillow to hoard and read over and over again. But she read them over and over anyway, chiding herself as she did so. What are you expecting, Roxie? she asked herself. It impressed her how forcefully his personality came through his words. He could almost be there, except that he was not, and they all felt the poorer for his absence.

"Do you think he misses us as much as we miss him?" Lissy asked her one night after prayers and before she blew out the lamp.

Roxanna sat on the bed, looking into Lissy's eyes, so like her own. "Oh, I am sure he is very busy with his canal venture, my love, and all the activities of his estates."

"Do you think if I told him I missed him, he would come sooner than March?" Lissy persisted, even as her eyes started to close.

"I think you ask too many questions!" she said, avoiding the issue.

Without question, she missed him. Even long before their precipitate marriage, she had enjoyed waking up in the dower house with the thought that perhaps if she worked on the renovation at Moreland, she might run into him during the course of the day. He always had something to say, some observation to make, that cheered her. True, he could be outrageous, but it was worth a blush to really laugh again.

As February began to slide toward March, she thought she understood why his letters were so businesslike: he obviously did not choose to further whatever relationship might have begun between them. The thought pained her a little, even as she scolded herself for thinking there would ever be more. She had made a marriage of convenience and that was all it was, barring one slip. Everyone's human, she thought, and then blushed. Maybe some of us more than others. But it was only a onetime moment, obviously of little importance to Lord Winn.

Or so she reasoned as she and Mrs. Howell busied themselves with some early spring cleaning, in the hopes that would bring an end to the eternal snows of 1817. And then it was March 5, a year since Anthony's death, and Lord Winn sent a note accompanying a bolt of burgundy dimity. "Dear Roxie, how about a walking dress of this? I found it in London and thought it would look especially nice on your back. More to follow. Winn." Two days later, a carter arrived with bolts of material, lavender, soft gray, blue and white, and a note pinned to one bolt of green fabric: "Is there enough for you and the girls? I can send more. I probably will. You know me. Winn."

Meggie laughed over that note. "Enough?" she asked, pointing to the bolts that they stashed in the linen room. "We could outfit an army from this. Someone ought to tell Lord Winn that current fashions don't require whole bolts. Well, Roxanna? You're wool-gathering again."

Guilty, Roxanna looked up from the note. "You know me," she read again as she dragged her attention back to Meggie. No, I don't know you, Lord Winn, she thought. And yet I know you awfully well. Lord, what a mull. "Yes, Meggie? I'm sorry. Say again?"

It was springtime material, but spring was still just a dream in the North Riding. Roxanna summoned a modiste anyway, and plotted and planned wardrobes for her and her daughters as the snow fell and the wind whistled around Moreland's well-insulated windows. When the weather broke, she promised herself a whole day in Darlington to look at hats and silk stockings.

When she finally completed the wallpaper and painting in Lord Winn's bedroom, she declared the renovation complete. True, the bedcovers and furniture were still definitely Queen Anne in a house more Regency now, but that could wait for a trip to the warehouses in Richmond. Curtains could wait, too. The matter interested her less and less. What was the point of renovation? She and the girls had their rooms completed, and Lord Winn was not selling Moreland. The other bedrooms would only remain empty.

And then it was March. Lissy triumphantly threw away her February calendar page. "Mama, he said he would come in March, didn't he?" she asked for the umpteenth time. She stood still only long enough for Roxie to button her nightgown and then ran to the window seat. "Do you think I will be able to see him from this window when he comes?"

Helen joined her. "Lissy, he might not come."

Lissy shook her head. "He said he would."

Oh dear, Roxie thought as she watched them both in the window seat. We have got to get over our melancholy. And we cannot spend all our days waiting for something to happen. Please, Lord, a break in the weather, she prayed that night.

She heard the wind howling as she shivered in bed and clutched her pillow close to her. Go to sleep, she told herself, even as she listened and dreaded the snow that would follow soon. But as she listened, she heard a different sound. The wind was coming up from the south, accompanied by the welcome drip of water from the long icicles outside the window. Spring was coming.

For two days, the winds blew warmer and gradually the ground began to emerge from the long sleep of a Yorkshire winter. Snow was everywhere still, but they could walk outside now and see the dark soil again. And here and there crocuses poked up through the snow.

"Come, girls," she said after breakfast. "Put on your oldest shoes. We are going walking."

She thought it would take some urging, but the girls were almost as restless as she was. The wind cut across the dale as they left the house, but it was warmer than the blizzards of January. Lissy tugged on her beloved red mittens and held up her hand.

"Mama, they almost do not fit!"

Roxanna smiled at her daughter, and examined her mitten. "That means a new pair next winter." She looked at Helen. "And for you, too?"

Helen nodded. "But let us not talk about next winter, Mama," she said. "Let us put it off, as you like to put off things."

They laughed together, grateful to be outside.

They passed the dower house, looking almost like a doll's house now, after the spaciousness of Moreland. "Do you know, Helen," she murmured, "I think I will ask Meggie if she would like to move in there."

"Why, Mama?" Helen asked. "She likes it with us."

"Every woman should have a home of her own," Roxanna said decisively. "Before she came here, Meggie only lived in rented rooms." She took her girls' hands and walked more purposefully toward the park beyond the house. "I will ask Lord Winn what he thinks."

It was really too cold to be walking long, but the meadow seemed to open up for them. And there in the distance were sheep. Lissy ran ahead, waving her arms. As Helen and Roxanna watched, she stopped and looked down at one sheep, then hurried back to her mother.

"Mama, it is grunting and grunting," she said, giving a demonstration that would have made Lord Winn laugh, Roxanna decided. "Is it sick?"

Roxanna shrugged. "Let us see." She hurried closer, and discovered the ewe deep in labor. She knelt in the mud beside the sheep and fingered its bedraggled wool, looking about for help. "Helen, see if you can find Tibbie or one of the shepherds," she asked as the ewe grunted, then panted softly, looking vaguely disturbed.

Helen was gone a long time and the wind blew colder. Lissy knelt beside her, grunting along with the ewe. Her nose was red and she shivered in the wind.

"This will never do," Roxanna said at last. "In for a penny . . . ," she muttered as she took off her cloak and rolled up her sleeve.

"Mama, what are you doing?" Lissy asked in astonishment as Roxanna inserted her arm into the ewe.

"Call it a courtesy," she said as she rummaged around and discovered a wonderful tangle of legs inside the ewe. The animal only looked back at her once and continued chewing placidly. "Goodness, Lissy, there are at least two lambs in there!"

Lissy leaned closer. "Mama! Do you know what to do?"

"I think I can figure out this puzzle," she grunted as she pulled on two legs, pushed back two others, then hooked her forefinger into an eye socket as another unborn lamb licked her wrist. "Stand back, Lissy! This may be like a cork in a bottle."

By the time Tibbie arrived, there were two lambs shaking themselves off and contemplating the ewe's udder. "Well, well, Mrs. Rand," he said as he squatted to watch her continued efforts. "No. You keep going. This last one ought to slide right out like an oyster. Grand work, Mrs. Rand! You'll put my shepherds out of business!"

As Roxanna sat back on her heels, her fingers aching, Lissy stared at the three lambs. She listened with satisfaction as the sheep made its odd purring noise and the lambs at the udder settled down to more serious matters.

"Mama, you are wonderful!" Helen declared as she ran up with a shepherd.

Roxanna accepted a piece of toweling from the man. She was bloody and covered with mud, but smiling with satisfaction. Spring had come to this harsh land at last, bringing new lambs. Perhaps it would bring Lord Winn back for a visit.

That evening Helen wrote a narrative to the marquess of her mother's exploits in the meadow, while Lissy drew a picture of the three lambs. Over her daughters' protests, Roxanna vetoed

Lissy's first picture of her arm in the sheep. "I think Lord Winn has sufficient imagination to figure out where lambs come from," she assured her children as she added her note about the dower house and Meggie, and sealed it with the pictures.

The next day was warmer, so while Lissy napped under Meggie's watchful eye, she and Helen rode their horses into the village to post the letter. The Empress Josephine was a well-mannered mare, Roxanna decided as they trotted along amiably. Lord Winn obviously knew his horses.

"Mama, have you ever seen a finer day?" Helen exclaimed, her face turned upward like a sunflower to the sky.

"Never, my dear," she agreed, struck all over again how different this year was from last year, when they were all claustrophobic in black and numb with Anthony's death. As they rode along, glorying in the North Riding spring, last year's tears and agony seemed to fold into the earth. She felt at peace finally, as if the disappearing snow was taking with it the unquiet in her heart. It had been a long year. She was glad it was over.

They returned to Moreland by way of the graveyard in Whitcomb parish. The snow was gone from Anthony's grave, and there were crocuses in bloom. They dismounted and came closer, admiring the beauty of the flowers against the scrollwork of the tombstone. Roxanna took Helen's hand and swallowed an enormous lump in her throat. "Helen, let us return tomorrow and plant daffodils," she said, speaking through her tears.

"Oh, yes, Mama, and then something else for summer." Helen's eyes were bright with tears, too, but she was smiling. "Papa would like that. Columbine, Mama."

Roxanna nodded and took her daughter by the shoulder as they turned away from the graveyard. And maybe woodbine, too, she thought, and holly later. There should be some part of Yorkshire for all of Anthony's seasons here. She looked back one last time at the crocuses, their petals giving way now in the sharp wind. "To everything there is a season," she thought, remembering a sermon given in the strength of his better days. This was yours, my love.

Lissy watched all week for the postman; Lord Winn did not disappoint her. While the others stood by, she opened a letter and pulled out a sketch of Roxanna, her eyes wide with disbelief, sitting up in bed and clutching her blankets as three lambs jumped over the footboard. Roxanna chuckled over the note at the bottom: " 'Little lamb, who untangled thee? Dost though know who untangled thee?' " she read. "Lord Winn, you should be shot for such a mangling of Blake!"

As the girls decided where to pin the picture in their room, Roxanna read the accompanying letter. He had given his whole-hearted approval of Meggie's removal to the solitary splendor of the dower house. "Heaven knows she deserves an occasional break from Lissy's enthusiasms," he wrote in his rapid scrawl. "It was good of you to think of it, Roxie." Her heart warmed as he informed her that he had settled three hundred pounds a year on Meggie Watson with his solicitor. "I'd say her service was above and beyond the call of duty, wouldn't you, wife?" he continued. *Wife,* she thought. *It sounds good.*

The rest of the letter brought a frown to her face. *Oh, dear, Helen was right,* she thought as she continued on the next page. "I fear I cannot return in March as I had promised," he wrote. "I must go to Northumberland by way of Carlisle, as we have another canal backer to cajole there. I wish it were not so. Please tell the girls how sorry I am. Perhaps I can visit later in the summer, when negotiations are settled. Winn."

That is somewhat indefinite, my lord, she thought as she scanned the last page again. *What would you rather I read into that?* She looked from the letter to the picture, wondering at the contradictions. *Are you as confused as I am? Likely,* she told herself. *But now comes the hard part.*

It could have been worse, but I am not sure how, she decided an hour later after she closed the door to the girls' room. Lissy was asleep now, tears drying on her face, crushed by her news of Lord Winn's nonarrival. She had stormed and wailed, then refused to sit in the window seat for her nighttime perusal of the Plain of York. Roxanna went to her own room and lay down on the bed. To her mind, Helen's reaction was worse. She had flinched at the news, then her shoulders drooped as she looked at Roxanna. "Mama, at least with Lord Winn we don't have so much to tuck away in our minds," she said quietly, then turned away to sit in her chair by the fire.

I suppose every family needs a realistic member, she thought as she stared at the ceiling. *Lissy and I hope and dream, and Helen keeps us tethered to the ground. I doubt she will ever put off things like I do, but oh, she can break my heart.* There was no point in blaming Lord Winn. He was a busy man, and once cut adrift from the loose ties of Moreland, quite in demand in his busy world. It was no wonder he had forgotten them. She would be a fool to think otherwise.

She went to the window for her ritual look across the wide plain. And he never promised you anything more, Roxanna, she told herself. Look what he has done already. She smiled to herself. It would be sufficient. Lonely, perhaps, but sufficient. "I shall close that book, too," she said and then chuckled. "Not that it was ever open very far, anyway."

In the morning, she wrote a proper letter expressing their regrets, but saying nothing that would cast blame, or express the deep disappointment of her daughters. As she left the bookroom to look for Tibbie, Helen ran up with a letter, too. "For Lord Winn," she said.

Roxanna took it. "I trust you said nothing to cause Lord Winn any discomfort," she said as Tibbie came into the hall, motioning for her to bring the letters.

Helen shook her head. "I don't think so, Mama. Mostly I had a question about Five Pence. Do you think he will have time to answer it?"

Roxanna shrugged, and handed both letters to Tibbie. "He's obviously a busy man, my dear. Thanks, Tibbie."

The last week in March saw the roads freed finally of mud from the thawing snow. It had taken no cajoling on her part to talk the girls into accompanying her to Darlington to select bedcovers and material for curtains in the almost-completed bedrooms. There had been the dresses to pick up from the modiste, too, and a careful look at bonnets, which rendered Lissy bored beyond belief. Only the bribe of luncheon in a real tearoom bought Roxanna enough time to purchase silk stockings and several lengths of ribbon to refurbish old dresses.

It was a good luncheon. Lissy ate everything brought to her, and even Helen finished most of her meal. As they waited for dessert, Roxanna played her final card in cheering up her daughters. "My dears, I was thinking that a month at Scarborough this summer would be something fine. What do you think?"

"Mama, the seashore!" Helen gasped. "Really?"

"I remember making such a promise last year," Roxanna replied. "What about you, Lissy?"

She hesitated. "But what if Lord Winn decides to visit while we are gone?"

Roxanna sighed inwardly. Oh, Lissy, let it go! I have. "Well, we can let him know our plans so he will not come then."

"But suppose that is the only time he can visit us?" Lissy argued, with all the maddening persistence of a four-year-old.

"Don't be a nod," Helen said, her voice firm. "Think of sand castles and pony rides along the beach. And raspberry ices, Mama?"

"Of course."

Lissy thought, and then nodded. "I like it."

"Very well," Roxanna said as the dessert arrived. "August, then, in Scarborough."

They rode home singing loud songs, to the amusement of the coachman, and glorying in the unexpected warmth of early spring. Even the news that they must return to the classroom with Meggie tomorrow did nothing to dilute her daughters' noisy triumph over winter. "For we have gotten lax in our studies, now that Meggie has moved to the dower house," she reminded them. "Tomorrow, it is spelling and penmanship again."

And thank goodness for that, Roxanna said in the morning as she waved her daughters off to the classroom Meggie had established in her upstairs bedroom at the dower house. She debated over her new dresses, then hurried instead into a faded muslin which had once been blue. Climbing tall ladders does not require much fashion, she thought as she draped the tape measure around her neck and pulled the ladder closer to the window in one of the empty bedrooms. Now that she had finally chosen the material, she needed to measure windows. I have put this off too long, she thought. Why do I do that?

"I wish you would not dangle yourself atop tall ladders."

She blinked—it couldn't be—then reached out for the top of the window to steady herself. "Lord Winn?" she asked, and then turned around slowly on her perch.

"I thought I was Fletch to you," the marquess said, leaning against the frame of the open doorway, still wearing his many caped riding coat and hat. He tossed his hat onto the bed. "Obviously my credit is a little lower with the females of the Drew/Rand family right now. Do get down, Roxie! You make me nervous."

She hiked up her skirts and climbed down the ladder. She stopped halfway down and smiled at him. "You came after all," she said softly.

She didn't know what it was about her smile that made him stand up straight and stare back at her. I don't know about your expression, she thought as she descended and shook her skirts out. I wonder if I am in trouble?

She decided she wasn't when the marquess shrugged out of his overcoat, tossed it after the hat, and took her in his arms. Well, that's a relief, was her last coherent sentence before he kissed her, held her off for a moment, then kissed her again. In another moment she was flooded with desire, drenched in it, craving his body even as he pulled away and went back to the door.

Drat, she thought, her hands stopped on her buttons. To her relief, he was only closing the door and locking it. She went back to the buttons again, wondering why, out of all her clothes, she had put on the dress with so many. He turned back to help her, but his fingers were shaking, too.

"Roxie, is this dress valuable to you?" he asked finally.

She shook her head. "It's years old."

"Good." He grasped the front of it and ripped it open, sending the buttons clattering to the floor. "Now then, Roxie."

It was an easy matter to wriggle out of her chemise and petticoat as he tugged off his boots. He looked up at her, his eyes admiring what he saw. "You've been eating better, my dear," he managed. "Lord, Roxie, you could almost be an eye-popper!"

She laughed, sat on his lap, and started on his shirt. "You say the most romantic things, Fletch."

After that, words drifted from her brain in odd little bursts. I'm glad that door is locked, she thought as she shoved aside a coat and hat, and rolls of wallpaper, and took the tape measure from her neck. No sheets on this bed, she thought as he laid her down onto it. "Frills," she muttered, then devoted her whole attention to more pressing matters.

"Frills, eh! I am a frill?" he asked later as she rested herself on him. "Don't move. You're fine. But frills?"

She closed her eyes in vast contentment. "I was merely pointing out that there are no sheets on this bed, and your head is resting on a pillow of wallpaper."

"And your bum is covered with goosebumps," he added in most unloverlike fashion, running his hand over her backside. "Can you reach my overcoat without moving?"

She did, and he pulled it over both of them, then dug in one of the pockets, taking out a folded sheet. "I honestly do not have time to be here," he explained.

"I'll move," she offered, remaining where she was.

"Don't you dare! Take a look at this letter."

She spread out the letter on his chest. "It is from Helen," she said, and looked into his eyes.

"Read it. You'll see my primary reason for this visit, all frills aside, Roxie dear."

She did as he said, then rested her head on his chest. "Thank you for coming, my lord," she murmured.

He picked up the letter. "What could I do? That part about 'getting used to disappointment' sliced me to the bone." He put his arms around her again, running his hand over her back. "And the thing is, she was so matter-of-fact. There's not an ounce of pity in that letter. I wish she could still be a child, despite all that's happened to her. That's why I had to come."

"Helen never deals in self-pity." Roxie kissed his chest absentmindedly. "I wish . . . well, I don't know what I wish. She will be so glad to see you."

He sighed and gently relocated her to the bed, sitting up to rummage for his watch, which he snapped open, shaking his head.

"It's nine-thirty in the morning, Roxie," he said, his voice filled with wonder. "I don't recall that I ever did this before so soon after breakfast." He grinned at her. "What about you?"

She grinned back, even as she reached for her chemise. "Well, vicars do not keep regular hours, my lord," she hedged, her face red. She giggled. "Anthony used to swear it helped the digestion."

They dressed quickly. "Drat, there's no mirror." The marquess complained as he held out his neckcloth.

"Let me help," she replied, tying it expertly. She paused halfway through. "How could you manage this?"

"Well, I took off my clothes . . ." he began, his eyes roguish.

"Lord Winn, you're risking your credit! You said you were busy."

"I am," he agreed as he tucked his shirt into his pants and looked for his waistcoat. "After Helen's letter came, I told my solicitor that we were by damn going to go to Carlisle another route, even if we had to ride all night in a post chaise—he hates inconvenience, Roxie."

She put her hand to her mouth, her eyes wide. "And now you will tell me you have left that poor man sitting downstairs in the parlor!"

He nodded. "Well, yes."

She burst out laughing. "You are a rascal!"

He held up his hands in self-defense. "I did not plan this! Really! You are the one who gave me that look from the ladder, Roxie." He let her help him into his coat, and ran his fingers through his hair. "I can just drop in on Helen and Lissy and say hello now."

He took her hand and she felt her heart flop about in her chest. "My dear, we need to consider our arrangement," he said.

She nodded. "It does bear serious thought."

"Write me," he urged as he grabbed up his hat and overcoat.

"I'll be at Carlisle this week, and then High Point in Northumberland. I want to know how you feel."

"I'm not sure I know," she protested.

He grabbed her hand again and kissed it, then pulled her close to him. "Roxie, you need to decide if I am to be an everyday husband or an occasional convenience. Good-bye, my dear." He opened the door, then looked back at her. "If you hurry, you can make it to your room and find another dress before my solicitor sends Mrs. Howell on a hunting expedition."

She dressed quickly in her room and then went to a back bedroom, where she watched the dower house as Lord Winn ran in, and then came out a few minutes later, carrying Lissy, Helen at his side. He kissed them both, waved good-bye, then rejoined the solicitor in the post chaise. In a moment they were gone from view, heading north toward the Pennines.

It was almost hard to conceive that he had even been there at all, so quick was the visit. Except for the fact that she felt hugely content and her buttons were spilled everywhere on the floor, Lord Winn's visit might have been a product of her imagination. She went back to the other bedroom, replacing the rolls of wallpaper and hunting for her tape measure. She found it, but sat on the bed, staring at her hands. It's a good question, Roxie. What do you want?

Chapter 17

It was a good question, and one that she asked herself several times every hour, no matter how involved she was with other matters. *What* do I want? became her refrain as she supervised the hanging of the curtains in that bedroom. What *do* I want? she asked herself, changing the emphasis as she listened to Helen practice her Scarlatti. What do I *want*? was the question that chased around in her head when she should have been paying attention to Lissy's somersaults in the orchard.

Her brain told her that it was much too soon after Anthony's death to have formed a rational opinion about another man. If you truly loved Anthony, her mind scolded, you wouldn't even have thoughts about another yet, even if he is your husband now. "Bother it," she said out loud in church that Sunday during the reading of the Gospel, which caused a few heads to turn in her direction. She retreated behind her prayer book to tell herself that was a rumdudgeon notion. You couldn't put a timetable on love, as if it were a mail coach.

But is this love? was the next logical question. She glared at the vicar, wondering why he was prosing on and on about the atonement and resurrection, when she was wrestling with the more weighty matters of existence. Without question, she enjoyed Lord Winn's body. She slid lower behind her prayer book, hoping the Lord God Almighty wouldn't be troubling Himself at the moment to monitor her unruly thoughts. And the interesting thing is, she considered when she stood to take communion, neither time did I compare Fletch to Anthony. Beyond the basics, their lovemaking was not alike. She glided up the aisle, her eyes on her folded hands. Anthony had been a leisurely man, restful almost in his patterns, while entirely satisfying. Fletch was an adventure, a tumult. Oh Lord, she thought as she opened her mouth for communion. I shall be struck dead here at the altar, and what a pity that will be.

The Lord did not strike her dead, but she knew better than to take any more chances. She forced herself to concentrate on more mundane matters, such as why Lissy was staring cross-eyed at the lady in the next pew, and was it fair that the man over by the window had shoulders as broad as Fletch's? She could almost feel Lord Winn's back under her hands . . .

"Drat," she whispered under her breath, causing Helen to look up at her with a startled expression.

"Mama," she warned in a low voice. "You should behave yourself."

It's too late for that, she thought mournfully. Much too late.

They walked home across the fields to Moreland, Lissy stopping to blow dandelion puffs and dance around in the warm breeze of late March, as unexpected as it was richly deserved by the hardy souls of the North Riding. She walked with her hand in Helen's, miserable because Lord Winn was not there, her mind a tumult because she could not speak to him and hear his lovely Yorkshire brogue, with all its old style words that she, a transplant to this shire, could never master without sounding fake. It pained her that she could not see him lounging about in that casual way of his, or playing the piano with his sleeves rolled up and that look of concentration on his face, his long legs tapping out the rhythm.

She stopped suddenly in the middle of the park. Helen smiled and let go of her mother's hand, flopping down in the new grass, while Lissy danced around them both. I am an idiot, she thought as she dropped down beside Helen. How could I ever have considered Lord Winn just a convenience? Oh, well, he is a magnificent convenience, but that is only part of it, she amended, stretching her arms over her head in the soft grass. He is also someone I like to talk to, to walk with, to tease, to flatter, to laugh with, to admire, to worry about. I am in love again.

I wonder when it happened? she thought as she held up her left hand and regarded her wedding ring. Have I been in love with him since I first saw him looking so dejected on my doorstep? Was it when he let me cry all over him while he was shaving? Or maybe when he got that determined look in his eye and said we were going to Scotland, no matter what.

"Mama, are you listening to me?"

Lissy was sitting on her, staring into her eyes. Roxie grabbed her and rolled over with her in the grass, growling, as Lissy shrieked and tried to leap away. Helen giggled and threw handfuls of grass at them both.

"Come, my dears," Roxie said finally as she stood up and brushed off the grass. "I know you are starving, Lissy, and I have a letter to write."

She wrote to Lord Winn after dinner, debating whether to post her message to Carlisle or Northumberland, and choosing the latter finally. I have already delayed a reply to a pressing question, she reasoned, and he may have left Carlisle for High Point. This way, it will find him, she assured herself as she applied a wafer. She gazed at the letter, a smile on her face. I suppose he will respond promptly with one of those silly sketches of me.

The letter was on its way in the morning, and Roxanna busied herself with more spring cleaning. Two or three days at most, she thought as she finished hemming the last curtain in the last bedroom. Perhaps he will even show up again. That would be the best of all.

When he did not return a reply that week, she put it down to business. By the end of the second week, she was trying not to think about it. By the end of the third week, she had a bigger problem than Lord Winn's apparent lack of interest in her declaration of love through the mail.

She noticed it first one morning when she woke with a

headache and the urge to throw up. "Lord, this is unkind," she moaned as she sat up in bed and eyed the washbasin, wondering if she could get to it in time. She made it only just, retching until she thought her liver and lights would appear in the basin, too. She crawled back into bed and threw the covers over her head.

She was feeling much better until Lissy ran into her room and bounced on the bed. The motion made her gorge rise again, except that there was nothing left to heave. "Oh, Lissy, not now!" she gasped, her hand over her mouth.

Lissy ended her with real surprise, then rested her head against her mother. Roxanna flinched at the pain in her breasts. I must be coming down with something, she thought as she carefully settled her little daughter against her.

"Mama, you promised to take us riding in the gig," Helen reminded her over breakfast. "Remember? Tibbie said there were new calves in the upper pasture."

"Well, then, let us get ready," Roxie declared as she pushed away her uneaten breakfast and forced down the rest of her tea. She stood by the table, nibbling on a piece of dried toast, and wondering what else she could do today to forget that Lord Winn was not interested anymore. She shrugged. Perhaps she would just take a nap that afternoon. She had been so sleepy lately, and it was a convenient way to pass time.

They found the calves in the upper pasture, and Tibbie there, too, admiring the herd. "This is more like, Lady Winn," he said. "It's always a pleasure to communicate good news to Lord Winn."

"Oh? And have you heard from him lately?" she asked, hoping her voice was casual.

"Aye, ma'am, think on," he replied. "Only yesterday I got a letter asking about spring planting."

"Where did he write you from?"

"Why . . . Winnfield, of course, ma'am. He's been back from Carlisle for these two weeks and more."

Tibbie eyed her speculatively, and she managed a smile in his direction. "I suppose we'll hear from him one of these days," she said. "Come, girls. You have lessons."

She was grateful that her daughters wanted to sit in the back of the gig, take off their stockings and shoes, and dangle their bare feet over the edge. That way they wouldn't see her tears and ask questions. She drove slowly, reminding herself that Lord Winn had been jittery about the married state, and adamant so many times about not wanting children. Certainly it followed that he really would not care to assume any other relationship with her except the one that now faced her. Whatever he had said that day in the unfinished bedroom had obviously been because his emotions were carried away temporarily. He had chosen not to respond to her letter, and she would have to live with that. I should have known, she thought. I should have been wiser. She dried her eyes on her sleeve. Perhaps Tibbie will find me some estate business to work on to keep me occupied. Does he need a barn built? a road constructed? I fear it will have to be a major project.

The bailiff was happy enough the next morning to send her to the village with an order for grain and a letter for Lord Winn's solicitor. Emma Winslow had brought them by the house after breakfast with the news that Tibbie was in bed with a cold.

"At least, that's what we think it is," she said as she handed Roxanna the letter. "Mind you, and wasn't my husband shaking with chills and fever when he came home yesterday?"

"I'm sorry," Roxanna said. She touched Emma's arm. "Well, you know, lots of soup with onions in it will mend him."

"Aye, ma'am, and a mustard plaster, think on."

She rode the Empress Josephine into the village and discharged Tibbie's business, riding slowly home, then dismounting and leading the mare because the motion was nauseating her again. Goodness, I hope this is not catching, she considered as she sat under a tree finally and let the reins drop. I wonder if it's what Tibbie has? The Empress cropped grass by the side of the road as Roxanna leaned back to watch.

I haven't felt this bad since I was expecting Felicity, she thought as nausea surged over her. Her eyes closed, and then she sucked in her breath and sat upright again. Surely not. She stared at the Empress, trying to remember when her last monthly had been. The end of February? The first part of March? Not that she had had any reason to keep records for the last few years. No need at all, Roxie, she thought, except that you and Lord Winn sported pretty heavily at the end of March. If you weren't such a nincompoop, you'd remember that so much fun does make babies.

"This is another unkind hand," she declared out loud, and then rested her forehead on her drawn-up knees. Mind you, Lord, I suppose someday I will appreciate the exquisite irony, she told God Almighty with some asperity, but not now. I have written a declaration of love to a man who doesn't want children, and who is content apparently to have a wife in Yorkshire to keep his relatives at bay so he can get on with his own life undisturbed. And now we've fetched a child. Lord, I am not laughing.

Her next thought was to write him immediately. She discarded that idiotic notion as fast as it came to her mind. How would it look, Roxie, to follow your letter of love with the casual announcement that in eight months he would be a father? He would think you had declared your love expeditiously, to blunt his wrath when the glad tidings become inevitable. He would think you dishonest. Better not to say anything.

She looked down at her belly in dismay. You can put this one off for only so long, Roxie. He'll have to know eventually, and then he will be furious. He will not believe that you really do love him to distraction.

I think I shall run away to Canada, she thought as she got up, held onto the tree until it stopped leaping around, then slowly mounted the Empress again. I shall move into the interior and become a shepherdess. We will change our names and join an Indian tribe.

She patted her belly. "Oh, well, little one," she said out loud, smiling briefly when the Empress pricked up her ears. "I am sure your father will be dreadfully upset with me." She rested her hand there. "It's not your fault, however, and I shall never blame you." And I will have something of your dear father forever, even if he did not choose to remain with us himself. It is better than nothing.

She was through crying by the time she returned to Moreland. The girls would have to know eventually, but it could wait several months at least. Thank goodness current fashions are kind to the expectant mother, she thought, and I never have been one to show early. Maybe I'll have thought of something by then, or at least started learning whatever language they speak in Canada. Perhaps Australia would be better.

Her disquieting thoughts kept her awake all night, and she braced herself for another session with the washbasin in the morning. She was still hanging over it, her face white and perspiring, when Mrs. Howell knocked on her door.

"Lady Winn, Emma Winslow is below. It seems that Tibbie is not well at all. Can you come downstairs?"

"Yes," she gasped, wiping the bile from her lips. "Give me a moment."

Give me three months, actually, she thought grimly as she dressed. I'll feel fine then, and ready to tackle dragons—maybe even Lord Winn. But I have ten minutes to look agreeable.

She shoved away her own discomfort when she opened the bookroom door on Emma Winslow, who leaped up from her chair, her eyes red.

"Lady Winn, Tibbie is terribly sick! I have summoned Dr. Clyde, and he tells me that influenza has broken out in Richmond!"

Roxanna took Mrs. Winslow by the hands, sat her down again, and calmly poured her a glass of sherry. "Surely it is too late in the season for influenza," she said, remembering other outbreaks. Anthony even had a funeral sermon just for the flu season, she remembered with a pang.

Mrs. Winslow sipped the sherry, then shook her head. "Those were my very words to Dr. Clyde, but he said it was entirely possible." She looked up at Roxanna. "Tibbie wondered if you could ride out to the west pasture this morning. They're dipping sheep today, and someone needs to supervise."

"Of course," Roxanna said. "Tell him not to worry about anything."

Mrs. Winslow retreated to her handkerchief again. "He's so concerned! It will be such a burden on you."

"I'll be fine, my dear," she replied, drawing strength from some reservoir she must have forgotten about. "I can check Tibbie's farm record from last year and see what needs to be done until he is well again. Tell him not to trouble himself."

Mrs. Winslow nodded, gave her a watery smile, and left. Roxanna sat back down in Lord Winn's swivel chair, holding very still against any sudden motion. She took a deep breath and reached for the farm records.

"Stay at Moreland, Lady Winn, and keep your circle of visitors small," Dr. Clyde told her three weeks later, stopping in on his way back to Richmond. His eyes were red-rimmed from lack of sleep, and he looked as though he slept in his clothes. "I only wanted to stop by here to tell you that. This is a wicked flu. Is everyone still well?"

"Everyone except Tibbie," she replied. He had found her in the stables after a long day in the fields, trying to get the energy to remove the Empress's saddle. "Oh, thank you, sir. I seem to be too tired to lift a saddle these days."

He peered at her closely, and put the back of his hand to her forehead. "You don't feel warm. Can you identify any other symptoms, Lady Winn?"

Oh, can I ever, she thought as she shook her head. "No, Dr.

Clyde. I am just tired." She managed what she thought was a rather fine smile. "Surely it will be better when Tibbie is about on the estate again."

He set down the saddle and removed the Empress's bridle, turning her into the loose box. "That'll be some time yet. You've written Lord Winn, of course," he said. "He needs to get you another bailiff."

"No, actually, I have not written him. He's a busy man, Dr. Clyde. We'll manage."

He walked with her to the back door, but shook his head when she invited him in to dinner. "I'm needed back in Richmond," he explained as he mounted his horse again. "And my wife said something about a bed, and clean clothes in a house I vaguely remember as my own. I think I even have children."

"Oh, dear," she said and held out her hand to him. "Take care, Dr. Clyde. There's nothing wrong with any of us here that won't keep."

She could not keep her eyes open over dinner, even through Lissy's lively chatter about Meggie's drawing lesson that morning, and Helen's description of their afternoon's expedition to the stream to find watercress. Silently she blessed Meggie Watson for her cheerful taking over of the girls so she could spend her days in the saddle seeing Moreland through the busy season of sowing, shearing, and calving.

Mrs. Howell approached her after dinner, when Helen had taken Lissy into the sitting room to practice a duet. "Lady Winn, I know how busy you are." She prefaced her remarks. "It's my sister, Mrs. Hamilton. You remember how she helped out at Christmas?"

Roxanna nodded, knowing what was coming next. "Is she ill?" she asked quietly.

The housekeeper nodded, tears in her eyes.

"Then you must go to her at once," Roxanna murmured, her arm around Mrs. Howell. "We will manage. I know I can ask Meggie to come back over here and help in the kitchen. Isn't there a scullery maid left?"

"Aye, ma'am, Sally," Mrs. Howell replied. "She can cook, too, even though she's young."

"Excellent! And you know, I imagine Helen could help, too," she said as they walked along together. Calm, calm, Roxie, she told herself. We can eat simply, and the dust can wait. "I think you should leave as soon as possible. Can the groom take you in the gig tomorrow morning?"

Mrs. Howell was gone after breakfast, waving her handkerchief from the front drive, and then sobbing into it. Roxie stood there a long while, wishing she had time to admire the handsome, full-leafed lane and the orchard close by, the apples large enough to be visible. She rested her hand lightly on her belly. She could feel the bulge now, as slight as it was. You must be a stubborn little one, she thought as she watched the gig retreat down the lane. Considering your father, why am I surprised at that? Here I have been riding and riding for weeks now, and I even fell off the Empress once. You must be well seated in there. Thank God for that.

She walked slowly to the dower house, wanting a word of comfort from Meggie. I really should tell her about the baby, she thought as she tapped on the door. She's so good with children. And with me. I'd like to put my head in Meggie's lap and make everything go away for a while.

There was no answer. She knocked again, louder this time. She stepped back finally and looked at the open windows in the upstairs bedrooms. "Meggie?" she called, cupping her hands around her mouth. "Meggie?"

In a moment she was wrenching open the front door and running up the stairs, her heart in her throat. She pounded on Meggie's door, then burst into the room, her eyes wide at the sight before her.

Meggie Watson looked up at her from the floor where she had fallen. She was shaking all over, and trying to speak. Roxanna threw herself down beside the nursemaid. She touched her forehead, drawing her hand away quickly, alarmed at the warmth there. Meggie could only shiver, and stare at her.

"Oh, my dear, not you, too?" she said as she helped the woman into her bed. "Don't try to speak. Just rest. I'll—I'll think of something."

Meggie died three days later, attended at the end by Helen because Roxie was supervising the first cutting of hay in the upper meadow. She used to enjoy watching the rhythm of the workers in the hayfield as they cut and stacked the hay. But now, influenza had ripped such a swath through the North Riding that she had to help pitch the hay into wains because there were too few men to work the fields. When she rode back that evening, her arms and back on fire from her exertions, she saw Dr. Clyde leaving the dower house.

"I'm sorry, Lady Winn," he said. "The flu is hardest on the young and the old."

"Oh, no," she whispered, too tired to work up more emotion. "Please tell me Meggie will be better."

"My dear, didn't you hear me? She is dead," he said. "Helen rode to tell me."

Her mind numb, she dragged herself into the dower house, where Helen and Lissy sat on the sofa, their arms around each other, both too stricken for tears. Wordlessly, she sank down at their feet and gathered them in her arms. Lissy said nothing, but burrowed in close to her, holding tight as though afraid she would disappear, too. Roxanna clung to her daughter, then touched Helen. "My dear, I am so sorry I was not here," she murmured.

Helen regarded her with those searching eyes so like Anthony's. "Mama, I think you should write to Lord Winn," she urged. "We need some help."

Roxanna shook her head. "Helen, we have been such a trouble to him for so long."

"Mama, don't you like him anymore?" Helen asked. "We have not sent letters or pictures in such a long time."

Oh, I love him, she thought. Nothing would make me happier at this minute than to crawl into his lap like Lissy here and turn all my miseries over to him. But I dare not. I am too much trouble, and he has already done more than any man could be expected to do, considering the nature of our agreement.

"I just want to carry on without bothering him," she said. It sounded lame, but it was the best she could do without tears.

There was no funeral for Meggie Watson. The epidemic had reached such a stage that the doctors forbade mourners to gather in large groups, for fear of passing on the contagion. It tore out her heart to watch Meggie's simple coffin bundled into a farm wagon and destined for the burying ground without anyone there to lament her passing. She stood with her daughters on the front steps as the wagon rolled away, acutely aware of Meggie's devotion, and wondering what to do now, with Mrs. Howell gone, and Tibbie still too ill to do more than sit up in bed and look distressed when she visited him.

She lay awake a long time that night, too tired to sleep, going over and over in her mind all the activities of the days and weeks that seemed never to end. What if I have left something out? she thought. She hoped it would rain, so she could find an excuse to stay inside, and not risk falling off the Empress again. How nice it would be to sit still, and really, how much safer. She knew she should not be in the saddle.

Thank God you are still so small, she thought as her hands rested on her belly. Perhaps she could write Lord Winn after all, and plead for help. She could assure him that he needn't come himself, but at least loan her a bailiff from another estate untroubled with illness. She reflected a moment and sighed. Since he had not been interested enough to answer that letter she sent to Northumberland, he probably would not come. And even if he did, he would never notice. Men really weren't so observant.

"Roxanna, you are a great looby," she said as she patted down her pillow and tried to find a cool spot. "How long can you keep this baby a secret?" She couldn't bring herself to voice her greatest fear, the one that dogged her all day and left her sleepless at night. When he found out, suppose Lord Winn was so angry that he divorced her? She knew he could do it. And then will I be at the mercy of my brother-in-law again?

The thought so unnerved her that she got out of bed and went to the window. She opened it and breathed deep of the fragrance from the park. Somewhere she could smell orange blossoms, and it calmed her. She stared at the moon, so full and benevolent, wondering how the night could look so serene when people were dying of influenza and her own life was a turmoil. Soon high summer would come. The flu could not hang on forever, and perhaps she would find the courage to tell Lord Winn, before he discovered it himself, or heard from others.

She climbed back in bed, trying to compose her jitters. Her eyes were finally closing when the door opened. Fletch, is that you? she thought, caught halfway between awake and dreaming. I wish I looked better.

Helen ran to the bed, her eyes wide with fear. Roxanna sat up and grabbed her daughter. "My dear, what is it?" she asked, holding her close.

"Mama! Lissy is so hot! And she is coughing like Meggie did." Helen started to cry, a helpless sound that made Roxanna suck in her breath. "Mama, I don't know what to do! Look what happened to Meggie!"

Roxanna closed her eyes in agony, seeing in her mind Helen standing helpless as Meggie died before her. She gathered her child close as she sobbed, even as she got out of bed, her heart and mind on Lissy. "Helen, you did everything you could. No one could have done more. Let us go see to Lissy now."

She compelled herself to walk slowly, her arm resting on Helen's shoulder, when she wanted to run into the other bedroom, grab Lissy, and run with her to the doctor's house. I will not panic, she told herself. She sat down on the bed, willing her hand to stop shaking, and touched Lissy's forehead.

It was so hot that Roxanna shuddered. Lissy's skin was oddly clammy, and as she sat staring down at her sweat-soaked hair, the child shivered and opened her eyes. She reached for Roxanna. "Mama, make me better," she whispered.

Roxanna grasped Lissy's hands, fearful of their feverish heat. God give me strength, she thought as she stared down at her daughter.

"Mama?" Helen asked, her voice filled with terror.

Enough of this, Roxanna, she told herself. "Don't worry, Helen," she said calmly. "I am sure that Lissy will be fine. Hand me that pitcher of water and a facecloth. Very good, my dear."

She wrung out a cool cloth for Lissy's face and then took her by the hand, kissing her fingers one by one. "Now you must try to sleep, my love," she told Lissy. "I'll be here with you. Helen, go to my bed. You need to sleep so you can help me tomorrow."

She held Lissy all night, crooning to her as she sobbed with the fever. In the morning she left Lissy in the care of the scullery maid and Helen, and hauled herself into the saddle for a half-day in the field, after sending the groom for Dr. Clyde.

She watched the farm laborers, some of them newly recovered from the flu, and then she did not care anymore. She turned the Empress toward Moreland, hoping that Tibbie would be well enough to take her place in the field. And if he was not, well, then, it didn't matter, not the harvest, or the animals. Nothing mattered but Lissy.

Dr. Clyde could promise nothing, and do little but offer fever powders of dubious value, and advice that might or might not bring about a change in Lissy's condition. He could only visit every other day, peek into the sickroom, and say "h'mmm" in that way of all doctors, and shake his head. As much as she clung to his visits as a sign of hope, she began to dread the familiar sound of his footsteps on the stairs.

"You're doing everything I would do," he assured her one afternoon as June began to turn into July with no change in Lissy's condition. He picked up Lissy's hand, frowning at her limpness. "Where's our old Lissy?" he asked, more to himself than to Roxanna. "This damnable flu just doesn't let go." He tried to smile, but it was a failed attempt. "And it preys on anxious mothers, too. Lady Winn, can you remember when you last slept?"

Roxanna stared at him stupidly, then shook her head. No, I cannot, she thought, or even when I last ate something. She could only look at him, as though he had the power to change the situation, and then look away, aghast at the helplessness in his eyes.

"Roxanna, you need some help here," he said. "I wish I could think of anyone who could help you that isn't already tending the sick."

"I just wish it would let go of her," Roxanna said as she squeezed out another cloth to wipe Lissy's body, feeling as wrung and pummeled as the rag she held. "She is so thin now."

Dr. Clyde could only nod. "Does she ever speak to you?" he asked, his voice low.

Roxanna nodded. "Sometimes. It doesn't always make sense." She glanced sideways at the doctor, and noticed how his own eyes were closing. Poor man, she thought. For two months and more now you have watched your patients sicken and die. She touched his hand, drawing back quickly when he gasped and leaped to his feet, startled out of his somnolence.

"Go home, Dr. Clyde," she said softly. "We'll manage here."

Manage what? she asked herself as he rode away, chin tipped down against his chest, swaying as though he already slept. She watched him from the upstairs window, wanting to call him back. What for? she thought. My child is dying and I can only wring out cool cloths and pretend that I am doing something to help her.

"Winn."

She turned back to Lissy, whose eyes were still closed. "What?" she asked, coming closer.

Lissy opened her eyes suddenly, and looked around as though she expected to see someone. "Winn," she repeated, then closed her eyes again to begin her cycle of coughing and then struggling to breathe. Roxanna held up her daughter so she could get an easier breath, breathing along with her until she felt light-headed and even more useless than before.

While Lissy dozed fitfully, Roxanna tiptoed from the room. She peeked in on Helen, but she was sleeping, too, exhausted from watching. Roxanna went downstairs, standing in front of the bookroom door for a long moment, as if wondering why she was there. Finally, she squared her shoulders and went inside. I have put this off too long, she thought as she reached for a sheet of paper and the inkwell. *Lissy wants him, too. I hope we will not be too much trouble, but I cannot face this alone.*

Chapter 18

In the thirty-eight—nearly thirty-nine—years that I have known you, brother, I disremember your ever asking my advice on any subject. Let me savor the moment."

Lord Winn looked up from the contemplation of his mother's favorite silverware pattern and into his sister's eyes.

"You're right, of course, Clarrie," he replied. "But damn it, why hasn't she written me?" He broke off a corner of the cinnamon bun on his plate and regarded it moodily before flicking it out the open window. "French cooks have no clue when it comes to cinnamon buns. Even Lissy would sniff at these. Why doesn't that stubborn woman write?"

Clarice patted her lips with her napkin and continued her perusal of him. "My dear brother, only think how fast this dear little creature has gone from widow to wife, and under what circumstances. She needs time."

"I know, I know," he said impatiently, leaning back in his chair. "But when I was there in March . . ." He paused. This isn't something to confess to a sister, he thought, then hurried on with the narration before he lost his nerve. "Well, she was awfully glad to see me." He smiled at the memory. "Awfully glad, Clarrie." He ran his fingers around the inside of his collar.

His sister reacted as he thought she would by increasing the candlepower of her stare. "Winn, you told me you were there not more than thirty minutes!" she declared.

"It's true," he confessed, feeling the blush travel upward from his navel to his hair follicles.

"And that part of the time you were visiting with Helen and Lissy?" she continued inexorably. "Winn! Really!"

Trust a big sister to make a grown man feel like a boy, and not a bright boy, either, he thought sourly. "Yes, really!" he retorted, out of sorts with Clarice and wondering why he had invited her to Winnfield. "We didn't waste a minute. Clarrie, must you smirk?"

Clarice laughed, and he directed his attention to the silver pattern again, disgusted with himself.

"I had no idea you were such a ladies' man," she murmured, a smile in her eyes.

"No, no!" he protested. "Not *any* lady's man, Clarrie. Just that lady's man. I don't know what it is about Roxie Rand." Well, yes I do know, he thought, but I'll be damned if I need to catalog a sexual primer for my older sister. I've never been so excited by a woman as I am by my own wife. "And you don't need to grin about it, Clarrie," he admonished.

She promptly wiped the smile off her face, but couldn't disguise it so easily in her eyes. "Brother, I am just remembering some comments from you earlier this year. Something about 'never wanting to be trapped in a matrimonial snare again.' Correct me if I am wrong," she concluded.

He could only sigh in exasperation. "Clarrie, cut line, won't you?" he declared. He took a turn about the breakfast room, pausing at the sideboard for a piece of bacon, and waving it at her. "I asked her to let me know how she felt about our relationship. I have heard nothing from that time to this!" He ate the bacon, wishing Clarice would not give him that feather-brained look. "Oh, what?" he snapped in irritation.

To his surprise, she went to him and kissed his cheek. "Winn, you're really dead in love, aren't you?"

He nodded, miserable. "I thought I loved Cynthia, but what I felt was only a pale cousin to this. And what's worse, I miss Lissy and Helen, too. This isn't fair!"

Suddenly the room seemed too small to hold him. He wanted to stride out of doors and walk for several miles until he felt more in control of himself. Roxie, I will have to go on my own forced marches if you do not come to the rescue, he thought grimly.

"I seem to remember also that you were pretty adamant about not wanting any children of your own, too," Clarice reminded him. "Did you ever mention that to Roxie?"

He thought a moment, chagrined. "Too many times, I fear," he confessed. "I really should go to Moreland, throw myself at her feet, and tell her I have been an idiot."

Clarice nodded, to his increased irritation. "You were pretty stupid, Winn," she agreed, her eyes merry. "Now don't poker up! Let me have the fun of scolding you, and then tell you that I will do whatever I can to further this relationship. Only ask, Winn."

He nodded then, grateful she was his sister. "Thanks, my dear," he said, flinging himself into his chair again. "I suppose I can go see her this fall, whether I hear from her or not."

"Why wait that long?"

He nodded. "Why, indeed? I'm too old to play games, Clarrie. I just wish this were her idea, too, and not mine alone."

Clarice was about to reply when the door opened. "My lord, the mail is here. Shall you read it now, or do you wish it in the bookroom?"

He waved his hand at the butler. "The bookroom, Spurgeon. No. Wait. Bring it here."

The butler set down the correspondence and left the room. Winn glanced at the pile, then looked away. "Bugger it," he muttered.

But Clarice was going through his letters. "Really, Winn, your language," she murmured as she sorted the mail. She let out a triumphant laugh and dangled a letter in front of his face. "Winn, does this handwriting look familiar?"

He pounced on the letter, ripping it open, filled with joy he had not felt since March. "She wrote, Clarrie, she wrote!" he declared in triumph as his eyes scanned the page.

As he read, his eyes eager, his heart pounding, the horror dawned on him slowly. He read the letter again, certain that he had missed a joke somewhere, a phrase that would turn the nightmare on the closely written page into a huge jest. After his third perusal, he stared at Clarice, who was regarding him with an expression that went from delight to fear as she watched his own face.

"Winn, what is it?" she demanded, when he could say nothing.

Wordless, he pushed the letter toward her, and leaped to his feet. He jerked the door open and leaned into the hall. "Spurgeon!" he shouted. "I need you immediately!"

He glanced back at Clarrie, who was on her feet now, her mouth open. "Clarrie, I had no idea," he said, feeling the tears start in his eyes. "Tibbie has been ill for months, Meggie Watson is dead, and Lissy . . . Oh, Clarrie!"

"Maybe it is not that serious," Clarice said, hurrying around the table to clutch his arm.

He took the letter from her. "Roxie would never tease about this. Those children are her life. And here I am at Winnfield. Damn you, Spurgeon! Where are you?"

It took him only a few minutes to pound upstairs and change into riding pants and his old campaigning boots, talking to Clarice as fast as he thought of things. "Can you follow me soon? I'll leave it to you to contact my bailiff and find someone to come along who can take over, at least temporarily. Can you bring along some servants, too? Damn it, where are my saddlebags?"

He stopped in the middle of the room, ready to scream. In a second Clarice was holding him close. His arms went around her and he sobbed into her hair. He could hear her murmuring something, but all he could see was Roxie's face, and then the letter, scarcely legible, written by someone exhausted and incoherent with worry. He cried at his own stupidity, havering around Winnfield like a mooncalf, full of self-pity and ill humor, when his wife needed him so badly.

I have left out so much, he thought as he snatched up the reins and threw himself into the saddle. He looked back at Clarice, a better sister than he ever realized before, who had run after him to the stables.

"Don't worry about anything," she was telling him as Ney danced about, impatient as he was to be off. "I'll write a little note to Fred, and organize things here. Chickering can pack your clothes, and I have a good idea what Roxie will be needing."

Roxie needs me, he thought as he blew a kiss to his sister and galloped from the stable yard, taking the fence cleanly. She needs me.

It became the refrain that kept him in the saddle mile after mile. He stopped at noon for a meal, then was too impatient to eat it, thinking of Lissy near death and Roxie watching at her bedside. He tossed a coin at the tavern keep as he snatched up some bread and beef and forked his leg over Ney again.

Snatches of her letter came back at him as he rode into the afternoon of a beautiful summer day. "If you can spare the time," and "Truly I do not wish to trouble you," harrowed him as Ney pounded along the Great North Road. All she can see is what a great lot of trouble she has been, he thought. She cannot fathom how much I love her and her daughters. I would do anything for you, my love, he thought. Pray God I do not have to bury your daughter for you. I do not know that even together we could bear that. I know I could never face it alone.

He reached the North Riding as the sun was low in the sky. His mind was on Roxie, but as Ney trotted along, Lord Winn wondered where the field laborers were. There should have been many of them on the roads at this hour, returning to their homes, but there were so few. This influenza has taken its toll, he reflected. He had seen the flu in Spain, and soldiers too exhausted to level a musket or drag themselves into the saddle. A man could be pronounced well by the impatient surgeons, but still die if he could not rest sufficiently.

He was weary of the saddle himself as Ney climbed steadily into the foothills of the Pennines. Just another mile, he thought. And then there was Moreland, the elms offering slanting shade to the estate's approach as the sun finally set. It was a different sight from the bare branches of March, more welcoming. He spurred Ney for a final effort. Where *was* everyone?

The groom was nowhere in sight as he ducked his head and rode Ney into the stable. Damn the man, he thought as he dismounted and hurried to remove his horse's saddle. Five Pence and the mare he had left for Roxie looked at him with interest. He glanced in their mangers, and cursed to see them empty of grain. The water troughs were dry, too. I will fire that man on the spot, he swore as he grained and watered all three horses. He will never work in this shire again.

The groom rode into the stable as he was preparing to leave for the house. Hot words were on Lord Winn's lips, but he watched from the gathering shadows as the man dragged himself from the saddle and leaned against his horse, scarcely able to stand. He stayed that way a long time, and then Lord Winn cleared his throat.

The groom glanced around as though his neck pained him, then sighed with relief. "Thank God you've come, my lord," he said, not letting go of his horse's mane.

Winn came out of the shadows, observing at close range the perspiration on the man's face, and the paleness of his skin. He took him by the arm. "Are you ill, too?" he asked, his angry words forgotten.

The groom nodded, shivered, and allowed Lord Winn to lead him to a perch on the grain bin. "We've all had it, my lord. Tibbie can just barely manage in the mornings, and I oversee in the afternoons." He protested when Lord Winn took the saddle from his horse, then could only stare dumbly, as though trying to gather strength for a trip up the stairs to his quarters.

"How long have you been doing this?" Winn asked as he stabled the groom's horse.

"Not long. Two weeks? Before that, Lady Winn was in the saddle all day, even after Felicity took sick. I don't know when she slept." He paused, too tired to say more.

Winn helped the groom to his quarters, promising to send

someone with food later. The man only shook his head and closed his eyes.

His mind deep with disquiet, Lord Winn ran into the house. It was dark, as though no one lived there. "Roxie?" he called, his voice tentative.

There was no answer. He hurried to the stairs, and could make out a little light on the first landing. He took the stairs two at a time, dreading what awaited him. A single candle flickered in a sconce at the top of the stairs, casting weird shadows on the slowly moving lace curtains. He hurried down the hall, calling Roxie's name.

And then Helen was standing in the hallway by the only room with a light in it.

"Helen," was all he said. With a sob she ran down the hall, her arms out, to fall into his welcoming embrace. He knelt and hugged her close, breathing in the dearness of her, grateful down to the depths of his soul that she was on her feet and appeared healthy.

Finally she pulled away from him a little and ran her hand over his face, as though she could not believe he was real. "You came," she said simply, and his heart turned over.

She took his hand then and led him to the room with the open door. "Mama," she said from the doorway. "Mama."

Roxanna was sitting in a chair by the bed, her head bowed forward as if in sleep. She jerked awake at Helen's quiet words and looked around wildly as he came forward and gripped her by the shoulders. She closed her eyes again, as though in prayer, then rested her cheek against his hand. "Thank you for coming," she whispered. "I am so tired."

He knelt beside her and took her hand. "Roxie, I left the moment I received your letter."

She opened her eyes, but her vision rested on the quiet form in the bed. "I didn't mean to trouble you . . ." she began, then shook her head and was silent.

"Who ever said you were trouble?" he whispered as he looked at Felicity, lying so unnaturally still.

She squeezed his hand and started to reply, but Lissy moved then, and she dropped his hand and reached for her daughter, touching her forehead. As he watched, she dipped a cloth in water, wrung it out, and carefully ran it over Lissy's bare little body, so still again under the sheet.

"She is so thin," he whispered. He touched her arm, wincing to see her ribs so prominent. "And so warm."

Roxanna finished her work, standing a moment over her daughter, breathing along with her, then sank into the chair again. "She does not eat much," she explained, her voice toneless. "Dr. Clyde says that the fever will go away eventually, but I do not know that Lissy can last long enough to find out."

She was silent again. He glanced at her to see silent tears coursing down her cheeks. Such hopeless tears, he thought. He touched her face, wondering if she had cried this way for Anthony. Of course you did, my darling, he thought as he took out his handkerchief. Is this never going to end for you?

The dimness of the room bothered him. "Can I light some candles?" he asked.

Roxanna shook her head. "The light bothers Lissy's eyes. Oh, Fletch, how kind of you to come," she said, as though just realizing that he was in the room.

"When did you last sleep, Roxie?" he asked as he pocketed his handkerchief.

"I can't remember exactly."

"When did you last eat?"

She shrugged and looked away, as though it was of little importance to her. "I think it was yesterday. Yes, I'm sure it was . . ." Her voice trailed off as she stared at her daughter. "I should eat, though. You see, Winn . . ." she began, and then stopped.

"What?" he asked.

"Nothing that can't keep." She directed her attention to her daughter again.

He rested his hand against Roxie's cheek a moment, then left the room, taking Helen with him. "Come, my dear, let's light some lamps downstairs. Can you cook?"

She smiled at him. "I've been learning. Sally is in the kitchen now, fixing some soup for us."

Below stairs, he shook hands with the scullery maid he only dimly remembered from Christmas, overriding her shyness by sticking his finger in the pot of soup, rolling his eyes, and pronouncing it excellent. It is tasty, he thought as he took up a spoon for a further dip from the pot. In a few years upon retirement, Mrs. Howell may have a worthy successor. He turned to Helen.

"Now, my dear, if you will set the table in the breakfast room, and Sally, if you will brew a pot of coffee as fine as that soup, I'll try to coax Lady Winn downstairs for a bite. Helen, can you watch Lissy while your mother eats?"

Helen nodded and glanced at Sally, who smiled back. "We've

both been doing that, sir. Sometimes Mama kicks up a fuss when we make her leave, but we insist at least once a day."

Lord Winn put his hands on the girls' shoulders. "I could have used you two at Waterloo," he said, his heart lifting as the light seemed to come back into their faces. "Come on, now, step to it. I'll get your mother downstairs."

While Helen set the table, humming softly to herself, he lit lamps in the breakfast room, entrance hall, and sitting room. He paused in the sitting room to blow dust off the piano lid and raise it. He played a tentative chord, pleased that the piano was still in tune. He looked at the music on the stand, seeing the little melody he had written earlier that spring for Helen. He played it, standing by the piano.

"I know that one by heart, Winn," Helen said from the doorway. "And I have been working on the Scarlatti, like you said."

He turned around to smile at her, pleased to note that she had brushed her hair and pulled it back into a bow. "Come, my dear. Let's go upstairs again and talk your mother into dinner. Do you think I will have any luck getting her to go to bed afterwards?"

"Not at all," Helen said. "She just sits in that chair and dozes."

"Not tonight she won't," he said firmly as he took her hand and walked down the hall. "I mean to do that in her place."

"She's stubborn," Helen said, her voice uncertain.

"So am I, dear. So am I."

He was prepared for real resistance, but Roxie offered little. He put it down to her general exhaustion. She nodded at his suggestion for dinner, and he had the good sense to agree with her rider that she return promptly to Lissy's room. "Of course, Roxie, anything you say. Isn't that what I promised the blacksmith?" he replied as he winked at Helen, who grinned back and seated herself in Roxie's chair.

Roxie, you've been losing weight, too, he thought as he took her by the hand and led her downstairs. The lights made her blink at first, but she gradually relaxed and allowed him to seat her at the table.

He looked at the table in pleasure. Helen had put out good china and crystal, and the place mats and napkins gleamed so white against the dark wood. It was a room of pleasant memories, too, of Felicity peeking around at him, waiting for cinnamon buns. And now . . . The pain of seeing Lissy lying so still upstairs washed over him again and he hung onto the back of the chair where he had seated Roxanna. The moment passed and he seated himself, nodding to Sally to serve the soup.

"You should have written me sooner," he said mildly as he sat and watched his wife eat, wondering at her ravaged beauty and its power over him. You are much too thin, but I am captured all over again, he thought. Beyond the misery of the moment, there was something different about her that he could not quite put his finger on. When she made no reply, he gave his attention to the soup, and then bullied Roxie into a second bowl, and a glass of sherry, too.

He poured himself another cup of coffee, preparing for an assault on Roxie's plans to return to Lissy's room. "Now then, my dear . . ." he began, and then stopped, looking at her. He grinned, raised the cup in a toast, and finished his coffee. So much for my strategy.

Roxie was asleep, her head nodding over the table, her hand still wrapped around the stem of the sherry glass. "You poor dear," he whispered as he got up quietly and eased the glass from her hand. He picked her up and carried her upstairs, marveling again how light she was. She smelled faintly of lavender, and his heart was full.

He thought she might wake when he laid her on her bed, but she only sighed and rested her hand on her stomach, relaxing completely as though she knew she could surrender to sleep, now that he was there. He lighted a branch of candles and the lamp beside the bed, looking around in appreciation at the new wallpaper and draperies. I could easily prefer this place to that slab of stone I live in, he told himself. I certainly prefer the company.

He removed her shoes, and considered leaving it at that, then changed his mind. Better to take the pins from her hair and divest her of her dress, he reasoned. He sat on the edge of the bed, taking the pins from her hair, spreading it out to flow over the pillow. Roxie slumbered on, captured by sleep. I could whistle "Lilliburlero" and accompany myself on the drums and you would not wake up, he thought, smiling to himself.

She parted company from her dress without a whimper. He pulled her arms from the sleeves, remembering how boneless she was that first morning in his bed, satiated with love. And now you are exhausted by Lissy's illness, he thought, fingering her wedding ring.

She looked more comfortable without her dress, but he continued, untying the cord that held up her petticoat. It was while he was sliding Roxie out of her petticoat that he noticed his wife had a little company.

"What's this, Roxie?" he asked out loud as he ran his hand

lightly over the slight bulge below her middle. "Oh, Roxie, no wonder you didn't want to write," he said as he rested his hand on her belly.

He sat back a moment, moved beyond words, then touched her again, delighting in the experience. *So we made a baby in March,* he thought, *and I can cup my hands around three and a half months of our child.* As he sat there, he felt the tiniest flutter under his fingers, like someone tapping lightly. "Oh, God," he breathed, and it was a prayer of gratitude.

The strength of the woman lying on the bed humbled him. *How could you do it?* he thought. *How could you take on Tibbie's work, and watch Lissy, and suffer Meggie's death? And all this time you were probably in the throes of morning sickness, if I can remember anything my sisters complained about. I think our child is determined to be born.*

Sitting there with his hand resting on his baby, he considered the matter. "In all this long agony, why didn't you say anything, my love?" he asked her sleeping body. He had his answer almost before the words were out of his mouth, and he could only wonder at his stupidity. *How many times have I insisted to you that I did not want children?* he berated himself. *You must be terrified that I will find out and be furious.*

"It can keep then," he said as he gently replaced her petticoat. "We can wait until Lissy is out of the woods. I can't wait to hear how you're going to bring up this subject, my dear wife!"

He laughed softly as he covered her with a sheet, kissed her cheek, and strolled out of the room on air. He was still smiling when he relieved Helen in the sickroom. "Go to bed, my dear," he whispered. "I'll watch tonight."

She stood up and allowed him to sit in her place, then sat down in his lap, leaning against him. "I missed you," she said softly. "We all did."

"Even your mother?" he asked, his eyes lively. He kissed the top of her head and settled Helen comfortably on his lap. He prepared for a long night of thinking and watching, his mind on the child lying so still in the bed, but his heart on the woman in the other room and her careful secret.

Chapter 19

Fortified with a pot of Sally's coffee and a Fielding novel, he kept awake all night. Around midnight, Helen staggered off to bed with a wave of her hand, and he returned his attention to the child before him.

Lissy slept in odd little spurts, muttering to herself, turning from side to side to find a cool place, and then sitting upright once to stare at him, speak nonsense, then lie back down. He made her drink the heavily sugared water on the nightstand, and sponged her down several times. Her skin was tight and dry, and warm enough to worry him. Just watching her was a draining process, he decided. No wonder Roxie looked like the walking dead.

His wholehearted admiration for his wife grew as the night dragged on. How on earth had Roxanna managed to tend Lissy and the estate, too? Whoever thinks women are weaker vessels never knew Roxie Rand, he thought. He counted the months on his fingers, and concluded that their son or daughter would be born around Christmas. Such a lovely gift.

As much as he loved Moreland now, he wanted his first child to be born in the family seat at Winnfield. We can spend our summers here, he told himself as he sat Lissy up to take her fever powders.

"Good girl," he said out loud, when she swallowed the bitter liquid without complaint. To his gratification, she opened her eyes at the sound of his voice and turned her head to stare at him. Her lovely eyes looked so wide now in her thin face that she seemed almost a caricature.

"Winn."

That was all she could manage, and it was such an effort that tears started in his eyes. As he laid her back down on the bed she tried to reach for his hand. He took her lightly by the fingers. "Hang on a little longer, my dear," he pleaded.

She slept then, and he dozed, too, waking before dawn to hear a carriage on the front drive. He stood up and stretched, his neck on fire from his awkward position in the chair. He pulled back the draperies to see, and could just make out the Manwaring carriage.

After a glance at Lissy, he tiptoed from the room and hurried down the stairs. He grabbed his sister and gave her a kiss as she came up the front steps.

"Honestly, Winn," she protested, a smile on her face. "We only parted company yesterday!"

"That's how glad I am to see you," he replied. He looked beyond her to the others leaving the carriage. "And you brought an army. Thank God for that. Clarrie, when was the last time I told you I loved you?"

Clarice grimaced. "It escapes my memory, brother." She introduced him to a tall young man who came next from the carriage. "Here is David Start, your new bailiff," she said as they shook hands. "Annie here will go to the kitchen or wherever she's needed, and Mrs. Mitchum is your housekeeper until the redoubtable Mrs. Howell returns." She handed a heavy basket to the bailiff. "Here we have lemons and jellies and potions galore. Lissy will not dare to remain sick."

He put his arm around her and led her into the house. "Such a lovely old place," Clarice murmured. "Is Roxie asleep?"

"Yes, and thank goodness for that," he said, helping her with her cloak. "Oh, Clarrie, she was burned right down to the socket."

"I can imagine."

He shook his head, amusement welling up in spite of the situation. "No, you really can't, my dear."

He only grinned at her quizzical expression, and then waited while she dispersed her help to various locations. She took the basket from the bailiff, and told him to wait there while she settled herself upstairs with Felicity. "And then the sun will be up, and Lord Winn will show you to Tibbie's house."

"Clarrie, you are a real general," Winn commented as they climbed the stairs. His sister only snorted and dug him in the ribs.

All joking ended as she stood silently over Lissy, shaking her head. "Flu is such a vile illness," she whispered, "never letting go until it is too late." She touched Lissy's arm and leaned over her. "Well, my dear, we shall see what can be done yet. Since you're a child of Roxie's, there's fight in you yet."

She removed her bonnet and allowed him to lead her to the next door. He opened it quietly. "Roxie's still asleep," he whispered, looking in on his wife, who lay in the same position he had left her in. "I wish she would stay in bed herself, but I am sure she will be up soon."

Clarice nodded. "Roxie would never stay in bed, but between the two of us, when she sees that we can manage, she might allow herself to rest."

He closed the door and leaned against it. "She really needs to rest, Clarrie. Roxie is expecting a baby." He grinned. "That March visit may have been brief, but it was potent, apparently."

She gasped and hugged him. "Winn! This is wonderful!"

He nodded, pleased to share the news with his sister. He put a finger to her lips. "I only discovered it last night when I removed her dress. Don't say a word. She has no idea that I know, and really, she doesn't show much."

Clarice took his arm as they walked back to Lissy's room. "I suspect she is afraid to tell you. I can't blame her."

"Nor can I, my dear," he agreed. "I shall have to dance very fast to repair my wounded credit. And Clarrie, I *am* delighted. In fact, I can't imagine why I had such a crack-brained notion about not wanting a child of my own."

Clarice touched his face and stood on tiptoe to kiss his cheek. "Brother, it was probably a combination of too much war at home *and* abroad." She went into Lissy's room. "Now go downstairs and show David Start what he is to do. Then go to bed yourself. I think yours will be the night shift."

"Oui, mon capitan," he said.

"Winn, you're a nuisance," she said affectionately as she bent over Lissy.

"Before I sleep, I think I will compose a little note to Lord Whitcomb," he said, his hand on the doorknob.

"Whatever for?"

"Call it pride. If we are to remain here, off and on, in the North Riding, it's time to mend that particular fence."

Clarice looked dubious. "Since when did you become a diplomat?"

He grinned and closed the door softly behind him.

When Roxanna opened her eyes, her room was bright with sunshine and there was a vase of roses on her nightstand. I must be dreaming, she thought. She sniffed the roses, grateful that her morning sickness had receded enough to permit pleasure again at sharp fragrances. She settled more comfortably on her side, her hand going almost automatically to her belly. The baby was moving now; she was sure of it.

She sat up then and threw back the covers. "Lissy!" she exclaimed.

"Lissy is being quite carefully watched, my dear," said an unfamiliar voice from the window seat.

Roxanna looked around quickly, and then smiled. "Oh, Lady Manwaring," she said, relieved to recognize her visitor.

"Clarice to you, Roxanna," said the woman as she set down her knitting. "Your husband is quite the bully. There I was, minding my own business on a visit to Winnfield, when your letter arrived. He drafted my services, plus those of a bailiff, housekeeper, and servant from his estate. Annie is watching Lissy."

"Thank God," Roxanna said as she lay down again. She wiggled out of her petticoat, which had twisted up around her waist. "Thank you for getting that dress off me last night."

"Oh, well, yes," Lady Manwaring replied, just a hint of laughter in her voice. "Now, my dear Roxanna, why don't you just go back to sleep? Annie is watching, and I will take over from her in an hour."

"You're sure? Where is Helen?"

"I'm sure. My brother—remember, he is a bully—convinced Helen to ride out with David Start, the new bailiff. She knows all the fields and can give him some real assistance." Clarice came closer. "Roxanna, you are raising a very capable daughter. Tell me your secret."

"She had no choice, the same as I," Roxanna said simply. She lay down again, and offered no objection when Clarice straightened her pillow. "Yes, Helen does know the estate. Heaven knows we've ridden around it enough lately. Fletch is right about Helen, of course."

Clarice laughed. "Well, don't ever tell him! That sort of confidence makes husbands intolerable." She touched Roxanna's cheek. "My dear, go back to sleep. There's nothing going on here right now that we cannot deal with."

Roxanna closed her eyes. I'll never sleep, she thought. When she woke, the afternoon sun was slanting in the window, and Clarice had been replaced by Lord Winn.

He sat in the chair by the bed, hand on his cheek, reading the book in his lap. She lay still, not wanting to attract his attention yet, and soaked in the familiar sight of his spectacles scooting out to the end of his rather long nose. He is a handsome man, she thought. I wonder if our baby will have green eyes, too?

"Fletch," she said, to get his attention.

He smiled at her, closed the book, and took off his spectacles. "Well, my love, you look less like a potter's field candidate now than you did yesterday. Feel better?"

"Oh, I do," she said. "My love," is it? she asked herself. He tugged the blanket a little higher on her shoulders and went to the fireplace to give the coals another stir. "How is Lissy?" she asked when he returned to her side, sitting on the bed this time. She wanted to touch him, to rest her hand on his leg to assure herself that he was there, but she did not. "I pray she is no worse."

"About the same. We're just continuing what you were doing so well, my dear. Dr. Clyde looked in on her, and pronounced us capable. I thought about asking him to look at you—"

"Oh, no!" she said hastily, eyes wide. "I am fine. Only tired."

He raised his eyebrows. "Don't like doctors, do we?" he asked.

"I am not the patient here," she said firmly.

"Of course you are not," he agreed, his voice serene. "You're not sick. You're just . . . tired."

"And now I must get up," she said.

"I'd rather you just rested," he said, putting his arm across her so she could not move.

She looked up at him. "Clarice is right. You are a bully," she whispered, and let him give her a hug. She clung to him, trying to press his strength into her own body, so thankful to have him here.

"I'm not going anywhere, my dear Roxie Rand," he assured her finally. "Plenty of time for this later."

Not after you find out, she thought as she released him. I have to tell you.

"Winn, I need to—"

But he was getting up now, and retrieving his book and spectacles from the chair.

"What you need is a hot bath. I promised Clarrie I would tell her when you woke up. The tub's already in front of the fireplace. I think she enlisted Inca runners to bring in hot water, so I will leave you now."

He was gone with a wave of his hand and a wink. When she made her appearance an hour later in Lissy's room, he was feeding Lissy. She stared at him and tiptoed closer, resting her hand on his shoulder in her surprise. How does he do that? she thought, watching the wonderful sight before her. Everything she had offered, Lissy had rejected, turning away. And here he was, spooning down oatmeal without a complaint.

"You're a wonder, Fletch," she marveled when Lissy finally closed her eyes and he lowered her back to the bed. "She wouldn't eat so much for me."

He set down the bowl. "My dear, as a former colonel commanding, I am not used to disobedience in the ranks. I think she knew I meant it when I ordered her to open up." He took her hand and leaned back, sniffing the air. "Ah. I love that lavender. If she will eat a little more each day and gather her strength, she might outlast the fever."

Roxanna nodded, her heart too full for words. Tell him, Roxanna, she thought, tell him now while he is mellow.

"Fletcher, you really should know something."

"What, my dear? That I am handsome and charming, and more than you ever dared dream of in a second husband?"

She laughed, then put her hand over her mouth when Lissy moved. "No! That you are aggravating and tyrannical and . . . and quite essential to my peace of mind right now," she finished in a rush, disappointed with herself that her courage failed, yet wanting to tell him how she felt at the moment.

He was about to reply when Mrs. Mitchum opened the door. "Lord Winn, there is someone below to see both of you," she whispered, her eyes on Felicity.

Winn raised his eyebrows. "Who, pray?"

"Lord Whitcomb," she replied. "I put him in the sitting room. Shall I tell him you will be down?"

Roxanna put her hands to her mouth and shook her head. Mrs. Mitchum looked at her, a question in her eyes, but Lord Winn only smiled at the housekeeper, as though this was the best news of the week. Roxanna stared at him in horror.

"Yes, Mrs. M. Tell him we'll be down directly," he said.

When Mrs. Mitchum closed the door, Roxanna leaped up and retreated to the far corner of the room. "I will not go down there," she said, her voice low with emotion.

"I think you should," Winn said, coming to her side and putting his arm around her. "You see, I wrote him this morning and told him what was going on here."

She wriggled from his grip, her eyes wide. "You did what?" she gasped. "Suppose he does something. Suppose . . ."

He took hold of her more firmly this time. "There is nothing by law that he can do, because you are my wife. Let me remind you that Felicity and Helen are his nieces. I think he has a right to know how they are. Don't you?"

She thought a moment, then nodded reluctantly. "Still, he frightens me," she said.

Winn put his arms around her. "I know, Roxie, I know. You're about to be reminded of one of the sterling benefits of marriage."

He tipped her chin up with his finger and looked right into her eyes. "You don't have to face things alone anymore."

There was nothing she could do except nod. He smiled and kissed her forehead. "Let's go face the lions, Roxie. I think you might also discover that they are not as frightening as you remember. At least, this is my suspicion."

She took his hand as they went down the stairs, clutching it tighter and tighter as they approached the sitting room, loosening her grip only when Fletch winced and declared, "If you cut off my circulation, I'll be minus fingers, too, my dear. How many parts can a man lose?"

She paused at the door for a deep breath. Helen was inside, playing Mozart, and it steadied her as much as Winn's hand on her shoulder.

"Excellent!" Winn said. "You always were one to ride toward the sound of guns, Roxie." He opened the doors. "Ah, Lord Whitcomb. Grand of you to come."

The door was open; there was nothing she could do but follow her husband inside, holding her breath until she felt light-headed, then letting it out slowly when Marshall Drew held out his hand to her. She hesitated, then felt the pressure of Lord Winn's fingers on her shoulder. *You are a bully,* she thought as she extended her hand finally and shook Lord Whitcomb's hand.

"Good evening, Marshall," she said, wishing that she could sound brave. I must say something. What's a conversational opener for a villain? "I'm glad you could hear how Helen has been progressing. That's lovely, my darling," she said to her daughter at the piano.

Helen beamed at her. "Shall I continue, Mama?"

Roxie felt herself relaxing. "Yes, of course." She indicated the sofa across the room. "Perhaps we could sit here?"

She sat as close to Winn as she could without climbing into his lap, recalling with painful clarity her last tête-à-tête with Lord Whitcomb in the vicarage. The memory left her unable to say anything. To her relief, her husband picked up the conversational baton and wielded it like a marshal. His voice was relaxed and genial, and she couldn't believe her ears.

"Lord Whitcomb, we wanted you to know how Lissy was. She seems to be gaining in strength, but it's still early days, I am afraid."

Whitcomb nodded. "We've had our share of influenza, too." He looked at her. "I heard that Tibbie was ill, but he must have recovered remarkably, Roxanna. Your fields are quite the envy."

Roxanna smiled in spite of herself and sat a little taller. "I was bailiff until a week or so ago," she said.

"You are to be commended then," Marshall Drew replied. He paused, then looked at Helen, who was concentrating on the sonatina. "She is well?"

"Yes, thank God," Roxanna said gratefully, warming to his concern. "The flu seems to pick and choose."

Marshall nodded. He rose. "I do not intend to stay long, of course, but I would like to see Lissy."

"Of course," Winn said, when she hesitated. "I do have a favor to ask of you first."

Lord Whitcomb smiled, and she further relaxed her grip on her husband. She remembered that smile, too, and was glad to see it again. "Whatever I can do, please know that I will."

"I haven't asked Roxanna yet, but I am certain she will agree. Will you take Helen back to Whitcomb for the rest of the week?"

Roxanna bit her lips to keep from screaming out loud and dug her fingernails into her husband's hand. He merely raised her hand to his lips and kissed her fingers.

But Winn was still speaking, as though he conversed with his best friend, and not the man who had tried to shame her and steal her daughters. "I'm sure you can see that Helen could use a change of scenery, and it would give Roxie some relief, too. Will you consider it?"

She held her breath, praying that Whitcomb would say no. To her amazement, tears came to his eyes. He looked away from them toward Helen, who was starting Scarlatti now, her head moving in time to the rhythm. He did not speak until he was firmly in control again.

"Yes, of course, Lord Winn," he replied. "I would be delighted, and I am sure I speak for Agnes, too." He turned to Roxie then. "If it is agreeable to you, Roxanna."

Suddenly she understood, and felt tears of her own. *And I thought I loved Fletcher Rand before,* she told herself as she looked at her brother-in-law. *I wonder if I would have the magnanimity to attempt what he is doing? Anthony would; surely I can do no less. One mustn't be outdone by one's husbands.*

"Yes, by all means, Marshall," she replied. "It would be a relief to me to know that Helen was in good hands while we are so occupied with Lissy right now."

Marshall sighed. "Very good. May I go invite Helen myself?"

She nodded. "Do tell her that we will let her know how Lissy goes on."

He went to the piano and sat next to her daughter, their heads together. She watched them and swallowed, reminded of other days.

"Does he resemble Anthony?" Winn asked quietly.

She nodded. "Sometimes it gives me a start." She looked at her husband. "When was the last time anyone told you that you are remarkable?"

It was his turn to blink and look away. "I never was remarkable before I met you, Roxanna," he said finally as Lord Whitcomb returned to the sofa.

He was smiling. "She agrees. I will send 'round my groom in the morning for her. Thank you."

"You're welcome," Roxanna said, when her husband seemed unable to respond. She took another deep breath and held out her hand to Lord Whitcomb. "Come, let me take you to Lissy. Fletch? I think Helen is stuck on that andantino. Can you untangle her, my dear?"

She climbed the stairs slowly with her brother-in-law, thinking her own thoughts, grateful for the gathering dusk, but more at peace than in months. They entered Lissy's room, where Mrs. Mitchum watched.

Roxanna remained in the doorway while he sat on the edge of Lissy's bed, touching her cheek, then kissing her forehead. He spoke softly to her, and she couldn't tell if Lissy was capable of response, but her heart went out to him. I can forgive, she thought. It costs nothing except a little pride, and the rewards are infinite.

Lord Whitcomb joined her in the doorway again and they went silently down the stairs. He paused at the bottom and took her hand. "Roxanna, please let me know how she goes on. If there is anything I can do . . ."

She smiled. "Remember her in your prayers, of course. Beyond that, we can only wait. Thank you for coming."

She opened the door for him. He looked back at her, some of the bleakness gone from his eyes. "Roxanna, I hope you can forgive me someday," he murmured.

"I will work on it," she promised. "Good night, Marshall."

She returned to the sitting room, standing in the doorway to watch her husband and Helen practice the andantino. I would like to hold moments like these in my hands forever, she thought as she stood there. I love him so much, and must face the blinding truth that if we can somehow go on this way, I will only love him more.

He turned around then at the piano bench and motioned her forward. She shook her head. "You two continue," she said. "Since everything seems to be in control, I will sit with Lissy for a while and then go to bed."

He nodded and blew her a kiss. "I can recommend the Fielding, if you like a ribald tale. Only don't lose my place. I'll be up to take over in an hour."

She smiled and turned away, but he called her back. "I meant to tell you, my love. David Start thinks you are a fine bailiff." He turned back to the piano and played a lavish chord while Helen giggled. "Yet another male shot from the saddle by Roxanna Rand. Good night, my dear."

By rights, the week that followed should have been a dreadful one, but it was not. She could only marvel what a little more sleep and the support of people who cared did for her outlook. The first night she woke up after midnight, her heart pounding, terrified that Lissy was alone. Snatching up a shawl, she ran to her daughter's room, only to discover Lissy sleeping and Lord Winn involved in Henry Fielding. He merely looked at her standing in the open doorway, put his finger in the place, and whispered, "Do I have to take you back to bed?"

That only gets me in trouble, she thought as she quietly closed the door behind her and returned to her room.

And while Lord Winn slept during the day, Clarice divided the time with her, making her eat, with a certain loving tyranny that made Roxanna suspect that all the Rands were cut from the same cloth. Annie cleaned, Mrs. Mitchum cooked and supervised, and Roxanna found herself with little to do except tend her daughter and rest.

Lord Winn joined her in Lissy's room in the afternoons, doing nothing more than sitting with his long legs propped up on the bed, reading aloud to Lissy from a book of nursery rhymes. "I am not sure she hears me," he explained, "but one never knows."

"I never took you for a reader of nursery rhymes," she said as she gathered herself comfortably in the chair and admired the way her husband's hair curled so neatly over his collar. He needed another haircut.

"There's probably a lot you don't suspect that I know, Mrs. Rand," he replied, a twinkle in his eyes. "Besides that, she's a little young for Fielding."

Clarice's husband, Lord Manwaring, arrived two days later in a post chaise, fortified with more lemons and oranges and another Fielding novel for his brother-in-law. He took his turn in the sickroom, too, moving with surprising agility for one so formidable.

"I wouldn't have it any other way, Roxanna," he insisted, when she assured him that they could manage without troubling him, too. "Clarice and I have been through enough of these sickroom dramas to easily outdistance you and Winn." He kissed her cheek. "Besides, m'dear, what are relatives for?"

What indeed? she asked herself as she tied on a bonnet for a stroll in the orchard at the end of the week. She thought then of her brothers in India, and those wretched card games they forced her to play, when they were all young together in Kent. I have been dealt such a hand this year, she thought as she admired the little apples. It was not a hand I would ever have chosen willingly, because of the force of circumstance, but I have done the best I could with it. I will have to face Lord Winn and tell him about the baby. If he chooses not to remain with us, I can manage that, too, because I have to. Fletch is always insisting that I never do things by halves, and he is right. There is no other way to live.

She looked across the Plain of York, hazy now in July's welcome warmth, a checkerboard of fields and pasture. I hope I am lucky enough to hang onto my husband and my daughters. When he says he does not want children, perhaps he does not mean it.

"Oh, I say, Roxanna," called Fred from the front steps. "Please hurry!"

She looked up, her nerves snapping suddenly at the unexpected tremor in his voice, shouting to her across the lawn. Please, God, she prayed silently, as he hurried toward her. She looked up at the open window in Lissy's room, and there was Fletcher, leaning out, his head bowed. "No," she said out loud. "It cannot be. We have all worked so hard."

She ran past her brother-in-law, and into the house, bursting into the room to stop in horror at the sight of Clarrie in tears, clutching her brother, who was sobbing, too. They stood in front of Lissy's bed, as though to hide death from view. "No," she insisted, as though there was no other word. "It cannot be."

Lord Manwaring pounded up the stairs behind her and stood, leaning against the door, trying to get his breath.

"Oh, I declare, you two," he said in disgust, shaking his head at his wife and brother-in-law. "Lissy, I hope you do not think all adults are cloth-witted. Maybe your mama has more sense."

Roxanna gasped and pushed aside her husband to gape at Lissy, who sat up in bed staring at all the commotion. She pursed her lips in that familiar way that made Roxanna sob out loud, and looked at her mother.

"All I did was ask for some food," she explained. Her voice

was rusty from little use, and her head wobbled from weakness, but she was completely coherent, and even a little impatient. As Roxanna put a shaking hand to her cool forehead, she smiled at her mother. "I really would like a cinnamon bun."

Clarice sobbed louder. Fletcher threw himself into a chair and stared at the ceiling, tears on his face. Roxanna found herself weeping, too, even as she clung to her daughter.

"Lissy, let me speak to Mrs. Mitchum about a cinnamon bun," said Lord Manwaring, picking up a bowl. "In the meantime, perhaps you would let me feed you this applesauce?"

Lissy nodded and opened her mouth obediently, like a little bird. Even Lord Manwaring had to pause a moment, and his voice was less assured. "It seems that we are the only sane people in the room. There is no accounting for relatives. How sorry I am that you had to learn this at such a tender age. Open wide for your Uncle Manwaring, Lissy."

"Well, my dear, let us take these glad tidings to Helen at Whitcomb," said Lord Winn as he helped her into the barouche. "I think I am sufficiently recovered not to make a cake of myself in front of Helen's uncle."

She smiled at him and scooted closer as he rested his arm across the back of the seat. "I know I cried enough for two," she said, then blushed. And heaven knows I have been eating enough for two lately. I simply *must* speak to this man.

She couldn't do it. They rode in silence, and soon Lord Winn was asleep. Dear tired man, she thought, and leaned back into his slack embrace, closing her eyes, too.

She woke as the carriage stopped at the steps of Whitcomb, then touched her husband's face to wake him. His eyes snapped open and he looked about wildly, then chuckled, embarrassed. "Roxie, let's go to bed when we're through here. I could sleep for a week."

She opened her mouth to speak and he kissed her suddenly.

"There," he said, satisfied with himself. "I have been wanting to do that—and other things—for considerably more than a week. Oh, yes, and to tell you that I love you, Roxie. Body and soul, heart and mind, through and through. Indefatigably, even, which will probably be a good thing, considering your unflagging interest in my various parts."

And so she was blushing fiery red as Lord Whitcomb came down the front steps, a question in his eyes. "Tell me it is good news," he demanded as Lord Winn helped her from the barouche.

She nodded and touched his arm. "It is, Marshall. The fever is gone. We wanted you and Helen to know right away."

Then Helen was there, throwing herself into her mother's arms, and hugging Lord Winn, who almost made a cake of himself again when he told her the welcome news.

"We will drive over tomorrow, if we may," Lord Whitcomb said. "May I keep Helen here until then? We're working on a little project for Lissy which we need to finish."

"Of course you may, Marshall," Roxanna said without any hesitation. "And you'll bring Agnes and stay to dinner?"

"With pleasure," he replied. He turned to Helen. "My dear, go inside and bring out our painting." He watched as she skipped inside, then took Roxanna's hand. "I really do owe the two of you an apology," he began, his voice low and hard to hear. He looked at Lord Winn. "My actions of this winter were reprehensible beyond belief. Even now I cannot imagine what was in my mind."

Roxanna covered his hand with her own and took a deep breath. "Marshall, I wish you would not harrow yourself up over this," she began.

"But Roxanna, I forced you to such a desperate act," he insisted as he released her hand.

She shook her head, wondering at the peace that came over her. "If you had not forced my hand, I would never have married Lord Winn. Now, that would have been horrible." She took her husband's hand. "I cannot imagine life without him now. Thank you, Marshall, for what you did. I am in *your* debt, for I love Fletcher Rand."

Lord Whitcomb stared at her, then smiled at Lord Winn, who swallowed and looked away. "Sir, you are a lucky man. Roxanna, we'll see you tomorrow for dinner."

He hurried back into the house, unable to continue. Roxanna found a handkerchief in her reticule and handed it to her husband, who blew his nose vigorously, wiped his eyes, and helped her back into the barouche. They rode in silence past the end of the lane and the vicarage now occupied by another, then Lord Winn called for the coachman to stop.

"We'll walk the rest of the way," he told Roxanna as he helped her down.

They started across the cow pasture. "Walking's good for you," he said, then stopped to take her by the shoulders. "Roxanna, if you love me so much, why didn't you write me in March?"

She stared at him. "But I did! I waited and waited for a reply." She sighed and put her arms around his neck. "Oh, dear! I knew I had waited too long, so I sent the letter to Northumberland, and not to Carlisle. Did you not receive it there?''

Lord Winn pulled her close to him, his arms tight around her. "Oh, no! Two days before we were to go to High Point, they were cleaning the chimneys there and someone managed to burn down that wretched pile. I never went to Northumberland."

She laughed and cried and tried to ignore the Ayrshire cows that were heading toward them, curious about this invasion of watering pots in the pasture. "So you never knew in March that I loved you amazingly?"

"Never knew," he repeated, his lips on her hair. "Suspected, but hell, that's not the same." He pulled her closer. "And, Roxie, excuse me for asking, but in such proximity as this, I cannot help but observe that someone has come between us."

She was silent for a long moment. "I was afraid to tell you, Fletch. Remember all those things you said about not wanting any children?"

He winced. "I did haver on, love."

"You did. When I did not hear from you, I assumed you had changed your mind about wanting to alter our relationship. I couldn't tell you about the baby then." She rested her head against his chest. "And you know how I like to put off bad news."

He pulled back from her and placed his hand lightly on her belly. "I said a lot of stupid things, didn't I? How kind you will be to overlook them. And I will overlook your procrastination," he added generously.

"You knew, didn't you?" she asked after a moment, her voice lively with good humor. "You have been so careful of me lately. How did you know?"

"Well, it became a little obvious when I separated you from your dress! I may be a cloth-head, dear wife, but when it moved under my hand—Roxie, what a feeling."

Roxanna kissed him. "You really don't mind?" she murmured.

"Mind? I think I can stand the strain of parenthood." He patted her belly. "I'm already so good at fathering. Why waste such an education? Do let me tell our daughters." He peered at her. "Do you mind if I call them that? They seem like my own."

She didn't mind. Somewhere in her heart, she knew Anthony wouldn't mind, either. "By all means, you tell them, my love."

They walked along slowly, and soon Moreland came in sight. Roxanna stopped, remembering her anxious walk last fall and her first view of the dower house. "In for a penny, Lord Winn," she said.

"In for ten pounds, Lady Winn and company."

Epilogue

Dear Clarrie and Fred,

Please know you two are the first with the news—Roxie was delivered of a son yesterday afternoon at 3:30 o'clock. He came out squalling and complaining and Roxie said he was just like me. You'll also be pleased to know, Clarrie, that I resisted the urge to tease her back just then. Poor dear, Roxie looked like she had been run over by a wagon. But I was brave. I either held her hand or rubbed her back through the whole ordeal, and only felt a little faint when I heard him cry for the first time.

We're going to name him Robert Newell Anthony Fletcher Winfrey, which seems quite a handle for something so small. He has Roxie's high-arched eyebrows and my green eyes, and he's long. Heaven knows where she stashed him all those nine months. Lissy and Helen are delighted. We've all taken a turn at changing nappies, but the menu will be Roxie's domain. Amabel wrote her last month about hiring a good wet nurse, but you know that Roxie does nothing by halves. Anyway, as Tibbie would say, "T'bonny lad is grazing on a good pasture."

And so are we all. By all means, please come for Christmas, as planned. Roxie will enlist us to do her work, and she can crack the whip from a chair by the fire while Rob dines.

How did I get so lucky, Clarrie? I'm giving Roxie an emerald necklace for Christmas. Don't tell her. As a joke, I've also framed a sketch I drew of Roxie giving Tibbie a ten-pound note in front of the dower house. Guess which she will prefer?

Love and Kisses from the Proud Papa,
Winn

P.S. Fred, should I wake up and act sympathetic during those 2 a.m. feedings, or just keep sleeping? Rush your reply, please.

W.

Miss Grimsley's
Oxford Career

*In memory of Jean Dugat,
my dear teacher*

Ay me! For aught that ever I could read,
Could ever hear by tale or history,
The course of true love never did run smooth.

—William Shakespeare
A Midsummer Night's Dream

Prologue

"It pains me to the quick to make this observation about my only son, but James, for a Gatewood, you are queer stirrups, indeed," said Lady Chesney.

This startling pronouncement was followed by a deep quaff of ratafia, and a look of deeper concern at the offspring who sat, legs crossed, eyes on a book.

James Gatewood looked up and smiled at his mother. It was a sweet smile, one full of lazy Gatewood charm that only served to irritate his parent and send her back to the ratafia for further fortification.

"Why you could not bring yourself to smile like that at Lady Susan Hinchcliffe, or Augusta Farnsworth, I will never understand! Son, you would tax the patience of a martyr!"

The smile deepened. After one more glance at his book, Lord Chesney laid aside the volume. "Dearest mother, that would be impossible. Martyrs are dead. That is why they are martyrs."

This observation served only to rouse Lady Chesney to greater heights. "And there you go again! You know very well that I meant saint!"

Her son laughed and picked up his book again, settling back into the chair.

Lady Chesney was not about to let a good topic wither for lack of nourishment. "How you can expect to find a wife in the Bodleian Library, I cannot fathom. James, wasn't once at Oxford enough? You're the only Gatewood in recent memory to . . . to immolate himself there, and look at the results!"

"Mother, do you perhaps mean, 'to immerse myself?' Or is this is a burning issue?" he teased. "And I do not expect to unearth a wife in the Bodleian. Indeed, it would be impossible, considering England's unenlightened state of national indifference to the education of females. I go there for scholarship."

Lady Chesney could only moan and reach for her handkerchief. "Other young men your age—your friends, I might add—are busy at their tailors, or bargaining for bloodstock at Tattersalls, or sitting in White's bow window like normal men!" She buried her face in her handkerchief and blew her nose. "I wish you would reconsider this off notion of yours. It is not too late!"

Lord Chesney only stood up, stretched, and reached over to ruffle her hair. He kissed her cheek and perched himself on the arm of her chair, his hand on her shoulder. He gave her a mild shake. "Mama, it isn't forever! I could not possibly turn down an appointment to All Souls. It is an honor I had not dreamed of, and I will read history there this year," he concluded, his voice firm.

The seriousness lasted no more time than it took to speak his intentions. Gatewood rested his cheek against his mother's hair. "Mama, look at it this way and take some consolation: at least I am not pursuing my fellowship in Shakespeare, too. I could, you know."

Lady Chesney shuddered. "You *will* remind me of your dratted double first!" She dabbed at her eyes. "When my set gathers for loo and we discuss the exploits of our sons, I have to endure Lady Whittington's bragging about that oafish lump she claims is Lord Whittington's and his exploits in Spain. Christine Dysart proses on and on about her dear Little Darnley's latest win at Newmarket. All I have to brag about is some pesky book you wrote about fairies and donkey's heads! Lud, it's enough to set me off my meals."

"*Midsummer Night's Dream,* Mama," Lord Chesney said patiently. "It's a rather good play, even if it is Shakespeare. And I only wrote a small commentary."

"Stuff!" Lady Chesney exclaimed. "You are a disgrace to all the Gatewoods who ever turned a card or made a wager. While we are having such fun, here you are, your nose eternally in a book."

Gatewood abandoned his station at his parent's elbow and took up a more defensive stance in front of the fireplace. "We made a bargain, Mama, you and Papa and I, remember? Papa is gone now, but I am holding you to the bargain. I will study this year at All Souls, and when the year is up, I promise to set up my nursery, and start riding to hounds, and gambling, and making my tailor's life miserable. Agreed?''

Lady Chesney sighed and nodded. ''That ought to redeem the family honor, although I've a mind to tell people, when they inquire where you are this year, that you are taking the Grand Tour on the Continent.''

''Mama! No one is taking the Grand Tour these days! Remember the Blockade?'' He regarded her with tender affection. ''Mama, when did you last look at a newspaper?''

Lady Chesney brushed aside world events with a wave of her handkerchief. ''Too much small print, my dear. Very well, I will not complain,'' she said, and complained, ''But you know that I do not approve. For the Lord's sake, you are the head of the family now!''

''I know, Mama, I know,'' he soothed.

''You will remember to send out your collars every now and then to be starched?''

''Of course, Mama.''

''I do not understand why you cannot take your father's valet with you to Oxford!''

''He would perish with boredom and kill me in my sleep, Mama,'' Gatewood said, the amusement creeping into his voice again. ''Besides that, Lord Winnfield has made him a wonderful offer of employment.''

''I suppose. At least promise me that you will not wear that beastly student's gown all the time. You are rumpled enough.''

''Certainly, Mama.''

Her tone softened. ''And write to me occasionally.''

''Yes, dearest. Oxford is not situated in the polar reaches.''

''It is dreadful unmodish, and you know it!''

''Dreadful slow,'' he agreed, with a twinkle in his eyes as he began a slow edge toward the door.

As his mother cast about for another argument, he reached the door, pausing with his hand poised above the handle, ready to bolt.

''I have hit upon it, Mama!'' Gatewood exclaimed as he turned the handle. ''You can tell your set that I have killed someone in a duel and must spend the year rusticating with relatives in Virginia. That ought to be sufficiently worthy of a true Gatewood!"

Lady Chesney puffed up for a resounding reply. Before it could leave her lips, her son was gone, laughing his way down the hall. "Oh, if you were only of an age for me to stop your quarterly allowance," she muttered.

She sprang to her feet, surprisingly agile for one of her bulk, and hurtled herself after him. All she saw was a pair of heels vanishing up the staircase. She shook her fist after him.

"It is my fervent wish that you meet your match at Oxford, you wicked, wicked, unnatural son!" she shouted, quite forgetting herself.

Her unnatural son's voice floated down from the second floor landing. "My dear, what could be safer than All Souls College?"

1

Master Ralph Grimsley tugged at his collar, sighed, and looked up at his sister. "Do you know, El, I do not think this interview will go well for either of us. That bagwig Snead don't much like to be corrected, especially by you."

" 'Doesn't,' " Ellen Grimsley corrected, her eyes on the saddled horse pawing the ground directly under the window where they sat. "And Papa hates above all things to be trapped by that prosing windpipe, especially when the fox has already been loosed."

As if to emphasize her words, the mellow tones of the hunting horn sounded through the open window. The wavering notes stretched out and then drifted away on the October breeze. Ellen shivered and pulled the window shut.

Ralph scrambled to his knees and pressed his nose against the windowpane. "Poor old fox," he said softly. He glanced at Ellen again. "There is a certain injustice to this system," he said.

Ellen smiled for the first time since Vicar Snead's arrival, charmed by the thought that her little brother, who was but twelve, sounded full grown. She thought of Gordon, incarcerated at Oxford, who had never sounded that mature at twelve, and likely never would. A certain injustice, she thought, her eyes on the closed door to the book room.

Ralph remained kneeling in the window seat, his nose pressed to the glass. In another moment, he was blowing on the glass and then writing his Latin vocabulary on the pane. "El, if I write it backwards, then people outside can read it forwards."

"You could," she agreed as she tucked in his shirttail and then tickled him. "But as the only animate object outside is Papa's horse, I think it would be a waste of good breath."

Ralph laughed, turned around, and sat next to her again, resting his head against her arm. He closed his eyes in satisfaction. "I'm glad it's Horry getting married and not you, El. Promise me that you will never marry."

"I promise," she said promptly, and then amended, a twinkle in her eyes. "But suppose I get a good offer? Mama is sure that if Horatia can bag the son of a baronet, then I ought at least to snare a vicar!"

Ralph frowned. "Well, as long as it's not Vicar Snead, that old priss." He brightened. "I think someone as fine as you could trip up a viscount at least."

"Silly!"

They were still smiling when the book room door opened and the vicar minced out. He smiled his gallows smile at the Grimsley progeny, his thin lips disappearing somewhere inside his mouth. Carefully he smoothed a finger across each eyebrow—his only good feature—and stood aside for the squire.

Ellen's heart sank lower into her boots. Triumph was etched all over the vicar's rather spongy features. Ellen, why do you not keep your mouth shut? she thought to herself. Why aren't you a more dutiful daughter?

The hunting horn sounded again, barely audible through the closed window. The squire lumbered to the window and pressed his nose against the glass in unknowing imitation of his younger son. The sigh that escaped him was plainly audible.

The vicar coughed and cleared his throat, recalling the squire to the proceedings at hand. "Squire Grimsley, I believe you have something to say to your daughter."

"My daughter?" the squire repeated absently. He opened the window and looked down at his horse.

Ellen bit her lip to keep back the laughter. Poor Vicar Snead! He hadn't been in the neighborhood long enough to know that one only asked easy questions of Squire Grimsley when the pack was loosed and the fox running fast. He would be hard put to remember any of his children, especially his daughters.

"Sir, your daughter!" the vicar repeated, when the squire stayed where he was, his hands resting on the glass as if he wanted to push through it, leap on the waiting horse, and gallop toward the sound of the horn.

"My daughter?" the squire said, as though the concept of parenthood were a new idea requiring further consideration.

"Ellen," Ralph added helpfully. "She's short for a Grimsley, and blond, Papa. I think she's pretty," he concluded, unable to resist, even as his sister kicked his foot.

"And you are impertinent," the vicar snapped. He cleared his throat again. "Your daughter, Miss Grimsley."

The squire waved his hand in the direction of the clergyman. "You have my permission, sir. Take her, she's yours."

The vicar gasped and turned the color of salmon. Ralph dissolved into helpless mirth.

The laughter recalled the squire to the distateful business at hand. He turned away from the window with a reluctance that was almost palpable. Ralph stopped laughing and scooted closer to his sister, who put her arm around him.

"Ellen, you will apologize to the vicar for your rudeness this morning during Ralph's lesson."

Ellen rose, wishing for the millionth time that she was tall like the other Grimsleys. She turned the full force of her cobalt blue eyes upon the vicar, who went even redder and seemed to have trouble with his collar suddenly. He tugged on it and made strangling noises that made Ralph shake.

"Mr. Snead," she began softly, "I do apologize for correcting you this morning when you said that Boston was the capital of the United States."

"And?" asked the vicar, running his finger around the offending collar as Ellen continued to regard him, a slight smile on her face.

"And?" she repeated.

"And you will not interfere again," the vicar concluded.

"I can't promise that," she said. "Best that you brush up on your geography, sir, before you lead any more young boys astray."

"Daughter!" roared the squire.

Ellen winced, but she stood her ground. "Papa, Boston is not the capital of the United States."

"No?" The squire rubbed his chin, his eyes on the vicar. "Well of course it is not! What do you say to this, sir?"

The vicar dabbed at the perspiration gathering on his upper lip. "She could have told me in private, sir."

Ralph sprang to his sister's defense. "Sir, as to that, I am sure she could not," he insisted. "Papa would never permit a *tête-à-tête* with a single gentleman such as yourself."

"Bother and nonsense," the vicar exclaimed. "I am her spiritual counselor, as long as she resides within the boundaries of my parish!" He turned to the squire and all but plucked at his pink coat. "Squire, I protest! Miss Grimsley corrects me in front of my other pupils. How does it look, sir?"

The squire forced his attention from the window to the domestic scene. "It looks to me, sir, as though you ought to take a good look at a map. Everyone knows that New York is the capital of the United States. Good day, vicar. Do come again when you can stay longer."

The vicar sniffed and patted his eyebrows again. "Very well, sir. I will withdraw now. Perhaps I shall compose a sermon from St. Paul about women not speaking in public!" He turned and strode majestically to the front door. The effect was marred when he closed the door upon his coattails and had to open it again to free himself.

The squire watched him go. "Our vicar is good evidence for the theory that all younger sons should be drowned at birth," he murmured, and then glanced at Ralph. "Present company excluded, of course."

Ralph grinned, pleased by his father's unexpected attention.

Ellen sat down in the window seat again. "Papa, the capital of the United States is Washington, D.C.!"

The squire, his family duties attended to, was at the window again. "That's not my fault," he said, and eyed his daughter. "What am I going to do with you, Ellen?" he asked.

"You could send me away to school, Papa," she said.

The squire roared with laughter and pinched her cheek. "You're the funny one," he said. "Lord, what use does a chit have for school? You had a governess for two years, my dear. That's enough. I have never heard that reading books will get you a husband." He looked about for his hat.

"But Papa, isn't there more to life than the getting of a husband?" she persisted.

He took his hat from Ralph and settled it on his head. He turned to her with a puzzled expression. "What else is there for chits?" he asked.

"But Papa," she began, and was cut off with a wag of the squire's finger in her face.

"None of that!" The squire took one last look out the window and hurried to the door. "From now on, you will stay out of the vicar's lessons. If you must walk into the village with Ralph, then visit your Aunt Shreve while your brother is at the vicarage." He frowned and took a few swings at imaginary enemies with his riding crop. "She's a dratted woman and a nuisance, but I can't have you hounding the vicar." He patted her cheek. "Even if he is a sorry excuse."

He had almost reached the door before other Grimsleys converged upon him like driverless coaches hurtling toward the same crossing. The squire looked about for a quick escape, but all routes were cut off.

Martha, towed along by one hand, cried the loudest, and hiccuped as her mother pulled her toward the squire. She appeared strangely splotchy about the face and neck.

"Spots, Mr. Grimsley!" Mama shrieked. "Spots!"

Squire Grimsley sighed and looked about for an escape while Ellen watched in amusement. " 'In sooth you 'scape not so,' " she murmured to Ralph, who nodded and smiled.

"*Taming of the Shrew*?" he asked, and she nodded, her hands on his shoulders, as they watched the rest of the Grimsleys unravel before their eyes. Even as she looked on, Horatia, her face pale, staggered toward the squire and sank into a chair, her hands covering her eyes.

"Sarah Siddons is warming up," Ralph whispered.

"She must wait her turn," Ellen whispered back. "Mama will win out."

"Spots!" Mama cried again. She tugged on her husband's arm. "Mr. Grimsley, this is serious business!"

The squire peered closer at his youngest child and then leaped back. " 'Pon my word, if it persists, won't she be a sight when she skips down the aisle in front of Horry, strewing around them little posies that I am supposed to pay a king's ransom for in December!"

Mrs. Grimsley glared at her husband until he stepped back again. Her eyes narrowed. "We are having a wedding in less than two months' time, Mr. Grimsley. This is no joking matter!'' She followed up her words by bursting into tears, noisy tears that cast Martha's efforts into the shade. The child ceased her wailing and stared up at her mother. Then her red-dotted face darkened again and she added her miseries to her mother's woe.

Ralph put his hands over his ears and then nudged his sister, who still sat in the window seat, transfixed by the spectacle before her. ''It is Horry's turn,'' he whispered. ''This will be good.''

''Hush, Ralph,'' Ellen whispered, as Horatia, her lovely face filled with misery, staggered to her feet and latched onto the lapels of her father's riding coat.

Like others of the Grimsley race, she was tall and possessed of a headful of guinea-gold curls that tickled Papa's nose and made him sneeze.

Wide-eyed, Ralph watched the tableau before him, then turned away. ''Dear me,'' he managed, his shoulders shaking.

Ellen put her finger to her lips. Was ever womankind plagued with such a helpless family, she thought, as she hurried to Martha and knelt in front of her little sister. Expertly she ran her hands over the bumps on Martha's face, then stood up.

''Mama, do take it down a peg.''

Mama only sobbed harder. ''You and your dreadful slang! *You* are not faced with a crisis of monumental proportions!'' Mama wept into her handkerchief. ''Spots!''

''It is worse and worse, Mama!'' Horatia burst out. ''Chevering says . . .''

''Nonsense!'' Ellen said, cutting off her sister in midsentence and resting her hand upon Martha's head. ''Mama, let us begin with Martha. Did you take a good look at her? A really good look?''

Mama wiped her eyes and squinted down at her littlest daughter. ''I think I know my own children, Ellen,'' she said, biting off her words.

Ellen knelt in front of her sister again, her hands firm on Martha's shoulders. ''Tell me truly, Martha. Have you been in Mama's chocolates again?''

Martha, a finger in her mouth, looked from one parent to the other and back to Ellen again. She scratched her stomach and nodded.

"There you have it, Mama. It is merely a rash and will likely be gone before noon." She gave her little sister a shake. "And you stay out of Mama's chocolates, miss! You know they are her 'ever-present help in trouble.' "

Mama wiped her streaming eyes. "Don't be sacrilegious, daughter! And speaking of that, wasn't that the vicar I saw leaving here in such a snit?"

Ellen nodded. Mama dabbed at her eyes again.

"And I had such hopes of him." Turned loose, Martha darted away. Mama sighed again. "My nerves, Ellen, my nerves!"

Ellen put her arms around her mother. "They are your closest companions, my dear," she soothed. "Mama, lie down now and think about this: you could invite Cousin Henrietta Colesnatch to stay with us for the duration of the wedding. You know how she loves to batten herself on relatives. She can watch Martha for you."

Mama opened her mouth to utter a protest, but she closed it instead and then regarded her daughter for a long moment. "I could do that, couldn't I?"

"You could, Mama," Ellen replied. "You could even go do it now. Cousin Henrietta could be here by tomorrow evening. She would spare no expense—as long as you paid the post chaise."

A thoughtful expression on her face, Mama followed her daughter Martha down the hall. Ellen turned her attention to Horatia, who still sobbed upon the squire's coat.

"My dear, what *is* the matter?" she asked. "Is Napoleon at the gates and no one told us?"

Horry cast her a watery glance. "It is worse than that." She clutched her father's lapels in both fists. "Papa, did you really promise Edwin's father that you would toast us with Fortaleza sherry?"

Papa stared at his eldest daughter. "I may have, Horry. What is the problem with that? You know we save the best for special occasions."

Horatia's eyes filled with tears again. "I have come from belowstairs," she announced dramatically. "Chevering tells me that there is no Fortaleza left. Furthermore, he says that with the Blockade, there is no way to get any more. Papa, I shall die!"

The squire blinked and removed his daughter's hands from his rumpled, sodden lapels. He took one last, longing look out the window. "Surely we can find some good Madeira."

Horatia threw herself onto the window seat, sobbing and drumming her feet on the cushions. "Papa, you promised!" she sobbed between fresh gusts of tears. "You promised Edwin's father that we would be toasted with Fortaleza. And now I have this note from Edwin informing me that his papa is so looking forward to a sip of the world's finest sherry! Papa, I am undone."

The squire blinked again. "You cannot suppose that Edwin would cry off over a dusty bottle of sherry, my dear! That is a particle of nonsense not worthy of even you!"

Horatia took no comfort from his bracing words. "You know very well that Sir Reginald fancies himself a specialist in wines."

She struggled into a sitting position and pressed her hand to her heart. "This will cast such a cloud upon my nuptials that I do not see how I can possibly face Sir Reginald." She returned to her tears and the handkerchief that Ralph handed her without a word.

Ralph watched in fascination. " 'I wouldn't have thought the old girl to have had so many tears in her,' " he whispered to his sister.

Ellen regarded him in amusement mingled with exasperation. "This is no time for *Macbeth,* you silly chub," she whispered back. She looked at her sister, pale and miserable in the window seat, and then glanced at Papa, who hovered over her with miserable solicitation.

A year ago, she would have been jealous of the attention Papa expended on Horry. I must have been growing up when I wasn't even aware of it, she thought. Someone in this family *has* to. She thought another moment and then made up her mind.

"Papa, doesn't Aunt Shreve have a bottle or two of that sherry? I seem to recall that Grandfather Grimsley divided that case in the will."

The squire made a face. "As he divided everything!" he exclaimed, his voice loud, his face red. "Do you think I would ask my sister for anything?" He pulled Horatia to her feet, his arm about her. "Horry, I think your precious Edwin can drink Madeira. And so can his father! Paltry little baronet," he concluded.

Ellen winced as Horatia increased the volume of her misery. Lord help us, in another minute she will be in strong hysterics, and Papa will storm and stamp, and Mama will come running in with hartshorn and burning feathers. Ellen took a deep breath.

"Papa, I can ask Aunt Shreve for a bottle of Fortaleza."

"You will never get it out of her," Papa insisted, "particularly if she knows it will be a favor to me!"

"I can manage," Ellen said quietly. "Hush, Horry. If your face gets splotchy, Edwin might reconsider."

Horatia gasped and ran to the mirror in the hall, turning her head this way and that to survey the ravages of tears on her face.

"You will look all of twenty, if you keep crying," Ellen said, her face devoid of all expression.

Horry gasped. "Twenty! Horrors!"

"Twenty," Ellen repeated, her voice firm. "Now, dry your eyes, Horry. I can solve this problem."

With a tight little nod, and one last teary-eyed entreaty of her papa, Horatia summoned her little brother to help her from the room. She smiled bravely and allowed him to lead her away.

The squire turned to his remaining daughter and grasped her by both hands. "Ellen, if you can carry this off, I will get you anything you want," he declared.

Ellen stood on tiptoe and kissed her tall parent's cheek. "Done, Papa, done. Better yet, I will return with *two* bottles of Fortaleza."

Papa closed his eyes in relief, hugging her to his ample bosom. He picked up his riding crop again and dashed out the door, leaving it wide open. In another moment, Ellen saw horse and rider thundering in the general direction of the last siren call of the hunting horn.

Ralph returned and flopped down on the window seat. "El, they wear me out," he complained when he could manage speech. "I think Horry is a perfect lamebrain to moon over that spotty Edwin. You would never do such a thing, would you?"

She shook her head, the laughter back in her eyes.

Ralph sat up, resting on one elbow. "Why did you promise

Papa two bottles of that dratted sherry? You know that Aunt
Shreve has not spoken to him since the reading of that will four
years ago. When I was but a child," he added.

Ellen burst into laughter. "And what are you now, my dear?"
she teased and took him by the hand, pulling him to his feet.
"Come. Let us do our best."

It meant retracing their steps from manor to village again for
the second time that morning, but neither Grimsley objected.
The air was crisp with autumn; the tantalizing fragrance of
burning leaves made brother and sister take a deep breath and
sigh together.

They looked at each other and laughed. There wasn't any need
to speak; they understood the Grimsleys too well. Papa saw no
further than hounds and horses; Mama darted from anxiety to
crisis; Horry was twined all around herself and her darling
noddy Edwin.

"There is hope for Martha," Ralph said finally, giving voice
to what his sister was thinking. "We shall give her a few years,
and see if she improves."

" 'A few years,' " Ellen mimicked. "By then you will have
abandoned me for Oxford and will not have a thought to spare
for either sister!"

"If Papa doesn't stick me in an office in the City with one
of Mama's brothers first," he said quietly and took her by the
hand. "You know Gordon is supposed to be the Oxford-
educated one."

They walked a moment in silence. Ralph squeezed her hand.
"Whatever the outcome, I will always have a thought for you,
El."

They continued in companionable silence. And I for you,
Ellen Grimsley thought as she looked down at her little brother.

He strode along at her side, his face half turned to the sun,
a smile in his eyes. His hair looked as it always did, as if he
had bounded out of bed, rushed to the stable and combed it with
a pitchfork.

But his freckles were fading. Mama had remarked over breakfast only this morning that his wrists were shooting out of his
cuffs and he was overdue a visit to Miss Simpson, who made
all the children's clothes.

Papa had come out of his hunting fog long enough to peer closer at his son. "Nay, wife, not this time," he had boomed out. " 'Tis time for Ralph to visit my tailor. He's too big to wear nankeen breeches anymore."

Ellen nodded, remembering the glow of pleasure on Ralph's face. Papa had noticed him. Perhaps when he wore long pants and a gentleman's riding boots, Papa would acknowledge that his younger son could be a scholar as well as a rider to hounds.

On a day as glorious as this autumn morning, anything was possible, Ellen decided. Perhaps Aunt Shreve would relinquish two bottles of Fortaleza without a murmur; perhaps Horatia would reconsider and let her be a bridesmaid after all, even if her small statue did upset the symmetry of the other, taller cousins and friends. Perhaps when the wedding was over and Horatia shot off, Mama would relax for a season and not scold and berate her younger daughter because she made no push to secure a husband for herself among the eligibles of the district.

I am too short for a Grimsley and I have no hunting instincts, she thought as they stood still and watched Papa race toward the hounds and riders that milled about on a distant, smoky hillside, waiting for the dogs to recapture the scent.

Brother and sister stood close together and watched the hunters. They leaned forward and listened and then smiled to each other when the hounds began to bay again. Soon the pack, followed by the pink-coated riders, disappeared over the hill.

The field was theirs again. Ralph sat down on a sun-warmed rock. "I will wait for you here, El," he declared, and then made a face. "After this morning, I haven't the fortitude for the scold Aunt Shreve is going to give you."

Ellen grinned. "Coward!"

Ralph nodded, unruffled. "Shakespeare would call me a 'whey-faced loon.' "

Ellen waved to him and hurried toward the village.

When she was out of sight, she slowed her steps. Why did I promise Papa that dratted Fortalelza? she thought.

She remembered the reading of Grandfather's will, with all the relatives assembled, black and sniffling, or at least holding handkerchief to nose in a show of sorrow.

Not that anyone had loved Grandfather overmuch before he

cocked up his toes. He was a testy old rip who pinched the
maids, scandalized his daughter and infuriated his son by
outliving his usefulness. To the best of her recollection, Ellen
was the only grandchild to mourn his loss. She missed his stories
of battles fought, creditors outrun, fortunes won and lost and
won again.

She missed him still, even four years after his death. At
eighteen, she still mourned the loss of the only relative who
had not gawked and gasped when she did not fulfill the promise
of her Grimsley heritage and grow to elegant heights. He had
not scolded her, as if complaints would add one inch to her
stature. He had thoughtfully matched his stride to hers and they
had walked and talked over the Cotswold hills until he died.

She thought again about the will, written in Grandpapa's
crabbed handwriting and changed and changed again as relatives
fell short of the mark. In a final show of pique against her father,
Grandfather had evenly divided all his possessions between his
only surviving son and daughter, right down to the half case
of Fortaleza.

Ellen closed her eyes, seeing again Papa storming out of the
solicitor's office, cheated out of lands and entitlements he felt
were rightfully his, muttering about the perfidy of a sister he
could name. Aunt Shreve, stung by his anger, had taken instant
exception to his blathering and closed her door to him.

"And mind you, Ellen Grimsley," Aunt Shreve said a half
hour later as Ellen sat in her aunt's cozy sitting room on Porter
Street. "Your father sets too great a store by Horatia's wedding
to that peabrained excuse of a son and heir to Sir Reginald Bland.
A baronet!"

She spat out the word, as if the tea she sipped suddenly displeased her. "What is that to anything? Grimsleys have managed
for centuries without titles in the family and done quite well
thank you. Does my brother do this so he can smile and nod
and play the fool and introduce his son-in-law, the son of a
baronet, to his horse-dealing cronies? I ask you."

Ellen knew better than to interrupt a Grimsley tirade, even
if this particular Grimsley had long been wedded and widowed
by a Shreve. She folded her hands patiently in her lap.

"And such a collection of foolish parts is our dear Edwin!"

Aunt Shreve said, not failing her niece. "Does anything ever go on behind those blue eyes of his, Ellen?"

"Oh, Aunt Shreve, you know that Horry loves Edwin. And if he is not over sharp, what is that to anyone in my family? They'll never notice."

Aunt Shreve took another sip of tea. "No, I suppose they will not. As long as he can sit a horse, I suppose everyone will overlook his other deficiencies." She peered over her spectacles at her niece. "Not for the first time have I wondered how you and Ralph came to be dropped down in the midst of that ignorant family, my dear. One could accuse your mother of shady dealings."

Ellen laughed. "Aunt Shreve! You know that my mother is perfectly respectable!"

Aunt Shreve managed a smile. "Respectable to the point of numbness. Setting all that aside, I trust you will do better than Edwin Bland, my dear."

Her niece sighed. "Mama claims that all I can hope for is Thomas Cornwell, particularly now since I have driven off the vicar."

Aunt Shreve winced. There was a long silence, which she finally broke when she had drained the rest of her tea. "Dear me," she said finally, "he of the protruding ears?"

"The very same," Ellen replied.

"Goodness, a lowering thought," Aunt Shreve murmured. They regarded each other, Aunt Shreve shuddered. "Now there is a young man with nothing to recommend him but his height!" She leaned forward. "I charge you to find some tiny little man. It will drive your father into bedlam."

"Aunt Shreve, you are absurd!" Ellen protested, laughing.

Her aunt smiled. "I know it. We can safely say that your father only got a half-share of the eccentricity, too! But seriously, my dear, you must get out of this place."

"How?" Ellen asked, and helped herself to another biscuit. She studied the tray in front of her, remembered the reason for her visit, and cleared her throat.

When she said nothing, Aunt Shreve snorted in impatience.

"What errand has your ridiculous father sent you on, child?" She chuckled and rubbed her hands together. "One would suspect you had come to me on some nefarious expedition, sent by my brother!''

Ellen was silent as the embarrassment spread up her shoulders and onto her face like a contagious disease.

"You have hit upon it, aunt," she murmured. "Papa made an extravagant promise at the last Assembly Ball that he would toast the happy couple with Fortaleza sherry, and now Sir Reginald won't rest unless it actually happens. You know what a connoisseur of wines he thinks himself." Ellen looked away, suddenly ashamed of her relatives. "You would think that the fate of nations hung upon this single issue."

Aunt Shreve was silent for a long moment that stretched into minutes. She poured herself another cup of tea and took it to the mantelpiece, where she sipped it and regarded her niece thoughtfully.

"My dear," she said finally, "what would irritate your father the most? I mean, what would really get his goat?"

Ellen smiled in spite of her own discomfort. "Probably to be forced to dance to your tune, Aunt. You know how he hates that." She laughed out loud, her embarrassment overcome. "He must have been a dreadful little brother."

"The worst," Aunt Shreve agreed absently, her mind intent upon the question she had posed.

"Papa even told me that he would give me anything I wanted, if I could talk you out of one dusty bottle of sherry," Ellen said, joining her aunt by the fireplace.

Aunt Shreve mused a moment more, and then looked her niece in the eye. "My dear, what is it you want more than anything?"

"Well, I would like to be one of Horry's bridesmaids, but even wishing won't help me grow six inches." She blushed at her aunt's shocked stare. "I . . . I upset the symmetry, Aunt."

"Upset the . . ." Aunt Shreve paced the length of the room and back.

"I don't mind, truly I don't," Ellen said quickly, her heart pounding at the look in Aunt Shreve's eyes. "I was thinking about teasing Papa for some hair ornaments." She fingered her cropped hair. "I don't need anything else, really. Oh, Aunt, don't look like that!"

Aunt Shreve was silent. When she spoke, her voice was even,

serious. "We can do better than that, much better. Did I not see you this morning, trailing in the wake of our vicar, one of God's greatest jokes upon the Church of England? Are you in trouble again for correcting him in Ralph's lessons?"

Ellen nodded. "He insisted that Boston was the capital of the United States of America." She shook her head. "Papa assured him that New York was the capital, and that is how the matter stands."

Aunt Shreve rolled her eyes and returned the teacup to the table with an audible click. She took her niece's hands in both of her own.

"Do I recall a conversation last week over tea where you told me your greatest wish was to go to Oxford like your brother Gordon?"

Ellen stared at her aunt, remembering her words. "Yes, but that was only in jest! It's impossible. Just wishful thinking. Besides that, Papa told me only an hour ago that I had all the education I needed and that my duty now was to find a husband. He would never permit it." Ellen laughed. "Not to mention the entire English educational establishment! Really, Aunt Shreve."

Aunt Shreve went to the bellpull and gave it a tug.

"Do you think he would change his mind for two bottles of Fortaleza? What about four bottles?"

Ellen stared at her aunt. "That would be the half case that Grandfather left you. Even the Prince Regent doesn't have four bottles of Fortaleza, I vow."

"I never could tolerate the stuff," Aunt Shreve confided, "although I would never tell your father that." She clapped her hands together. "I would love to see the look on your father's face when you present him with my half case and tell him that his sister will take it all back unless he allows you to go to Oxford!"

Ellen sat down. "What do you mean?"

"I know that Oxford University itself is out of the question, and more's the pity. I ask you, what possible polluting effect would females have upon the quadrangles of Oriel or Balliol? But setting that aside, as we must, have you not heard of Miss Dignam's Select Female Academy? Miss Dignam is an old and

dear friend of mine, for all that we have not seen each other
in years. And I believe the academy is even located on the High
Street. You could admire any number of spires and crockets
and see that clever round library from your window.''

''Do you mean the Radcliffe Camera?'' Ellen asked, her eyes
wide. ''Papa would never . . .''

''I believe he would, my dear, for four bottles of Fortaleza
and relief from Horatia's endless tears.'' Aunt Shreve went to
her escritoire and took out paper and pen. '' 'Dear Charles,' ''
she began, and then crumpled the paper. ''He has never been
'Dear Charles.' 'Charles' will suffice.'' She thought another
moment, smiled and wrote a note, sealing it with wax and
handing it to her niece. ''Take that to your ridiculous father
and start packing, my dear!''

2

I am a perfect beast, Ellen thought as she leaned back against the cushions in the post chaise and rested her eyes on the late-October scenery. I should be missing them all so much, and I am not.

She thought a moment and then smiled to herself. I will miss Ralph. He had hugged her for a few moments longer than the others. "I shall think of you often, El," he had whispered when the others had already turned back to the house, and Mama and Horry had resumed their argument over hothouse flowers or potted plants for the wedding.

"I will miss you, too," she replied. "I will write you and tell you all about the colleges."

"About Oriel, if you please," he urged, letting go of his sister and straightening his new waistcoat, sewn by the squire's own tailor.

"Do you wish to be an Oriel man someday?" she teased, keeping her tone light to discourage the tears that threatened to fall.

"I do, above all things," he replied fervently. "And then I will hope for an appointment to All Souls, where I will read literature and eventually become a scholar of renown."

Ellen kissed him on both cheeks. "And I will be your secretary?" she teased.

Ralph shook his head. "No, El; you will be *my* teacher." He looked across the fields stripped bare by winter. "At least, that is how it should be."

"But it is not, my dear," she said.

He stood on the front steps, waving goodbye until he was only a small figure. "I will write you often," she whispered to the glass.

Horatia had been properly appreciative of the Fortaleza, although she did not change her mind about her bridesmaids. "You are a perfect dear to do this, Ellen, and I am fully aware

of what I owe you," she declared, tears glistening on the ends
of her lashes as she clutched the dusty bottles of sherry to her
breast. "After the wedding, I will tell you just where to stand
so that you may catch my bouquet. Mama will be so thrilled."

Papa had turned shades of scarlet, crimson and a deep magenta
that worried them all when Ellen brought the Fortaleza to him
and declared that she would spend the winter at Miss Dignam's
Select Female Academy in Oxford as her reward. Horatia sat
him down and Mama loosened his waistcoat, while Ellen
propped his feet on the hassock and Ralph stood close by with
a pillow for his neck.

When he had control of his faculties, the squire fired off a
fierce note to his sister in the village, demanding an explanation
of Ellen's strange request, and declaring that it was absurd and
out of the question. Aunt Shreve sent her reply in the form of
her footman, who demanded the return of the Fortaleza. He
stood there, his hands outstretched, while Horatia sobbed and
Mama scolded. Papa had no choice but to relent and then
collapse in his armchair, overcome by the rigors of maintaining
domestic tranquillity.

"You are the most unnatural Grimsley!" he declared for the
next two weeks, each time he encountered her in a hallway or
at meals. He even began to eye his wife askance, as if to accuse
that virtuous and boring woman of some misdeed that had landed
someone else's child in the Grimsley bassinet some eighteen
years previous. The result of his mutterings had been a lively
argument between the parents that kept everyone tiptoeing about
the manor until a truce was declared and the squire readmitted
to his bedroom.

Ellen bore it all calmly, ignoring Papa's pointed stares and
Mama's torrent of advice, larded with admonition and fore-
boding. "You know, Ellen, that Dr. Spender Chumley over
in Larch lectured on the subject of females damaging their brains
with overmuch study," she warned. "He claims that the brain
enlarges and creates a curiously shaped head that is not attractive
in any way."

This information sent Horatia rushing to the mirror to examine
the shape of her own head.

Ellen laughed out loud. "Horry, you haven't a fear in the
world," she said. "I don't think two consecutive thoughts have

ever encountered each other in that space between your ears.''

''And thank goodness for that,'' Horatia declared. ''I would not wish to risk deformity.'' She looked at her mother, her eyes filled with anxiety. ''Mama, surely dancing lessons do not come under the category of study that Dr. Chumley speaks of?''

''They wouldn't dare,'' Ellen replied.

She was packed by the end of the week, but the November rains came early that year. She was forced to fidget and pace about the house another week until the roads were passable again.

She endured one final visit from Thomas Cornwell, who dropped by after a day at the Grain Exchange in Morely, full of news about the price of corn and the effect of war on his bankbook.

No use in telling Mama to send down the news that she had a headache.

''Ellen, you never have a headache,'' Mama said. ''Now go downstairs and do your duty!''

''But Mama!'' she protested.

Mama only stared at her as her lower lip began to quiver. ''If I have to play the hostess and sit for hours in the parlor while he talks on and on about rye and barley, I will go distracted.''

Ellen dug her heels in. ''Mama, this is the man you paint in such rosy colors for me! Now I find that you can scarcely tolerate his conversation!''

''My dear Ellen,'' said Mama as she held the door open for her daughter. ''Once you are well married to Thomas Cornwell, you needn't listen to him!''

And so she had listened until the rains began again and darkness settled in, and she had no choice but to invite him to dinner. By the time he left after a game of whist in the sitting room, she knew everything about this year's rye and barley crop (the most promising in the last ten years) and the total number of pigs transported to market.

And now my head does truly ache, Ellen thought as she walked Cornwell to the door, careful to keep her distance, dreading the moment when he would clear his throat and look at her expectantly.

So far she had managed to avoid his kisses. For a small stipend from her quarterly allowance, Ralph usually presented himself in the front hall in time to dampen the Romeo in Thomas Cornwell.

But this time Ralph had been dragged to the sewing room to try on the new waistcoat Horry had commissioned just for the wedding. Cornwell cleared his throat on cue.

"I will miss you dreadfully, Ellen," he said, and gazed at her, his eyes hopeful.

This is my cue, Ellen thought. Instead, she held out her hand and smiled up at the big farmer. "Mr. Cornwell, I am sure that your rye and barley will keep you feverishly busy this winter."

He dropped to his knees in front of her as she grabbed his elbow and tried to tug him to his feet. "Marry me, Ellen, and make me the happiest man in Oxfordshire!"

"Get up," she hissed. "This will never do."

"Only say yes and I will get up," he pleaded, following her on his knees across the hallway.

Mama, her arms full of deep green fabric, hurried into the hall. She stopped, her eyes enormous, and stared at Thomas Cornwell. Ellen looked at her in desperation.

Mama sighed. "Mr. Cornwell, this will never do! I cannot possibly contemplate another wedding right now! Do get off your knees and save this for the spring."

His face red from his exertions, Cornwell scrambled to his feet. "Yes, Mrs. Grimsley," he said as he accepted the hat and coat that the wooden-faced butler was holding out. "Ellen, I will write," he declared, hand to his heart, as she opened the door and ushered him into the rain. He stuck his head back in the door, his face redder still. "Provided that is not too forward."

Ellen shook her head. "I think it is, Mr. Cornwell," she said, her voice low, even though Mama had already retreated from the front hall. "I will see you at Christmas." She closed the door on his protestations of love.

Ellen endured another week of Mama's tears and good advice. "You will be sharing rooms with Fanny Bland, our own dear Edwin's older sister. That is the only thing about this havey-cavey business that sets my mind at ease. Fanny is all that is proper and she will keep an eye on you."

"Yes, Mama."

"And you will not go out of doors unaccompanied, or have anything to do with the students in the colleges."

"No, Mama."

"You will do nothing to call attention to yourself."

"Never, Mama."

She spoke so quickly that Mama looked at her and frowned, but made no further comment beyond a martyr's sigh and a sad shake of her head.

Ellen found herself walking to the road during that interminable week of impassable roads, testing the gravel, willing the sodden skies to brighten.

The postman met her one morning with a letter of welcome from Miss Dignam and a list of her classes. I will take French and embroidery? she asked herself, letter in hand, as she walked slowly back to the house. She turned the letter over, hopeful of further enlightenment. Surely there was some mistake. She wanted to take geography and geometry, too, if it was offered.

She folded the letter. Surely I can discuss this with the headmistress when I arrive, she thought.

Mama could spare none of the maids to accompany her to Oxford. Papa was forced to prevail upon his sister to act as escort. Aunt Shreve accepted with alacrity, declaring it a pleasure and presenting the squire with two more forgotten bottles of Fortaleza, to his great amazement and grudging approval.

"There now," she declared. "Charles, you have enough Fortaleza to toast Horatia, and her first child, and Ralph's entrance into Oxford—if you have the unexpected good sense to send him there instead of to a beastly counting house in the City. You can also celebrate Gordon's leaving of Oxford eventually, if that should ever happen before we are too gnarled to pop a cork."

Brother and sister had declared a wary truce and were sitting knee to knee over the tea table in Aunt Shreve's house. Ellen cast anxious glances at her papa throughout the interview.

He surprised his daughter by managing a ponderous joke. "What, no bottle for Ellen?" he asked. "She may marry someday, if we can force her nose out of books, or if she is not off exploring the world in a birchbark canoe."

Aunt Shrive smiled at her favorite niece. "I wasn't going to tell you this, Charles, but years ago Father gave me a bottle of Palais Royal brandy.''

The squire choked on his tea. ''Good God,'' he exclaimed when he could breathe again. ''I doubt there is another bottle in England!''

''Quite likely,'' his sister agreed as she poured more tea. ''I am depending upon Ellen to make a fabulous alliance.'' She set down the cup and fixed her brother with the stare that had made him writhe when they were growing up. ''*When* she is good and ready, Charles. Then I will open the Palais Royal.''

Thinking back on that artless disclosure, Ellen laughed softly to herself. Mama declares that since I scared off the vicar, the best I can hope for is Thomas Cornwell. Horatia claims that she can find me someone among her darling Edwin's circle of rattlebrained acquaintances. She shook her head. None of these paragons would be worth Palais Royal. I suppose I must make the exertion on my own.

Aunt Shreve joined her in the village and they continued east across rolling fields shorn of sheep that dotted the landscape in other seasons. The trees had all molted their leaves in great piles, leaving skeletal branches that bore no promise of spring in the near future. ''Bare ruined choirs, where late the sweet birds sang,'' she thought, her mind upon Ralph and his everlasting Shakespeare.

''Perhaps I should study Shakespeare, in honor of Ralph,'' she said out loud. She dug in her reticule for the letter from Miss Dignam and held it out to her aunt. ''See here, Aunt, they have me down for nothing more strenuous than French and embroidery. I believe that I will request geography and Shakespeare, at least. I am not afraid of scholarship.''

Aunt Shreve put on her spectacles and read the letter. She leaned back, the look on her face telling Ellen that she was choosing her words with care.

''My dear, I hope you will not be too disappointed if Miss Dignam's falls short of your expectations,'' she began. ''I have never been there, but I do not know that study for women is serious anywhere.''

Ellen waved her hand and reclaimed the letter. ''Oh, that is all right, Aunt. If they only teach the tragedies of Shakespeare and not the more ribald comedies, I can be forgiving!''

The sun broke through the weight of autumn clouds by late afternoon and their entrance into Oxford. The post chaise had slowed to the movement of farm carts that trundled toward the ford of the Thames called, in true scholar's eccentricity, the Isis, while it wound around the university town.

"It is only when I travel this road behind loads of potatoes, onions, and pigs that I wonder why anyone saw fit to establish a university in this place," Aunt Shreve grumbled. "If this is the center of the universe, then I am Marie Antoinette, head and all!"

Aunt Shreve was poised to say more in the same vein as they inched along, but the look on her niece's face stopped her complaints. She tapped on the glass, and rolled it down as the post chaise stopped.

"Mind that you pause and pull off when you reach the top of this hill, Coachman," she ordered.

They continued in silence broken only by the squawk of geese in the cart ahead. In a few minutes, the carriage pulled out of the line of traffic and stopped.

"Get out the stretch yourself," Aunt Shreve suggested. "And do go to the top of that rise."

"You needn't let me slow you down," Ellen protested. "Surely the view can wait."

"No, it cannot," Aunt Shreve insisted. She motioned to the carriage door, where the post boy stood to open it.

Ellen stepped out, grateful—even though she had objected— for the chance to walk about for a moment. She walked to the top of the gently sloping rise, looked toward the east, and loved her aunt all the more.

The sun was going down over Oxford, throwing streams of molten fire upon honey-colored walls and spires. Ellen held her breath at the sight and then let it out slowly. There was Great Tom, and the spires of Magdalen, grace notes to the elegant architectural humor of the Radcliffe Camera and behind it, the Bodleian Library. The river flowed under bridges as inspired as the buildings that lined it on both sides.

From her elevation, Ellen gazed, hand to eyes, into college quadrangles where the grass was still green, protected by the

warmth of centuries-old stone. She clapped her hands in delight.
Oxford was a city the color of honey, and a veritable honey-
comb itself of colleges, quadrangles, and churches.

The sky turned lavender as she watched, and then a more
somber purple. We will have rain tonight, she thought, but it
will be special rain because it falls upon Oxford.

"Excuse me, Miss, if I appear forward, but are you in some
trouble with your post chaise?"

Ellen whirled around. Papers in hand, a man sat upon a rock
near the crest of the hill where she stood. She had not noticed
him in his black student's robe because he blended in so well
with the shadows that were lengthening across the copse.

"Oh, no, sir. We are fine," she said, putting her hands behind
her back as though she had been caught pilfering a candy jar.
"My aunt merely wanted me to have a look at the city before
we drove in."

The man got to his feet. He was taller even than the tallest
Grimsley. His hair was ordinary brown and untidy, and the wind
was picking it up and tousling it further. Ellen felt the need to
put her hand to her bonnet.

The breeze caught the student's gown and it billowed about
him, making him appear larger yet. The wind tugged at the
papers in his hand. As she watched, he tore them up and held
them in both palms to the wind like an offering. The scraps
swirled up and out of sight.

"Good riddance," he said and came closer.

He had an elegant face, at odds with the untidiness of his hair,
with high cheekbones, a straight nose and eyes as dark as his
gown. She noticed that his ears lay nicely flat against his head,
and she smiled as she thought of Thomas Cornwell.

"I amuse you?" he asked, giving her a little nod that passed
for a bow.

"No, it is someone else. You have excellent ears, sir," she
said, and then put her hand to her mouth. "I mean, I was
thinking of someone who is not so blessed. Oh, dear, that was
a strange thing to say!"

He laughed and tossed away the remaining scraps of paper
that still rested in his palm. He gave her a real bow, and he
was more graceful than she would have thought, considering

his height. Suddenly she felt out of place and much younger than eighteen.

"Do you come up here to commune with nature, sir?" she asked.

He shook his head. "I come here to walk off my letters from home."

She thought of her own home, and found this reasonable. "I expect I would like to do the same thing," she said. "Do your parents smother you, too, and worry and prose on and on?"

He gave a shout of laughter, grabbed her hand and kissed it, bowing again. "Are you a Sybil, or perhaps a Cassandra, to divine this? I would not have thought there were other parents in all of England like my mother, but perhaps I was wrong. James Gatewood at your service, miss."

She smiled and withdrew her hand from his. "I am Ellen Grimsley, sir."

"Ellen?" he asked. "Prosaic name, but lovely."

"I do not mind that it is ordinary," she replied, twinkling her eyes at him for no reason that she could discern. "It could have been much worse." She hesitated, looking at the student. Something about his open countenance seemed to invite confidence. "It could have been Zephyr."

"Zephyr?" he asked in amusement. "Oh, surely not!"

"Zephyr indeed. It happens that a horse named Zephyr won at Newmarket the day I was born. My papa is horse mad, sir," she sighed, and then grinned as he laughed. "But Mama, who seldom prevails, prevailed from her bed of confinement, for which I am grateful."

He nodded in perfect understanding. "As it is, I suppose now you have brothers who tease you and call you Nellie, but that must be preferable to Zeph."

"Indeed, it must be," she agreed. She looked around at the carriage and made a motion to leave.

He grabbed up his books by the rock, falling in step with her as she retraced her way to the carriage below. She glanced at his books, noting North's *Treatise on Government,* and a copy of Paine's *The Crisis.*

He followed her glance. "I should be studying, but it looked . like a fine afternoon."

"And you are 'a summer soldier and a sunshine patriot,'" when the weather is mellow?" she teased.

He raised one eyebrow. "You are a spy, sent by my don," he teased in turn, "come to find out why Lord . . . in the Lord's name I am not buried in scholarship."

She shook her head. "I am no spy, and that's all I know of Thomas Paine," she confessed. "I found the pamphlet at a church rumble sale, but Mama snatched it away and told me it was wicked."

"And well she did, Miss Grimsley," he said with a smile. "You might have attempted a nursery room revolt. But wicked? No."

"You're teasing me," she observed. "Sir, I do not joke about books."

"*Touché.* Nor do I, Miss Grimsley," he replied. "Perhaps I can loan you my copy. Are you staying in town?"

She nodded. "I will be matriculating at Miss Digman's Select Female Academy."

"I never heard the word matriculation used in the same breath as Miss Dignam's," he said. "I had thought the most strenuous course there to be French knots."

"I am sure it is not so," she said quickly. "I have great plans." She was silent a moment. "I have greater plans than my brother, and he is a student here . . . under duress."

"That happens to some," he replied. "And what is this scholar's name?"

"It is Gordon, and he is in his first year at University College," she replied. "He does not know how lucky he is."

"They seldom do," Gatewood murmured. He was silent then as they continued down the hill together.

As they came closer to the carriage, Ellen stopped in confusion. "Excuse me, sir, for being so forward. I really shouldn't be talking with strangers."

"Neither should I," he said, and twinkled his eyes at her. "But as I did not think you would do me any harm, I chanced it. Good day, Miss Ellen Grimsley. I trust you will find Oxford to your liking."

She nodded and smiled up at him. "I am sure that I shall."

He continued toward the main road. Ellen looked at the post chaise and called to him.

He turned, a look of interest in his lively eyes.

"My Aunt Shreve was teasing me a moment ago, but tell me, sir, is Oxford really the center of the universe?"

He came back to stand beside her. She noted the shabbiness of his coat under the student gown and his collar frayed around the edges. He did not appear to have shaved that morning, and his eyes were tired. He was silent a moment, considering her question, and then the good cheer reappeared. He shifted his books to his other arm and touched her arm lightly.

"I will give you an Oxford answer, Miss Grimsley," he said. "The answer to that question depends entirely upon where you are standing."

"Well, then, sir, where are you standing now?" she persisted. "I really must know."

He looked down at her, his expression hard to read. "I would say that from where I am standing right now, yes, and yes again, Miss Grimsley. Good day."

And then he was gone, taking long strides down the hill toward the town. She thought he whistled as he hurried along.

Ellen watched him for a moment, and then returned to the carriage. "I just met the strangest man," she said to her aunt, who had been admiring the view from the other window. "A student, I think."

Aunt Shreve turned and followed Ellen's gaze. "That fellow over there? He certainly has a broad set of shoulders to recommend him."

"Aunt!"

"I may be a widow twenty years and my children grown, my dear, but I can admire," Aunt Shreve replied. "Come, come, Ellen. You have had your look at Oxford. What do you think?"

"His ears are flat."

Aunt Shreve stared at her in consternation and then burst into laughters. "My dear, I do not open bottles of Palais Royal for flat ears!"

"I am only teasing, Aunt," Ellen replied. "I think Oxford is splendid. I also think that words do not describe it." She leaned forward and touched her aunt on the knee. "Thank you, Aunt Shreve. Even if Papa only allows me to stay here until Horry's wedding, it will be enough."

As they drove across the bridge, the clouds settled lower, resting on the highest spires as the honey-colored buildings turned gray again. When the cold rain began, Ellen wondered if the tall student had reached his chambers in time. Then she put him from her mind as the magnificence of Oxford surrounded her.

Gorden Grimsley, black-gowned and even handsomer than she remembered, paced in front of the fireplace in Miss Dignam's sitting room. Ellen shook the rain from her cloak and only had time to lay it aside before her brother grabbed her in a bear hug and kissed her soundly on both cheeks.

He had an appreciative audience. As he whirled her around and she shrieked in protest, Ellen made the observation that Gordon Grimsley rarely did anything without an audience.

The sitting room was occupied by young ladies who had all suspended whatever activity they were engaged in to watch— cards clutched tight in nerveless fingers; stitches dropped; pages unturned; words arrested in midsentence. As she stood in the circle of his arms, Ellen Grimsley noted that her brother had lost none of his effect on females, even the select females of Miss Dignam's Academy.

"Gordon, really," she whispered. "You've never been so glad to see me before!"

He winked at her and nodded to a dry husk of a woman bearing down on them from the other side of the room. He spoke out of the side of his mouth. "I do not think she will suffer me much longer in her sitting room."

"And no wonder," Ellen whispered back. "Gordon, you are incorrigible."

"Yes, thank the Lord," he agreed. He turned then and bowed to the lady approaching. The bow was so elegant that several of the young ladies sighed. Ellen put her hand to her mouth to smother her laughter. Trust Gordon to put his best foot forward.

"Ellen," he was saying, "it gives me great pleasure to introduce to you Miss Dignam, your headmistress. Miss Dignam, this is my little sister, Ellen."

Ellen grasped the woman's cool, dry hand, opened her mouth to speak, and then closed it when the woman only touched her hand and then hurried past her to embrace Aunt Shreve.

"Eugenia, how long has it been?" she exclaimed, lips stretched tight over protruding teeth in what must be a smile.

The students in the room continued to gape. Gordon looked at them in amusement. "Perhaps they never knew a dragon to have friends," he whispered to his sister.

While they watched the reunion, Gordon took his sister by the arm. "I have spoken a meal for the three of us at The Mitre." He grinned. "Providing you can fork over the blunt."

"Gordon, it is only just past the quarter. Are your pockets to let already?"

"Always," he agreed cheerfully. "I was hoping you would be bringing some reinforcements from home." He looked around to make sure that his aunt could not hear him. "I am planning to toddle over to London this weekend with a new friend of mine."

"Gordon, that is a long way to go. What about your studies?"

He shrugged and flashed that lopsided grin of his that only made her more wary. "I'll get by."

There wasn't time for a reply. In another moment, Aunt Shreve, her arm about Miss Dignam, had returned to her side. "Come, my dears," she announced, "Miss Dignam has given us leave to go to—The Mitre, is it, Gordon? I promised to have you back here by nine o'clock, and indeed, Gordon has his own curfew."

Again that careless shrug. Ellen frowned, dreading the uneasiness that was already stirring her stomach around.

"I am entirely at your service, ladies," Gordon said as he made a final bow, to the accompaniment of an entire row of sighs from the students grouped on the sofa.

"Gordon, you are utterly shameless!" Ellen scolded as they bundled up against the drizzle and hurried along the street to Cornmarket. "I think you are a dreadful flirt."

"I must second the notion," Aunt Shreve agreed as they entered the inn and surrendered their cloaks to the serving girl. She smiled at her handsome nephew. "And I also must acknowledge that you received an unfair amount of the Grimsley charm." She took him by the arm as they walked into a private parlor. "I would advise you not to waste it on your aunt and sister. We know you too well."

The first course was ready as soon as they were seated. They ate in hungry silence and then Gordon pushed back his plate. "Sister, I could not believe my own eyes when I received that letter from Mama, telling me that you would be attending Miss Dignam's Academy. Have you let your brains leak out? If Papa offered me anything I wanted for two bottles of sherry, this place would be low on my list."

He smiled at the waiter, who set the next course in front of him. "I can't imagine anyone comes up to Oxford without vast coercion, El."

"You're a dunce, Gordon," she said, without missing a bite.

He slammed down his fork. "Don't keep me in suspense, sister! Did or did not Papa say something to you about my joining that cavalry regiment?"

Ellen stared at her brother. "He did no such thing, Gordon, and you know it. I remember well the terms of the agreement he forged with you when you came up here only one month ago. You are to acquit yourself at Oxford for a year, through all the terms, and then he would think about it."

Gordon picked up the fork again and dragged it around the food on his plate. "Think about it!" he burst out. "While he's thinking about it, the war will end in Spain and I will have missed all the fun!"

"It cannot be otherwise," Ellen replied. "Now tell me what you have learned thus far at your college."

He gave her a blank stare and continued picking over his food, his lips tight together and the frown line between his eyes deeply pronounced.

Aunt Shreve picked up the ball of conversation. "My dears, whenever I see you two together, I am struck by your resemblance to one another."

Ellen smiled at her aunt and took a closer look at her elder brother. They had the same fair hair and blue eyes, but to her mind, there the resemblance stopped. She observed her brother in profile, admiring the regularity of his features, and wondering why they were so different in temperament, inclination and goal. I would give the world to walk these halls and quads, and Gordon cannot wait to leave it.

Her own pleasure in the meal dissolved. She ate what was put before her, and wished herself elsewhere. Gordon, when he recovered from his sulks, kept up a witty conversation with Aunt Shreve that earned him a kiss on the cheek as he escorted them back to the school, and a handful of guineas.

"Your mother thought you might be in need," Aunt Shreve said. "She says that is all you will have until the quarter, so practice economy, my dear."

Gordon grinned and kissed them goodnight. The bell in Magdalen Tower tolled, and then another and another. "I'll be in touch, Ellen," he said as his lips brushed her cheek.

Aunt Shreve watched him go. "I worry for him," was all she said as they opened the door and were greeted by Miss Dignam.

"I will show you to your room," she said, handing Ellen a candlestick.

"One moment, Miss Dignam, if you please," Ellen said. She set down the candle and reached in her reticule for the letter. "Miss Dignam, if you please, could I change these classes in embroidery and French for geography, and perhaps geometry? I would like that, and I know that I can keep up."

Miss Dignam blinked. "We do not offer such things here! We find that a little Italian and a little French, and watercolors or embroidery are enough. Geometry? Goodness, child, these subjects are not for females."

"Do you mean I cannot study them here?"

"Precisely." Miss Dignam permitted herself a smile. "If you continue with us next year, the older students study the improving poetry of John Donne. But only with their parents' approval," she emphasized, "and only if it does not excite them."

"I had no idea," Aunt Shreve said in a faint voice.

"Oh, yes, my dear Eugenia. We follow the same pattern with the modern composers such as Beethoven." Miss Dignam gestured toward the stairs. "Come, my dear, you will have a strenuous day tomorrow. We have been studying the different shades of blue and green in watercolors, and you must attempt to catch up with us. I recommend that you retire."

Ellen kissed her aunt goodnight and quietly climbed the stairs behind the headmistress. Miss Dignam opened a door and peered in.

"You are sharing chambers with Fanny Bland," she whispered. "She is an unexceptional girl, and all that is proper. I believe you are already acquainted?"

Fanny made no sound. Ellen said goodnight to Miss Dignam, undressed in the dark, and crept into bed. The sheets were cold and stiff, as if Miss Dignam had added starch to the rinse water. Ellen huddled into a ball and ducked her head under the covers as the tears began to fall.

When she finished crying, she blew her nose quietly and tucked her hand under her cheek. "Things always look better in the morning," she said, her voice soft.

As she drifted toward sleep, she thought again of the student on the hill. She had already forgotten his name, but she could not forget the independent way he strode down the hill. You look so free, she said to herself as she watched the shadows cross the window and the moon change.

I want to be free, too.

Ellen was almost asleep when she heard the sound of pebbles hitting against the window. She did not move, imagining that the sound came from some other part of the hall. She closed her eyes.

The sound continued, little scourings of sound against the window. After debating with herself another moment, she rose silently from her bed and tiptoed to the window. She opened it and leaned out.

Gordon stood below, his hands cupped around his mouth.

"I thought you were deaf, my dear."

Ellen leaned her elbows on the windowsill. "What on earth do you want, Gordon? Don't you have a curfew?"

He laughed softly. "I can climb the wall, silly! We're leaving for London in the morning. Loan me ten pounds. I know Mama must have sent you some money. Be a sweet thing, Ellen."

She leaned farther out. "I dare not!" she called down to him.

"I'll win it back at faro," he assured, his voice sharpening with that impatient edge to it that reminded her of Papa. "Don't be so missish, El."

"Oh, very well," she grumbled as she groped about on the dressing table. She counted out some coins and tossed them down to her brother one story below. He caught the money expertly and pocketed it. He bowed elaborately and walked backward down the deserted street, facing her.

"I'll win it back, and with interest, El. Don't you worry about a thing."

Ellen stayed at the window until he was gone. She turned to her bed. The girl in the other bed was sitting up, watching her.

"Why, hello, Fanny," Ellen said, smiling. "I'm sorry I woke you."

Fanny rested herself on one elbow. She squinted into the gloom and then smiled, showing all her teeth. "I'm telling Miss Dignam in the morning."

3

Thanks to Gordon's late-night entreaty and Fanny Bland's spite, Ellen spent her first morning at Miss Dignam's Select Female Academy sitting on a hard chair writing, "I will practice decorum as a virtue whilst I reside in Oxford," one hundred times.

No matter that she had pleaded with Miss Dignam that Gordon was her brother and in need of assistance. Miss Dignam only pursed her lips in a thin line. "We have a front door," she said, and held up her hand when Ellen opened her mouth. "And he can plan ahead next time before curfew!"

When Ellen tried to speak again, Miss Dignam forgot herself so far as to put her hands on her hips and exclaim, "Miss Grimsley, are you always so difficult?"

Ellen closed her mouth and glanced at Fanny Bland, who had pounced on her as soon as Aunt Shreve had said her farewells with hugs and kisses. Fanny was smiling.

Ellen raised her chin higher. "I have been told I am rather more trouble," she said in her clear voice. "You can ask anyone in the district. I am certain Fanny would be happy to furnish you with names and directions. She takes such an interest in me."

The smile left Fanny's face.

Miss Dignam chose not to pursue the conversation. "Fanny, please conduct Miss Grimsley to an empty classroom, where she can pursue her morning's labors," she said.

Ellen waited until Miss Dignam had closed her office door behind them. "Fanny Bland, you are a fine friend!" she declared. "And to think I was looking forward to being your rooming companion."

Fanny sniffed. "I don't know why you ever entertained that notion. You might have fooled me, except that Edwin wrote to warn me that you were a coming little snip who thought nothing of correcting people like our good vicar."

With a sinking feeling, Ellen remembered that Vicar Snead was a distant cousin to the Blands. "Lead on, Fanny," she said, eyes ahead. "I will take my punishment."

Fanny blinked in surprise at Ellen's unexpected capitulation, but led her into the empty classroom. She supplied her with pen and ink and moved to the door. Ellen stopped her.

"Tell me, Fanny, what is the capital of the United States?"

Fanny fiddled with the doorknob, a look of intense concentration troubling her face for a small moment. "I do believe it is Philadelphia," she replied. "Yes, I am certain of it."

Ellen only sighed and turned to the blank page before her. "I am sure you are right," she murmured.

She finished writing her sentences before noon and was composing a letter home, begging someone to come and get her, when Miss Dignam swept into the room. She held out her hand for the sheaf of papers and checked them, her eyes growing wider and wider as she scanned the closely written sheets. She jabbed the offending papers with her fingers and thrust them under Ellen's nose.

"My dear Miss Grimsley, I do not know why I ever allowed your dear aunt to enroll you here!"

Mystified, Ellen took the sheets and stared at them, her cheeks growing rosy. From number fifty on, when her mind began to grow numb, she had written, "I will practice boredom as a virtue whilst I reside in Oxford."

Without a word, she accepted another sheet of paper and bent her head over her labors once more. Miss Dignam watched in silence for a moment. "And while you are at it, compose an essay on the folly of disobedience," she said before she made her majestic progress from the room.

The dinner hour came and went. As her stomach rumbled, Ellen breathed in the fragrance of beef roast and gravy, boiled mutton and the sharper odor of mint sauce. Never mind that she had always regarded boiled mutton as penance; she could have eaten a plateful and held out her dish for more.

But no one else came to rescue her from her sentences. "Ellen Grimsley has been sentenced to starvation," she said out loud, and giggled, despite her misery.

There was a tap at the door, scarcely audible, and Ellen stifled her laughter, fearful that too much enjoyment during punishment would lead to more sentences, and perhaps a thesis on the folly of mirth.

"Yes?" she asked.

A maid stuck her head in the doorway. She looked around, and seeing no one else in the room, whisked herself inside and closed the door behind her quickly. She held out a small package, done up in white paper and tied with a silver bow.

"For you, miss, at least, if you are Miss Grimsley," said the maid, when Ellen made no move to take the gift.

"I am Miss Grimsley, but tell me, who is this from?"

The maid looked about her again and came closer. "He was a tall gentleman, a student I am sure, but older than some. He came to call, but Miss Dignam had left word with the footman that you were in the middle of an 'improving punishment.' " The maid leaned closer, cupping her mouth with her hand, in the event that the walls had ears. "At least, that is what she always calls it. I don't know that it ever improved anyone."

"Did he leave his name?" Ellen asked, thinking of Gordon. "Was he tall and blond, and rather fine to look at?"

The maid shook his head. "No, miss, not a bit of it." She perched herself on a desk. "But that's only the half of it. I shoved him out, and then who do I see poking about the kitchen door a half hour later but the same gentleman!"

"And?" Ellen prompted.

"And he handed me this package and told me to sneak it to you, and mind that I was not to let the dragon see it."

Ellen slid the ribbon off the package and opened it. Inside was a box of chocolates. "Wagoner's Chocolates," she read, and looked at the maid. "Tell me, is that a local emporium?"

The maid nodded. "It's the best candy shop in Oxford."

Ellen opened the box, inhaling the comforting odor. With inkstained fingers, she picked up the small card.

" 'Courage. Jim,' " she read out loud. She turned the card over. Nothing more.

"How singular," she said, as she popped a chocolate into her mouth. She held out the box to the maid, who protested at first and then took a piece. They sat in companionable silence in the room that had somehow become less depressing.

Ellen sighed. "I am sure it is a mistake, but oh, how pleasant," she said as she selected another piece. "I love nougat centers." She wiped her fingers on the wrapping paper. "I suppose we should not eat any more. I am sure these are intended for one of the other students. If we do not stop soon, that will mean another hundred sentences." She laughed out loud. "I will remember that gluttony is a deadly sin whilst I reside at Oxford."

The maid giggled and shook her head when Ellen offered her another candy. "It's no mistake, miss," she said, accepting a second piece when Ellen continued to hold out the box to her. "He said it was for Ellen Grimsley."

Ellen shrugged. "How many Ellen Grimsleys can there be in Oxford?"

Then she remembered the tall gentleman on the hill yesterday afternoon. "Tall, and with brown hair and . . . and . . ." she said, trying to think of how to describe that look of interest in his eyes.

"Wondrous broad shoulders," the maid continued, and then blushed. "At least, that's what I noticed."

"You and my aunt! James . . . James Gatewood," Ellen said, her mind full again of the student with the easy air about him. "I don't suppose you ever wrote sentences, James Gatewood," she said under her breath.

"Beg pardon, miss?" the maid asked, her hand poised over the open box again.

"Oh, nothing, nothing, although I do not think he should waste the ready on such expensive chocolates. Do have another. I intend to. What is your name?"

"Becky, miss. Becky Speed."

"Well, Becky Speed, thank you for rescuing me from starvation. Let us each take one more, and then hide this box behind that row of books. I would hate for Miss Dignam or the odious Fanny Bland to suspect we had enjoyed a pleasant moment."

When Miss Dignam entered the room ten minutes later, Becky Speed was gone, the chocolate was hidden, and Ellen was finishing the last sentence of her essay with a flourish.

Miss Dignam sniffed the air. "I smell chocolate," she accused.

Ellen looked up from her work. "I cannot imagine," she

exclaimed with an air of wide-eyed innocence that would never have fooled Gordon, but seemed to suffice for Miss Dignam.

The headmistress accepted the essay and additional sentences and then arranged her lips in some semblance of a smile. "Very well, Miss Grimsley. Virtue is as virtue does. Come along with me now. It is time for embroidery."

An hour later, Ellen looked up from a tangle of embroidery threads, filled with the desire to return to the sentences and the hidden box of chocolates. Miss Dignam had introduced her to a roomful of Fanny Blands, students who, from the whispers behind their hands and the looks they gave each other, had already been introduced to Ellen by Miss Bland herself.

Ellen dug her toes into the carpet during Miss Dignam's introduction, accepted the basket of tangled threads with the admonition to make order out of chaos, and scurried to the remotest corner of the room.

The whispers reached her then and her ears burned, even as her heart ached. "She thought to study Shakespeare and geometry. Imagine that!" "A petty squire's daughter with no more breeding than to lean out her bedroom window and toss money down to someone she claims is her brother." "Dreadfully fast." "Frightfully wild."

The tangle of threads blurred as she worked on them. In another moment, they disappeared altogether. She folded her hands in her lap, bowed over the threads and cried.

The others in the room were silent then. When they began to speak again, it was to each other, as though they had effectively shouldered her aside and cut her off from all further notice. She might not have been in the room.

The afternoon dragged on. Doggedly, Ellen kept her head bent over her work, unraveling twisted strands and wishing herself elsewhere, anywhere. She longed for a seat by the window, where at least she could look out occasionally. As it was, she saw nothing except the backs of the other girls, and heard nothing except the impartial tolling of Oxford's bells. The clamor thrilled her to the bone, even as it mocked her and reminded her that she had no part of it.

After a cheerless dinner of boiled mutton and potatoes, she longed for Gordon to return. She sat in the parlor with the others, her head down, her eyes politely neutral.

Gordon had never been her favorite brother, although they were so close in age. He had teased her, bullied her, and tormented her throughout their shared childhood. But sitting there in misery in Miss Dignam's parlor, she would have given the earth for a glimpse of him.

When the clock struck seven times and still he had not made his appearance, Ellen remembered that he had taken himself off to London. *Where you will likely get into huge trouble,* she thought, *and cause Papa such misery that you will get no closer to the fighting in Spain than the pier at Brighton.*

Gordon, why are you not more prudent, she thought, as she shifted in her chair, careful not to draw attention to herself, but weary beyond words with sitting.

Visitors arrived and were admitted to the sitting room. Some of them were parents, and others were young men from the different colleges. Parents chatted amiably enough with their offspring, but the young men writhed and squirmed under the cold eye of Miss Dignam, who sat in one corner and played solitaire.

Ellen observed the couples with some compassion, despite her own misery. While she did not exactly wish herself back in the company of Thomas Cornwell and his big ears and stupifying conversation, she wished that someone would come for her.

After another hour of quiet observation, she was grateful that no one had chosen to visit her. With increasing amusement, she watched how Miss Dignam slapped her cards down and cleared her throat whenever any young man went so far as even to gaze overlong into the eyes of one of her select females.

It would take a man of supreme courage to carry on a court-ship under such daunting circumstances, Ellen decided as the evening drew to its weary conclusion. *I wonder that anyone attempts it,* she thought. *The desire to perpetuate the human species is stronger than I imagined.*

For one tiny moment, she wished that James Gatewood would announce himself to the butler and drop in long enough for her to thank him for the chocolates. When he did not, she realized that his kindness had been an impulsive whim, now forgotten. *And I had better forget it,* she thought.

At last the final guest left. Miss Dignam nodded to Becky

Speed, who bolted the front door and took the Bible from the bookcase. Miss Dignam accepted the Bible, and then peered slowly around the room until her eyes lighted on Ellen, sitting in the corner and trying to make herself small. The headmistress thumbed through the pages, stopped at Ecclesiastes and cleared her throat.

While the other girls knotted fringes, crocheted, or embroidered, Miss Dignam read chapter one, slowing down on the last two verses: " 'And I gave my heart to know wisdom, and to know madness and folly. I perceived also that this is vexation of spirit. For in much wisdom is much grief: and he that increaseth knowledge increases folly.' "

Miss Dignam closed the book. Ellen looked up at the sudden sound in the quiet room to see Miss Dignam's eyes boring into her.

"And that, my dear Miss Grimsley, is how the preacher disposes of wisdom. It brings only sorrow and grief. I am certain that we can all echo the sentiments of Ecclesiastes."

She looked around the room as the girls nodded. Her eyes fell again on Ellen. "And you, my dear?" she asked.

Ellen considered the question. She thought about the dreadful day she had endured, relieved only by the kindness of a servant and a box of chocolates. She thought of Gordon, likely making a cake of himself in London and ignoring the riches that were here at Oxford. She took a deep breath and threw herself into the breech once more.

"I am equally certain, in this instance, that Ecclesiastes could not be farther from the truth, Miss Dignam," she replied, quietly, her hands tight together in her lap.

Miss Dignam gasped and gathered the Bible closer to her, as though Ellen would spring from her chair, snatch it from her, and trample the Holy Writ underfoot.

"And now you will criticize the Bible?" she said as the other students looked at each other with varying expressions of amusement and horror.

Ellen, her face pale, stood up. "No, I do not argue with the Bible!" she declared, her voice low and intense. "I merely put forward the suggestion that in the many years and years of its translation that possibly, just possibly, there might be an error in the text? Surely God does not wish us to glory in ignorance.''

She looked around her and slowly sat down, numbed by the blank expressions of the select females of Miss Dignam's academy. Don't you ever have a thought that is original? she wanted to ask, but did not.

Instead, Ellen rose again and went to the door, her back straight. She paused in front of Miss Dignam, who still clutched her Bible. ''I suppose this will mean more sentences,'' Ellen said, her eyes straight ahead.

''Two hundred more,'' snapped Miss Dignam, ''plus an essay on 'Why I Have Decided to Follow the Teaching in Ecclesiates.' ''

As she went slowly and quietly up the stairs, candle in hand, Ellen smiled as she reflected that with her sentences and essay, she was possibly getting a better education than the girls who untangled yarn and fretted over watercolors.

She looked back down the stairs where the other girls stood, whispering to each other. ''I shall think upon this assignment and create a truly masterful essay,'' she said quietly.

Fanny Bland treated her to prickly silence as they both prepared for bed. Ellen sighed, said her prayers in mutinous fashion, and leaped between chilly sheets, pulling the blankets up tight around her chin.

Fanny remained where she was beside her bed for another pious five minutes while Ellen lay with her hands behind her head, staring at the ceiling. She was drifting off to sleep when Fanny finally crawled into her own bed, muttering something about those who don't take much time for God.

Ellen only gritted her teeth and resisted the urge to declare that she kept her prayers economical so the Lord God Almighty could spend His valuable time helping the troops in Spain or guarding sailors on the high seas. She lay quiet, her eyes shut tight, composing another letter home in her mind, pleading with them to rescue her from her own folly. In a moment, she slept.

The tedium of that weekend was unparalleled in Ellen's memory. Her hopes of at least a walk beyond the front door of the academy were dashed by Miss Dignam's upraised eyebrows and the assignment of one hundred more sentences, on top of the two hundred, at her suggestion of a stroll down the High Street. " 'I will remember to conduct myself with decorum at all times,' " Miss Dignam had pronounced, and left her to the empty classroom and the chocolates.

The other young ladies were permitted a repairing lease around the extensive gardens behind the academy. Her head bent over the paper, Ellen smiled with unholy delight at the sudden rumble of thunder, followed by the drumming of rain and the shrieks of the select females assembled outdoors to walk about. She popped another chocolate in her mouth, raised her pen high in salute to the soggy students, and labored on, finishing each sentence with a flourish that bordered on insolence.

Becky Speed joined her, scooting into the room and closing the door quietly almost before Ellen realized that she was not alone. She smiled and held out the chocolate box. Becky accepted with a curtsy and sat on the desk, her legs swinging, as she nibbled around the nougat center until the chocolate was gone.

"I wish that I could write," she said at last, shaking her head over the last chocolate in the box and then changing her mind when Ellen insisted.

Ellen tucked the empty box behind the bookcase again. "It would be an easy matter to teach you," she said.

Becky shook her head and got down off the desk. "Miss Dignam says I don't have any need to learn how. She says it would put me above my station."

Ellen eyed her thoughtfully. "I suppose it would, but where would be the harm in that?" She perched herself on the teacher's desk. "Perhaps you could become a bookkeeper's assistant, or run your own shop. A candy shop."

The girls giggled together.

"I would like that," Becky said. "I could help my mum provide for us."

Ellen took out the remaining sheet of paper. "Then sit yourself down, Miss Speed," she said, raising her eyebrows in an imitation of Miss Dignam that made Becky smile. "You could become rich at the Female Academy, writing sentences for the wicked!"

They were part way through the alphabet when Ellen heard

Miss Dignam's measured tread in the hallway. Becky leaped to her feet and began to ply the feather duster around the bookcase with such vigor that she sneezed. Ellen grabbed up the pages of the letters and words A through K, sat upon them, and continued with her sentences.

Miss Dignam opened the door slowly. She did not hurl it open as she had the day before, intent upon surprising Ellen at some misdeed. The expression on her face as she peered over Ellen's shoulder, while grim, had not yesterday's suspicion. Ellen held her breath, too afraid to look at Becky, who continued to dust with all the energy of a troop movement.

Miss Dignam cleared her throat and Ellen looked up, biting her lip to keep from exclaiming. Miss Dignam was smiling. She handed Ellen the essay on Ecclesiastes that had been part of yesterday's punishment.

"Well written, Miss Grimsley, well written, indeed," she said, "even if I do not precisely agree with your argument."

"Why thank you," Ellen stammered, taking the paper in trembling fingers, amazed at Miss Dignam's sudden about-face.

"I have marked a few places where it might be improved upon," Miss Dignam continued, "but it was an excellent piece of expository writing. You are to be commended."

Ellen could only stare as Miss Dignam took a seat beside her. "I believe we can continue to expect writing of a similar quality from you, Miss Grimsley." She paused, as if composing herself for an apology. Ellen waited, holding her breath.

The apology did not come, but Miss Dignam continued in a voice that was almost human. "My dear, I had no idea of your family's connections here at Oxford," she said at last, and paused, obviously waiting for some comment from Ellen.

Ellen racked her brain for an Oxford connection other than Gordon, who, if suspicion served her right, was setting no records at University College.

But Miss Dignam expected some response. Ellen swallowed the lump in her throat, hoped fervently that no stray chocolate still clung to her teeth, and smiled. "Yes, Miss Dignam, our ties here are exemplary," she said, crossing her fingers behind her back, totally at sea.

Miss Dignam only nodded and smiled back. "I have never

before had the honor of admitting Lord Chesney to my sitting room, but there he was this morning, for a quarter hour and more, telling me about your abilities! I could only agree with him, of course," she said, and reached out a bony hand to pat Ellen's knee. "Naughty girl! You should have told me of such an illustrious connection!"

Ellen continued to smile, even as she searched her brain. Lord Chesney? Surely she has me confused with someone else, was her first thought. No one in our entire family knows a lord, she thought. The only titled gentleman of her acquaintance was Fanny Bland's insufferable father, and he was only a paltry baronet.

Her own confusion was amply covered by Miss Dignam.

"Goodness, child, Lord Chesney is one of All Souls' most distinguished Fellows! Surely you are aware of that?"

"Well, no, ma'am," Ellen said honestly. "Lord . . . er . . . Chesney is a modest man. I have never once heard him to sound his own horn," she finished. That, at least, was honest enough.

"How true that is," Miss Dignam agreed. "He is the epitome of good breeding and all that is correct."

In the small silence that followed, Ellen ventured a question. "Tell me, did he explain yesterday the nature of his visit?" she asked, hoping that any information Miss Dignam would drop would give her a clue.

"He said that he was interested in your progress, and hoped that I would have good reports to make of you."

"How . . . kind," Ellen said faintly. "Of course, Lord Chesney has always been kind. He is probably one of the kindest gentlemen of my acquaintance," she offered, fervently praying that a just God would not strike her dead on the spot.

Miss Dignam managed another indulgent laugh and rose. She shook her finger at Ellen, but there was no malice in the gesture. "Naughty girl!" she said again. "We will see that you are not a disappointment to his lordship."

"Yes, certainly. Of course," Ellen said, hoping for a quick and merciful end to this strange interview.

Miss Dignam gestured toward the papers on the desk. "When you have finished those silly little sentences, bring them to me, and we will discuss your future plans here at the academy. Lord

Chesney assures me that he is deeply interested in your progress.''

Miss Dignam overlooked Ellen's open-mouthed amazement and left the room in all her majesty, closing the door quietly behind her.

Ellen stared at Becky, who stopped dusting and hurried to her side. ''I get the feeling that you have no idea who Lord Chesney is,'' she said, as Ellen continued to stare at the closed door.

''You are right enough,'' Ellen said finally. She frowned and drummed her fingernails on the desk. ''Although I have my suspicions. I think it is my brother Gordon, up to some trick.''

''But hasn't Miss Dignam seen Gordon?'' Becky asked.

''Then it must be a fellow student he has coerced into this little prank,'' Ellen said. ''Gordon, when I see you . . .''

She took her time over the sentences, in no hurry to see Miss Dignam again so soon. Lord Chesney? Father had never mentioned such a personage. Papa's cronies were other well-heeled squires like himself, men dedicated to the hunt and little else. And Aunt Shreve prided herself on her small circle of friends, all of them well-known to Ellen.

Her interview an hour later with Miss Dignam left her shaking her head. Gone was the animosity of yesterday. The formidable headmistress might have been a different person as she informed Ellen that, beginning on Monday, she would study geography with the older students, and that perhaps a scholar could be found to tutor her in one or two of Shakespeare's more proper plays.

Ellen hurried from the headmistress's office when the interview ended. She closed the door behind her and leaned against it for a brief moment, baffled by Miss Dignam's startling bonhomie. I shall ask Gordon, she thought as she hurried to her room. Surely he will be back tomorrow. Her heart warmed toward him. Can it be that he has done something that will make this dungeon tolerable for me? Gordon, you are a dear.

Sunday came, but no Gordon. Marching in ranks of two, the students traveled at a slow and decorous pace down the High Street to St. Mary's for church at eleven of the clock. It was the parish church at Oxford's center, and there were many students in attendance. Ellen looked them over, wondering which man was Lord Chesney. Miss Dignam had mentioned All Souls College. "Rare air, indeed," Ellen murmured as she listened to the priest's responses. "What does it all mean?"

Surely Gordon would return on Monday. The next morning she sat politely through a lecture on geography, her mind wandering about, as the instructor, a spinsterly don with a permanent blush, spoke at length on the products of the Low Countries and What It All Meant to England.

Evening came and still Gordon did not make his appearance. Ellen stood at her bedroom window, looking down into the street, willing him to appear. Her uneasiness grew until her head began to ache. What kind of trouble had Gordon gotten himself into in the middle of London? She had heard tales of Newgate, and Bow Street Runners, and flats and cheats and gaming hells, and assorted lowlife on the prowl for young men less wise in the ways of the world than they thought themselves.

She thought, too, of James Gatewood. Already she was having difficulty remembering his face, seen only briefly that afternoon of her entrance into Oxford. He had not returned after delivering the candy. She had told herself that she would not think about him anymore, but she did, as she stood at the window and chafed after Gordon.

"And what would you do if James Gatewood were here?" she asked herself. "Tumble all your troubles into his lap?"

She would never do that, but as she considered the matter, she had a feeling that his lap was big enough to carry them all. How she had come by this knowledge, she could not tell, but it was the one warm thought in an evening of fret and worry.

She was walking from geography next morning, chewing on her lip and wondering where she had misplaced her pathetic bit of embroidery for the afternoon's class, when she heard someone hissing at her.

Startled, Ellen looked around. There was no one but Becky Speed, watering the plants by the stairwell. She came closer.

"Thank goodness, miss," Becky said. "There's someone here who wants to see you in the worst way."

The maid set down the watering can, looked both ways, and darted for the door that led belowstairs. Ellen followed, after a careful look of her own.

And there was Gordon, sitting at the servant's dining table, rubbing his head as though it hurt. He looked up when Ellen came clattering down the stairs, and winced as she shrieked, "Gordon!" and threw her arms around him.

"Have a care, sister," he pleaded, holding his head with both hands. "My head is screwed on upside down."

Flashing a grateful look at Becky, Ellen sat down close to her brother. She sniffed the air around him and drew back slightly. He smelled as though he had not changed his linen since their last meeting. His face was a rough field of whiskery stubble and he smelled of gin, sweat, and stale tobacco.

He acknowledged her presence with a gusty sigh and then rested his head on the table again. "Lord, Ellen," he croaked, "you don't know what I have been through."

His eyes were red puddles in his pale face. Ellen waited for him to speak, waited for some explanation.

The realization of what had happened dawned on her. "Gordon," she said, her voice over-loud. She shook his arm. "You didn't lose all your money?"

"Softly, softly," he pleaded, clutching his hair this time. "Every farthing, El. And then there I was in the gutter, looking up at this huge watchman." He sat up at the memory and groaned.

Ellen stared at him, her eyes wide. "Papa would be aghast," she said.

The look he fixed on her had nothing in it of exhaustion or alcoholic muddle. "He's not going to hear about it from me *or* you," he said, clipping his words off and then sinking his head to the table again, as though gathering strength for his next thought.

She waited for him to speak. Becky plunked a cup of tea on the table and pushed it close to his nose. "I found him out by the back door," she whispered to Ellen. "I thought he was your brother."

Ellen gave her a grateful look. "Becky, you're a wonder."

Becky only smiled. "I . . . had a brother once, miss."

Ellen pushed the cup closer. In another moment, the odor reached Gordon's nostrils. He sat up and took a sip. "You're as bad as Mama," he grumbled. "El, tea doesn't cure everything."

Ellen touched his arm. "It helps, Gordon. Now you have

merely to tighten your belt until the next quarter rolls around and . . .''

Gordon let out a sound between a wail and a moan and turned his face away. "El, you don't know the half of it," he said. "I needed that money to pay the student who has been writing my essays for me. He won't continue without more blunt, and I lost it all!"

Ellen stared at him as the words sank into her brain. "Good heavens, brother, do you mean . . . ?"

Wearily, Gordon propped his head on his hand. "Every week he writes the essay that I read on Saturday mornings. He wrote the last one on credit, and said he wouldn't write any more until I coughed up the guineas." He fumbled in his pocket and pulled out a wrinkled letter. "And what do I find under my door but this note from the warden himself! I missed last Saturday's essay, and if I do not produce an acceptable essay this Saturday, he will write Father."

The silence stretched between them. Gordon took another sip of tea. "Then Papa will summon me home and I will never be any closer to Spain than I am right now!"

Ellen sat in silence, thinking to herself that it was no time to trot out her childhood scolds and remind him that it was only what he deserved. She touched his hair, matted and dirty from the London gutter. "Can you not write your essay now? It is only Tuesday. Surely . . ."

He groaned again and drained the rest of the tea. "El, you dolt," he said. "I am trying to tell you that I have never written an essay in my life!"

As tears filled his eyes, she realized it was also not the time to vent her own anger at his good fortune in an Oxford career. For he will not see it that way, she thought.

"You have attended the lectures," she began. "That ought to be some help in writing an essay."

"Yes, I attend the lectures," he said. "I take notes while that dreary don drones on about this or that, and then I turn my notes over to my friend and he writes the essay."

He eyed his sister, and as she stared back, the look in his face changed and became more thoughtful. He brushed the hair back from his eyes but his glance did not waver from her face.

Ellen had seen that expression before, but not in years. She shook her head. "I don't care what you are thinking, but the answer is no, you provoking brother."

He did not appear to hear her words. A grim smile played about his lips. "I have just had a brilliant idea, El. It's a real hay-burner, and I am astounded that I could think of it, considering how I feel right now."

She knew better than to say anything, but pursed her lips into a thin line.

When she made no comment, he took her by the arm.

"Ellen, you're going to attend that lecture in my place and write my essay."

"I am not!" she declared. "You can go to your lecture and . . ."

He shook his head. "Not like this, El. It starts in half an hour, and I can't even hold up my head. Can you fathom the trouble I would get into from the warden if he saw me like this? No, Ellen, you'll be as safe as houses."

"You can't possibly be serious," she said, her voice soaring into the upper registers.

He winced. "Trust me, El."

4

"I wouldn't trust you if you were the last Grimsley alive," she declared indignantly, even as Becky Speed put her finger to her lips and Gordon flinched at her bracing tones. "Especially if you were the last Grimsley alive."

She moved closer to her brother, her face inches from his. "We are not children in the nursery anymore, and I cannot be coerced! You must think I am fearful stupid," she hissed.

To his credit, Gordon shook his head vigorously, which only caused him to moan and clutch it in both hands, as though he wished to wrench it off. "No, never that," he gasped. "I ask you to help because *I* am fearful stupid," he continued, changing his tack as he watched the suspicion grow in her eyes. "You owe me no favors. And I am certain you can think of countless injustices that would render such sisterly goodwill impossible."

"I can," she agreed, with feeling. "If you give me leave of twenty seconds or so, I will name ten or twelve, brother."

He shook his head more carefully this time, and took her by the hand before she could get out of his vicinity. "Ellen, I am desperate," he said, his voice soft, pleading.

"Well, I suppose you are," she replied, at a momentary loss over his apparent abandonment of the argument. She regarded him in silence for a long moment.

That they did resemble one another, she would not deny. Her fingers strayed to her own blond hair, cut almost as short as his, and just as curly. She sighed. Even this similarity would fool no one.

"It won't work, Gordon," she began. No sooner were the words out of her mouth than she knew she would do what he asked.

After a lifetime of careful strategy with his little sister, Gordon knew it, too. He sat up, still cradling his head, his eyes alert for the first time.

"Under ordinary circumstances, I would agree with you," he said, his tone normal as he watched her closely for adverse reactions. "But we are dealing with my don, who is probably more ancient than the Magna Carta, and nearsighted to boot."

Ellen bit her lip, but she listened, wondering why she was listening even as she did so. Drat all brothers, she thought to herself. They should be buried at birth and dug up at twenty-one.

"You need merely to swathe yourself in my student's gown," Gordon said. He took another sip of the refilled teacup that Becky had placed at his elbow, along with a plate of ginger-snaps. "Sit away from the window, where the room is lightest, and he will never know."

"Gordon, when I walk in, he will observe how short I am!" Ellen insisted.

Gordon was calm now, in control. "No, he won't, sister. You will be seated long before he arrives. I swear he forgets every week where our assigned meeting place is. All you have to do is take notes now and then, say 'hmmm' and 'ahh,' in all the right places, and remain seated until he leaves. Nothing could be simpler."

"The gown will not be sufficient," she grumbled, casting about for argument. "You know very well I will be found out the moment I attempt to cross the quadrangle in my dress and your gown."

"I already considered that," he replied, and nodded gingerly toward a bundle near the back door. Becky hurried to fetch it. Gordon opened the bundle and pulled out a pair of trousers and a frilled shirt.

Ellen shook her head. "I couldn't possibly," she said. "Besides, Gordon, I will not fit into your clothes!"

He eyed her patiently, fondly. "These belong to the chap I share my quarters with, El. He's a little taller than you, but not by much. And here are his shoes and stockings. Come on, El, what do you say?"

She snatched the clothes from him and held them to her. "I should leave you to your fate, brother," she began. "You brought this all upon yourself, you know."

"I know," he agreed, his voice contrite. He got down on one knee and looked up at her.

Tears started in her eyes, and she touched the top of his head. Why should I "wink at your discords," she thought. And here I am, quoting the Bard like Ralph. Why should I be an instrument to hurry you ultimately to Spain? She straightened her shoulders and turned to Becky.

"Becky, can you get this bundle to my room? I must beg off from embroidery with Miss Dignam."

Becky nodded and dashed away with the bundle. Gordon rose, resting his hands on the table. "Just this once, Ellen," he said. "Then perhaps you can show me how to write a scholarly essay."

"Perhaps I can. Wait for me here."

She met Miss Dignam in the hall and made no effort to disguise her agitation. Her heart in her shoes, she hoped her face looked as pale as it felt. She put her hand to her forehead, gratified that her fingers shook.

"Miss Dignam, I must beg your excuse from embroidery," she said. It was an easy matter for tears to stand out on her long lashes. It was an art she had learned from Horatia. Her chin quivered and Miss Dignam succumbed.

"My dear! You must go lie down!" the headmistress exclaimed. "Are you well?"

Ellen shook her head. She looked about to make sure that no one lingered to listen, and stood on her tiptoes. "It is a female matter, Miss Dignam."

The headmistress colored and patted Ellen's arm. "Go lie down, my dear," she repeated. "Shall Becky create a tisane for you?"

"If she will bring me a warming pan for my feet, that will suffice," Ellen said, her voice faltering as she considered the enormity of her deception. And dare I drag Becky into this mess? she thought as she walked slowly up the stairs.

With Becky's help, she dressed quickly in the shirt and trousers. The shoes were too large, but Becky stuffed them with tissue paper.

While Ellen fiddled with her hair, biting her lips and scarcely daring to look herself in the eye, Becky arranged her pillows and extra blankets into a facsimile of a person and pulled the comforter up high. She went to the window.

"Thank the Lord it is raining," Becky said. "You will have the hood up over your face." She sniffed the air. "If only you did not smell of lavender, Miss Grimsley."

Ellen turned away from the mirror. "That is the least of our worries." She strode up and down the room. "Oh, Becky, I cannot begin to walk like a man."

"Turn your toes out more," suggested the maid. "Let your arms swing."

"I look like Jack Tar!" Ellen protested after several more trips up and down the small chamber.

Becky shrugged. "Better that than a schoolroom miss. Now, throw out your chest. No, no, you had better not do that, Miss Grimsley!"

"I will clutch Gordon's gown tight about me, I assure you," she said, and then sighed and pulled on a dress over the shirt and trousers. She swung an engulfing shawl of Norwich silk about her shoulders. "Lead on, Becky Speed," she said, her eyes straight ahead.

The students had all taken themselves to the classrooms on the main floor. With Becky in the lead, Ellen hurried down the back stairs.

In the servants' hall, Gordon sat up when he saw her. He watched in appreciative silence as she removed the shawl and dress and held out her hand for his student's robe. He draped it around her slim shoulders. "One could wish you had broader shoulders," he began, but shut up when she glared at him. "It was only a wish." He sniffed at her hair. "Perhaps Old Ancient of Days has no more sense of smell than of sight," he said, more to himself than to her. "He will think me Queer Nabs indeed."

Ellen opened her mouth for a retort, but thought better of it. She waited a moment until she had command over her voice. "Tell me what it is we are studying today, Gordon, if you can think that far."

The wounded look he fixed upon her was small recompense for the murder in her heart. "It is to be Shakespeare, of course."

"Could you not narrow it down at least to the comedies,

tragedies, or histories?'' she snapped, grabbing the tablet and pencil he held out to her and stuffing them in one of the deep pockets of the gown.

''It is the one about fairies and donkeys' heads and a chap named Puck. I suspect it is a comedy,'' he said, opening the back door for her. ''Of course, come to think of it, that sounds like government, and so it could be a history.''

''How wise of you, dear brother,'' she said.

He returned her frown with the smile that had always caused Mama to indulge him. Ellen laughed in spite of herself. Filled with more charity, she followed him into the street and took his arm.

He stopped and removed her hand from his arm. ''Really, my dear, how does this look?'' he asked. ''That sort of thing will never do in public.''

They hurried across the High Street. Swept with rain, it was nearly devoid of all students. Ellen glanced back at the Female Academy. No one watched from the windows. She could only breathe a sigh of thanks to the patron saint of students, whoever he was, and hurry after her brother.

He slowed down for her on the curb and ushered her into one the narrow alleyways that led into the heart of the university. Gordon kept his head down against the rain, but Ellen raised her face to the sky, looking about her at the spires and ancient walls.

''I never thought to be here,'' she said and stopped to admire the high walls that dripped rain. ''Where does that little door lead?'' she asked, pointing.

''To All Souls, El, holy ground indeed. Now hurry up and keep your face down. Lord, I never thought a beautiful sister to be a handicap before.''

She stopped again, and smiled up at him. ''Gordon, that's quite the nicest thing you ever said to me!''

''Well, it's true,'' he replied gruffly, his eyes on the street ahead of them. ''Once you got rid of your baby chins and freckles, you were the prettiest chit in the district. And I'm not just saying that,'' he hastened to add. ''I mean it. Now, quit gawking and step lively.''

They hurried down another narrow lane and another, robes clutched tight against the wind and rain. Gordon paused for a moment, waved her off, and was quietly sick down another alley.

As she waited for him, a group of students passed, looked at him, and winked at her. Her heart in her stomach, Ellen grinned and winked back. Mama will flail me alive, she thought, when the students offered some ribald advice to Gordon, pale and shaken.

Mama must never know, she thought and rubbed her arm in the unfamiliar linen shirt. Gordon had tied the neck cloth about her, and it seemed to tighten like a hangman's noose. Surely I will not be sentenced to appear before a firing squad if I am discovered, Ellen thought. Perhaps they will only transport me to Botany Bay. She tugged at the collar, wishing her imagination less lively.

Another brisk five minutes brought them to University Quadrangle. Gordon stood outside the door and turned to his sister. "El, go up the first flight of stairs, down the hall to your left. It's the last room on the left." He took her hand. "He'll do all the talking. He always does."

She squeezed his hand. "Gordon, I think I do owe you a favor."

"What?" he asked, surprised.

"Silly! For sending someone called Lord Chesney to Miss Dignam. You certainly convinced her that we have high connections here, and he—whoever he was—saw to it that I was moved into geography instead of watercolors. And she says I will have a Shakespeare tutor."

He continued to stare at her. "El, have your wits gone wandering? I don't know any Lord Chesney. Must be one of Aunt Shreve's eccentric connections. You know how she is about not letting her left hand know what her right hand does."

"Yes, but . . ."

"But nothing, El." He grinned at her suddenly. "Besides, El, you know I never exert myself for my sisters! Perhaps you have a benefactor. I wish I had one. Now, go on."

He opened the door for her and leaned against the frame, his expression warning her that in another moment he would be on his hands and knees by the gutter again. She hurried inside the quad and shut the door after her.

She held her breath and looked about her. The rain had turned the honey-colored stone a dismal gray. The trees were bare, the grass the faded tan of autumn. The only sound was the rain that rumbled through the gutters and gargoyles and spewed onto the ground. She sighed and clutched her gown about her. It was the most beautiful place she had ever seen. "University College," she whispered, unmindful of the rain that pelted her. "Founded by Alfred the Great. Home of scholars these thousand years."

With a laugh in her throat, she ran across the quad toward the hall, remembering to keep her toes turned out. The steps to the second floor were worn and uneven. She mounted them slowly, not so much fearful of her footing as mindful of the thousands who had trod them before her. She breathed deep of air that smelled of old wood, new ideas, candlewax, and somewhere, books in leather covers.

The room was empty, as Gordon had predicted. A fire struggled in the grate. She spent a moment in front of it, warming her hands, and then tugged the straight-backed chair into the shadow and away from the window, with its wavy panes of leaded glass that admitted little light anyway. She took out her pad and pencil and waited.

In a few minutes, she heard someone climbing the stairs slowly, as she had done, a step at a time. The steps down the hall were measured and sure, as if they had walked this way for centuries at least. She smiled to herself as the person stopped frequently, as though to peer into each room. Gordon had said tht his don was forgetful. I wonder how many students he has misplaced over the years, she thought. I wonder, are they still waiting?

She saw a mental image of rows and rows of dusty skeletons waiting in each room, pencils still caught in bony fingers. She laughed out loud, and then stopped when Gordon's don crossed the threshold and stood there, peering at her.

She would not have thought such a thing possible, but the man was shorter than she. His scholar's gown swept the floor as he entered the room. He raised his shoulders at the sound of the fabric dragging along the floor, rather like a barnyard fowl attempting flight and then thinking better of it. He had no hair on his head, and drops of rain glistened there and on his spectacles.

Still observing her, he brushed his hand across his head and dried his glasses on the hem of his dusty robe. The results did not satisfy him, so he removed a handkerchief from some inner pocket and tried again.

"Better, much better," he murmured and then sniffed the air in Ellen's general vicinity. He frowned and peered at her, squinting through nearsighted eyes.

"Lavender, eh?" he asked. "The new mode at University College? How odd is this younger generation."

Ellen cleared her throat and returned some noncommittal reply, careful to utter it in lower tones, with some semblance of Gordon's style. She sat forward, ready to capture his every word.

The don perched himself on the room's only table and gathered his robes about him like a crow folding its feathers. Ellen looked on in fascination, waiting for him to turn around and around and settle himself. She smiled at the absurdity of this, her fear gone.

He frowned. "My dear Grimsley, is this some special occasion? Is there something particular you wish from me?"

Ellen stared at him, her eyes wide, her fear returning. What had she done wrong?

"See here, sir. This is the first time you have come to drink from the font of knowledge with pencil *and* paper." He withdrew a slim volume in red morocco from another pocket. "Dare I to hope that you have even read *Midsummer Night's Dream?*"

"I have, sir," she answered, grateful that only two weeks ago she and Ralph had hidden themselves in the buttery and read the play aloud to each other while Horry sobbed over the fit of her wedding dress, Mama lamented the dearness of beeswax candles, and Papa, booted and dressed in his hunting clothes, shook his fist at the heavens because of the rain.

"For we need a good laugh, El," Ralph had insisted. "And what could be funnier than lovers?"

"I have indeed, sir," she repeated. "It is a favorite of mine."

The don grabbed his book to his meager chest in a gesture of extreme surprise. "Next you will tell me something profound, Grimsley, and then I will know I am in the wrong room."

Ellen had the wisdom to be silent.

The don waited another moment, then opened the book. "Very well, then, since you have no more profundities, let us begin this romp, Grimsley. Let us see 'what fools these mortals be.' "

When she set down her pencil two hours later, sighing with satisfaction, Ellen was in complete charity with her brother. For two hours, she had listened to the under-sized scrawny don transform himself into all the characters wandering about in that enchanted forest.

She regarded the little man with feeling close to affection. He was Pyramus; he was Chink; he was the haughty Hyppolita, the confused Helena. He was lover and rustic; fond father, foolish maid. He was an absurd little bald man, undeniably prissy, and stuffy with old ideas. He was the very soul of education, and she would have followed him anywhere.

"I understand this play," she said softly, her words not even intended for his ears.

He heard her, though, and smiled. "Then, Grimsley, you can tell me what it is about, can't you? You can be the first scholar I have instructed this day who is not more concerned about his stomach, or his imagined injuries, or his paper due, his book unread. Tell me then, sir."

Ellen took a deep breath. "It is about the absurdity of love."

The don closed his book and whisked it out of sight in his pocket. "Grimsley, you astound me. Yes, yes! It is about the absurdity of love." He pointed his finger at her. "Do you understand the absurdity of love?"

"I know nothing of it, nothing at all, sir," she confessed, and hesitated, looking up at him.

"Yes?" asked the don, leaning forward. "What else?"

"Perhaps I was wrong. I confess that I know even less than when you began to read," she said, looking down at her hands. "I said I understood the play, but I do not. My ignorance is nearly complete, and somehow, this does not bother me." Ellen looked at him. "Have I failed?"

Her heart nearly stopped when the don hopped off his perch and strode to the window, throwing it wide. He leaned out for a deep breath, a beatific expression on his face, and turned toward her again. "Grimsley, my lad, you have succeeded! Such ignorance is the essence of education. I must have misjudged you.''

Ellen looked at him in confusion.

''My dear Grimsley, armed as you are with this supreme ignorance, and an obvious love for the play, what should you do about it? Think hard, lad, and we will see if there is hope for you?''

She thought hard. I could answer this odd question with a smile and shrug, as Gordon would, or I could be honest.

''I would seek to find out more, sir,'' she replied quietly.

''Why?'' he challenged.

The word hung in the air and seemed to settle on her shoulders.

''Because I wish to know more, even if for no other purpose than to satisfy myself,'' she replied.

The don smiled and nodded. ''Then education is served, lad,'' was all he said as he adjusted his gown and went to the door. ''I can recommend a course to follow.''

''Sir, please do,'' she said, rising to her feet and following him.

''Grimsley, how short you are today,'' the don said.

Ellen held her breath, but he did not pursue this line of reasoning.

''In the Bodleian you will find a book. It is called *Commentary and Notes on A Midsummer Night's Dream*. I suggest you read it and make it the basis of your paper for Saturday's reading.'' He shook his finger at her. ''Which, I must add with sorrow, you neglected to attend last week. I am certain the gods mourned. Redeem yourself, lad, with this little work of Lord Chesney's.''

She sat down again. ''Lord Chesney? *The* Lord Chesney?''

''There is only one from that shatterbrained family.'' The don shook his head and bowed his head. ''Sad what happened to him. England has lost a great Shakespeare scholar.''

''He is dead?'' Ellen gasped, her mind filled with even more confusion. Was that the mysterious Lord Chesney who sat in Miss Dignam's parlor only two days ago and changed the course of her Oxford stay? ''I do not understand.''

''He is dead in English literature, Grimsley! What could be

worse? I hear he is even now a fellow at All Souls and reading history.'' The don made a face, as though he had uttered a foul word. ''I fear he will become a Philistine after all.''

He brightened then. ''But he is young, Grimsley. Perhaps there is hope. Such wisdom! Such sagacity! We can only pray that he will yet return to his own special analysis of the Bard. Such piquancy! Such wit!''

He paused, as if so much exclamation had wound him down like a top. His voice was milder when he spoke again. ''Good day, Grimsley. I await your paper this Saturday with something close to bated breath.'' He cast his eyes upon Ellen, squinting at her. ''I hope you will leave off the lavender. And do grow, Grimsley, between now and Saturday.''

He closed the door behind him. Ellen stared after him, shaking her head and then smothering her laughter with her hands. Such a funny stick, she thought, recalling Gordon's dire warnings.

She went slowly down the stairs, trailing her hand along the bannister. How many have done this before me, she thought, as she felt the years of polish, the roughness of the wood worn smooth by hands and time. No matter than no one believed any longer that Alfred the Great himself had established this seat of learning. She lowered herself to the bottom step and leaned against the railing, content to summon the sight of king and scholars, gathered together at this oxen ford, thirsty for knowledge in an age when few knew anything.

''Not so different from now,'' she said, and rose.

The rain pelted down, drenching the quadrangle, driving the few remaining leaves to the ground and the students indoors. She tucked her tablet into her pocket and walked slowly toward the door in the wall. She looked back once at the hall she had left and raised her hand. It was an absurd gesture, but there was no one around to see her salute to stones and wood and scholarship.

Ellen peered about her, but Gordon was nowhere in sight. She had not expected to see him, especially with the rain pouring down and his inner workings in such a muddle. She was glad of the solitude. She wanted to think for a moment of what she had learned. Her own inclination ran more to geography, cartography and mathematics, but she had read Shakespeare to humor Ralph. The scrawny little don—I don't even know his name, she thought—had awakened her to the vigor of Shakespeare. She clasped her hands together and looked down at them. "Like Adam, I have been touched by the finger of God," she whispered.

The rain did not let up. She walked faster. I should return to Miss Dignam's, she thought, but I must go to the Bodleian for that book by the mysterious Lord Chesney. Ellen glanced at the little door that led into All Souls quadrangle. The don said Lord Chesney was a fellow there. She paused a moment, and then hurried faster. The mystery would keep for drier weather.

A quick run through deepening puddles brought her to the Bodleian Library. She stood at the entrance a moment, amazed at what she was about to do, took a deep breath, and entered.

The odor of books was overpowering. It made her mouth water as she stared about her, admiring row upon row of handsomely carved bookshelves, busts of Oxford's better-known graduates, and the plastered, ornamental ceiling that seemed to go on forever.

All was silent. She tiptoed into the main reading room and let out her breath in a sigh of relief. The library was almost empty. A few students sat here and there, some studying, more sleeping, others gazing out the window with a thoughtful expression. The smell of wet wool competed with the odor of books.

I should remove this cloak, she thought, but I dare not. She clutched it tighter about her, sloshed in soggy shoes to the librarian, and in her gruffest voice, asked for Lord Chesney's book.

It was brought to her in a moment with the admonition to keep it dry. Keeping her head down, she nodded her thanks and looked for a safe place to read. Beyond the rows of shelves that flanked the main room's middle section was an area with tables and small desks lining the walls. She hurried to one of the desks, sat down, and began to read, careful to keep her sodden cloak high around her face.

She was deep in the first chapter when she heard footsteps behind her and felt a firm hand on her shoulder. She stiffened, not daring to turn around.

"That's my carrel, lad," said a familiar voice. "Best you move into the center tables."

She knew without even looking over her shoulder that it was James Gatewood. There was just the trace of London in his voice that she remembered from their brief meeting on the hill. Without a word she got up and moved to a table.

From the corner of her eyes, she watched as Gatewood took off his cloak, draped it over the back of his chair, and looked with a sour expression at the wet chair she had vacated. He removed a neck scarf and dried off the seat. In another moment, he was tipped back in the chair with his feet propped up on the desk.

Ellen put her hand to her mouth to hide the laughter. Mama would cough up nails if I sat like that, she thought. Oh, what am I saying? She would twirl about and expire if she knew I was sitting in the Bodleian Library in borrowed trousers.

She looked down at herself. Her legs were primly together, as she always sat. After a quick glance about, she pulled back the cloak and crossed her legs, resting her ankles on her knee and leaning back slightly in her chair. Her face flamed. Good Lord, I am vulgar, she thought, but my goodness, this is comfortable.

She picked up the book again and in another moment was captivated by Lord Chesney's remarkable wit and cynicism as he deftly skewered the young lovers in *Midsummer Night's Dream* and served them up to the reader on a platter of impeccable scholarship. She laughed out loud at Lord Chesney's description of Helena as "Befuddled, bemused and outwitted by love, that great leveler. Why should she be different than we? Do we laugh at her, or ourselves?"

"Shhh!" said James Gatewood, finger to his lips. "Lad, this is a library, not a theatrical amusement," he whispered.

"But it is Shakespeare, sir," Ellen replied, lowering her tones, hoping she sounded more masculine than she felt as she clutched the cloak more tightly about her face.

Gatewood only smiled and nodded, to her relief, and returned to his reading.

Ellen dug the paper and pencil from her pocket and bent her head over her notes, writing as rapidly as possible. The rain had stopped. Soon scholars would be returning to the library. She wrote faster.

She did not notice the mouse until it ran right by her hand, took a quick glance at Chesney's *Commentary*, and scurried off the end of the table.

Ellen gasped, screamed and leaped onto the chair, grabbing her cloak about her. Starting in surprise, Gatewood tipped too far back in his chair and tumbled himself to the floor. He lay on his back, his face red, his eyes indignant.

He scrambled to his feet and gripped her tight by the arm. "Scared of a little mouse, eh, lad?" he declared as he yanked her off the chair. "Lord, is this 'the gift and flower' of English youth? God help us!"

She stumbled against him. As her breasts brushed his arm, Gatewood flinched and drew back, gaping down at her with open-mouthed amazement. Before she could say a word, he ripped the cloak from her face and stared at her.

"Blast and damn, Ellen Grimsley," he said in a voice much too loud for the Bodleian Library. "Grimsley, Grimsley, Grimsley," echoed in the vault overhead.

He hastily released his hold on her, touched her face with the back of his hand in the oddest, most tender gesture, and then looked up as the librarian bore down on them.

She remained silent as he whirled her about and clamped his arm around her shoulders, quick-marching her toward the exit.

"Smartly now, Miss Grimsley, you rascal," he whispered. "I think we can beat him to that door!"

5

It was a near-run thing. As he propelled her toward the side door, she pushed it open and stumbled through. Gatewood slapped her sharply on the hip and turned to face the librarian, who was red-faced from his pursuit of them across the main floor.

"I can deal with this upstart noisebox," Gatewood said and closed the door behind him. Without another word, he grabbed her by the hand and tugged her along the alley into the nearest doorway, where they stood as the rain began again.

Ellen couldn't bring herself to look at James Gatewood. She stared down at her hands, embarrassed beyond words.

Gatewood cleared his throat. "Miss Grimsley, in my wildest imaginings, I never thought to be ejected from the Bodleian."

She looked up, fearful of his wrath, into smiling eyes. "I am so sorry. Will your reputation suffer damage?" she asked in all seriousness.

"Probably." He laughed and leaned against the wet stones. "Lord, Miss Grimsley, you look like a drowned rat. Or mouse, in your case. Which reminds me. I must brave the Bodleian again." He stepped from the protection of the doorway and into the rain.

Ellen grabbed for his hand. "I must have my notes, sir. Oh, please, can you fetch them?"

He kissed her wet hand, and dashed back into the library. Ellen drew her gown around her again and huddled in the doorway. She thought at first she would run. In another moment she could be across the High Street and safe in the kitchen belowstairs at Miss Dignam's. But that would mean abandoning her notes and leaving Gordon to his well-deserved fate on Saturday, and she could not do that.

Since when have I become so scrupulous about casting Gordon to the fates? she asked herself. Let us be honest, Ellen. You want your notes back. You want to write that paper.

Gatewood was back then, his cloak draped about his shoulders this time and her notes in his hand. He glanced at them as he handed them to her. "I noticed Chesney's *Commentary* on the table."

She accepted the notes. "I wish you could have smuggled that out for me, sir. I had only just begun it."

"Please call me Jim," he said promptly. "And I will call you . . ." he paused and looked her over as she blushed. "Somehow, Miss Grimsley, or even Ellen—it is Ellen, isn't it?—sounds misplaced for someone in trousers."

She grimaced as she pocketed the notes. "I am supposed to be Gordon Grimsley."

" 'Worse and worse it grows,' " he quoted, his eyes twinkling again. "I scarcely need remind you that women, even women in their brothers' trousers, are not allowed to undertake serious scholarship in the Bodleian. Or any scholarship, for that matter."

When she made no reply, he looked beyond her into the rain, the smile gone from his eyes. "And more's the pity, I suspect."

She looked at him then. "Well, thank you, sir." Her teeth began to chatter and she shivered.

He put his arm around her and pulled her into the rain again. "Bundle up, Mr. Gordon Grimsley," he said, speaking loudly to be heard about the thundering downpour. "I feel the need of a pint."

She stared at him, her eyes wide. "Sir, I have never been in the taproom of a tavern!"

He only laughed and tugged her along. "Then you should not have got yourself into a pair of trousers, Miss Grimsley!"

She pulled back. "Sir! I should think that you could wish to see the back of me, after the embarrassment I just caused you."

He released her and they stood regarding each other in the pouring rain. "I suppose you are right," he said slowly. "After all, scholarship is a stodgy thing, is it not? No?" He did not put his arm about her again, but started walking toward the High Street.

The fact that he did not look back to see if she followed piqued her own interest, and she trailed after him. In another moment, he slowed down and walked by her side.

"I confess to curiosity, Miss Grimsley," he continued. He seemed unaware of the turn their brief acquaintance had just taken in the rain and the narrow alley. "From my knowledge, I have never before encountered a female in the Bodleian. As you are the first, and I may claim some slight acquaintance, I thought I should ask you."

"Yes, but a tavern?"

He continued his slow meander down the alley, unmindful of the rain. "If I escort you to Miss Dignam's, I fear you would be in the suds indeed, unless that dragon's ideas of females and academe have changed. I would have no leave to find out more." He bowed. "And as a student, is not my task to find out more? I ask you, Miss Grimsley."

"Ellen," she said involuntarily.

"Not a chance," he replied as quickly. "I will call you . . . oh, let me see, how about . . . I will call you Scholastica."

"Please don't," she said. "Surely you cannot call that an improvement over Ellen."

"Does Ellen need improving?" he asked. "Ah, well, since you were deep in Chesney's *Commentary* on the fairies and lovers, I will call you Hermia."

She stopped in the middle of a puddle and clapped her hands. "Do you like *Midsummer Night's Dream* too?"

He took her by the elbow and steered her down another alley. "I am excessively fond of it, fair Hermia. As I am also excessively wet, let us discuss this indoors."

In another moment she was seated in a high-backed settle in a smokey corner, her hands wrapped around a battered pint pot. Gatewood sat next to her, turning himself to face her, and effectively shielding her from others in the room. He twitched the cloak back from her face and just looked at her until she turned away and took a deep quaff of the ale.

She coughed as the fumes rose and circled through her brain. "This is a vile brew!" she gasped, when she could talk.

"Yes, isn't it?" Gatewood replied. "You would be amazed how inspirational it can be in the eleventh hour before a paper is due." He leaned closer, lowering his voice. "I have it on good authority that Lord Chesney himself wrote much of his *Commentary* at this very table."

Ellen opened her mouth to ask him about Lord Chesney, but

Gatewood was off and running. "My dear Hermia, please tell me—if it isn't too much trouble—what you were doing in the Bodleian? I suspect that Miss Dignam's is slow indeed, but isn't the Bodleian rather a risk?"

Ellen nodded and frowned into the ale as she swirled the pot around and around. "I told Gordon it would not work, but he was suffering the ill effects of a weekend in London, and I said that I would write his Saturday paper for him." She laughed and shook her head. "I should never listen to Gordon."

Gatewood only smiled and took another drink. Ellen took him by the arm. "But, think, Jim! I actually attended his tutorial!" She let go of his arm, but she could not keep the enthusiasm from her voice. "I have been merely a dabbler in the Bard—it is Ralph who is enamored of him—but never before did I realize that Shakespeare could be such fun!" She subsided then, her face red. "I suppose I get carried away."

"Not at all," Gatewood said. "I like the way enthusiasm makes your eyes shine. Most chits only look that way when you pay them a compliment, and even then, they are not sincere." His voice trailed off and he leaned back against the settle, staring at the wall straight ahead. "How on earth did you fool your brother's instructor. And by the way, who is Ralph?"

"He is my younger brother," she said, the animation coming into her voice again. "He is taking lessons from the vicar, a prosing bagwig who thinks the capital of the United States is New York City."

"Ignorant clergy," Gatewood said. "They should all be lined up and shot. Your brother would be better served at Winchester, or Eton."

"Papa will not hear of it. He says Ralph can do well enough with Mr. Snead." She sighed and took another cautious sip. "He has plans to send Ralph into the City to work with one of Mama's brothers—she has prodigious many. Gordon is here at University College because he is the oldest son and Papa wants him to be a gentleman."

Gatewood laughed, and then sobered immediately. "No, no, go on," he said. "From what I already suspect of the infamous Gordon, this is not his inclination."

"Indeed, no! He wants more than anything to take up with

a cavalry regiment in Spain. But he promised Papa a year at Oxford, and provided he acquits himself well, he may yet buy his colors.'' Ellen set aside her cloak, wringing water out of it under the table. ''Have you ever noticed, sir, that life is not fair?''

''It has come to my attention on occasion,'' he said. ''Are there others in your family? Are they satisfied?''

Ellen smiled. ''Horatia is prodigious happy, sir.''

''Jim,'' he said automatically, not taking his eyes from her face, which she considered somewhat forward. She put his manners down to the ale he was steadily consuming.

''Jim, then,'' she amended. ''She is soon to marry the son of a baronet.'' Her eyes widened as she looked at Gatewood. ''He is worth almost four thousand a year. Imagine!''

''I cannot,'' Gatewood replied, his eyes as merry as hers.

''So Horatia is happy.''

''And what about Ellen?'' he asked, when the silence stretched on and she returned to her own pint pot.

''Mama is determined that she will do as well as Horry, but Ellen is not so sure. She would prefer to map unknown continents,'' she said, her voice subdued. She thought a moment more and then set down the pint pot with some force. ''Is marriage the destiny of women, sir, I ask you?''

''I fear it must be, Hermia,'' James Gatewood said, a smile playing around his lips. ''We all have our little duties.''

''Even you?''

''Even me.''

Ellen sighed and reached for her cloak again. ''I thought as much.'' She paused and stroked the sodden material. ''But I have had my afternoon at University College, sir—Jim, and I have learned so much about Shakespeare!''

''Ah, yes, we have returned at last to the issue. How did you fool your instructor?'' he asked again.

She peered at Gatewood, the admiration strong in her voice. ''My goodness, sir, you are so good at keeping the thread of the conversation.''

''Jim,'' he said again. ''Well, of course, fair Hermia. That is what they teach us here at Oxford, don't you know. We learn to detect false argument, to build an unassailable case, and to be, above all else, objective.'' He ran a lazy finger down her cheek, even as she leaned away from him. "Not in a million years could any man alive mistake you for your brother."

"Do you know my brother?" she asked. "I am sorry for you."

"I . . . well, I know who he is now," he said.

If he was evasive, she overlooked it. Her eyes were merry as she also overlooked his forward behavior. "I sat in the shadows, sir, and to tell the truth, I think the old man was remarkably shortsighted. And sir, he was so small!"

Jim sat up straight again, his eyes filled with remembrance. "You can only be describing Hemphill. No bigger than a minute, and with a funny way of hunching up his shoulders to keep his gown from dragging?"

"The very same," she said, as she eyed the pint pot and pushed it away from her. "He was all the characters for *Midsummer Night's Dream.*"

"And his Pyramus has a lisp," Jim continued, draining the rest of his ale. He struck a pose in the narrow booth. " 'Thuth die I, thuth, thuth thuth.' "

Ellen joined in his laughter. "Yeth, you have hit it, thir," she said, a twinkle in her eyes to match his. "And now I must go."

He inclined his head to her. "So you should."

She reached for her cloak, draping it about her shoulders again and feeling the pocket to make sure that her notes at least were dry. "I could wish for Chesney's *Commentary*, but I believe that I can recall enough to write Gordon's paper."

Gatewood edged his way out of the booth, keeping between Ellen and the other patrons while she gathered her cloak tight about her again. She had taken no more than one step toward the door when Gatewood propelled her back into the booth, put his finger to his lips and practically sat on her.

Mystified, she craned her neck around to see what had caused this strange behavior, spotted her brother, and ducked her head until only one eye peeked out from under Gatewood's arm.

She held her breath as Gordon crossed the floor, listing about as though the tavern itself moved. Supporting him was another student, dressed also in black and no more able to navigate the perils of a public house. Ellen let out a gusty sigh.

"Oh, if I could only wring his neck," she muttered. "Do get off me, Jim."

Gatewood moved slightly. "Wring his neck?" he whispered. "You are much too kind."

She only looked at him, noting that his eyes were the warmest shade of brown and quite close to her own. They even had little gold flecks in them.

"He is a ridiculous brother," she whispered back.

"I suppose he is." He turned around and watched the two young men cross to a distant bench and throw themselves down like rag dolls. He moved over to give her more room. "And here I have just rescued him and that other young chap—he is, regrettably, a relation of mine—from the pitfalls of London. Ingratitude."

They looked at each other. "It appears that my brother and your relative are keeping low company."

Gatewood smiled. "It does. That was where I was this weekend, by the way, Hermia. I went on a rescue mission to London to wrest two rascals from the Watch. Did you wonder why I did not follow up that clandestine box of chocolates?"

She took another glance at her brother, who leaned over the table, head resting against the wood, eyes closed. "They were delightful and you were very kind," she said as he ushered her from the tavern and into the rain again.

"But I do not understand why you did it," she added as he threw an arm over her shoulders and steered her around the larger puddles.

"I came to pay a visit, and a cheeky little maid informed me that you were suffering the indignity of Miss Dignam's personal attention. In situations like that, only chocolates will do."

Before she could ask any more questions, he was hurrying her across the High Street. He paused under the awning of a greengrocer's to shake the rain from his gown. He held out his hand to Ellen and she grasped it.

"I had better leave you here," he said. "I must return to the Bodleian where Machiavelli awaits." He made a face. "I confess to no love for the labyrinthine mind of the politician."

"Then why do you study him?" she asked. "Surely you can do whatever you wish. You are a man."

"No, actually, I cannot," he replied, after a moment's re-

flection. "I have made my own bargain with my late father."
He sighed. "And my mother, who likes to worry." He shook
her hand, but did not release it. "Perhaps your brother and I are
more alike than you know. Good day, my dear. Do stay dry."

She watched him cross the street again, and ran after him.
"Oh, wait!" she called.

He turned. "If you get a putrid sore throat or a racking cough,
I will refuse to claim any responsibility beyond a posy or two
on your grave."

She stopped in front of him, shy suddenly, wondering why
she had pursued him. She held out her hand this time. "I just
wanted to thank you again for quite the nicest afternoon I have
ever spent," she said, her voice low. "Thank you for not
betraying me in the library."

He bowed over her hand, and the rain from his hood dripped
onto her wrist. "I will advise the librarian to engage the services
of a good mouser. I will even return poor Chesney's
Commentary to the stacks for you."

A cart rumbled by, splattering them both. Without a word,
he lifted her onto the sidewalk and closer to him. "I can think
of no greater misfortune to a father than that his dear daughter
Ellen be struck and killed by a passing poultry cart when he
thought her safe and bored at Miss Dignam's. It is not the sort
of news that parents thrive on, I suspect," Gatewood said, his
voice lively with amusement. "I suppose I must pay a visit to
Miss Dignam's horrible sitting room when we are both dry and
you do not look like a heroine out of a bad novel!"

"Promise?" she asked, releasing her grip on his hand.

"If I am able. I wish to read your paper before that ungrateful brother of yours acquires it."

"I will begin it tonight," she said, and looked both ways
before stepping into the street. "I have other qestions, sir, many
others! Who is Lord Chesney? I have something perfectly
diverting to tell you about him, and I don't even know who he
is." She leaned forward for one last confidence. "I think he
is my benefactor. Imagine that!"

"I cannot. Of course, Chesney is a raving eccentric." Gatewood held up his hand to stop her flood of questions. "Even
Chesney can wait, fair Hermia. Good day, for the second or
third time."

Ellen laughed and waved her hand to him as she splashed across the street again and hurried to the shallow steps that led to the servants' entrance. When she looked back across the High, he was still standing there, watching her. He blew her a kiss as she ran down the stairs.

Becky Speed was watching her at the window. When Ellen clambered down the stairs, the maid flung the door open wide and pulled her into the pantry. She thrust a bundle of clothes at Ellen, and whispered at her to hurry and change.

"It is almost dinner time, Miss," she said as she closed the door to the pantry and helped Ellen off with her soaking wet cloak.

Without a word, Ellen hurried out of her clothes. She gathered them into a sodden bundle and tiptoed up the back stairs. She just had time to throw them under her bed and rearrange herself and the pillows before Fanny opened the door.

Ellen snapped her eyes shut, wishing that she could look pale and interesting, instead of rosy from her exertions. She was mindful of her damp hair that curled so outrageously around her face. Her heart was pounding loud enough for Fanny to hear it, she thought. She patted the lump of papers under her pillow, grateful that her notes were dry.

She made no comment as Fanny came closer to the bed. Even with her eyes shut tight, Ellen could almost see Fanny peering at her down the length of her long Bland nose. And probably regarding me with vast suspicion, Ellen thought. For a small moment she considered her years and years of diligent honesty and cast them aside.

She opened her eyes slowly. "Fanny, is that you?" she asked, her voice cracking as she sought for just the right tone between mere discomfort and Fatal Illness.

"Of course it is," Fanny snapped. "Who else would it be?" she said, her voice still harsh, but troubled now with a faint uncertainty. "Ellen?"

Ellen sighed and tugged at her damp hair. "Fanny, 'tis laudable perspiration. Thank God the fever has broke," she said.

Fanny took it all in. She gaped at Ellen's damp hair, and the red spots of color in each cheek. "I had no idea," she said, lowering her voice. Her tones took on a reverent quality that almost made Ellen choke. "Are you feeling more the thing now, Ellen?"

Ellen nodded. With a gesture that she hoped was casual, she tugged the blankets up higher around her throat, covering her day dress. "Thank you for your concern, Fanny dear," she replied. "Please assure Miss Dignam that I will be right as a trivet by morning."

Fanny Bland was all solicitation. "Can I get you a tisane?" she offered. "May I bathe your temples with lavender water?"

Ellen shook her head and touched Fanny's hand. "Just let me rest in peace," she said, careful not to look Fanny in the eye. She coughed for good effect, and closed her eyes again.

She could hear Fanny by the bed. She heard the rustle of skirts, a sudden sniffling, and was thoroughly ashamed. In another moment, Fanny closed the door quietly behind her.

Ellen, how can you stoop so low, she thought as she sat up in bed. Depressing, boring, vindictive old Fanny Bland is actually worried about you.

After a moment spent in minor repentance, Ellen stripped off her dress and leaped into her nightgown. She retrieved the notes from under her pillow and smoothed them out. She toweled her hair dry, felt pangs of hunger, and decided that her penance would include no dinner that night.

Besides, she considered as she flopped back on the bed with her arms flung wide, I have such food for thought. She lay there in the semidarkness, her mind busy on *Midsummer Night's Dream* and the whimsy of love.

Morning brought Miss Dignam to her bedside. Dutifully, Ellen—her fingers crossed under the covers, stuck out her tongue upon command and coughed as directed.

"You seem to be recovering nicely," Miss Dignam assured her. "Goodness, but you certainly gave our dear Fanny a start yesterday!" She shook her finger playfully in Ellen's face. "Now, you rest today. I am sure you can catch up with your embroidery tomorrow. We are exploring the variety of the French knot today. I feel that one of your mental acuity can easily conquer that subject tomorrow while we go on to daisy chains." She held up her hand when Ellen tried to speak. "No protests, my dear!"

"No, Miss Dignam," Ellen said.

After Miss Dignam left the room, Fanny followed in her wake with her bag of neatly arranged embroidery threads. When the door closed, Ellen sat cross-legged on her bed and spread out the closely written notes she had taken during the tutorial and in the library. Pages in hand, she bit back her disappointment about the *Commentary*. Her notes were thorough, as far as they went, but the page was blank after the mouse scare, when her pencil drew a line like a startled eyebrow across the rest of the sheet.

"I suppose Vicar Snead would tell me that is what comes of spurious scholarship," she muttered.

As she sat wondering what course to take now, a servant scratched at the door.

Becky Speed opened the door, a parcel in her hands. Her eyes danced with excitement as she held out the package to Ellen.

"Here you are, Miss Grimsley," she said, her voice breathless as though she had run up three flights of stairs. "You cannot imagine who this is from!"

"Lord Chesney?" Ellen asked.

Becky shook her head. "Oh, I do not think so. He didn't look much like a lord. No, it was that student who brought you the chocolates last week. There I was, beating out the hall rug over the front railing, when he runs across the High, saying something about being late for a tutorial, and tossed me this package."

Ellen pushed aside her notes. "It must be James Gatewood." She leaned toward Becky. "He is an original item, Becky, and heavens, I caused him such monstrous trouble yesterday."

Becky frowned and backed toward the door. "Perhaps it is some sort of incendiary device, ma'am. Perhaps you should not open it."

Ellen tugged off the brown paper. "Goose! He wasn't *that* angry!" She paused, the wrapping in her hands. "Goodness knows he could have been. No, he was rather sweet about the whole thing. Heavens knows why. When I think . . ."

She stopped, embarrassed, and looked at the books that came spilling from the wrapping. "Becky, it is Chesney's *Commentary*!" She opened the slim volume. "And look, it hasn't even been cut yet!"

A note fell from the book. " 'Fair Hermia, if Miss Dignam's Select Female Academy is as disapproving of mice as it is of all forms of scholarship and original thought, you will not be interrupted as you study this work,' " she read. " 'The other book should provide further insight.' "

"What a kind man," Ellen said as she opened the other volume in her lap. "Becky, I do not think he can afford to give me books. He does not appear entirely prosperous."

"There is more writing on the back of that note," Becky said.

Ellen turned it over. "I hope you have not discarded your breeches and student gown. The larger volume must be returned to me at All Souls. Behave yourself. Jim."

Becky sucked in her breath. "Cheeky sort, Miss Grimsley."

"Not at all," Ellen protested. "I would say that he is more like a big brother." She considered Gordon in all his drunken splendor, sprawled across the table in the tavern. "At least, the kind of big brother that does one some good."

The servant came closer again and looked about the room. "Do you still have . . ."

"The breeches and cloak? Oh, my, yes. I hung them in the dressing room far in the back. Fanny will only find them if she pokes her long nose amongst my possessions, and why should she?"

Ellen put the books on the desk and turned back to her notes. She rested her cheek on her hand. "I will return the book, Becky, but then I will be done with this business. It can only get me in trouble of the worst kind. Then I would be dragged home to a purgatory of addressing wedding invitations, and listening to Horry moan and groan each time some piddling little detail went awry."

Becky's face fell. "But don't you love weddings, Miss Grimsley?"

"I daresay I might someday, but Horatia's is rather a trial."

She opened the book, but her mind was far away. It was more than just foolish, brainless Horatia. The trial was also Mama, looking her over so carefully when she thought Ellen was not aware, wondering if there was such an advantageous alliance in her younger daughter's future.

"Bother it," she muttered as she pulled out her letter opener and slit the pages of Chesney's *Commentary*. In another moment, she was deep in Shakespeare's enchanted Athenian forest, smiling over Lord Chesney's wise remarks and wondering about the man who wrote them. By the end of the day, when Gordon's essay had become a rough reality, she had created in her mind a picture of her benefactor.

He must be a kindly older man, probably someone with children of his own that he had seen through the trials of love, she thought, as she lit the lamp and continued copying her draft onto better paper. He can only be one of Aunt Shreve's friends. Papa doesn't know anyone this intelligent.

She put down her pen. James Gatewood says that Lord Chesney is a fellow at All Souls, so how can he be old? It is all too strange, she decided.

She sat in her room, waiting for Gordon to announce his presence below. Jates Gatewood had promised he would visit her and read the paper, so she waited for him, too. No Gordon, no Gatewood.

"Men are selfish beasts," she decided as she tied on her sleeping cap and blew out the candle.

Chesney's *Commentary* lay on the desk beside her bed. Moonglow streaked across it, setting the gold lettering on the spine shimmering. Ellen picked it up, settling the book on her stomach. "But for this excellent bit of insight, I forgive you, Jim Gatewood."

Gatewood did not darken Miss Grimsley's door the next day. Ellen's mind wandered through her geography teacher's tight-lipped description of the French countryside. During the interminable lecture, which dealt more on the evils of Napoleon than on the geography of France, she was tempted to ask why it was necessary to be so censorious about flora and fauna. Surely one cannot blame flowering shrubs for the rise of That Beast From Corsica, she thought.

She fared no better in embroidery, tangling her threads until Fanny was forced to desert her own neat sampler and help her. Ellen gritted her teeth, smiled sweetly at Fanny, and edged her chair closer to the window. She could see the spire of All Souls, located as it was just across the street. She was no wiser about the whereabouts of James Gatewood.

His gown rumpled as though he had slept in it, his eyes bulging from the exertion of running, Gordon darkened her door that evening. She met him in the sitting room under the agate eyes and wooden countenance of Miss Dignam. Without a word of greeting, he snatched the manuscript from her lap. He rifled through the pages and then sighed with relief, flinging himself into a chair.

"Ten pages! Thank God!" he exclaimed. "I had forgotten to tell you that the paper had to be between eight and ten pages." He counted the pages again, smiled and stuffed it in his pocket.

Ellen started forward in her chair, mindful of Miss Dignam's eyes on her. "But don't you wish to read what I have written, Gordon?"

"Oh, Lord, no," he said, and shook his head. "I am sure I could not understand one word, anyway. All that matters is that it is ten pages long." He leaned forward then and tugged at the short curls framing her face, curls she had spent all afternoon taming, in the hopes that someone would arrive to appreciate them. "Someday, I will do you a great favor, sister," he said and then laughed. "I'll start by telling you that your curls make you look like a poodle! Really, El."

She stuck out her tongue at him, and he laughed and leaped out of his chair in pretend fear. He dashed to the door, ignoring the quelling look Miss Dignam cast in his direction as she smacked down her playing cards.

Ellen hurried to his side. "At least let me know how it goes when you read the paper, you beast! You owe me that."

He tweaked another curl. "I will report promptly. Lord, El, did you do all those curls for me, or do you have a beau already? Someone stuffy and studious?"

"Of course not," she denied, her face rosy. "I did them for . . . for Lord Chesney!" She laughed at the look on his face and pushed him. "I am beginning to wonder if my benefactor really exists. Well, go on, if you must."

He left, after a kiss in the air by her cheek and a wave in her general direction. Ellen walked slowly back to her room. I will never compose another page for so ungrateful a brother, she thought, as she ran her hand along the stair railing. I wonder how many other select females have felt so full of the dismals.

She would never attempt the Bodleian again, as much as it beckoned. She sat at her desk, chin in hand, and gazed across the street to the spires of Oxford.

It might as well be on the moon, she thought, for all the good it does me.

6

Ellen steeled herself for another dreadful weekend. She lay in bed and watched Fanny primping in front of the mirror, raving on about the treat in store for her.

"Really, Ellen, if you had paid more attention to your embroidery this week, I am sure that Miss Dignam would have permitted you a stroll down the High Street with an unexceptionable beau."

She paused and turned around, her smile arch. "Provided you could find an unexceptionable beau, Ellen. I have my doubts."

She turned back to the mirror, and Ellen stuck her tongue out. "I am not sure that it is to my taste to be shepherded about in the company of a beau *and* a servant, not to mention the other couples in attendance," Ellen replied, keeping her voice light.

Fanny refused to be ruffled. She shook her head and clucked her tongue at her reflection. "Ellen, you are a faster little piece than I ever thought. Countenance, Ellen, countenance."

With a wave of her gloved hand, she was gone. Ellen threw her pillow at Fanny as the door closed, and then pulled the covers over her head. She thought about home, and even about Thomas Cornwell. At least if she were home, they could stroll about the gardens, or play cards in the library without the ubiquitous presence of a maid or footman. And if he was poor company, well, at least he was company, and she knew his faults.

She could ride when she chose, and walk to the village with Ralph, talking about Great Ideas. Here there was nothing but the prospect of another day spent at the embroidery hoop.

She was almost asleep again, when Becky Speed knocked and stuck her head inside the room. "Miss Grimsley, come quick! You have a visitor."

"Go away," Ellen said, her voice muffled under the bed clothes.

"It is Mr. James Gatewood, and he has never looked so good," Becky said. She ran into the room and pulled the covers off Ellen, who sat up in surprise.

"You mean his hair is combed?" she asked, and then laughed. "Well, I suppose such a momentous event calls for my presence, if for no other reason than to verify it."

She dressed quickly, running a comb through her tousled curls, grateful for once for naturally curly hair. She patted on her lavender cologne while Becky buttoned her up the back. "He said he didn't have much time," the servant said.

Ellen hurried down the stairs and threw herself into the sitting room.

James Gatewood whirled around from his contemplation of the view out the front window and put up a hand to stop her. "Whoa, fair Hermia! Where is the fire?"

Ellen twinkled her eyes at him. "Becky said you did not have much time, and I wanted to see how you looked with your hair combed."

He threw back his head and laughed until Ellen blushed. He turned around slowly, for her benefit. "Every hair in place, my dear. Note that the gown is pressed and I have on a starched collar." He put his hand over his heart. "I promised my mother that I would go to such exertions occasionally. It was one of the terms of the agreement."

"Agreement?" she asked.

It was Gatewood's turn to blush. "I did not really mean to mention that, but here it is: I promised Mama a year only at All Souls, and then I would go into the . . ." He paused and frowned, as if searching for the right words. He brightened. " . . . into the family business."

Ellen sat down and patted the seat beside her. Gatewood joined her, and she noticed that he smelled quite pleasantly of French cologne. "And what, sir, is the family business?"

"Horse trading," he replied, not batting an eye. "And window dressing," he added.

"Such odd occupations," she said.

"Someone must do them," he replied. "It is my lot in life to be a horse trader and a window dresser."

He regarded her for a moment, and she was aware how

patched-up was her own hurried appearance. "I slept late," she said in self-defense.

But there was nothing in his eyes of complaint. It was a warm expression he fixed on her, one that mde her stomach jump a little.

"I think you are charming," he said, "even with the wrong shoes on, and the marks of the bedspread still on your face."

Ellen gasped and looked down at her feet, where one brown shoe and one black one peeked out from under her dress. She touched her cheek. "Oh, dear!"

He leaned back on the couch, stretching out his legs, enjoying the moment. Without thinking, Ellen socked him in the stomach. "You are no gentleman!" she protested, laughing. "You remind me more of my brothers, and I will treat you that way."

"Brothers, eh?" he teased, when he could breathe again. "I don't know who to pity more: you or them."

The bells of Oxford sounded the hour. Gatewood glanced out the window. "I would love to discuss your family, but I am late. Do you have a copy of your *Midsummer Night's Dream* paper? I would love to read it."

"I did not have time to make another copy."

Gatewood shook his head. "My dear Miss Grimsley, always keep a copy. That is the first rule of the writer."

"It is only a paper for Gordon," she protested.

"Still and all, madam, scholarship demands it, and there is no telling who might try to gyp you." He rose and put on his gloves again. "I shall be forced to attend Gordon's University College reading this morning then, won't I?"

Ellen stood up, too, careful to keep her shoes under her dress. "I wish I could accompany you."

He looked down at her, a lazy smile playing about his face. "I wish you could, too." The smile vanished. "It seems unfair."

He took her hand and squeezed it. She looked up at him in surprise, and then smiled her sunniest smile.

"It doesn't matter." She let him hold her hand. "I am going to cry uncle soon and ask Papa to come and get me." Unexpected tears filled her eyes, replacing the smile. "Oxford it not what I thought it was, and I was a silly nod to harbor expectations."

"You are leaving?" he said, his voice as serious as hers. He only tightened his grip on her hand. "Do reconsider, Hermia. The Bodleian will be so dull with only the mice to entertain me."

She smiled then, and turned loose his hand, which she was gripping just as tight. "Still, sir, it has made me wiser."

He was standing so close that she could have kissed him. The thought made her blush again, even as she wondered where such an idea had come from. She stepped back, and clasped her hands behind her.

"You'll be late to the lecture, Jim," she said, her voice soft.

"So I shall be." He kissed her cheek. "Courage, fair Hermia," he said, and quoted, " 'Do not doubt that saints attend thee.' "

"*Hamlet,*" she said, "and badly altered, I might add."

He laughed and touched her cheek where he had kissed her.

And then he was gone. She stood in the doorway until he vanished down the alley that led to the interior of Oxford and University College.

Fanny and the other students returned before noon from their stroll about Oxford, rosy from the cold and glowing with news. Ellen looked up from her embroidery as Fanny entered the room. Fanny removed her hat and unbuttoned her pelisse. She went to the fireplace to warm her hands.

"Guess who we saw, running and jumping about on Cornmarket Street like a rabid dog?" she said at last.

"The Duke of Wellington," Ellen said promptly, her eyes on her embroidery.

"Silly! It was your brother!" Fanny shook her head in disapproval at the memory. "He accosted me, Ellen, and grabbed me by the shoulders and said he had news for you. Imagine." She looked down her long nose at Ellen. "Perhaps someone taught him how to write his own name, or tally beyond his fingers."

Ellen tightened her lips, counted to ten, and then smiled sweetly into her roommate's smug face. "Capital! Perhaps we should recommend Oxford to your brother Edwin, so he can learn these skills, too. It must be grievous indeed for Edwin to have to take off his shoes to do higher math at the Grain Exchange."

Fanny turned white about the mouth. "You're going to wish

you hadn't said that,'' she exclaimed, and then cast about for
something else. She raised her chin. "At least I, unlike you,
am to be a bridesmaid for my dear Edwin and your feather-
brain of a sister. Too bad such ignorance seems to run in your
family!'' She grabbed up her own embroidery and flounced from
the room, slamming the door after her.

"Sticks and stones may break my bones,'' Ellen muttered.
She refused to let her mind dwell on Fanny's rudeness. "Or
my own,'' she said out loud, grinning to herself. "That was
a repartee worthy of Ralph.''

She looked out the window, wondering when Gordon would
appear, wondering if her paper had really been such a success.

In a few moments she saw him meandering along, hands
shoved deep into his pockets, whistling. She tapped on the
window to get his attention. When he looked up, he pointed
down the street. Ellen shook her head, but he only shrugged
his shoulders and grinned at her, pantomiming a pint of ale in
one hand.

"Drat you, Gordon,'' she said as she ran down the stairs and
out the front door. She took him by the arm. "Not one step
farther until you tell me how it went,'' she said, out of breath.

Gordon looked around him. "Really, El, how does this
look?'' he complained. "I was merely going to celebrate the
successful outcome of this morning's work,'' he said. "And
then I was going to come back to Miss Dragon's Female
Hothouse and tell all.''

Ellen tugged him back to the academy. "That won't do,
Gordon. I know you too well. Tell me first, and then go to the
Cock and Hen.''

He gave her a look of compounded suspicion, surprise, and
hurt feelings. "Really, El. How did you know it was the Cock
and Hen?'' he accused, assuming that exalted air he used on
occasion when he wanted to remind her that she was the younger
sibling. "El, one would think you had been there yourself.
You're not keeping low company here in Oxford, are you?''
he asked, on the attack. "On the sly from Miss Dignam?''

Even though his dart hit home, she refused to acknowledge
it to him. "The lowest company I keep is yours, brother,'' she
said. "Now come in here. You owe me that.''

When she released her grip on his gown, Gordon Grimsley

carefully shook out its folds and followed her into the school, muttering something about little sisters who haven't a penny's worth of dignity to their name.

He followed her into the parlor, head high. When she closed the door behind them, he grabbed her and whirled her about, setting her down again and kissing her cheek with a loud smack.

"We did it, El. My paper was a smashing success!"

"Whose paper?" she asked quietly, but he did not hear her as he continued to dance about the room with her. He stopped finally, and flopped down on the settee.

"El, you should have been there. I rose to read my paper, and everyone was rummaging around and making vulgar noises. You know, the usual bits of nonsense at the Saturday readings."

She didn't know, but she nodded. "Go on."

He rose to his feet and struck a pose by the fireplace. "By the second page, everyone was silent," he said, his eyes bright. "Even the dons and fellows were hanging on my every word."

Ellen sighed with pleasure. "Magnificent, Gordon," she said.

He bowed. "It was, rather." He hurried forward then, and grasped her hands. "But the best part was the end, El. When the last word died away, the room was dead silent. And then everyone began to applaud."

"No!" she gasped, her eyes wide, the color rushing to her cheeks.

"Yes! And they stood up!" He threw himself in the chair across from her. "I never knew I could do so well!"

She frowned at her brother, who lolled in the chair, head back, eyes closed, a silly smile on his face. "I am the one who wrote the paper, Gordon," she reminded him.

He opened his eyes. "Oh, yes, quite," he said. "Wish you could have been there, dear, to see my triumph."

She chose to overlook his enthusiasm, and wondered for only a moment about the depression that settled over her.

It lasted only long enough for Gordon to sit upright and leap to his feet again. "El, here's the best part! Lord Chesney was there, and he singled me out for a conversation!"

"No!" she exclaimed again, her hands to her face. "Gordon, for heaven's sake, tell me what he looks like. What did he say?"

Gordon looked at her and shrugged. "Well, he was tall, and had brown hair."

Ellen pounded the armchair. "Can't you be more specific? That could be almost anyone in England!"

"I suppose you are right," he said and smiled. "He really looked like a lord."

Ellen sighed and took a turn about the room. "Gordon, you have never met a lord. How would you know?"

"Well, he had a certain air about him."

"So does the village tannery back home, Gordon."

He tried to stare her into capitulation, but he blinked first. "He had a Londoner's accent, I think. Sounded like a real aristo." He frowned and tried to think. "Black robe . . . what else is there?" He brightened. "He did have a rather magnificent gold watch fob."

Ellen sat down beside him. "So does James Gatewood, Gordon, and he is nothing out of the ordinary. Far from it, in fact."

Gordon grinned and tweaked her curls before she could draw away. "Silly! What do you expect here at Oxford? That Lord Chesney will wear his House of Lords getup or employ slave girls to dance in front of him and toss out rose petals? Lord, Ellen, sometimes you are almost as ridiculous as Horatia. Or me," he added, to soften the blow.

She took his words in good grace and considered their merit. What did she expect, after all? "And I suppose you will tell me that he puts his trousers on one leg at a time."

"He probably does, El," he said, and put his arm around her. He leaned closer. "I think he must tie his own neckcloths, too. Between you and me, it didn't look so expert."

He glanced toward the door that led to freedom and the tavern, and ran his tongue over his lips. Ellen tugged on his arm.

"One thing more, Gordon, before you abandon yourself to the Cock and Hen—or whatever that place is called—you said he had some conversation with you."

He slapped his forehead. "Oh, Lord, did he ever!" He took both of her hands in his. "El, you need to write me another paper."

She withdrew her hands from his grasp as though they burned. "Not this sister, Gordon! I swore I would not do that again." She eyed him until he blinked again. "Particularly since you seem to forget who wrote that first paper."

She might as well not have bothered to speak. "El, he told me I should write a paper on *Measure for Measure.*" Gordon rose and took his stand by the fireplace again. "He wants to know what I think about it! El, is it a play?"

"Yes, you block, it is a play," she said quietly. "Perhaps it is time you learned to write your own papers at University College."

His eyes grew round as he stared at her in horror. "Ellen! Don't abandon me now! It's just one more paper, and soon the winter vacation will be upon us and maybe, just maybe, Papa will change his mind and buy me a pair of colors."

When she made no reply, he fell on both knees and clasped his hands together. "Sister, have a heart!" He thought a moment, and sidled closer to her on his knees. "Didn't you just tell me that you owed Lord Chesney for your own improved treatment here?"

"I suppose I did, Gordon," she said at last. "Although what that has to do with . . ."

Gordon Grimsley had no time for sisterly riders. He let go of her hands and leaped to his feet. "I knew you would not fail me! I promise to attend my tutorial and take exemplary notes this time."

She nodded, already regretting her decision. "At the very least, you can give me back my *Midsummer Night's Dream* paper."

He shook his head. "I wish that I could, but Lord Chesney asked me for it, and what could I do?"

"What indeed?" she asked. "Gordon, you are the biggest flat that ever drew breath. Yes, I will write your stupid paper for the honor of the Grimsleys, and you had better hang on to the original this time."

He kissed her cheek. "Ellen, you are a great goer! Remind me to do something nice for you sometime."

The look she gave him sent him backing toward the door. He had almost escaped into the hall when she called to him.

"Gordon, I want you to take a note to James Gatewood at All Souls," she said, hurrying to the escritoire. She wrote quickly. "Tell him that I will return that one book that he loaned me, and tell him that I have a few questions about *Measure for Measure.* Maybe he will help me."

"I don't know, El," he said doubtfully, the letter between his fingers. "Gatewood doesn't sound at all the thing. Didn't you tell me that he comes from a long line of horse traders? I know that Papa is horse-mad, but I am not sure he would approve."

"Find someone to deliver that note, or I won't write your paper," she said.

He gave her a wounded look. "Lord, El, you can be difficult. Why did I never see this before? Very well, I will deliver it to the porter at All Souls, but that is all. Suppose I run into Lord Chesney there? He would ask me something about Shakespeare, and then we would be in such a fix."

"No, Gordon, *you* would be in such a fix," she amended pointedly.

He could not have heard her. He opened the door and stood there in the hallway, shaking his head over the perfidy of sisters until she wanted to yank the hairs out of his head one at a time.

As he regarded her, the gleam came back into his eyes. "El, you should have heard the applause I got," he said as he closed the door behind him.

"Ungrateful wretch," she muttered under her breath.

She took the noontime meal in thoughtful silence, considering *Measure for Measure,* and wondering why Lord Chesney would request a paper on that play, of all plays. She had never read it, and had only the vaguest notion of the plot.

After luncheon, she hurried to the academy library, a skimpy affair with one rack of books that were all split leather bindings and mouldy paper. *Measure for Measure* was not numbered among the Shakespeare collection.

Miss Dignam, noting the library door open—a rare thing in her academy—came into the room with a glare of suspicious inquiry in her face.

Ellen had perched herself on a stool, her knees drawn up to her chin. She brightened to see Miss Dignam, and got down off her roost.

"Miss Dignam, tell me please, does the academy possess a copy of *Measure for Measure*?"

Miss Dignam had shut the door behind her. "Miss Grimsley, that is most decidedly *not* a play for select females," she said, lowering her voice to a hiss. She gestured toward the bookcase. "I will tolerate *Romeo and Juliet* because, heaven knows, young girls need to see what happens when they disobey their parents . . ."

"I don't think that is precisely the message Shakespeare intended," Ellen murmured.

Miss Dignam frowned down at her. "It is the message *I* intend, Miss Grimsley!" she declared. "*Hamlet* is tolerable, I suppose, because who among us will ever actually meet a Dane? And *Macbeth*, well, *Macbeth* is questionable, what with ladies walking about in their nightgowns. But there will be no *Measure for Measure* in this academy," she concluded, shaking her head vigorously at the thought. "I honestly do not know where you get your ideas, Miss Grimsley."

Ellen threw up her hands in exasperation. "Miss Dignam, have you ever read *Measure for Measure*?"

Miss Dignam sucked in her breath as though she had been shot. "Of course not! I have it on good authority that it is no play for a lady to read, and that is enough for me!"

Ellen was forced to listen to the improving tirade that followed. With her fingers crossed behind her back, she promised never to stray into those less-accepted works of the Bard, and beat a hasty retreat when Miss Dignam paused for breath.

Miss Dignam followed her into the hall. "Miss Grimsley, I recommend a turn about the garden to work off your excess zeal for scholarship of a questionable sort."

"Yes, Miss Dignam," she replied, and hurried upstairs before Miss Dignam dredged up another argument.

Fanny was seated at the dressing table, examining the spots on her face up close in the mirror. She leaped back when Ellen bounded into the room.

"Lord, can't you knock?" she protested.

"It's my room, too, Fanny," Ellen said over her shoulder as she hurried into the dressing room she shared with her roommate.

She pulled aside her clothes to find the scholar's gown and the shirt and breeches. She peered closer, a frown on her face.

Surely she had not left that shirt all bunched up like that. She thought she remembered shaking it out before putting it on the hook behind her other clothes, but there it was, thrown in a ball on the floor of the closet. She put it on the hook again and grabbed up her sewing basket.

To her relief, Fanny was gathering up her embroidery. "Some of us have been invited to Lady Willa Casterby's apartment to complete our assignment." She smiled in triumph. "Too bad that you were not included."

"Yes, a pity," Ellen agreed, flopping down on her bed. "I do not know how I shall endure this slight." She laughed and rested on one elbow. "Think how convenient this will make it for you to talk about me. Think how I would retard the conversation, were I there."

Fanny uttered an unladylike oath she never learned at Miss Dignam's Select Female Academy and slammed the door behind her. Ellen was off the bed and back into the dressing room as soon as Fanny's footsteps receded down the hall. She took off her dress, pulled on the shirt and breeches, and put her dress on again.

Ellen looked in the mirror and laughed. "Lord, I am as fubsy as Fanny, with all these clothes on," she said. She threw a shawl around her shoulders to hide the lumps, and then folded the scholar's robe as small as she could and stuffed it in her embroidery basket. She snatched up the book she was to return.

Becky Speed was polishing silver in the servants' quarters when Ellen tiptoed silently down the stairs. She looked up in surprise. "Miss Grimsley! I thought you said you were not going to try that again!"

Ellen made a face as she struggled to unbutton her dress. "I was not, but Gordon has found himself backed into a corner and needs my help. This one last time," she finished, biting off each word.

Becky finished unbuttoning her. "You may say that, but I think you like writing those papers."

Ellen nodded. "You have found me out, Becky. I suppose I do."

In another moment, she was wrapped in the scholar's gown and across the High Street. She took a deep breath and turned the handle on the small door that opened onto All Souls quadrangle.

She crossed the quad quickly, head down, hardly allowing herself a look around at the peaceful grandeur that was All Souls in early December. She ran into the hall and stepped up to the porter's tall desk, standing on tiptoe and keeping her head down at the same time.

If the porter was surprised to see an undergraduate before him, and one so short, he did not let on. He scarcely glanced up from the paper he was reading, and inclined his head in her direction.

"Yes, young master?" he inquired mildly.

"The way to James Gatewood's apartment, please," she said, her voice gruff.

"Gatewood. Gatewood. Oh, yes, Gatewood!" the porter said, a smile wreathing his face. "Up the stairs and to the right. Look for the nameplate."

Ellen nodded and ran up the shallow steps, holding her breath when a group of scholars passed her. They were speaking in Latin. She rolled her eyes. I have died and gone to heaven, she thought. Surely there is no place in all of England like All Souls, maybe not in all the world.

One of the men said something in Latin and the rest laughed. Ellen hugged herself. Only Ralph would understand how exciting it was to be in a place where scholars joked in Latin.

She took the hall at a half-trot, looking at the nameplates, exclaiming to herself over the viscounts and earls and other distinguished names she recognized from the scraps of London news that occasionally made their way into the Grimsley household.

James Gatewood. There it was, an ordinary piece of paper stuck in the holder. She peered closer. The ink looked hardly dry. Trust James to forget about such details, she thought as she timidly knocked.

The door opened and James stood there, dressed in a shabby shirt without a neckcloth and breeches that looked slept in. His waistcoat was unbuttoned and his shoes were off.

"Hermia," he said, keeping his voice low. "To what do I owe this pleasure? Come in, come in."

She hurried into the room. "I sent Gordon with a message," she stammered, her face red.

He shrugged, a smile on his face. "I think we know Gordon well enough to suspect the outcome of that, my dear. I am glad I am here."

Ellen looked about her in delight. Books lined the room, filling each bookcase to overflowing. They rested on the broad window ledges, and jostled each other on every flat surface. The desk was covered with papers, the wastebasket crammed to capacity.

"You are fearsome untidy," she said, clutching the book she was returning, as if afraid to turn it loose in this room.

"It is the despair of my mother," he agreed. "But what is the point of putting away a book, when you know you will only be needing it again sometime next week, or the month after?"

She laughed. "I can't imagine, James." She held out the book to him. "I wanted to return this book, as you requested. I have kept Chesney's *Commentary*, because you said I should."

"So I did," he said, taking the book from her and adding it to the pile on the chair by the desk. "By the way, I heard your brother's presentation this morning. That essay was something fine, indeed." He shook his head. "You should have seen Gordoon basking in all that acclaim."

He noted the mulish look in her eyes. "Acclaim that should have been yours?"

She nodded, and then laughed in embarrassment. "But that wasn't why I wrote the paper, Jim, and not why I have come now."

James gestured to a chair by the fireplace, removing the books in it and sitting down across from her. "Why have you come, Hermia? I hoped you would, but I did not expect to see you, not really."

She clasped her hands in front of her. "I know I should not be here, but the worst thing has happened, James."

"There was an earthquake, and no one told me?"

She laughed, despite her agitation. "Are you never serious?"

"I am usually too serious," he said firmly, "except where you are concerned. And if I get too serious, I will send you into the Bodleian again to hunt for mice, so I can have another laugh."

"It is Lord Chesney, James," she said, when he had fallen into his familiar pattern of just looking at her in silence, his eyes appreciative. "He was at the lecture, too, and he has asked my looby brother for another paper!"

"Such a troublesome man is Lord Chesney," Gatewood commented. "It is a wonder that any of us tolerate him."

He went to a cabinet by the fireplace and removed some cheese. He sliced it and put it onto a cheese fork and handed it to her. "Turn that slowly while I toast the bread."

She did as he asked, watching the cheese change color and begin to bubble. In another minute, she slid the cheese onto the toast he held out to her and accepted it gratefully. He poured her some tea and then toasted some cheese for himself.

"Now, is that better?" he asked when she finished, and was sitting cross-legged by the fire.

"Oh, much, Jim, but it has not solved my problem. I am supposed to write a commentary on *Measure for Measure*, and I daren't chance another tutorial, or try the Bodleian. I don't even have a copy of the play, and there is not one at Miss Dignam's. In fact, she was aghast that I would think of reading it." She looked at him as he sat beside her in front of the fireplace. "What is the matter with *Measure for Measure*?"

He went to a particularly abundant bookcase and stood there a long moment, his eyes skimming each row. He pulled several more books from the shelf.

"You may borrow these, Ellen, and this copy of the play. They might answer some of your questions." He chuckled. "Knowing your mind, though, I expect they will only raise more questions, but that is the essence of scholarship, so we shall be satisfied."

She opened the first book, which was stenciled with a heavy crest and the word Chesney scrawled across the top. She looked at him, her eyes puzzled.

He took it from her, swallowed, and returned it without batting an eye. "Dear me, it appears that I have acquired some of the mysterious Lord Chesney's books. We have been known to raid each other's libraries."

She opened another book and another. All were stenciled with the same crest. She closed the books and raised laughing eyes at him. "You are a bit of a rascal, Jim! Don't you think you ought to return his books?"

He crossed his heart. "As soon as you have finished with them, I pledge that they will be returned to Lord Chesney. There, is that good enough, you little Puritan?"

She nodded. "I would hate for Lord Chesney to lose track of his books. Perhaps you should check his shelves for books of your own, James. Ralph and I are forever getting our books mixed up."

"I will do it this very afternoon," he said. "Of course, Chesney is such a raving eccentric that he probably won't even remember that he loaned them."

She laughed and hugged the books to her. Her eyes grew troubled then, and he sat down beside her on the floor again.

"What's the matter, my dear?" he asked, his voice soft.

"I am so tired of getting all my information secondhand. What am I supposed to look for in *Measure for Measure*?" she asked. "What is there that Gordon is supposed to discover?"

Gatewood settled himself against the dressed stones of the fireplace, where he could see her better. "Merely whatever speaks to you about the play, fair Hermia," he said. "It is called one of Shakespeare's 'problem' plays. It is the story of sexual blackmail, simply put. See if you can uncover a new way of looking at it, something no critic has ever even considered." He shifted slightly, resting his arm on his knee. "I wonder that Lord Chesney would choose such a topic, but then, he is a different sort of fellow."

"You know him well?" she asked, her face fiery red from Gatewood's plain words.

"About as well as one person can know another," he replied, moving away from the warmth of the fireplace. "We have always been friends. He's a bit of a rascal, I think, but harmless enough."

She was silent a moment, staring into the flames. "I will write this one paper, and then no other, as I am leaving," she said. "One would almost think that Lord Chesney engineered this to keep me here, with the assignment of this paper to Gordon."

"I did not know you were leaving," he said quickly. "Didn't you tell me that . . . that Lord Chesney had smoothed things over at Miss Dignam's?"

She shrugged. 'I am enjoying my geography class, thanks to his lordship, but I want more, Jim. The other girls laugh at me, and I begin to think I am as much a raving eccentric as Chesney himself.''

He smiled and took her hand. ''What is it you really want, Ellen?''

She looked around from habit, to make sure that no one was listening, and he chuckled. ''I want to map the world, Jim! I want to ride in an ascension balloon all across Europe and visit every country there is, learning languages and customs. And when I am done, I am going to write the most marvelous books about what I have seen. Books for young ladies who aren't as fortunate as I am.'' She stopped, embarrassed. ''Well, you did ask.''

''So I did,'' he replied, and gazed into the fireplace. He looked at her, his eyes piercing. ''And what if you cannot do any of these things?''

Ellen rested her chin on her knees. ''I will probably just return home and marry Thomas Cornwell, or someone else my Papa has in mind, someone with horses and property and a seat on the Grain Exchange. That's probably what will happen. I'm not a fool.''

Gatewood was silent then, his face unreadable. Ellen watched him for a moment and then got to her feet. She touched the books in her arms. ''But right now, I will write about Shakespeare, and probably remember these days as the best of my life. Thank you, James Gatewood.''

She went to the door and let herself out while he still sat on the floor. She was at the top of the stairs when he bounded out of the room, grabbed her around the waist and kissed her.

She didn't struggle to get away, because she didn't want to. She let him kiss her, and kissed him back, wishing that her arms were not full of Shakespeare.

He stepped back from her. ''That is for luck, Ellen,'' he said, his voice unsteady. ''Make it a wonderful paper.''

Hands in his pockets, he backed down the hall and into his room again. She heard him whistling before he closed the door.

7

She began *Measure for Measure* in earnest the following morning. When geography was over, and she had learned all she cared to know about the exports of Portugal, Ellen ignored the summons to luncheon and seated herself at her desk.

Chin in hand, she gazed out the window to the spires of All Souls across the street. If I were to tell James Gatewood that I had just come from an hour's enlightenment on the kinds and varieties of cork and its implications in the society we live in, I could probably have heard him laughing from here to All Souls, she thought. Scholarship is strangely served at Miss Dignam's.

And then she thought no more of James Gatewood, because thinking of him made her blush.

How extremely odd it was that he had kissed her. She could fathom no reason for it, not really. He knew she was the daughter of a squire, and a man of some substance in the shire. Ellen stirred restlessly in her chair and opened the play before her. Wasn't James Gatewood descended from a long line of window dressers and horse traders? Surely he could not think himself in any way eligible. She knew that a certain number of openings in some of the colleges were saved for poor students, but he was not in the same class with her.

She closed the book again, considering the matter. As she had created her own fiction about Lord Chesney, she could do the same for Gatewood. He was probably an only son, whose proud but respectable yeoman family had scrimped and saved for years to afford him this one year at All Souls. She sighed. Perhaps it was a parish effort. She knew that appointments to All Souls were rare, indeed. Perhaps Gatewood's entire parish had banded together to see that he received this chance to make something of himself.

She frowned. It did not fadge. Although he generally looked

undeniably rumpled, his clothes were of excellent quality, and there was nothing seedy about him. His personal library was huge, and he was a friend of Lord Chesney.

Ellen brightened again and reopened the book before her. Perhaps James Gatewood was another of Lord Chesney's projects. It would be so like Lord Chesney in his bounteous eccentricity to help a poor but honest son of his retainers.

Lord Chesney. Now there was an unknown quantity, indeed, she thought. I know only that he is a peculiar eccentric who loves the plays of Shakespeare. He has taken it upon himself to interest himself in the Grimsley family. Beyond that, I have nothing but idle speculation. I don't even know what he looks like, she thought, as Lord Chesney crossed the stage of her mind and followed Jim Gatewood into the wings.

The boards were cleared for Shakespeare.

She read rapidly, almost finished the play while the others were at the dining table, and then stretched out for the repairing nap that Miss Dignam considered essential before her minions tackled the intricacies of embroidery.

Fanny Bland had eyed her with vast suspicion as she flounced into the room they shared and laid herself down. Ellen ignored her, beyond a glance and an unvoiced question at Fanny's self-satisfied expression.

It was an expression she remembered from their shared childhood, when the older Fanny had taken such delight in seeing that Ellen was constantly in trouble. Horatia had always been content to follow after the insufferable Edwin and listen to him prose on and on about horses and the proper management of a Cotswold farm. Fanny had made her own fun by tripping up Ellen with her infernal tattling.

The memory rankled, even though they were too old for that sort of childish devilment. Pointedly, Ellen turned her chair slightly to avoid Fanny's smirk.

She was unprepared for embroidery, and had to endure Miss Dignam's icy stares, and the laughter of the other girls as she struggled to follow the simplest instructions. Her mind was full of the trials of Isabella and her impetuous brother, Claudio, arrested by Angelo, a petty bureaucrat. As her eyes paid attention to Miss Dignam's explanation of feather-stitching, her mind was full of Isabella's awful dilemma, and the price Angelo wanted from her for Claudio's life.

I would never surrender my virginity for the safety of my brother, she thought, red-faced, as she fumbled with the threads and knots in her lap, not daring to raise her eyes to Miss Dignam's barely banked wrath.

Well, not for Gordon, anyway, she concluded, as, tongue between her teeth, she hurried through another lopsided row of daisy chains.

For Ralph? Well, possibly. The thought made her laugh out loud, and brought Miss Dignam over to stand in front of her, staring down.

"You find this abomination of a sampler amusing?" Miss Dignam thundered, as the room grew quiet.

Ellen paled and swallowed. "No, Miss Dignam," she whispered. 'I was merely thinking of something else."

"Shakespeare," Fanny offered, and then laughed at Ellen's discomfort. "One of those questionable plays, I do not doubt."

Miss Dignam snatched the sampler from Ellen's nerveless fingers and waved it about the room as the other girls laughed. "Miss Grimsley, it is a continuing mystery to me why Lord Chesney is so interested in your progress here," she said as she picked out the offending threads and thrust the project back in Ellen's lap.

"It is a mystery to me, too," Ellen said, and then flinched when Miss Dignam frosted her with a head-to-toe stare.

"I'll thank you not to add impertinence to your numerous— and growing—list of character deficiencies, Miss Grimsley," the headmistress said.

Ellen raised startled eyes. "I meant no impertinence," she stammered. "I . . . I don't understand his interest, either, Miss Dignam. I meant nothing more."

But Miss Dignam had turned her back on her and was admiring Fanny's beautiful row of daisy chains.

Ellen sighed and vowed to do better. By the time the endless class was over, her back ached and her head was pounding.

In the peace of her room, a quiet contemplation of the armload of books that James Gatewood had loaned her did nothing to restore her confidence. It was as he had said: they raised more questions than they answered. She stared hard at the books, willing them to tell her more about *Measure for Measure*. Her scrutiny yielded nothing except a greater headache, and the gnawing discomfort that she, or Gordon, at any rate, was about to be weighed in the balance and found wanting.

She leaned back in her chair and stared at the ceiling. "What is it that Lord Chesney—bless his quirky heart—expects that Gordon will discover from this play?" she asked out loud.

The answer came to her so fast that she thudded all four chair legs back onto the floor. Her heart pounding, she looked at the books of commentary on the desk in front of her and closed them one by one. She stacked them to one side and took out a piece of paper. Lord Chesney expects more from Gordon— the wonder scholar—than stale, revisited ideas. And James Gatewood expects more from me, she thought, opening the play again and dipping her pen in the inkwell. I will not merely shake my head over this frank and enormously engaging play and declare it a "problem" like other Shakespeare students. I will turn it on its head.

She wrote steadily until the dinner bell chimed in the hall. With a yawn, Ellen got to her feet, stretching her arms over her head, and then pressing her hand to the small of her back. Scholarship is tedious business, she decided as she went slowly down the stairs, her mind full of *Measure for Measure*.

The small talk at the dinner table flowed all around as she ate thoughtfully, chewing over Isabella's plight and Shakespeare's intentions with the same interest that she awarded the beef roast and kidney pie. She sat impatiently through all the courses, with their accompanying dreary gossip about the royal family and Beau Brummell's latest witticisms, eager to be back at her desk.

After Miss Dignam finally released the diners, Ellen scurried into the library and surveyed again with dismay the pitifully few copies of Shakespeare's plays. "This will never do," she declared firmly as she hurried upstairs.

In another moment she had composed a hasty scrawl to James Gatewood, fellow, All Souls. It was a plea for a copy of Shakespeare's complete works, if he possessed such a volume,

plus the return of his commentaries. " 'I have decided to attempt
original scholarship,' " she wrote. " 'Should you wish to know
more, then don't miss Gordon's Saturday recitation. Regards,
El.' " She signed her name with a flourish.

She summoned the footman and sent him downstairs with the
books, the note, a shilling, and the admonition to jettison the
books and swallow the note if Miss Dignam should happen by.
The footman merely grinned and bowed.

Ellen expected no reply that evening, but she waited, anyway,
hopeful that the footman would find Gatewood in his quarters
and possessing just the volume she required.

Her wishes were rewarded an hour later by a tap on the door.
Fanny looked up from her contemplation of her face in the
mirror, but turned away with a sniff when Becky Speed came
into the room.

"Miss Grimsley," she said breathlessly, as Fanny turned to
regard her again. "The footman said I was to give this to you."

She handed Ellen a cumbersome folio edition of Shakespeare's
complete works.

It was a beautiful work in and of itself, bound in soft morocco
leather, with gold leafing. She carried it to her desk and took
out the note stuck into it.

Jim had returned her own note, and added his own scrawl
to her words. " 'I can hardly wait to hear the pearls of wisdom
that will drop from Gordon's lips. Yrs., Jim.' "

She laughed and followed the arrow at the bottom of the page.
" 'P.S.,' " she read silently. " 'I suppose I shouldn't have
kissed you on the stairs like that, but it seemed like a good idea
at the time.' "

She blushed and read the postscript again, wondering for the
first time if James Gatewood was as wild an eccentric as his
friend Lord Chesney. She crumpled the note in her hand, putting
it in the back of her desk drawer. She looked over her shoulder
to see Fanny regarding her thoughtfully.

"Little secrets?" was Fanny's only comment as she began
to dab witch hazel on her face.

Ellen's eyes were as wide and innocent as Fanny's. "Fanny,
you know my life is an open book," she said as she gathered
together her papers and arranged them neatly on her desk.

"Besides, I have never known a time when you could not find out my business. I have no secrets, Fanny."

Fanny turned an unhealthy red and set her lips in a firm line. Ellen prepared for bed, retrieving her flannel nightgown from the chair close to the fire where she had draped it. She climbed into it quickly in the chilly room, grateful for its warmth, not caring that Fanny thought her tacky for leaving her gown on the chair for all to see.

In perfect charity with God, she knelt longer beside her bed for prayers this time. And God bless Jim Gatewood and his wonderful library, she prayed silently. After a moment's consideration, Ellen rested her cheek on the bed. And help him to find someone who doesn't mind a little disorder, and who is not above scolding him to dress tidy occasionally. Heaven knows, he shows to advantage when he does.

Ellen raised herself up on her knees and clasped her hands together again. There was no sense in bothering the Lord Omnipotent about James Gatewood's less-than-perfect personal habits. And bless Mama and Papa and Martha and Horatia and Ralph, and even Gordon, she concluded, and then hopped into bed.

Fanny blew out the lamp. Ellen sighed and closed her eyes, grateful to be away from her desk, even as her mind tossed about scenes and plots from Shakespeare's plays to support the theory that was going to startle University College on Saturday.

"Did you hear me, Ellen?"

She opened her eyes. Fanny was speaking in her usual querulous tones.

"No, I'm sorry, Fanny. What did you say?"

"Merely that I was going home this weekend to be fitted for my bridesmaid dress."

There was an edge of triumph in Fanny's voice. Ellen felt tears sting at her eyelids, and she scrubbed them away. Horatia had chosen the most beautiful deep green for her bridesmaids. Ellen had lingered over the bolts and bolts of specially dyed lawn that Mama had purchased, wishing that she could grow six inches and be symmetrical enough to march in the bridal procession.

Ellen raised herself up on one elbow and looked through the

gloom at Fanny. "I hope you have a good time," she said softly. "I wish I could be a bridesmaid, too. Goodnight, Fanny."

"Oh, well, thank you, Ellen," said Fanny, the surprise showing in her voice. She cleared her throat in a way that sounded vaguely like embarrassment to Ellen. "Is there . . . is there anyone you want me to say hello to for you?"

Ellen thought a moment, and remembered her conversation with James Gatewood in his chambers. She took a deep breath. "If you should happen to see Tom Cornwell, tell him hello for me."

"I will, Ellen."

She closed her eyes again, surprised at the tears that still threatened, even though her artless words had disarmed Fanny for the time being. Tom Cornwell was likely her destiny. She had said as much to Jim. She clutched her pillow in her arms, enjoying the comfort of it, and wishing for the briefest moment that James Gatewood's arms were still around her and that silly armload of books on the All Souls stairwell. Perhaps Thomas will hold me like that someday, she thought, and dabbed at her eyes. Maybe, if and when we are married, he will become someone I can love and respect.

Soon she would be returning for Horatia's wedding, and she could see him again. Perhaps he would be more to her liking, then, if she looked at him seriously in the light of a possible husband. Someone to share my bed with, she thought as she rested her head against the pillow. Someone with enough money for Papa, and living close by for Mama.

What about me? she thought. What does he have that I will need? Her tears flowed faster. Would he understand if I wanted to travel, and learn to make maps, and write guidebooks? Would he loan me books, and give me chocolates when I was desperate, rescue me from the Bodleian, and make me a little tipsy in a tavern?

She turned her face into the pillow so Fanny could not hear her. Will Thomas Cornwell, with his big ears and horse talk, and conversations about the Grain Exchange, even have a clue about me, Ellen Grimsley?

When she heard Fanny breathing slowly and evenly, Ellen left her bed and sat at her desk again, parting the curtains so she could see the moon rise over the spires of Oxford. Her hand gripped the curtains. "It is only across the street, but I can never reach it," she said softly. "Oh, God, it is so unjust."

She touched the pages in front of her. There would be this final paper for Gordon, and no more. She would go home before she made a fool of herself, and tell Mama that she was ready for Thomas Cornwell and his clumsy attentions. If she had any regrets, she would bury them in the back of her mind, stuffed out of sight like the shirt, breeches, and scholar's gown that hung in the dressing room.

Fanny left after morning classes in the company of a maiden aunt who was returning home to the Cotswolds from London. "I will remember you to your family," she told Ellen over her shoulder as she followed the footman downstairs with her trunk.

"Thank you, Fanny," Ellen said. She waited impatiently by the front door while Fanny stood there, trying to remember if she had forgotten anything.

As soon as Fanny left, Ellen darted upstairs again, spreading her pages and notes across both beds and walking around them, rearranging ideas as she considered what she was doing. Using *Measure for Measure* as her starting point, she would prove, play by play, that many of the plays of Shakespeare were written by a woman.

"Surely no man can know the mind of a woman so well," she said out loud, and then repeated her words as she wrote them down. "I will prove it and prove it until there can be no argument," she said, looking around her at the garden of notes planted everywhere.

"What do you think of my idea?" she asked Becky Speed later when the maid came in.

"I think you are going to find yourself in the middle of a muddle," the maid said frankly. "How long will it be until someone asks Gordon an intelligent question—begging your pardon, ma'am—and he stands there like a half-wit?"

"There is that risk," Ellen agreed. "But what is that you have there?" she asked, eager to change the subject, because Becky had hit on the target of her own fears.

From her contemplation of the clutter about her, Becky brightened and held out the box. "More chocolates, Miss, and don't we know who they are from?"

Ellen clapped her hands. "Jim Gatewood is probably spending

money he does not have, but oh, how thoughtful!'' She opened the box, sniffing the contents, and pulled out a note. " 'If chocolates be the food of scholarship, eat on,' " she read, and laughed. "He is never serious where Shakespeare is concerned. What a mangle of a quote."

Ellen popped a chocolate in her mouth and held out the box to Becky. "I am to be interrupted only if the building is burning down," she told the maid. "If Miss Dignam should cut up stiff that I am missing embroidery, tell her . . . oh . . . tell her that Lord Chesney has given me a particular assignment that I must fulfill. She won't believe it for long, but at least I should have the paper in hand before she gets too suspicious."

She was back at Shakespeare before Becky let herself out quietly.

That evening, Gordon delivered his notes to her from his weekly tutorial. "We discussed *Measure for Measure,*" he said, stretching out his hands to the sitting room fire. "Lord, I do not know how Shakespeare comes up with such rattlebrained plots. I am sure I do not have a sister like Isabella, who would surrender her . . . well, you know . . . for me."

Ellen only glanced up from his notes and smiled her best gallows smile, the one reserved for brothers. "You are absolutely right, Gordon."

An uncomfortable silence followed that Gordon broke finally by putting his arm cautiously about his sister. "Well, El, some day when I am a general you will look back on all this and laugh."

"I doubt it," she replied. "You have put us both in such a spot, brother, that I may never forgive you. Goodnight. Come back Friday for the paper."

She left him standing, open-mouthed, by the fireplace.

She finished the paper Friday morning, when the candles had burnt out and the sun was struggling over the barren, winter-swept hills. Her eyes burned and her back was sore. With a sigh, Ellen gathered her night's work and took it to the window. She perched on the window seat and watched the sun rise. She looked down at the closely written pages in her hands. *I could have done better,* she thought, tracing the words with her finger. Flipping to the last page, she read the ending again.

"Oh, it is good," she whispered out loud.

In another moment, she was seated at her desk again, writing out a fair copy for Gordon. When she finished, she added a note, admonishing him to read it through first before he sprang it on himself in front of an audience of scholars, and summoned the footman. Her eyes drooping with exhaustion, she gave him Gordon's directions and another shilling.

Back in her room again, she finished the box of chocolates and fell asleep in the middle of a pile of notes.

When she woke, the room was tidy again and Becky was just stacking the last of her notes and first draft in neat piles on the floor. Ellen sat up and rubbed her eyes.

"Best burn them, Becky," she said. "I would only get in trouble if Fanny chanced upon them and put two and two together."

"Very well, Miss," Becky said, "although it seems a shame after all your work."

She attended her classes that day, nodding off over the geography of Cyprus and then struggling in vain to make sense of her embroidery. She could only bow her head in misery over the scathing criticism that Miss Dignam rained down upon her head. With her eyes closed, she even dozed a little, waking up when Miss Dignam shook her and demanded to know how in the world she expected to find a husband if she knew so little about the domestic arts.

"I . . . I don't know that I have ever given it much thought," she managed finally when the headmistress just stood there, hands on hips, glaring at her. Finally she raised her own cool blue eyes to Miss Dignam's red face. "I shall have to trust Papa to find someone among his horsey acquaintances who will have me with all my faults. He will probably want to examine my teeth and watch my gait about the paddock. After all, what can a girl expect?"

The other students in the room gasped.

"Miss Grimsley, go to your room," Miss Dignam ordered, her voice perfectly awful.

Ellen went, grateful to collapse in sleep upon her bed again. She was still sleeping the next day when Becky shook her awake.

"Miss Grimsley! Gordon is below, and I have never seen him so excited!"

She sat up and stuffed her feet into her shoes, looking about for a shawl to hide the wrinkles in the dress she had slept in. "I am amazed that Miss Dignam let him in."

"Oh, she does not know. He is belowstairs in the kitchen."

Ellen followed the maid down the servants' stairs and into the kitchen, where Gordon strode about like a caged animal. When he saw his sister, he ran to her, lifted her off her feet and whirled her around.

"El, I have been declared a Shakespeare prodigy!" he crowed, ignoring her request to set her down.

"How lovely for you, Gordon," she said, when he finally stopped whirling her about like a top.

He smiled modestly. "Of course, I'm not sure what a prodigy is, El, but since everyone was standing on their feet and applauding—the ones who weren't cheering, anyway—I guess it is a good thing."

Ellen sat down and merely regarded her brother in silence until he recalled himself and sat beside her.

"Well, tell me," she said, when he just sat there grinning.

With a laugh, he leaned back in his chair. "I was almost scared spitless when I read your conclusion about Shakespeare being written by a woman."

"Gordon! I told you to read the paper over first!" she scolded.

He ducked his head in embarrassment. "I meant to, really I did, but the men in the next room were holding a mouse race, and when that was done, we went to the Cock and Hen, and there just wasn't time. You understand, El."

"Of course," she replied promptly. "Never let education interfere with the business at hand."

"I knew you would understand. Well, when I finished my paper, you could have heard a pin drop. And then someone started applauding, and others were on their feet cheering me. It's the greatest feeling, El."

She could think of nothing to say except hot words that she would regret later, so she had the wisdom to knot her hands in her lap, grit her teeth, and be silent.

Gordon touched her arm. "The best part, El, the best part of all! Someone had invited the Vice Chancellor of Oxford. Come to think of it, he was sitting beside Lord Chesney." Gordon grinned at the memory. "He told me I was a credit to my family and the whole nation."

Ellen leaned forward. "Did Lord Chesney seem to enjoy it?"

"Oh, El! He's the one who called me a Shakespeare prodigy." He closed his eyes, a dreamy expression on his face. "Gordon Grimsley, boy genius, England's gift to the world. El, everyone should have a sister like you."

She swallowed the tears that threatened. "Did . . . did you see James Gatewood?"

He frowned. "I don't know this Gatewood chap you are always going on about." He shrugged. "Who cares? Lord Chesney was pleased, and so was my warden, and I can't think anything else matters."

"I don't suppose it does. Did you get the copy back?"

He slapped his forehead in contrition. "Would you believe that Lord Chesney insisted upon having this one, too?"

Ellen uttered an exclamation of disgust. "Gordon, I particularly told you not to let that happen! I was too tired to write out another copy, and see here, I told Becky to burn my notes and rough copy, so there is nothing left."

He looked at her with an expression that wavered between pity at her shortcomings and brotherly condescension. "I don't see how you can possibly blame me for that, El. Besides, what can it matter? What can he possibly do with those papers?" He put his arm around her. "And what use can you have for them, sis?"

She nodded slowly. "I suppose you are right, although it does make me uneasy that I have no copies of anything."

He laughed and tugged at her curls. "Great Godfrey, El, what were you planning? To publish a book of your collected essays?" He gave her a hug and pulled her toward the door. "Who do you think would ever read a stodgy old Shakespeare collection by the world-renowned Ellen Grimsley?"

It did sound unlikely, put that way. Ellen felt her face grow red. Was I honestly imagining that I would ever publish those works someday, she asked herself as Gordon prattled on about inanities, and finally took out his watch.

"I'm off, El," he declared finally. "Some of the chaps are hosting a dinner for me." He puffed out his chest. "I've become a credit to University College, don't you know."

"Gordon, what you are is a fool," she said, not mincing her words and softening none of the sting.

He only looked at her fondly and kissed her cheek. "Yes, ain't I?" he agreed, all amiable complacency. "Maybe it will be enough to get me sprung early from this pile."

"Either that, or it will make you so valuable that University College—and Papa—will never let you go."

He stopped and looked at her with an expression close to horror. "Lord, I never thought of that, El!" he squeaked, his voice suddenly raised into the upper registers by the prospect of a life of study. "Whatever you do, sister, do not make the next essay so brilliant, will you?"

He opened the door. She put her hand out and closed it again. "What essay, Gordon?" she asked, her voice quiet. "I am writing no more essays for you."

His face lost its usual healthy glow and he swallowed several times. "See here, El. You must," he managed, when he could speak.

"I don't have to do anything of the sort," she retorted. "And I am thinking of applying to Papa to spring *me* from this pile."

He gripped her arm. "El, you must help me."

"Oh, must I? I suppose you will tell me that Lord Chesney insists upon another essay," she said, opening the door for him.

He closed it this time. "As a matter of fact, he did, El, and he wants this one to be about . . ." He paused to reflect, rolling his eyes. "Dash it all, something about a storm, and more of them damned fairies, or sprites. Lord C. went on and on about 'brave new world,' whatever the devil that means."

"*The Tempest,* you block," she said, and opened the door again. "Very well, but no more after this one, Gordon. I have done enough for you."

He only smiled, but she did not like that smile.

8

If she expected a visit from Jim Gatewood that afternoon, she was mistaken. For someone who seemed so interested in her progress, for someone so willing to help, he was notable by his absence.

Even Ellen's first official expedition outside the academy in the company of a maid, footman, and other select females failed to rouse her from her disappointment.

What is it that I expect? Ellen thought as she walked along the High Street with the other students. With a blush, she looked away from her own reflection in a shop window. I want his approbation, she thought. I want him to tell me what a fine job I did on this essay. She looked down the street to the spires of All Souls.

It could be that I just want to see him.

The thought made her pause in the middle of the street. The other Christmas shoppers hurried around her, looking back in irritation.

"Ellen! Hurry up!" called one of the girls. "You are becoming a trial!"

The afternoon was cold, the kind of blue-gray cold that she was familiar with from her own corner of the Cotswolds, the cold that burrowed in between the shoulder blades and never let go until spring. Ellen tugged her woolen scarf tighter about her neck and shoved her hands deep into the pockets of her pelisse. Dutifully she followed the others from store to store along the High, exclaiming over ribbons and fancies until she was heartily bored.

A reminder from one of the other students about the closeness of Christmas inspired her to find a doll for Martha, a strand of coral beads for Horry, and grey kid gloves for Mama. Papa would content himself with his favorite pipe tobacco. She felt disinclined to buy anything for Gordon, and turned her interests to Ralph.

"We must go to the bookstore," she said as the others were starting back. "I think it is not far," she coaxed, when the girls groaned and began a litany of complaints about their feet, the weather, and the weight of their packages, at least the ones that the footman, burdened as he was, was unable to carry.

"I have to find something for my brother," Ellen declared. She gave her scarf another yank. "Just . . . go on," she ordered, "and leave Becky Speed with me. Surely that's proper enough."

Grateful not to have to surrender their footman, the others agreed. In a moment they were hurrying toward the warmth of Miss Dignam's asylum.

Ellen tucked her arm in Becky's. "I'm sorry," she apologized, "but suppose I am punished next week for some misdeed or another and cannot escape to finish my Christmas obligations? I would hate to disappoint Ralph."

Becky only smiled, even though her nose was red from the cold. "If we cut through the alleys, we will be there quicker."

They hurried through Oxford University's alleys. Soon Ellen saw Fletcher's sign, swaying in the stiffening breeze. They ducked inside, and Ellen sighed with pleasure. The walls from floor to ceiling bulged with books of all types and sizes. Clerks scurried like sailors up and down the ladders that moved on tracks the length of the narrow store.

A clerk appeared at her side.

"I say, can you show me a copy of Shakespeare's complete works?" Ellen asked, when her mouth had thawed sufficiently to permit the formation of words again.

He disappeared, climbed a ladder, and retrieved a duplicate of the copy James Gatewood had sent to Miss Dignam's last week. He quoted her a price that made her eyes open wide.

"Mercy on us," she exclaimed. "I haven't near enough!"

Disappointed, the clerk whisked the book away before she could sully it with one more glance. Ellen whispered to Becky, "Oh, I am so embarrassed! James Gatewood paid a small fortune for that book he sent me. I had no idea it was so dear. Becky, that was probably all his money in the world!"

The maid eyed her doubtfully. "Surely not, miss. Surely Mr. Gatewood has other resources." She thought a moment. "Well, perhaps he does not, considering the state he is always in when we see him." She giggled behind her well-darned mittens. "He always looks like he came backward through the shrubbery, doesn't he?"

"And I am afraid he has gone to awful expense for me," Ellen said mournfully, thinking of the beautiful book on her desk with "Good luck!" scrawled across both inside pages.

After another moment spent in real discomfort, Ellen settled on a more modest volume of Shakespeare's histories and let the clerk carry it away to be wrapped in brown paper.

"I must remember never to petition James Gatewood for books," she said out loud, and then glanced at Becky. "I feel that for my penance I should write that sentence one hundred times. Oh, dear!"

Becky took the package from the clerk. "Well, it can't be helped now, Miss Grimsley."

"I suppose it cannot," Ellen said.

The wind outside Fletcher's staggered them backward. Snow was falling. Ellen linked arms with the maid and they turned, heads down, into the wind.

It fairly carried them along, swooping and dodging through Oxford's warren of alleys and hidden streets. Ellen's dress whirled up around her knees, and she could only be grateful that no one else was abroad on such a chilly afternoon to witness such a brazen display.

Almost no one. She was turning to attempt some remark to Becky as they struggled along, when suddenly James Gatewood separated them and put his arms through theirs.

"What a duo of silly chits you are," he said mildly, as the wind ruffled through his already untidy hair. "I expected that England's next preeminent Shakespeare scholar would have the wit to keep warm."

Ellen giggled despite her misery. "We are on Christmas errands," she shouted above the wind.

"You'll only get a lump of coal from me, if you do not seek shelter soon," he shouted back, still cheerful.

Becky tugged at his other arm. "Please, sir, I live only one street over. We could duck in there for a moment to get warm."

Gatewood smiled at the maid. "Capital notion, my dear!" he declared. "How glad I am to know that one of you has a

particle of sense.'' He laughed out loud when Ellen dug him
in the ribs. "My dear, if the shoe fits . . ."

He had to duck his head to get through the low doorway into
the Speed house, a narrow set of quarters built along the same
lines as the bookstore. A woman who looked very much like
Becky Speed was sitting beside a thin, sunken-faced man with
no expression who lay on a daybed close to the fire. She blew
a kiss to Becky and took in the situation at a glance, rising to
her feet.

"Come close to the fire," she said, gesturing toward the small
mound of coal that glowed in the grate. After a slight hesitation,
she hurried to the cupboard on the dark side of the little room
and took out two china cups.

In another moment, Ellen was sipping the weak tea. She
smiled her appreciation. The woman beamed back as Becky put
her arm around her.

"Mr. Gatewood, Miss Grimsley, this is my mother," Becky
said, and then tilted her head toward the man on the daybed.
"And my father. He was a stone mason, and fell from the walls
of Magdalen while making repairs last year." Her voice faltered
and she tightened her grip on her mother. "We think he can
understand us."

Gatewood hesitated not a moment. He walked to the daybed
and sat down in the spot Mrs. Speed had vacated. "Then we
thank you for your hospitality, Mr. Speed," he said, his voice
gentle.

Beyond a slight movement of his head, Mr. Speed lay still.

With increased appreciation, Ellen watched James Gatewood
as he sat where he was, addressing pleasantries to the man who
could not answer him. She turned away and found herself
looking at Mrs. Speed, who was watching Gatewood.

Becky kissed her mother's cheek as Mrs. Speed began to dab
at her eyes with her apron. "I think he reminds Mama of
Tommy, who went to Spain to war and never came home."

"Becky, I am so sorry," Ellen said. Her throat felt scratchy
and her eyelids burned. She sipped her tea-flavored hot water,
her heart troubled. *And Spain is where Gordon thinks he must
go,* she thought. *I was so unkind to him this afternoon.*

In another moment, Mrs. Speed directed her attention to the
fireplace. Carefully she took out two more lumps of coal from

the nearly empty pasteboard box that served as a coal scuttle and arranged them on the little fire with all the skill of a bricklayer. Ellen's eyes clouded over as she remembered the maids at home tumbling coal into the grate, careless of it.

Gatewood remained by Becky's father until the man closed his eyes and relaxed in sleep. He looked at Ellen then, who had removed her pelisse and was sitting close to the fire, her hands extended to it.

"You look so nice in a dress," he whispered, so none of the Speeds could hear him. "Much more flattering than a scholar's gown."

She raised her eyes from her contemplation of the struggling little fire, as though she had not heard his small compliment. "James, I think they intend to have us for supper."

He sat close beside her. "We can't put them to that embarrassment," he said softly, "even though I would like to sit with you by the fire a little longer."

"Well, you cannot," she said, and then glanced at his face. "You could come to Miss Dignam's parlor some evening."

"No, I could not," he replied enigmatically and then changed the subject by wrapping his scarf about his neck again and pulling on his gloves. "Mrs. Speed, Becky: Thank you so much for rescuing us from the storm, but I must return this waif to Miss Dragon's."

Becky giggled. Ellen couldn't help but notice the look of relief on Mrs. Speed's face.

"If you must," Mrs. Speed began.

James held out his hand. "We must. Miss Grimsley is so often in and out of trouble that it would not be wise to tempt the Fates. Good day to you all. Here, Ellen, let me help you."

Becky reached for her cloak again. James shook his head. "I can see Miss Grimsley home. After all, I am going in that direction too."

Ellen buttoned her pelisse and stood still while James wrapped the muffler about her neck. She held out her hand to Becky. "I am sure I will be fine." She frowned. "Becky, wasn't this your half-day, anyway?"

Becky nodded. "I didn't mind the shopping this afternoon. I love to look in shop windows, even if I do not buy."

"Mind you hurry then, Miss Grimsley," Mrs. Speed said

as she opened the door. The snow blew in and nearly extinguished the exhausted fire. "I wouldn't want your cold or sore throat laid at my door!"

Ellen smiled and touched the woman's arm. "I am never sick," she declared. "It is a sore trial to my mother, who thinks I would be more interesting if I could languish a bit, like my sister."

They said goodbye and set out, arm in arm, through the alleys. It was too cold to talk. Ellen clutched Ralph's present to her, grateful that the footman had taken the others on ahead.

After walking in silence through the winter twilight, James stopped, pulling Ellen up short. "I, for one, am grateful you are never sick," he said, speaking distinctly to be heard above the wind. He started walking again.

She looked up at him in amusement. "Well, thank you, sir!" she declared.

"Seriously, El," he replied, "think how handy that will be when you are slogging through the malarial rain forests of Brazil, or the frozen steppes—God help us—of Siberia. The world was never explored by weak people."

Ellen stopped this time. "You don't think I am foolish, like all my relatives do, and Miss Dignam, and Fanny Bland, and Vicar Snead?"

He tugged her into motion again. "I don't think you are foolish," he said quietly. "Not at all, Ellen Grimsley. You may be a little ahead of your time, but so was Galileo."

"You put me in august company," she shouted over the wind.

"It's where you belong." He stopped at the top of the steps to the female academy and rang the bell. "The only difficulty I foresee is finding a husband obliging enough to let you traipse off around the world."

"It is a problem," she agreed, rubbing her hands together, and taking a firmer grip on her package. "He will have to be quite wealthy and excruciatingly patient." She laughed and extended her hand. "Should you ever meet anyone like that, please send him calling to Miss Dignam's! Thank you for your escort, sir."

He only leaned forward and kissed her cheek. "If it were any colder, we would be stuck together right now, and then

Miss Dignam would have you writing thousands of sentences,'' he murmured, his voice close to her ear.

She smiled and touched his face. The door opened, and the footman stood there, grinning at them.

"One moment."

Gatewood took her arm and led her down the steps again. "We have not even had time to discuss your much-applauded essay."

"Did you like it?" she asked, wishing the footman would close the door again. He just stood there, leaning against the frame, whistling softly to himself.

"Like's not the word, Ellen. It was a masterpiece," he replied. He took her hand again. "Meet me tomorrow afternoon at the bridge at the end of the High. We'll go punting. Wear your scholar's gown, of course."

She stared at him. "But it's snowing! And cold!"

He looked up at the sky. "See the stars peeking through over there? It will be clear tomorrow. And this is a perfect time to punt. No one will bother us while we discuss your next paper."

"But . . ."

Gatewood was already backing away down the street. He waved to her, and ran across the street to the All Souls entrance.

Ellen stood there a moment until she heard the footman clearing his throat. She turned back to Miss Dignam's, shaking her head. James Gatewood was an odd one indeed, she thought. He must be almost as eccentric as Lord Chesney. It's no wonder those two are friends.

Ellen woke in the morning to sunlight streaming through the curtains. With a sigh of contentment she snuggled deeper into the pillow and regarded that portion of sky she could see from her bed. It was a beautiful, crackling blue, untroubled by a single cloud.

For a moment, she wished herself home, where the upstairs maid would bring her cinnamon toast and hot chocolate, and she and Horatia would share her bed and plan their lives. Her smile faded. Horatia's life was already planned, and soon she would be married to Edwin Bland, the silly son of a sillier baronet.

And then Horry will be a wife, and likely a mother, and I

will be an aunt, she thought. We will forget we were ever sisters who giggled over life in bed on Sunday mornings.

Ellen turned over on her stomach and lay there, her face pressed into the pillow. There was an ache somewhere in her body as she thought of Gatewood's words of last night. Would she ever really slog through malarial swamps or conquer frozen steppes? It seemed unlikely.

She rested her chin in her hands. I wonder if Thomas Cornwell has ever been up to London, she thought. He has seen no more of the world than I have, but the difference is, he doesn't care if his horizons extend no farther than the farthest Cotswold hill. His only interest in the horizon would be to own it and sow it. Tom's idea of an excursion would be a trip here to Oxford, and even then, he would only come here because it was a market center, and not because it was the seat of all learning and wisdom.

Ellen sat up cross-legged in bed, her pillow propped behind her, wondering at the feeling of homesickness that washed over her suddenly. At home they would be rushing around, getting ready for the ride into the village and church, steeling themselves for the prospect of another of Vicar Snead's stupifying sermons.

In the afternoon, Mama would knot lace in the sitting room and carry on about the neighbors, while Papa, his mind and heart on horses as always, would pace the floor from sofa to window and back again, chafing because it was Sunday and Mama would allow little else. As soon as he settled himself in a chair, Martha would climb into his lap and they would both fall asleep.

They were silly, idle people, but she missed them, and loved them in her own way. And they loved her, Ellen thought suddenly. Mama thinks that Thomas Cornwell is the best choice for me.

The pang of homesickness did not go away as she thought of Horatia, sitting close to the fire, deep in loving silence with her ridiculous fiance. Ralph would find an excuse to steal from the room to the company of his beloved Shakepeare.

Shakespeare. Ellen rolled her eyes and plopped her hands in her lap. "Dear Willie of Avon," she said, "you are rapidly becoming my greatest trial in life."

She looked around, feeling foolish that she had spoken out loud, and in such decisive tones, and then remembered that Fanny Bland was away until tomorrow. She tightened her lips, seeing in her mind's eye Fanny and the other symmetrical bridesmaids, giggling with each other as they received their final fitting of that divine deep green lawn.

Mama and Horry had gone round and round over the tiny puffed sleeves and low-cut neckline. "But my dear, it will be winter!" Mama had protested. "They will have to carry warming pans instead of nosegays!"

"I hope you all come down with galloping consumption and putrid sore throats and chilblains," Ellen declared, looking at Fanny's bed, all tidily made up with not a single wrinkle. "And frostbite," she added for good measure.

But none of those things would likely happen. The tall, elegant bridesmaids would march down the aisle, Horry would be shot off, and Ellen would be left to keep the younger children in line and see that Martha did not eat too many sweets. And when it was all over, Mama would look her over once or twice and ask her how she felt about Thomas Cornwell. "Such a nice young man, and from such a good family," Mama would say.

What a pity that James Gatewood was so ineligible, Ellen thought, and then smiled at the idea of the casual Mr. Gatewood, in his shabby collars and wrinkled clothes, bowing over Mama's hand. It would never do. Even if he combed his hair and pressed his clothes, he would still be just a horse trader's son.

A pity, Ellen thought. We could probably have dealt so well together. The notion made her blush. What was she thinking? Mama would never understand what she saw in him. Ellen was not sure herself, except that she felt better when he was around.

Ellen wrapped herself tight in her blankets again. It could not be love, at any rate, she thought. Horatia had informed her that love was a feeling of total delight. Horry had never mentioned the restlessness that Ellen felt when she was away from James Gatewood, or the feeling of wanting to tidy him, and organize his life, and bully him into eating better than toasted cheese and rather bad tea.

It must be infatuation, she decided as she threw back the covers and pulled on her robe. She headed for the dressing room, but got no farther than the window. She sat at her desk and looked out at the lovely spires of Oxford. *I suppose I am also a little bit in love with Oxford, too.* She smiled to herself. *Like her infatuation with James Gatewood, it would have to pass, and quickly, too, for her own peace of mind.*

Church was a quiet business. Many of the older parishioners from Oxford's center had stayed indoors, kept there by the bracing cold that brought a bloom to Ellen's cheeks. She sniffed the air appreciatively as they walked from church in decorous ranks of two. The fragrance of wood smoke, captured and held in the bowl-shaped valley by the cold, competed with musty smells off the River Isis and cooking odors from every hearth. Ellen knew it was her imagination, but she thought she could smell the delicious aroma of leather bindings on old books.

Ellen thought twice, and then three times, about sneaking out of Miss Dignam's after the noon meal. *I can have no business out of this building with James Gatewood,* she told herself as she picked up her embroidery basket and gazed at it in dismay. How was it that those threads seemed to knot and tangle of their own accord? *I declare it is perverse,* she thought, *a conspiracy to remind me of my failings.*

She tried not to think about the scholar's gown hanging in the back of the dressing room, hidden from prying eyes. Ellen looked out the window then, and her resolve weakened. The sky was so blue, a dramatic backdrop for the honey-colored stones, mellow with age, that made up many of Oxford's colleges. Resolutely, Ellen turned away from the window and took her embroidery basket onto her lap.

After a futile half hour spent trying to follow each errant thread to its source, she dropped the basket at her feet and kicked it under the desk. She looked in the direction of the dressing room and got slowly to her feet.

No one was about as she crept down the backstairs, the scholar's gown draped over her arm, shirt and breeches underneath her dress.

Becky was the only servant in sight, the rest having taken themselves off for the afternoon, away from Miss Dignam's crotchets. The maid scrubbed the pans in the scullery, looking up with a smile when Ellen stepped out of her dress and fluffed her wilted shirt points.

Becky dried her hands and hurried to shake out Ellen's dress and hide it in the broom closet. "Where are you going today?" she asked as Ellen pulled on the scholar's gown.

"James Gatewood has some harebrained scheme about punting on the River Isis," Ellen said. "I think he is crazy."

"No, Miss Grimsley, he is wonderful," Becky said, her eyes shining.

Ellen stared at her. "Whatever do you mean?"

Becky dabbed at her eyes with her apron. "This morning, the beadle from the parish came tapping on our door. Behind him was a coal wagon. He backed that wagon up to the cellar window and shoveled in a mound of coal that still has the neighbors wondering."

"My word," said Ellen, her voice soft. "And you think it was James Gatewood?"

"Who else?" Becky asked. "When I woke up, Mama was crying, and piling coal on the grate until I thought she had taken leave of her senses."

Ellen sat down at the table. "I simply do not understand where he finds the money for his philanthropies. Horse trading must pay beyond my wildest imaginings."

"There's more, Miss Grimsley," Becky said as she plunged her hands back into the dishwater. "The beadle told us that as soon as the coal gets low, we are to notify him. Miss Grimsley, we will be warm all winter!"

Ellen felt tears prickling her eyes. "I will definitely confront him with this evidence of his kindness," she said.

"If you think it won't embarrass him," Becky said.

"It won't hurt to embarrass James Gatewood," Ellen replied as she opened the door and peered out. "Sometimes I have the distinct impression that he is not giving me straight answers."

The afternoon was clear and cold, the street deserted. Ellen huddled in her scholar's gown and hurried down the High to the bridge. The street was icy so she took her time, asking herself again what she was doing outdoors tempting fate like this. Only the knowledge that Miss Dignam insisted on quiet Sunday afternoons, spent in meditation of some sin or another, kept her going. No one would miss her.

"Watch your step, Hermia."

She looked down from the bridge. James Gatewood stood halfway up the little steps that led to a small landing on the river's edge. He held out his hand to her and she gripped it.

"This is insane," was her only comment as he helped her down the ice-covered steps.

"Yes, isn't it?" he agreed cheerfully. "Consider it advance training for an adventure at the North Pole, grim Miss Grimsley. Your sleigh awaits."

He gestured toward a punt that bobbed on the choppy water. Ellen chewed her lips and looked back at Gatewood doubtfully.

"Trust me, Ellen," he said.

"I should not," she said promptly, wondering at her own wildness. She would never be so brazen at home, where her most forward act had been a stroll unchaperoned in the shrubbery with Thomas Cornwell. Not that her virtue was ever in any danger from Thomas. All he could talk about was the price of grain. "No, I should not," she repeated.

"That is up to you," he replied, and held out his hand to help her into the punt.

She hesitated and then took hold of his hand again. He made no comment, but regarded her with an expression she had not noticed before. There was none of the casual amusement in his eyes that she had become familiar with in their brief acquaintance. He was serious about something, and she did not entirely understand.

"You'll not regret it," he said as he followed her into the boat and picked up the pole.

She was silent as she settled herself into the little craft. His was not a statement that seemed to require comment. In some inscrutable way that was currently beyond her understanding, she sensed that he meant much more than he actually said.

I should change the subject, she thought, as the stillness between them became uncomfortable, and then blushed. There was no subject to change.

Gatewood poled in silence into the middle of the stream. Gradually, the somber, almost sad expression left his face. He concentrated on punting into the stream and down the river. Soon he was humming to himself.

Ellen leaned back against the cushion and watched him. How odd it was to be on the river in December. She had read in feverish novels about punting on the Isis in warm, romantic summer, with a picnic hamper and champagne, and a hero with burning eyes. She smiled. James Gatewood's eyes looked a bit red, as though he had not slept much recently, and it was so cold that her nose tingled.

He looked back at her and smiled. "Open that basket," he said, indicating the wicker basket midway between them.

She lifted the lid. A dark green bottle nestled in the straw, with two glasses tucked stem to lip beside it. She smiled up at Gatewood.

"You, sir, are a complete hand."

"Champagne is, I believe, a requirement for a punt on the Isis," he replied. "If it is not frozen, we will be in luck."

She popped the cork and poured them each a glass. He accepted it without missing a push against the pole as they glided along. He raised his glass to her.

"And now, Miss Grimsley, shall I tell you what I think of *Measure for Measure*?"

When he finished, the bottle was half empty. The warm glow in her stomach had traveled down to her fingers and toes, leaving her slightly piffled and charitable to the world at large that drifted by.

"Your ending was particularly adroit," he was saying as he accepted a refill. "I own that I felt sorry for Gordon. He is, I regret to say, too dense by half to realize that you wrote the whole thing in jest. I am sure he still thinks that Shakespeare really was a woman."

Ellen joined in his laughter. Gatewood drained his glass and held it out again, but Ellen shook her head and tapped the cork more firmly into the bottle. "You have had enough, sir," she said

"You are a bit of a tyrant," he replied, tossing the glass over his shoulder. It bobbed on the current and then sank beneath the waves. "But I will tolerate this heavy-handed cruelty if you will tell me: what is your next assignment?"

Ellen made a face. "Gordon has committed me to *The Tempest.*" She regarded her glass of champagne, wrinkling her nose as the bubbles rose. She swirled the liquid around and around. "Tell me what you think, sir. I believe I will write this paper as a travel guide to the New World. You know, something along the lines of Hakluyt's *Navigations, Voyages, Traffiques and Discoveries.*" She frowned. "That is, provided I can find a copy of that work among the moldly, unused stacks of the female academy."

"And if you cannot, I . . ."

She held up her hand, sloshing the champagne from the glass. "You will not—repeat not—invest in such a book at Fletcher's, James!"

"But it gives me pleasure," he said simply, as if that was all the argument there was to consider. "And besides, Hakluyt was a Christ Church man."

"Let us see how pleased you will be when you have run through your quarterly stipend and there is no bread and cheese to be had," she retorted.

"My dear Miss Grimsley," he began, his voice filled with dignity that sounded almost ducal to her ears, "I happen to know that Lord Chesney possesses the Hakluyt collection in his library. I will beg the loan of one volume for you. He is a Shakespeare scholar of such renown that he could never resist a plea on behalf of the Bard." He held up his hand this time to ward off her objections. "Not a word, Miss Grimsley. In this, I insist. You will have the book by tomorrow noon."

Ellen did not argue. She drew her cloak tighter about her shoulders. The afternoon sun was beginning to dip behind the hills. She looked up at Gatewood, who was smiling down at her.

"I have an idea for another paper," she began, picking her way among half-formed thoughts. "It is for me alone, I suppose."

"Some topic that Lord Chesney has not poked his long nose into?" he asked.

She looked at him quickly. "Oh, do not think that I am ungrateful for all he has done, and I have truly enjoyed writing those papers. I have learned so much. This is just an idea of my own."

"I would like to hear it."

"Only promise you will not tell Lord Chesney," she insisted.

"I promise," he said. "But why not?"

"Maybe I will surprise him with it. Maybe I will even sign my name to this one."

"Bravo, fair Hermia," said Gatewood. He steadied the punt and turned his full attention to her. "Speak on."

She clasped her hands over her knees. "Let us pretend that Romeo got Friar Lawrence's message in time to rescue Juliet from 'yon Caple's monument.'" She nodded toward James, her eyes merry. "And then . . ."

"Let me guess," he interrupted, and laughed out loud, missing a beat with the pole and setting the little craft rocking. "Excuse that! And they both live happily ever after. Only, perhaps they don't?"

Ellen clapped her hands. "Exactly!"

"Oh, ho!" Gatewood chortled. "Imagine the possibilities of domestic discomfort in the palazzo of Mr. and Mrs. Romeo Montague. Now why did I never think of that?"

"You are not the Shakespeare scholar."

"Alas, yes."

Ellen put the bottle back in the wicker basket. "That title belongs to your friend, Lord Chesney. By the way, sir, why do you not bring him along sometime? I owe him so much and would like to thank him in person for smoothing my way here."

"He is a bit shy around women, Ellen," James said.

"Well, I would be shy, too, I am sure," Ellen said. "Imagine meeting an actual marquess! I am sure that beyond expressing my thanks, I would be quite intimidated and have nothing of significance to say."

"Surely you could think of something," he coaxed.

"No," Ellen said with a shake of her head. "I am sure I could never be comfortable around a peer."

"You could, Ellen, you could," Gatewood said, his voice suddenly serious. "He's not so fearsome."

"Too rare for me!" She said with a wave of her hand. "Still, I would like to tell him goodbye, and thank him."

"Goodbye? Are you still intent upon leaving?"

"Yes. When this paper is done, I am writing to Papa to come and get me," she said.

"Giving up?" he asked quietly.

She nodded, and met his eyes. "Exactly so. All I want is Oxford University, and I cannot have it. I write papers, and others get the applause."

"I never thought applause was your motive," Gatewood said.

She shook her head. "It is not. Oh, James, I fear that I would grow bitter if I stayed around Gordon and watched him squander the riches here." She shook her head. "No, it's high time I returned home. Christmas is coming, and then there is a wedding to prepare for. I am needed at home."

Gatewood poled toward the bridge in silence for several moments. "I understand your bitterness," he said at last.

"You couldn't possibly," she burst out. "You have this university education spread before you like a feast, and I never will!"

"I didn't mean it that way," he retorted. "I am saying that I know what it is to feel the weight of family responsibility." He leaned on the pole and gazed across the river. "I am reminded in frequent letters that I should be home, too."

Ellen looked away, embarrassed with herself for reminding him of his own meager condition. She imagined the drain of his education on his parents' limited resources and she was ashamed.

"I am sorry," she said, her voice soft.

The sun was behind the hills now, and she shivered. "I really don't belong here."

"I think you do," was all he said as he poled the boat alongside the landing.

She could think of nothing to say as Gatewood helped her out of the punt. He held her hand and helped her up the steps, which were now sheathed in shadow. She felt disinclined to let go, even when her footing was sure.

They walked slowly up the High Street in awkward silence. Finally Gatewood nudged her shoulder. "Tell me something, El." He let go of her hand as others appeared on the street. "It's about your paper on *Romeo and Juliet*. Do your parents have a happy marriage?"

She stared at him, startled at his astounding question. After a moment's thought, she smiled, her good humor restored. "You are wondering where is my authority for a paper on marriage?"

"I suppose I am."

"Yes, they do, I think," she said. "I have never given it much thought until lately. Ah me, perhaps I am homesick."

He stopped and gestured grandly toward Miss Dignam's. "What? You can have all this and be homesick?"

"Silly!" She clasped his hand again when the people passed, and unconsciously slowed her steps as the academy loomed closer and closer. "My parents are pretentious and silly, but they love each other. Mama will humor Papa when the weather is rainy and he cannot ride, and he will listen to her silly stories about the neighbors. But sometimes she is afraid when he storms and stomps about."

"Can that be love?" he asked in amazement, with a twinkle in the eyes that looked so tired.

She smiled. "I think it is. They know each other so well, faults and all, and it does not disgust them. And that is how my Romeo and Juliet will be."

"Ellen, you astound me," Gatewood said finally. "I never suspected you for a cynic, my dear." He touched her under the chin.

"No, sir, I am a realist," she replied quietly. "I hope to be as fortunate as they, some day. It may not seem like much, but perhaps it is. How will I know until I am there myself?"

Gatewood put her arm through his as he helped her down the steps leading to the servants' entrance. "Perhaps you will be more fortunate, Hermia."

She took her arm from his and opened the door, her mind on Thomas Cornwell. "Who can tell? I suspect that one must work at success in marriage, as in any other venture. Good night, Jim. Take care."

He kissed her fingers and hurried up the steps without a backward glance.

She watched him go, listening to his footsteps as he crossed the empty street, and then went into the servants' quarters.

Becky met her at the door of the scullery, her eyes wide. "Miss Grimsley, do you know what time it is?"

"Why, no," she said, startled.

"Miss Dignam has already summoned all the young ladies for Psalms in the sitting room," Becky said as she hurried Ellen toward the stairs.

Ellen stared at her. "It is that late?"

"Oh, hurry, Miss Grimsley!"

Ellen gathered her robe about her and took the steps two at a time. She opened the door into the main hallway and looked about. Young ladies, armed with needlework, were headed toward the parlor. Ellen closed the door to a crack. When the last girl had passed, she opened the door and ran to the back stairs.

To her relief, the upper hall was deserted. She tiptoed down the corridor to her room and threw open the door.

Fanny was seated at her desk. She looked up in surprise at Ellen, who stood before her in shirt, breeches and scholar's gown. The only sounds in the room were Fanny's sharp intake of breath and Ellen's gasp of dismay.

Her whole body numb, Ellen closed the door. She clasped her hands in front of her.

"Well, say something," she said at last, when Fanny continued to regard her in silence.

Still Fanny said nothing. After a moment's observation, she rose from her chair and walked around Ellen, who followed her with her eyes.

"Charming," she ventured at last.

Ellen felt the tears start in her eyes. "Are you going to tell Miss Dignam?"

"Of course I am," Fanny replied, unable to keep the triumph from her voice.

Ellen closed her eyes and thought of the papers yet to be written, and Lord Chesney's disappointment.

"When?" she croaked.

Fanny laughed, but there was no mirth in the sound.

"When I am good and ready, Ellen Grimsley."

9

Ellen undressed in miserable silence while Fanny busied herself at her desk. Shivering in her chemise and drawers, Ellen balled up the breeches, shirt, and cloak and threw them in a corner of the dressing room. Her face set, wooden, she pulled on a dress, and ran her fingers through her tangled hair. She followed Fanny downstairs to the sitting room, where she bowed her head and waited for the ax to fall.

It did not. Fanny said nothing to the headmistress then. Other than peering at them over the top of her spectacles for being late, Miss Dignam addressed herself to the Psalms and then dismissed the girls to their rooms.

Ellen got slowly to her feet. She glanced back to see Fanny and Miss Dignam in earnest conversation. Her heart plummeted to her shoes and stayed there between her toes, as her stomach began to ache. She pressed her hand against her middle, wondering what would happen next.

As she slowly mounted the steps, she heard Fanny and Miss Dignam laughing. In another moment, Fanny was beside her.

"You look so pale, Ellen," Fanny observed with a smirk.

"Did . . . did you tell?"

"Not yet," Fanny said. "I will just let you stew and fret this week. Let us see if you choose to make any more cutting remarks about my brother. I advise you to hold your tongue, Ellen, if it isn't too much trouble."

She stopped on the landing and grasped Ellen by the arm. "Do you know, Ellen, I had not thought . . . When my father gets wind of this, I wonder if he will be so happy to see a connection between our two families."

"No, Fanny!" Ellen pleaded, her voice low.

It was as though Fanny had not heard. She released Ellen and gave her a little push. "And, Ellen, Edwin always does what Papa asks."

Ellen held her tongue, silently taking back every spiteful

remark she had ever made to Fanny, following Fanny with her eyes. The ache in her stomach did not go away. Soon her head throbbed in sympathy.

Nothing escaped Fanny's sharp eyes during the endless week. She was watching when Ellen, with trembling fingers, opened the package from James Gatewood and took out Chesney's volume of Hakluyt's *Navigations and Voyages.*

"It is for geography," Ellen lied as she tried to make the book disappear on her cluttered desk.

"Silly me," Fanny said calmly. "I had thought we were studying Portugal and Spain this week."

Ellen swallowed her misery in *The Tempest,* working on it by the light of a single candle after Fanny snored in her bed. She could not sleep; the evils of the situation she had placed herself in revolved around and around in her head until sleep was out of the question. She drowned her own uneasiness in the misfortunes of the Duke of Venice, turning his adventures into a travel guide to the New World that was witty, urbane, and written in the middle of her own despair.

Several frantic notes to Gordon, delivered on the sly by Becky or the footman, evoked no response. As she sat, numb, through geography or struggled through embroidery, all she could think was that Gordon, safe in the knowledge that she would do his work for him, had gone to London again. Wretched brother, more stupid sister, she thought over and over as she sat at her desk, hand pressed to her forehead, as the words poured from her like nervous perspiration.

She did not know if Fanny had truly made the connection between her writings and Gordon's university triumphs. She shuddered to think of the scandal that would errupt of Gordon were dismissed for cheating. She blamed him for putting her in this delicate situation, and blamed herself more for succumbing to her own vanity and writing those clever imaginings that now threatened to choke them both.

Each day dragged past and still Fanny said nothing. Ellen found herself existing in an unfamiliar world of perpetual fright as she waited for Fanny to take Miss Dignam aside and tattle to the headmistress about the student clothes and gown that were still balled up into a corner of the dressing room. She would be sent home, her reputation in tatters. Ellen knew Fanny Bland well enough to know that, once home, Fanny would continue her malicious work, spreading tales about girls who go away to school and turn into fast pieces who dress in trousers so they can follow men about.

Only one note of brightness illuminated the grim picture: Thomas Cornwell would be so disgusted that Ellen need never fear again that he would offer for her.

It was little consolation. As the hounds of her imagination snapped at her heels, Ellen kept them at bay by plunging into the second paper, on *Romeo and Juliet*. While she kept busy writing, she could almost dismiss her own miseries. Late at night, when her stomach ached and her eyes burned with unshed tears, Ellen wove a fanciful comedy about a young couple, miraculously spared, who are too young and gradually find themselves wondering what they saw in each other in the first place. As the candle guttered out early Saturday morning, she penned the last word, blotted it dry, and then rested her face against the warm wood of the desk.

With a sigh, she put the paper in the desk drawer with the one on *The Tempest* that Gordon wanted. She frowned as she closed the drawer. It was Saturday morning, and Gordon had not made an effort to retrieve his paper.

It will serve you right if you miss the reading, Gordon Grimsley, she thought as she quietly stood up, rubbed the small of her back, and carried her notes and rough drafts of both papers to the fireplace. Fanny stirred as the paper flamed up and crackled, but did not waken. When her scholarship was nothing but ashes, Ellen crawled into bed. Once Gordon's paper was gone from her desk drawer, there was nothing to connect her with the writing of it.

She woke an hour later to the sound of knocking. Fanny opened the door to let in Becky Speed, who carried a brass can of hot water, which she set down at the dressing table.

"It's about time," Fanny said as Becky poured the water into a ceramic basin.

"Sorry, miss," Becky said and bobbed a curtsy.

Fanny turned to the washbasin. The maid came closer to Ellen's bed. "Gordon," she mouthed, so Fanny would not hear, and pointed down toward the lower reaches of the academy.

Ellen rose up on one elbow and looked Becky in the eye. She

pointed to the desk and pantomimed opening the drawer. Becky nodded and tiptoed across the floor. Quietly, her eyes on Fanny, the maid opened the drawer and took out its contents.

She had almost reached the door when Fanny, her face soapy, turned around to watch her progress. Fanny's head came up and her eyes narrowed as she stared at the papers in the maid's hand. She looked at Ellen and then back at Becky, a smile spreading slowly across her damp face.

"Wait right there," she commanded.

Becky froze where she was, the papers tight in her hand. Ellen lay back and closed her eyes as she felt the blood drain from her face. Once she saw the title, there was no way Fanny could mistake the connection between Gordon and the papers.

Fanny held out her hand for the papers as Becky backed up against the door. As Ellen held her breath, Fanny began to rub her eyes.

"Drat!" she exclaimed and turned around for a towel to wipe the soap from her face.

In the moment she turned, Becky threw open the door and ran down the stairs. Fanny, clad only in her chemise and petticoat, could only stare out the door and watch.

Ellen sighed, and thanked the Lord who watches out for miserable sinners that Fanny Bland was too much of a lady to go charging half-naked after the maid.

"That was for Gordon, wasn't it?" Fanny exclaimed, whirling on Ellen. "And don't try to weasel out of it, Ellen Grimsley. You've been doing something for your brother, haven't you?"

Ellen made no reply, other than to get out of bed, and tug down her nightgown, her mind made up. She ignored Fanny's questions as she crossed to the dressing room and calmly removed the scholar's gown. Deliberately she shook it out and laid it across her bed.

With a smile on her pale face, she touched its folds one last time. Moving fast to take advantage of Fanny's amazement at her brazen behavior after a week of miserable cowardice, Ellen pulled on the frilled shirt and breeches.

"Do you know, Fanny," she commented as she smoothed out the dark hose she had hidden in her bureau drawer, "these garments are so comfortable. I think that men have been keeping such a secret from us. If we knew how wondrous liberating trousers were, we would have worn them years ago. It's such fun to sit with your legs wide apart, or propped up on a desk.''

Fanny sputtered and wiped the soap from her face. Ellen scuffed her feet into the shoes, touching them up with the corner of the bedspread. "Of course, I don't doubt, Fanny, that when you marry, you'll wear the pants. If you marry."

"You . . . you . . ." was all Fanny could say as Ellen swirled the student's gown around her with a flourish.

"Brilliant repartee," Ellen said as she bowed elaborately to her roommate and closed the door behind her.

She wasted no time in the hall, but darted down the back stairs, running past several other students, who shrieked and leaped out of the way. Her face set, her mind working a million miles an hour, she ran to the front door and out into the High.

As she raced across the street, the gown flapping in the stiff breeze, she looked back at her second-floor window where Fanny stood, beating on the frame. She sighed and thanked the Lord again. In another moment she would be protected by Oxford's warren of alleys and safe from immediate discovery.

Once out of sight of Miss Dignam's Select Female Academy, she slowed to a fast walk, breathing hard. To her knowledge, Fanny had no idea which college Gordon attended. University was only one of many colleges that required Saturday papers of its first-year students. With any luck at all, Fanny and Miss Dignam would take some time finding her.

"And I will hear my paper read," she said out loud, unmindful of the students who stared at her when she spoke so emphatically and grinned at each other.

She knew they would find her. It was only a matter of contacting the Vice Chancellor and searching the student enrollments for each college. Perhaps by then, if Gordon were toward the first readers, she would have heard her paper delivered. There would be the humiliation of discovery and then Papa would be summoned. She would go home in disgrace.

"But I *will* hear my paper first," she whispered as she paused on the steps of University College's lecture hall. It would be something to remember through the dreary winter months at home, and all the months of her life to come, when she was tending Thomas Cornwell's children and running his manor, subordinating all her wishes and dreams to others' needs.

The hall was still empty. Quietly she sat down in one of the side pews, toward the back. Her stomach pained her. She winced at the pain and shoved her elbow against her middle, looking about at the serenity of the hall, with its stained glass windows and fine-grained wood. The peace of it filled her, and she forgot her own misery.

Her chin went up as she looked about. I am sitting in the lecture hall at University College, she thought. I will hear my paper read.

Time passed. Even the slightest noise from outside the massive doors made her start in surprise. The unheated hall was frigid and she could see her breath. She shivered and tucked her hands up under her armpits. The familiar ache began in her forehead.

Soon the students began to file in, laughing and chatting with one another. Some of them carried papers, and others, the ones who looked at ease, carried nothing more than gloves. The sound of their good humor filled the hall and echoed around it.

Tears started in Ellen's eyes. They don't even know what they have here, she thought, as she dashed the tears away and made herself small in her corner pew.

She saw Gordon in the circle of his friends, his back straight, his eyes triumphant, as he clutched her paper. She peered closer. Just as she had thought. Becky had taken both essays from the drawer, and thank goodness for that. There was nothing left in her room to connect her with the papers. Whatever else there was had gone up the chimney hours before when she burned her notes. With any luck at all, she could get the *Romeo and Juliet* paper back from Gordon and tuck it away, to be hauled out and looked at in years to come.

Not that I will ever need a reminder of this day, she thought, with a slight smile. To her relief, Gordon sat far up front. Her smile broadened. In all her memory, Gordon Grimsley had never sat up front for any event requiring his attention.

The students all rose as the warden, dean, and fellows entered the hall in stately fashion and settled themselves behind the rostrum. Ellen nearly laughed out loud. His hair combed, and his shirt points reasonably starched, James Gatewood sat with them. He crossed his legs in that careless way that she so envied, and looked out across the audience.

She wondered why he was there. Sitting next to him was a distinguished gentleman, with deep creases etched in his face like sculpted marble. As she watched, the two men put their heads together and exchanged a pleasantry that set them both laughing.

Ellen looked back at the open door. If there were time, she would get that *Romeo and Juliet* paper from Gordon and share it with James Gatewood. It was the least she could do for him. Dear James, without your help, I would never have had the books I needed. Someday I will find a way to repay you, she thought, as the chaplain asked them all to kneel for prayer.

The prayer was long and in Latin. When it ended, the students seated themselves, coughed, and shuffled papers until the warden called them all to order.

"Young masters," he began, "you all know why we are here." He looked around and beamed at the faculty seated behind him. "We applaud your eagerness to rise at this disgraceful hour on a Saturday, God help us, and contribute to the stamping out of ignorance."

The scholars laughed; it was the polite, appreciative mirth for a joke heard often. Some of them sat up straighter in anticipation of their own ordeal to come.

The readings began in no discernible order that Ellen could make out. She jumped in fright as the massive doors were closed behind her. The student sitting closest to her looked at her in surprise, and then looked away, bored, as the next student rose to speak.

The hour dragged along. Some of the papers were witty, brilliant even, and Ellen applauded along with the other students in appreciation. Others were pedestrian and stilted, the kind of paper that Gordon would have written, had he been compelled to do his own work, she thought. The reminder of her own iniquity in the matter of Gordon's success came back again as she shivered and drew her gown tighter about her slight shoulders.

"Gordon Grimsley."

At the warden's announcement, the students whispered to each and then were silent, expectant, as her brother rose and walked slowly to the podium, papers in hand.

Ellen smiled, forgetting her own discomfort at the sight of

her handsome brother mounting the podium, his back so straight, his head upright. I should be so jealous, she thought as he arranged the papers in front of him. He has caused me considerable anxiety and anguish over this. She shook her head. It was enough to be there.

" '*The Tempest,* ' " he announced in carrying tones. " 'A Travel Guide to the New World of English Literature.' "

Ellen beamed at the sounds of appreciation from Gordon's audience. It *was* a good title. She had labored over it when her stomach ached and she was so exhausted she had to lay her head on her books to rest for a few minutes each hour.

His voice carried well in the medieval hall. She listened, tears gleaming on her cheeks, as her useless brother made her happier than she could ever remember. No, she thought, I was this happy once before, and that was in James Gatewood's chambers at All Souls, eating toasted bread and cheese and talking about Great Ideas.

The thought of Gatewood turned her attention to him. She looked at his face, pleased to see the delight in his animated eyes, even from this distance. She only wished that he did not still look so tired, as though he slept no more than she did. What can be troubling you, sir? she thought, her mind miles away from Gordon. Did you truly give away all your quarterly allowance to buy me books, and now you are hungry?

She turned her attention to Gordon again. The door opened behind her, but she was caught up all over again in the magic of Shakespeare and did not feel the puff of colder air until it spread over the hall and then diminished as the door closed again.

Out of the corner of her eye, she saw the porter, note in hand, hurrying toward the podium. Ellen watched in mounting uneasiness as the man handed it to the college warden and then stepped back respectfully, his hands behind his back.

She sucked in her breath as the warden rose behind Gordon and put a heavy hand on his shoulder.

Surprised, Gordon stopped in midsentence.

"Stand to one side, lad," the warden said.

The students looked at each other and began to whisper among themselves. Ellen swallowed several times and felt the blood drain from her face.

The warden looked down at the paper in his hand and shook his head over it. He looked out across the audience, his eyes searching as the silence deepened and filled the hall.

"Ellen Grimsley, come forward at once."

She did not move.

The warden continued his search of the hall, his lips set in a firmer line. His voice was softer, but carried with it command.

"Miss Grimsley, we will find you in this hall, of this you can have no doubt."

The students burst into excited chatter, looking about them. Someone laughed. Gatewood had uncrossed his legs. His hands were on the arms of his chair, as though he were about to rise himself.

You cannot do that, she thought suddenly. Any connection betweeen us would be worse than my discovery in the Bodleian. It would ruin you.

She leaped to her feet, propelled there by sheer nerves, and stood clutching the pew in front of her.

"Ellen!" Gordon gasped. "What the devil are you doing here?"

She stood as tall as she could and drew the cloak tighter around her as the hall fell immediately silent. "I wanted to hear the paper, Gordon. That is all."

The voices buzzed again as she forced herself to walk into the center aisle and stand there, her back straight.

The warden was shaking his head. "No, that is not all, Miss Grimsley. I have it on good authority that you are the author of these papers that Master Grimsley has been favoring us with week after week."

The talk rose to a roar that hushed with a wave of the warden's hand.

Ellen clasped her hands in front of her, marveling how cold they felt. She waited for the warden to speak.

"Did you write these papers, Miss Grimsley? Speak up now."

The full knowledge of what she had done descended with a thump on her shoulders. As she watched the warden leave the podium and start toward her, she realized that admission of the truth would mean Gorden's immediate dismissal from University College. And no cavalry regiment would ever allow him to buy a pair of colors.

She lowered her eyes to the stone floor as the warden approached. Isn't that what you want, Ellen Grimsley? she asked herself calmly. It's Gordon's fault and blame entirely. He was lazy and he ought to be made to suffer for his sins.

She looked up at Gordon, his face as white as hers, his mouth open to speak, his hands tight around the papers. The look in his eyes was naked, pleading.

James Gatewood had not stood up yet, but he was perched on the edge of the chair, his eyes on her face. She managed a smile at him, which the warden misinterpreted as he came closer.

"This is hardly a smiling matter, Miss Grimsley," he thundered. "Did you or did not not write those papers?"

Ellen closed her eyes for an instant and then raised her chin higher.

"Of course I did, sir."

It took the warden several moments to quiet the lecture hall. Gatewood was on his feet now, starting toward her. She shook her head and he stopped. Gordon clutched the podium and bowed his head.

The warden was directly in front of her. He towered over her like a bird of prey in his long robe with the velvet bands on the sleeves. He waved the note under her nose.

"You wrote them?" he asked again, the incredulity in his voice unmistakable. "Impossible! Females cannot do such work!"

It stung worse than she had imagined it would. How dare this man think that because she was a woman, she was incapable of scholarship? But so he would have to think, she decided. One last glance at Gordon convinced her. She managed a slight smile.

"Yes, sir, I did. If you knew my brother's wretched hand-writing, you would understand why he came to me and begged me to make fair copies of his Saturday talks. I did not think it would hurt. I came only because I wanted to hear him read one."

Several students began to laugh. The scholar closest to her nudged another and remarked how he wished he had a beautiful sister with good handwriting so conveniently at hand.

The warden did not smile. His agate eyes remained un-readable, even as his lips relaxed slightly. He shook his head.

"I have knowledge from Miss Aloysia Dignam of her Select

Female Academy that you are the author of these papers, Miss Grimsley.''

Ellen swallowed again and took a step toward the warden.

"Prove it," she said, her voice loud and clear, even as her legs trembled and would scarcely hold her up.

The warden stared at her, his mouth open. He looked over his shoulder at the podium. This time, the tall man next to James Gatewood rose to his feet.

Everyone rose. Ellen blinked in surprise. Who was this man? Majestically, he strode down the aisle. The warden bowed as he approached and stood in front of Ellen Grimsley, whose knees had begun to shake by now.

He looked at her long and hard, and then turned his attention to the warden.

"She has admitted to no guilt. This ends the matter, sir, as far as the scholarship is concerned." He looked back up at the aisle at Gordon, who had not relaxed his grip on the podium. "An Oxford man would never lie about such a thing. If Gordon Grimsley makes no disclaimer, then we will not question you further. Sir?"

Wordlessly, Gordon shook his head and then bowed it again.

"Then here the matter rests, Warden." The man turned his attention to Ellen again. "Miss Grimsley, I am Vice Chancellor of Oxford University. It is my duty, in very deed it is my heartfelt pleasure, to expel you from these premises. Please go and do not return."

Without a word, or another glance at the podium, Ellen turned and fled the hall. The door was heavy and she thought she would never get it open, but in another moment, she was in the quadrangle of University College. Miss Dignam, nostrils flaring, eyes blazing, took her by the arm and hurried her across what seemed like acres and acres of wintry stubble. Ellen looked back once at the entrance hall. Some of the students had opened the narrow medieval windows and stared out at her. Someone waved.

She turned away in shame as tears of rage ran down her face.

Miss Dignam gave her arm a good shake. "It's very well that you feel humiliated, Ellen Grimsley," she exclaimed. "I don't know what this will do to the reputation of my school!"

Ellen shook herself free, sobbing out loud in frustration and anger. She looked back once more. "I am better than all of you foolish scholars who waste your time," she shouted. "Some day this will change!"

The wind carried her words away over the walls of the quadrangle as though she had not spoken them.

Fanny said nothing to her as Miss Dignam escorted her to her room. She sat at her desk, cool and tidy as usual, looking down her long nose at Ellen's rumpled gown and her tear-streaked face. She met the rebellion in Ellen's eyes for one brief moment, then looked away, her face pale.

Miss Dignam marched Ellen over to her desk and plumped her down. "You will remain in this room until your father comes to get you, Miss Grimsley. I have already sent for him. I do not doubt that he will be here soon." The headmistress rolled her eyes and fanned herself with her hand. "I cannot imagine what possessed you to dress so indecently and parade yourself in front of all those students."

Ellen sighed. Thank God Miss Dignam had made no mention of the papers. "I wanted to hear Gordon read," she repeated stubbornly.

Fanny was turning around now, and frowning. "But Ellen wrote those papers!" she exclaimed.

"Absurd!" Miss Dignam snapped. She slammed the door behind her.

"You wrote those papers, Ellen Grimsley," Fanny said quietly as Miss Dignam's footsteps retreated down the hall.

"You will have to prove it, Fanny," she replied, her eyes boring into the view of Oxford before her.

Fanny jumped up and crossed the room to Ellen's desk, jerking open the drawer. It was empty. She ran her hands over the books on Ellen's desk, searching for stray papers, going at last in frustration to the fireplace, where she stood, her fists clenched, looking down at the piles of ashes.

"You burned your notes. All of them. Didn't you?" she asked.

"I have nothing to say," Ellen said. After one last look, she tugged at the curtain pull and removed the panorama of Oxford from her sight. She changed clothes, and lay down on her bed, her face to the wall. In another moment, she slept.

10

Squire Grimsley, even more red-faced and pop-eyed than usual, was there by morning. He was standing over her bed, his riding crop twitching against his leg, when she woke.

White-faced, Ellen sat up. The squire pulled a chair to the bed and sank into it as he unbuttoned his mud-flecked coat. He looked over his shoulder at Fanny Bland, who sat at her desk, studiously ignoring them both.

"Fanny, find someplace else to sit," he said and stared at her until she gathered up her embroidery and swept out of the room, shutting the door with a decisive click that bordered on the insolent.

The squire turned back to his daughter. He said nothing for several minutes, until Ellen wanted to dig her toes into the mattress.

He sighed finally and leaned back in the chair. "I can be grateful, I suppose, that you did not tease me with one of those 'But Papa, you don't understand,' arguments that Horatia favors."

"I really don't have anything to say, Papa," Ellen managed at last. Her tongue felt too large for her mouth, as though it would impede her very speech and breath.

"Well, I do, Ellen," he replied, and glanced around to make sure that the door was shut.

When he finished a half hour later, his face was as white as hers. He was looking out the window at the view she had renounced the day before, and from the way his knuckles were stretched so tight against the draperies, it obviously brought him little pleasure.

"A scandal like this could ruin a family, Ellen," he was saying, almost more to himself than to her. "A man's daughter parades herself around a university in breeches? Good God, what does this tell about her parents, her upbringing?"

Ellen could only stare, dry-eyed at last, at his broad back.

Why is it so wrong to want to learn, she wanted to cry out. Why must I sneak around to study? Why can I not use the library and the study halls, listen to the lectures and ask questions of dons and fellows?

"Well, what do you think of that?" Papa was asking her.

"I am sorry, I was not listening," she stammered.

The riding crop crashed on the desk. "Have you even heard a word I have said, daughter?" he raged.

Ellen burst into tears again.

Papa snorted in frustration and dragged his damp handkerchief back out of his pocket.

"Come on, Ellen, perhaps in time Thomas will get over this unfortunate bit of high spirits," he said. "Goodness knows he would still be in the dark, if someone had not send an anonymous letter from Oxford."

"What!" Ellen gasped, clutching the handkerchief. She sank back down in the bed, resisting the urge to pull the blankets over her head and retreat. "Who could have done that?" she asked, only to know the answer already. Fanny must have told him, meddling, jealous Fanny.

But Papa was talking. She forced herself to listen.

" . . . and he almost insisted that I let him come along, daughter. I told him it was still a family matter." The squire sat down again, this time not meeting her eyes. "He said, 'All the more reason I should be there.' "

Ellen was silent, digesting this oblique bit of information. "What has Thomas Cornwell to do with our family?" she asked finally, knowing the squire's answer before he spoke, and dreading it.

"Well, we have been talking, these past few weeks," was all he said, his voice unsure for the first time since their gruelling interview began.

"Did you tell him I would marry him?" she asked quietly.

The squire nodded, taking in the distress on her face that she did not try to hide. "Ah, daughter, we all have to do things in life that we don't relish!" he burst out, when she did not speak.

"Not marriage!" she exclaimed, sitting up straight. "You don't need the money, do you, Papa?"

He shook his head and then looked at her. "Think of the land,

Ellen! He may not have a title like Horry's future father-in-law, or that Bland prestige, but he has land.'' He threw up his hands. ''We can join the farms for twice the profit, and I'll get that little parcel of land over by Lowerby that I have had my eyes on for years.''

''You would do that to me?'' was all she said. ''Papa, I don't love Thomas Cornwell. I don't even like him.''

''What does love have to do with our discussion?'' the squire said, after several long moments dragged by in silence. ''What indeed? Get your clothes on, Ellen. We're going home.''

''How could you, Papa?'' she whispered.

''Because it is my right!'' he raged.

He left the room, but she lay where she was, contemplating the ruin of her life, and all because she had written a few paltry papers.

A moment's reflection convinced her that the papers had nothing to do with it. While she had been away at Oxford, Papa had schemed and meddled with the Cornwells until all she had to do was return home and in a few weeks slide into Horatia's wedding gown, still warm from the Bland wedding. Papa would likely exchange a few acres of his own for those acres of the Cornwell's he had been coveting, and the deed would be done. It had nothing to do with Oxford, except that her sojourn there, if only for a few weeks, had let Papa wheel and deal to his heart's content.

She thought of the papers, particularly the unread paper on *Romeo and Juliet*, wondering again if Gordon still kept it, or if Lord Chesney has appropriated it in all the excitement yesterday in University College Hall, or if Lord Chesney had even been there. She closed her eyes against the humiliation still so fresh in her mind. Pray God Lord Chesney was not there.

''I did so want *you* to see that paper, Jim Gatewood,'' she said softly as she pulled on her clothes and checked the room one last time to see if she had forgotten anything. ''I wish I could have said goodbye, and thank you.''

The books lay on the desk. She picked up the Hakluyt book, turning its old and mellow pages, breathing deep of the fragrance of worn leather, ink, and rag paper from an earlier century or two. She wrote a hasty note to the footman, asking him to see that this was returned to its owner, and then crammed the complete words of Shakespeare into her little trunk, along with Chesney's *Commentary and Notes on A Midsummer Night's Dream*. She could give Gatewood's gifts to Ralph. Better he should have them than she should see them mock her from her bookshelf.

If Cornwell's house even had a bookshelf.

She was dressed and downstairs in a matter of minutes. No one was in the halls and she tiptoed along them, but she heard doors open as she passed, and knew that the other inmates of the academy were staring at her. The knowledge burned, but she did not turn around to confront their rudeness.

The door to Miss Dignam's office was closed. She regarded it for a moment, then sat in the straight-backed chair against the wall. She gazed across the hall at the art Miss Dignam chose to hang where students awaiting reprimand could see it. The print was an old one of Hogarth's illustrating the course of life open to young ladies who choose to be disobedient, fractious, and disagreeable.

Hogarth had limned his topic well, but as Ellen stared at it, she couldn't help suspecting that A Fate Worse Than Death might be more tolerable than waking up each morning for the rest of her life and seeing Thomas Cornwell snoring beside her.

She listened to the low murmur of voices inside Miss Dignam's *sanctum sanctorum* and was startled to hear the sound of laughter.

"Sadists," she muttered under her breath, and then sighed with weariness. She had slept only after a night of tossing about. All she wanted now was to endure one final scold from Miss Dignam, pull her cloak up about her ears, and go home to her own bed. It couldn't come soon enough.

The door opened. She jumped in spite of herself as Miss Dignam stepped into the hall, her face wreathed in smiles. Ellen blinked in surprise and slowly rose to her feet.

"Good morning, my dear," Miss Dignam said, her smile at its toothiest as she closed the door behind her. "I trust you slept well."

"Quite badly, actually," Ellen said, her eyes wide with wonder at the spectacle before her.

"Very good, my dear, very good. Come along inside, if you will."

This is worse and worse, Ellen thought. Only a case-hardened veteran of the French Revolution could smile that way as the blade dropped. She put up her hand as Miss Dignam started to open the door again. "Miss Dignam, were you in France during the Revolution?"

It was Miss Dignam's turn to stare, and then laugh indulgently. "Ellen, what won't you say?"

Ellen shook her head to clear it and followed Miss Dignam into her office. Her father, all rage and animosity vanished, looked back at her. Her jaw dropped in amazement as she glanced at the occupant in the easy chair by the window, who sat so carelessly with his legs crossed.

"Jim!" she exclaimed. "How did you get dragged into this?"

Miss Dignam tittered behind her hand. "It appears you two *have* already met. My lord, you are a naughty, naughty boy! Ellen, let me introduce James Gatewood, Lord Chesney, of Chesney, Hertfordshire, and Chesney Hall, London."

Ellen could only stare in stupified silence.

Gatewood stirred himself. "I think I am a bit of a surprise to her," he commented to the squire, who nodded and laughed in appreciation, goodwill written all over his florid face.

"Ah, that you are, your worship," Squire Grimsley said. "One hardly ever finds Ellen at a loss for words." He paused, and then stumbled into the conversation again as Gatewood opened his mouth to speak. "Not that she is a chatterbox, or a gossip monger, my lord. Oh, no! She's the soul of circumspection and the delight of her mother and me."

Ellen stared at her father. Less than fifteen minutes ago he had given her the scold of her life, and so much as sentenced her to endless matrimony with the worst bore in the county. Now he was all smiles and good cheer.

Miss Dignam was no better. She nodded and bobbed her head until Ellen grew almost dizzy with watching. "My best pupil ever," she declared, even as she dabbed at her eyes. "I will miss her more than I can say, my lord."

"You . . . you never told me," she began, and stopped, plopping into the chair by the door because her legs would not hold her up.

"No, I didn't, did I?" Gatewood began. He blushed and stared down at his hands. "I really owe you an explanation, but would prefer to reserve it for some more private moment."

"Oh, la, my lord, we can arrange that in a moment," simpered Miss Dignam.

She cleared her throat and then poked the squire, who scrambled to his feet, giving Ellen a broad wink. "Miss Dignam, we can easily retreat to the sitting room and you can tell me again your theories on education."

Ellen stared at her father, who had never once, in all the years of their acquaintance, come within a ten-foot pole of theories of any kind. Here he was, bowing and scraping and making a perfect cake of himself, where only minutes before he had been hard as nails.

And then she understood, and was filled with the greatest humiliation she had ever known. The misery she had inflicted upon herself yesterday in University College's lecture hall held no candle to this new agony that washed over her and left her drained. It was the humiliation of being ashamed of her family.

As they watched her, Gatewood's eyes hopeful, Miss Dignam and her father eager to please, Ellen felt the bile rise in her throat. All her life she had known the security of being the daughter of a prosperous squire from a prosperous county. There was comfort in knowing that no matter how she personally regarded each family member's silliness and vanities, they were unknown to others. The Grimsleys name in Oxfordshire was enough.

And now, here was this new squire she had never seen before, twittering about Lord Chesney like a moth to a flame. In one introduction to Lord Chesney, Papa had gone from respected man in his own little sphere to a very small frog in a very large pond. The knowledge caused her unspeakable embarrassment.

She looked at Lord Chesney, who was on his feet by now, running his fingers through his tousled hair. His face was agitated; unlike the others, Gatewood had seen the look in her eyes and understood what it meant.

"See here, Ellen, I am sorry," he began, only to be interrupted by the squire.

"No, lad, no! I mean, your worship. It was only a high-spirited prank on your part!" The squire laughed, showing all his teeth. "Ellen doesn't mind, do you, my dear?"

"I mind greatly," she said, her voice low. "Why didn't you

tell me who you were? Why did you lead me on down a path that you must have known would end as it did yesterday?"

"I . . ."

The squire could see that the tide was not turning in Lord Chesney's favor. He chucked his daughter under the chin, choosing not to notice when she drew back from him and made herself smaller in the chair. "Ellen! It's all right and tight! Lord Chesney has explained that you wrote those silly papers that Gordon read! Miss Dignam and I would never tell a soul, so your secret is safe."

Ellen noted that, to his credit, Lord Chesney winced at her father's artless confession.

"You are wrong, Papa," she said, her voice rising slightly. "Gordon should be expelled from university for what he did, and there is no censure great enough for my part in it. We did a disservice to this great university." She turned her fine eyes on James Gatewood, who by now was at the window again and chewing on his fingernails. "I do not know why you took such an interest in my scholarship, sir . . ."

"He is a lord, Ellen, not a sir!" her father hissed at her.

"Sir," she continued, her voice cool even as her face flamed. "Who are you? A duke? an earl? a marquess? a viscount? The Lord God Almighty?"

"Ellen!" the squire groaned. He leaped to his feet. "My lord, she does not mean any of this."

"I am sure she means all of it, sir," he replied, "and I, for one, do not blame her." He crossed the room to stand before Ellen, who rose slowly to her feet. "We share a weakness, Ellen. It is scholarship. It has gotten you in trouble, and I was the author of your humiliation."

"I am sure she can overlook this little fault," the squire said magnanimously.

Ellen said nothing. Papa, you are such a toady, she thought. I am so ashamed.

But Lord Chesney was speaking. "I am a marquess, Ellen. I am worth a bit more than Edwin Bland's four thousand a year, although I have never had the feeling that such trivia mattered to you. I am also somewhat shy. That was why I created this fiction. I had a feeling that you might not care for a marquess over much. Was I wrong?"

"Nonsense!" the squire brayed. "Ellen knows what's good for her." He laughed out loud and Miss Dignam joined in.

"Oh, God, Papa, please stop," Ellen begged. She edged toward the door. She held out her hand to James Gatewood. "Goodbye, sir. I . . . I . . . cannot say that I am sorry to have written those papers, but I am embarrassed that you have seen us as we really are."

He took her hand. "I love you, Ellen."

She froze, even as her father clapped a meaty hand on the marquess' shoulder.

"Well said, your worship," he exclaimed. "Do you know, Ellen, he has already talked to me this morning about settlements, and Gordon is even to have a cavalry regiment of Lord Chesney's choosing. I call that magnanimous."

"I call it foolish," Ellen said, withdrawing her hand from Gatewood's. "Good day, my lord. I hope you choke on your scholarship."

"Ellen!" the squire gasped, and then turned it aside with a little laugh. "She'll come around, your worship."

"Possibly," Lord Chesney replied. "If you'll excuse us, Squire?"

Before she could protest, Gatewood took her by the hand and dragged her into the hall. He pushed her against the wall and grasped her by both shoulders.

"I didn't mean any of this to happen, Ellen. You must believe that," he said, his voice urgent. Doors were opening all along the hallway. He looked around in annoyance. "God, I hate this place!" He sighed, and released her to run a finger around his shabby collar. "See here, I've never proposed before, and I am sure I have done it all wrong, Ellen. But I love you. Will you marry me?"

She said nothing. He pulled her close and kissed her, his arms tight around her. To her ultimate humiliation, she found herself kissing him back. Her fingers were in his untidy hair, smoothing it, caressing him.

When the buttons on his coat began to dig into her breast, she came back to herself. With a shock, she leaped back, took a deep breath, made a fist and struck him on the face.

He reeled back in surprise, his hand to his flaming cheek. They stared at each other, breathing hard. Her humiliation complete, Ellen felt the tears starting behind her eyelids. She stamped her foot.

"I hope I never, ever see you again, Jim Gatewood!" she sobbed.

He said nothing for the longest moment. She watched his face, waiting for some sign of repugnance, some indication of his disgust of her after her shameless kiss and then that dreadful punch that still seemed to echo in the hall. Instead, he reached in his pocket and gave her his handkerchief.

She blew her nose vigorously. "I'll . . . I'll have this laundered and returned to All Souls," she said, her voice stiff.

He smiled then, even as a bruise of impressive proportions began to form on his cheek. "Are your knuckles all right?" he asked, his voice mild. "That was quite a facer from someone of such unsymmetrical proportions."

She looked down at her hand, with the knuckles cracked and bleeding, and dabbed at it with the handkerchief. She was unable to think of a thing to say, except to stammer again that she would return the handkerchief.

Lord Chesney shook his head, and then winced and clapped his hand to his cheek again.

Ellen writhed with inward embarrassment.

"No need, my dear," he said as he started backing toward the outside door. "I'll be seeing you in a couple of weeks."

"I doubt that!" she declared and blew her nose again.

"Doubt it not, fair Hermia," he said as he continued down the hall, backing away from her. "Your father has invited me to Horatia's wedding, and I accepted with great alacrity and greater pleasure."

"He didn't!" she wailed.

"He did! See you soon, you dreadful wench." He paused with his hand on the doorknob. "Do you know, I am relieved that you are such a pugilist."

She sobbed harder, whether in rage or humiliation she could not tell.

"I need never fear that harm will come to me while we are mapping the world, fair Hermia!"

11

Her knuckles throbbed all the way home and Ellen welcomed the pain. "Maybe if it hurts bad enough, you will remember not to be so stupid in future," she told herself as she sucked on the swollen joints.

She could not imagine what had possessed her to deliver such a wallop to James Gatew . . . to Lord Chesney. Even if Mama was a flibbertigibbet of the first stare, Ellen had been raised with great circumspection. She knew better than to flirt with young men, or to even sit down in a chair recently vacated by one, because it would still be warm. That she should cut loose so entirely as to assault a marquess was a continuing astonishment to her as she rode in solitary splendor through magnificent scenery turned sour by her mood.

It was a relief that her Papa had ridden his horse to Oxford, and was therefore compelled to arrange a post chaise for his daughter. Ellen curled up in one corner of the vehicle and tucked her chin into her cloak, grateful that there was no need of conversation, except that mighty scold that she dumped upon her own head like hot coals and ashes.

Oh, how could Papa invite Lord Chesney to the wedding! She started to twist her hands together, uttering a yelp of pain when she encountered her knuckles. It was too bad, utterly too bad. He will see us at our worst: Papa chafing and swearing if the weather is too inclement for at least one canter about the countryside each day; Mama even more unmanageable than usual, with her silly spasms over the tiniest slipup in her plans.

And Horry, Horatia would be worse than useless, mooning about the house as soon as Edwin—with many a backward glance and thrown kisses—nudged his horse down the lane. Either that, or some of the reality of marriage will have set in and she will be scared spitless and cowering in her dressing room.

Ellen retreated farther into her cloak. *And then Mama will give her improving lectures on the evils of men in general, and reassure us that all will be well, or at least, as good as can be, considering that it is woman's lot in life to suffer.* Ellen shuddered. *It is a wonder to me,* she thought, *that someone would really want to be mauled about in that way. Horry is stupider than even I suspected.*

She reflected on that thought, and felt her cheeks grow red. She hadn't minded a bit when James Gatewood had grabbed her by both shoulders and kissed her so soundly. In fact, she recalled with some personal irritation that the worst part about the whole, regrettable incident was the nagging feeling that she couldn't get close enough to him. *And did I really thrust myself against him? Oh, dear, I hope he did not notice.*

There, she had thought the unthinkable. *Good Lord, Ellen, you are a worse ninnyhammer than your sister,* she thought. Nice girls didn't reflect on those rather impish thoughts that had raced through her mind as she clung like a barnacle to James Gatewood.

"Lord Chesney, not Jim Gatewood any more," she said out loud. "It is Lord Chesney, and he has done you a bit of no good."

So he had. For weeks and weeks he had led her to believe he was someone he was not. He had placed her in several compromising situations that would have sent Mama into terminal spasms, should she ever find out.

Or had he? Ellen drew her knees up and rested her chin on them as the post chaise swayed along. She had been in no danger from Lord Chesney's designs, or so Mama would put it. They had spent an afternoon together in his chambers, and another on the river, discussing Shakespeare and nourishing each other's minds. It was the kind of conversation she envied among the scholars of Oxford, that equal exchange of thoughts and views.

"I wonder if men and women will ever be permitted such freedom of thought," she asked out loud. "I . . . I guess I was lucky."

She smiled at the memory and then sobered as she thought about the rest of her family. Ralph would acquit himself well, this she knew. Lord Chesney—no, Jim Gatewood—would be captivated by her little brother and his serious approach to scholarship. Should he come for the wedding, she would see that Jim and Ralph saw plenty of each other during the days before the wedding. And Martha? It would be her duty to keep Martha out of the chocolates.

She let her mind rest a moment, and then laughed out loud. "Ellen, you are a true idiot," she said. "You will be safely out of this ridiculous infatuation when Jim sees your family as they really are. No need to apologize for them. Just let him see for himself."

She nodded to her reflection in the window glass. In a short space, he will be so disgusted that he will probably beat a hasty retreat even before Horry's nuptials. End of problem.

The thought did not relieve her as she had imagined it would. For no reason that she could discern, she burst into tears.

Her eyes were long since dry by the time she tapped on the glass and stopped the post chaise before they turned off the main road and traveled down the lane. Papa reined in his horse and leaned toward the carriage as she rolled down the window.

"Papa, I forbid you to mention one word of this affair to anyone," she ordered, keeping her knees tight together so they would not quake at this unheard-of insistence by daughter to father.

"Oh, you do?" he asked. To her relief, his voice was mellow. Obviously Squire Grimsley was still basking in the idea of an alliance far beyond his wildest dreams.

It was on the tip of her tongue to assure him that such an event would never come to pass, but she let it go, and smiled sweetly up at him instead. "Yes, Papa, I insist! It is Horry's big day, and nothing is settled, and it would be the height of rudeness for us to trumpet these imaginings about the countryside."

"I suppose so," he agreed, his voice filled with reluctance. He brightened. "But I shall have to say something to Mama, or she will think only the worst about my sudden trip to Oxford." He frowned and shook his riding crop at her. "And you are still a scamp, Ellen Grimsley."

"Yes, Papa," she said, and there was no subterfuge in her voice. "I was. But I mean to reform."

"Very well, miss. Now, roll up that window before

pneumonia carries you off and I can never tell my comrades that I am closely related to the Marchioness of Chesney!''

She sighed and did as he said. I hope he will not take it too badly when I continue to refuse Jim's offer of marriage, she thought as they proceeded down the lane. I suppose I had better consider Thomas Cornwell more seriously.

Ellen was happier to see them all than she would have thought possible. Horatia was as silly as ever; Mama as nervous. Ralph wanted to discuss Great Ideas, and Martha nosed about for sweets. As she stood in the hallway, still clad in her traveling cloak and hiding her swollen knuckles, Ellen could only regard them with affection.

"I have missed you all," she said simply, and wondered why she felt like tears again.

Mama's chin trembled. "I hope you were not in terrible trouble in Oxford, my dear, else why would Mr. Grimsley rush off in such a hurry?" She rested her hand against her forehead. "I have been imagining the worst."

" 'Tis nothing, my dearest," the squire soothed. "Let us discuss this matter in private."

Mama nodded and watched him retreat down the hall, whistling to himself as he swatted at the potted plants with his riding crop. "He is in rare good humor," she observed, then turned to her daughter again. "Ellen, it is too bad! Your papa refuses to spend one more penny on food for the reception, and I have told him it is not enough."

"And he is being a perfect beast about the music in the church," Horry added, handkerchief to her eyes, too. "He insists on all his favorite hymns, and you know how old-fashioned they are!"

Ellen took off her bonnet and tossed it to Ralph, who grinned and beat his own retreat before the Grimsley females began to weep in earnest. Slowly Ellen unbuttoned her pelisse and smiled upon her sister and mother. Last week, I would have been so impatient with you both, she thought.

Tears came to her own eyes as she embraced them, urging them not to fret, telling them that she would make things right with Papa. She hugged her silly mother and sister, deeply cognizant of the fact that even their combined foolishness did not equal the enormity of her own folly.

"There now, Mama, I am certain I can convince Papa to lay out some more blunt for refreshments. Now, go along and hear what he has to tell you."

"I wish you would not use such dreadful cant," Mama scolded, but she did as Ellen said.

Ellen turned to Horatia. "Horry dearest, all you have to do is slip in one of two of Papa's own favorite hymns, and he will allow you the rest, you know he will. Don't be a goose."

"Do you think so?" Horatia asked.

"I know so."

Horatia blew her nose. She was silent a moment as they walked arm in arm toward the stairs. She stopped suddenly to more closely observe her sister.

"Ellen, you act as though you had something on Papa."

"It could be that I do, my dear."

"Oh, tell!"

Ellen laughed, even though she did not feel particularly jolly. "It is nothing that cannot wait. Come, dearest, and let me hear your plans."

She lay wide awake in bed late that night, long after Horry had yawned for the last time and taken herself off to her own room, eyes bright with wedding plans. Ellen thought about dinner, and turned restlessly onto her side. Mama, bursting with Papa's news but sworn to secrecy, was all smiles and dimples from first course to last.

It is bad of me to encourage her, Ellen thought, as she turned to her other side and flipped around the pillow for a cool spot. I should tell them all flat out that I have no intention in the world of marrying Lord Chesney.

Or do I? She hugged her pillow to her, thinking of James, head thrown back, laughing at something she had said that afternoon in his chambers. James with his feet propped up so negligently at his carrel in the Bodleian. James poling so expertly on the river rimmed with ice, a glass of champagne in one gloved hand, and good ideas tumbling out of his head. James that first afternoon on the hill overlooking Oxford, letting his shredded letter blow into the wind.

With a shake of her head, she got out of bed and stood by the window. It had always been her favorite view, that long expanse of valley before her, wooded, and with streams flowing.

Now it was merely cold and wind-scoured. The trees had surrendered all their leaves and the streams were clogged with ice. The distant hills that were so invitingly purple in the summer were only dim, dark shapes now. She closed her eyes, wishing with all her heart that she could open them upon the Oxford landscape.

She rested her cheek against the curtain. "I shall write an essay on the permanence of impermanent things," she decided as she allowed the tears stifled since her homecoming to flow. "After all, what are the quads, halls, chapels, and libraries except symbols of ideas that will never die?"

But there would be no time for essays, not in these hectic days before the wedding. She glanced at the large volume of Shakespeare on her desk, a gift from James Gatewood. She had not given it to Ralph yet. Perhaps it could wait another day or two, when the reality of being home, and all that it meant, set in with a vengeance.

If it ever does, she thought as she crawled back into bed. I have changed. It was only a paltry few weeks, but I have changed.

Whether it was for the better, she could not tell. And as the sound of her fist against James Gatewood's face echoed through her head, she knew that she could not possibly have improved. How could I have done that? she asked again. I have never been that angry at anyone before, and here I thought I liked him.

Earlier that evening, she had approached Horatia cautiously, when they were both sitting on her bed, asking if she had ever felt angry enough to strike Edwin Bland. Horry's eyes had widened as her hand went to her mouth. "Mercy, Ellen, of course not! He is my true and only love!"

"Don't you ever get angry at him?" Ellen had asked.

"I couldn't possibly. Edwin is everything that is proper and right."

"Oh."

Ellen sighed in the dark. Whatever it was she felt for James Gatewood obviously wasn't true love, then. She blushed. Dear me, she thought, it is much worse. Last year, Mama had sat them both down one afternoon when they had the house to them-

selves. With blushes and long pauses, Mama had divulged some
of the mystery surrounding the male sex. Mama had warned
them about the "animal instincts in men."

Do women have such base instincts? Ellen asked herself. Dear
me, I wish there was someone I could ask. She scrunched herself
into a ball and pulled the blankets over her head, reflecting on
this compounding of her sins. She would never marry Lord
Chesney, no matter what Mama and Papa thought, so the matter
of her base instincts would likely never surface to trouble her.
And if she married Thomas Cornwell? Ellen shook her head.
She had not the remotest wish to plant either a facer or a kiss
upon him, so the matter could be considered safely closed.
Cornwell would likely never inspire those tempting thoughts
that had filled her head and now left her ashamed.

Still, Jim's lips had been so warm and . . . she cast about
for the right words to describe his kiss. She decided after much
thought that there was no single adjective. Gatewood's kiss had
been a complexity of many feelings. I felt that he and I were
doing something that no one else in the world had ever done
before, she thought. I didn't give a rap who saw us. The only
thing that mattered was Jim.

Ellen burrowed deeper in her bed. "Miss Grimsley," she
began, her voice muffled by the covers, "you will begin by
not thinking of him as 'Jim' anymore. He is Lord Chesney, a
peer of the realm, who thinks himself in love. A Christmas visit
with his own kind will wake him up, I am sure."

That thought was a bucket of cold water on her nervous
imaginings. He would never show up for the wedding. A little
cool-eyed reflection of his own would show him the wisdom
of staying far away from Squire Grimsley's manor. He might
feel honor-bound to send a gift, but he would not bring it in
person, she convinced herself.

It should have been a reassuring thought, but it wasn't. She
dwelt upon it long enough for the monotony of that single idea
to send her off to sleep finally.

In the morning, she disappointed Ralph by insisting that her
walk into the village be solitary.

"My dear, since I am not returning to Oxford, we have ages
and ages to discuss Shakespeare," she told him as she pulled

on her gloves. She touched his cheek. "On my desk is an early Christmas present to you. That should distract you sufficiently for me to have a comfortable chat with Aunt Shreve."

She watched her brother hurry up the stairs. Tears welled up suddenly as she thought of the "Good Luck" Jim Gatewood had scrawled across both inside pages. She dabbed furtively at her eyes, looking around to make sure that she was not seen. *I simply must get over this lacrimosity,* she thought, as she let herself out of the house.

With the door carefully closed against the servants, and a comforting fire in the hearth, Ellen told her aunt everything that had happened during her brief Oxford career, leaving out no detail, no matter how gory. When she finished, Aunt Shreve merely sat there, a slight smile on her face, as Ellen stirred up the coals in the fireplace.

"I gather then that I do not need to sacrifice my one remaining bottle of Palais Royal just yet."

"It seems so, Aunt," Ellen replied quietly, her chin on her palm, as she stared into the flames that briefly rose and then died because there was nothing left to feed upon. "It would never have worked. I have been a fool, and I freely admit it."

Aunt Shreve took Ellen by the hand. "But I must know, my dear: did you enjoy writing those papers?"

Ellen laughed out loud, her misery shoved aside for the moment. "I did! It was glorious fun. I only wish I had them to show you, Aunt."

"Perhaps you can ask Lord Chesney about that when he arrives for the wedding," Aunt Shreve suggested.

"He will not come," Ellen said. "I am sure of it."

"You will not think me foolish if I beg to differ with you?" her aunt asked, a twinkle in her eyes.

"He will not come," she said again. "I know it. Let us find another subject to discuss, Aunt."

They did, touching upon the weather, Horry's wedding, the approaching Yuletide, and the visits of Aunt Shreve's own children, one of whom was symmetrical enough to be in Horry's bridal party.

"Tell me, Aunt," she said suddenly, during a lull in trivia. "Do you know anything about the marquesses of Chesney?"

"It hardly matters," Aunt Shreve replied, her dimple much in evidence. "He will not come."

"Aunt! I am merely . . . curious."

"Go to the bookcase. My dear Walter used to enjoy thumbing through *Great Families of England*. I believe our copy is up to date within ten years."

Ellen found the book. Perching herself on the arm of Aunt Shreve's chair, she turned to the section on Hertfordshire. Aunt Shreve peered at the book, too. "Hertfordshire, is it? Excellent country. I wonder, does he hunt?"

"Only for mice in the Bodleian," Ellen murmured. She ran her fingers down the page. "Let us see: Casewell, Charterus, Chesmouth, Chesney." She read to herself and then looked up. "It is an old title, Aunt. Dear me, they appear to own half of Hertfordshire!"

"It is a small shire," Aunt Shreve commented, a smile playing about her lips. "Why, in Northumberland, that would be merely a farm."

"Aunt! It would not! And why in heaven's name would anyone want a seat in Northumberland?"

"Why indeed? Dreadful slow place!"

"You are quizzing me," Ellen said mildly. "They have been a distinguished family, too. Look here, there have been ministers to the crown, ambassadors, and any number of soldiers."

"But not recently," Aunt Shreve said as she scanned the page along with her niece.

"No. They appear to have done nothing of merit for at least one hundred years." Ellen closed the book and put it back on the shelf. She leaned against the bookcase. "Jim—Lord Chesney—claimed he was descended from a long line of 'window dressers and horse traders.'"

Aunt Shreve nodded. "Perhaps, of late, the Chesneys have been more concerned with cutting a dash at Brooks and Watier's, and racing horses at Newmarket. Do you suppose that was what he meant?"

"Likely it was." Ellen made a face. "Even then, Aunt, he is much too exalted for the likes of the Grimsleys."

Aunt Shreve shook her head. "I don't know, my dear. From what you have told me, James Gatewood is neither exalted nor common. He sounds like a rare gem to me. Do excuse the pun."

Ellen groaned. "How vulgar, Aunt!"

"Yes, indeed." She peered at her niece more closely. "I own I do not precisely understand what your objection is to this paragon."

"He is no paragon," Ellen said quickly. "He is deceitful."

Aunt Shreve considered this. "Perhaps he must protect himself. You mentioned some remarks of yours that were somewhat disparaging of the peerage. Could it be that you are too proud? And do you suppose, my dear niece, that this man has been hounded for his wealth by females with more on their minds than scholarship? Is he handsome?"

"Well, no, but he does have quite a nice smile," Ellen admitted. "In fact, it is a very nice smile. And he has an air about him . . ."

She stopped and then laughed at herself. "Listen to me. You would almost think I cared. But I do not!" she added hastily. "He was so untruthful."

"And you, a little too proud?" Aunt Shreve asked again, more gently this time.

"How odd that I should feel too proud for a marquess," Ellen mused, and then took a turn about the room, stopping in front of her aunt. "Actually, Aunt Shreve, I think I just wish to control my own destiny. I see how wrapped up in Edwin Horatia is, as though she had no mind of her own." Her chin went up. "I intend to resist this."

"Well, resist away," said Aunt Shreve. She idly picked at some lint on her sleeve. "As your dear Uncle Walter would say to me, 'This is moot, Jeanie, moot indeed.' For after all, Ellen, he will not come."

"He will not come."

By the time Christmas was little more than a memory of too much egg nog and not enough sleep, Ellen had resigned herself to the fact that Lord Chesney had really changed his mind. There had been no communication with Papa from the Marquess of Chesney, not even to reaffirm the day of the wedding and give assurances of his own arrival. Papa's optimism in the face of his daughter's good fortune dwindled and expressed itself only in an occasional weak smile in Ellen's direction.

Ellen kept her feelings to herself. As the house began to fill up with relatives and close friends come to witness this first

Grimsley wedding, she occupied herself with keeping Mama and the cook far away from each other. By judicious council and earnest appeal, Ellen managed to keep Cook's threats to resign down to a minimum of a crisis per day.

Gordon returned from London, where he had spent Christmas with one of Aunt Shreve's sons. Ellen had her own doubts that Giles Shreve had actually invited Gordon, but she did applaud her brother's newly acquired wisdom in staying away from the wrath of the squire. As it was, the squire only frowned at him, threatened vaguely "to have a few words with you, my boy," and soon forgot his Oxford misadventures after Gordon's present of a new riding crop and a spanking dash across the landscape with his eldest son. He returned, charitable and forgiving.

Sensing that the coolness between himself and his sister had not warmed appreciably, Gordon trod a narrow line with Ellen. He tested the waters gradually.

She interrupted him one afternoon in the library, where he had gone to sleep off a massive luncheon. He sat upright when she entered the room to return several books to the shelves.

"Best sofa in the house, Ellen," he ventured.

"It ought to be," she replied crisply. "No one uses this room except me and Ralph."

"I wouldn't, either," he assured her. "It's just that this place is filled with kin, and where there is not a relative sitting, there is a present or two."

Ellen smiled and shelved the books. She prepared to leave the library, but he stopped her.

"El, guess who I saw in London?" he asked.

"Dick Whittington and his cat? King Arthur, or perhaps Sir Gawain?" she asked in turn.

"No, silly! I do not run with a royal crowd! No, it was Lord Chesney."

"Oh?" she replied, raising her eyebrows. "And what makes you think I am interested?"

"Well, I thought you might be." He lay down again. "Sorry I brought it up."

She remained at the door. "Well, he wasn't in trouble or anything, was he?" she asked, keeping her tone casual.

"Lord, no! He was in Tattersall's with a bunch of his friends. D'ye know, he looks different when he is not in that old student's gown. I almost did not recognize him in real clothes."

"Did he see you?"

Gordon shook his head. "I thought it best not to announce myself. El, it wasn't auction day at Tat's, but they had pulled out a regular show of the most beautiful bits of bone and blood I ever saw. Lord Chesney must run with a plummy crowd, El. You'd never know it to look at him."

"There is a lot you'd never know about Lord Chesney by looking at him," she replied and turned the door handle. She looked back at her brother. "How . . . how did he appear?"

"Bored! I don't think I ever saw anyone looking so bored. I think if I had that line of thoroughbreds to choose from, I would at least try to appear interested."

"Gordon, it is not given to everyone to be horse-mad," she reminded him.

"Still . . ."

He closed his eyes. Ellen let herself out of the library and ran straight into the arms of Thomas Cornwell.

"Oh! Beg pardon!" she stammered, and would have stepped back, but the door was closed.

His face fiery, Cornwell leapt aside. "You . . . your butler said I could come on in, Ellen," he said. He took her by the hand and swallowed several times. "We have been away for Christmas, or I would have been here sooner."

Wordless, she stared up at Thomas Cornwell, noting the way his ears stuck out, and the way his chin and his nose seemed to be growing toward each other. This is my destiny, she thought. I am safe from my baser instincts.

She held out her hand. "How do you find yourself, Thomas?" she asked.

"Well, I just look down, and there I am, Ellen," he replied, puzzled.

He still held his hat in his hand, and he turned it around and around, worrying the brim into a shapeless mass. "I want to talk with your father," he managed at last.

Ellen groaned inwardly and took Thomas by the arm, leading him away from the library door, and any possible encounter with Gordon, who would only tease. "Thomas, I think this is not a good time, what with Horatia to be married in two days and a houseful of guests."

He thought about that for a long moment, considering the pros, cons, logistics, strategy, and implications until Ellen wanted to tear her hair. "I suppose you are right," he said at last, the words dragged out of him. "I should wait until after the wedding?"

"I think that would be an excellent idea."

She guided him toward the door, and in another minute he found himself on the outside steps, almost without being aware how he got there.

"I missed you, Ellen," he said simply as she started to close the door. He fumbled in his pocket and handed her a folded piece of paper, his face turning scarlet. He jumped back down the steps as though they burned through the soles of his thick boots. "It's just a little something I wrote."

Mystified, she opened the paper as he backed into the yard and stumbled against his horse.

" 'Bye, Ellen," he whispered as he vaulted into the saddle and tore off down the lane.

She closed the door and leaned against it, looking at the soggy page before her. Her eyes misted over. Thomas Cornwell, sturdy yeoman, wealthy landowner, son of the soil, had written her a love poem.

She read it through once, twice, noting the misspellings and splotches where he bore down too hard with his pen or repeated himself. She marveled at the variety of ways he found to rhyme "love," but felt no urge to laugh at the bumbling effort she held in her hand.

"Dear me," was all she could say as she refolded the poem. "This will never do."

That afternoon, Papa took her aside and asked if she thought Lord Chesney was really coming. "For if he is not, we can use the best guest room right now."

"I think he is not coming, Papa," she said. Her hand went to the poem in her pocket.

Papa could only shake his head. "And I was so sure he would."

She was spared the necessity of further conversation on a painful subject when Mama called, her voice edged with hysteria.

Papa looked up at the first-floor landing. "Ellen," he began, his eyes on the sewing room door. "I think I should go check and see if that roan of mine has dropped her foal yet."

Ellen couldn't resist. "Papa, you told me the foal wasn't due for another six weeks!"

Mama called out again for Ellen. Papa started down the hall at a gallop. "You can't be too careful!" he shouted over his shoulder.

She found Mama in the sewing room with two bridesmaids, who shivered in their sketchy gowns. Fanny Bland glared at her as she rubbed her arms to tame the goosebumps.

"Hello, Fanny," Ellen said as she hurried to Mama, who was by now sobbing helplessly into her handkerchief. "Mama! Whatever is the matter?"

Mama leaned against her daughter and gestured feebly with her free hand. "Look you there. Maria Edgerly has grown two inches taller since she was measured for her gown." Mama sobbed into Ellen's shoulder. "Can you think of a more beastly trick to play upon me?"

The bridesmaid in question burst into noisy tears and fled the room. Fanny looked on in silence, her eyes ahead, her own expression stony, as Mama followed Maria down the hall, calling after her.

Ellen turned to Fanny, waiting for a cutting remark. She dreaded the sight of that arch look that would signal to her that Fanny had been busy spreading the news of Ellen's Oxford career about the countryside. To her surprise, there was no expression on Fanny's face beyond a vague sadness.

"Fanny, I trust you had a pleasant Christmas," Ellen said cautiously.

"Well enough, thank you," Fanny said, and nothing more.

Ellen looked at her in confusion. Her amazement grew as she watched tears well up in Fanny's eyes and spill down her cheeks.

"Why, Fanny Bland, whatever is the matter?" she asked in surprise. She held up her hand to help Fanny down from the chair she stood on.

Fanny sank into the chair and dabbed at her eyes, even as she shivered in her skimpy dress. She sniffed once or twice, not looking at Ellen.

"Did Thomas Cornwell . . . did he bring a poem to you?" she asked.

Ellen nodded. It was on her lips to relieve the tension by joking about the misspellings and primitive rhyme pattern, but something in Fanny's expression prevented her. "He did."

Fanny could not bring herself to look at Ellen. "I have known Thomas Cornwell for years and years, even as you. He brought that poem to my house yesterday morning and made me go over it with him. He wanted every word right. I . . . I couldn't bring myself to correct any of it, because it seemed perfect just the way it was."

Fanny's face crumpled up and she sobbed into her handkerchief. Ellen watched in bewilderment until the truth came crashing down around her. Boring, vindictive, spiteful Fanny Bland, was in love with boring, well-meaning, earnest Thomas Cornwell.

I wonder, does this account for your unkindness to me Ellen thought as she watched the spectacle before her. During my miserable stay at Miss Dignam's, you were jealous. Oh, Fanny. Slowly she sat down next to Fanny and touched her shoulder. Fanny did not pull away, but only sobbed harder.

"And I know he came to propose yesterday, be . . . because he told me he was going to," Fanny blubbered. "He tells me everything!"

Ellen handed her another handkerchief. "Well, he did not," she said. "I sent him away because it really wasn't a good time. Oh, Fanny, don't cry! Surely we can work something out!"

"I don't know what," Fanny sobbed. "It isn't fair, Ellen, that you should be brilliant and beautiful, and have Thomas Cornwell, too."

Ellen gasped. "I am not beautiful, Fanny!"

"Thomas thinks you are!"

"Thomas Cornwell is all about in his head," Ellen said, only to blink in surprise when Fanny turned on her.

"Take that back, Ellen Grimsley," she snapped. "Thomas Cornwell is the most wonderful man in Oxfordshire."

She retreated into her handkerchief again and Ellen apologized, wondering if everyone within hearing distance had gone lunatic and she was the only sane person. She heard the doorbell jingle.

"You'll have to excuse me, Fanny," she said, eager to flee the sewing room. "Mama is having a fit somewhere, Papa has escaped, Horry is not speaking to any of us, and I don't know where the butler is."

She hurried down the stairs, only to stop and stare at Lord Chesney coming toward her, a certain spring in his step. Squire Grimsley trailed along behind him, smiling and bowing whenever the marquess looked his way. Ellen gulped and searched about for an avenue of retreat, but there was none.

"Look who has arrived," Papa was saying, as though he had gone personally to fetch the marquess. He wagged a playful finger at his daughter. "And you thought he would not come!"

Ellen blushed. Papa, stop! she wanted to shout. Do not play the mushroom to this man. You demean yourself and embarrass me.

Lord Chesney only smiled. "You thought I would not come? After that fond farewell in Oxford?"

"Silly me," was all she could manage as Lord Chesney took full advantage of her confusion, wrapped his arms about her, and kissed her thoroughly.

He was still cold, but he smelled of woodsmoke and the outdoors, two of her favorite things. She had no intention of kissing him back, but there he stood with his arms around her, his lips upon hers. What was she to do?

"Merry Christmas," he murmured a moment later, his lips in her hair. "I was hoping you had not forgotten me entirely."

"No, no," she stammered, out of sorts with herself again, and recalling with painful clarity the result of their last kiss. She turned her head slightly to stare at the fading bruise of greenish-yellow on his cheekbone. "How ever did you explain that to your relatives?" she asked.

"I occasionally tell the truth when it suits me," he replied, touching his cheek. "I told them that a young woman I rescued from the Bodleian library slapped me silly for proposing marriage. They laughed for days and dismissed it as one of my more harebrained eccentricities.'' He bowed. ''Your secret is safe. No one believes me.''

She laughed in spite of herself, just as the front door slammed open and rapid footsteps pounded toward them. Surprised, she peeked around the marquess's arm in time to see Thomas Cornwell, face white, eyes ablaze, grab Gatewood by the shoulder.

''Oh horrors,'' she said, freeing herself from the marquess. ''Thomas, if you . . .''

He did. Without a word, and to the vast amazement of the squire and the marquess, Thomas Cornwell stripped off his glove, slapped Lord Chesney hard across the face with it, and dropped it in front of him.

12

Ellen gasped, as the marquess reeled from the force of the blow. The squire staggered to a chair and clutched his head in both hands. His fist clenched, Thomas Cornwell struck a pose.

Gingerly, Lord Chesney put his hand to his eye, which had caught a finger of the glove and was starting to water. He looked down at the glove in front of him. "My dear sir, you have dropped your glove."

Thomas frowned and stared down too, as if seeing the glove for the first time.

"Isn't that how it is done?" he asked, whatever fire raging in him banked by Gatewood's calm.

"I wouldn't know," Gatewood said. His hand still to his face, he bent down to retrieve the glove.

"It is a challenge, my lord, a challenge to a duel to the death for the hand of Ellen!" declared Cornwell, as though he had just recalled a phrase read in a bad novel and memorized it over too much brandy.

"Her hand?" Gatewood inquired. He dabbed at his eye. "My intentions go far beyond her hand, sir. Tell me, you must be Thomas Cornwell."

Cornwell nodded and accepted the glove. "Yes, my lord. I have loved Ellen for years and years."

"A tedious business, indeed," the marquess said. "I congratulate you on your stamina."

Cornwell grinned.

"Well, I like that!" Ellen declared.

Her bracing words recalled Cornwell to the matter at hand. "Sir, I demand satisfaction!"

The marquess pursed his lips as though engaged in deep thought, and shook his head. "I've never dueled before, sir. I wouldn't begin to know how to go about it."

It was Cornwell's turn to stare. "But I thought . . . I assumed

. . . don't you marquesses and dukes and earls and such know all about that sort of thing?''

Gatewood shook his head with vigor, and quickly put his hand to his eye again. ''It's not one of the rules for membership in the peerage, Mr. Cornwell. I really haven't a clue, and would rather not fight at a wedding. Bad form, don't you know.''

By now, the hall was filled with spectators. Fanny Bland, her eyes red and rabbity from weeping, had heard the commotion and come out on the second-floor landing.

Ellen looked from Thomas Cornwell to Lord Chesney. She took a deep breath. ''Alas, Thomas, you wouldn't want to kill this helpless man who is much more at home in libraries.''

''Well, I like that!'' exclaimed the marquess in turn, a smile playing around his lips.

She ignored him and stepped between the two men. ''It was a lovely thought, Thomas,'' she said, resting her hand lightly on his coat lapel. Fanny burst into noisy tears. ''There are times when I think a duel would greatly improve the marquess.''

''Daughter!'' the squire exclaimed. ''She doesn't mean a word of it, your worship.''

Ellen colored with embarrassment. She patted Thomas Cornwell's lapel one last time and stepped in closer to the marquess, crossing her fingers behind her back where he could definitely see them. ''Thomas, I have promised myself to Lord Chesney.''

Fanny stopped sniffling. The squire sighed with relief.

''I mean, if you have any regard for me, you wouldn't want to kill the object of my affection, now, would you?''

''Not a convincing argument, Ellen,'' the marquess whispered in her ear. ''Think of the temptation.''

It was Thomas's turn to frown and purse his lips. ''I suppose I do not.''

The marquess stuck out his hand. ''I like your style, Cornwell, I really do.''

Cornwell grinned and shook hands. He turned suddenly serious. ''But you had better be good to her, my lord.''

''I aim to make her happiness my sole object in life.''

There was a commotion on the upstairs landing. Fanny Bland, prosaic old Fanny, had fainted and was draped over the railing.

Ellen took Thomas by the arm again. "Thomas, be a dear and see Fanny home," she whispered.

He nodded, his eyes on the second-floor landing. He took the steps two at a time. In another moment, he had picked up Fanny—a substantial handful—as though she were a bag of feathers. He came down the stairs carefully with his burden.

"If you should ever change your mind, Ellen," he said, "I'd be happy to shoot this fribble."

Lord Chesney raised his eyebrows as Thomas stalked away, Fanny lolling in his arms. "I've never been accused of being a fribble," he complained. "Come to think of it, I've never been challenged to a duel before. And I thought the country would be slow. Ellen, you have made me a happy man."

She could tell by the twinkle in his eyes that he was about to burst into sustained and uncontrolled merriment that would be difficult to explain to Papa, who was eyeing them both with an expression bordering on ecstasy. She took the marquess by the arm and marched him into the book room.

He tried to take her in his arms again, but she warded him off. "I didn't mean a word of it, Jim," she protested.

He didn't take the news badly. "Ellen, do you mean to ruin my new year entirely?" he asked.

"I hadn't planned on it."

"You won't mind then, if I propose to you occasionally during the coming year?"

"Well, I . . ."

"Just to keep in practice?"

"Be serious, Jim!"

"I am!"

"You are not!"

"Oh, yes I am!"

Ellen opened her mouth and then closed it again, embarrassed. Here I am, worrying about the impression my family is going to make on this man, and I sound like Martha brangling with Ralph. Her chin went up. "Very well, sir, you may do as you choose. As I am not returning to Oxford, I doubt our acquaintance will extend much beyond this wedding."

Lord Chesney only nodded, and looked thoughtful. Ellen watched him with suspicion.

"You are scheming something, I know it!" she declared flatly.

He merely bowed and opened the bookroom door. "My dear, let me set the record straight. The Marquess of Chesney never schemes. As a matter of fact, he hardly ever gets angry."

"Thank the Lord for that," she retorted, preceding him through the door.

"What he *does* do is get even."

She couldn't even be sure he had said that.

The house was crammed with relatives and it was easy to avoid the marquess, especially as her father kept dragging that obliging man from uncle to cousin to aunt, introducing him as "His worship, Ellen's future husband, even though we are to keep it under the hatches."

She cringed at her Papa's bad manners with one part of her mind and heart, while the other part applauded his vulgarity, convinced that a steady application would soon send the marquess screaming into the night.

But James Gatewood was made of sterner stuff. He bore the toadying and vulgar stares with aplomb. To her amazement, he even seemed to enjoy himself with the younger cousins in a bloody duel to the death with jackstraws, while the older members of the family yawned over cards.

"I like him, Ellen," Horatia ventured to say, when she could tear herself away from Edwin and his slack-jawed devotion.

Ellen set down the bridesmaid's dress she was hemming. "He is an unprincipled rogue, Horry!"

"He could never be that," Horatia declared, "else you never would have fallen in love!"

Ellen picked up the dress again, struck by her sister's words. "Do you know, Horry, that is quite the nicest compliment from you."

Horry merely patted her arm and rose to return to Edwin, who looked bewildered, sitting by himself. "I know you would never love a rake."

She watched her sister return to Edwin and sit on the low stool at his feet. She observed with some amusement the way Horry looked up at her husband-to-be with such adoration and trust. I am sure I am not in love, she thought, attending to her hemming again and wondering why it was coming out so uneven. Of course, I am not so sure that Jim would find it comfortable to have me crouch at his feet like a spaniel. I know I would not care for it.

She raised her eyes to the marquess, who was sitting on the floor with her rowdy cousins, Martha in his lap, as she shook the jackstraws. If our common touch does not disgust you, Lord Chesney, than I suppose you will be harder to dissuade than I thought, she considered.

As she watched him, he turned and winked at her. To her further disgust, she winked back.

Because the house was full, Lord Chesney was condemned to room with Ralph. He accepted his sentence with a cheeriness that amazed Mama.

"I would have thought that such an exalted personage would be picky about his bedmates," Mama whispered to her as they handed out candles to the relatives and bid them goodnight.

"Mama, do not call him exalted! You act as though he were a member of the Blessed Trinity!"

"I am sure I do not!" Mama protested. "It wouldn't hurt you to appear a little more lover-like, my dear."

Ellen rubbed at the frown between her eyes. "Mama, this is Horry's big occasion. I will not turn it into a circus, not for anyone."

"Yes, but you have scarcely said more than five words to him all evening."

"No, I have not," she agreed quietly. What she really wanted was a turn about the shrubbery with Lord Chesney, to assure him once again that she had no intention of marrying him. But the shrubbery was cold this time of year. She sighed. And the house was full of relatives.

She caught up with Ralph and Lord Chesney on the stairs, heads together, engaged in earnest conversation. "Jim," she called out, "I mean, Lord Chesney."

"I still prefer Jim," Gatewood replied, stopping and handing Ralph the candle they shared. "Go on, lad. I'll join you in a minute." He turned to Ellen. "I trust you are not planning to apologize for the accommodations, as your father has done, this half hour and more. Ralph and I have been discussing *Hamlet*, and the scene in Act V that Shakespeare did not write and should have, in Ralph's opinion.''

"Will you have him write a paper?" she asked as he trailed her down the hall to the lesser-used third-floor landing. She sat down on the steps and drew her knees up to her chin.

"I believe I will. If his scholarship is sound, it could be an excellent essay to secure him entrance into Winchester, my old school.''

"Papa would never allow it," she said. "He says Ralph is to go to my uncle's counting house in the City.''

"We shall see, dear Ellen, light of my life.''

"You have got to stop talking like that. I crossed my fingers behind my back when I told that fib to Thomas.''

"So you did," he agreed, his good humor intact. He touched her lips with his fingers before she could draw away. "That mulish look on your face tells me that I had better change the subject. My dear, I do not have to cross my fingers to tell you that your paper on *Romeo and Juliet* has no equal for wit and sarcasm. Even Dean Jonathan Swift—*requiescat in pacem*— would agree with me, I am sure. It is a classic.''

"I would like to have it back.''

He shook his head. "I did not bring it." He took her by the hand. "And why, may I ask, did you give your complete Shakespeare to Ralph?''

She would not look him in the eye. "I probably will not have any use for it here at home.''

"Not even to press flowers?" he asked lightly, and then sobered immediately. "That was rude of me. Excuse it. No use?''

She shook her head.

"That remains to be seen," he said. "Come, my dear, and kiss me quick. Tomorrow is going to be an awful day, I assure you. Desserts will burn, flowers in the church will wither, relatives will fall out with one another and the weather will turn sour." He laughed. "At least I need not fight a duel, too. And Horry will probably finally realize that marrying her elegant blockhead means going to bed with him.''

"Jim!"

He looked about elaborately. "No one heard me."

When she refused to kiss him, he pecked her on the cheek and strode down the hall to Ralph's room, humming softly under his breath.

The tune sounded like a wedding processional.

The day began precisely as Lord Chesney had predicted on the third-floor landing the night before. The desecration of burned pudding permeated the entire house, and Mama was finally forced to lie down and sob out her misery in the lap of her sister, who had been through a similar ordeal the year before. Horatia stalked about the house, her face pale, her expression wooden. Gordon was quarreling with his cousins in the stables and Martha sulked in her room because she had to share her toys.

Only Ralph appeared content. Ellen found him in the library, sitting cross-legged on the sofa with her folio open to *Hamlet*, and scribbling notes at a furious rate. He spared her only a grunt of recognition and then turned back to his labors.

With a snort of her own, Ellen pulled on her sturdiest boots and cloak and headed for the shrubbery. Her head throbbed with the odor of burned pudding and the quarrels of fractious relatives. Soon Fanny and the others would be there for a final fitting. She did not think she could bear either Fanny's gloom or her malice. "And I do not know which is worse," she muttered to herself as she set out for a brisk walk.

She was scarcely out of sight of the house when a familiar figure came toward her, wrapped in overcoat and muffler, but with his untidy hair blowing in the wind.

"You should wear a hat," she scolded as James Gatewood approached her, bowed, and linked his arm through hers.

"I only lose them. The warden at All Souls thinks that I should sit on them, and then I would know where they are."

He stopped and looked her in the eye. "I have not yet proposed for the day, madam." He went down on one knee. "My dear, would you make me the happiest man alive and consent to share my bed and board?"

"Never," she replied.

He grinned. "Oh, well. Failing that, will you marry me?"

She gasped, and then laughed in spite of herself. She tugged on his arm, looking about to make sure that no one saw them. "Now, get up before the moisture soaks through your buckskins and you come down with a dreadful cold, and I am forced to nurse you long after the wedding is over."

"Very well," he replied, rising and taking her arm again. "Now where was I?"

"I refuse to remind you."

He laughed, and Ellen was forced to smile.

"Do you really intend to propose every day?" she asked.

"Perhaps not every day," he said. "Who knows but that some day the element of surprise might prosper my wooing?" He touched her hand. "But yes, that is my intention."

They walked in silence, arm in arm through the shrubbery. "This is not good weather for lovemaking," he commented. "Think how much better it will be in Oxford this spring."

"I am not returning to Oxford," she insisted.

"Oh?" he said in that irritating way of his. "Which reminds me somehow. This would be a good time to puff up my consequence with you a little. Do you know what the Genuine-Article Lord Chesney has gone and done? He's such a good fellow."

"What has that eccentric man done now?" she asked in mock seriousness. "Dare you repeat it?"

"I do believe he has established a trust fund at Oxford University covering all the workers injured on college property. The idea has caught on amongst all the colleges, and soon there will be a sizable endowment. I believe Adam Speed's family will be the first to benefit."

Ellen stood still and took hold of Gatewood's other hand, too. She could not speak for a moment, and even then, she could not look him in the eye. "What would England be without her eccentrics?"

He raised her gloved hand to his lips. "Merely a stodgy little island with indifferent food." He continued on, kindly overlooking her sniffles. "Who knows what he will do next?"

"I wouldn't even hazard a guess."

They walked in companionable silence through the woods, Ellen lost in thought. Without realizing it, she leaned her head against Lord Chesney's arm as they walked along, wondering how she could face the house again. There was the wedding rehearsal tonight, full of unexplored peril.

She stopped walking. "Why do weddings have to be such uncomfortable events?" she asked the sky. "Oh, beg pardon," she said. "I didn't mean to hang about you like that."

"I didn't mind."

He led her to a fallen tree and sat her down. "Wedding giving you the blue devils?"

Ellen nodded. "I wonder that anyone does it." She brightened. "Perhaps Papa will pay me to elope some day."

"You wouldn't!" the marquess declared.

"Of course not, silly," she said. "What, would I deprive all my relatives of food and high drama?" She scuffed her boots in the spongy soil. "And now Horry is impossible, just as you predicted. I made some offhand remark about Edwin this morning, and she turned ten shades of pale and bolted to her room like a rabbit. She definitely has cold feet." She blushed. "But this is hardly a subject to discuss with you."

He nudged her shoulder when she appeared disinclined to continue. "There was a time when we could talk about anything."

"And I was pretty foolish in Oxford," she replied. She rose. "I must go back and enter the lists again. Come at your own risk. Oh, I shall be so grateful when this wedding is over and . . ."

" . . . and I go away?" he concluded.

She considered him, sitting there on the log. "Yes, Lord Chesney. You don't belong here. I come from a family of toadies, fools, and mushrooms. We really don't improve upon further acquaintance."

She started to walk, leaving him behind. There, she thought as she hurried to the house, if that doesn't tell James Gatewood the time of day, I do not know what will.

It was a simple matter to avoid him for the rest of the day. Ralph emerged from the library only long enough to beg Cook for two sandwiches, milk for him and ale for Lord Chesney, and plague Ellen for more paper.

"It is famous, sister," he said, fairly jumping up and down

in his excitement. "I am writing another scene for Act V. Lord Chesney has such incredible ideas."

"Yes, he does," she said quietly. As Ralph almost danced away, she wanted to call after him, to tell him not to build up his hopes. It's the counting house for you, Ralph, and country obscurity for me. And Gordon will squander one last term at Oxford, and then didn't Lord Chesney promise him a cavalry regiment? Heaven knows why. Life is decidedly unfair.

Icy rain was falling that evening as the wedding party adjourned to the chapel in the village for the rehearsal. Mama had insisted that the bridesmaids wear their gowns so she could take one last look at the hems. The girls shivered in their low-cut dresses with the skimpy sleeves. Martha ran in and out of the door with her basket of flower petals until the back of the chapel was quite damp with icy rain. Horry observed the chaos in perfect misery, staying far away from Edwin, who looked like a puppy without a home.

Sir Reginald Bland was there, splendidly overdressed as usual, and looking about him with disdain at all the others who did not preface their names with "sir." Ellen experienced one moment of pleasure when her father introduced the august Sir Reginald to Lord Chesney. She felt mean enough to relish the way he wilted and sat down in the chapel, quiet for the rest of the evening. She sat down, too, grateful to be a mere onlooker.

"Ellen, Ellen, we need you right now," Mama was saying.

She looked around. Mama was motioning furiously to her from the back of the church.

"See here, Ellen, you must stand in for Horatia," Mama said. "It is a tradition that the bride not participate in the rehearsal." She pushed Ellen closer to Papa, who was gazing wearily at his pocket watch.

There was a commotion from the front of the church. The relatives who had come to watch ceased their chatter and looked up with interest. Mama sank into the nearest pew and began to fan herself, even though she could see her breath when she spoke.

"Edwin has fainted, depend upon it," she said in a toneless voice.

So he had, right among the potted plants. Best man Thomas Cornwell, his ears as red as his face, grasped him under the armpits and draped him across the choir seats closer to the altar. Horry charged down the aisle in tears, waving her smelling salts in one hand.

"Well, thank goodness for that," Ellen said to Papa as Horry passed them. "I was beginning to wonder if she was going to avoid Edwin for the rest of their engagement."

Papa only chuckled. "I seem to recall a scene like this some twenty years ago," he said.

"Papa, not you!" Ellen exclaimed, her eyes bright.

He nodded, and tucked her arm closer in his. "Ah, well, Ellen, somehow these things are accomplished. Are you ready for a stroll down the aisle?"

In perfect charity with her father, Ellen watched Martha romp down the aisle in front of them, swinging her empty flower basket like a censer. The bridesmaids, sneezing in earnest now, followed slowly. She started next, minding her steps in time with the music and Papa's dreadful sense of rhythm. They lurched down the aisle together, ignoring the snickers of the cousins in the front pews.

And there by the altar was the Marquess of Chesney, standing in for Edwin, who by now was sitting up in the choir seats, an expression of complete befuddlement on his already vacuous face. Horry chafed his wrists and uttered little cries of concern.

Ellen rolled her eyes and the marquess winked at her. She turned her attention to Thomas Cornwell, the best man, who gazed with something close to rapture upon Fanny Bland, even though her eyes were red and her nose ran.

With only a minimum of confusion, Papa gave her away to the greatest rascal in the peerage and they knelt together in front of the altar.

"I only hope I am not wearing the shoes with the holes in the sole," he whispered in her ear.

"You really should take better care of yourself, Jim," she hissed back.

"Ellen, make me the happiest man alive and marry me," he whispered.

"Not on your life," she whispered back. "And don't you

think for one minute that this charade gives you any special privileges. We are mere stand-ins.''

"Do you mean I cannot ravish you in front of all these guests? You can certainly put a damper on a wedding rehearsal, Ellen.''

She burst into laughter as the priest glared at her. "Sorry, Father Mackey,'' she said, and choked down her merriment.

"That's better,'' the marquess said. "Have a little countenance, Ellen, on this serious occasion. Lord, my knees ache! Sorry, Father.''

The priest stood there with his book, glaring down at the happy couple, while Mama inspected all the bridesmaids, and scrutinized Thomas Cornwell, the best man, until his ears turned scarlet again. In a voice that made the priest wince, she ordered Martha to stop her fidgeting, and pronounced the tableau before her acceptable.

The organist wheezed into the recessional. Martha bolted down the aisle, followed by the bridesmaids, coughing and sneezing. Ellen Grimsley and James Gatewood turned and started down the aisle. In another moment they stood in the freezing vestibule.

"Thank God that is over,'' said the marquess to Cornwell. He snatched up a shawl from the back bench and thrust it at the best man. "Here. Put this around Miss Bland before she freezes solid.''

Thomas did as he was bid, and then scampered back to Lord Chesney's side. "You don't think it would be monstrous improper if I cuddled her a little?'' he asked. "After all, she is so cold.''

"I think it an admirable stroke, Thomas.''

Cornwell drew himself up to his full height and started back toward the bridesmaids, a man with a mission. Ellen watched his stately progress and tugged Fanny aside. "Fanny, let him take you home in his carriage,'' she whispered, her eyes on the approaching farmer, who had stopped to straighten his neck-cloth and gird his loins. "And if you should happen to lean up against him, or . . . or put your hand on his knee, all the better.''

"Ellen! That is so improper!'' Fanny declared. "My mother would be mortified!''

"Your mother is not here,'' Ellen reminded her. "Now blow

your nose." She gave Fanny a little shove into Thomas's arms, crossed her fingers and hoped for the best.

She was still smiling as she buttoned up Martha and led her to the waiting carriage. She handed her up to the Marquess of Chesney, who sat Martha on his lap and made room for Ellen.

The carriage filled up with relatives and there was no opportunity to talk, much to Ellen's relief. She longed for her bed, and the peace and quiet of an empty house in which to think about her own future. But she was to share her bed with one of Mama's interminable nieces, and aunts and uncles fairly hung from the rafters. She leaned against the marquess again.

"Ellen," he began, his voice low, gentle.

She put her finger to her lips. "Don't say anything now."

He nodded and stared out the window, his eyes serious. He said nothing to her in the house beyond a formal good night.

She thought of him as she climbed into bed and curled up against her cousin who was already asleep. This wedding can't be over soon enough, she thought, as her eyelids drooped. When the house is empty, and Gordon back at Oxford, I should make some plans of my own.

Aunt Shreve had talked of spending the spring at Royal Tunbridge Wells. Perhaps if I tease her enough, she will allow me to accompany her, Ellen thought. Tunbridge Wells was in the opposite direction from Oxford. I must not think of Oxford again, she told herself.

The wedding day dawned bitter cold, but mercifully clear. Ellen hopped on bare feet by the icy window, gazing out at the beautiful morning until Mama stuck her head in the door and scolded her to hurry up and dress.

She did as she was told, grateful to pull on her favorite dark blue wool dress. And to think I wanted to be a bridesmaid, she recalled. I think I would rather be warm.

She sat at the dressing table for a longer minute than usual, staring into her own face. It is a pretty face, she decided, after a careful scrutiny. I have excellent pores and all my teeth. My mouth is a trifle large, but it's the only one I have. She brushed her blond hair until it stood in little curls all over her head. Seriously, what does he see in me?

Horatia was a ravishingly lovely bride, with her blond hair,

elegant height, and enormous brown eyes. Ellen smiled at her
sister as she twirled around in her satin dress with the net
overskirt and the bodice studded with seed pearls. So what if
she was not over bright, and Edwin Bland equally dense? They
loved each other, and that seemed to be enough for them. I
wonder if it would be enough for me, Ellen thought as she
attached Horry's train and gave her a last hug.

The church was no warmer, but it was full of relatives and
village friends, all come to see Horatia Grimsley married to
Edwin Bland. Even the flowers that only last night had looked
so sorely put upon by the cold had taken on new bloom for the
occasion.

Aunt Shreve patted the bench beside her as Ellen looked about
the chapel. She moved over to make room.

"Should we leave room for Lord Chesney?" Aunt Shreve
asked. "I don't see him anywhere."

Ellen scooted over, searching the chapel for the marquess.
Perhaps he has allowed discretion to overtake valor and has fled
the scene. Thank goodness for that, she thought.

Aunt Shreve nudged her and nodded with her head in the
direction of the vestibule. Ellen smiled. She could see Martha,
her flower basket clutched tight, sitting on the steps next to the
marquess, who was whispering in her ear. Martha chewed on
her lower lip and threatened tears until the marquess said
something magical. She brightened and sat up straight again,
allowing him to reposition her little headpiece more firmly. She
leaned against him as the organist began to play, the picture
of contentment.

I have leaned against him like that myself, Ellen thought. She
looked down at her prayer book. And I must admit that once
you have done that, it's easier to stand up on your own. Bless
you, Jim Gatewood.

And then it was almost time for Mama, weeping noisily, to
be led to her seat in the front. Ellen sat where she was in the
back, watching the scene unfold in the vestibule, where the
symmetrical bridesmaids sniffled and blew their noses one last
time.

Another word and a pat, and the marquess left Martha
standing in front of the line with her chin up and a determined

smile on her face. He strode down the aisle, searched her out, genuflected outside the pew and slid in just as the groomsman led Mama toward the front.

There was still a little room on the other side of Aunt Shreve, but she seemed oblivious and would not move any more. The marquess was compelled to put his arm around Ellen to find space in the pew. Ellen found herself tucked in tight next to him and her head against his chest this time.

"Sorry to discommode you, James," she whispered as Mama came down the aisle and was seated.

He merely smiled down at her. "I'm happy as a clam," he replied. He sniffed her hair. "Lavender is my favorite, El. How did you know?"

She tried to think of something witty, but Martha was venturing down the aisle, and her little sister had Lord Chesney's full attention.

Ellen watched him keep time with his head as Martha stepped carefully in rhythm, counting out loud, her eyes straight ahead. When she saw him, he made a sowing motion with his hand. Martha looked down at her full basket, as if remembering it for the first time. In another moment, she had moved past them and was strewing rose petals like a professional.

Gatewood's ear was close to her face. She whispered in it, "However did you get her to move? She looked decidedly stubborn in the vestibule."

He smiled, his eyes still on Martha. "Yes, stubbornness runs in the females of your family, doesn't it? I promised her she wouldn't have to be a flower girl at our wedding unless she *really* wanted to, because the aisle is twice as long and much more frightening. She said she would think about it. Which reminds me, will you marry me?"

"No," she said forcefully, and then stood up as Horatia, a vision of net and satin, floated down the aisle with Papa.

The pew was so crowded that Lord Chesney was forced to put his arm around Ellen's waist and hold her close as the bridal party passed. She should have remonstrated with him, but his hand was warm on her waist, comforting. She told herself that she leaned against him only because she had no choice.

Edwin did not faint. Horatia responded distinctly in the

affirmative to each query from Father Mackey. Thomas handed over the wedding ring as though he had been performing such a delicate task with regularity on his farm. Hardly any of the bridesmaids sneezed, and Mama cried enough for everyone.

It was a beautiful wedding.

The reception was Mama's crowning glory. Each little biscuit, petit four, macaroon, mint, and marchpane fruit performed to perfection and disappeared in short order.

As Ellen was returning from one of her many trips to the kitchen, Mama accosted her, glowing from the warmth of the hearth and too much rack punch. "My dear, yours will be even grander," she beamed.

"Mama, about that . . ." Ellen attempted, but her mother had turned her attention to another of the guests, full of compliments and good cheer.

Cooler heads will prevail tomorrow, Ellen thought grimly, as she waved farewell and godspeed to cousins, aunts, and uncles with a wary eye on the weather, which was turning blustery.

And here was James Gatewood, overcoat buttoned up, still hatless, descending the staircase with Ralph close by. "Have Ellen take a look at your conclusion," he was saying. "If she makes any suggestions, I can recommend them to you."

"Where shall I send it when it is done?" Ralph asked, waving the papers in his hand.

"Send them with Ellen when she returns to Oxford," he replied, and set down his portmanteau long enough to shake Ralph's hand. "It's been a pleasure, Ralph. Not only are you a budding Shakespeare scholar like your sister, but you don't snore." He bent down closer to Ralph and whispered loudly. "Does she snore?"

"I don't think so, my lord."

"Ah, better and better," he replied.

Ellen put her hands on her hips and glared at him. "Are you finally leaving, my lord?" she asked, her voice frosty.

"And not a moment too soon, from the looks of things," he replied, the picture of good cheer. "I'll see you in Oxford inside of a week, Ellen," he said as she opened the front door for him.

"Oh, no, you won't," she replied. "I am going to ask Aunt Shreve if I can accompany her to Tunbridge Wells." She held out her hand. "Goodbye."

"Until next week," he said again as he shook her hand, and then kissed her fingers one by one.

She jerked her hand back and stamped her foot. "Don't you understand a word I have been saying?"

But he was gone then, hurrying toward the elegant post chaise with the crest on the door that awaited him.

Ellen slammed the front door louder than she intended to, and thought she heard laughter in the driveway. "That man is a total distraction," she said out loud to her father, who had come into the hall with more of Mama's brothers and sisters. "Do you know, Papa, he still thinks I am returning to Oxford. Imagine!"

It was Papa's turn to look thoughtful, and everywhere but at her. "Well, daughter, we did discuss this, the marquess and I. He has secured a place for you at St. Hilda's Hall."

"What?"

"Exactly so, my dear," Papa said hastily, watching the storm about to break on her face. "Says it's much more a challenge than Miss Dignam's."

"You see, El, you can take my paper to him after all," beamed Ralph.

"And keep an eye on Gordon, that rascal," Papa added. "I knew you would be pleased."

13

She was not pleased, not at all, but as Ellen mutinously tossed her clothes back in her trunk a week later and sat upon it while Ralph strapped down the lid, she was hard pressed to understand why.

The only girl in the neighborhood who did not envy her good fortune at snaring Lord Chesney was Fanny Bland, who had discovered love of the bucolic sort with Thomas Cornwell. She dropped in, two days after Horry's nuptials, to blush and giggle and entreat Ellen to be her bridesmaid in two months' time.

"For had you not thrown us together, I am sure I would still be correcting those dreadful poems which he now writes to me," Fanny exclaimed, patting her bulging reticule.

While Ellen owned that it was kind of Fanny to change her opinion, she could only wonder at the miracle love had wrought. And with Thomas Cornwell. "Love is indeed blind," she said to the closed door after Fanny had exchanged a few more pleasantries that required little attention in return and floated out the door, intent upon other such visits about the neighborhood.

The news of Lord Chesney's intentions traveled on seven league boots about the district, even though the issue was far from resolved, at least by Ellen. Ladies who never would have come otherwise, came to visit Mama to drink tea and exclaim over the Grimsleys' good fortune. Ellen could see no other purpose for their visits than to take a peek at her and wonder what on earth a peer of the realm saw to enamor him to Squire Grimsley's singular daughter.

I am sure they do not go away satisfied, Ellen thought, as she watched Mama lead the last gaggle out to their carriages, amid laughter behind gloved hands and heads-together communication, and more backward glances at the house.

"I mean, Aunt Shreve, he is offering me the sun, moon, and

stars, a house in London, a manor in Hertfordshire, one more house in Bath, I believe, and the worship of countless modistes and milliners,'' she said one afternoon as she took another turn around her aunt's parlor. ''And I almost think I love him, although it doesn't seem to be the kind of love that Mama and Horry think best.''

''Thank the Lord for that,'' Aunt Shreve murmured under her breath. She poured her favorite niece another cup of tea as Ellen paused in her restless circuit. ''If you wear a path in my carpet, I shall petition my brother for a new one, and won't that irritate him,'' she said, smiling a little. ''I believe I will do it.'' She patted the sofa beside her. ''Come, sit down. You begin to wear *me* out.''

Ellen could only continue her traverse about the room. ''Try and try as I might, I cannot seem to reconcile my objections. No more do I understand them,'' she admitted, sinking down at the window seat and staring out at the fast-waning afternoon. ''Oh, Aunt, what is the matter with me?''

She looked at her aunt, noticing the compassion that rendered her features even more dear. ''You do know what is troubling me, don't you?'' she asked quietly.

''I think I do, my dear,'' was all Aunt Shreve said.

''Then tell me!'' Ellen demanded, leaping up.

''No, I will not,'' Aunt Shreve said decisively. ''You must discover this for yourself.'' She rose and went to the window herself. ''For I discovered it myself, when I was but a little older than you.'' She touched her niece's hair. ''Every woman's response is different, my dear, and you must find your own way through this particular dilemma.''

''That's no help,'' Ellen declared crossly.

Aunt Shreve only embraced her, kissed her cheek, and offered her a biscuit.

I wish I could solve all my problems with biscuits and tea, she thought as she sat at her desk in St. Hilda's Hall and gazed out upon another afternoon sky.

She looked down at the sheet of problems before her and sighed with pleasure. Two problems to go, and a glance had already told her that she could do them. There would be geometry to follow the algebra, and then tomorrow, more Shakespeare. They were studying the comedies in all their ribald glory, and a paper was due.

Ellen looked around her room with undiminished pleasure, even after nearly a month in residence. The chamber was much like Gatewood's chamber at All Souls, with its narrow mullioned windows, dark wainscoting, and ample bookcases. The headmistress at St. Hilda's, an intense woman with an air of great competence about her, had said that the school had once formed part of a medieval hall that had risen to the status of college and moved closer to the main cluster on High Street.

"And so, Miss Grimsley, the women have indeed moved into Oxford," Miss Medford had declared the afternoon of Ellen's introduction to St. Hilda's. "And we will not be easily dislodged, no matter what our current status."

She had ushered Ellen into her quarters, hiding a smile when she opened the door upon a veritable flower shop. "I believe you have an admirer," was all she said as she ushered Ellen into her room.

Ellen had looked about her in delight that immediately turned to chagrin. She could only shake her head and ask, "How do people like that have access to flowers in January?"

Miss Medford laughed and clapped her hands. "I suppose in summer he will bring you shaved ice brought from the Andes by Inca runners." She coughed delicately. "Lord Chesney has become one of our most enthusiastic benefactors of late. Perhaps he will endow a chair of horticulture."

Ellen laughed and sat on the bed. "Miss Medford, let me tell you this at once. Lord Chesney is of the opinion that I should marry him, but I have no such intention."

Miss Medford only inclined her head, a smile on her face. "So he told me."

"What?"

"He said that you regarded him with complete indifference and . . ."

" 'Complete indifference?' " Ellen interrupted, without even meaning to. "Well, I do not know if I would go that far . . . yes, yes, I would! Complete indifference. Pray excuse the interruption, Miss Medford."

"Certainly. I assured him that we at St. Hilda's Hall would

keep you sufficiently challenged so that you would never have the opportunity to repine either lost or unrequited love."

"And what did his lordship say to that?" Ellen asked, a smile playing around her lips.

"He laughed long and hard."

"He would! That is so entirely in character."

"And when he was quite recovered, he offered his services here, should we ever wish an occasional lecture on Shakespeare."

"Which you accepted?"

"Of course! My dear, in scholarly circles, Lord Chesney is renowned." She moved to the door. "We accepted his offer gladly, and leave it to you two adults to sort out your own private difficulties." She picked up a nosegay of tea roses by the door. "I expect he will prove difficult to argue with, but that, Miss Grimsley, is your problem."

Ellen dealt with the distraction of Lord Chesney in womanly, time-honored fashion: she avoided him. It was an easy matter at first. Her first morning's work at St. Hilda's quickly showed her that this little hall so modestly situated on one of Oxford's more quiet streets far exceeded the mild scholarship available to the unwary of Miss Dignam's Select Female Academy.

Coming as she did in the middle of the school year meant serious catching up. To the balm of her somewhat bruised and trampled-upon scruples, it was no prevarication to send down the upstairs maid with a note stating that she could not leave her studies when Lord Chesney came to call.

It was more difficult to avoid the summons to his maiden lecture on the nature and study of Shakespeare. She tried in vain to resist when she heard he would be discussing *Much Ado About Nothing*, her favorite comedy. She succumbed during the middle of his lecture, sneaking in and sitting down in the back of the hall.

He took no notice of her capitulation other than to raise his eyebrows and make more sure that his voice carried to the back of the hall where she sat.

Following the lecture, he was remarkably fleet in walking with rapid dignity to the back of the hall and bowing over her hand, which she had reluctantly extended.

"I trust you are still in harmony with Hero and Beatrice, even though I may have muddled their motives," he commented, strolling with her from the hall.

"You did not muddle them at all," she replied. "And you needn't fish for compliments from me. I know you too well, Lord Chesney."

"Jim to you," he added. "I wish you would marry me."

"It was a masterful lecture," she said, ignoring his little aside. She wished he would not stand so close, which made it difficult to resist the urge to straighten his neckcloth. "I took copious notes."

"To what purpose?" he asked, holding the door for her.

She stopped walking and turned to face him. "To refute every argument," she said, looking directly into his eyes for the first time. "I couldn't have agreed less with your conclusion."

"Then write your own, Ellen, and let me see it when it is done."

"I shall," she replied.

He took her hand before she could leave. "I haven't proposed yet today," he began when she cut him off.

"You just did, Jim! And you also sent a note with the flowers this morning."

"I thought I did that yesterday," he replied. "Love is making me absentminded."

She shook her finger in his face. "It is doing nothing of the kind! You are the most calculating man I ever met! And try to deny that your lecture today was given to incite me to a response."

He held up his hands in a gesture of surrender, laughing. "Am I so base, fair Hermia?"

She couldn't help but smile. "You are! But I will write your silly paper. And sent Ralph's with it when I am done."

He tucked his arm in hers and headed with her across St. Hilda's small quad. "Ah! I was wondering when you would hear from that enthusiastic young fellow. Did you make any changes in his addition to *Hamlet*?"

"Only a very few. At times he sounded more like Fielding than Shakespeare, so I aged his words a bit. That was all." She sighed and tucked her notebook closer to her. "I only wish he could be here."

"He could, you know. You could marry me and we could make a home for him here in Oxford. I think your father would not object."

She stopped again. "He would not object because he is a toady! He will do whatever you say." Tears welled up in her eyes and she angrily brushed them away. "Jim, do stop this proposing! I have not the heart for it."

He only put his arm about her and continued walking. "I couldn't possibly stop proposing, Ellen. I love you." He took her by both shoulders. "Can you look me in the eyes and tell me that you don't harbor some small sentiment in my direction?"

She raised her eyes to his and then lowered them quickly. "Perhaps some small sentiment, but I am sure that is nothing more than friendship." She tugged at his neckcloth. "I wish that you would take a look in the mirror before you venture out of your room! Hold still a moment."

Her eyes serious, she straightened his neckcloth and gave it a pat. "There now, you are much more presentable. Now, sir, I ask you to leave me in peace to make my own muddles here at St. Hilda's."

He looked down at her, his eyes equally serious. "I can help you through your muddles."

"I know you can," she replied quietly. "But don't, please. I don't need your help."

There, she had said it. I hope I have not wounded you beyond repair, she thought, as she waved a hand to him and ran the rest of the way across the quadrangle. Requiring your assistance in all matters will make me a cripple.

The daily flowers became weekly flowers, accompanied by a note requesting marriage, which she ignored. She applied herself to her studies and watched January slide effortlessly into February. If she slept less well than usual, or found herself picking over her food, she put it down to the general melancholy that always struck after Christmas, and would abate, she knew, with the arrival of spring.

For I truly do not need you, Lord Chesney, she told herself. I have you to thank for St. Hilda's, but I have come to apply myself to scholarship.

She was not alone at St. Hilda's in her search for knowledge, but she soon discovered a difference between her and the other students. Most of them were daughters from good families, but daughters of clergymen and teachers, without much hope of excellent marriages to ease their paths through life. Several had told her that when the term ended, they would apply as governesses in England's greatest houses. Two were planning to follow cleric brothers to mission posts in distant reaches of the realm. One other was engaged to a vicar from Yorkshire and seeking only additional polish before her own wedding.

Ellen took it all in, puzzled over what it meant, and continued her Shakespeare papers. As they accumulated in a small stack on her desk, she debated whether to send them to Lord Chesney, as she had sent on Ralph's paper. She dissected all the comedies with particular care, but found herself wishing to bounce them off Gatewood's sounding board.

"But I have said I do not need any help," she told herself as she folded the last comedy paper.

In the morning Ralph stood before her, looking defiant and smelling faintly of pig.

The headmistress, concern showing in the frown on her face, had wakened Ellen from a sound sleep and ushered her into the sitting room where Ralph waited, muddy and tired. "My dear, the cook found him curled up on the doormat at the servants' entrance. He insists upon seeing you."

"Ralph!" she exclaimed, hugging him, and then stepping back from the odor that drifted up, even in the cold room. "How on earth did you get here?"

"In Papa's pig wagon," he said. "He was sending a load to slaughter in Morely. I hid in the back as far as the slaughterhouse and walked the rest of the way."

She hugged him again. "But . . . but why, Ralph?"

He began to cry, rubbing at the tears that coursed down his cheeks and streaking his face with mud. "Papa is sending me to Uncle Breezly's counting house in London! Oh, Ellen, I want to study! If I go there, it will only be a lifetime of columns and figures."

She held him close as he sobbed, flogging herself for not

warning him sooner of his fate, so he could wear around to the idea before the shock of Papa's demand sent him running away from home in dead winter.

"Perhaps it will not be so bad, my dear," she soothed. "You know that Mama's brother has no sons. In no time, you could head the whole business."

He only cried harder. "Ellen, I do not want that! I want to study and learn, and maybe teach someday."

"Ralph, Papa has probably intended this for years. It is not a bad plan," she said, feeling traitorous to the brother she held so tight in her arms.

He stopped crying with an effort, and wiped his coat sleeve across his eyes. "It is not my idea, Ellen," he said as he turned away. "If you will not help me, I don't know what I will do."

She sat back on her heels, looking at him. "You're so young," she murmured.

"I am old enough to be in school," he replied in that decisive tone that reminded her of Papa. "Vicar Snead and I only meet to argue nowadays. Please, Ellen!" he begged.

"What can I do?" she asked, knowing the answer even before he said it, and dreading it.

"You can petition Lord Chesney."

"Ralph, I cannot!" she protested. "Especially not after I told him that I did not want his help."

Ralph only shrugged. "*I* need his help, Ellen. Isn't that good enough?"

She looked at her brother, tired and dirty. You don't understand, she wanted to shout. How can I prove my independence of him—paltry as it is—if I am forever rushing to him for help the moment a crisis looms?

"We could send a note round to Gordon," she offered. "Maybe he would have a good idea."

The look that Ralph fixed on her was one full of scorn. "Ellen, you know that Gordon seldom has any ideas, and never any good ones."

She could only agree. It was true. Gordon had come to her only the day before, asking for money. "Gordon, it is still six weeks before the next quarter," she had said, and sent him away, his pockets still to let.

And even if they did go to Gordon, what would he do but pat Ralph on the shoulder and tell him to hurry home, and maybe Papa wouldn't even know he was missing.

After another moment's thought and misgivings of the severest sort, Ellen seated herself at the escritoire. With a firm hand that belied the writhing of her insides, she scrawled a hasty note to Lord Chesney, All Souls College, and directed the footman to deliver it at once.

"I only hope that note finds him in," she said to Ralph as she opened the door.

Ralph blinked. "Where else would he be at this time of the morning? It's only quarter past six, Ellen."

"Good Lord, he will be furious," Ellen said. "It will serve us right if he does not come at all."

She had expected some difficulty in getting Miss Medford's permission to take Ralph upstairs, but it was given easily enough. With her hand on his head, but standing well back from his somewhat soiled person, Ellen accepted the headmistress's consent, and the provision of an immediate bath.

"I only hope you left a note for Papa," Ellen said as she led Ralph up the stairs to her room.

"Well, I did not," he replied, his defiance lessened by the great weariness that seemed to settle on him with each step. "If he is so wise, let him figure it out."

"Oh, Ralph!"

He turned on her at the top of the stairs, his face white with exhaustion, and something else. She recognized the desperation in his voice, the sudden flash of his eyes. "Ellen, this is my future we are talking about," he said, his voice low, pleading. "Surely you, of all people, understand this."

She did. Ellen put her arm around him, thinking of the strange charity she had felt for her father the night of the wedding rehearsal as they walked down the aisle together, and her despair the next day when he informed her that she would go to St. Hilda's. Why do those we love the most put us out so much? she asked herself as she threw caution downwind and hugged her brother.

"Perhaps Lord Chesney will think of something, Ralph."

A few minutes later, she closed the door to her dressing room.

The maids, all smiles, had set up the tin tub, pouring in cans and cans of hot water, and left a liberal offering of soap there for Ralph, who was noisily splashing. She sat down at her desk and pulled back the curtains on a still Oxford morning.

Although she missed her intimate view of the High Street, she was growing fonder of the sight outside her windows here at St. Hilda's, overlooking as it did the river and the deer park of Magdalen College. The trees were yet bare, but she was patient with nature. In a few weeks' time, there would be the temptation of lime green cascading from the willows along the river. Even if it snowed again, those vanguards of spring would exhibit their early bravery and be followed by wisteria and then hawthorn hedges in bloom. Flowers would poke up from every window box at Oxford.

But now it was still winter and too early for many to be about except the farmers, bringing produce from nearby farms for the great markets of Oxford. And there, coming toward St. Hilda's, was a student running.

She looked closer and rose to her feet. It was James Gatewood, his student's robe thrown over his shoulders, his shirt open-throated without benefit of neckcloth.

I wonder why he is in such a hurry, she thought as she patted her hair and wished she had found time for more than a robe pulled on over her nightdress.

As she wondered, she heard the front door flung open, hurried voices, and then Gatewood on the stairs. In another moment, her door burst open and he threw himself into the room.

Before she could assure him that there wasn't any real emergency, he had pulled her off her feet and had gathered her close. His heart beat rapidly from his exertions and he could do little else except hold her tight and try to catch his breath.

When he could speak, all he did was bury his face in her neck and murmur "Ellen," over and over until she began to wonder what she had written in that hasty note that could have led him to this fevered response.

She thought that when he caught his breath he would set her on her feet again, but he carried her to the armchair and held her close on his lap, his arms tight around her. While her first instinct was to push away, she relaxed in his arms, struck by the same feeling of total absorption that had so preoccupied her when he kissed her at Miss Dignam's. It was a wonderful feeling of complete safety; she did not want it ever to end.

And then, when she felt almost limp with well-being, he took her by the shoulders and held her off from him a little.

"Ellen, are you all right? You appear sound. Was it bad news from home? I came as quickly as I could. Please tell me."

She touched his cheek, moved beyond words. He must have been in the middle of shaving when the note came, for he had shaved half of his face, and merely wiped the lather off the other side. Surely nothing in her note had indicated great trouble, but he had come immediately to her side. In wordless amazement at his love, she could only touch her forehead to his and then pull back a little to regard him seriously.

He smoothed down her hair. "When I receive notes at 6:30 that read, 'Please help me,' I am most attentive," he said at last.

"Now when have you ever received a note like that before?" she quizzed, to cover her own embarrassment.

"This is the first, and I pray the last, at least from you. You have me a turn, Ellen. Now, what is the matter? You appear sound of wind and limb." He straightened the lace around her robes's collar which he had rumpled. "I don't know when I have seen flannel show to such advantage before."

She got off his lap and seated herself at the chair to her desk. "It is Ralph. He arrived on my doorstep this morning."

"Ralph!" he exclaimed and then laughed softly, almost to himself. "I am relieved it is no worse than that. And what, pray tell, precipitated what I assume is a clandestine flight from the home fires?"

"Papa told him that he is to go to Uncle Breezly's counting house in the City." She spread her hands out, palms up, in her lap. "Snd he has come to me for help, I who am helpless to give it." She blushed. "He asked most urgently that I petition you."

Gatewood leaned back in the armchair, stretching his long legs out in front of him. "And you didn't want to, did you?"

"You know I did not, Lord Chesney," she said, her voice even.

"Jim."

"Jim then," she said impatiently. "You might recall my recent plea to be left alone to make my own blunders."

"I seem to recall something of the sort," he admitted, a slight smile on his face. "Where is this rascal?"

She pointed toward the dressing room. "He spent the night in Papa's pig wagon and was a bit ripe. I thought him overdue for a bath."

He went to the door of the dressing room and knocked before sticking his head in. He closed the door behind him. In a few minutes he emerged with Ralph in tow. Ralph was clad in another of her robes, the look of wounded pride on his face daring her to make a single comment. He held a sheaf of papers, creased many times, which he handed to Lord Chesney.

"Sorry it smells like pigs," he said, seating himself on Ellen's bed. "I had no idea that pigs could be such nasty customers in close quarters."

Ellen laughed for the first time. "Ralph! And I suppose you will tell me that you brought no change of clothing."

He shook his head. "I . . . I'm afraid I just bolted."

Lord Chesney looked up from the papers in his hand. "So now you have tackled *Macbeth*," he said, holding a page out at arm's length and wrinkling his nose. " 'A drum, a drum, the pigs doth come.' "

Ralph laughed out loud. "No, it doesn't say that! But yes, I have written about *Macbeth*. And I have other papers. Oh, sir, I don't want to go to a counting house! Please say that I will not have to."

Gatewood held up his hands as if to ward off an invasion. "Whoa, lad! How can what I say have any bearing?"

Ralph gave him a pitying look, such as a bright lad would give one whose wits had gone wandering. "My lord, let me tell you plainly. My papa will always dance to your tune, and it happens I need your help."

"Ralph!" Ellen exclaimed, her face fiery.

"You know it, El, I know it," Ralph replied calmly. "I cannot bear a counting house. I would rather study. My lord," he added with a gasp, as if finally amazed at his own temerity.

"Lad, your sister is rather at outs with me. I think my stock is not so high with her."

"It is my father, my lord, and he is the one who matters."

Ellen stared at her little brother, and felt a chill ripple down her spine. "How calculating you are, Ralph," she said slowly, as her heart began to break. "And yet I am sure you are right. From father to son and on down through the generations. I wonder that women are not put upon hillsides to die at birth." She stood up. "You two must obviously decide this for yourselves."

"Ellen . . ." Gatewood began.

She cut him off, close to tears. "Ralph is right. A little blunt, I vow, but his plain speaking is what I need." She stalked into the dressing room and pulled out the student's gown, breeches, and shirt she had cleaned and pressed and saved to look at. "Ralph, you had better change into these. Take him with you, Lord Chesney. He will be welcome where I am not. I am sure you have a lecture to attend, or to deliver."

"In Latin, for a fact," he said with a wry face, as if trying to cover up for a blunder of huge proportions. "Ellen . . ."

She continued, her face wooden. "I am sure that the two of you will think of something. Ralph will be a charge upon you, but then, I could have thought of no solution, could I?" She choked back her tears. "Go on, Ralph. I am sure that Lord Chesney will make all things right and tight with Papa. Good day to both of you."

She held the door open and they left, but not without a long backward glance from James Gatewood.

"Ellen, my dear, it can't rest here," he said, his face more serious than she had ever seen it.

"No, I think it cannot," she replied. She managed a smile. "Thank you for your help, sir. And you, Ralph, I owe you more than I can say, for your plain speaking."

She closed the door on them. There was no sound in the hallway for the longest moment, and then she heard slow footsteps on the stairs, descending.

14

Ellen sat at her desk, watching them move slowly down the street, Gatewood's hand clapped on her brother's shoulder, their heads together. Miss Medford must have allowed Ralph to change in one of the other rooms, because he wore the student's clothing she had thrust at him so angrily. Oh, Ralph! she thought, as the tears began to fall. How could I be so hateful to you for only speaking the truth? What is the matter with me?

She sobbed, hating herself. All her short life, she had known it was a man's world, and now, suddenly, it mattered. Ralph would get his school, Gordon his cavalry regiment. She would likely be bullocked into a marriage with the marquess. I think I love him, she thought through her tears, but that doesn't matter. I will likely marry him anyway, because I am a woman and my opinion counts for nothing.

The unfairness of it smote her like a blow from a fist. She rested her head on her desk and cried until she was dry of tears. She ignored the summons to class and then to luncheon, and continued at her desk, wondering why she had been so foolish as to object to matriculation at St. Hilda's, or to scold Lord Chesney for pressing so hard. It didn't matter what she thought. He would get what he wanted.

She took out her math book and stared at the equations on the page before her. Soon it would be time for algebra. She could not waste this entire day.

After an hour of staring at the numbers that had no meaning for her, she looked up from the book and rested her chin on her hand. The dratted fact is that I love him, she thought. She sighed. Perhaps I only think I do. I feel none of that deference that Horry feels for Edwin Blockhead, and none of the fear that Mama shows to Papa. If Jim Gatewood were in the wrong I would never hesitate to tell him so. And I could never hang on his words like Horry. I suppose what I feel is not love after all.

She paced the room in real dissatisfaction with herself. All this wretched day wants is a visit from Gordon to make it complete, she thought. He will ask for money again, or some little favor to smooth his path here. Perhaps he, too, will demand that I petition the marquess for something or other. " 'El, you need only ask,' " she said in bitter imitation of her older brother. " 'He will dance to your tune.' " It seemed only fitting that Gordon would constitute another of the plagues of Egypt that seemed to be dropping on her doorstep in unwelcome heaps.

With that thought as consolation, she was not surprised when Miss Medford stopped her after class and said that she had a visitor in the sitting room.

Gordon rose with an easy smile at her entrance. He looked at her face, and frowned. "The bloom off the roses today, Ellen?"

She sat down and faced him. "What is it you want, Gordon?" she asked, her voice controlled.

"Why, nothing," he replied, surprised in his reply. "I merely wanted to tell you that I had a visit this morning from Ralph and Lord Chesney, who thought that as head of the family here in Oxford, I ought to know." He laughed. "Lord, I can't imagine what good he thought that would do, but so he came. They've gone home."

Ellen clapped her hands together in exasperation. "I wish Ralph would not have dragged him into this! Don't you find it embarrassing that Lord Chesney has to help us out of muddles?"

Gordon shrugged, as though he had not considered the matter before. "I expect he will be my brother-in-law before too long. Might as well put the man to good use. After all, he loves you."

"How . . . how do you know?" she asked.

"He told me." Gordon smiled and took her hands in his, stopping their agitated motion. "I told him he's crazy to love someone so book-mad and more stubborn than Balaam's ass, but it didn't deter him. Besides, what are you going to do except marry?"

"I . . . I have plans," she said.

He got up and went to the window. "Still going to map the world, and write guidebooks, and travel the seven seas? Really,

El! Maybe you should grow up. You can't do any of those things, because you are a woman.''

She opened her mouth to protest, and then closed it. Gordon, her foolish, spendthrift, care-for-nobody brother, had hit the mark.

He turned to face her. "I know I'm not as smart as you are, sister, but I think there ought to be a purpose for everything, even all this education. What's your purpose? You know you're not going to be a governess, and we don't have any missionary connections, thank the Lord, so you can't go toddling off to India and cholera epidemics. What's the reason for all this? Or maybe you don't know."

She joined him at the window. "I thought perhaps I would start a day school for young girls of the lower classes. If some of them could learn such rudimentary skills as reading, writing, and ciphering, they could find better employment."

It sounded stupid to her ears. To her relief, Gordon did not laugh. "Wonderful, sister, but how will you finance such a venture, for it will never turn a penny on its own. Even I know that. And you know Papa will never lay down any blunt on a scheme like that."

There was so much truth in what Gordon said that Ellen could not look at him. She stared out the window, seeing nothing, thinking suddenly of Aunt Shreve's strange words: "You must find your own way through this particular dilemma, as all women must."

She shivered and rubbed her arms. This was the dilemma that Aunt Shreve meant, this realization that all her plans and ideas meant little in the reality of her female situation. She rested her forehead against the cold windowpane, scarcely feeling Gordon's hand on her arm.

She looked at her brother. "This is not the Middle Ages, is it, Gordon? I mean, I could say no to this marriage scheme that Papa and Lord Chesney have hatched between them, couldn't I?"

He nodded. "You could." And then he had to look away. "But you know that Mama and Papa both have ways of making you want to change your mind."

She leaned against his arm, filled with more charity than she would have thought possible for this author of her misery. "Papa would rant and rave and storm about the house. And Mama . . . Mama would sniff and turn pale and take to her bed, and call me an ungrateful daughter, and prophesy the almshouse for all of us."

He nodded again, his arm about her shoulders now. "Or call me an ungrateful son because I wanted nothing to do with Oxford."

Ellen hugged him. He started in surprise, and then embraced her.

"Gordon, I am so wicked to think that you were such a fool for not wanting to be here!" She looked up at her brother, tears glistening on her eyelashes. "It never was your style, even though I thought it should be."

He could only nod his head again in complete agreement. "Poor El! I was the one sentenced to Oxford, when you wanted to go."

"But you, at least, have only to endure the rest of this term," she reminded him. There was no bitterness in her voice anymore. "And then you will be where you want to be."

"Perhaps," was all he said, his own voice subdued.

She hugged him again and then stepped back to regard him. "I have neglected you of late, Gordon. How have your studies gone at University College?"

He smiled faintly. "No more standing ovations on Saturday mornings, if that's what you mean. The warden has decided that Shakespeare was a fluke with me, and is willing to suffer my mediocrity on Milton. I have done all right, for all that it's my own work now." He cleared his throat, and studied the pattern in the carpet for a long moment. "Ellen, I'm sorry for the trouble I caused you."

She only shrugged. "You'll note that I wasn't really dragged into those damnable papers kicking and screaming. It doesn't matter any more, if it ever did. I'll never forget those weeks." She stopped, not able to bring herself to say anything to Gordon about that wonderful afternoon spent in Gatewood's chambers, discussing Shakespeare like equals, or the December punt on the half-frozen Isis. She would have those private memories to shore her up for years to come.

"Well, what do you think?"

Gordon was still talking, and she hadn't heard a word.

"What?" she asked. "Excuse my vapor on the brain."

"I was just inquiring politely as to the possibility of your changing your mind about a small loan until the quarter."

"No! Gordon, you are yet a rascal!"

He grinned and grabbed for his cap as he backed out the door. He paused. "I thought that since you were mellowing a bit, that I would try. I suppose I will have to come up with my own money-making scheme, won't I?"

"I suppose you will," she agreed, no anger in her voice, but only an emotion she could not quite put her finger on.

Still he stood in the doorway, turning his cap around and around in his hands. "Ellen, you're a right one. If you really can't stomach a proposal from Lord Chesney, I'll stand by you with our parents." He clapped the hat on his head. "But I, for one, would like a warm brother-in-law who has elastic purse strings."

He was gone then, slamming the door behind him. She stood at the window and blew him a kiss. Gordon, you will always be a rascal, she thought. She leaned against the window again. And you, Ralph, are a bit of a Machiavelli where your own interests are paramount. Neither of you have measured up to any of my ideals of what brothers should be, I suppose, but then, no one has measured up lately, not even me.

She returned to her room and her books. Ellen sat down at her desk and thoughtfully fingered the stack of Shakespeare essays she had written in the last few weeks. She walked with them to the fireplace.

"Ellen, you could toss these on the flames right now and be done with them," she told herself. "Or you could keep them for your own children, or your nieces and nephews to find, yellowing in a trunk someday, or lining mouse nests. Or you could give them to Lord Chesney," she said out loud. "That may have been all he wanted from you in the first place."

She stopped. That was unfair. Her face red again, and not from the nearness of the flames, she remembered the look in his eyes when he threw open the door and grabbed her. There was nothing of a calculating scholar in that instant. He was a man desperate with worry for his love.

She wavered in front of the flames, holding out the pages until her fingernails started to hurt. She could not bring herself to drop them.

"No," she said decisively. "These are mine, at least for the moment." She put the pages back on her desk and went to the dressing room for her warmest cloak.

A walk will do me good, she decided, as she joined the other students who were setting out for their weekly expedition to Fletcher's Book Shop. On the way downstairs, she stuffed her essays into a box, scrawled "Lord Chesney, All Souls College," on top and thrust it at the porter, with instructions.

Ellen breathed deep in the brisk air and listened with half an ear to the talk of the others as they hurried along. Soon she did not listen at all, because the talk centered on end-of-term plans. Susan was cajoled into stripping off her glove to give them a glimpse of the ring her missionary-fiancé had sent from India. Millicent and Augusta compared notes on the great houses they had already been contracted to teach in, and speculated on the probability of finding eligible vicars in the district.

"What about you, Ellen?" one of them was saying as they walked along companionably, arm in arm. "We hear rumors . . ."

There was a pause, and smiles all around. Ellen could only shake her head. Have we no conversation that does not revolve around men? she wanted to ask. Is everything we do dependent upon their good will?

The questions remained unasked because she already knew the answers.

It was an easy matter to see the other girls inside Fletcher's, and then duck over to the next block and knock on a low door. As she waited for it to open, she noted a new window box, and earth freshly turned, as if lying in wait for a long-promised spring.

The door opened; Becky Speed stood there, dishcloth in hand, her mouth open in surprise.

"Miss Grimsley!" she managed at last, and took hold of Ellen's arm. "Do come in! How glad I am this is my half-day! Mama, you cannot guess who has come to visit us."

In a few minutes, Ellen was seated before a respectable fire, with a cup of strong tea in her hand.

"None of that hot water now, Miss," Mrs. Speed was saying. "It's real tea, and I even have sugar, should you want it."

Ellen shook her head. Her eyes took in the new coat of whitewash in the room, and two sagging, comfortable armchairs close to Mr. Speed's daybed.

Becky followed Ellen's gaze with her own eyes, and raised her chin. "We were able to redeem them from the money-lender's," she said. "Papa loves to have us close by. I think he even knows we are there," she added, and took her mother's hand in her own. "And there is tea."

Ellen sipped her tea, her eyes on Mrs. Speed, who had lost that pinched look.

Becky brought her mother's hand to her cheek. "And doesn't my mum look fine as fivepence?" she asked, her eyes sparkling. "Since Papa now has that pension from the university, Mama has given herself permission to eat something besides bread and hot water."

"Is he better?" Ellen asked quietly.

Becky sat down beside her father. "Nay, Miss Grimsley, and he will likely not improve. But think on this: we have had a doctor in to tell us that himself, so now at least we don't have to wonder if there was something else we could have done."

Mrs. Speed touched Ellen's arm. "Cheer up, miss. There's some comfort in knowing that."

"I suppose there is," Ellen replied. *I refuse to embarrass these good women by tears,* she told herself. *They don't pity themselves, and I should not.*

She sat back in the chair and watched Becky hovering about the inert form of her father, wiping his face, arranging his hands more comfortably on the blanket. *Without a complaint, they have taken their lot in life and made it something whole and dignified. I think there is a lesson in this for me.*

She leaned forward suddenly, nearly spilling her tea. "Tell me, Becky. If you could, would you attend a school—let us say an evening school—where you could learn to read, write, and cipher?"

"I am sure I could not afford such a wonder," Becky replied.

"But if you could, Becky, would you?"

Becky straightened the blankets around her father slowly, carefully. "I . . . I suppose I would."

"And what would you do with your education?"

Becky sat down in the chair across from her. "It's all wild speculation, miss," she protested.

"Perhaps now it is, but tell me, what would you do?"

Becky closed her eyes, a dreamy smile on her face. "I would get a position in a little shop, someplace where the master wants a bit of clerking, and tidying up, and bookkeeping." She opened her eyes and shook out the dish cloth. "And I'd never darken Miss Dignam's door again!"

"What an admirable course," Ellen agreed.

But Becky wasn't through. "And with a position like that, I could probably find myself a fellow, maybe a tradesman or journeyman who could use a little of the money I saved to help himself into his own business." She blushed. "Stranger things have happened, miss, stranger things."

Ellen set her cup down with a decisive click. "How right you are, Becky." She rose and held out her hand to Mrs. Speed. "Thank you for your hospitality."

Mrs. Speed clung to her hand. "If I'm not too brash and all, will you be seeing Lord Chesney?" she asked, her eyes anxious.

Here it comes, thought Ellen, here is the petition that everyone, me and my brother included, wants. "Yes, I probably will," she replied.

Mrs. Speed kissed her cheek. "Don't mean to be forward, but that's for Lord Chesney, miss. Tell him 'thank you from the Speeds.'"

"Anything more?" she asked, her heart lifting.

Mrs. Speed shook her head. "We can't think of anything we need. Lord Chesney has thought of it all. Just tell him 'thank you.'"

"And I shall," Ellen whispered as she quietly let herself out of the house and hurried around the corner to the bookshop. Oh, I shall, she thought as she joined the others. And when he proposes, I will say yes this time, and Becky will have her school.

And what will I have? she asked herself as she hurried to keep up with the others. A husband who loves me. She stopped, and the others bumped into her. But do I love him?

She shook her head and hurried on, ignoring the questioning looks of the others. *I wish I knew what love really was.*

Ellen did not expect to see James Gatewood the next day, not if he had truly been cadged into escorting Ralph home to plead his case for Winchester with her father. She steeled herself against the knowledge that the days would seem infinitely long until she heard from Gatewood again. *I shall take the Speeds as my example, and learn to wait and hope with a little dignity,* she resolved.

But it was not enough. Her studies in Shakespeare and mathematics that only the day before had meant the earth to her, she merely endured now. She waited to see Gatewood's familiar figure striding down the street toward St. Hilda's, straightening his neckcloth as he came, pausing to look in a shop window to see if there was any use in running his fingers through his hair again.

My dear James Gatewood, you are a true Genuine Article, she thought. *We will spend our days together here at Oxford, and I will hope to keep you tidier than you are at present, and you will be free to devote yourself entirely to Shakespeare. And I shall run an evening school for girls like Becky.*

Her impatience grew as the week crawled by and Gatewood did not appear. When the flowers he sent every Wednesday arrived, she hurried downstairs, looking among the hot house roses for the note he always sent each Wednesday that read simply, "Marry me."

There was no note this time. *Perhaps it fell off,* she told herself, as she carried the flowers to her room and searched through the roses again. No note. And no word on Ralph's success.

And then on Friday, when classes were over and she was harrowing up a furrow in the carpet, pacing back and forth in front of the window, she saw James Gatewood strolling down the street toward St Hilda's.

Only the greatest force of will prevented her from throwing open the window and shouting a greeting to him. Instead, she took a long look at herself in the mirror, wishing that her color were not so high.

Her heart beating at twice its normal speed and threatening

to leap out of her throat, Ellen answered the maid's knock and walked slowly down the stairs.

He waited for her at the bottom, extending his arm to her. "Come, my dear Miss Grimsley," he said. "At the cost of a wall of books, and probably a new wing on this fine, old hall, I have extracted permission from Miss Medford to take you walking in the Physic Garden." He smiled at her, that slow, lazy smile, and her heart slid down into her shoes. "Ostensibly, it is in pursuit of knowledge. We are to admire and exclaim over the gateway, which was designed by Mr. Inigo Jones himself."

She tucked her arm in his. "And so we shall, my lord, Jim."

"Much better."

He was silent as they walked toward the garden. They had traveled a block when Ellen stopped. "You must tell me about Ralph. I cannot wait for the Physic Garden!"

"Postponement of gratification is a sign of maturity, Ellen," he said mildly. "It is high time we all grew up."

She ignored him. "What about Ralph?"

He stopped and faced her, his hands on her shoulders, unmindful of the tradesmen and students who passed and looked back, smiling.

"He is to go to Uncle Breezly's counting house."

She stared at him, her mouth open.

"A good thing it is still winter, else there would be a fly down your throat."

Her eyes filled with tears. "He had his heart so set on Winchester," she managed, and then hurried to keep up with Jim as he lengthened his stride.

"So he did. It won't do Ralph any harm to be incarcerated in a counting house for this spring and summer." He gave her a little nudge with his shoulder. "Your father—Ellen, he does improve upon further acquaintance—your father and I both agree that he should have ample time to think about his future while totting up Uncle B's columns."

He paused before the entrance to the Physic Garden, and pointed to the gate. "Magnificent example of Inigo Jones's art. Memorize it for Miss Medford, and follow me, my dear."

"But I don't understand," she said, out of breath, as she hurried after him.

"Oh, beg pardon," he said, slowing down and taking her by the hand this time. "Neither did Ralph. He cut up a bit ugly, in fact. Your father and I agree, especially after that display of temper, that a counting house right now is just the thing for Ralph. If he is still of the opinion that it must be Shakespeare and nothing else, he will be granted admission to Winchester this fall."

"Oh, my," was all Ellen could say.

"The two papers he wrote were excellent," the marquess continued. "With that, and the fact that I am a trustee of that fine old institution, I foresee no difficulties for your brother."

She squeezed his hand and he smiled, but said nothing more as they strolled about the garden, which contained nothing of interest in early March beyond a few bare stalks of one mysterious plant or another, and the ragged remnants of apothecary herbs.

She waited for him to protest his love again, and declare himself as he had done on a regular basis any number of times these past few weeks. When he did not, the flutter of anticipation in Ellen's stomach turned into a gnawing pain.

He led her finally to a bench and sat her down. He did not sit, but paced the ground in front of her. "We discussed you, too, my dear. Squire Grimsley enumerated your numerous virtues and undeniably beautiful parts." He chuckled and sat down beside her. "I had to remind him that you are stubborn and willful and tenacious, when it comes to scholarship."

She turned her face away from the quizzical look in his eyes. "Then you don't love me after all," she said slowly, wishing that the bench were closer to the gate, and she could leap up and disappear in a crowd of shoppers on the street.

"I didn't say that, Ellen," he exclaimed, his hand on her arm. "And don't bolt, please. I'm not done by half."

She winced at his words, but sat where she was.

"I merely state that I am well-acquainted with your faults, as well as your virtues." He leaned forward and rested his elbows on his knees, looking straight ahead. "And it happens that I share some of them." He glanced at her. "Don't look so stricken! What do you think love is?"

"I have been asking myself that for some time now," she replied finally, when the silence threatened to overwhelm her.

She turned to face him. "Horry is Edwin's lapdog, and Mama is so afraid of Papa's bad humor that she does not give him sound advice when he needs it. They are my only examples, and it is not too satisfactory."

The tears spilled onto her cheeks, and the marquess made no comment about them as he handed her his handkerchief. "No, it is not too satisfactory, if this is your glimpse of married love."

She blushed. "I suppose we should not be having this discussion, Jim," she said quietly.

"On the contrary, I contend that more couples should have this conversation before they do something rash and irrevocable."

His words chilled her to the bone. She could not look at him. He has changed his mind, she thought, and the idea filled her head almost to bursting. She forced herself to listen to him.

"Do you know what my example has been, Ellen? A father who married for convenience and thought nothing of keeping his light skirts on the family premises." He stood up then, and walked to the edge of the garden path. "God, how humiliating it was for my mother!"

"I . . . I had no idea," Ellen said.

He shrugged. "She is a silly, vain woman, with no ideas beyond the latest fashions and the arrangements of furniture. But I contend that no one, no matter how frivolous, deserves to be hurt like that. I vowed I would never do it, and I shall not."

He sat down again. "So here we are, with your silly notions, and mine." He took her hand. "How cold your fingers are! Where are your gloves?"

She shook her head, unable to speak. He kissed her fingers. "And we must add another ingredient to this witch's brew, Ellen. I can't tell you how I have been hounded and chased by delicate females of impeccable background who would love to partake of the Gatewood monetary benevolence. And all their family members."

Ellen closed her eyes. "Go ahead, Jim, add Ralph and Gordon to your list. Gordon has probably petitioned you, has he not?" she said, her voice scarcely a whisper.

Gatewood smiled. "Oh, my, yes. But since that first time

a couple of weeks ago, we have enjoyed several illuminating conversations. Do you know, my dear, he wears well with repeated conversations."

"Gordon?" she asked, her eyes wide with amazement. "My brother Gordon?"

"Yes, Gordon," he said. "Possibly you have not given him his due. Ah, well. I even heard from Horatia this week, who expects me to make Edwin a peer of the realm or something. Oh, Ellen, come back!"

She bolted from the bench, her whole goal in life to reach Inigo Jones's gateway. Propriety would keep them from continuing this conversation, once they were in the street. And I thought to petition him for myself, she said to herself as she hurried along the path. Lord take me for a fool.

He had her by the arm then, pulling her around to face him. "I'm not finished, Ellen," he said, his voice low, pleading, nothing in it of disgust. "Ellen! People are always going to be asking me for things! It is my lot in life." He gave her a little shake. "When this term is over, I am finished at All Souls."

"What?" she asked, hardly believing her ears.

"There won't be another year here, or two more years, or a lifetime of sweet scholarship. I am the head of a large, silly, demanding family. I am the Gatewood freak of nature because I do not enjoy their idle pastimes."

He watched her closely to make sure she would not run, and then pulled her down onto a bench near the gate. "You're going to hear all of this, my dear Ellen."

She only nodded.

"Now, lean against me like a good girl," he said. "That's much better. My relatives all laugh at me and wring their hands over me, and wonder when I will have the good sense to become like them. They are distraught because I do not gamble and race horses, and dip snuff to perfection, and moon about because my tailor doesn't put enough buckram wadding in my coats."

"It's hard to believe," she murmured.

"Believe it," he said, his arm tight around her shoulders. "If you were to marry me, you would be marrying into a sillier family than the one you belong to. They would wear you out with their demands and petitions. You might even extend that disgust to me. That is what I greatly fear."

She leaned away from him just to straighten her skirt, and he quickly took his arm from around her shoulders. "I thought I had hoped too much," he said, his voice low. He got to his feet. "My dear, let me walk you back to St. Hilda's." He kissed her hand and held it for a lingering moment. "And now the term is almost up. My property manager has done yeoman's duty this year, overseeing the estates, but he has assured me in numerous correspondences that he is retiring in June. I have to go back to Hertfordshire and learn how to manage land, crops, tenants, sheep, and cattle."

"Country life is not so onerous," Ellen said. She tried to take his arm again, but he had moved away.

He looked back at her and stuffed his hands in his pockets. "You see, there wouldn't be any trips to explore and map the world, Ellen. There won't be much leisure to study, either." He chuckled without any mirth. "I am destined to become a gentleman farmer who falls asleep over his soup at dinner because he is so tired. And when I am in London, I will be expected to spend my time in frivolity, or endure the constant remarks of my stupid relatives."

"Sticks and stones, my lord . . ."

He nodded. "I know. I know. But, you know, El, the constant niggling and wrangling wears away at me, until it becomes easier to forget I ever had any dreams of my own."

Ellen joined him then and walked along in silence beside him. How stupid I have been about men, she thought. She hesitated, and then linked her arm through his. He looked at her in surprise.

"Forgive me," she said suddenly.

"For what?" Gatewood asked.

"For feeling sorry for myself because I am a woman. Forgive me for thinking you were so lucky and independent, and could do whatever you wanted because you are a man."

He was silent for the length of the block. "Forgiven," he said finally, his voice unsure. "Forgiven time and time again, my dear."

The streets were almost empty of shoppers now as people

hurried home to dinner. She slowed her steps, willing him to propose to her again.

He walked with her in silence up the shallow steps of St. Hilda's worn smooth by centuries of scholars. He took her hand at the top and she held her breath.

"Ellen, thank you for hearing me out." He kissed her hand and pressed it briefly against his chest. "And thank you for being such a welcome addition to my life this year at Oxford."

He cleared his throat and she slowly let out her breath. Oh, please, she thought.

"Well, let us part as friends, my very dear Ellen Grimsley, who has such plans to take the world apart and reassemble it. I wish I could help you, but my time will never be my own."

He turned to go, stepping down until his face was hidden by the lengthening shadows of early evening. "April will be a busy month at All Souls. Let us do meet again in May before the term ends."

"But . . ."

"Goodbye."

15

If there was ever a worse April on record in the British Isles, Ellen Grimsley didn't know of it. Usually it was her favorite month. She did not even mind drinking the horrible black brew that Mama inflicted on all her children in April to flush the miseries of winter out of their systems. She tolerated the rain because it was not a freezing rain anymore, and it would inevitably lead to a flowering of the English countryside, an event of such heart-breaking sweetness that Ellen knew she could never live anywhere else, even if she did travel the world.

But this April was different, preoccupied as she was by the greatest misery she had ever known. The rain was only rain, colder and more pelting this year, filling the gutters, drizzling down the windows, contributing to a general dampness in the air that did nothing to relieve the ache in her heart.

He still sent her flowers every Wednesday, but there was never a note anymore. She could only wonder if James Gatewood harbored some affection still, or had merely neglected to tell the florist to discontinue the standing order in his rush to put her out of his mind and heart.

Her studies were sawdust and dry toast. She stared at her books for hours, deriving no information from the pages. Once, during geometry, she looked up from the meaningless page to see Miss Medford regarding her, a worried frown on her face. Ellen wanted to throw herself on her knees in front of the headmistress and sob out her misery, but she merely turned the page, and attempted to apply the wisdom of Pythagoras.

Walks were little help. The favorite route from St. Hilda's took them by a small house with a sign in the window, "To let." Blowing trash from a long winter had accumulated on the front steps, in perfect harmony with a shutter that banged back and forth, and the windows bereft of curtains that stared back like hollow eyes.

She felt like that empty house, abandoned, neglected, dark.

She would always turn away from it when they passed, and then would be drawn to look back, and suffer all over again. And then she would return to her room, only to stare at the flowers and ask herself over and over, "Why didn't I say yes when he asked me?"

It became the last question she asked herself each night before she blew out her candle, and the first thing she thought of each morning. And from the way her head ached and her stomach hurt, it must have bothered her in her sleep, too.

Letters from home were no balm to her wounds. Ralph mailed back the student's gown and breeches she had sent him off in. "It's not safe for me to keep them here, especially since I will soon be with Uncle Breezly," he had written. "And I think I know what they mean to you."

Horry wrote too, all misspellings and enthusiasm for the married state. She dropped a hint about a blessed event far in the future, and hoped that Ellen would stroll the aisle soon enough with Lord Chesney so that she could participate without embarrassment.

Ellen sent no reply to either letter. What could she say? She dreaded her return home, and the disappointment that her unwelcome news would cause. Mama would give her no peace, compelling her to go over and over again all that she had said and done to disgust Lord Chesney. Papa would storm and rage and call her ungrateful.

When the pain was too great to bear, Ellen tried the other tack, convincing herself that she never loved him anyway, and they never would have suited. "I would surely have been a disappointment to Lord Chesney," she told herself each night as part of her consoling catechism. "Even if his family is silly, they are still peers. I would be so out of place. It is better this way. And besides, I'm still not so sure that I loved him."

Then why don't you feel any better? she asked herself one afternoon when the sky was bluer than blue and the willows along the river had finally burst into bloom. She could see the Isis from her window. With a pang, she observed that students were already out punting.

I wonder if he even thinks of me, Ellen thought as she leaned her elbows on the open window and watched the little boats drift past. He is probably too busy.

When the maid knocked on the door, she jumped. "Someone to see you below, miss," the maid said, and giggled behind her hand.

Ellen leaped to her feet, patting at her hair and cramming her feet into her slippers. She straightened her dress on the way down the stairs, regretting that it was her least attractive kerseymere.

Gordon waited below. "Oh," she said from the doorway. "It's you."

He smiled. "Who did you expect, the chancellor of the exchequer?"

She shook her head.

"Speaking of which, dear El, are you sure you won't make me a small loan?"

"Gordon! The quarter has only begun!" she exclaimed, irritated out of her lethargy. "How can you possibly be under the hatches?"

"It's an easy matter when your chambermate is practically a faro dealer," he grumbled. "I shall never turn a card with him again. Ellen, it is a matter of a gambling debt. Surely you will help."

He named the sum, and she paled. "Good Lord, I have not half that amount, Gordon. Whatever were you thinking?" she said.

"I was thinking that I would eventually get lucky," he said.

"Oh, Gordon."

He regarded her low state. "Really, El, can't you do any better than that? I expected at least a resounding scold, and all you can do is look hangdog and tell me 'Oh, Gordon.' "

When she said nothing, he took her by the arm. "Come on, El, let's escape from the halls of academe." He overrode the excuse already forming on her lips. "I saw Miss Medford when I came in, and she suggested that I do this very thing. Said you were blue-deviled about something."

The afternoon was warm, and she did not shiver, even though Gordon wouldn't give her a moment to grab up a pelisse, or even a bonnet. He held her hand, content to stroll along.

"What do you say we turn into the Physic Garden?" he asked.

Tears came to her eyes and she pulled back on his hand. "I couldn't possibly go there," she said.

"Very well, then, Ellen," he said, his voice less certain. "My word, you remind me of Lord Chesney. I've never seen anyone so down in the dumps."

Her eyes flew to his face. "Have you seen him lately?"

"Only this morning."

"I had no idea you visited him."

He smiled at her confusion. "Oh, I've been doing that off and on for some weeks now." He laughed. "And now you're going to ask me whose idea that was! Well, it was his at first, but now I go because I like his company. Do you know, El, he's quite an engaging sort, when one looks beyond all that blasted scholarship."

"I know," she whispered and then humiliated herself by bursting into tears.

If she had done that six months ago, Gordon would have turned and fled, or laughed in her face. Instead, he pulled her into the shelter of an alley and held her close, patting her back until her tears stopped.

"Poor dear," he said. "I suppose you will tell me now that Lord Chesney has changed his mind."

She nodded, and blew her nose vigorously on the handkerchief he gave her. "He teased and teased all term," she wailed, "proposing over and over, and then when I finally thought it would be a good idea, he didn't."

"Scurvy rascal," Gordon said mildly, kissing her cheek. "No wonder he hasn't been much fun lately. I go to his chamber for good conversation and better ale, and he stares into the fire and doesn't hear half of what I say."

"I think I love him," she said, sniffing back her tears, "but how will I ever know for sure now?"

"Well, you could propose to him," Gordon suggested.

"I could never!" she gasped.

They stared back toward St. Hilda's. "I'm fresh out of ideas, El," Gordon said finally. "You know ideas aren't my strong suit. Now, if you want me to call him out, or something . . ."

Ellen put her hand on his arm. "No, don't do anything, Gordon," she said hastily. "And I'm sorry I cannot help you with that gambling debt. I'll give you what I have."

He shook his head. "No, not necessary. I think I have a better idea." He grinned and kissed her cheek again. "Maybe if I hang around with you or Lord Mope-in-the-Muck, I'll have good ideas on a regular basis!''

"Better you should apply to Papa," she suggested.

He shook his head vigorously. "That is the last thing I want to do, El. He might change his mind and make me stay here another year. I mean, the war in Spain could be *over* before I am sprung from this place!"

"What a pity," she said, her mind other places than Gordon's troubles. As she stood in the doorway and watched him saunter down the street, she thought she should have questioned him more closely about his brilliant idea. "I must be in my dotage to think that Gordon Grimsley would hatch a real scheme," she muttered as she climbed the stairs.

The Wednesday flowers were waiting for her on the table outside her door. She sniffed the roses, vowing that she would not look for a note, even as her eyes searched the bouquet.

She dropped the flowers on her desk. "Maybe I *should* propose to him," she said, looking at the roses. But even as she said it, she knew she would never do it.

"If I just had the nerve," she whispered. "Aunt Shreve was right. I am too proud."

She dismissed Gordon from her mind, and only wished it were as easy to dismiss James Gatewood, who traveled lightly through her dreams and occupied her waking hours. She chided herself for her foolishness, knowing that it was well within her power to make his life easier. "If only I had accepted him when I had the opportunity," became the sentence that she wrote over and over in her mind, in atonement for a misdeed greater than any she ever committed at Miss Dignam's.

But as the days passed and no word came from All Souls, she knew it was time to gather what dignity remained and consider what she would say to her parents in less than a month.

The thought of facing them caused her heart to leap about in her throat. If I were a man, I would take the king's shilling and beat Gordon to Spain, she thought. Or failing that, it is too bad I am not missionary-minded. I would rather preach to a thousand Hindus than to look Mama in the eye and tell her that I said "no" once too often to the marquess.

She was considering the merits of Australia over Canada one evening long after lights-out, when someone pounded up the stairs and banged on her door. Ellen sat up in bed when Becky Speed, breathing hard, threw open the door.

Becky grabbed her by the shoulders. "Oh, Ellen, the worst thing has happened!" she said, and then sank down in a chair to catch her breath.

Ellen was out of bed and on her knees in an instant beside the maid. "Is it your father? Oh, please say it is not so."

Her hands clutching her sides, Becky shook her head. "It's Gordon," she managed to say finally. "He's going to fight a duel!"

Ellen sat down on the floor. "You can't be serious," she said. "Even he is not that foolish."

"Oh, yes he is, Miss Grimsley, begging your pardon," Becky said.

Ellen clutched Becky's hands. "Tell me everything you know," she demanded. "I can only hope we are not too late."

Becky leaned forward, tears in her eyes. "It was something I overheard from one of the students at Miss Dignam's. She was telling the other girls that her brother was dueling with pistols tomorrow morning along the river with his chambermate, someone named Grimsley who owed him money."

Ellen felt her whole body go numb. She nodded. "Go on."

Becky shook her head. "That's all I heard. The duel is to be somewhere along the river tomorrow morning. Probably it will be at sunrise, don't you think?"

Ellen nodded again as she let go of the maid's hand. "I wish I knew what to do," she said slowly. "There's not time to contact my father." She shuddered. "I wouldn't dare anyway."

Becky cleared her throat. "Perhaps if you got word to Lord Chesney he could . . ."

"No!" Ellen said. "I won't do that! I cannot plague that man with one more problem."

Becky only looked at her. "But you must, Miss Grimsley. He can find out what is going on and stop Gordon, you know he can."

Ellen looked at Becky in silence. Jim would find Gordon and settle the problem. "I don't have any choice, do I?" she asked, more to herself than to Becky, who was already heading for the dressing room.

"If you put on that student gown again and hurry, you might

be able to get into All Souls before the porter closes the gate
for the night,'' Becky said as she rummaged through Ellen's
clothing. "Here, miss, and don't waste a minute!"

Ellen stripped off her nightgown and dressed herself in shirt
and breeches, painfully aware that these were the clothes that
Gordon had lifted originally from his chambermate, the same
student who was out to avenge a debt of honor with a duel now.
She threw the gown around her shoulders and tiptoed down the
back stairs, Becky on her heels.

They walked swiftly away from St. Hilda's, mindful of the
night watchman who strolled the quiet streets. "How did you
get away from Miss Dignam's?'' she whispered as they hurried
along.

"I hope they still think I am in the kitchen washing dishes,"
she whispered back. Her voice faltered. "If they do not, then
I am out of a job.''

"Oh, Becky!''

Rapid walking, and a pause in a darkened alley as the night
watchman passed, brought them to All Souls' door. Holding
her breath, Ellen turned the handle. Locked. She looked back
at Becky in dismay. They ran around to the side door. Locked.

Ellen looked up at the wall surrounding the quad. The ivy
that climbed it was only beginning to flourish again, but maybe
with a little help . . . She turned to Becky.

"Help me up on your shoulders," she commanded.

Becky crouched and Ellen climbed onto her back, clutching
the ivy on the wall as she stood upright on the maid's shoulders.
She grasped the ivy more firmly and pulled herself up and over,
dropping down into a muddy patch of daffodils.

"Gordon, you had better appreciate what I am doing for
you,'' she muttered, as she scraped off the worst of the mud
and crept around the perimeter of the quad, careful to stay out
of the moonlight.

She tried the handle to the hall door, sighing in audible relief
when it creaked and turned. She peeked in. The porter still sat
at his tall desk, his eyes closed, his head drooping. She opened
the door an inch at a time, holding her breath, and then crept
on her hands and knees across the stone floor to the stairway,
which was shrouded in welcome darkness.

The upstairs hall was dark. Ellen removed her shoes and

padded quietly along the floor, pausing at each door to squint at the name plate.

There it was, third door from the stairwell. Taking a deep breath, and wishing herself anywhere but at James Gatewood's door, she knocked.

No one answered. She knocked louder. To her ears, the sound seemed to reverberate like a bass drum across the fellows hall, over the quad and down to the High Street itself. "Gordon, the things I must do for you," she muttered through clenched teeth as she knocked again.

She was about to consider the possibility of going outside and trying to climb in a window when she heard slow steps on the other side of the door.

"This better be really good, Lambeth," she heard as she pressed her ear to the door.

The door swung open. James Gatewood, clad in a nightshirt, stared at her.

"You're definitely not Lord Lambeth," he murmured finally, and grabbed her by the arm, pulling her inside, and then looking up and down the hall before he quietly closed the door. "Ellen, what on earth . . ."

He looked down and rolled his eyes. "One moment," he said, and disappeared into the next room.

Ellen looked around the chamber, lit as it was by the remnants of a fire in the grate. Her heart sank as she took in the crates of books already packed, and the half-empty shelves.

Gatewood returned wearing a robe and carrying a lamp, which he held in front of her face. "Just wanted to make sure I wasn't dreaming," he explained.

"I wish you were," she said, grateful that the shadowy room covered her own embarrassment. "I swore I would never plague you again, and I know you are busy . . ." she began. "Oh, Jim, it's the worst thing!"

He sighed and scratched his head. "Can't be, my dear. We've already been through the worst thing."

She looked up at his words, her eyes hopeful, but he was making himself comfortable in his armchair. He motioned to the other one.

"How bad can it be?" he asked, a slight smile on his face as she seated herself on the edge of the chair.

"Gordon is involved in a duel tomorrow morning, Jim," she said, keeping her voice low to mask her own agitation. "You've got to find out where and stop him. please."

"What?" he shouted, leaping to his feet. He pulled her up by the shoulders until her feet were off the ground. "He couldn't possibly do anything that harebrained at Oxford, not even Gordon!"

She opened her mouth to insist that he set her down, when there was a banging on the wall. A faint voice, "Go to hell, Gatewood," came through the wall.

He set her down and pounded the wall with his fist. "Eat rocks, Lambeth," Gatewood yelled back. "That should stop him. Now, what is this?"

"It is Gordon," she repeated. "Becky heard one of Miss Dignam's students to say that her brother was going to fight a duel tomorrow—oh, Lord, this morning—with someone named Grimsley who owed him a gambling debt." She burst into tears. "And I would not let him have any money when he came to me."

Without a word, he picked her up more gently this time and sat her on his lap. "Neither would I," he muttered into her hair as he kissed the top of her head. "Now, dry your tears, my dear. I'll go find your dratted brother." He rubbed her arm. "With any luck at all, this will not get to the ears of the warden or, God help us, the Vice Chancellor."

She sat up in his lap. I could propose now, she thought, as she put her hands against his chest. Oh, but this is decidedly the wrong time. Drat Gordon, anyway.

"Yes, by all means, please do what you can."

He put her off his lap and stood up. "You stay here while I get dressed." He hurried to the other room and then looked back. "How did you get in here in the first place?"

"I climbed the wall, Jim," she said.

He burst into laughter, which precipitated another bang on the wall. "Ellen, you need someone to take care of you," he said as he ran across the room and banged back. "For someone who can't matriculate at good old Ox U, you certainly have performed a time-honored custom." He ruffled her hair as he hurried past to his bedroom. "Did you land in the daffodils or the shrubbery?"

She laughed and then put her hand over her mouth, and waited for Lambeth to object. When he did not, she came closer to the bed chamber. "I should be going, Jim," she whispered.

In a moment, Gatewood stood before her in his buckskins and a half-buttoned shirt. "Indeed you should, but unless you are a prodigious climber, you will need some help getting back over the wall." He tucked in his shirt, ran his fingers through his hair and grabbed up his student's cloak.

"Surely you could just open the gate from the inside?" she asked.

"And how are we to convince the porter to hand over his keys?" He grinned. "Ellen, you really don't look like a man. By the way, how did you get past the porter in the first place, or dare I ask?"

Ellen's chin went up. "I crawled on my hands and knees. Oh, the things I have done for Gordon this night!"

Gatewood reached for her hand and blew out the lamp. "Come, my dear, and let us save your witless brother."

The hall was still deserted. They crept down the stairs and peered into the main hall. The porter, very much awake, was reading his paper.

"This will be a bit tricky," Gatewood said, his arm tight around Ellen. "Let me go first. I will engage him in some idle chatter while you creep out the way you came in, right up against the desk where he cannot see you."

"I hope you have a brilliant explanation if he sees me," she said, getting down on all fours again.

Gatewood flashed his lazy smile. "Oh, I will let you think of something. You're a creative person."

As unconcerned as if it were midday, Gatewood sauntered up to the desk and leaned his elbow on the high counter. "Can't sleep, Wilson," he said. "I do believe I'll take a turn about the quad."

"Certainly, my lord. Would you wish me to unlock the gate?"

The picture of casual unconcern, Gatewood shrugged and shuffled his feet as Ellen crawled past him. "I think not. If a walk about the quad doesn't wear me out, then I'll reconsider. Good evening to you, Wilson." He chuckled. "Or should I say, 'Good morning?' "

"Aye, my lord."

He strolled through the doorway into the dark, and grabbed up

Ellen by the back of her cloak as she crouched in the shadows. "Now let us stay in the shadows and casually stroll toward the daffodils. My Lord, Ellen, did you do all this damage?"

She looked in dismay at the flower bed. "Surely not!" she declared. "I expect that others have sneaked in after me."

He shook his head. "Nay, my love, most of us go over the back, where there are no flowers." He nudged her shoulder. "You can store that bit of All Souls wisdom for future reference."

"I doubt I'll come this way again," she replied, her voice crisp.

He laughed, cutting it short as he glanced back at the porter's light. He cupped his hands and knelt down in the flower bed. "Up you get, Ellen."

In another moment she had scrambled to the top of the wall. Becky, her face upturned and anxious, watched from the other side. Ellen looked down at Lord Chesney. "Thank you, Jim. Do please find Gordon."

"It will be my total duty tonight," he replied, his tone affable, as though he had all the time in the world. "Now I will stroll back to the porter and ask him to let me out the main gate. Scram now, before someone sees you."

Still she balanced on top of the wall. "You will let me know the outcome?"

"I'll let you know." He chuckled. "I don't think that even the long-suffering and vastly tolerant Miss Medford would applaud this excursion of yours."

He blew a kiss to her and started back to the porter's hall.

"Jim, wait!" she whispered.

He turned around.

I love you, she wanted to shout, but Becky was calling to her from the other side of the wall. "Just . . . thank you."

He bowed. Ellen let herself down until she was dangling by her hands, and then dropped quietly to the pavement.

Becky grabbed her hand and they started at a fast trot for St. Hilda's. Quietly they crept into the servant's entrance again, where the door still hung slightly ajar. Becky released her hand.

"I have to hurry back to Miss Dignam's." She hesitated, then leaned closer. "Did he propose tonight, Miss Grimsley?"

Ellen stared at her in surprise. "Why, no, he did not, Becky," she said slowly. "And I don't think he's going to."

"I just wondered. What a pity," the maid said as she let herself out the door.

Wearily Ellen climbed the stairs. She stuffed the student's cloak under her bed and pulled on her nightgown again. No, he did not propose, nor would he ever. Drat you, James Gatewood, she thought as she tied on her sleeping cap again. You're going to be noble and spare me from a lifetime of inanity at the hands of your ignorant relatives. She sighed and threw herself back on the pillow, pulling the blankets up to her chin. And I am so practiced in dealing with inane relatives!

She rooted about for a comfortable spot and tucked her hand under her cheek. You'll choose some brainless wonder who will fit right into your family, like Horry did. What a dreadful waste of you and me.

She was beyond tears. She thought about Jim, and then about Gordon, and still was wondering which of them was more irritating when her eyes closed.

She was awake just after dawn and standing at the open window, listening with her whole heart for the sound of gunfire. All she heard were the bells of Oxford, reminding scholars of another day. Likely Jim had found Gordon and talked him out of this infantile silliness. They were probably eating breakfast together right now in one of the old inns that flanked the Isis.

Ellen dressed slowly, wondering how long it would be before her thoughtless brother remembered to send a message that all was well. Probably Gatewood would relieve his financial difficulties and sent Gordon Grimsley on his way rejoicing. What my brother really wants is one of Papa's canings, she thought, her lips set in a mutinous pout that lasted all the way to the breakfast table.

Ellen had scarcely filled her plate and seated herself at the table when the footman approached her chair. "There is a young person outside to see you," he announced, his face impassive.

Her mind alive with sudden worry, she nodded her apologies to Miss Medford and forced herself to walk slowly into the hall.

Becky pounced on her as soon as the door was shut. The maid grabbed Ellen's hand, tugging her toward the outside door.

"Miss Grimsley, you must come quick. Gordon has shot Lord Chesney!"

16

Without a word, Ellen gathered up her skirts and ran out the door, close on Becky's heels. Her mind was a blank as they raced toward the river, where the morning mist was just beginning to clear.

She ran until her sides began to ache, and then she saw them down by the river, Gordon seated on the grass with Jim Gatewood's head in his lap. There was blood everywhere.

"Dear God, Becky," she breathed as they approached the scene. "Do you know what happened?"

Becky stopped to catch her breath. "Only that Lord Chesney got in the way to prevent them from firing upon each other. There was a scuffle, and the other dueler fled." She averted her eyes from the bloody ground. "I don't see how it could have happened, but it did."

Ellen threw herself down beside Gordon, who looked up, his face ashen. "El, please believe I had no idea . . ." He looked down at the unconscious marquess sprawled across his lap. "Perhaps you should take my place. I will see about a surgeon."

Gordon moved aside and Ellen cradled Lord Chesney's head in her lap. She rested her hand on his chest and was rewarded with a steady heartbeat. That's something, she thought, as she gingerly touched the blood-soaked sleeve. Working carefully, her lips tight together, she widened the tear in the fabric and laid bare his arm.

The wound bled, but as she dabbed at it with the remnants of the sleeve, the bleeding stopped. She gathered Gatewood close in her arms and pressed the cloth to the wound. "Jim," she whispered, "I do not suppose you thought your Oxford year would end like this."

His eyes fluttered open and slowly focused on her face. He studied it and managed a lopsided grin. "I know I have not died," he said finally, "because I know better than anyone that you are not an angel, Ellen."

"No, I am not," she agreed, grateful that he had command of his faculties, even though he did seem to be rubbing his cheek against her bosom in rather an unseemly fashion as she held him close. The feeling was not unpleasant; quite the contrary.

He winced as he reached up to touch her cheek and continue his perusal of her face. "You know, Ellen, as care-for-nobody as my relatives are, not one of them has ever used me for target practice."

"I am sure it was a mistake," she murmured, overcome with shame. "Gordon would never . . ."

She looked up. Gordon and the proprietor of the nearby inn were hurrying toward them, arguing loud and long.

The marquess winced again. "Do tell them to quiet down," he pleaded. "And not to pound so hard on the grass. Godfrey, but I am uncomfortable."

He turned his cheek against her bosom again. "Perhaps not too uncomfortable," he amended.

She put her finger to her lips and the landlord was silent. Gatewood motioned him closer with a nod of his head. "Bend down, my good man."

"Yes, my lord."

With a grunt and a creak of stays the landlord moved close. "I can have the constable here in a shake."

Gatewood shook his head. "That is precisely what I do not wish," he said, his voice scarcely more than a whisper. "And if word of this should get out, I will never lift another tankard in your inn. I will also tell everyone at All Souls, Balliol, and Oriel to avoid your place as they would the plague."

"Yes, your worshipful sir," the landlord gasped as he worked his way to his feet again. "But someone ought to make an example of young chubs what duel."

"I will deal with him," the marquess said. He closed his eyes. "Now if you would send for Mr. Charris, the surgeon at the corner of New and St. Giles, you will make me a happy man."

"Done already," the landlord assured him. He glared at Gordon. "You are sure you do not wish the constable?"

"Positive," Gatewood said. "Leave us alone for a moment, will you?"

The landlord took his ponderous way toward the inn while Gordon climbed the bank and sat there, head in his hands.

Ellen looked down at the marquess. "There is never going to be a right time for this," she said, tracing her finger along his cheek.

"For what?" Gatewood asked. He opened his eyes and then closed them again, as though the sunlight were too bright.

"I will simply have to jettison my pride and get it over with, won't I?"

"Ellen, you are making no sense at all," he protested, "or else I am in such a shape that I do not know good sense when I hear it."

"That is likely the case," she said, and took a deep breath. "Will you marry me, please, sir, so I can protect you from my family?"

The marquess smiled, but did not open his eyes. "Novel idea," he said, and his words slurred together. "Discuss it later. Not at my best . . ." He relaxed in her arms as his head lolled to one side.

She touched his pale lips with her finger. "Now was that a yes or a no, my lord?" she asked him. She glanced over at Gordon, who was watching her with a slight smile on his face. Her eyes grew thoughtful. *I wonder. Oh, surely not.*

Gordon convinced her to return to St. Hilda's. "The landlord and I will see him to a bed here, El," he assured her. "It will be bad enough if Papa gets wind of this, but if he finds out that you were involved, I am sure it will be quite twenty years before he allows me out of my room for excursions farther than the necessary."

"It would serve you right," she said, careful not to disturb the marquess as she kissed his forehead and gently lowered him to the ground. "Gordon, you are the greatest menace to world peace and the future of western civilization that I ever heard of."

He grinned. "El, I didn't know you cared!"

She sighed in exasperation. "Oh, for the Lord's sake! Loan me your cloak. I daren't face Miss Medford with blood all over my dress. And wherever did you get such a cape?"

He swirled it about her shoulders. "Thought it would be just the thing for a duel."

"Gordon, you try me!" Ellen declared, her voice unsteady.

She knelt beside the marquess again, who still slumbered among the dandelions, a peaceful expression on his face. "James, you certainly need me," she said, and touched his cheek.

Becky did not feel inclined to chatter, so they walked in silence away from the river. The mist had cleared. "What a perfect spot for a duel," Ellen ventured at last, her eyes on Becky's face. "I don't know how Gordon could have planned it better."

"Beg pardon, miss?" Becky asked, her eyes innocent.

Ellen shook her head. "Perhaps I am entirely too suspicious."

She looked back at the riverbank. A man carrying a black satchel hurried down the slope, accompanied by two boys with a litter. She waited until they had picked up the marquess and laid him on the litter before she continued down the street.

Gordon, looking contrite beyond relief, stood before her that evening as the students took the air in St. Hilda's quadrangle. "He is resting in testy discomfort at All Souls," he reported, and then cleared his throat. "He begs me to invite you to 'one more intrigue.' "

She regarded her brother with vast suspicion. "Gordon, you are a rogue, and I will do no such thing."

He held up his hands. "Those were his very words, so help me! Lord, but you are suspicious! I am to collect you from St. Hilda's before dawn in two days and meet him at Magdalen College."

"And I suppose he will line us up against the wall there and shoot us!"

"Nothing of the sort," Gordon protested. "See here, El, he's much more of a gentleman, even if he looks like a ragbag half the time. Which reminds me. You are to wear your breeches and student robe."

"This will be the last time," she warned.

He nodded. "Funny, but those were Lord Chesney's words, too. And dashed if he didn't wag his finger at me, just as you are doing now." He grinned and hugged her about the waist. "You two will be the death of me."

"Don't you ever use that expression again, Gordon," she said. "It makes me shudder."

To say the next two days crawled by would have been a gross understatement. Ellen finally turned the clock in her room to the wall because the hands refused to move, no matter how hard she watched them. The nights were much too long, the days even longer. She sleepwalked through her assignments like Lady Macbeth, wondering that she had ever thought scholarship so important.

All the flowers in the room suffered at her hands as she strewed petals about, wondering, "Love me, love me not."

He couldn't possibly love her, not after that fiasco at the riverbank. James Gatewood had suffered nothing but aggravation, irritation, and now blood loss at the hands of her family. He couldn't possibly love her.

And yet, even if his eyes were slightly out of focus at the riverbank, there had been such a light in them. Ellen tugged another handful of petals from a rose, groaned, and tossed the whole vase away.

She would like to have slept the night of April 30, but it wasn't even a consideration. She tossed about on her bed, alternating between tears and laughter, certain that she was in love. She blew her nose and wiped her eyes, thinking of Horatia and her lapdog love for Edwin.

Horry, you have it all wrong, she thought. Love is aggravation and worry, complete contentment, and the worst sort of discomfort. I wonder that anyone falls in love.

She thought of James Gatewood with his head in her lap, nuzzling her breast. I wonder how anyone can help but fall in love.

She was dressed and waiting for Gordon on the steps before dawn. Miss Medford was going to cut up stiff when she knocked on her door for breakfast and found the room empty, but it didn't matter; she was going home soon. Ellen gazed out across the spires of Oxford, still silhouetted in black, timeless monuments to the best efforts of spirit and soul. She did not feel sad. Oxford might be a dream unattainable now, but perhaps one of her granddaughters or great granddaughters would enter those halls and seat herself without fear or disguise in the lecture rooms.

"Stranger things have happened," she said as she watched Gordon come toward her.

The streets were full of students, all heading toward Magdalen College. Ellen looked at her brother, a question in her eyes.

"It is May Day," he reminded her. "I think even I am glad to be here for this moment." He took her hand. "And especially with you."

"Why, Gordon," she said. "One would think you almost cared."

"Don't let it swell your brainbox, sister," he replied, his voice light. He grew serious then. "I never did really thank you for standing by me during that dreadful Saturday reading. You could so easily have betrayed me. And I would have deserved it."

She smiled, remembering less of the misery and more of the pleasure at actually being there—if only for a brief time—listening to the exchange of ideas, some of them her own. "It was nothing, Gordon. Maybe we have both learned a few home truths this year that you cannot find in books."

Still serious, he linked his arm through hers.

Lord Chesney, looking unusually dashing with his arm in a sling, was waiting for them on the chapel steps. He looked up at Magdalen Tower and held out his good hand for Ellen.

"Let us carol in the May, my darling Hermia," he said, and kissed her fingers. "You may come, too, Gordon, if you are not afraid that I will do you injury. 'Tis a long way to the ground from the top."

Gordon took his sister's other hand. "I will stand on this side of her." He looked more closely at the marquess. "Are you sure that you are equal to this climb, my lord?" he asked.

"I think I can put one doddering foot in front of the other," the marquess replied. "Come, my love. You too, Gordon."

Almost afraid to speak, Ellen followed her marquess up the narrow staircase, the wood worn smooth by the progress of centuries. They paused for breath part way up.

She put her hand to his chest. "Are you able to continue, Jim?" she asked. "You lost a lot of blood, I think."

He shrugged. "Less than you would suppose. It looked worse than it was, so your brother assures me. One could almost suspect he shot me for maximum effect and little damage."

Gordon coughed and looked away.

"And note how romantic I look with this sling. I have given out so many explanations of how I came by it that it would require your calculating mind to keep them all straight."

She laughed and let him lead her up the tower with the other pilgrims to spring.

Near the top, they paused again on the crowded landing. The

marquess held her close, his good arm about her waist. He didn't look at her, but instead stared upward where they could glimpse the white-ruffed Magdalen students and choirboys waiting.

"Tell me, Ellen," he asked, his voice casual. "Did you mean what you said the other morning, or was I delirious?"

"I meant what I said," she told him, her voice firm. "I love you and I want to marry you above all things. And I only propose once, my lord."

"Then I accept, with all deliberate speed," he said.

Gordon let out a crack of laughter. "Thank the Lord for that," he exclaimed. "I was beginning to fear that I would have to shoot you again."

"What!" roared the marquess, his voice rising several octaves.

Ellen only looked at her brother. "I wondered, Gordon," she murmured. "And Becky was in on this, wasn't she? I did wonder."

He grinned. "I cannot tell a lie, at least not right now. So was my chambermate, who is still suffering from the ill effects of seeing all that blood. I did assure him that I would not shoot anything that Ellen would miss."

"My blushes, Gordon! Give him my condolences," the marquess said drily as he tightened his hold on Ellen.

"That was the best scheme I could devise on short notice."

The marquess could only stare. "But Gordon, you shot me!"

Gordon nodded. "I am an excellent marksman, my lord, so it wasn't as tricky as you might think. You were really quite safe."

The marquess groaned and Gordon threw up his hands in exasperation.

"How else was I to get Ellen's attention? And yours, too, I might add. I never saw such a gaggle of slow-tops as you two! One would think I had to do everything," he added virtuously.

"Yes. Well," was all the erudite and articulate Lord Chesney could manage as he sank down on the landing, his face a shade less sanguine. He pulled Ellen down with him. "My darling Ellen, do you realize that your brother is certifiable?"

Ellen considered the question for a moment, and kissed the marquess. "He *is* rather a good shot, Jim."

The marquess could only pull Ellen closer to him.

"Gordon . . ." he began.

But Gordon had gone farther up the tower. When he was safely out of reach, he looked back down. "You two would probably rather be alone," he said generously, shouting above the sweet soprano of the boys' choir that suddenly burst forth in full harmony as the sun cleared the tops of the hills.

Ellen snuggled closer to her marquess, unmindful of the strange looks she was getting from the students crowded around them on the landing. She kissed his cheek and whispered in his ear, "These students think we are queer stirrups, indeed."

"Oh, we don't care. Listen, Ellen. It is the most beautiful sound."

Her head pressed to his chest, she smiled at the wonderful rhythm of Lord Chesney's generous heart. There would never be any opportunity to explore the world beyond Hertfordshire, most likely. She and Lord Chesney would be too busy managing the silliness of his family or hers, or finding creative ways to help others. There would be that night school and Becky would find a better future, even as she had done. It was enough; it was more than enough.

Arms around each other, they listened as the choir caroled in the May from the top of Magdalen. " 'Like to the lark at break of day arising from sullen earth, sings hymns at heaven's gate,' " he said softly, his lips to her ear. "You'll not object if I occasionally quote the man who brought us together?"

"You know I won't."

When the last crystal notes faded into the morning light, Ellen sighed in complete contentment, but did not stir from the marquess's side. Gordon started down from the tower and blew a kiss to them in passing.

"I am so glad you are sending him off to Spain," she said as the other students stepped around them on the way down the rickety stairs.

Gatewood pulled away from her a little, the better to see her face. "Who said anything about Spain, my love? You are apparently laboring under the same misconception as your brother." He chuckled wickedly.

"Jim, what have you done?"

"I told you once that I seldom get angry, but I invariably get even," he replied, his voice serene. "I believe what I actually said was that he would go into an excellent regiment of my choosing.''

"Yes, yes, the Ninth Hussars. You said so," she interrupted.

"They are not *all* in Spain. Part of the regiment is reluctantly posted in Canada, keeping peace among polar bears and French voyageurs, I don't doubt. That is where your rascal brother is going."

She burst into laughter. "You are a sly dog!"

"I have been trained by masters this year," he replied. "He will suffer a boring but relatively safe incarceration in Canada."

He turned serious as he took her hand again. "I have discovered that I have too much regard for your scapegrace brother to willingly send him to the slaughter in Europe. Better he should stay alive and have many, many years to improve his faulty character."

Tears came to her eyes. "And Ralph will have Winchester."

"If he wants it."

She kissed his hand. "You are a wonder."

He shook his head in mock seriousness. "I do not know what I can do about Edwin Bland, though. I am afraid he will always remain a blockhead, and there are entirely too many of them in the peerage already to warrant the inclusion of another, even if it *was* in my power. Edwin will have to blunder on by himself. Perhaps he can purchase a title like his father."

The stairs were clear, but they did not move. "Why did you change your mind?" Ellen asked. "I know too well that you had decided against marrying me. You were going to be noble and spare me from your ridiculous family."

He rested his chin on her head. "Oh, I was honor bound. You see, I have just received the most amazing proposal . . ."

"Be serious!"

"It's strange. I have a letter in my pocket from Lady Susan Hinchcliffe. You will meet her soon, I fear. Anyway, it was full of misspellings and vapidity, expressing her delight that I was soon to be sprung from the halls of academe. She is as beautiful as she is brainless, and probably even now considers herself just the fitting ornament for the Gatewood family tree."

He kissed her head and was silent a moment. "I just couldn't do it, fair Hermia. I want a wife who will argue with me and challenge my mind and chide me when I get lazy or discouraged. Oh, and someone to make me glad for nighttime and quiet afternoons.''

She blushed. ''I have base instincts, my lord. You really ought to know.''

He kissed her again. ''Thank goodness for that.''

''You don't mind?'' she asked, her eyes wide.

''Lord, no!'' He grinned. ''Mine are pretty base, too. We'll just not tell the world.''

''I would never!''

He laughed. ''There is something else. I am relying on my father-in-law to help me find a new bailiff and perhaps an estate manager.''

''That is one thing he is very good at, Jim,'' she said. She touched his face. ''It will not be so bad in the country. And if you feel that you will miss Lady Susan, I give you leave now to change your mind.'' She clung to his good arm and leaned against him shamelessly.

''I wouldn't dare!'' he insisted. ''Gordon would blow my head off!''

He kissed her, leaving her breathless and agitated, and without a doubt that he had already forgotten Lady Susan Hinchliffe.

Gordon started up the stairwell again. ''Really, you two! What would Mama say?''

''Mama would be beside herself with joy,'' Ellen murmured. She unwrapped herself from the marquess and helped him to his feet. He put his arm around her.

''Let me lean on you, if you don't mind. That kiss made me dizzy.''

''You may lean all you choose, sir.''

They started slowly down the stairs. ''I thought you would enjoy listening to the choir from here,'' he said.

''What choir?'' she asked innocently.

''Witcracker! I should kiss you soundly for that, but I fear we would tumble down the stairs.''

They descended carefully. She stopped halfway down. ''Of course, you know why I am marrying you.''

''Hmm?''

''How else am I ever to get my Shakespeare papers back? Do you know, I have been wondering what became of them.''

He pulled her down again on the stairs. ''In the grip

of my base instincts, I almost forgot. Ah, yes, the book.''

"Book?" she asked, not daring to say more.

"In a wild flight of optimism, I gathered your essays and some of my own together, plus those ones of Gordon's—they must bear his name, I fear—and Ralph's. My publisher went wild with joy."

Ellen clapped her hands.

"Only yesterday, still clutched in the grip of fancy, I had them print 'Lord and Lady Chesney,' and 'Gordon and Ralph Grimsley' on the cover and spine. And you know how printers hate to change type, once it is set."

"Oh, Jim!" She kissed him, holding his face between her hands. They kissed until Gordon called up the stairwell again.

"Come on," the marquess grumbled. "Such a lot of stairs. I think that next May we will come here, but we will listen to the choir from the ground." He twinkled his eyes at her. "Something tells me that you might not feel up to all these stairs by this time next year."

"James!"

"Yes, James! My dear, in all your wondering what good your education is, you overlooked a most important reality, one that is not exalted or lofty, perhaps, but which will likely bring us both joy in years to come. When you educate a woman, you educate a family."

He kissed her hand and tucked it against his chest. "I could wish you the acclaim you deserve in the world of scholarship, but the time isn't here yet. I do promise to stand up every year in the House of Lords and rail on and on about the need for equal education for women. They will declare me a nuisance, but blast and damn, who cares?"

"Who, indeed?" she agreed.

"And I suspect you have some ideas of your own on how— outside of general marital conviviality—I can best be put to use. I rest assured that you will correct me if I am wrong."

"I will think of something, my dear."

* * * * * * * * * * * * * * * *

In 1878, the first women's college was established as part of Oxford University. Not until 1920 were women granted degrees.